for Lenn and Lura Latham

Basic Musicianship for Classroom Teachers

A Creative Musical Approach

Charles R. Hoffer
Indiana University

Marjorie Latham Hoffer
Monroe County Community School Corporation

Wadsworth Publishing Company, Inc.
Belmont, California

Music Editor: Edward Eldredge

Designer: Gary A. Head

ISBN 0-534-00394-X

L. C. Cat. Card No. 74-27856

Printed in the United States of America

1 2 3 4 5 6 7 8 9 10–80 79 78 77 76

The Wadsworth Music Series

Music Literature

A Concise Introduction to Music Listening by Charles R. Hoffer

A Concise Introduction to Music Listening Record Album by Charles R. Hoffer

A Study Guide for a Concise Introduction to Music Listening by Charles R. Hoffer

The Understanding of Music, Third Edition by Charles R. Hoffer

A Study Guide and Score for The Understanding of Music, Third Edition by Charles R. Hoffer

The Understanding of Music Record Album by Charles R. Hoffer

The Search for Musical Understanding by Robert W. Buggert and Charles B. Fowler

The Musical Experience, Second Edition by John Gillespie

The Musical Experience Record Album by John Gillespie

Music Foundations

Basic Concepts in Music by Gary M. Martin

Basic Resources for Learning Music, Second Edition by Alice Snyder Knuth and William E. Knuth

Foundations in Music Theory, Second Edition with Programed Exercises by Leon Dallin

Basic Piano for Adults by Helene Robinson

Intermediate Piano for Adults, Volume 1 by Helene Robinson

Musical Beginnings for Teachers and Students by Gary M. Martin

Basic Musicianship for Classroom Teachers by Charles R. Hoffer and Marjorie Latham Hoffer

Music Skills

Introduction to Music Reading by William Thomson

Keyboard Harmony: a Comprehensive Approach to Musicianship by Isabel Lehmer

Keyboard Skills: Sight Reading, Transposition, Harmonization, Improvisation by Winifred K. Chastek

Master Themes for Sight Singing and Dictation by Winifred K. Chastek

Music Dictation: a Stereo-Taped Series by Robert G. Olson

Music Literature for Analysis and Study by Charles W. Walton

Steps to Singing for Voice Classes by Royal Stanton

Techniques for Beginning Conductors by Allan Ross

Music Theory

Harmony and Melody, Volume 1: The Diatonic Style by Elie Siegmeister

Harmony and Melody, Volume 2: Modulation, Chromatic and Modern Styles by Elie Siegmeister

A Workbook for Harmony and Melody, Volume 1 by Elie Siegmeister

A Workbook for Harmony and Melody, Volume 2 by Elie Siegmeister

A Comprehensive Anthology of Music Forms, Volume 1 by David Ward-Steinman and Susan Ward-Steinman

A Comprehensive Anthology of Music Forms, Volume 2 by David Ward-Steinman and Susan Ward-Steinman

Music Education

A Concise Introduction to Teaching Elementary School Music by William O. Hughes

Music in the Education of Children, Third Edition by Bessie R. Swanson

Singing with Children, Second Edition by Robert E. Nye, Bernice T. Nye, Neva Aubin, and George Kyme

Teaching Music in the Secondary Schools, Second Edition by Charles R. Hoffer

Contents

Contents of Sound sheets

Side 1

1. "Tallis' Canon" with beat; "Tallis' Canon" four-part round: Nona McCown, soprano

2. Beethoven, Symphony No. 7, second movement (excerpt)

3. "Good Night" with meter; "Scotland's Burning" with meter: Nona McCown, soprano

4. "Camel Caravan": children's voices; clarinets

5. "Early One Morning"; "Hanukah": Nona McCown, soprano; guitar

6. "Die Musici" two-part round: children's voices

7. "All the Pretty Little Horses": Nona McCown, soprano; guitar

8. "Drill, Ye Tarriers": Mark Reina, baritone; piano

9. Improvisation lead-in (rhythmic); improvisation lead-in (melodic)

Side 2

1. Major and minor scales

2. Britten, *The Young Person's Guide to the Orchestra*, beginning and fugue

3. Schubert, "The Trout": Nona McCown, soprano; Lois Pardue, piano

4. "Rise Up, O Flame" in minor and in major: Nona McCown, soprano; guitar

5. Chords

6. Chord progressions

Side 3

1. "Now All the Woods Are Sleeping": Nona McCown, soprano and alto; Michael Schwartzkopf, tenor; Mark Reina, bass; piano

2. Schubert, Quintet in A Major, Op. 114, "The Trout," fourth movement (excerpts)

3. Compound and simple meters

4. "Dogie Song": Hal Hedlund, tenor; guitar (Recorded by permission of Follett Publishing Company. Copyright © 1966 by Follett Publishing Company.)

5. Brahms, "Cradle Song of the Virgin" Op. 91 No. 2 (excerpt): Sandra Mathias, soprano; Marjorie Hoffer, viola; Barbara Roberts, piano

6. "Summer Has Come": June Browne, soprano; Bruce Foote, baritone; oboe, drum, piano (Recorded by permission of Follett Publishing Company. Copyright © 1966 by Follett Publishing Company.)

Side 4

1. "Shenandoah": Mark Reina, baritone; piano

2. "Waters Ripple and Flow": children's voices; piano

3. Pentatonic scales and modes

4. "Gaelic Lullaby": Marilyn Powell, soprano; guitar (Recorded by permission of Follett Publishing Company. Copyright © 1966 by Follett Publishing Company.) "Navajo Happy Song": Ataloa of the Chickasaw Nation, singer and tomtom (Recorded by permission of Follett Publishing Company. Copyright © 1966 by Follett Publishing Company.)

5. "Scarborough Fair": Nona McCown, soprano; guitar

6. Dello Joio, "Anatomy Lesson": Nancy Carr, soprano; piano (Recorded by permission of Follett Publishing Company. Copyright © 1966 by Follett Publishing Company.)

7. "Chester": Mark Reina, baritone; piano. "Havah Nagilah": Nona McCown, soprano; piano

Other Performers

Guitar	Nona McCown
Percussion	Steve Hanna
Piano	Lois Pardue
Children	John Hattery
	Doug Lathom
	Chiara Mickel
	Heather Mickel
	Jennifer Mickel
Violin, Viola	Marjorie Hoffer
Clarinets	Charles Hoffer
	Allan Hoffer
Recording Engineer	Steve Hanna
	Gilfoy Sound Studio, Inc.
	Bloomington, Indiana

Preface

This book presents the musical information and skills that are relevant for elementary education students. It does not attempt to present methods for teaching music. Instead, its purpose is to develop the readers' musicianship, so that they will increase their own enjoyment of music and be able to inspire musical growth in the children they teach.

The book relates the learning to musical sounds, rather than limiting it to a cerebral, visual effort. For example, major scales are learned through working with songs in which these scales are featured. Rhythm and beats are introduced through spoken word patterns and immediately applied in a song. Throughout the book, musical knowledge and skills are gained through performing and analyzing actual pieces of music.

As an aid to performance and analysis, many of the songs and several musical exercises are presented on the two recordings included with this book. The songs are selected to provide variety: the styles differ; the vocal types include men's, women's, and children's voices; and the accompaniments involve the varied tone qualities of piano, guitar, autoharp, rhythm instruments, and the standard orchestral instruments. The recordings are useful both as a learning aid and as a source for later listening experiences appropriate for children in the classroom.

The readers not only learn musicianship by experiencing music; they also are encouraged to be musically creative. Although these creative efforts may not produce compositions in the usual sense of the word, they encourage the students to learn about music by manipulating and experimenting with its sounds. All but two chapters contain graded suggestions for creative activities.

The various aspects of musicianship are presented in a carefully ordered sequence that avoids cramming too much information into the first few chapters. Later chapters expand and reinforce the concepts presented earlier. Musical terms are defined as soon as they appear in the text. Every effort has been made to avoid detailed discussions of those technical points that are of limited value to elementary school teachers.

Because several approaches to music reading are presented—rhythmic syllables, conventional counting, sol-fa syllables, hand signs, and numbers—instructors may emphasize whatever methods they prefer.

An attempt has been made to present the most interesting song material from the repertoire in the elementary basal series books. Folk songs and songs from Broadway musicals and other sources are also included.

The book seeks to develop the student's skills on one melody instrument (recorder) and one harmony instrument (autoharp). These are the least expensive, the most quickly learned, and the most widely used of their respective types. Piano and guitar are also presented so that students with a previous knowledge of those instruments can play them in addition to the recorder and autoharp. (Normally the time in the course is too short to allow for mastery of piano or guitar unless the student has had prior experience with them.) The piano is mentioned often because its visual and tactile features aid in learning music.

Each chapter concludes with review exercises. These provide students with practice material on which they can work outside of the class period.

We are grateful to the School of Music of Indiana University for the use of its library. We would also like to thank the following persons for their reviews of the manuscript: Frances Madachy, Southern Oregon College; Alice Bartels, Moorhead State College; Susan Matych-Hager, Siena Heights College; Gary M. Martin, University of Oregon; and Jane M. Eby, Mankato State College.

Charles Hoffer
Marjorie Hoffer

1   *Beat, Tempo, and Note Values*

Music is an art that exists in the dimension of time, not space. Songs and symphonies progress in time from beginning to end. The sense of motion that occurs as the music progresses through time is described as *rhythm*. Rhythm includes several different aspects. The most important is the *beat*. Beat and rhythm are not synonyms. The beat is the recurrent throb or pulse that makes you want to tap your foot. It's an important part of almost all the music you hear and sing, because it gives a feeling of ordered movement to the music.

A sensing of the beat is necessary if you are to understand rhythm. The beat in music is like your heartbeat in two ways. 1) Both are usually regular. They can be all fast or all slow or all medium speed, but they occur regularly within that speed. 2) Like your heartbeat, the music beat is felt rather than heard; we know it's there even when there is nothing tapping it for us. To feel your heartbeat, touch your throat with your fingers at one side of your voicebox (larynx) and your thumb at the other. Press backward gently until you can feel the strong pulse in your throat. Notice that it is both regular and silent.

When sounds occur at regular intervals, they draw attention to the beat. Nowhere is a beat more evident than in the chants and cheers shouted at athletic events. In the following cheer, each beat is marked with a straight vertical line. The beat is steady, with a single speed maintained throughout the cheer. Try saying or chanting the words so that the feeling of the beat inside you is as strong and secure as possible. Move your arm, tap your foot, or in some other physical way indicate that you feel the beat. Be vigorous about it! (Granted, your amount of expression may depend on where you are and how extroverted you are.)

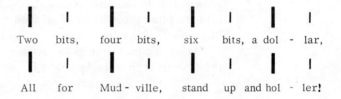

The beat in music is seldom as obvious as it is in a cheer. But it's there, and it's steady. The following song, "Tallis' Canon," contains one note on each beat throughout the entire piece—a rare occurrence in music. The song is presented in music notation, even though it has not been explained yet, because it will accustom you to seeing musical symbols and provide you with the music for later reference.

Tallis' Canon (*Recorded*)

Thomas Ken, 1695   Thomas Tallis, c. 1567

All praise to thee, my God, this night, For
all the bless-ings of the light. Keep me, O keep me,
King of kings, be-neath thine own al-might-y wings.

Listen as the instructor sings the song. Then lightly tap the beat in some manner as you sing it. The song will be more musical if, beginning with the word "praise," you gently emphasize every fourth note.

Before you start to sing this or any other song on your own, establish a beat speed that seems appropriate for the song words. The rate of speed at which the beats occur is called the *tempo*. When you have established a comfortable tempo for a song you want to perform, clap or at least think several consecutive beats before the song begins. For "Tallis' Canon" clap out three beats and then sing "All" on the fourth beat without interrupting the rhythmic flow you have established. As soon as you have learned the song, try singing it as a *round*. A round is a simple form of *canon* in which different performers begin the same song at different times. In "Tallis' Canon" and other songs of this type, numbers often indicate when each group of singers should begin. The overlapping effect is pleasing when rhythmic accuracy is observed in every part.

To help you learn this song and establish the feeling of the beat, one of the records included with this book contains "Tallis' Canon." First the song is presented with the beats sounded, and then it is performed as a four-part round. Like the other songs included on these records, this one is designated by the word "Recorded" above the music.

Many tempo markings are written in Italian. A list of the most common of these words is given in Appendix B.

Quarter Notes

A *note* is a printed symbol that indicates by its appearance how long a sound should last and by its vertical position how high or low the sound should be. The notes in the foregoing song consist of an egg-shaped *head* connected to a vertical line called the *stem*. This note—a dark head attached to a stem—is called a *quarter note*. The direction of the stem (pointing either up or down, as in "Tallis' Canon") does not affect the duration or sound of the note. A quarter note is most often assigned to represent one beat, but other types of notes can also represent one beat.

The duration of a musical sound is not measured by the clock. Instead, it is figured in relation to the beat. The sound may last for just one beat, or it may continue for a longer or shorter period of time. In any case, its duration is judged according to regularly occurring beats.

The duration of a note is called its *value*. Notes of different appearance have different values. If note values are arranged in order from longest to shortest, or vice versa, a 2:1 ratio is maintained between each note and the one next to it. Each note value is twice or half as long as its neighbor in such a series. The 2:1 ratio is one of the basic concepts in understanding rhythm and its notation.

This concept is evident in the hymn "Old Hundredth," which is sung (with different words) as the doxology in many churches. The sources of the words and music of a song are indicated in the upper left and right corners, respectively. The symbols above the notes are suggestions for accompaniment. They will be explained in chapter 10, and you will be encouraged to return to this and other songs at that time.

Old Hundredth

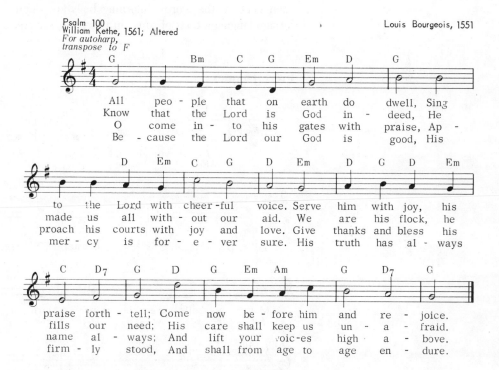

Half Notes

There are several quarter notes in "Old Hundredth," but you can also see notes that have an empty head. This note with a stem and a white, hollow head is a *half note*. It lasts twice as long as a quarter note, which means that it lasts for two beats if a quarter note lasts for one beat.

Establish a comfortable tempo, and then sing "Old Hundredth" while continuing to tap the beat, which is represented by a quarter note. Be sure to sustain the half note for two full beats, right up to the start of the next sound. If you clap the note values, leave your hands together for the duration of the half note, and bounce them slightly when the beat occurs midway through the note. This helps you to figure the note's length exactly.

Eighth Notes

The 2:1 ratio of rhythmic values is also apparent in the type of note that is only half as long as a quarter note. It is an *eighth* note, and it looks like a quarter note with a *flag* added to the end of the stem. If there are two or more consecutive eighth notes, their flags are often combined into a straight *beam* connecting the ends of the stems.

Traditionally, vocal music has been written with flagged eighth notes whenever each has its own syllable, and with beamed eighth notes whenever they share a syllable. Beamed notes are easier to read because they can be visually grouped into beats. This way of writing them, therefore, has gained favor in recent years, even when each note has its own syllable.

The round "Frère Jacques" contains the three note values presented in this chapter. The first ten notes in the song are quarter notes and coincide exactly with the beat. The word "John" lasts for two beats. Be sure to sing two *equal* notes for each beat on the words "morning bells are ringing." (For help in pronouncing foreign language texts of songs in this book, see Appendix C.)

Frère Jacques

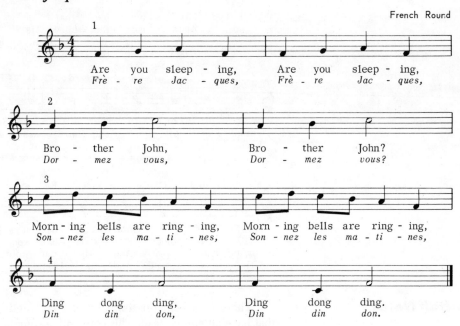

French Round

Tap the beat as you sing, and check your performance for rhythmic evenness and accuracy.

Patterns involving quarter and eighth notes are often present in music. One of the records included with this book contains a portion of Beethoven's Symphony No. 7. Notice the pattern ♩ ♫ | ♩ ♩ that is sounded over and over.

"Bingo" contains only eighth and quarter notes. It starts with an unstressed note called a *pickup*. "Tallis' Canon" also starts with an unstressed note, and that is why you were advised to emphasize the second word of that song. (When a pickup lasts for exactly one beat, as in "Tallis' Canon," it is called an *upbeat*.) As you sing "Bingo," again put more emphasis on the second word of the song than on the first.

Bingo

When you have learned the song, try varying it. Omit all sound when you come to the letter "B" in the spelling of the dog's name. The next time omit both the "B" and the "I." Continue in this way until no spelling is left. If the class can't start singing exactly together after the silences, a beat-clap can be temporarily substituted for each missing letter. Soon, however, the beat should become so strongly felt that no external cue is needed to bring the singers in together after a period of no sound. Such a silence should be considered active, conveying the sensation of an ongoing beat; it should not be dead.

Experiment with different tempos for this song. A moderately slow speed suggests melancholy, while a fast tempo sounds crisp and vigorous. Remember that the note values should remain in proportion to one another at every tempo.

Rhythmic Ostinato

For further variety, try adding a rhythmic *ostinato* to the song. An ostinato, related to the word "obstinate," is a persistent rhythmic or melodic pattern that is repeated several times in succession. Here are two rhythmic ostinatos that can be clapped throughout the song "Bingo":

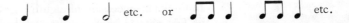

When clapping a half note, remember to keep the hands close together and move them slightly on the beat midway through the note.

Rhythmic Syllables

In addition to clapping rhythms when a song is being learned, it is often helpful to say syllables to reinforce the pattern. Almost any set of syllables is satisfactory for this, and several systems are currently in use. One of the more frequently used methods specifies "ta" for a beat, or quarter note; "ti" (pronounced "tee") for the division of the beat, or eighth note; and "ta-ah" for two beats, or a half note.

Look at "The Goose," noticing first the note values. Then tap the rhythm of the song. Next read through the song with rhythmic syllables, then with the regular words. Finally, listen to the melody of the song and sing it.

The Goose

German Folk Song

1. Once there was a sly old fox who stole a plump fat goose,
Stole a plump fat goose, But the farm - er caught him, now he's
locked in the ca - boose, _____ But the farm - er caught him, now he's
locked in the ca - boose, Locked in the ca - boose.
The ca - boose. The ca - boose.

2. Once there was a crocodile who snapped at all he saw,
   Snapped at all he saw.
   Till he crunched a rock and got a toothache in his jaw, *(2 times)*
   Toothache in his jaw. In his jaw. In his jaw.

3. Once a silly young hyena laughed at ev'ryone,
   Laughed at ev'ryone.
   Then he haw-hawed at a tiger, Tiger made him run, *(2 times)*
   Tiger made him run. Made him run. Made him run.

Reprinted from *Eleven Choruses for Treble Voices* by Milton Kaye. © 1962 by Silver Burdett Company. Used by permission.

In the long succession of eighth notes in "The Goose," feel the beat occurring on the first note in each pair of eighths. Remember that the beam combines the eighth notes into a group that lasts as long as one quarter note, which is one beat in this song. Your eye can tell at once where the beats occur in such a series. Perform the eighth notes evenly, sustain each half note for two full beats, and hold each quarter note for one beat.

"The Goose" is easily adapted to echo effects, such as *echo clapping*, in which the teacher and the class, or two sections of the class, imitate one another in clapping out rhythms. The teacher can clap the rhythm from the beginning of the song up to the first word "goose," with the class clapping the echoing rhythm more softly on "stole a plump fat goose." Toward the end of the song there is a double echo ("locked in the caboose" twice and "the caboose" twice). The level of softness at these points should be changed accordingly. The various levels should be noticeable in both the clapping and the singing. Listen to be sure the soft singing sounds alive and interesting.

On the first appearance of the word "caboose," notice that three notes are encompassed by a curved line. This is a *slur*, which indicates that two or more notes, moving higher or lower, are to be sung on a single syllable without a break. The long line at the end of the first word "caboose" means that the syllable is to be sustained while all the notes above it are being sounded.

At this point you have experienced the three most common note values. Their relative durations are illustrated in the chart below. The passing of time is indicated by arrows, although arrows do not appear in actual music.

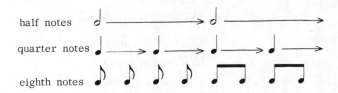

To develop the ability to read and perform rhythms, clap your hands or tap your foot, or tap one hand on a solid surface to represent an even, steady beat. Assume that each tap represents a quarter note (♩). Now refer again to the chart and read the top line rhythmically, by continuing your hand- or foot-tapping and also saying "Ta-ah, ta-ah" through four beats. You have now produced two half notes. Using the syllable "ta" for every note, or adopting another system of your choice, try the other lines, making your hand beat at the same speed for each line. Notice that the syllables get closer together as the note values get shorter, but the beat continues evenly.

Exercises

1. Practice reading the following patterns rhythmically several times, while maintaining a steady beat by clapping or tapping your foot.

2. Write the rhythmic pattern for the first six notes in the chorus of "Jingle Bells."

3. Practice changing from one note value to another as you say rhythmic syllables. To help you keep your place, the beats are marked off into groups of four.

Syllables
Beat

Syllables

Beat

4. Imitate short rhythmic patterns that another student or the instructor performs for you.

Review Questions

1. The beat is one aspect of _____. Usually it is (steady/irregular) and is more (felt/heard) than (felt/heard).

2. The word tempo refers to:

   a) a type of canon

   b) a type of round

   c) the speed of the beats

   d) the sense of the music moving in terms of time

   e) the recurrent pulse or throb in the music

3. a) Name this note: _____

   b) Name this note: _____

   c) Name this note: _____

4. To what do the words "value of a note" refer?

5. The ratio in the types of note values is:

   a) 4:1

   b) 3:1

   c) 2:1

   d) 1:1

   e) variable

6. It makes no difference in duration whether eighth notes have stems or flags. (T or F)

7. What is an ostinato?

8. What is a slur in music?

2 Meter and Rests

It is not enough merely to perform a piece of music with regularly placed beats—the music would be uninteresting for both the performer and the listener. The beats usually remain even, but certain ones are emphasized. This emphasis is a natural human tendency. When a person hears identical sounds repeated—a ticking clock, for example—the mind tends to group the sounds into patterns so that some seem louder than others. In music, the grouping of sounds into a pattern of emphasized beats is called *meter*. A stressed beat usually indicates the start of the pattern.

Every meter pattern is written with a "fence" or *barline* on each side of it. The area between two barlines is a *measure*. (It is also sometimes called a *bar*.)

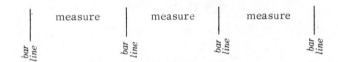

In two-beat, or *duple*, meter, each measure contains all the notes that occur during this beat pattern:

| BEAT beat | BEAT beat | BEAT beat | etc.

In three-beat, or *triple*, meter, each measure follows this pattern:

| BEAT beat beat | BEAT beat beat | BEAT beat beat | etc.

The songs in chapter 1 are in four-beat, or *quadruple*, meter:

| BEAT beat beat beat | BEAT beat beat beat | etc.

Meter Signatures

The meter is usually indicated at the beginning of the piece by numbers or symbols called a *meter signature*, or *time signature*. Two numbers, one above the other, can usually be interpreted as follows: the upper number tells how many beats are in each measure, and the bottom number tells what kind of note gets one beat. A "4" on the bottom stands for a quarter-note beat, a "2" for a half-note beat, and an "8" for an eighth-note beat. Exceptions to this interpretation of meter signatures will be discussed as the need arises.

The songs in the early chapters of this book maintain a quarter note as the beat and change only the number of beats per measure. At first, therefore, you will be dealing with $\frac{2}{4}$, $\frac{3}{4}$, and $\frac{4}{4}$ meter signatures. The latter signature is sometimes called *common time* and is abbreviated with a "C" at the beginning of the piece.

Although they are written one above the other and a line of the music staff separates them, the two numbers in a meter signature are not a fraction. They do not represent a portion of anything. They tell "how many" and "what kind" in regard to the beat, but many different values are possible within that meter. A $\frac{3}{4}$ meter signature, for example, says that each measure contains three quarter notes *or their equivalent in other note values.*

The single note pickup that occurs at the beginning of "Tallis' Canon," "Old Hundredth," and "Bingo" appears to be an exception—a shorter measure than is indicated by the meter signature. But it is actually a continuation of the final measure of the song. In every case, the first and last incomplete "measures" add up to the proper number of beats for one full measure.

An upbeat begins the following round. You can tell from the meter signature that there are three beats in each measure and that a quarter note lasts for one beat. Each half note, therefore, lasts for two beats. Tapping the beat may help you sustain the half notes for their proper duration, especially when the phrases are being sung at different times as a round. In music, a *phrase* is a group of notes that belong together as a musical idea, like a phrase in language. In fact, musical phrases in vocal music conform to the verbal phrases, as you can see by comparing the song text with the melody.

Good Night (*Recorded*)

"The Ash Grove" is also in triple meter with an upbeat. The symbol at the end of the second line (:||) is a *repeat sign*, directing the performer to repeat the preceding section of music immediately, with different words if they are indicated. Notice, too, that all of the eighth-note pairs are slurred. Keep the rhythm exact as you sing them. A slight stress on the first beat of each measure will help you feel the meter. Listen to your singing, however, to be sure the stress does not detract from the effect of the music.

At one spot in "The Ash Grove" the regularity of the beat should be suspended. The ⌒ is a *fermata*, or *hold*, which means that the beat should be delayed slightly until the performer feels the music should return to its regular tempo.

The Ash Grove

John Oxenford   Welsh Folk Song

The ash grove, how_ grace-ful, how plain-ly_'tis_ speak-ing,
When o - ver its_branch-es, the sun-light_is_ break-ing,

The wind through it_ play - ing has lan - guage for me.
A host of_ kind_ fac - es is gaz-ing at me.

The friends of_my_ child-hood a - gain are_be - fore me,

Fond mem - o - ries_ wak - en as free-ly I roam.

With soft whis-pers_ la - den, its leaves rus-tle_ o'er me;

The ash grove,_the_ ash grove that shel - tered my home.

Here is a song in quadruple meter that contains an unusually long slur. Keep a steady beat throughout the song. The long dotted line in the last word of the first verse indicates to the singer that the word is not completed yet; only one syllable of it is being sustained during the slur.

Unto Us a Boy Is Born

15th Century   1582

Un - to us a boy is born! King of all cre -
Now may Ma - ry's son who came long a - go to

a - tion, came he to a world for - lorn, the
love us, lead us all with hearts a - flame un -

Lord of ev - 'ry na - - - - tion.
to the joys a - bove_____ us.

"Scotland's Burning" is a lively round in duple meter. Sing this song with vigor, in the style indicated by the words. A strong emphasis on the first beat of every measure is appropriate here. Measures 1, 3, 5, and 7 are imitated exactly by measures 2, 4, 6, and 8. This provides a good opportunity for echo clapping. There should be no interruption to the flow of the beat.

Scotland's Burning (*Recorded*)

Traditional Round

Scot-land's burn-ing, Scot-land's burn-ing, Look out, Look out,

Fire! Fire! Fire! Fire! Pour on wa-ter, Pour on wa-ter!

To review the concept of meter, listen to the performance of "Good Night" and "Scotland's Burning" on the record. The first beat of each measure is sounded more heavily. Listen once, then hear the songs again while tapping the beat. Give more emphasis to the first beat of each measure as you tap or sing.

Conducting

An effective way to experience meter and tempo visually and physically is to conduct the beat patterns. These are the standardized arm motions by which a conductor indicates the tempo and metrical pattern of the music. The first beat of each measure always goes straight down and is called the *downbeat*. The last beat of each measure always moves upward and is logically called the *upbeat*. It prepares for the downward motion of the next beat. When there are two beats in a measure, the motion goes "down-up," like this:

Trace this pattern in the air several times, bouncing your arm slightly on each beat to show the exact instant at which the beat occurs—at the X's in the diagram. Notice that there is a slight hook to the right in the two-beat pattern. Also notice that the second beat is not quite as large as the first. In conducting, the arm should move very little at the wrist and elbow; the motion comes from the shoulder. The palm of the hand faces the floor. When you can conduct the pattern with precision, sing "Scotland's Burning" while you conduct.

When you are directing other people, you must give a *preparatory beat* so that the performers will feel the tempo and begin exactly together. If the sound is to begin on the first beat, conduct the preceding silent beat in the correct tempo so that everyone will be ready. Practice leading other people in the singing of

"Scotland's Burning." Think the tempo to yourself beforehand, then give the silent motion for the second beat.

The conducting patterns for other meters will be presented in later chapters.

The Whole Note

A new note value appears in "Camel Caravan." It is a white note with no stem, and it is called a *whole note* (o). It lasts four times as long as a quarter note. If a quarter note lasts for one beat, therefore, the whole note lasts for four beats. In rhythmic syllables the duration is "ta-ah-ah-ah." As you sing this song, space the beats farther apart than usual so that the piece will move slowly. The music should sound heavy and labored, to suggest hard work and a slow procession over miles of desert.

Camel Caravan (*Recorded*)

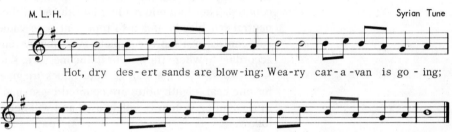

As soon as the melody becomes familiar to you, try these two melodic ostinato parts. Repeat each phrase several times.

For a most effective performance, the class can be divided into two sections. The people assigned to Ostinato I begin singing alone and softly, as if from a distance. After one phrase, the singers on Ostinato II join in with their part, a little louder. The melody enters as soon as the Ostinato II part has sung one phrase. The song gets gradually louder up to the word "slowly" to give the effect of the caravan coming closer. As the procession moves farther away, the song becomes more and more quiet to the end. When the melody stops, the two ostinato parts continue together for one phrase, then Ostinato II drops out to let Ostinato I finish the song very softly, as it began. Listen to the effect in the recorded version.

Rests

So far the songs in this book have had notes sounding throughout the piece. But silences are also important in music, and these silences must be measured as precisely as sounds. A silence in music is called a *rest*. Rests are named and measured like their counterparts in notes. In the following chart, the arrows again represent the passing of time, but they do not appear in actual music.

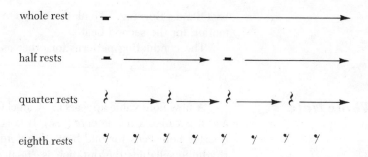

The whole rest is a black rectangle hanging from the fourth (next-to-top) line of the staff. The half rest is a black rectangle sitting on top of the middle line of the staff. You can tell them apart by remembering that the *half* rest is the one on the *half*-way line. The eighth rest looks somewhat like a "7." The flag on the rest is similar to the flag on an eighth-note stem.

"The Wells Fargo Wagon" contains three types of rests: the eighth, quarter, and half. It also contains rhythms that can be better understood if the beats are counted. The rhythmic reading introduced in the preceding chapter used only the neutral syllables ta and ti to represent note values. When you understand meter, you can learn a more complete counting system in which sounds are identified according to where they occur in the measure. Each beat note is numbered (e.g., "1 — 2 — 3 — 4 —"), and other note values are given syllables. If a quarter note lasts for one beat, eighth notes are counted by saying "and" or "an" after the number. This counting system is widely used and will help you understand the rhythms that follow.

The Wells Fargo Wagon
from *The Music Man*

Ward sent me a bath-tub and a cross-cut saw. O - ho, the
R. sent us a can - non for the court - house square.

Wells Far - go Wag - on is a - com - in' now, Is it a
I don't know

pre - paid sur - prise or C. O. D.? It could be
how I can ev - er wait to see. It could be

cur - tains or dish - es or a dou-ble boil-er or it could be
sum-pin' for some - one who is no re - la-tion or it could be

sum - pin' spe - cial just for me._____

© 1957, 1959 Frank Music Corp. and Rinimer Corporation. Used by permission.

The first full measure of "The Wells Fargo Wagon" can be counted:

Practice clapping the beat and saying this rhythm, first with the rhythmic syllables and then with the actual words of the song text.

Now notice the pickup containing three eighth notes. To perform the pattern, first clap a series of quarter note beats. Continue this while saying the counts for a complete measure of eighth notes: "1 and 2 and 3 and 4 and." Now whisper only the first five eighth notes of that measure, and start speaking aloud on the "and" after "3": "(1 and 2 and 3) and *four* and. . . ." Be sure to keep the beat steady. Next say the song words: "(1 and 2 and 3) O-*ho*, the. . . ." Go through the song once or twice, saying the words precisely according to their note values.

Notice that the rests are not dead spots in the music. They are essential to the character of the song, especially in the last line. When you sing, keep your mind actively involved with the progress of the song by counting the rests. It helps to keep a finger or foot tapping the beat.

Measure 12 contains a half note and a quarter note with a curved line connecting them. The line looks like a slur, but when it occurs between two notes of the same pitch, it is called a *tie*. It forms one note that lasts as long as the combined durations of the two tied notes.

Syncopation

"The Wells Fargo Wagon" contains a feature not found in the songs previously presented: the rhythmic emphasis does not always coincide with the beat. Look at the second complete measure. It begins with an eighth rest instead of with the emphasized sound that the listener expects. "Com-," the most emphasized note in the measure, starts not on the beat, but halfway through it. The removal of the accent where it is expected and/or the addition of emphasis where it is *not* expected is called *syncopation*. It is found seven times in "The Wells Fargo Wagon." In addition to the ⁊ ♩ ♪ pattern found in measures 2, 6, 18, and 22, there is syncopation on "birthday" in measure 10, on "grapefruit" in measure 13, and on "Tampa" in measure 14.

When performing music with rests in it, be sure that the span of the rest is actually silent. It's a temptation to let the preceding note sound too long, so that the music loses clarity and becomes "muddy." Remember, too, that the word *rest* in this sense does not mean a relaxation of mental attention. The beat should be felt just as intensely during periods of silence as it is during periods of sound.

Creating Rhythmic Patterns

Now is a good time to put to use your knowledge of note and rest values, meters, and measures by creating some short musical phrases out of rhythmic patterns. First, think in terms of only a few measures, perhaps four, and save longer efforts for later. Second, start with quarter notes and then change to enough other notes and rests to keep the pattern from sounding dull. (A string of eight quarter notes won't do!) Third, give the pattern a satisfying conclusion so that it doesn't seem to end "up in the air."

When you can clap or tap your pattern and are reasonably satisfied with it, write it down in notation. Then ask other members of the class to perform it. If they have trouble, check to see that you have notated correctly what you had in mind, then check to see if the other students are really performing accurately what you have written. If other class members have created patterns of the same length, these patterns can be performed simultaneously.

Make your pattern more interesting by assigning some sounds in addition to clapping. Suggest that your performers stomp their feet, slap knees or desks, snap their fingers, and click their tongues to add variety to the sound of the pattern. Words—even nonsense words—can be assigned to the notes. Use your imagination!

Exercises

1. Clap or tap the following measures several times by maintaining a steady beat and saying the appropriate rhythmic syllables. Several of the patterns contain syncopation.

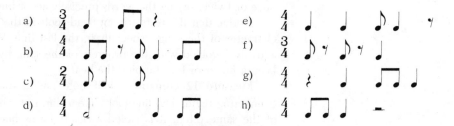

2. Write in the *one rest* that will correctly complete the measure. Then produce the patterns in the same manner as in exercise 1.

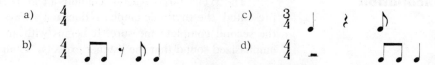

e) $\frac{4}{4}$ ♫ ♫ ' ♪ ♪   g) $\frac{4}{4}$ ' ♪ ♫ ♩ ♪

f) $\frac{4}{4}$ ♩ ♪ ♪ ♩   h) $\frac{2}{4}$ ♩

3. Which measures contain syncopation? Clap or tap the patterns in the same manner as in exercise 1.

a) $\frac{2}{4}$ ♫ ♫   c) $\frac{3}{4}$ ♩ ♩ ♫

b) $\frac{2}{4}$ ♫ ♫   d) $\frac{4}{4}$ ♫ ♫ ♪ ♩ ♪

Review Questions

1. How many beats may be expected in the following measures?

a) $\frac{3}{4}$ _____

b) $\frac{2}{4}$ _____

c) $\mathbf{C}$ _____

2. Define the word *meter* as it is used in music.

3. Match the term to the correct definition.

Two beats to a measure	Triple meter
Three beats to a measure	Quadruple meter
Four beats to a measure	Duple meter

4. What does the bottom number in a meter signature usually indicate?

5. a) What does this sign mean: ‖ ?
   b) What does this sign mean: ⌢ ?

6. Draw the pattern for conducting two beats per measure. Label the downbeat and upbeat.

7. Match the rest with its corresponding note.

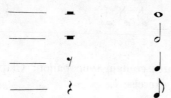

8. What is the difference between a tie and a slur?

9. What is syncopation?

3   *Pitch Notation, Singing, and Playing the Recorder*

In the first two chapters you learned about rhythm—its notation and its feel. *Pitch* refers to the highness or lowness of a sound. Unfortunately, "high" and "low" have nothing to do with height as far as the production of sound is concerned.

The sensation of pitch is created by the frequency of vibrations in whatever is making the sound: a string, a column of air in a wind instrument, a set of human vocal cords. On a string instrument you can often see the strings vibrate. They appear blurred as they sound, because the vibrating motion of the string is so fast. The faster the frequency of vibration, the higher in pitch the sound is, and the slower the frequency, the lower the pitch. The notes in most children's songs range in pitch from about 256 to 650 vibrations per second.

"Hot Cross Buns" has just three different pitches, and they are the same ones that begin "Three Blind Mice."

Hot Cross Buns

Traditional Song

Hot Cross Buns! Hot Cross Buns! One a pen-ny, two a pen-ny, Hot Cross Buns!

Before you try to sing "Hot Cross Buns," tap the beat and say the words in rhythm. When you feel secure about the rhythm, sing the song by memory or in imitation of your instructor.

Now, without looking at the notation of "Hot Cross Buns," take a piece of paper and draw a picture of the relative position of the pitches of the song. Use short lines to indicate each note. Since the pitches of the song are rather close to one another, don't make too much vertical distance between the short lines. Think of the pitch levels as steps. Be sure that notes on the same pitch are kept on the same plane on the drawing.

Next, compare your drawing with the notation of "Hot Cross Buns." Do the lines on your drawing move higher and lower, as they do in the notation? They should, because a primary function of music notation is to provide a visual representation of the various pitch levels.

The Staff

A *staff* is the five lines and four spaces on which the notes are placed. Notes are written on both the spaces and the lines of the staff. In this respect, conventional notation differs from your drawing, in which all notes were associated with lines.

The staff provides fixed reference points to tell the performer how far one note is from another. In musical terms, the distance from one pitch to another is called an *interval*.

19

In some ways a music staff is like a graph. Unlike most graphs, however, it appears with many symbols that are exclusive to music notation. One unique symbol is the *clef* sign. *Clef* is French for *key,* and the clef sign is a key, or clue, in the sense that it reveals the exact pitches that should be sounded. The range of available pitches is wide, and the range of a staff is relatively narrow, so musicians have devised a system of clefs to show what portion of the overall pitch range each staff is to represent. Unless there is a clef sign, the notes on a staff have no specific pitches, only relative position.

The Treble Clef

The *treble clef* sign is the curving figure seen at the beginning of each of the songs presented so far in this book. The inside curl of the treble clef curves around the second line, which is the note G. In fact, sometimes the treble clef is called the *G clef.* The other note names in the treble clef can be figured out from G. Only the first seven letters of the alphabet are used in designating pitches. To ascend above G, the seven letters are repeated. The descending order of pitches moves backwards through the same seven letters of the alphabet.

"Hot Cross Buns" begins not on G but on the line above it. Since both lines and spaces are used in notating pitch, the space above G is assigned to A and the next line above that is assigned to B. The first three notes of "Hot Cross Buns," therefore, are B A G. To reinforce the relationship of these note names and their appearance on the staff, sing the song again, not with the words but with note names.

To be sure your rhythm is accurate, sing the song while conducting the two-beat pattern presented in chapter 2.

Singing Pitches Accurately

Just as a camera must be in focus if the picture is to be clear and worth seeing, pitches must be in tune if the music is to be pleasing and worth hearing. The correct rendering of pitches is essentially a matter of *listening.* Be especially careful to establish the first pitch of a song accurately.

A pitch pipe is helpful for sounding a desired pitch if no piano or other melodic instrument is available. The most useful pitch pipe is a circular device with thirteen holes around its circumference. Each hole contains a reed mechanism that is activated when blown. Each pitch is clearly identified by letter name and by its position on a miniature staff. To keep track of a hole that you may need to refer to again in a short time, cradle the pitch pipe in the palm of your hand and keep your thumb and index finger over the holes on either side of the desired pitch. If singing is to occur with a melody instrument of some type, the starting note should be given by that instrument, not by a pitch pipe.

To help you match the pitch of an instrument or another singer, give attention to the interval of an *octave*—the pitch distance between pitches with the same letter name (E to the next closest E, G to the next closest G, and so on). The blending of sound on this interval is so good that it is sometimes hard to tell which octave is being sounded. It is advisable for females to sing a treble-clef song in the octave that the music specifies. Adult males should sing it only *one* octave lower than written. Although the songs in this book are reasonably pitched, it may require a little effort from a person who sings infrequently to maintain the right octave. This will become easier with practice.

When you sing, you may find it easier to listen to yourself if you put a hand or finger over your ear. This action seems to focus the sounds clearly in your mind and ear, and yet it also allows you to hear what else is happening in the music. Another device to help you hear your own singing is the tape recorder. Even an inexpensive cassette machine can provide a rather clear reproduction of pitch, although it may be inadequate to reproduce other aspects of music. You can record the performance of a song from the recording in the book while you sing along with it. This procedure will permit an objective analysis of your pitch and rhythmic accuracy.

Basic Singing Technique

Good vocal technique promotes accuracy and ease of singing. Although singing is a "natural" activity, the voice seems to sound best when these simple procedures are followed:

1. Sit or stand straight, with your chest high, but keep your shoulders relaxed. Well-aligned posture with an expanded rib cage is necessary to allow enough room for the air in the lungs, and it permits better control of the flow of air. Lifting the shoulders does not help, because it adds no more air capacity and usually creates tension.

2. Inhale deeply, as if you are filling the abdominal area with air. This means that the abdominal wall should move *out* as air is taken in. As a phrase of music is sung, the wall gradually moves in, and this is the action that expels the air. The chest should remain high as the abdomen moves in.

3. Keep your throat open and relaxed. This contributes to the clear, natural sound of good singing. Trying to sing with a tense throat is like trying to run with tense leg muscles; the effort is labored and ineffective. You should sing *through* your voice box (larynx) and not *with* it. The effort and focus of attention in singing should involve the abdomen, not the throat.

4. Let the sound roll out; do not force it. This "spinning" of the tone helps prevent the fuzziness and distortion that often are produced by forcing. The stream of air should be concentrated and released economically. Singing requires a good amount of air in the lungs, but only a small amount is necessary to produce the sound.

To practice these four singing steps—and they should be practiced a little each day—turn back to "Unto Us a Boy Is Born" on page 11. Concentrate at first on the last three measures that contain the long slur. Think through the four steps in order, then sing the nine slurred notes, using only the sound *ah*. Check to see that you follow through each step. Then sing the phrase with other vowels (*oo, oh, ee, ay,* and so on). Listen for pitch accuracy as well as good vocal tone. When you sing the song with words, be sure to maintain a steady stream of sound, except at those points where you take a breath. It is the continuity of sound on pitches that makes the difference between singing and speaking.

"Early One Morning" is a good song in which to practice correct singing technique. The melody in each of the five phrases ascends to a higher point near the middle and then drops down to approximately the same level as the starting pitch. The moving eighth notes give the song a feeling of momentum and fluency. Keep an open, relaxed throat and maintain good breath support through each phrase. You can practice this song by singing with the recording.

Early One Morning (*Recorded*)

English Folk Song

1. Ear - ly one morn - ing, just as the sun was ris - ing,
2. Sang the poor maid of her sor - row and sad - ness,

I heard a maid sing in the val - ley be - low,
The poor maid sang in the val - ley be - low,

Oh! don't de - ceive me, oh! nev - er leave me,

How could you treat a poor maid - en so?

Playing the Recorder

The recorder is a simple wind instrument that can sound most of the pitches of the songs in this book. It has a light and gentle tone quality. Recorders come in several sizes, but the soprano is the most practical for classroom use.

Recorders are constructed with two slightly different fingering systems: the Baroque, or English, and the German. The Baroque recorder has double holes for the lower fingers of the right hand. When optional fingerings are available for a particular note, the final choice should be determined by which fingering results in the most accurate pitch. Fortunately, only a few notes are significantly different between the two systems. With the exception of these notes, only one fingering is presented in this book for each note.

To play the soprano recorder, insert it slightly between the lips, holding it at a 45° angle to the body. Place the tongue against the back of the upper teeth or the rounded part of the gum just above the teeth. Start each tone with the syllable "doo" and a *light* breath pressure. The first three fingers of the left hand cover the upper holes, and the left thumb covers the hole at the back of the recorder. The right thumb supports the instrument, and the four right-hand fingers control the four lowest holes. The ball of the finger, not the tip, should cover the hole.

To produce the note B on the soprano recorder, cover the hole underneath the instrument with the thumb of the left hand and the hole nearest the mouthpiece with the index finger of the left hand. Cover the hole so that the fingerprint is centered. The fingerings on wind instruments are often indicated by fingering charts in which the covered holes are represented by small black circles and the uncovered holes by white circles. For example, the note B can be shown in this way:

Play B and sustain it, to be sure the sound is pleasant and clear. The sound you are producing (and the sound of all the notes you will play on the recorder) is an octave higher than the printed pitch. The sound is written lower so that its range will not extend so far above the staff, and the notes will be easier to read.

When you can produce the pitch B easily and clearly, play a series of eighth or quarter notes at a steady tempo. Next try to play these patterns:

Then, with another class member, make up various rhythmic patterns on the pitch B. Either imitate each other's patterns or verbally specify rhythms for the other person to play. For example, "Play four eighth notes, rest for a beat, and play a quarter note."

The basic fingerings of the recorder follow a simple principle. As each hole is covered, moving from the mouthpiece toward the other end, the air column is lengthened, and the sound is lowered in pitch. Therefore, the next several notes below B are logical and easy to learn. The note A is fingered when the hole below B is covered. The note G is fingered when the hole below A is covered.

Remember that air moving through a pipe will escape at the first available opening, so there usually can be no openings between the source of the air and the lowest covered hole. When you cover the hole for G, you must also cover the holes for A, B, and the thumb. Otherwise the instrument may squeak or emit no sound.

Each note will be distinct from its predecessor when you form the "doo" at the start of each sound. This is called *tonguing*. You can slur two or more different pitches on the recorder by playing them with one continuous breath after the initial tongue action. In notation for wind instruments, all notes are tongued unless marked with a slur or tie. Slurs are not so common in songs, however, so when you play vocal music on the recorder you may rely on your own judgment as to whether to tongue or to slur certain passages.

Tonguing requires coordination between fingers and tongue. This is not hard to achieve if the music moves at a slow or moderate tempo. To tongue when there is a change of note, concentrate on covering or uncovering a hole at the exact moment you execute the "doo" syllable. Practice tonguing B–A–G–A–B a few times to gain this coordination.

When you can play the notes G, A, and B easily, play the song "Hot Cross Buns." If you wish, you may play it from memory or "by ear" by picking out the tune as you play it. But be sure that you know the name of each note and can recognize it when you see it in notation.

Sightreading

There may be occasions when you need to play or sing by reading music without hearing it first. That is called *sightreading*—the ability to perform unfamiliar music without rehearsing or studying it beforehand. It means interpreting the notation accurately without stopping to make corrections or experiment with what lies ahead. Sightreading requires keeping a steady beat, reading somewhat ahead of each note, and correctly reacting to the visual symbols as the music moves along.

Try sightreading the following musical phrases on the recorder:

Now try playing a familiar song by ear: "Mary Had a Little Lamb." Begin on B, and remain on B when you reach the spot where the melody customarily goes higher than that note. When you have played the song by ear to your satisfaction, write it in notation. Do the written symbols conform to the sound of the music as you played it? If you aren't sure, ask someone to check your work.

Two-Part Songs

The following Polish carol is arranged for two voice parts. The melody is in the upper notes. When you have learned to sing it, see if you can maintain the part while the instructor sings the lower notes.

In a Manger

bove, in   cho - rus   ho - ly, An - gels sing un - to our Lord.
praise with cho - rus   ho - ly, Sing with joy un - to our Lord.

When two parts share one staff, two note heads can share one stem if their rhythmic values are the same. If their values are different, a stem going up represents the upper part and a stem going down represents the lower part. If both parts are to sing the same pitch, as in measure 4 and the last measure, the single head has two stems.

"In a Manger" is effective with a simple *descant* played on the recorder. A descant is a separate melodic line that is intended to complement an existing melody. A descant is usually higher than the main melody.

To play the following three-note descant on the recorder, two new notes need to be introduced. They are C and D:

Although the fingering for D may appear to violate the principle of "longer pipe/lower pitch," this is not true. When the thumb hole is opened, the recorder overblows an octave higher. The instrument thereby adds a second "layer" of pitches for which the longer pipe/lower pitch principle still operates.

Here is a descant to "In a Manger":

When you play the descant, be sure that the quarter rests are actually silent. Notice that the last three rests occur at the ends of the musical phrases. Because the descant here helps reinforce the phrases established in the melody, observance of the rests is important. They do more than just indicate the places at which the recorder player can take a breath.

Now that you know the five notes G A B C D on the recorder, you can play "Camel Caravan" on page 13. To review the note names before you play the piece, establish a slow, steady beat and then *say* the letter names at the speed they occur in the song: B–B–, BC BA G A, etc.

Next notice the four phrases, each of which is two measures long. As you play the song on the recorder, make a slight break at the end of each phrase by stopping the flow of air briefly with the tongue.

Dynamics

"Camel Caravan" is most effective when performed with varying levels of loudness and softness. This feature of music is called *dynamics*. Play "Camel Caravan" with the same dynamics that were suggested when the song was first presented: begin softly, get louder to the word "slowly," then get gradually softer to the end of the song. In playing a recorder, as in singing, an increased amount of breath pressure produces a louder sound. Practice the song until you can play it with controlled dynamic changes and good phrasing, as well as with the correct pitches and rhythms.

Creating Patterns with Dynamics

In the preceding chapter you created rhythmic patterns. Patterns can also be created with dynamics. Assume that you are performing eight quarter notes in succession, and decide on a pattern of dynamic changes for these eight notes. If you use more than two dynamic levels, loud and soft, you can add even more interest to the series of sounds.

Now combine the creative activities of chapter 2 and this chapter. Think up a new short rhythmic pattern and add to it a pattern of dynamic changes. You may wish to involve other types of sound in addition to voice or recorder: a clap, finger snap, or other distinctive sound that will occur at a particular point. Write out your dynamic-rhythmic pattern for performance by members of the class.

Exercises

1. Practice saying the pitch names in the following exercises. Then say the names in rhythm. Next play the exercises on the recorder and, finally, sing the exercise on a neutral syllable.

2. Clap or tap the rhythmic patterns of these exercises. Next sing them on a neutral syllable, then sing them with the pitch names.

3. Sightread the following phrases.

Review Questions

1. Name the following pitches.

2. To what aspect of music does *pitch* refer?

3. An interval is:

   a) the distance from one pitch to another

   b) the five lines and four spaces on which notes are placed

   c) the symbol that indicates the exact pitches

   d) a long rest or gap

   e) the general pitch area of a song

4. The treble clef is sometimes called the _____ clef.

5. Identify which measures contain octaves.

6. What are the four basic steps in producing a good singing tone?

7. What is a descant?

8. In music, the word *dynamics* refers to:

   a) the quality of two pitches sounded simultaneously

   b) the speed of the music

   c) the underlying rhythmic pattern

   d) unpleasant sounding pitches

   e) the levels of loudness and softness

4 The Keyboard and Intervals

Knowledge of the piano keyboard is a helpful visual aid for anyone who wants to understand pitch. Furthermore, several simple melody instruments are based on a keyboard arrangement (for example, the sets of tuned metal bars, such as resonator bells, that are struck with a mallet and are found in most music classrooms). Since pitch itself is intangible, a visible representation of different pitches is useful, and the keyboard is uniquely able to provide this.

The black keys of the piano are found in groups of twos and threes. All white keys are identified in relation to these groups of black keys. For example, every C on the piano is a white key immediately to the left of a two-black-key group; every F is a white key immediately to the left of a three-black-key group. The white keys are named in order from left to right, using the letters A to G:

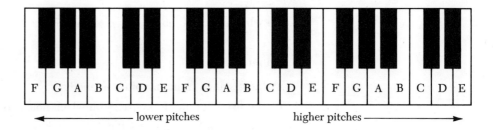

F G A B C D E F G A B C D E F G A B C D E

◄─── lower pitches   higher pitches ───►

Sharps and Flats

Some note names require a modifying symbol in addition to the letter name. There are three symbols that modify the pitch of a note:

Sharp	(♯)	a symbol placed before a note to raise the pitch one *half step*, which is the smallest pitch difference possible on the piano
Flat	(♭)	a symbol placed before a note to lower the pitch one half step
Natural	(♮)	a symbol placed before a note to indicate that it is neither raised nor lowered. This symbol cancels a sharp or flat previously applied to the note.

To find the sharp of any white key on the piano, find the black key touching it on the *right*. To find the flat of any white key, find the black key touching it on the *left*. If there is no black key on the side where you are looking, the nearest white key in that direction is the sharp or flat.

On the keyboard below, notice that each black key has two names: for example, the key called G♯ (because it is to the right of G) or A♭ (because it is to the left of A).

28

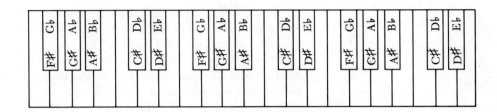

Middle C is the C nearest the middle of the piano keyboard, and it is the note that occurs midway between the staffs of the two most common clefs: the treble and the bass. The bass clef is pictured beneath middle C in the following example, and its pitches can be computed downward from middle C. Knowing the placement of middle C and using it as a guide, you can look at any note on either staff and find on the piano the exact tone it represents.

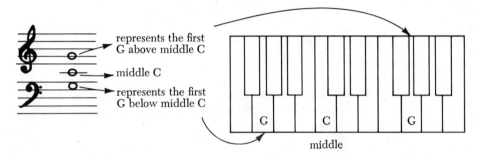

Notice that middle C is too low to be placed on the treble clef staff and too high to be written on the bass clef staff. Its placement is indicated by a *leger line*. Leger lines are the short horizontal lines indicating the pitch of notes too high or too low to be written on the regular staff. Leger lines, which extend the range of the staff, are placed exactly as far apart as the staff lines. Some notes, like the following, require more than one leger line:

The pitch names of notes involving leger lines are computed in the same way as notes on the staff.

Transposition

Refer again to "Hot Cross Buns" on page 19. The first note of the song is a B—the first B above (to the right of) middle C. When you have found it at the piano, play the song with the correct notes and rhythms. Then move to the same three pitches in a higher or lower range and play the song a few more times at different pitch levels. The note names are the same, but if you were to write them on a staff, they would have to be placed differently or another clef would have to be used. Performing or writing notes at a pitch level different from the original is called *transposition*.

For another experiment in transposition, play the song with other note combinations: E D C or A G F or the group of three black keys called A♯ G♯ F♯ (or their alternative names, B♭ A♭ G♭). These patterns involve only white keys or only black keys. Many other patterns are possible, however, if you want to start on a different note and then combine white and black keys. Try starting on various notes and let your ear guide you as to which notes you should play to maintain the same pitch relationships for this three-note song. As you experiment, name the notes as you play them, so that you will learn them more quickly.

The following German folk song contains only five different pitches and three note values. Play it on the piano and sing it until you can easily remember the tune. Then transpose the song by starting on other pitches and keeping the original pitch relationships. Try starting on G instead of D for a different pitch level that also involves only the white keys of the piano. You might also start on A, inserting an F♯ where required, or start on C and include a B♭ where it is needed.

Es Regnet
It's Raining

The tie that appears twice in "Es Regnet" is observed when singing in German and disregarded when singing in English. What note value would be given to the C if the verse were not translated into English?

The notes in the printed version of the song—G A B C D—are those you have learned on the recorder. Play the song on that instrument and select repeated phrases that can appropriately be played more softly the second time to achieve an echo effect. Experiment with soft playing on the piano, too, so that you can learn to control the dynamic levels on the keyboard.

Piano-playing will be easier for you if you find a comfortable fingering for each phrase—not a one-finger technique, but a method that allows you to use adjacent fingers on consecutive notes wherever possible, or that lets you cover several notes by extending the distance between your thumb and little finger. This gives you greater facility and produces a smoother and more musical effect. Because most of the songs in this book have notes that lie above middle C, you will probably prefer to play them with your right hand. The left hand will become involved when the songs are accompanied on the piano.

Key Signatures

One feature of music notation needs to be explained before you play the other songs you have learned in the first three chapters of this book. In many songs, certain notes should be sounded with a sharp or flat whenever they occur. To prevent clutter in the song notation and to give the musician useful information before he begins to perform it, these sharps or flats are pictured together in a group at the beginning of the song. This grouping is called the *key signature.* It is explained further in chapter 8 and charts of all key signatures can be seen on pages 82–83 and 90. For now, you need to remember two things: 1) The line or space occupied by any given sharp or flat goes through the center of the symbol. 2) The sharps or flats of the key signature affect all notes bearing that letter *throughout the piece,* unless the composer indicates that he wants a change later in the song. When a sharp, flat, or natural occurs in the body of the piece, indicating a departure from the key signature, the symbol is called an *accidental. An accidental applies only to the measure in which it appears, but it is valid for the remainder of that measure unless canceled.* For example, the second F in this measure is F♯ even though no sharp sign appears before it.

But the F in the second measure is F natural because it is in another measure and has no sharp in front of it.

Look at "Tallis' Canon" on page 2. The key signature consists of one sharp on the top staff line, which is F. The F♯ in the key signature applies to every F in the song, so the notes on the words "to" and "thine" are both F♯ (the black key), not F♮ (the white key). "Frère Jacques," on page 4, has one flat in the key signature, and this changes every B to a B♭ throughout that song. Practice playing these two songs on the piano. Sing the note names (including any sharps or flats) occasionally as you play to help you learn them more accurately.

Whole and Half Steps

In chapter 3 the different pitch levels were called *steps.* This is more than a picturesque analogy—it is a legitimate musical term suggesting the position of a given pitch in relation to the adjacent pitches. A *half step* (sometimes called a *semitone*) is the smallest pitch change that can occur between two notes on the piano. It is found between every pair of adjacent black and white keys, and between every pair of white keys unseparated by a black key. The pitch difference in a *whole step* equals two half steps. Play several pairs of whole and half steps at the piano, naming the notes in each pair and listening carefully to the relationship between them. Then have a friend play some examples for you to identify by ear. See also if you can specify a whole or half step when given only the note names, such as D and E♭, F and G, C♯ and B. Such drill will help you sing in tune, read music accurately, and notate what you hear.

The seven letters assigned to musical pitches and the lines and spaces on the staff do not represent equidistant intervals. As you can see on the keyboard, the pitches E to F and B to C are each only a half step apart. Likewise, there are places in every seven consecutive steps on the staff where an adjacent line and space represent only a half step—for example, E to F and B to C when no accidentals are involved. The presence of a sharp or flat shifts the points at which the half steps occur. For this reason, it's *always* necessary to check the key signature before starting to perform a piece. An oversight here can change the sound of the music quite radically. To become better aware of half and whole steps, go through "Tallis' Canon" (page 2) and write in whether adjacent notes are a whole or half step apart.

Here is a song that can be played exclusively on the white keys because there are no sharps or flats in the key signature and no accidentals within the piece.

Alleluia

Al - le - lu - ia,   Al - le - lu - ia,   Al - le - lu- ia.

Arrange the fingering so that the hand lies comfortably over the notes in each phrase (each measure in this song). Play adjacent notes with consecutive fingers, spreading the hand between thumb and little finger to make a smooth transition from middle C to the higher C.

With two other persons, sing the song as a round.

Conducting Four-Beat Meter

The conducting pattern for four beats per measure is as follows:

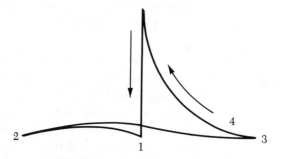

or down, left, right, up. Notice that beat 1 goes down and beat 4 (the last beat of the measure) goes up, like the first and last beats in duple meter. For precision, maintain the slight bounce of the hand exactly on the beat. Sing "Alleluia" again, this time with the four-beat conducting pattern.

Polyphonic Music

A similar song, in the sense that a second part imitates the first and both can be played on the white keys of the piano, is "Thanks Be to God." Two characteristics of this song make it a canon rather than a round. 1) The two parts do not begin on the same pitch—the second part is five steps lower throughout the song. 2) The parts are adjusted at the end so they finish together. The sounding of two equally important voices is called *polyphony,* a term for music in which two or more distinct lines contrast with one another.

Thanks Be to God

For clarity and ease of reading, the two parts are written on two staves, in contrast to the two-part song written on a single staff on page 24. The upper part performs only the notes on the upper staff in each pair, and the lower part keeps to the lower staff; the staves should not be performed consecutively from the top of the page to the bottom. Notice that the music is notated so that simultaneous sounds are aligned vertically in each set of bracketed staves.

Play the upper (soprano) part on the piano, then the lower (alto) part. The half steps will occur between the notes B C (found only in the upper part), and E F (found only in the lower part). Notice that those are the only two white key pairs that are not separated by a black key. Their closeness of pitch can be seen on the keyboard and is taken care of by the tuning of the instrument.

The whole rest in the first measure of the alto part is important. This silence permits the starting of the soprano line to be heard clearly, and calls more attention to the later start of the alto on the same melody exactly five steps lower. This one-measure lag continues throughout the song until the last two measures, where the parts are adjusted to end together.

You can play the upper part of "Thanks Be to God" on the recorder after you learn one new note:

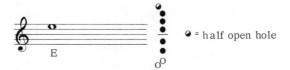

The high E requires a half-hole fingering: the thumb of the left hand only partially covers the hole. Slide the thumb down slightly to accomplish this.

Now try the song with various combinations of voices and instruments: two voices, voice and recorder, voice and piano, recorder and piano, or piano on both parts. Decide which combination best emphasizes the equality and independence of the parts. Conduct the song with the four-beat pattern you used for the "Alleluia" on page 32.

A polyphonic song in three-beat meter, with two melodies that are not at all alike, begins on page 41.

Chromatic Notes

"Hanukah" is another two-part song, but neither melody imitates the other.

Hanukah *(Recorded)*

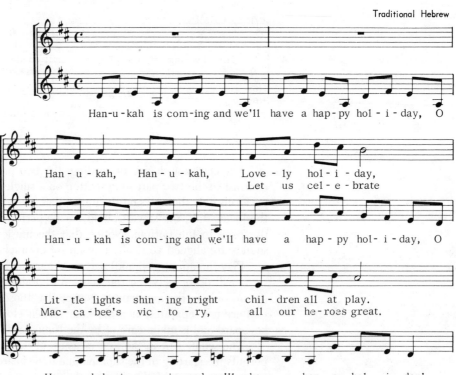

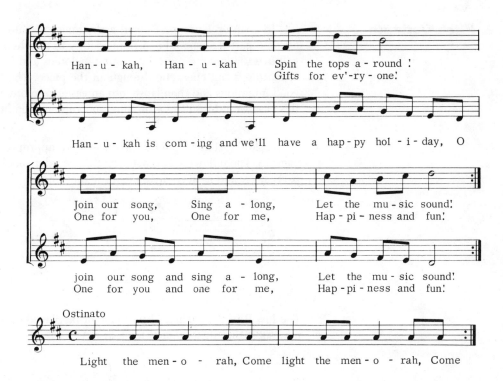

There are accidentals in the lower part of "Hanukah." In measure 5 you see the C♮, which is a departure from the C♯ indicated by the key signature. Immediately after the C♮ the C♯ is reinstated to produce a short series of consecutive half steps. Such a passage is called *chromatic*, from the Greek word for *color*. Play just these three notes slowly on the piano a few times until you become accustomed to reading the accidentals and hearing the sound of the consecutive half steps. Sing the three notes, also, to be sure you can produce the slight pitch differences accurately with your voice.

Now play and sing the whole measure with even eighth notes, repeating the measure until you can perform it easily. Observe that an accidental appears *before* the note in music notation (♯♩) but *after* the note if it is spoken or written with letters (C♯).

Next try the parts of the whole song separately, playing and/or singing each, until you feel secure enough to maintain either one while someone else performs the other part. Singing with each part on the recorded version may help. Each part is presented separately, and then combined.

"Hanukah" should be performed with vigor. Keep the notes short and emphasize those that occur on the beat. This will produce the appropriate feeling of gaiety without the need for excessive speed. In fact, a controlled and vigorous style will achieve a better musical effect here than an attempt to just "go fast."

Pitch Ostinato

In chapter 1 you performed a rhythmic ostinato. "Hanukah" has a one-pitch ostinato part that should contribute subtly to the rhythmic drive. If it is too loud it will overshadow the more interesting melodies and become irritating. So keep the ostinato soft but energetic throughout the piece. The tendency is to start out with good intentions and then lapse into an easier or more commonplace style, which in this case would result in a droning, monotonous rendition.

A slow sustained pitch ostinato is more appropriate for "Camel Caravan" on page 13. The following two notes on the recorder should be learned for the ostinato parts suggested as accompaniment for the song:

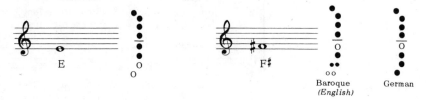

The low B in the Ostinato I part cannot be played on the soprano recorder, so you may substitute the higher B for that note:

Now try the song with recorders playing all three parts. The ostinato parts begin and end the song alone, as suggested on page 13, so those performers will have an especially long time in which to increase and decrease the dynamic level of their respective parts. Again, work for controlled dynamic changes and careful phrasing in all three parts.

Creating Patterns with Pitches

Another element of music—pitch—has now been added to the resources of rhythm and dynamics. So far you have practiced eight pitches on the recorder, and you have probably tried more than that number on the piano. For your first creative effort, however, success is more likely if the number of pitches is limited. So begin with only G, A, B, and D.

First play these pitches on the recorder or piano so that you have them in mind. Second, experiment in your mind with short phrases, not more than sixteen notes in length. Don't attempt to "fish out" a tune on the recorder or piano, because creating music is not a process of looking for something but of thinking. Third, when you have a phrase of pitches clearly thought out, put it on the staff. You may want to place just dots on the paper at this point; rhythmic values can be added later. For example, your paper might look like this:

Fourth, play the phrase on the recorder or piano to make certain you have written down what you had in mind.

At this point you can add the rhythm and dynamics. Be sure to include a meter signature and bar lines. Perhaps your pitch phrase has further potential. To find out, write a second rhythm for it with different dynamics as well. Here are two versions of the pitches shown in the example above.

Exercises

1. Clap the following phrases, say them with rhythmic syllables, then sing them with pitch names.

2. Play these phrases on the piano and recorder.

3. Clap, play, then sing these phrases on a neutral syllable.

4. Practice these recorder fingering exercises.

Review Questions

1. Match the symbol with its function.

   ♭   raises a pitch one half step
   ♮   lowers a pitch one half step
   ♯   cancels a previous sharp or flat

2. The key with the arrow pointing to it can be given two different note names. What are they?

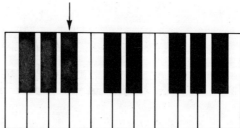

3. What are leger lines?

4. *Transposition* in music means to:

    a) play a piece on a different instrument

    b) perform the song at a different pitch level

    c) change one or two pitches in a song

    d) move a song from treble to bass clef

    e) change the written notes but retain the same pitch (e.g. B♭ to A♯)

5. What is the function of a key signature?

6. What are accidentals?

7. Which intervals are half steps or semitones?

8. Draw the pattern for conducting four beats in a measure.

9. The characteristic feature of polyphonic music is:

    a) two or more equally important parts or lines

    b) two or more performers on a part

    c) two or more clefs used in the notation

    d) two or more languages sung in the work

    e) two melodies now joined together to form one longer melody

5 Dotted Notes and Sixteenths

The rhythms of the songs presented so far can be pictured by four basic note values—by whole, half, quarter, and eighth notes. Often, however, a composer wants a sound to last for a duration *in between* these note values. It's possible to lengthen a note by writing after it another note of the same pitch and connecting the two notes with a tie (as is done in "Wells Fargo Wagon" on page 14 in measures 10, 12, 14, and 27).

Dotted Notes

An easier way to lengthen a note value, however, is merely to add a dot. The system works in this way: *A dot to the right of a note head adds half again as much value to the existing note.* The value of a dot changes, therefore, depending on the value of the note with which it appears. Assuming in each case below that a quarter note lasts for one beat, the duration of each dotted note is:

$$\text{♩.} = \text{♩} + \text{♪} = 1 + \tfrac{1}{2} = 1\tfrac{1}{2} \text{ beats}$$

$$\text{𝅗𝅥.} = \text{𝅗𝅥} + \text{♩} = 2 + 1 = 3 \text{ beats}$$

$$\text{𝅝.} = \text{𝅝} + \text{𝅗𝅥} = 4 + 2 = 6 \text{ beats}$$

Dotted notes are related to one another in the same way that nondotted notes are related—both kinds of note values reveal a 2:1 ratio. Compare the following chart with the one on page 7:

"Sing and Rejoice" is a simple round that contains three dotted half notes. You can tell from the bottom number of the meter signature that a quarter note lasts for one beat. A half note in this song, therefore, lasts for two beats. The dot beside it adds half of that two beats (one beat), for a total of three beats on that note. To double check, look at one of the measures containing a dotted half note. The top number of the meter signature indicates that each measure should contain three beats, so the duration of one measure is correctly consumed by that single three-beat note value.

Sing and Rejoice

Play this round on the piano, then on the recorder, observing the new note, low D.

Three recorders can play this round effectively. To produce the slurs, do not tongue "doo" at the beginning of the second note. Merely change fingers while keeping a steady stream of breath. The first note of each slur is tongued, but the slur connects subsequent notes to the first without a break.

In "The Inch Worm," the first portion (the verse) contains three dotted half notes. The melody is characterized by several wide intervals, many of them the distance of a fourth or wider. Look now at the refrain, which contains two simultaneous melodies that are equally important. How many intervals of a fourth or wider appear in "The Inch Worm" melody of the refrain? Notice that there is no interval wider than a third in the other voice part of the refrain. This provides contrast in melodic character and a good balance between the two lines of polyphony.

Observe, too, the notation for *first* and *second endings*. The first ending is a temporary closing section that leads back to a repetition of the same music. In this song, it includes everything between the repeat signs (‖:   :‖). A different ending (the second) concludes the section and leads on to new material if the music continues.

The underscored words in the upper part of the refrain show the verbal emphasis that is necessary if the meter is to be maintained.

The Inch Worm

"Die Musici" includes dotted quarter notes.

Die Musici (*Recorded*)
Music Alone Shall Live

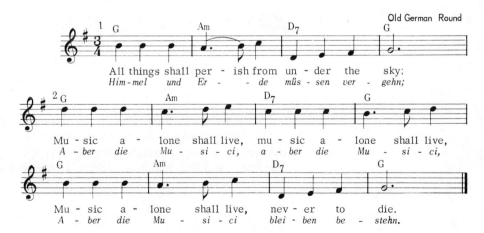

Old German Round

All things shall per - ish from un - der the sky;
Him - mel und Er - de müs - sen ver - gehn;

Mu - sic a - lone shall live, mu - sic a - lone shall live,
A - ber die Mu - si - ci, a - ber die Mu - si - ci,

Mu - sic a - lone shall live, nev - er to die.
A - ber die Mu - si - ci blei - ben be - stehn.

The meter signature of "Die Musici" indicates that a quarter note lasts for one beat. The dot adds half of that amount (a half beat). To perform the dotted quarter note correctly, giving it the correct 1½ beats, sustain the note *beyond* the starting of the next beat, as if the dotted note were tied instead:

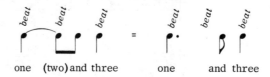

Play "Die Musici" on the piano and as a two-part round on recorders. Check the accuracy of your performance by listening to the recorded version. Because the third line of the song exactly duplicates the first, it would be ineffective to start a third part at that point.

Another round, in Latin, includes the same dotted half and dotted quarter note values as the preceding German round.

Dona Nobis Pacem
Grant Us Peace

To play "Dona Nobis Pacem" on the recorder you need to become familiar with the fingering for three new notes. Because it requires fewer pitch changes than the melody, a simple ostinato part will help you learn each note more thoroughly. The first new note is middle C. This note may be difficult to play at first, but if you blow gently and evenly it will sound.

Play the following ostinato part three times while someone sings the complete round or plays it on the piano.

Now try a slightly more interesting ostinato with an additional new note.

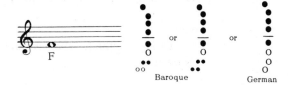

Again play the revised ostinato line three times as accompaniment to the main melody.

A final new note for this song is:

Try the following ostinato part, then play it three times with the original round.

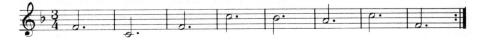

For more challenge, try to play the main melody on the recorder. Keep a steady beat and give special attention to the rhythmic accuracy of the dotted half and dotted quarter notes. Remember to slur without the "doo" articulation of the tongue after the first note of each slur. Tongue only on the unslurred notes.

Sixteenth Notes

One common note value has not yet been encountered in the songs in this book. It is the sixteenth note (♪), which is only half as long as an eighth note. In a chart of note values its duration compares as follows:

The sixteenth rest resembles an eighth rest, except that it has two flags instead of one: ꓽ

Various rhythmic syllables can be used for sixteenth notes. Among them are the following:

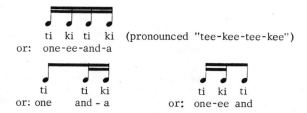

To help you feel the relationship between quarter, eighth, and sixteenth notes, perform the following exercise several times in succession while you clap or tap and say the counting or rhythmic syllables:

The dotted eighth and sixteenth (♪.♪) is a common pattern that is often performed inaccurately. Notice how the combination is notated for ease of reading: the sixteenth note shares one beam in common with the adjoining eighth note, and its other flag is open-ended. (The figure ⌣♪♪ is visually more helpful, but it takes up more space and is seldom encountered in actual notation.) The two-note dotted pattern lasts as long as one quarter note or four sixteenth notes. In fact, all three rhythms occur consecutively in measures 3 and 4 of the next song. Read the phrase rhythmically while tapping a steady quarter note beat and saying rhythmic syllables on each note:

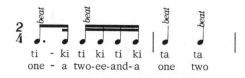

Notice that this two-measure pattern appears four times, consuming eight of the sixteen measures in "All the Pretty Little Horses." Repetition and fanciful imagery are common in lullabies.

On the recording notice the difference between two even eighth notes, as on the words "Hush - a," and the dotted-eighth and sixteenth notes, as on the words "Go to."

All the Pretty Little Horses (*Recorded*)

"Drill, Ye Tarriers" contains many sixteenth note combinations. Read the rhythm of the entire song with neutral syllables, counts, or rhythmic syllables until you feel secure with it. You may also want to clap or tap the rhythm.

Drill, Ye Tarriers (*Recorded*)

twen-ty tar-ri-ers a-work-ing at the rock, And the
tell you sure__ he's a blame__ mean__ man; Last__
Goff was short__ one__ buck,__ he__ found;"What__

boss comes a-long and he says, "Keep still, And
week a__ prema-ture__ blast went off, And a
for?" says__ he; then__ this re-ply, "You're

come down heav-y on the cast iron drill."
mile in the air__ went__ Big Jim Goff.
docked for the time__ you were up in the sky."

So drill, ye tar-ri-ers, drill, And drill, ye tar-ri-ers,

drill! Oh, it's work all day for sug-ar in your tay,

Down be-yond the rail-way, And drill, ye tar-ri-ers, drill!

Word association may help you to remember and execute rhythmic patterns. Any four-syllable word with an accented first syllable will do for sixteenths—"drom-e-dar-y," "al-a-bas-ter," "wa-ter-mel-on," and many more. Even the combinations can be linked with the words of songs you have learned. "Tar-ri-ers" from "Drill, Ye Tarriers" can be a musical reminder of the ♩♩♩ pattern.

"Drill, Ye Tarriers" is a song from the nineteenth century when the railroads were being built. The word "tay" in the chorus means *tea*. The word "tarriers" has been given several explanations. One is that the beards of the immigrant Irish laborers resembled terrier coats; another is that the railroad work required the men to dig and burrow like terriers; still another is that the men were being rebuked by an impatient foreman for "tarrying" or dawdling over their work. Whatever the derivation of the word, the song has strong rhythmic drive, and this is apparent in the recording. Notice, too, the precision with which the various sixteenth note patterns are sung.

When you can sing the song with accuracy and confidence, try to devise a rhythmic ostinato. The text gives two clues about the type of rhythmic accompaniment that might be appropriate. 1) This is a work song, so the accompanying patterns should be repetitive—almost monotonous—since a simple, steady rhythm historically kept work crews together when they were engaged in hard physical labor. 2) The accompanying part should be simple so it will not detract from the text of the song. The story requires the listener's undivided attention if he is to appreciate the catchy ending. A fancy rhythm would suit neither the demands of the narrative nor the characters described in the story.

Chorale

A *chorale* is a hymn based on a straightforward melody that is sung by the congregation during a service. Traditionally there are additional parts for the choir and organ. The following chorale features the dotted eighth and sixteenth pattern. This particular melody is called the "St. Anthony Chorale," and it appears in a piece composed by Franz Joseph Haydn. A century later, in the 1870s, Johannes Brahms used the melody as the basis for an orchestral composition of his own.

As you sing this chorale, make a special effort to observe rhythmic accuracy on the dotted patterns.

Song of Praise

© 1966 Follett Publishing Company. Used by permission.

In the second section of this chorale, at the first repeat sign, there is a compositional technique called *sequence:* a short melodic figure is repeated at increasingly higher or lower pitch levels. The pattern begins on D, moves up to E in the next measure, then up to F♯ in the third measure. Almost immediately afterward, the same figure starts on C, moves down to B in the next measure, and down to A in the third measure. A sequence usually contains at least three successive appearances of the pattern, but more than that number is less common because, if overdone, a sequence loses its effect.

Double Dotted Notes

It's possible to have a *double dotted* note, as in the following march. The second dot adds half the value of the first dot, which is already adding half the value of the note. So the second dot adds one-fourth the value of the note. In the following illustration, it is assumed that a quarter note lasts for one beat, as it does in "Men of Harlech."

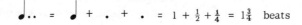

Men of Harlech

"Men of Harlech" is highly effective when the double dotted patterns are maintained throughout the song. The temptation, when performing ♩.. ♪, is to even out the two notes into a simple ♩. ♪ pattern. To prevent this, think a background of four sixteenth notes within every quarter-note beat, and wait to add the short note until it jibes perfectly with the proper background sixteenth note.

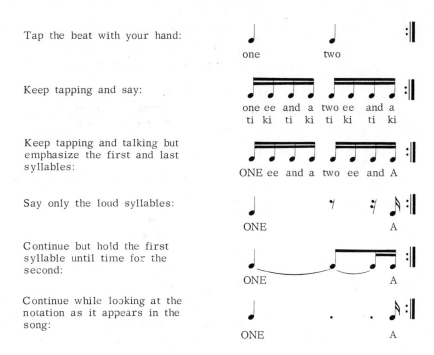

Tap the beat with your hand:

one   two

Keep tapping and say:

one ee and a two ee and a
ti ki ti ki ti ki ti ki

Keep tapping and talking but emphasize the first and last syllables:

ONE ee and a two ee and A

Say only the loud syllables:

ONE   A

Continue but hold the first syllable until time for the second:

ONE   A

Continue while looking at the notation as it appears in the song:

ONE   A

As you can see in measure 12 of "Men of Harlech," rests may be dotted, as well as notes. The most common dotted rests are shown below, with an acceptable alternative notation.

Dotted sixteenth notes are possible, but are rare in the songs that are most appropriate for classroom use.

Here are two last bits of advice in regard to dot usage. 1) Do not confuse a dot *under* or *over* the note head with the dot on the right side that lengthens a note. The dot above or below the note actually makes it shorter, creating a different style, usually called *staccato*. 2) A dot should not extend the duration of a note or rest into the next measure. To extend a sound or silence over the bar line, write a tie for continued sound or a new rest for continued silence:

THIS: $\frac{4}{4}$ ⬭ | 𝅗𝅥 ▬ | NOT THIS: $\frac{4}{4}$ ⬭· | ▬ |

(6 beats)   (2 beats)

THIS: $\frac{2}{4}$ ♩ 𝄽 | ▬ | NOT THIS: $\frac{2}{4}$ ♩ ▬ | 𝄽 |

(3 beats) (1 beat)

Creating More Complex Patterns

The old saying that "Necessity is the mother of invention" is true. Limitations often bring forth imaginative efforts—the development of the "sight gag" in the old silent movies is one example. Let's see if some prescribed limitations will encourage imaginative thinking on your part.

Here are specifications for a creative exercise:

Length: 8 measures

Meter: $\frac{3}{4}$

Rhythms, with frequency of usage:

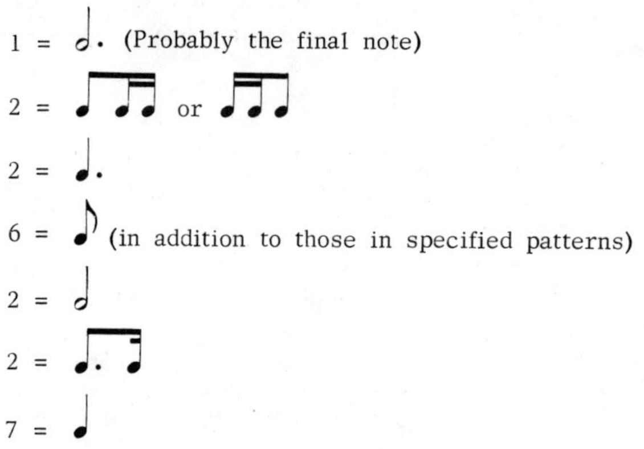

1 = 𝅗𝅥. (Probably the final note)

2 = ♩♫ or ♩♫

2 = ♩.

6 = ♪ (in addition to those in specified patterns)

2 = 𝅗𝅥

2 = ♩. ♪

7 = ♩

Pitches: C F G A B♭

Final pitch: F

Dynamics: 2 measures soft

2 measures loud

4 measures moderate

Two approaches seem equally workable. You may want to follow the procedures suggested in chapter 4: determine the pitches and then work out the rhythm. Or you may prefer to think out the rhythmic pattern first, making sure you include the specified note values and patterns.

When your exercise is completed, play it on the recorder or piano. Finally, sing it on a neutral syllable.

Exercises

1. Execute the following rhythmic patterns with a neutral syllable, rhythmic syllables, or counting. Then clap or tap the pattern.

a)
b)
c)
d)
e)

2. Fill in the *one note* needed to complete the measure.

3. On the staff below, transpose "Sing and Rejoice" (page 41) so that all its
pitches are one step lower. Then play the transposed version on the recorder or
piano.

4. Practice the following phrases on the recorder and/or piano.

5. Select a poem and say it to yourself rhythmically, noticing the patterns of
stressed and unstressed syllables. Write the patterns in rhythmic notation.

Review Questions   1. What is a slur in music?

2. A dot to the right of a note adds _____ to the value of the note.

3. a) A 𝅘𝅥𝅭 equals _____ ♪ notes.

   b) A ♪. equals _____ ♬ notes.

   c) A 𝅗𝅥. equals _____ ♪ notes or _____ 𝅘𝅥 notes.

4. Fill in the *one note* needed to complete the measure.

5. a) What rhythmic syllables may be applied to 𝅘𝅥𝅘𝅥𝅘𝅥𝅘𝅥?

   b) What counting syllables may be applied to 𝅘𝅥𝅘𝅥𝅘𝅥𝅘𝅥?

   c) What words might help a person to execute 𝅘𝅥𝅘𝅥𝅘𝅥𝅘𝅥?

6. What is a chorale?

7. A sequence is:

   a) the immediate repetition of a melodic pattern
   b) the delayed repetition of a melodic pattern
   c) the repetition of a melodic pattern at a different pitch level
   d) the repetition of a melodic pattern with different rhythmic values
   e) the slight alteration of a melodic pattern when it is repeated

8. What does a dot over or under a note indicate?

9. Describe the appearance and function of the two repeat signs.

6 Tone Quality and Playing the Autoharp

Every musical instrument has a characteristic sound that makes it unique. The human voice is equally distinctive, whether speaking or singing. Simple rhythm and melody instruments, available in most classrooms, provide a good introduction to differences in sound. The chance to experiment with instruments can contribute significantly to an understanding of tone quality, sometimes referred to as tone color or *timbre*.

Rhythm Instruments

The most common rhythm instruments—those that produce no specific pitches—are described below.

Drum	A stretched skin or membrane struck with the fingers or a beater.
Castanets	Two small, hollow, wooden cup-shaped pieces attached to a handle and sounded by a whip-like motion of the player's wrist, or struck against the palm of the hand or leg, or held in one hand and tapped together by the fingers of the other hand.
Claves (Clah-vays)	Two wooden blocks, one of which is held between the base of the thumb and ends of the fingers and struck with the other.
Coconut shells	Two hollowed half-spheres, struck together on the open ends, hit singly on a flat surface, or struck on the outside with a mallet.
Cymbals	Large metal discs struck together or suspended singly and hit with a mallet or brush.
Finger cymbals	Small metal discs struck against one another on their edges for a metallic, bell-like sound.
Guiro (Guee-roh or Wee-roh)	A notched gourd scraped across the notches by a stick.
Maracas	Rattles, often in pairs, that are shaken to produce the sound of moving pellets.
Rhythm sticks	Two dowel rods that are hit against one another.
Tambourine	A skin or membrane stretched across a wood hoop that has metal discs around its edge; these produce a jangling sound when the instrument is shaken, struck on the center with the knuckles, tapped with the fingers, or played with mallets.
Tone or Temple blocks	Wooden blocks struck with a mallet for a hollow, resonant sound.

55

Triangle	A three-sided suspended metal frame struck with a beater to produce a clear metallic sound.
Sandblocks	Sandpaper stretched over wooden blocks to cause a raspy effect when scraped against one another.
Sleigh or Jingle bells	Small spherical bells attached to a strap or frame and shaken for a light jingling effect.

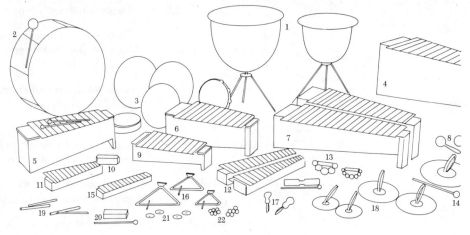

1	Kettle drums	9	Soprano xylophone	17	Castanets
2	Bass drum	10	Box rattle	18	Hanging cymbals
3	Tambours (hand drum)	11	Alto glockenspeil	19	Claves
4	Bass xylophone	12	Alto-soprano glockenspeil	20	Wood block
5	Alto metallophone	13	Bell spray	21	Finger cymbal
6	Alto xylophone	14	Felt head beater	22	Sleigh bells
7	Alto-soprano xylophone	15	Soprano glockenspeil		
8	Gourd	16	Triangles		

Interesting sound effects can be produced by the body alone. They include such sounds as tongue-clucking, finger snapping, and clapping hands together or on the thighs. Singing and whistling also qualify, but such sounds are pitched. Experiment with echo rhythms produced by the body: analyze the tone quality of each, then imitate one another's rhythms and notate them.

Experiment also with the sounds of commonplace objects. Keep a list of the most distinctive sounds produced from unlikely sources.

Melody Instruments

Melody instruments produce definite pitches. They include:

Glockenspiel and bells	Metal strips arranged in keyboard fashion and slightly upraised from their supporting frame; struck with a mallet. In a set of resonator bells, each bar is mounted on a separate hollow block which can be removed from the special box in which the set is stored.
Xylophone	Similar to the glockenspiel except for its wooden bars, which are mounted on resonating devices.
Recorder, songflute, and flutophone	Wind instruments on which holes are covered to alter the length of the air column and thereby change the pitch.
Piano	Keyboard instrument capable of producing 88 pitches.

Accompanying Instruments

Other instruments produce pitches, but in the classroom they are generally used to accompany singing because they can produce several notes simultaneously. These instruments, in addition to the piano, are:

Autoharp	Metal strings stretched across a frame and strummed to produce a group of sounds determined by a pushbutton mechanism regulated by the other hand.
Ukulele and guitar	Strings stretched on a hollow wooden body for resonance and plucked or strummed with the fingers.

Orff Instruments

Many classrooms today have instruments especially developed for elementary school children under the direction of the contemporary German composer Carl Orff. Among these instruments are metallophones and xylophones of different sizes, as well as medieval types of string instruments and several of the rhythm instruments mentioned earlier in this chapter. The main features of these instruments are the fine quality of their sound and their adaptability for classroom use. For example, the bars on the metallophones and xylophones can be removed so that an unwanted pitch will not be sounded accidentally by the student.

Enriching a Song with Rhythm Instruments

Three contrasting songs will illustrate how to judge which rhythm instruments can best be played with each song. The emphasis is on the choice of appropriate tone color rather than specific rhythmic patterns.

In "Drill, Ye Tarriers" on page 47, the words speak of "rock," "cast iron drill," and "blast." The quality of the accompanying instruments, therefore, should be metallic, heavy, and rough. A recorder tone quality would be inappropriate. Experiment with various sound effects until you find a quality that matches both the subject of the song and the rhythmic patterns you have chosen for your ostinato.

"The Peddler" offers magic charms, potions, and enchanted objects to believing buyers. Such words suggest an exotic and somewhat Arabian influence, so the instrumental accompaniment should be light and delicate—perhaps involving triangle, finger cymbals, and tambourine. Make up a rhythmic ostinato of appropriate tone colors to enhance the mood of the song. Write it down so the class can perform it. Notice that several accidentals appear in the music. In the refrain, the word "Aida" is pronounced EYE•da.

The Peddler

© 1966 Follett Publishing Company. Used by permission.

The preceding two songs, one about railroad workers and the other about a seller of magic, require different tone qualities in the accompanying instruments. A third type of tone quality is suggested by "Giddap, Old Dobbin." The most obvious suggestion is a horse's clip-clop, which can be produced in at least four ways: 1) tap on a tone block or on temple blocks; 2) hold a broad-rimmed heavy paper cup in each hand and hit the two open ends together; 3) round the hands as if holding an orange in each one, and clap the empty hands together by hitting only on their edges; 4) tap coconut shells on a desk top or hit the halves together.

Giddap, Old Dobbin

B. P. K. and M. T. K.

Beatrice P. Krone
and Max T. Krone

© 1966 Follett Publishing Company. Used by permission.

Four times in the first half of the song (this is the verse, or stanza, in contrast to the refrain), a syllable starts before the listener expects it, and then it's tied over into the beat on which it "should" have occurred. These alterations, described in chapter 2, produce syncopation by creating a conflict between what is felt (the beat) and what is actually heard (the note). The examples in "Giddap, Old Dobbin" are in measures 2, 4, 6, and 7. Practice reading the pattern in three stages, beginning with the preliminary step of eliminating the tie:

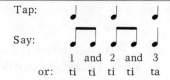

```
Tap:    ♩    ♩    ♩
Say:   ♫    ♫    ♩
       1  and 2 and 3
   or: ti  ti ti ti ta
```

Next add the tie, eliminating the syllable on the quarter note because it is now a continuation of the preceding sound:

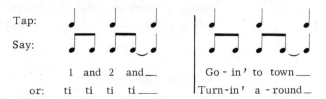

```
Tap:     ♩    ♩    ♩   |   ♩    ♩    ♩
Say:   ♫    ♫   ♫  |  ♫    ♫   ♫
       1  and 2  and__  | Go - in' to town__
   or: ti  ti ti ti __  | Turn-in' a - round__
```

The fourth example of syncopation in the verse is similar. Say it first without the tie, then with it, as written:

```
Tap:    ♩    ♩    ♩  |   ♩    ♩    ♩  |   ♩    ♩    ♩
Say:   ♩   ♫   ♩  |  ♩   ♫  ♩ |  ♩   ♫  ♩
       1   2 and 3  |  1   2 and__ | miles to go__
   or: ta  ti ti ta |  ta  ti ti __ |
```

When you have learned the song, get together with another person or group and sing the verse and refrain simultaneously; they fit together nicely. The sign *D.S.* (*dal Segno*) *al Fine* means to return to the sign 𝄋 and sing to the Fine (FEE-nay, meaning *end*). The note head on the word "Whoa!" is an X to indicate that it is spoken, not sung.

'round.   clip, clop, clip, clop,   clip, clip, clop.   Whoa!

fore sun - down.   *Whistle* _____   Whoa!
fore sun - down.

Enriching a Song with the Autoharp

Earlier in this chapter the autoharp was described as an instrument with metal strings stretched across a frame. These are strummed with one hand while the other determines the choice of note combinations by pressing a pushbutton. With its long side toward the player, the autoharp is usually laid on the lap or a flat surface, although a seated player can cradle it in an upright position in one arm and press the buttons with that same hand. Each button represents a different chord. A *chord* is the simultaneous sounding of three or more pitches. When a button is pushed, it depresses a set of felt bars that deaden the unwanted strings. For example, when the F button is pushed, only the pitches that make up the F chord are allowed to vibrate when the instrument is strummed.

To tune an autoharp, compare the pitch of a given string with its counterpart on a pitch pipe, piano, or other instrument with a fixed pitch. Place the tuning key down squarely on the tuning pin and turn it slowly to the right to raise the pitch and to the left to lower it. When you have tuned one note—a C, for example—to a standard pitch, tune every C on the autoharp, in its respective octave, before you move to a different note. If you have a "good ear," you can slowly strum a complete chord that includes the tuned strings, identify the pitches that need adjustment, and then strum another chord that has some of the same notes in it, checking the new strings against those already tuned.

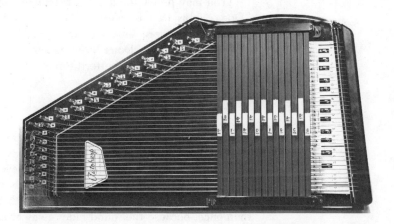

It's advisable to strum the autoharp with your most dexterous hand. If you are right-handed, therefore, you will have to cross your right hand over your left in order to strum at the most advantageous spot—midway along the strings' length. Newer models are being constructed for the convenience of right-handed players.

The number of chord bars on an autoharp determines how much variety of chord selection is possible on that instrument. The chord symbols suggested for the songs in this book assume that a 15-bar autoharp is available to the player.

The tone of the autoharp can be varied somewhat by the type of pick that is used for strumming. A felt pick gives a softer and less metallic sound than a plastic pick. If neither is available, another item, such as an eraser or paper clip, can be substituted to produce the desired tone quality.

Different types and speeds of strumming give further variety. Although the best tone is achieved by strumming near the middle of the instrument, you can play to the right side of the chord bars for a thinner sound. The motion of your hand, wherever it is strumming, can be confined to the short, higher-pitched strings or to the lower, more resonant strings, or it can encompass the whole range of pitches for a more brilliant effect. For the heavy first beat of the measure, you can strum a short firm stroke over a few low notes, then play the less emphasized beats with a lighter strum over the higher pitches. It's also possible to extend the thumb and index finger apart and then pluck the strings with a pinching motion that draws the thumb and index finger together.

The speed with which you repeat the strumming strokes depends on the character of the piece. For a peppy song, frequent repetition of the chords helps to maintain a brisk tempo. If the music is quiet and introspective, it's advisable to strum less often. In any case, the rhythm of the strumming must relate to the music.

An instrumental accompaniment is seldom heard with a round because the singers' parts automatically supply the desired chords as the various sections join in the song. Sometimes, however, an instrumental accompaniment helps the singers stay in tune. Furthermore, most short rounds can be accompanied with only one chord, so they provide a good opportunity for the beginning player to become accustomed to the autoharp. (A list of such songs is found in the Index.) For "Frère Jacques" on page 4, hold down the F (not F7) button on the autoharp and strum according to your feeling of the beat. You may want to establish either of the following beat speeds:

Fre - re   Jac - ques   or   Fre - re   Jac - ques

You may prefer to alter the rhythmic pattern for variety. Longer rounds, like "Dona Nobis Pacem" on page 44, can involve chord changes because the longer phrases allow more time for new chords to be introduced and resolved to the "home" chord. Play "Dona Nobis Pacem" with a change of chord on each measure, repeating this harmonic pattern three times:

To accompany songs with the autoharp when chord symbols are given, merely push the button indicated and strum at appropriate times. Because chord symbols are provided only when a chord changes, several strums can be made even though only one symbol appears. For example, only one chord symbol is provided for the first two measures of "Simple Gifts," but that chord needs to be strummed more than once, because the sound fades away after a few beats.

Although the meaning of chord symbols has not been explained—that will come in chapter 10—you can now accompany some of the songs you sing by pressing the autoharp chord buttons that are presented in the music.

"Simple Gifts" is an example of the music of the "Shaking Quakers," or Shakers, who brought their religion from England to the United States in 1774. They were noted for their simplicity and piety, and for the style of dancing (or "devotional exercises") with which they dramatized their songs. Their inclination toward movement is explained in this traditional Shaker poem:

With every gift I will unite, and join in sweet devotion;
To worship God is my delight, with hands and feet in motion.

Simple Gifts

American Shaker Song

'Tis the gift to be sim-ple, 'Tis the gift to be free, 'Tis the gift to come down where we ought to be, And when we find our-selves in the place just_right 'Twill_ be in the val-ley of love and de-light. When true sim-plic-i-ty is gained, To bow and to bend we will not be a-shamed. To turn,_to_turn,_will_ be our de-light And by turn-ing, turn-ing we come 'round right.

The tone quality of a recorder fits well with the sentiment of "Simple Gifts." Practice playing the song on that instrument after you have learned to sing it. Then follow the printed chord symbols as you accompany yourself on the autoharp.

"Simple Gifts" has been rewritten for orchestra in the ballet music *Appalachian Spring* by Aaron Copland. Listen to the orchestral version after you have learned the song and compare the two arrangements. Listening to recordings of different instruments and voice combinations is an excellent way to become familiar with various tone qualities.

Orchestral Instruments: Related Listening

To become acquainted with the tone qualities of orchestral instruments, there is no better work than *The Young Person's Guide to the Orchestra* by Benjamin Britten, a contemporary English composer. In spite of its title, the work is not juvenile in any sense, as you can tell by listening to the recorded portion. For the *theme*—the central melody of an instrumental work—Britten chose a melody by the most esteemed English composer of the seventeenth century, Henry Purcell. The Italian words indicate the appropriate tempo and style for the music—it is to be played "brightly, majestically, and broadly."

(Recorded)

Allegro maestoso e largamente

The first section of Britten's work presents variations based on the theme. The full orchestra is heard first. Next the woodwinds are featured. This group of instruments includes the flute, oboe, clarinet, and bassoon. All of them originally were made of wood, and all except the flute use reeds to produce sound. (The flute is sounded by blowing across a hole in the pipe.) Following the woodwinds come the brasses: trumpet, French horn, trombone, and tuba. They are made of metal, and sound is produced on them by "buzzing" the lips on a cup-shaped mouthpiece. Featured next are the strings: the violin, viola, cello, string bass, and harp. Except for the harp, which is plucked, sound is produced on these instruments by drawing a bow across the strings. The first portion of the music closes by featuring the percussion section. This group includes a wide variety of instruments that produce sound when they are struck or shaken—drums, triangle, and all the rhythm instruments mentioned earlier in this chapter.

Having presented the full orchestra and each group, or "family," of instruments, Britten proceeds through each section from the highest- to the lowest-pitched instruments—the order in which the instruments are cited in the preceding paragraph. Each instrument, even the kettledrums (timpani), is given a solo. The last section of the work is a fugue, a form that will be discussed in the next chapter. The music closes with the full orchestra sounding Purcell's theme.

Creating by Improvising

Improvising is the process of making up music as it is being performed. *Composing*, on the other hand, is the development of a musical work over a period of time. A composed work is written down before it is performed. Both processes have their virtues. Composed works are more carefully planned and remain stable. Improvised pieces reflect more the feeling of the moment and are "fresher" in that they differ with each performance.

Improvising is usually limited to short pieces or sections. Seldom are the musical ideas made up "out of thin air." Instead, improvisation is carried on under guidelines dictated by the particular style of music. These guidelines help the performer by limiting the large number of choices he would have if given complete musical freedom.

One way to learn to improvise is to provide an "answer" to a short phrase. This can be accomplished with rhythm alone:

Instructor
(claps or plays on rhythm instrument)   Student

The answer should *not* be a repetition of what the instructor clapped or played. It should be original. An additional rhythmic phrase to which you can respond is presented on the recording accompanying this book.

When the attempts at improvising rhythmic patterns seem successful, try improvising with pitches. Select only three pitches for the first try—perhaps E, G, and A. If resonator bells are available, move these three bars away from the others so that there is no possibility of hitting unintended pitches. On the piano, place the right thumb on E and the index and second fingers on G and A. Unless you are rather accomplished on the recorder, it is better to use bells or piano for the initial attempts at improvising. An additional pitch phrase to which you can improvise responses is provided on the recording.

The statement-answer technique can be applied again:

Instructor   Student

As you become more experienced at improvising, the phrases can be made longer and more complex.

Exercises

1. Play these patterns on one or more rhythm instruments.

2. Practice singing and playing these phrases.

3. Name the notes while fingering them silently on the recorder, then play the phrases.

Review Questions

1. What is timbre?

2. Briefly describe the following instruments.

   a) cymbals:

   b) claves:

   c) tambourine:

   d) maracas:

   e) melody bells:

   f) autoharp:

3. If you see *D.S. al Fine* in a song, you should _____
   _____.

4. The simultaneous sounding of three pitches is a:

   a) figure

   b) sequence

   c) chord

   d) timbre

   e) trio

5. How can you vary the tone quality of an autoharp?

6. List the instruments that belong to the woodwind family.

   a)

   b)

   c)

   d)

7. List the instruments that belong to the brass family.

   a)

   b)

   c)

   d)

8. List the instruments that belong to the string family.

a)

b)

c)

d)

9. What characteristic do percussion instruments have in common?

7 *Dynamics and Form*

Much of the expressiveness of music is derived from skillful control of dynamics. This term was explained on page 26, and you have produced changes of dynamics in your singing and in your playing of the recorder.

Certain terms and symbols should be recognized by everyone who wants to read music. The terminology for dynamic levels is given here with the basic Italian terms and abbreviations.

p (piano)	= soft		*f (forte)*	= loud
pp (pianissimo)	= very soft		*ff (fortissimo)*	= very loud
	mp = (mezzo piano)	= moderately soft		
	mf = (mezzo forte)	= moderately loud		

A gradual change from one dynamic level to another can be indicated by either words or symbols:

cresc. or *crescendo*	or	◁‾‾‾	= gradually louder
decresc. or *decrescendo*	or	‾‾‾▷	= gradually softer
dim. or *diminuendo*	or	‾‾‾▷	= gradually softer

Indications of dynamic level are not absolute, because a person's impression of loudness or softness depends on 1) what is occurring elsewhere in the music at the same time, 2) what tone qualities are being heard, and 3) what precedes and follows the particular place in the music. When you perform you should exaggerate the differences in dynamic level, because your awareness of the level you are trying to produce tempts you to assume you are communicating your own impressions satisfactorily to the listener. Be sure, then, that you as a performer can actually *hear* the different dynamic shadings you are trying to make.

Look again at "The Goose" on page 6 and pencil in some appropriate dynamic markings, perhaps the following:

(mp)	Once there was a sly old fox who stole a plump fat goose,
(p)	Stole a plump fat goose.
(f)	But the farmer caught him, now he's locked in the caboose,
(mf)	But the farmer caught him, now he's locked in the caboose,
(mp)	Locked in the caboose,
(p)	The caboose,
(pp)	The caboose.

Select dynamics that enhance both the words and the music. For example, in the text above, words about slyness and sneakiness should be somewhat soft. But when the farmer grabs the thief, loudness and the element of surprise help to support the narrative. Sing the song with the indicated dynamic levels and see if it isn't more effective.

68

This interpretation of "The Goose" points up another principle in the selection of appropriate dynamics: when a phrase is repeated immediately with identical words and music, the dynamic level should vary. Exact repetition can quickly become boring, especially when it occurs as frequently as it does in this song.

Maintain a good tone quality at all times, no matter what the dynamic level. The temptation is to sing with a harsh, forced sound in an attempt to achieve a convincing *forte* and with a weak and flabby sound when trying to sing *piano*. Remember that *forte* singing should retain a rich and appealing tone quality, and *piano* singing should sound intense and alive. Application of the vocal techniques described in chapter 3 will help maintain the musical qualities of the voice at every dynamic level.

In "The Goose," the echo effect of the words suggests that each musical phrase should have a consistent dynamic level throughout, with an abrupt increase or decrease in level between the phrases. The dynamics are *terraced* into distinct planes or levels.

In "Camel Caravan," however, the laborious procession, slowly advancing and receding, suggests gradual changes of dynamic level. The words do not tell a story with moments of surprise or sudden intensity. Instead, they create a mood in which the only change is created by the effect of slowly shifting distances. From beginning to end, the dynamic marking on the music might be merely:

For "Camel Caravan," select rhythm instruments that create an Arabian effect—perhaps finger cymbals, triangle, tambourine, and drum. Now sing the song with the rhythm instruments and the ostinato parts, all producing the long crescendo and diminuendo. When these dynamics are controlled and even, with consistently good tone quality in all voices and instruments, the effect is interesting and musical.

The following two rounds also are appropriate for a gradual crescendo and diminuendo. The pitch level of the melody reaches its highest point near the middle of each song, and this suggests an increase in loudness to that point. The controlled fluctuation of dynamics in a round creates an interesting wave-like effect, because the ebb and flow of the sound moves from one section to another as the music progresses.

The Wind in the Willows

The wind in the wil-lows sigh-ing like a sol-i-tar-y soul a-lone.

Ah, Poor Bird

Ah, poor bird, Take your flight, Far a-bove the sor-rows of this dark night.

You already know how to play on the recorder all the notes in "Ah, Poor Bird." By learning one new note you can also play "The Wind in the Willows." The note is high C♯:

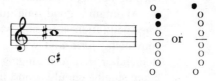

Form

An awareness of *form* in music requires a memory for musical phrases and the ability to distinguish between segments that are the same as, or different from, musical material heard earlier. Musical form is the overall design of repetition and contrast on which a composition is based. Because it gives you an overview of the music, recognizing the form of a piece can help you interpret it.

When analyzing form, the first phrase or first section (depending on whether the piece is short or long) is labeled *a* or *A*. The next portion, if the music is different, is labeled *b* or *B*. If a later portion is different from both of these, it is called *c* or *C*, and so on. Portions that are slightly different, but are not actually new material, are called *b′* (b prime) or whatever letter applies.

Many pieces of good music do not fit neatly into formal schemes, and this is to be expected, since composers are free to structure their works in any way they wish. Furthermore, musicians sometimes disagree in their judgments of phrase length and other factors that bear on the labeling of a form. Nevertheless, some of the songs in this book can reasonably be described as follows, with the number representing the number of measures in each phrase. Introductions (as in "Camel Caravan" or "Hanukah") which merely establish an ostinato part are not counted in the formal structure.

"Hot Cross Buns" (page 19)	2 2 2 2 *a a b a*
"Ash Grove" (page 11)	8 8 8 8 *a a b a*
"Hanukah" (page 35)	2 2 2 2 *a b a c*
"Now All the Woods Are Sleeping" (page 99)	2 2 2 2 2 *a b c a b c′*
"The Peddler" (page 58)	4 4 4 4 *a b b c c*
"Simple Gifts" (page 63)	4 4 4 4 *a a′ b a′*
"Tangalayo" (page 71)	4 4 4 4 4 *a a′ b b′ a a′*

"Tangalayo" has a balanced three-part form in which contrasting material is sandwiched between two appearances of the original material. *D.C. al Fine* stands for *da Capo al Fine*, meaning "return to the beginning and continue to the *Fine*." This type of repetition produces an overall *a b a* form.

Tangalayo

Tan - ga - lay - o! Come, lit - tle don - key,
come; Tan - ga - lay - o! Come, lit - tle don - key come.
My don - key walk, my don - key balk, my don - key,
he has such a fun - ny talk! My don - key go, my don - key
stop, my don - key look a - round and then he drop!

First establish the rhythms of "Tangalayo" by clapping, tapping, or saying them with syllables. Observe the rests, because they delineate the phrases and contribute to the vigor of the song by enforcing short note values. When you can sing the song with accuracy and spirit, choose rhythm instruments—perhaps maracas, claves, and bongo drums—with which to play ostinato parts derived from the rhythms of the song.

Rounds are generally *through-composed,* with new material throughout, because repeated material would not create the pitch variety that is necessary when all the voice parts are singing at the same time. See if you can find at least four other through-composed songs (not rounds) in one of the elementary series books.

Some songs are obviously irregular in form. Others have a *coda* (Italian for *tail*). This is a final portion of music that is somewhat different from the preceding structure.

Fugue

As pointed out in the discussion of *The Young Person's Guide to the Orchestra* (chapter 6), the final section of that work is a *fugue* (pronounced "fewg"). A fugue is like a round in that a melody, called the *subject,* is imitated in several other lines. The fugue is more sophisticated, however, because it adds a *countersubject* and much *free material* in addition to the subject. The subject for Britten's fugue first appears in the piccolo and flute, with a tempo marking that means *very fast.*

The countersubject consists of several short phrases, including this adaptation of the Purcell theme:

After they play the countersubject, the piccolo and flutes have free material that contrasts with the music of the other parts. Other instruments are also given a chance to play the subject as they enter, and they appear in the same order in which they were presented in the first half of the work. When all the parts have played the subject and countersubject, the *exposition* of the fugue is completed. For the rest of the fugue the subject and countersubject are interspersed with free material.

This work is an excellent one for learning the sounds of orchestral instruments because each has its turn playing the subject. Listen to the recording and notice each instrument as it enters: piccolo and flute, oboe, clarinet, bassoon, violin, viola, cello, string bass, harp, French horn, trumpet, trombone and tuba, and percussion. The fugue closes with the opening theme and the fugue subject sounding together as the music reaches a climax of sound.

Art Song

There is a type of song in which the sound of the piano is considered essential to the effectiveness of the music. Franz Schubert wrote more than six hundred of these songs, called by the German word *lieder*, or *art songs*. They are pieces showing a close unity between words and music, and the piano accompaniment is imaginatively constructed to contribute to the mood of the song. One of Schubert's best-known art songs is "The Trout." It is included in the records so that you can hear how the piano accompaniment enhances the melody by suggesting a darting fish and rippling water. You may find the music easier to sing if you chant the words with their proper rhythms before you try to sing the melody.

Die Forelle (*Recorded*)
The Trout

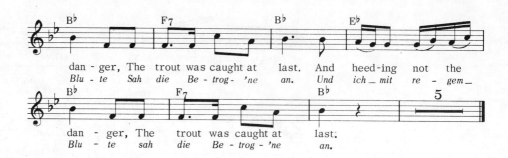

dan - ger, The trout was caught at   last.   And   heed-ing   not   the
Blu - te Sah   die   Be - trog - 'ne   an.   Und   ich _ mit   re - gem _

dan - ger, The   trout was caught at   last;
Blu - te sah   die   Be - trog - 'ne   an.

A measure containing only a long horizontal beam with a figure above it (see beginning and end of "The Trout") indicates a rest for that many measures. To keep your place during so long a silence, count to yourself as follows, assuming there are two beats per measure as in this song: "ONE two, TWO two, THREE two, FOUR two, FIVE two." In other words, substitute the measure number for the "one" in each meter pattern. Remember that the number appearing with the horizontal beam refers to the total number of silent *measures*, not just to individual silent *beats*.

Related Listening

Franz Schubert must have liked the melody he composed for "The Trout," because in 1819 he used it as a theme for one movement of a quintet for piano and four strings: violin, viola, cello, and string bass. This combination of string instruments is a bit unusual because the customary choice consists of two violins, viola, and cello. The title of the work is Quintet in A Major, Op. 114. (The word *major* will be explained in chapter 8.) The letters *Op.* stand for *opus*, the Latin word for *work*. Composers often assigned a number to each of their compositions. This quintet was number 114 in Schubert's list. Like many extended compositions, this one is divided into movements. A *movement* is a sizable independent section of a musical work.

The fourth movement is the only one of the five that contains the "Trout" melody. The form of the movement is called *theme and variations*. Each variation is rather easy to follow, and most of them are about one minute in length. The opening phrases of each variation are presented on the records included in this book.

The theme is presented by the violin.

Violin

The first variation features the piano playing a decorated version of the theme.

Piano

The second variation presents the theme in the viola, while the violin plays a decorated contrasting melody above the theme.

In the third variation the melody is carried by the low strings—the cello and the bass. The piano plays rapidly moving thirty-second notes (♪), each of which is only half the length of a sixteenth note.

The mood of the music changes in the fourth variation, becoming somber and dramatic. The "Trout" theme is still strongly implied, however.

The fifth variation more closely resembles the original "Trout" melody. The rhythm is decorated a bit and the theme is heard in the cello, while the piano adds contrasting figures.

The theme returns very clearly in the last variation. The piano plays the same darting figure that is heard in the accompaniment of the song and gives the feel of a trout playing in a stream.

As you listen to the fourth movement of the "Trout" Quintet, however, you should not be trying to picture a swimming trout. The musical point of this work is what Schubert does with sounds: for example, the manner in which he slightly alters the theme for each variation, manipulates the contrasting figures, and changes the character in the fourth variation.

If you have trouble keeping the theme in mind as you listen, once or twice (but not every time) sing "The Trout" to yourself as you listen. It fits quite closely with the music of the Quintet.

Creating Variations

Since Schubert has provided such a good example of a theme and variations, it seems appropriate to explore that principle of creating music. So far in this book, the elements of pitch, rhythm, dynamics, and tone quality have been introduced. Each will be the basis for a variation on a theme.

Here are the specifications for a theme and its variations:

1. Theme: eight measures in length, simple, easy to remember, and playable on the recorder
   Pitches: D E F♯ G A B C
   Meter and note values: free choice, but keep it *simple*
   Dynamics: at least two levels
2. One variation involving "decoration" of the pitches of the theme
3. One variation involving changes of rhythm
4. One variation utilizing different tone qualities, including some simple rhythm instruments

Write out your musical creation so that it can be performed.

Exercises

1. Sing the round "Ah, Poor Bird" (page 69) with these dynamic markings:

   a) ———————————— to measure 3 and ———————————— to the end.

   b) first measure *p*, second measure *mf*, third *f*, and fourth *mf*.

2. Practice these recorder exercises.

3. Sing these phrases with the note names, then check your singing by playing the exercises on the recorder.

Review Questions

1. *Cresc.* means to:

   a) slow down

   b) get louder

   c) get softer

   d) punch out the note with more emphasis

   e) change the tone quality

2. The full name of the piano is *pianoforte,* which means_____

   _____.

3. Form in music refers to_____

   _____.

4. What does the term *through-composed* mean?

5. What is a coda?

6. The main theme of a fugue is called the
    a) subject
    b) countersubject
    c) figure
    d) major
    e) melody

7. A close unity between words and music is a feature of the _____ song.

8. Describe some ways in which Schubert varies the theme in his "Trout" Quintet.

8 Major Scales and Key Signatures

Sing the opening phrase of the Christmas carol "Joy to the World." If you have the melody clearly in mind, make a simple graph-like representation of the pitches, much as you were asked to do at the beginning of chapter 3. Next, number the pitches of the phrase. Start with 8 and go backwards through the numbers, because the pitches descend and the letter names, therefore, go backwards in the alphabet. (Assign 8 to the word "Joy," 7 to "to," and so on until "come," which is numbered 1.)

Now, using your drawing and your memory of the pitches, decide which distances between the pitches are half steps and which are whole steps. Is the distance between 8 and 7 the same as between 7 and 6? Sing back and forth between the two numbers or words if you are in doubt.

Major Scale

What you will discover by doing this is the pattern of the *major scale*. A *scale* is a series of pitches ascending or descending in a prescribed pattern of intervals. If your efforts with "Joy to the World" result in whole steps between 1-2, 2-3, 4-5, 5-6, and 6-7 with half steps between 3-4 and 7-8, you have perceived the pattern of the major scale correctly.

It is important to understand the various aspects of music, including scale patterns, in terms of sound. If you need to recall the sound of the descending major scale, you can think of "Joy to the World." If you want to think of the ascending pattern, refer to the opening phrase of another Christmas carol, "The First Noël," beginning on the third note of the song.

A scale usually consists of eight pitches, the eighth pitch having the same letter name as the first. A scale can be built on any note, which is then called the *tonal center, tonic,* or *keynote.* Consecutive numbers are often applied to the steps of a scale to indicate the relationship of the notes to one another. Here is a scale with C as its keynote. Play it on the piano, both ascending and descending, to become accustomed to its sound.

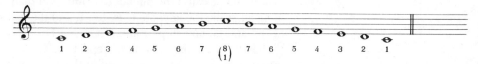

When eight-note scales are written on the staff, they use each line and space—every letter—between the low and high keynote. For example, there cannot be an F and an F♯ in the same scale, because some other letter would then be left out entirely.

As you discovered at the beginning of this chapter, a major scale has this pattern of whole and half steps:

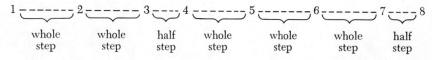

79

To help you remember the pattern, think of the initials W W H W W W H.

A scale can also be pictured as a flight of steps. The steps are not of equal height, however. In a major scale the interval between steps 3-4 and 7-8 is only a half step. Listen also to the major scales recorded for this book. The scales begin on different keynotes, but the pattern of whole and half steps remains the same.

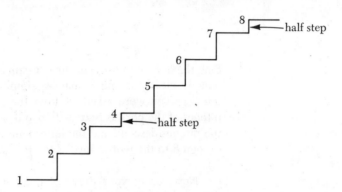

Play the C major scale again on the piano and observe the arrangement of the piano keys at the points where the half steps occur. At E-F and B-C there is no black key between the two adjacent white keys. This indicates that the white keys there are tuned a half step apart, rather than a whole step. Playing any scale on the piano is an excellent way to see and hear the interval relationships of that scale.

Let's return to the two Christmas carols again and this time examine them in notation. The complete major scale has been bracketed in each excerpt. Only the first phrase is presented because the songs are well known.

D is the keynote (step 1) in both of these examples, and the key signature indicates that two sharps, F♯ and C♯, are necessary to make the music sound major. Those sharps cause the pitches to conform to the pattern of whole and half steps for a major scale: the keynote D is step 1, and the half steps occur between steps 3 and 4 (F♯ and G) and steps 7 and 8 (C♯ and D).

Here is a song in which steps 1, 3, 5, and 8 are prominent. The text is a paraphrase of Psalm 23 as found in the Scottish Psalter of about 1650. The words and usage are quaint, but they add a simple charm to the music.

Brother James' Air

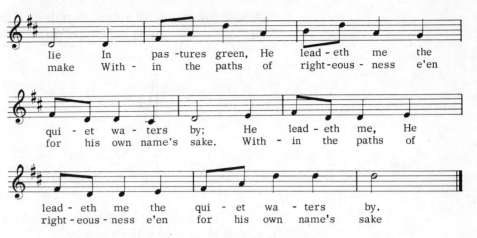

lie In pas -tures green, He lead - eth me the
make With - in the paths of right-eous - ness e'en

qui - et wa - ters by; He lead - eth me, He
for his own name's sake. With - in the paths of

lead - eth me the qui - et wa - ters by.
right - eous - ness e'en for his own name's sake

3. Yea, though I walk in death's dark vale,
   Yet will I fear no ill;
   For thou art with me and thy rod
   And staff me comfort still;
   For thou art with me and thy rod
   And staff me comfort still.

4. My table thou hast furnished
   In presence of my foes;
   My head thou dost with oil anoint
   And my cup overflows;
   My head thou dost with oil anoint
   And my cup overflows.

5. Goodness and mercy all my life
   Shall surely follow me;
   And in God's house forevermore
   My dwelling place shall be;
   And in God's house forevermore
   My dwelling place shall be.

You can play "Brother James' Air" on the recorder with the addition of one new note:

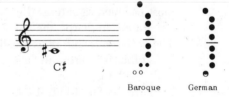

C♯

Baroque   German

This C♯ on German recorders requires a half-hole fingering: the little finger of the right hand only partially covers the lowest hole. Practice this technique by playing low D and C♯ alternately, rolling or leaning the little finger downward onto the upper edge of the hole from above. Also practice approaching the C♯ from C♮, rolling the same finger upward from its position over the C hole.

The triple meter of "Brother James' Air" requires a three-beat conducting pattern:

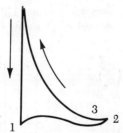

The first beat again moves downward and the last beat of the measure goes upward. To direct the upbeat of this or any other song, think the tempo of the silent beats that occur just before the upbeat, then direct them and begin the first note of the song at the proper spot in that preparatory measure. "Brother James' Air" should be started like this:

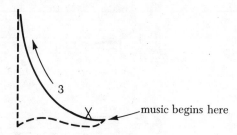

music begins here

Practice this preparation procedure several times, until you can direct the beginning of the song with confidence.

The key of "Brother James' Air" is D major, because the notes want to center around and end on D. *Key* is the effect created when several pitches are related to the same tonal center. If these tones are rearranged to form a scale, the starting note of the scale (step 1) is also the name of the key.

Determining the Key by its Signature

As pointed out in chapter 4, the key signature is the group of sharps or flats placed after the clef at the beginning of the staff. Every sharp or flat in the key signature applies to its particular note throughout the piece unless the composer later cancels it with a natural sign. The key signature indicates the tonal center of a composition. Awareness of the tonal center helps you sing in tune—with better pitch—because it enables you to anticipate the relationship of the notes to one another.

How can you determine the tonal center? It's a good idea to memorize the most common signatures. But you can figure out the major keys as follows: If the signature is in sharps, the last sharp to the right is always step 7 of the major scale. The keynote, therefore, is a half step above this last sharp.

If the signature is in flats, the last flat to the right is always step 4 of the major scale. Either count down to the first step or count up to the eighth step, and that is the keynote. Short cut: if there is more than one flat, the major keynote will have the same name as the next-to-last flat in the signature.

The only major key signature not covered by these rules contains no sharps or flats. It is C major.

The key signatures for all major keys are given below. Notice that sharps and flats cannot appear together in the same key signature. Notice also that the order in which flats appear in a signature is exactly the reverse of the order of sharps. Reading from left to right in a key signature, the order of sharps is F♯, C♯, G♯, D♯, A♯, E♯, and B♯; the order of flats is B♭, E♭, A♭, D♭, G♭, C♭, and F♭. (The first four flats spell *bead*. The sharps can be remembered by an acronym: *Fat cows get drowsy after eating breakfast.*)

name of major Key	C	G	D	A	E	B	F♯	C♯

| name of major Key | C | F | B♭ | E♭ | A♭ | D♭ | G♭ | C♭ |

Although the bass clef has been mentioned only once so far (on page 29), it is pictured here so that you can see the customary placement of sharps and flats in both clefs. The relationship of the various keys to one another can be observed in the circle of fifths which is pictured and explained in Appendix F.

Sol-Fa Syllables

Syllables, as well as numbers, can designate specific steps of the scale. The most common syllabic system is *do, re, mi, fa, sol, la, ti,* and *do.* It is derived from the Latin words of a medieval hymn to John the Baptist. Each line of the hymn began on a different step of the scale. The S in *Sancte* is combined with the I in *Ioannes* and pronounced *see.* Today, *si* has become *ti* and *ut* is *do.*

<u>Ut</u> *queant laxis*
<u>re</u>*sonare fibris*
<u>Mi</u>*ra gestorum*
<u>fa</u>*muli tuorum,*
<u>Sol</u>*ve polluti*
<u>la</u>*bii reatum,*
<u>Sa</u>*ncte* <u>I</u>*oannes.*

In the musical *The Sound of Music,* Maria introduces the children to the song "Do Re Mi," in which they give each syllable of the scale a familiar English meaning. As in the ancient hymn, each syllable begins on a progressively higher step of the scale.

The title of the next song, *"Solmisation,"* refers to the process of singing with syllables. The presence of *sol mi* is evident in the word. Sometimes this technique is called *solfège* (in French) or *solfeggio* (in Italian), both terms being derived from the syllables *sol fa.*

Solmisation

Luigi Cherubini
(1760-1842)

Do do sol la mi fa sol! Oh, sing a song, You can sing it loud and long. And you nev-er will be wrong If you sing *la ti ti do.* The gam-ut you can

run,   And then your song is   done.   *Ti   do   sol   mi   sol   do!*

From *Making Music Your Own.* © 1971 General Learning Corporation. Used by permission.

Sing "Solmisation" as a round. What is its key? Remember that every key name must have two features: the letter name of the key center (including any qualifying sharp or flat), and the term *major* or *minor*. Minor scales and keys will be discussed in the next chapter.

There are several systems of hand signals by which scale steps can be indicated visually. One of the most frequently used is the Curwen-Kodály system, which is pictured more completely in Appendix E.

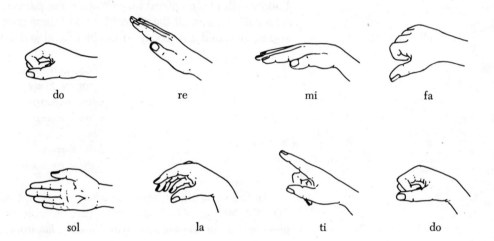

Look at "Solmisation" again. Without singing, figure out the appropriate hand signs for the sol-fa syllables. Then sing at least the first four measures while forming the hand signals.

Basic Intervals

You have had experience in hearing the difference between a whole and a half step, and to that extent you have been judging intervals. A whole step or a half step is called a *second* because the two notes in either pair are on an adjacent line and space when written on a staff, and they are named with adjacent letters of the alphabet. If either note moves a step farther away, the interval increases to a third, and so on. The name of an interval is determined by the number of letters encompassed between the two notes, *counting both the lower tone and the higher tone.* The names are not fractions in any sense.

In the following example of intervals, one pitch remains constant:

Prime, or   Second   Third   Fourth   Fifth   Sixth   Seventh   Octave
unison

Intervals can be computed either upward or downward, and their names remain the same whether the two pitches are heard separately or together. The presence of a sharp or flat doesn't change the basic name of the interval. It affects only the qualifying term that is coupled with the name, and that is a more technical distinction than is necessary for the scope of this book.

Certain memory aids are helpful for anyone who wants to identify intervals quickly by ear. "I've Been Working on the Railroad" opens with a fourth that is reiterated a few times before another pitch is introduced. "My Bonnie Lies over the Ocean" begins with a sixth; "America the Beautiful" features a third on the word "beautiful" after the upbeat; and the table grace, or round, "For Health and Strength," starts with an octave. "Happiness" is a song that is familiar to many people. Identify the intervals in the first two lines, and then learn to sing it.

Happiness

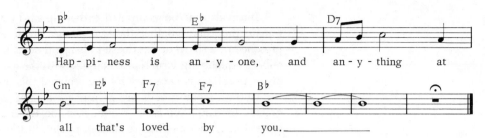

Hap - pi - ness   is   an - y - one,   and   an - y - thing   at

all   that's   loved   by   you._____

Creating a Rondo

A *rondo* is a piece of music in which one melody returns several times, with other melodies interspersed between its appearances. It can be represented symbolically as *a b a c a* and so on.

A simple rondo is created when a rhythmic or melodic pattern is alternated with new musical material. Clap or play on a rhythm instrument the rhythmic pattern of the first five measures of the "Song of Praise" (page 49). Alternate appearances of this rhythmic pattern with the patterns of other songs that contain two or four beats in a measure. Be sure to select a different rhythmic pattern for each contrasting phrase.

Another way to create a rondo is to invent a four-measure rhythmic or melodic pattern, and then improvise the contrasting sections. Each improvised section should be somewhat different from the others.

You can add further variety to a rondo by selecting different keys for different sections. Create a simple four-measure phrase in G major. Perform the *b* section (either composed or improvised) in D major and the *c* section in C major. Follow the rondo pattern of *a b a c a b a.*

Exercises

1. Silently read through these phrases while forming the hand signs. Then sing the phrases as you form the hand signs.

2. Practice these exercises on the piano, recorder, or bells.

3. Draw the pattern for conducting three beats in a measure.

Review Questions

1. Name these intervals.

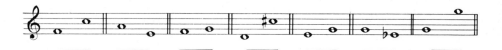

2. Identify the major keynote of these key signatures.

3. Using either a key signature or accidentals, write a major scale on the note D, ascending and descending through eight notes. Below each note write the scale step number and its sol-fa syllable.

4. Write the key signatures for these major keys: F, E♭, G.

5. The half steps appear in the major scale between ___ / ___ and ___ / ___.

6. What is the preparatory beat in conducting?

7. What does the word *key* mean in music?

8. The sol-fa syllables are useful in learning music because they:

   a) specify pitches

   b) indicate the relationship of pitches in a key

   c) aid in counting music

   d) all of the above

   e) none of the above

9. What is the main characteristic of a rondo?

9

Minor Scales and Key Signatures

In your study of this book you have already sung several songs in minor keys: "Camel Caravan," "Drill, Ye Tarriers," "The Peddler," "The Wind in the Willows," and "Ah, Poor Bird." The varied styles of these pieces are evidence that a song in a minor key does not necessarily sound "sad." A piece is not minor because of its mood but because of its specific pitch patterns.

Minor Scales

A *minor scale* is the pattern created when the third step above the keynote is lowered. Other tones in a minor scale also may be lowered, but a lowered third step is a consistent feature of the minor keys. The basic tone relationships in a minor piece are these:

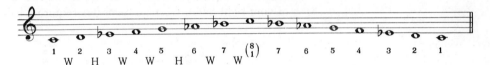

This is *natural* or *pure* minor, in which steps 3, 6, and 7 are lowered a half step from their position in the corresponding major scale. In the diagram below, the dotted lines show at what pitch steps 3, 6, and 7 would be heard if the scale were major.

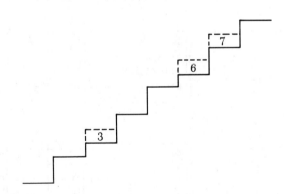

Listen to the natural minor scales on the records so that you become familiar with their characteristic tonal pattern.

To apply sol-fa syllables or hand signals to songs in minor keys, you must remember that step 1 in a minor scale is *la*, not *do*. The eight-step natural minor scale, then, is: *la ti do re mi fa sol la*. The half steps occur between *ti-do* and *mi-fa* (2-3 and 5-6). The reason for this difference in syllables representing major and minor is that the distance from one syllable to another is unchangeable. *Do-re-mi* signifies two whole steps, which fits the start of a major scale. But *la-ti-do* signifies one whole step and one half step, so it applies to the start of a minor scale.

89

Numbers, on the other hand, can be applied to either major or minor scales so that "1" represents step 1, regardless of the intervals that follow.

Here is a round in the key of C minor. Unlike many rounds, the parts enter at every measure instead of at the end of a textual phrase.

Rise Up, O Flame *(Recorded)*

You can play "Rise Up, O Flame" on the recorder if you learn low E♭. Baroque recorders require you to uncover one of the two small holes under the third finger of your right hand; German recorders require a half-hole technique.

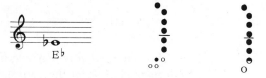

Minor Key Signatures

The key signature of a minor piece follows the pattern of natural minor. Here are the signatures for all minor keys:

Compare this chart with the chart of major key signatures on pages 82–83. Notice that each minor key has three more flats than the major key built on the same note. These additional flats (or cancelled sharps) represent the lowered steps 3, 6, and 7 of natural minor.

A key signature must account for every sharp or flat in the key, even though a few pitches may be missing from the melody, as in "Rise Up, O Flame," which is lacking the A flats and B flats indicated in the signature. But a complete key

Minor Scales and Key Signatures   **91**

signature gives the musician necessary information about the piece, and the addition of chords or an added voice part (such as a descant) is certain to involve the pitches unused in the melody.

Relative Keys

Every key signature does double duty, because it can represent either a major or a minor key. Major and minor keys represented by the same signature are *relative* to one another. To determine what key is intended by a particular signature, look at the song notation and see what note it seems to center around, especially at the beginning and end of the piece. If the note is a half step above the last sharp, or if it is the interval of a fourth below the last flat, that is the keynote for a major key. But if the note is three half steps below what would be the major key center, the piece is in minor and the note you are figuring with is the key center.

Here are some of the common key signatures with the names of the major and minor keys they represent. Notice that the minor key center is always three half steps below the major key center with the same signature. It is advisable to memorize the most common pairs of related keys.

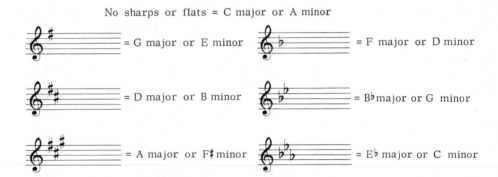

Songs in Natural Minor

The following round involves all the notes of the natural minor scale. The key is easily determined, since the keynote begins and ends the piece. The composer is Benjamin Britten, whose *The Young Person's Guide to the Orchestra* was recommended as a listening activity in chapter 6. "Old Abram Brown" should be sung with a gradual crescendo to "more" and a decrescendo from that point to the end.

Old Abram Brown

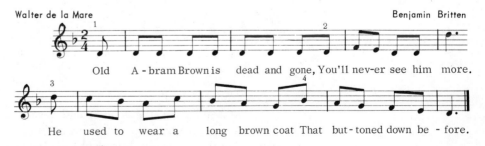

From *Friday Afternoons.* Copyright 1936 Boosey & Co., Ltd.; renewed 1963. Used by permission of Boosey & Hawkes, Inc. Text from *Tom Tiddler's Ground* by Walter de la Mare.

In the same key is "O Come, O Come, Emmanuel," an early hymn based on a style of vocal writing called *plainsong, plainchant,* or *Gregorian chant.* It consists of a simple, smooth-flowing line without accompaniment or added vocal parts. Its rhythms and pitches move subtly to sound like the inflections of speech and to support the meaning of the Latin text. True plainsong should be notated without bar lines, meter signature, or conventional note values. The song "Of the Father's Love Begotten" (page 138) is also derived from plainsong and is notated without a meter signature. In the fourth line of "O Come, O Come, Emmanuel," a shift to G major is implied, but the key of E minor returns in the last line.

Veni, Veni, Emmanuel
O Come, O Come, Emmanuel

"Don Gato" is a cat (*gato* in Spanish means *cat* or *tomcat*) who enjoys a wide spectrum of emotional experiences, as outlined in the narrative of the following song. Again the key center is evident from the first and last notes of the piece.

Don Gato

English Words by
Margaret Marks

Mexican Folk Song

1. Oh, Se-ñor Don Ga-to was a cat,— On a high, red
2. "I a-dore you!" wrote the la-dy cat,— Who was fluff-y,

roof Don Ga-to sat.— He went there to read a let-ter *meow,meow*
white, and nice and fat.— There was not a sweet-er kit-ty,

meow, Where the read-ing light was bet-ter, *meow, meow   meow.*
In the coun-try or the cit-y,

'Twas a love note for Don Ga-to!_____
And she said she'd wed Don Ga-to!_____

3. Oh, Don Gato jumped so happily
He fell off the roof and broke his knee,
Broke his ribs and all his whiskers,
And his little solar plexus,
"¡Ay caramba!" cried Don Gato!

4. Then the doctors all came on the run
Just to see if something could be done,
And they held a consultation,
About how to save their patient,
How to save Señor Don Gato!

5. But in spite of everything they tried
Poor Señor Don Gato up and died,
Oh, it wasn't very merry,
Going to he cemetery,
For the ending of Don Gato!

6. When the funeral passed the market square
Such a smell of fish was in the air
Though his burial was slated,
He became re-animated!
He came back to life, Don Gato!

From *Making Music Your Own.* © 1971 General Learning Corporation. Used by permission.

Answering the following questions will give you an overview of "Don Gato."

1. In what key is the song?
2. How is phrase 5 similar to phrases 1 and 2?
3. What is the form of the song?
4. What compositional technique can be seen and heard in phrases 3 and 4?

Harmonic Minor Scale

Sometimes a melody in a minor key has an alteration in the seventh step of the scale. When the seventh step is raised, the new arrangement of steps is called a *harmonic minor* scale. Composers sometimes prefer to raise the seventh step so that it gives a feeling of "leading into" the keynote (step 8) above it, and certain harmonies seem to reinforce the key more convincingly if that note is raised within a chord. Variations of the sol-fa syllables are available for indicating such accidentals (see Appendix E). For present purposes, it is acceptable to say "sharp *sol*" for the pitch deviation. Listen to the harmonic minor scale on the record, and notice the wide gap between steps 6 and 7.

The carol "Pat-a-Pan" demonstrates the sound of the raised seventh step, which is F♯ in the key of G minor.

Pat-a-Pan

Bernard de la Monnoye
Transl. M. L. H.

Burgundian French Carol

Wil- lie, take your lit - tle drum; Rob-in, bring your flute and come! We will join you as you play, Tu-re-lu-re-lu, pat-a-pat-a-pan, We will join you as you play, And we'll cel-e-brate this day.

Guil-laume prends ton tam-bou-rin, Toi, prends ta flû - te, Ro - bin; Au son de ces in-stru-ments, Tu-re-lu-re-lu, pat-a-pat-a-pan, Au son de ces in-stru-ments, Je di-rai No-ë gaî - ment.

2. People in the olden days
   Gave the King of Kings their praise,
   Playing music in this way.
   Tu-re-lu-re-lu, pat-a-pat-a-pan.
   Playing music in this way
   Let us do as much as they.

3. Man and God are now as one,
   They are merged like flute and drum.
   When you hear the music play,
   Tu-re-lu-re-lu, pat-a-pat-a-pan,
   When you hear the music play,
   Sing and dance for joy today!

2. *C'était la mode autrefois
   De louer le Roi des rois,
   Au son de ces instruments,
   Tu-re-lu-re-lu, pat-a-pat-a-pan,
   Au son de ces instruments
   Il nous en faut faire autant.*

3. *L'homme et Dieu sont plus d'accord
   Que la flûte et le tambour.
   Au son de ces instruments,
   Tu-re-lu-re-lu, pat-a-pat-a-pan,
   Au son de ces instruments,
   Chantons, dansons, sautons en.*

The Hebrew melody "Yigdal" ("The God of Abraham Praise") includes the seventh step both ways—as D in the first two lines where the melody sounds like G major, and as D♯ near the end where the effect of E minor is stronger.

The God of Abraham Praise
Yigdal

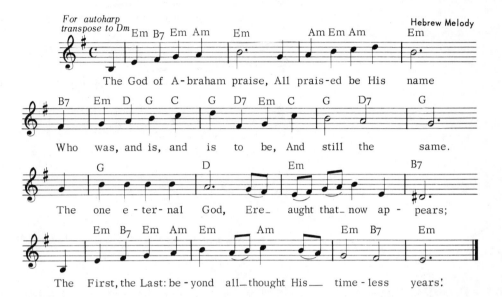

The raised seventh step and other deviations from the natural minor key signature must be written into the piece as accidentals. They are not incorporated into the key signature.

Occasionally a song in a minor key ends with a chord in which the lowered third step—the consistent feature of minor keys—is raised a half step to make the piece appear to end in a major key. This is called a *Picardy third* and is found in the following lullaby. "A la nanita nana," based on a Spanish folk melody, features not only a Picardy third but an entire middle section in a major key. The piece begins in D minor, changes to D major, then returns to D minor, with a final F♯ that again suggests D major.

A la nanita nana

English Words by
Beth Landis

Spanish Folk Melody

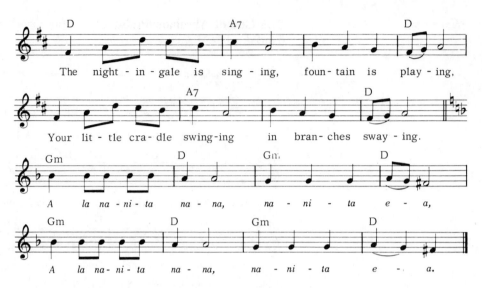

The night-in-gale is sing-ing, foun-tain is play-ing,

Your lit-tle cra-dle swing-ing in bran-ches sway-ing.

A la na-ni-ta na-na, na-ni-ta e - a,

A la na-ni-ta na-na, na-ni-ta e - a.

Words by Beth Landis. © 1966 by Holt, Rinehart and Winston, Inc. Used by permission.

Parallel Keys

The two key signatures within "A la nanita nana" point up the relationship between *parallel* major and minor keys—those that share the same starting note but have different key signatures. To make the transition from D minor to D major at measure 9, the B♭ is cancelled by the B♮ to raise step 6; the F♯ is added to raise step 3; and the C♯ is added to raise step 7. The process is not as complex as it appears, because the three steps are accomplished merely by choosing the correct key signature. Relative major and minor keys represent the opposite situation—they are pairs that share the same key signature but have different starting notes. The chart on page 91 dealt with relative, rather than parallel, major/minor key combinations.

As an experiment in hearing the difference between parallel major and minor keys, convert "Rise Up, O Flame" (page 90) into major by changing one note: raise every E♭ to E♮, and sing the song in C major instead of C minor. Then listen to the two versions on the record. The effect of the major key is quite different. Which tonality, or key, do you prefer for this particular song?

For further experience with minor keys, choose two of the minor songs presented so far in this book and sing them again. Identify the key center, name the eight tones of the scale by letter name, and say the notes of the song with scale step numbers and syllables. Practice some phrases with the hand signs.

Creating in Major and Minor

In chapter 7 you created variations by changing pitches, rhythms, tone quality, and dynamics. You can vary another aspect: the key can be major or minor, which, of course, is a pitch change of sorts.

First, create an eight- to sixteen-measure melody in a minor key. Concentrate on the quality of the melody, and keep the rhythm uncomplicated. Write down the melody and check it by playing it on the recorder or piano.

Next, retain the melody but change it to major.

Decide which version you like best. Make the preferred version into a more finished composition by adding dynamics and some suggestions for enrichment by rhythm or melody instruments. For example, you might write a simple descant of two or three pitches. Or you can create a simple rhythmic ostinato.

Exercises

1. Read through these phrases silently while using the hand signs. Then form hand signs while singing the phrases.

2. Practice these exercises on the piano, recorder, or bells.

3. Say the following patterns with rhythmic syllables or counting, then clap, tap, or play them on an instrument.

Review Questions

1. Identify the minor keynote of these key signatures.

2. Using either a key signature or appropriate accidentals, write a natural minor scale on the note F, ascending and descending. Below each note write the scale step number and indicate whether there is a whole step (W) or half step (H) between adjacent pitches.

3. Write these three minor key signatures: g, b, c.

4. What should you look for in determining whether a song is in a major or a minor key?

5. What scale degree is changed, and in what way, when a natural minor is altered into a harmonic minor scale?

6. What is the difference between relative and parallel keys?

10   *Harmonizing a Song and Playing the Guitar*

Hearing a melody without any accompanying music is like watching a play performed without scenery or costumes: it's all right, but a richer setting provides a more convincing and enjoyable experience. Most songs seem more satisfying when they are *harmonized* by the addition of an accompanying part. *Harmony* is the effect created when pitches are sounded at the same time. When notated, harmony is indicated by notes written vertically, one above another.

Vocal Harmony Parts

One way to provide harmony for a vocal melody is simply to add one or more voice parts to it. "Now All the Woods Are Sleeping" is a hymn with an added part below the main melody.

Nun Ruhen Alle Wälder (*Recorded*)
Now All the Woods Are Sleeping

Paul Gerhardt
Transl. M. L. H.

Heinrick Isaac c. 1510
Harmonized by J.S. Bach

"Now All the Woods Are Sleeping" is an excellent example of a chorale—a type of hymn described on page 49. Johann Sebastian Bach harmonized more than three hundred chorale melodies, writing them for four voice parts: *soprano, alto, tenor,* and *bass* (SATB). He incorporated many chorales into other compositions, as well. The melody of this chorale appears at two different places in his *St. Matthew Passion,* each time with different words. (A *passion* deals with the suffering of a martyr.) To sound authentic, a chorale should be sung with dignity. Listen to the recording of "Now All the Woods Are Sleeping." First the soprano line is heard alone, then the alto. A third version presents the chorale in its SATB form.

Although a choir of mixed—men's and women's—voices is most often divided into SATB parts, other vocal combinations are possible: SSA indicates two soprano parts and one alto part; SAB refers to soprano, alto, baritone; and TTBB means two tenor parts, baritone, and bass. Full chords rarely can be achieved in elementary school choral classes. The voices at this age are not spread over a wide pitch range, and elementary school children are sometimes unable to maintain a part when several different sections are singing simultaneously.

Rounds are a good introduction to part-singing because all sections perform the same music. The harmony is produced with little effort, merely through the delayed entrances. *Part songs,* on the other hand, are songs having one or more different parts in addition to the melody. If the second part is a contrasting line with melodic quality of its own, the combination of melodic lines is called *counterpoint.* An easy introduction to counterpoint is the simultaneous singing of two songs—"Three Blind Mice" and "Frère Jacques," for example, or the two contrasting verses of "Giddap, Old Dobbin" (page 60) and "Oh Give Me the Hills" (page 121). But contrapuntal (counterpoint) music is seldom that obvious. Most part songs are not contrapuntal, because the secondary part—like a descant that is sung or played on the recorder—is subordinate to the main melody.

"The Virgin's Cradle Hymn" contains two harmony parts, one below and one above the melody. The upper part is for recorder. The lowest part tends to move with either the recorder part or the melody. The range of the three parts is rather narrow; never are they more than an octave apart. The song is well suited to this SSA format.

The Virgin's Cradle Hymn

If _____ thou sleep _ not, Moth - er mourn - eth, Sing - ing as her
Si _____ non dor - mis, _____ ma - ter plo - - rat In - ter fil - a

wheel she turn - eth: Come, soft slum - ber, balm - i - ly! _____
can - tans o - rat, Blan - de, ven - ni, som - nu - le. _____

The tonal characteristics of "The Virgin's Cradle Hymn" are interesting. The sixth step of the key—the note C—never appears in the melody. At times the song seems to be in G major, but then it shifts to the relative key of E minor, which shares the same key signature. The alternation of major and minor characteristics is found in many Spanish songs, including the lullaby "A la nanita nana" in the preceding chapter. In that song, however, the two keys are parallel, sharing the same key center (D) but not the same key signature.

In "The Virgin's Cradle Hymn," notice the G♯, or Picardy third, at the phrase ending in measure 10 and again at the end of the piece. Both measures imply a brief change from E minor to the parallel key of E major.

To play G♯ on the recorder, use this fingering:

Triads and Primary Chords

In chapter 6, a chord was defined as any combination of three or more tones sounded simultaneously. A *triad* is a specific kind of chord, with three tones that are each a third apart.

At the piano, find the notes C E G. First play them as a melody (one after another) and then as harmony (all three played at once). Now assume you are in the key of C major. What syllables and scale step numbers go with the notes C E G in this key? Be careful—they are not *do re mi* or 1 2 3. You have now played and identified the pitches of a triad.

Triads are of several types, depending on how far apart the notes, or *chord members,* are from one another. A *major triad* contains the interval of a wide third (two whole steps) from the root to the next higher chord member, with a narrow third (three half steps) above that. In a *minor triad* the narrow third is directly above the root, with the wide third on top. Listen to the recording of major and minor triads and notice the difference in their sound.

Another term is important to the understanding of harmony: the *root* is the pitch on which a chord is built, and it sounds like the basic note from which the intervals ascend when the chord is in its simplest form. The root is not necessarily the first step of the scale, because a chord can be constructed on any step. Nor does it have to be the lowest pitch sounding in the chord, because the notes can be rearranged by assigning one or more to a different octave.

Because a triad can be built on any step of a major or minor scale, each triad is identified by Roman numeral—I, VI, II, V, etc.—according to the scale step number of its root. Certain triads appear more frequently than others, however, especially in the songs found most often in children's music books. Here are the three most common triads, called *primary chords*, written to show how their roots are related to the scale. The key of this example is C major.

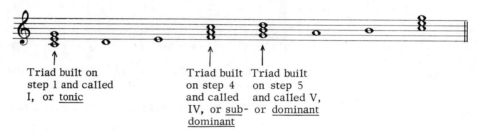

Triad built on step 1 and called I, or <u>tonic</u>

Triad built on step 4 and called IV, or <u>sub-dominant</u>

Triad built on step 5 and called V, or <u>dominant</u>

Primary chords in a minor key are determined in a similar manner, with one slight change. The dominant chord in a minor key usually sounds better when the seventh scale step (the middle note of the V triad) is raised one half step. In E minor, for example, this alteration produces the following series of primary chords:

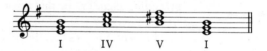

A *seventh chord* is a chord of four pitches, each a third apart. The notes G B D F are an example. The root in this case is G. If this seventh chord appears in C major, the root G is the fifth, or dominant, step of the C major scale, and the chord is called a *dominant seventh*. The term "seventh" here does not mean that there are seven notes in the chord or that the root is step 7 of the scale. It refers to the interval between the root and the top note. Count the distance for yourself in the G B D F example, and listen to the sound of a seventh chord on the record.

The tonic triad acts as "home base;" the harmony moves to and from this center. Almost all songs end on the tonic chord; unless it is sounded the music seems incomplete. The tonic triad is usually preceded by the dominant, because this chord progression gives the music a strong feeling of conclusion. The subdominant chord sometimes moves to the tonic, but this progression does not create as strong an effect of conclusion or repose.

The folk song "The Orchestra" can be harmonized with only two primary chords: the tonic and the dominant seventh. The song may be performed as a round, with each group singing all five parts consecutively but entering with the violin part at different times. Another possibility is to assign a single part to each group of singers, letting each "instrument" be heard alone before it joins forces with the instruments that have been heard previously.

The simultaneous sounding of all five parts creates complete harmony in itself, making accompanying chords unnecessary. But the suggestion of the I and V^7 chords is so strong, especially in the roots sounded by the drum part, that the process of chord selection is made extremely simple.

Write Roman numerals and chord letter names over the violin part at the beginning of each measure, then accompany the song on the piano or autoharp.

The Orchestra

Austrian Folk Song

The vi - o - lin's sing - ing, la

The clar-i - net, the clar-i - net goes

Oh the trum - pet oh the trum - pet, ta - ta -

The horn, the horn it

The drum drum drum thrum thrum I'm

la la la la la la la la la, The vi - o - lin's

du - a du - a du - a du - a det, The clar-i - net, the

ta ta ta ta ta ta ta ta ta ta ta, The trum- pet oh the

sounds for - lorn, The horn, the

pound - ing the drum, Five, one, one,

sing - ing   la   la la   la la   la la   la.

clar - i - net   goes   du - a   du - a   du - a   det.

trum - pet   ta ta   ta ta ta   ta ta   ta   ta.

horn   it   sounds   for - lorn.

five,   five,   five,   five,   five,   one.

Inverted Chords

An *inverted chord* is one which does not have its root sounding as the lowest tone. The notes in a chord can be inverted (put into a different order from bottom to top) without changing the name of the chord.

Look at the following chord progressions and mark all the inverted triads by writing "inv." under each. Here is a clue: check the lowest note in each chord to see if it is the scale step indicated by the Roman numeral. The first four examples are in the key of F major, in which step 1 is F, step 4 is Bb, and step 5 is C. The last two examples are in the relative key of D minor to help you become accustomed to the sound of minor chords.

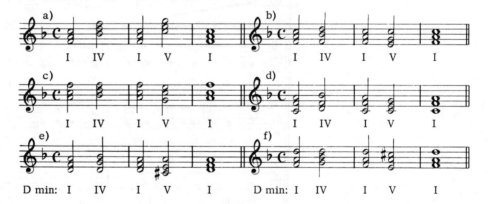

Play the examples on the piano, or get two people to perform the lines with you, playing on instruments or singing in three-part harmony. Listen to the examples on the record to be sure you are performing them accurately. Notice that the last five examples sound better than the first one. Inverting some of the chords makes the progressions smoother, because the chord tones lie closer to the notes that precede and follow them. The leaps are gone.

Knowledge of the bass clef is necessary for understanding the notation for the full range of pitch available on the piano and autoharp. The bass clef is also called the F clef, because its curve starts on the fourth line (F), and its two dots are on either side of the F line. The bass clef indicates specific pitches as follows, with the treble clef above it and the note middle C in common, for comparison of the two pitch ranges:

When treble and bass cleffs appear together, the two staffs form a *grand staff*.

Refer again to the six chord progressions on page 104. At the piano, play the written notes with your right hand, and the chord roots with your left hand. This will familiarize you with the sound of notes in the bass-clef range, and you will be creating the richer sound of four-part harmony. The chords will no longer be inverted, because the lowest sound in every chord is now the root. Notice, too, that in each chord the root is *doubled*—it appears in two different octaves.

Fitting Chords with a Melody

Because many songs include chord symbols with the notation, it is possible to harmonize a song without understanding the choice of chords. When chord symbols are not provided, however, it is usually rather easy to select appropriate chords if you follow a few simple procedures.

Suppose you are deciding which chords might accompany this phrase:

First, look at the key signature to determine the key. It has no sharps or flats, so it is either C major or A minor. Since the notes C, E, and G occur frequently and there is no A or G♯, C major appears to be the logical choice.

Next, determine the notes in the primary chords of C major. The I or tonic triad is C-E G, the IV or subdominant triad is F-A-C, and the V⁷ or dominant seventh chord is G-B-D-F.

Then determine which notes in the melody are the most important in terms of being longer and/or occurring on the beat. In the first measure the first note (C) is on the beat, while the second note (D) is not.

Finally, select chords in which the most important melody note is present. If a melodic note is a member of two primary chords, look at the other pitches in the measure to see which chord is implied. For example, an F occurs on the first beat of measure 2, but the other notes in the measure are D and B. A G-B-D-F (V⁷) chord would be more logical here than one beat of F-A-C (IV), which would have to change on the next quarter note.

Generally, the following choice of chords works well:

scale step in melody		chord
1, 3, or 5		I
5, 7, 2, (or 4)°	use	V⁷
4, 6, or 1		IV

°Depending on its context in the melody.

"Harvest Song" opens with a strong 1 3 5 8 melodic pattern, and succeeding phrases also outline particular chords. Learn the melody, then write in the chord symbol (C, F, or G^7) that best fits each two-beat (or half-measure) segment of the melody.

Harvest Song

Danish Folk Song

It is possible, of course, to accompany songs "by ear" without the aid of notation. This is a slow process and not recommended if singers must sit and wait for the accompanist to figure out what chords to play! Playing by ear is educational when you are alone, however, because by experimenting over a period of time you can gain a sense of which chords to select.

Playing Chords on the Piano

To play chords on the piano you must depress three or more keys at the same time. For ease in outlining chords for casual accompaniment, inversion is a useful technique. (For more serious efforts, chord inversions should be manipulated carefully for maximum effectiveness.) In this progression of primary chords the inverted IV and V^7 allow the hand to maintain its basic position.

Notice that the V^7 chords contain only three notes. The fifth above the root is not essential to the effectiveness of seventh chords, and it can be omitted to simplify the keyboard player's part.

Practice each hand of the example separately, using any fingering that seems comfortable. Combine hands when you feel you can do so. In actual solo playing and accompanying, both hands seldom play identical groups of notes because the sound becomes too "thick." But for practice in note reading and finger dexterity, such duplication is useful. Such chords as those in the example are called *block chords.*

Look again at the "Harvest Song" (page 106) for which you wrote chord symbols. On the piano, play an accompaniment of block chords to fit the melody. The key, meter, and half-note rhythm will be the same as in the example on this page, but the order in which the chords appear will be different. The block-chord style is appropriate for "Harvest Song," which conveys the imagery of a hard-working peasant culture.

Many songs are more interesting when the harmony part is "dressed up" a little by spreading out the pitches of the chord in different rhythmic patterns. For example, in *The Music Man,* the song "Goodnight, My Someone" (which appears in this book on page 119) is accompanied very simply by sounding the pitches of the chord consecutively rather than simultaneously. In fact, the part is so easy that it can be performed by someone with minimal music background. Learn to play it and, after you have learned the song, sing it with the accompanying part.

Goodnight, My Someone (Accompaniment)

The song can be harmonized on the piano with many other patterns. One pattern, popular in the time of Mozart, is the *Alberti bass*.

Another type is called "waltz" accompaniment:

Or the accompaniment can be syncopated:

Creating Autoharp Accompaniments

The chord bars of the autoharp are labeled to correspond to the three most common chord types: Maj = major, min = minor, and sev = seventh. Each chord is built on a specific root note, and both its letter name and the chord type appear on the button. A major triad can occur in a minor key, and vice versa. For example, in the chart of primary chords on page 102, the key is major and so are the I, IV, and V triads, because the interval above the root is a wide third and the interval above that is a narrow third. Now build triads above steps 2, 3, and 6; you will find they are minor triads, with the narrow third on the bottom. In a minor key, there is a similar availability of major and minor triads above the various roots.

For the player's convenience, the chord bars are arranged so that chords I, IV, and V[7] in the keys of C, G, F, B♭, A minor, and D minor (on a fifteen-bar autoharp) lie comfortably under three adjacent fingers of the left hand. The index finger is on I, the next finger is on V, and the ring finger is on IV. To acquaint yourself with the sound of the harmonies and the feel of the instrument, play various rhythms of I IV V in the six keys cited above. The classified index lists the songs in this book that can be accompanied by one, two, or three primary chords; by other chords in addition to I, IV and V; and by *altered* chords—those containing accidentals not indicated by the key signature. Work out varied accompaniments for selected songs from the list.

For a special effect, press more than one bar, and fewer notes will sound. For example, to produce only the notes C and G, press both the C major and C minor chord bars. The former blocks out all E♭ strings and the latter blocks out the E♮ strings. Oriental or American Indian music is sometimes effective when accompanied by the open, or "empty," sound of a fifth produced in this way. Try the "Navajo Happy Song" on page 145 with an introduction and coda (concluding section) of open fifths on D and A, produced by depressing both the D minor and D major chord bars. Then sing the song one step higher than it is written. (This transposition is necessary to accommodate the limited chords available on the autoharp.)

Guitar

The guitar is a six-stringed plucked instrument with frets, which are crosswise ridges set at half-step intervals to indicate the placement of the fingers for various pitches. The notes on a guitar sound an octave lower than they are written. A guitar is tuned to these pitches:

Guitar notation, with its pictures of finger placement, is called *tablature*. Here is the tablature for the tonic and dominant seventh chords in D major. The sign "o" means an *open string* with no fingers pressing down on it, and an "x" means that the string should not be strummed for that particular chord. Notice that the lowest note (the one farthest left) in each diagram is the root of the chord. The numbers indicate fingerings, with the index finger called "1."

Practice the D and A⁷ chords until you can find the notes easily with your left hand. Then accompany yourself on "He's Got the Whole World in His Hands."

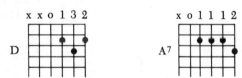

He's Got the Whole World in His Hands

Black Spiritual

in His— hands, He's got the whole world   in   His   hands.

3. He's got you and me, brother, in His hands, (3 times)
   He's got the whole world in His hands.

Experience with the following chord, which is IV in the key of D major, will enable you to play additional songs in that key.

When you are comfortable with the fingering for the G chord, try to accompany "The Goose" on page 6. Pay special attention to the dynamic levels suggested by the song text. Then add the same three chords to two other songs in D major: "Brother James' Air" (page 80) and "Hanukah" (page 34).

The following chart shows how to play the three primary chords in the keys of C, G, F, and D major, and in the minor keys of A, D, E, and G. Practice strumming the chord progression I IV V^7 I in different keys, working for fluency and for variety of tone color, style, and dynamic level.

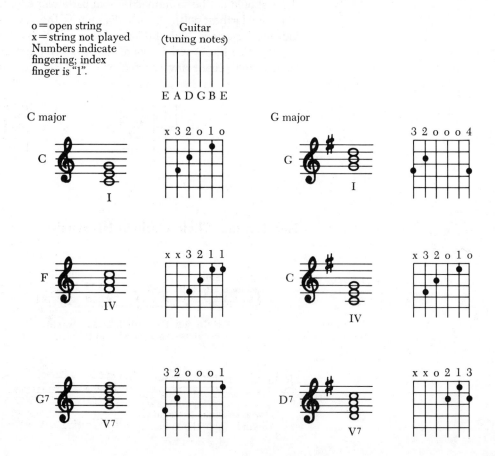

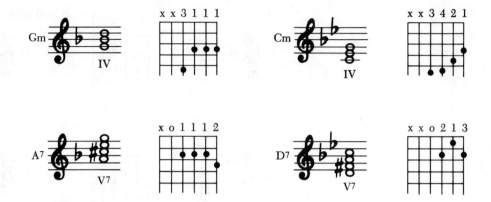

Use these chords to harmonize some of the songs in this book, following the given chord progressions or experimenting with other harmonies. (The songs are listed in the classified index according to their harmonizations.) Work with other songs, too, letting your ear tell you what chords sound best. Sometimes the note occurring on a heavy beat in the melody is not a member of the chord that happens to sound best at that point. But almost always, the melody changes to a note that *is* a member of the chord being sounded, and the result is a good blending of sound between melody and harmony.

There are two approaches to chord selection for a song you want to harmonize. You can change the finger pattern to accommodate the key of the song, or you can transpose the key of the song to accommodate a fingering pattern you have learned. Be sure the new key does not put the melody beyond your singing range, however.

To figure out the fingerings for chords not shown on the preceding charts, remember that the crosswise ridges (frets) are set a half step apart from one another. You can compute each pitch name according to its distance above the open string.

Exercises

1. Determine the chords that can harmonize "Dona Nobis Pacem" (page 44). Write the appropriate chord symbol and letter name for each chord, changing only at the beginning of each measure. Check your harmonization by playing it on the autoharp while singing the melody. Because this is a round, the harmonization for the first eight measures should also fit the succeeding eight-measure segments.

2. Determine the chords that can harmonize "Brother James' Air" (page 80). Write the appropriate chord symbol and letter name for each chord. Check your harmonization by playing it on the autoharp while singing the melody.

3. Notate the harmonization you developed for "Dona Nobis Pacem" by writing block chords on the grand staff for performance by piano.

4. Working from the harmonization for "Brother James' Air," add musical interest by writing something other than block chords.

5. Write out the first line of the harmonization for "Dona Nobis Pacem" for guitar. Write the chords in notation and in tablature.

1. What does the word *harmony* mean in music?

2. An adult chorus of mixed voices contains four voice parts: _____,
   _____, _____, and _____.

3. What is the pitch pattern in most chords?

   a) every other note—A C E

   b) consecutive notes—A B C

   c) two adjacent notes and one a third away—A B D

   d) every fourth note—A D G

   e) no particular pattern

4. Is the root of a chord always the lowest pitch sounded in the chord?

5. What are the three primary chords in a key?

6. A seventh chord is so named because it

   a) is built on the seventh step of the scale

   b) contains seven notes

   c) has an interval of a seventh from its root to the top note

   d) appears about one-seventh of the time in the song

   e) harmonizes the seventh scale degree

7. Which chords are inverted?

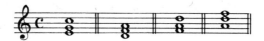

8. a) What chord most often harmonizes the seventh scale step?

   b) What chord most often harmonizes the sixth scale step?

9. What is tablature in music?

10. What does the term *open string* mean in string or guitar music?

11 Compound Meter

As was briefly mentioned in the first discussion of rhythmic notation, the quarter note is not the only note value that can represent a beat. Almost any kind of note can do this, as long as the meter signature provides this information. Furthermore, no matter what type of note represents one beat, the relative note values remain unchanged; an eighth note is twice as long as a sixteenth, half as long as a quarter, and so on.

The $\frac{6}{8}$ meter signature is an example of a non-quarter beat value. This particular meter can indicate six beats in a measure, with an eighth note lasting for one beat. This is the correct interpretation of the meter signature when the tempo is slow enough to allow an unhurried pace for each eighth note.

Such a tempo is evident in "Sleep and Rest," a lullaby by Mozart (1756–1791). Before you try to sing it or play it on the recorder, piano, or bells, look through the music and lightly pencil a slash mark over the six places in each measure where an eighth note beat occurs. The first and fourth beats should be the heaviest. As an example, four of the measures should look like this:

When you have completed the slash marks, sing the song while tapping the eighth note beat. Give extra emphasis to the first and fourth eighth notes in each measure, and notice the gentle rocking effect that results.

Sleep and Rest

W. A. Mozart

Sleep O my dar-ling and rest,— Birds are a-sleep in their nest,— Gar-den and mea-dow are still!— Bees hum no more on the hill.— In through the win-dow so bright— Shines the moon's sil-ver-y

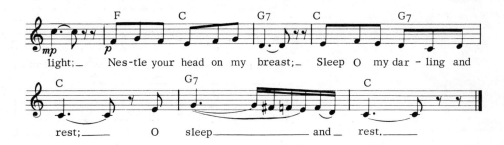

light;— Nes-tle your head on my breast;— Sleep O my dar-ling and

rest;—— O sleep———— and — rest.——

Tempo Considerations

Often 6/8 meter is taken at a faster tempo than that found in Mozart's "Sleep and Rest." An example is "Seventy-Six Trombones" from *The Music Man* by Meredith Willson. Try singing just to the repeat sign for now.

Seventy-Six Trombones

Meredith Willson

Sev-en-ty-six trom-bones led the big pa-rade,—
Sev-en-ty-six trom-bones caught the morn-ing sun,—

With a hun-dred and ten cor-nets close at hand.——— They were
With a hun-dred and ten cor-nets right be-hind.——— There were

fol-lowed by rows and rows of the fin-est vir-tu-o-
more than a thou-sand reeds spring-ing up— like— weeds,

sos, The cream of ev-'ry fa-mous band.— ev-'ry shape and
There were horns of

kind.— There were cop-per bot-tom tim-pa-ni in horse
fif-ty mount-ed can-non in the bat-

pla-toons,— Thun-der-ing, thun-der-ing, all a-long the way.
ter-y,— Thun-der-ing, thun-der-ing, loud-er than be-fore.

Dou-ble bell eu-pho-ni-ums and big bas-soons,——

Each bas-soon— hav-ing his big fat say. There were

It is clear that the eighth note in "Seventy-Six Trombones" no longer represents the beat. What type of note does last for one beat (on the words "-six trom-bones," for example)? A dotted quarter note. Why? Because the song is in *compound meter.* The main characteristic of compound meter is that its beat subdivides into three background pulses, rather than the two that have been typical of the meter signatures so far presented.

A dotted note represents the beat because it can be divided into threes:

$$\text{♩.} \; = \; \text{♩} \; + \; \text{♪} \; = \; \text{♪} \; \text{♪} \; \text{♪}$$

(The beat note cannot be a quarter note because that divides into only two eighth notes, and it cannot be a half note because that divides into four eighth notes.) Look at "Seventy-Six Trombones" again, and notice the frequent appearance of dotted quarter notes and the beams grouping three eighth notes together.

To establish the feeling of compound meter and the relationship among its note values, clap or tap the following pattern several times in succession:

Moderately fast

Then clap or tap the $\frac{9}{8}$ pattern at two tempos, first slowly with the eighth note as the beat value, then faster with the dotted-quarter note as the beat value.

The difference between compound meter and *simple meter*—meter that subdivides into two background pulses—is shown in the chart below:

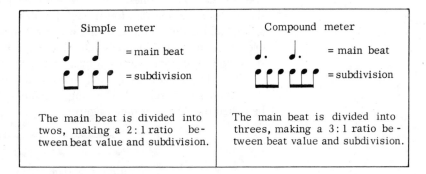

Simple meter	Compound meter
The main beat is divided into twos, making a 2:1 ratio between beat value and subdivision.	The main beat is divided into threes, making a 3:1 ratio between beat value and subdivision.

One way to contrast the two types of meters is to tap the following pattern, keeping the speed of the beat the same, as on the recording:

(Repeat several times)

There are several systems for counting compound meter. But because tempo has such a significant effect on how the rhythm is perceived, it seems best to count all the subdivisions with consecutive numbers and to let the feel of the music determine whether those shorter note values are the beats or the subdivisions of the beats:

Another advantage of this counting system is that the eighth note divides into two sixteenths. It is easy to insert "and" after each number to accommodate the sixteenth notes.

Go back to "Seventy-Six Trombones" and say the counts while clapping or tapping the beat. When you can do that successfully, sing the entire song with the words.

Compound meter signatures must be figured out somewhat differently than simple meter signatures. The bottom number of a meter signature is supposed to tell what kind of note lasts for one beat. But there's no system for indicating in the meter signature that the beat note is dotted. (The standard bottom numbers, 2, 4, and 8, represent undotted notes.) In compound meter, therefore, the bottom number describes not the value of the beat itself, but the value of the beat *subdivision.* The top number tells how many of these subdivisions occur in a measure.

Now you can understand the meter signature for "Seventy-Six Trombones." Since each beat subdivision is an eighth note, 8 is the bottom number. There are six of these subdivisions in each measure, so 6 is the top number.

How can you tell if a meter signature indicates compound or simple meter? The top number of a compound meter signature is divisible by three, so any signatures with 6, 9, or 12 as the top number are compound. (Numbers larger than 12 are rare.) All other top numbers except for 3 indicate simple signatures. The number 3 in a meter signature is ambiguous, and it will be discussed shortly.

When reading rhythms in compound meter, it's important to visually group the notes and rests together into bunches representing each beat. Refer again to "Seventy-Six Trombones." Mark a slash over each eighth note, making longer slashes over the first and fourth eighth notes in each measure. Next draw a circle around all the notes and rests that occur within each beat. This will accustom your eye to grouping the symbols into the larger beats. Then sing or play the song, stressing the beginning of each beat to accentuate the feel of compound meter.

The "Dogie Song" is also in ⁶⁄₈ meter with a dotted quarter note as the beat, but the tempo is more relaxed. The song contains a slightly different rhythm that might be called the "Am-ster-dam" figure:

The first eighth note is lengthened and the second is shortened. The pattern can be understood as a derivation of the following rhythmic figures:

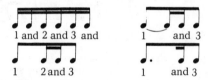

To feel the difference between this pattern and the strict eighth note subdivisions, read the following measures rhythmically:

As you sing the "Dogie Song" or listen to the recorded version of it, visually group the notes into the larger beats.

Dogie Song (*Recorded*)

1. As   I   was a - walk - ing   one   morn - ing for pleas - ure,
2. It's   ear- ly in spring that   we   round up the do - gies,

In *The Music Man*, "Seventy-Six Trombones" is cleverly transformed into a lullaby by changing the meter, style, and dynamic level. The pitches remain the same in the two songs, but the change of rhythm creates an entirely new effect. Compare "Goodnight, My Someone" with "Seventy-Six Trombones" through the phrase "There were horns of ev'ry shape and kind."

Goodnight, My Someone

bright - est light   For good - night, my love, for good - night. ___

___ Sweet   dreams be   yours, dear, if dreams there be; sweet

dreams to   car - ry you close   to   me.   I   wish   they may and I

wish   they   might.   Now good - night, my   Some - one, good - night.

Waltz Tempo

If the tempo of "Goodnight, My Someone" is increased somewhat, it becomes too fast to feel comfortable with a beat on every quarter note. It wants to fall into compound meter, instead, with a beat on every third quarter note. The new beat note contains three quarter notes, so it has to be a dotted half note. The dotted half note is the basis for waltz rhythm. Waltzes are traditionally written in $\frac{3}{4}$ meter, but a slow tempo for such music would be stodgy. The custom, therefore, is to perform waltzes with only one beat ♩. per measure, which produces compound meter.

The round, "Lovely Evening," is a song of this type. Let it swing with one beat per measure, to keep the music interesting and to suggest the to-and-fro motion of a large, pealing bell. Accentuate the "d" on the "ding dongs" for a bell-like effect, and enrich the song with ostinato parts involving bell-type rhythm and melody instruments.

Lovely Evening

German Round

Oh, how love - ly is the eve - ning, is the eve - ning,
O wie wohl ist mir am A - bend, mir am A - bend,

When the bells are sweet - ly ring - ing, sweet - ly ring - ing;
Wenn zur Ruh die Gloc - ken läu - ten, Gloc - ken läu - ten;

Ding,   dong,   ding,   dong,   ding,   dong.
Bim,   bam,   bim,   bam,   bim,   bam.

"Oh Give Me the Hills" is similar—it is written in $\frac{3}{4}$ but feels more comfortable with one beat per measure. Like "Giddap, Old Dobbin," in chapter 6, the verse and refrain are to be sung consecutively and then simultaneously. When they are performed at the same time, they produce counterpoint.

Oh Give Me the Hills

2nd and 3rd Stanzas by
Beatrice P. Krone

Miners' Song

1. Oh give me the hills and the ring of the drills,

And the rich sil - ver ore in the ground, _____

Where sel - dom is heard a dis - cour - ag - ing word

And man - y true friends will be found. _____

2. Oh give me a land where a man ____ may stand

And watch the clouds in a sky ____ of blue,

Though work - ing a - way at the ore in the ground,

His dreams may come true. _____

3. Oh give me the hills in a far west - ern land,

3. Oh give me the hills in a far west - ern land,

"Goodnight, My Someone," "Lovely Evening," and "Oh Give Me the Hills," are examples of music in $\frac{3}{4}$ meter in which the beat—a dotted half note—gives a compound effect. Other songs with a $\frac{3}{4}$ signature sound best in simple meter, with three beats to a measure and a quarter note as the beat. You can tell whether a song should be perceived as compound or simple meter mainly by considering the tempo and style of the music. Some songs will sound listless and drab with three beats in a measure, while others will seem hurried and superficial with fewer beats per measure. Your own inclination also affects your perception of the meter of songs that seem to be "in between."

Other Compound Meter Signatures

The German carol "Joseph Dearest, Joseph Mild" is also in compound meter, even though the bottom number of the meter signature (4) usually means a quarter note is the beat value. Remember that when the top number of a meter signature is divisible by 3—a 3, 6, 9, or 12—there is a good chance that the piece can be appropriately performed in compound meter.

Joseph Dearest, Joseph Mild

lit - tle child.   God   will give   you   your   re - ward   in
child   di - vine,   God's pure light   on   thee   will shine   from
Kin - de - lein,   *Gott der   will*   *dein* *Loh - ner sein*   *Im*

heav'n a - bove." So   prays the   moth - er   Mar -   y.
heav'n a - bove,   As   we   both   rock   the   ba -   by."
Him - mel - reich," *Der* *Jung - frau Sohn* *Ma -   ri -   a.*

The foregoing carol dates back to about 1500. Johannes Brahms (1833–1897) wrote a lovely arrangement of it for contralto, piano, and viola. (*Contralto* is the lowest range of the female voice.) Listen to the first half of Brahms' version of the carol on the recording, noticing the feel of the meter and the techniques by which he conveys the style of the music.

"Masters in This Hall" is in compound meter also, but it has four beats per measure. Scan the music before you sing it, to be sure you understand where the beats occur in each measure. This medieval song was arranged by the English composer Gustav Holst (1874–1934).

Masters in This Hall

Mas-ters in this hall, ___ Hear ye news to - day ___

Brought from o - ver-sea, ___ And ev - er I you pray:

Now - ell! Now - ell! Now - ell! Now - ell sing we clear! Holp-en

are all folk on earth, __ Born __ is God's Son so dear:

Now - ell! Now - ell! Now - ell! Now - ell sing we loud! God to -

day hath poor folk raised __ And __ cast a - down the proud.

Combining Simple and Compound Meters

The similarities and differences between $\frac{3}{4}$ and $\frac{6}{8}$ meters are interesting and significant. Both have six eighth notes, or their equivalent, in each measure. But the feel of the two meters is different, as you can tell by reading the rhythm of each example below. Tap your hand for each beat and say "ta" for each note, proceeding from one measure to the other without pause. At first, maintain the beat at the same tempo throughout; the eighth notes will vary in speed. Then read the measures again while keeping the eighth notes steady. You will notice that the beat varies from one meter to the other.

The grouping of subdivisions is clearer when the notes have beams instead of flags. The two measures above are written more clearly here:

For *West Side Story* Leonard Bernstein composed a song called "America" that alternates $\frac{6}{8}$ and $\frac{3}{4}$ meter with almost every measure. The music is in the style of a *huapango*, a festive dance from the Caribbean. The speed of the eighth notes is constant, so each measure takes an equal amount of time. But the beat shifts, so that the combination of the $\frac{6}{8}$ measure, with two beats, and the $\frac{3}{4}$ measure, with three, produces a unique pattern of accents. Practice saying the words rapidly before you try to sing the song. The alternating sentiments about America in the text represent the bickering between two groups of Puerto Rican girls with differing opinions.

America

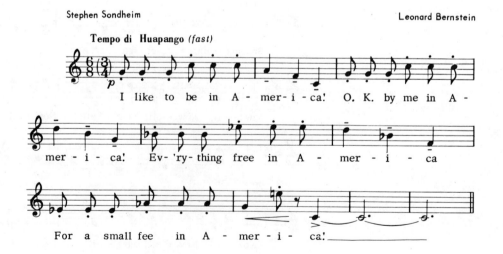

1. I like the cit - y of San Juan.___ I know a boat you can get on._____ Hun-dreds of flow - ers in full bloom.___ *(nearly spoken)* Hun-dreds of peo-ple in each room.___ Au - to - mo-bile in A - mer - i - ca, Chro - mi - um steel in A - mer - i - ca, Wi - re spoke wheel in A - mer - i - ca, Ver - y big deal in A - mer - i - ca! mer - i - ca!_____

2. I'll drive a Buick through San Juan
   If there's a road you can drive on.
   I'll give my cousins a free ride.
   How you get all of them inside?
   Immigrant goes to America,
   Many hellos in America,
   Nobody knows in America,
   Puerto Rico's in America!

3. I'll bring a T.V. to San Juan.
   If there's a current to turn on!
   I'll give them new washing machine.
   What have they got there to keep clean?
   I like the shores of America!
   Comfort is yours in America!
   Knobs on the doors in America,
   Wall-to-wall floors in America!

Conducting Patterns for Six Beats and One Beat

When compound meters have two, three, or four beats per measure, they are conducted the same way that two, three, or four beats would be conducted in simple meters. Conducting six beats in a measure is necessary for a song like "Sleep and Rest" that moves somewhat slowly. The pattern for six beats in a measure is:

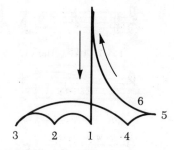

When a meter moves quickly enough, it is not feasible to conduct each beat in the measure. Instead, only one beat per measure is conducted. The pattern for one beat is:

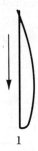

In this pattern the upward motion is not a separate movement but a rebound of the hand from the bounce occurring on the beat.

Creating Music in Compound Meters

Create a simple eight-measure rhythmic pattern in $\frac{6}{8}$ or $\frac{9}{8}$ meter, then build a set of variations on that pattern. Vary it first by changing some notes into rests. Second, add pitches to the pattern to form a melody. Third, if the melody is in major, change it to minor, or vice versa. Fourth, alter the rhythmic pattern by rewriting it in simple meter. This can be accomplished by removing a few notes, changing note values, or both.

Exercises

1. Clap, tap, and count the following patterns.

2. Play the following phrases on the recorder or piano.

3. Rewrite the first two measures of "Joseph Dearest, Joseph Mild" in $\frac{6}{8}$ meter so that the music will still sound the same.

Review Questions

1. Add the *one* note or rest that correctly completes the measure.

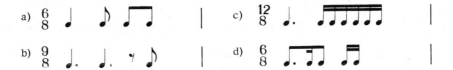

2. What is the basic difference between simple and compound meter?

3. A song has a meter signature of $\frac{3}{4}$. How can you determine whether a quarter note or a dotted half note should represent the beat?

4. Assume that the tempo is the same for these two measures. Which one will consume more time? Why?

5. Draw the conducting pattern for six beats in a measure.

12 Less Common Meters and Borrowed Patterns

The songs in simple meter that we have examined so far have been written with a quarter note as the beat value. Although this is the most conventional choice, other beat values are possible.

Alla Breve

In past centuries, *breve* (pronounced BREV) referred to a half note. The term *alla breve*, therefore, means *according to the breve*, or assigning a half note to represent the beat. Today the term is synonymous with $\frac{2}{2}$ meter, which is often called *cut time*. Its symbol ₵ is similar to the C abbreviation for $\frac{4}{4}$, or *common time*. The vertical slash means that both numbers, not just the upper one, have been cut in half in the transition from common to cut time, so cut time is $\frac{2}{2}$, not $\frac{2}{4}$ meter. In the illustration below, identical measures are interpreted both ways:

There is no overriding reason for the fact that different note values can represent the beat. When compared with notation having a quarter note beat, cut time tends to look less cluttered on the page, but that is not particularly important. Because the composer is free to choose any of several different note values to represent the beat, the performer's ability to interpret the various meter signatures is a necessary part of learning music.

Establish a two-beat pattern in a moderate tempo and say the note values with rhythmic syllables before you try to perform the piece as written. Remember that although every value will be decreased, the 2:1 ratio among the values is maintained.

"Sakura" is a Japanese song about cherry blossoms, which symbolize spring and the beauty of Japan. The cherry trees planted around the Tidal Basin in Washington, D.C., for example, were presented to the United States as a gesture of friendship from the Japanese people.

Sakura

Japanese Folk Song

From *Folk Music Festival in Hawaii* by John M. Kelly, Jr. Used by permission of Boston Music Company, Boston, copyright owners.

"Sakura" can be harmonized in A minor, but steps 5 and 7 (D and G) are missing from the melody, so the type of scale is uncertain. The form of the song is more clear-cut. When analyzed in two-measure phrases, the form is *a b c b c a d*.

"Sing" moves with the same meter and tempo as "Sakura," but its character is completely different. "Sing" sounds casual and light-hearted, largely because of the many rests and the extremely short vocal phrases. The song appears to be improvised on the spot, with snatches of thought developing into longer phrases as the music progresses. The piano part is printed here to indicate what happens musically during the vocal silences. The dynamics should of course support the words, beginning softly and increasing in intensity, with a softer level on the *la la* refrain.

Sing

J. R.   Moderately   Joe Raposo

$\frac{3}{2}$ Meter

It's possible to have a half-note beat with three or another number of beats per measure. At first glance, $\frac{3}{2}$ meter might seem to be just another version of $\frac{6}{4}$. But $\frac{3}{2}$ is simple meter and $\frac{6}{4}$ is compound. There is a difference in the feel of the two meters, like that between $\frac{3}{4}$ and $\frac{6}{8}$, as demonstrated on page 124. The following chart illustrates the difference between two meters that have a background of quarter notes:

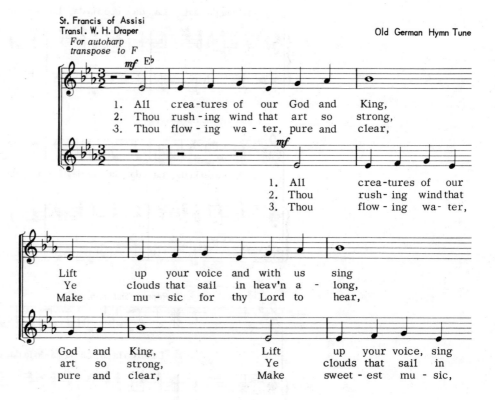

Read the rhythms as you did on page 124, saying "ta" for each note and alternating the two measures without pause. When you keep the beat speed constant, the quarter notes will vary. When you keep the quarter notes constant, the beat speed (or tempo) will vary.

The next song is in $\frac{3}{2}$ meter and features two parts that imitate each other throughout most of the song. An echo effect can be created near the end by singing the second of each repeated phrase at a soft dynamic level. The final "Alleluia" should be rich and full, to create a confident ending.

All Creatures of Our God and King

"All Creatures of Our God and King" can be played on the recorder. For A♭, finger G♯ (page 101). The high E♭ is:

Notice that it is like low E♭ except that the thumb and index finger of the left hand are raised. In the lower part of the song, move to D in the next-to-last measure one count early, to replace the low B♭ which the soprano recorder cannot play.

Asymmetrical Meters

A meter is *asymmetrical* when the placement of stressed beats in the pattern does not divide the measure into equal portions. In $\frac{5}{4}$ meter, neither 1 2 3 4 5 nor 1 2 3 4 5 produces a balanced rhythmic feel. In $\frac{7}{4}$ meter, the increased number of options still does not create a sense of symmetry: 1 2 3 4 5 6 7, 1 2 3 4 5 6 7, 1 2 3 4 5 6 7, or 1 2 3 4 5 6 7.

"Hippopotamus" is written in $\frac{5}{4}$ meter. The piece is more musical when there is emphasis on the first beat of each measure and the tempo moves sufficiently to give a "swing" to the rhythm. A dragging, labored tempo might be descriptive of the animal's size and lumbering movement, but the result would be musically dull. Try to find a compromise tempo that is not too lilting to be descriptive, and not too stodgy to be interesting. Be sure to make the note values identical in length, even though some are emphasized more than others.

Hippopotamus

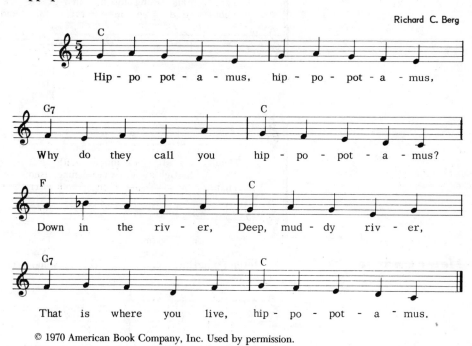

© 1970 American Book Company, Inc. Used by permission.

The five-beat conducting pattern varies, because the secondary accent in a measure can occur on the third or fourth beat of the five. In the word "hippopotamus," the third syllable gets the secondary stress, while in the phrase "Down in the river," the fourth syllable receives secondary emphasis. In the conducting options below, the larger motion to the right occurs on the beat of secondary stress (from beat 3 to 4 in the illustration on the left and from beat 2 to 3 on the right):

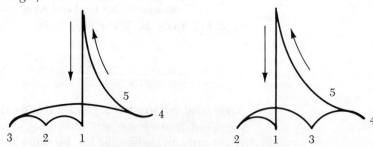

Try to fit the text of "Hippopotamus" to other meters by composing different note values and matching accented syllables with the natural stresses of the rhythms. Rewrite the song in $\frac{2}{4}$, $\frac{3}{4}$, and $\frac{4}{4}$ meter. For extra challenge, use a half note as the beat value in your notation, making your meter signatures $\frac{2}{2}$, $\frac{3}{2}$, and $\frac{4}{2}$.

Another example of asymmetrical meter is found in some West Indian music. Although the meter signature looks easy enough, the rhythm does not follow the usual rules. The eight rapidly moving notes in each measure are most often arranged into three unequal groups.

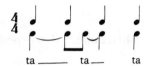

One way to learn the pattern is to count at a quick speed: 1 2 3 4 5 6 7 8. Be sure to make all the eighth notes equal in duration.

Another way to interpret such a pattern is to think of four quarter note beats per measure and regard the rhythmic deviations as syncopation:

This interpretation adapts well to measures in which the eighth note rhythm changes to a grouping of 2 + 2 + 2 + 2.

Typically, however, the calypso rhythm is felt as three unequal beats per measure. Before you try to sing the song, make sure you can say the words while tapping the main beats of the pattern.

Meter Change

Meter sometimes changes within a song. "Here We Come A-Wassailing" begins in $\frac{6}{8}$ and changes to $\frac{2}{2}$ at the refrain. The $\frac{6}{8}$ section should be in a brisk two beats per measure. Keep the same tempo by maintaining the same beat speed for both sections, and notice how the style changes from a skipping to a march-like effect.

Here We Come A-Wassailing

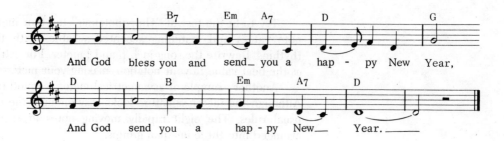

And God   bless you   and   send_ you a   hap - py New   Year,

And God   send you   a   hap - py New_   Year._____

Mixed Meters

Mixed meter occurs when the meter signature changes several times in a piece of music or within a particular phrase. Sometimes meters change to allow freer expression of the words or mood than is possible in a strict metrical pattern. This is true of the American folk song "Shenandoah." In the second complete measure, for example, "you" could be held a beat longer to make it conform to a meter of four beats, but the song would seem stiffer and less expressive. To increase your flexibility in looking ahead and adjusting to quick meter changes, try to conduct the piece as you sing it or as you listen to the recording.

Shenandoah (*Recorded*)

Mixed meters also result from the use of irregular or asymmetrical rhythmic patterns. Such patterns are found in the folk music of Bulgaria, Greece, and Turkey. They are also found in such Latin American music as the huapango which was presented in Bernstein's "America" in the preceding chapter. The first three measures of "Summer Has Come" reveal a $\frac{5}{8}$, $\frac{5}{8}$, $\frac{6}{8}$ metrical pattern that is repeated before the appearance of a second section in $\frac{2}{4}$. The melody consists of short phrases that move mostly by step within a narrow range. As you can hear in the recorded version, the opening lines are quite free and slow. The last half of the song is in a conventional $\frac{2}{4}$ meter.

Summer Has Come (*Recorded*)
Yaz Geldi

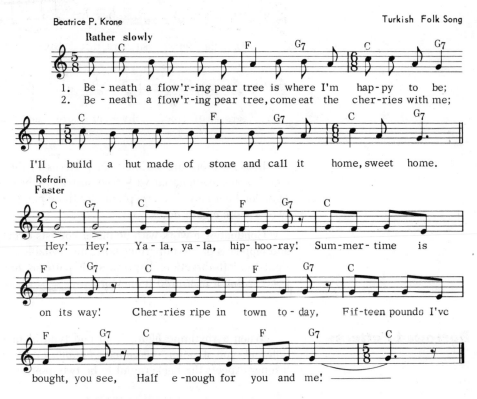

Beatrice P. Krone

Turkish Folk Song

1. Be - neath a flow'r-ing pear tree is where I'm hap-py to be;
2. Be - neath a flow'r-ing pear tree, come eat the cher-ries with me;

I'll build a hut made of stone and call it home, sweet home.

Refrain
Faster

Hey! Hey! Ya-la, ya-la, hip-hoo-ray! Sum-mer-time is

on its way! Cher-ries ripe in town to-day, Fif-teen pounds I've

bought, you see, Half e-nough for you and me! —————

© 1966 Follett Publishing Company. Used by permission.

Nonmetrical Music

A song with no meter signature at all is this hymn derived from plainsong. As mentioned in chapter 9, this early form of chant had only the most subtle rhythmic nuances, which followed the inflections of the text rather than a metrical scheme. For this reason, many modern interpretations of plainsong, including the following, also omit the meter signature. Stress the accented syllables of the important words only enough so the rhythm does not bog down.

Of the Father's Love Begotten

Prudentius; 4th Century
For autoharp
transpose to F

12th Century

Because there are no metrical patterns in the preceding chant, most of the eighth notes are notated with flags instead of beams, to avoid the appearance of rigid combinations. The exceptions are those points at which one syllable is sung to two or more eighth notes.

Conducting a work with no meter consists largely of indicating flowing motion and emphasis of the important notes and syllables. There is no attempt to indicate right-and-left direction, because such patterns imply the placement of specific beats within a measured framework.

Borrowed Patterns

When a rhythmic figure from one type of meter appears in a piece with a different type of meter, it is called a *borrowed pattern*. In the following example the listener expects the background to be two quarter notes:

A borrowed pattern might be inserted like this:

Notice that the borrowed pattern is identified by a numeral indicating how many notes are replacing the customary pattern. In the example above, there are three quarter notes in place of the usual two. This is a *triplet*—a group of three equal notes to be performed in place of more or fewer of the same kind. The rhythmic syllables can be "trip-let-ti" or "triple-ti."

Once to Every Man and Nation

James Russell Lowell

T. J. Williams

For autoharp
transpose to Dm

The following Slovakian folk song features another borrowed triplet figure, this time consisting of three eighth notes in place of the two that are normal in the meter. Again the figure "3" is required in the notation. Listen to the recording of this song to check your singing of the triplet.

Waters Ripple and Flow (*Recorded*)

Margaret Fishback

Slovakian Folk Song

For autoharp
transpose to F
Smoothly

From *Making Music Your Own.* © 1971 General Learning Corporation. Used by permission.

Borrowed patterns may involve any number of notes, not just three. The pattern may insert *fewer* than the expected number of notes, as well as more than that number. Also, the borrowed portion can span more than one beat.

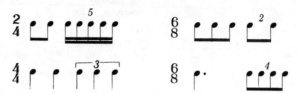

Creating Music with Mixed Meters and Borrowed Patterns

Create an eight-measure rhythmic phrase in which the meter changes every two measures. Use no borrowed patterns at this point. You may have two, three, or four beats per measure in simple and/or compound meter. When the pattern is determined, write it down and decide what instruments will play the pattern. Play a drum on the downbeat of each measure to emphasize the mixed metrical patterns.

Rewrite your rhythmic phrase to include several borrowed patterns, and decide what changes, if any, you might recommend in the use of instruments.

Exercises

1. Rewrite one of the following phrases with a different beat note but retain all the relative rhythmic values so the music sounds the same. Then play the phrases on the recorder or piano.

Review Questions

1. Fill in the *one* note or rest needed to complete the measure.

2. What meter signatures are written when the music is in cut time or *alla breve?*

3. What meter signature gives exactly the same directive as **C** ?

4. A meter signature such as $\frac{5}{4}$ is called:

   a) mixed
   b) irregular
   c) asymmetrical
   d) *alla breve*
   e) changed

5. Draw one of the two suggested patterns for conducting $\frac{5}{4}$ meter.

6. If the meter of a song changes several times, the meter is called:

   a) mixed
   b) irregular
   c) asymmetrical
   d) *alla breve*
   e) common

7. All music must have a meter. (T or F)

8. What is a borrowed rhythmic pattern?

9. How many equal notes does a triplet contain?

13 *Pentatonic Scale and Modes*

Although the major and minor scale patterns predominate in the music of Europe and America, they are by no means the only patterns that exist. In fact, much recently created music is not in major or minor. This chapter examines alternative scale patterns.

Pentatonic Scale

A *pentatonic* scale consists of five different pitches within an octave. The most common pentatonic scale contains no half steps—each tone in the scale is either one or one-and-a-half steps away from its neighbor. The tonal arrangement can be duplicated easily by playing only the black keys on the piano. The pentatonic pattern can start on any note, white or black, as long as the typical arrangement is preserved. All-white-key arrangements are F G A C D or C D F G A, C D E G A or G A C D E, and G A B D E or D E G A B. Listen to the pentatonic scales that have been recorded for this book.

Strictly speaking, a pentatonic melody has no tonal center, although when one note predominates, the song is sometimes accompanied by chords that treat it as if it were major or minor. Sometimes, too, sol-fa syllables are assigned to the various steps as if they were derived from major or minor keys. It is more accurate, however, to call the "tonal center" of a pentatonic melody its *final*, to avoid the implication that a pentatonic melody is somehow an incomplete or faulty version of a major or minor tonality.

The ambiguity of its tonal center makes the pentatonic scale an excellent framework in which to experiment and improvise. No matter in what order the notes of a pentatonic scale are sounded, the resulting melody seems acceptable, because it lacks the strong pull to a key center created by half steps. Any note makes an appropriate final, so anything the experimenter produces sounds good, especially if the choice of tone colors and rhythms is interesting. If children are to play resonator bells for melodic improvisation in a pentatonic setting, it's best to give them only the five bars on which they are to play, so they won't be confused by the presence of other notes.

The spiritual "Poor Wayfaring Stranger" has a final of D and a key signature of one flat, as if the key were D minor, but there is no E or B♭ in the melody. The notes are F G A C D. (The pentatonic scale can begin with either the two whole steps or the three whole steps, so the arrangement C D F G A is also valid here. But most often the scales are cited with the three whole steps first.)

The first note of "Poor Wayfaring Stranger" begins on the "and" of beat 2. Prepare in this way, thinking a half note for each beat: "*(one* and *two)* AND *THREE* AND." Then "*(one* and *two)* I'm *just* a. . . ."

Poor Wayfaring Stranger

Southern White Spiritual

"Poor Wayfaring Stranger" is easily harmonized with two triads: D minor and G minor. Experiment on the autoharp to create an accompaniment with these chords. If the first or second note of the measure is G, play the G minor triad throughout the measure. Otherwise, play D minor. Strum three times (once per beat) in each measure.

"Gaelic Lullaby" is another pentatonic song with a final of D, but it has no F or B, so its scale is C D E G A. The compound meter contributes an appropriate rocking motion. Notice the smooth singing style of the soloist on the recording.

Gaelic Lullaby (*Recorded*)

Gaelic Folk Song

The harmonizations implied by "Gaelic Lullaby" are much more ambiguous than those suggested by "Poor Wayfaring Stranger." Of the three triads—D minor, G minor, and A minor—almost any chord selection fits "Gaelic Lullaby." In fact, either the D minor or G minor triad can be sounded exclusively throughout the song. For more variety, however, try the following order of triads with the song, and decide which of the five harmonizations you prefer. Play two chords in each measure. (The measures are numbered in the chart below.)

	1		2		3		4		5		6		7		8	
two triads only	Gm	Am	Gm	Am	Gm	Am	Gm	Am	Gm	Am	Gm	Am	Gm	Am	Gm	Gm
two triads only	Dm	Gm	Dm	Gm	Dm	Gm	Gm	Dm	Dm	Gm	Dm	Gm	Dm	Gm	Dm	Dm
three triads	Dm	Am	Dm	Am	Dm	Am	Gm	Dm	Dm	Am	Gm	Am	Dm	Am	Dm	Dm

The following American cowboy song has a pentatonic scale of F G A C D with a final of F, ⁶⁄₈ meter with an upbeat, and a text in which the cowboy addresses himself to the dogies (motherless calves) in his care. The same features are also present in the "Dogie Song" in chapter 11. In that song the cowboy is urging the animals to move, while in the "Night Herding Song" he's trying to quiet them. Singing on the range had a varied purpose: it soothed the cattle, warned off possible predators, and helped ease the cowboy's loneliness.

Night Herding Song

American Cowboy Song

1. Oh, slow up, do-gies, quit rov-ing a-round,
2. I've cir-cle herd-ed and night herd-ed too,

You have wan-dered and tram-pled all o-ver the ground;
But to keep you to-geth-er, that's what I can't do;

Oh, graze a-long, do-gies, and feed kind-a slow,
My horse is leg wea-ry, and I'm aw-ful tired,

And don't for ev-er be on the go. Oh,
But if you get a-way, I am sure to get fired. Bunch

move slow, do-gies, move slow,__ Hi-oh, hi-oh,__ hi-oh!____
up, lit-tle do-gies, bunch up,__ Hi-oh, hi-oh,__ hi-oh!____

"Little David" is based on a pentatonic scale of F G A C D with a final of F, and the song is in duple meter. The text refers to an Old Testament character, but with only the sketchiest attempt at narrative, and the words suggest a leader/solo part to be answered by a recurrent group response. The music features syncopation in the frequent ♪♩♪ figure, which can be the basis for an effective ostinato part.

Little David

Black Spiritual

Lit-tle Da-vid, play on your harp, Hal - le - lu! Hal - le -

lu! Lit-tle Da - vid, play on your harp, Hal - le - lu!

1. Lit-tle Da - vid was a shep-herd boy; he slew Go-li- ath and
2. Old Dan-iel in the li - on's den; but he came out all
3. Lit-tle Da-vid was a might-y King; and all the peo - ple

sang for joy._____ Lit-tle Da-vid, play on your harp, Hal - le -
whole a - gain._____
came to sing._____

lu! Hal - le - lu! Lit-tle Da-vid, play on your harp, Hal-le - lu!

American Indian songs are often pentatonic. The "Navajo Happy Song" is an example that shows the wide pitch range and persistent rhythmic patterns found in such music. The recording, sung by Ataloa of the Chickasaw Nation, demonstrates an authentic Indian style. Notice the tone quality and subtle deviations of pitch and rhythm that make this style distinctive. Of the five three-measure phrases, which are identical or similar? Create a rhythmic ostinato to accompany the song.

Navajo Happy Song (*Recorded*)

With Strong Rhythm   Navajo Indian Song

Hai yo, hai yo ip si nai yo, Hai yo,

hai yo ip si nai—— yo,   Hai—— yo,   hai yo ip si

nai yo,   Hai yo,   hai yo ip si nai yo!

Hay nah yay nah yo.   Hai!

Songs based on pentatonic scales are found in many parts of the world, including the Orient, Africa, Scotland ("Auld Lang Syne"), and Canada ("Land of the Silver Birch"). In all pentatonic songs, remember that it is the *melody* that consists of the five scale tones; the accompanying chords or added vocal parts (such as a descant) almost always inject the missing notes to make the music sound typically major or minor. A list of pentatonic songs is presented in the classified index.

Modes

Modes are certain eight-tone scales that ascend and descend in specified patterns of whole and half steps. Major and minor scales were originally modes, but the term *mode* today usually excludes them.

The modes, sometimes called "church modes" or "ecclesiastical modes," dominated European music for a thousand years and have regained new popularity today. The sound of these modes can be duplicated by playing certain consecutive white keys on the piano: D to D for the *dorian* mode, E to E for the *phrygian*, F to F for the *lydian*, and G to G for *mixolydian*. Each of these modes is presented on the records for this book. A mode can be transposed by starting it on any desired note, but its pattern of whole and half steps must conform to the white-key model cited above. It is estimated that about two-thirds of American folk music is in a major key and that the remaining one-third is equally divided among the minor key and the dorian and mixolydian modes.

The song "Scarborough Fair" is in dorian mode, with a final of D as in the white-key example above. The song should move in a swaying style, with two rather slow beats per measure. Simon and Garfunkel made a popular arrangement of this song which was a hit a few years ago. It is a *ballad*—a song that tells a story. Because of time limitations only the first two verses are included on the recording.

Scarborough Fair (*Recorded*)

English Ballad

1. Are   you go - ing to   Scar - bor - ough fair,
2. Tell her to make me   a   cam - -bric   shirt,
3. Tell her to wash it   in   yon - -der   well,

Re - mem - ber me_____ to
With - out any seam___ or
Where never spring wa - ter nor

one who lives there,
nee - dle work, For once she was a true love of mine.
rain ev - er fell,

4. Tell her to dry it on yonder thorn,
   Parsley, sage, rosemary and thyme;
   Which never bore blossom since Adam was born,
   And then she'll be a true love of mine.

5. O, will you find me an acre of land,
   Parsley, sage, rosemary and thyme;
   Between the sea foam and the sea sand,
   Or never be a true lover of mine.

6. O, will you plough it with a lamb's horn,
   Parsley, sage, rosemary and thyme;
   And sow it all over with one peppercorn,
   Or never be a true lover of mine.

7. O, will you reap it with a sickle of leather,
   Parsley, sage, rosemary and thyme;
   And tie it all up with a peacock's feather,
   Or never be a true lover of mine.

8. And when you have done and finished your work,
   Parsley, sage, rosemary and thyme;
   Then come to me for your cambric shirt,
   And you shall be a true love of mine.

The dorian mode sounds like a minor scale except for one note: the sixth step is higher in the dorian than it is in the minor scale. The natural minor scale pattern, illustrated on page 89, is W H W W H W W; the dorian pattern is W H W W W H W. A composer or arranger has two options when selecting a key signature for a dorian melody. One option is to write the key signature for the minor key that centers on the same note as the mode, and then raise the sixth step by inserting an accidental whenever step 6 occurs in the music. Another option is to write one more sharp (or one less flat) than is found in the comparable minor key signature, and not have to worry about raising step 6 by means of accidentals. The arranger of "Scarborough Fair" has chosen the former option, raising step 6 to B♮ by means of an accidental in the music.

The French carol "Sing We All Noel" is notated in the same way. The key signature is G minor, and the final of the mode is G, so step 6 (E♭) must be raised to E♮ within the song, to provide the dorian flavor.

Noel Nouvelet
Sing We All Noel

French Carol

Sing we all No - el, Glad tid - ings_ now we tell,
No - ël nou - ve - let, No - ël chan - tons i - ci,

Thanks to God we bring, Our song to_ God we sing!
De - vo - tés gens, cri - ons a_ Dieu mer - ci!

Sing we No - el   for Christ is born, the   king, No - el!
Chan - tons No - ël   pour   le Roi nou - ve - let, No - el!

Sing we No - el   for Christ is born, No - el!
Chan - tons No - ël   pour   le Roi nou - ve - let!

Sing we all No - el, Glad   tid - ings_ now we   tell!
No - ël nou - ve - let, No - ël chan - tons i - ci!

The mixolydian mode sounds major except for its lowered seventh step. The pattern of intervals, like the white key pattern G to G, is W W H W W W H W.

Every Night When the Sun Goes In

American

Ev - ry   night_____ when the sun goes in,_____

Ev' - ry night_____ when the sun goes   in,_____

Ev' - ry night_____ when the sun   goes   in,_____

I hang down my   head_____ and morn - ful   cry._____

"Old Joe Clarke" is another folk song with the characteristic lowered seventh step of the mixolydian mode. The song bears the key signature of F major, with the lowered seventh step, the E♭, indicated by an accidental every time it appears in the music, with the exception of the next-to-last notes of lines 2 and 4.

Old Joe Clarke

American Folk Song

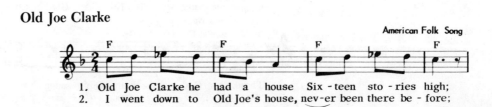

1. Old Joe Clarke he had a house Six - teen sto - ries high;
2. I went down to Old Joe's house, nev - er been there be - fore;

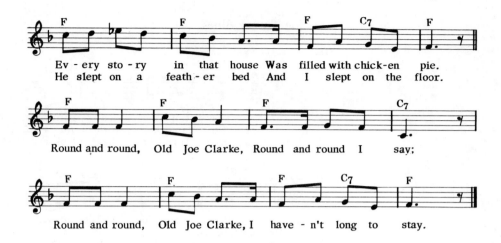

The lydian mode is not common, but one contemporary song will illustrate its characteristic sound. "An Old Christmas Greeting" is a round, and it should be sung in a bright and bouncy manner.

An Old Christmas Greeting

Jon Polifrone

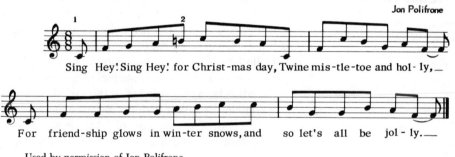

Used by permission of Jon Polifrone.

Blues

Blues music is characterized by syncopation, certain "slides" of the voice, a gloomy text, a form of *a a b*, and blue notes in the melody. *Blue notes* are the pitches that result when the third, fifth, or seventh steps of the major scale are lowered one half step. In C major, the notes E, G, and B in blues would occasionally be E♭, G♭, and B♭. The lowered pitches of the melody are harmonized with major chords, so that an E♭ in the melody may sound against an E♮ in the harmony. This causes a clash of pitch that adds a certain "flavor" to the blues.

"Joe Turner Blues" is in the key of C major. It contains only one blue note—the lowered third step, E♭. If this note were at its normal pitch, the melody would be pentatonic, because the fourth and seventh steps are not present. The harmony follows a typical blues progression: four measures of I, two of IV, two more of I, two of V7, and a return to I for two measures. In a major key, all of these primary chords are major. Perform the song with a rather brisk four beats per measure.

Joe Turner Blues

American Blues

1. They tell me— Joe Turn-er's— come and gone,—
2. He came here— with for-ty— links of chain,—
3. Joe Turn-er,— he took my— man a-way,—

They tell me— Joe Turn-er's— come and gone.—
He came here— with for-ty— links of chain.—
Joe Turn-er,— he took my— man a-way.—

He left me— here to sing _____ this _____ song.

Atonal Music

Some pieces are in neither a key nor a mode. If there is no sense of key center or final, the music is *atonal*, which means *without tonality*. Few songs are completely atonal, but a number of contemporary songs are very free in terms of tonality. "Anatomy Lesson," by the contemporary American composer Norman Dello Joio, is a good introduction to such music. The melody centers around C, but the piano accompaniment includes many accidentals and suggests continual deviation from the basic key of the melody, which seems to be C major even though it contains E♭ rather than E♮. Because the accompanying piano part is so important to the harmonic character of "Anatomy Lesson," the complete song is recorded. Sing with the recording to see how well you can maintain the melodic intervals against the unusual harmonic background.

Anatomy Lesson (*Recorded*)

Ilo Orleans

Norman Dello Joio

Flowing and Frisky (¢ 𝅗𝅥 = 66)

mf

⑤

mf

My bod-y is a po-em,— my bod-y's full of rhymes;

"Anatomy Lesson" contains considerable *dissonance,* which is the effect created when simultaneous pitches create an impression of tension. The opposite effect is *consonance*—an impression of pleasantness and compatibility. Judgments concerning consonance and dissonance are subjective, because different people perceive music in different ways, depending on their knowledge, past experience, and willingness to accept new experiences. Another factor influencing their judgment is the proportion of consonance and dissonance that is considered normal in the music of their culture.

Learn the melody of "Anatomy Lesson" and sing it with the accompaniment, noticing the effect created by the dissonance. When three or more pitches are sounded together, the result is still a chord, whether the notes are consonant or dissonant. There are four measures in which a chord in the piano part sounds both a G♮ and a G♯ for a dissonant effect. In measure 31, the five notes can be rearranged in ascending order (D G C F B) to create a chord built on fourths instead of the customary thirds. The first chords in measure 21 are similar, with the notes D G C F B♭, but the pitches are clustered together rather than strung out from bottom to top.

Measure 32 adds another note, A, to the five-note chord in the preceding measure. In fact, if an E were present, every letter of the musical alphabet would be represented in one collection of simultaneous sounds. The presence of so many notes in the chord allows a variety of interpretations. The top A, if placed at the beginning of the line-up for purposes of analysis, creates a series of fourths (A D G C F B). In another order, the same notes form a chord of thirds (G B D F A C) or seconds (F G A B C D) or fifths (B F C G D A). Because so many interpretations are possible, the most realistic analysis of such a chord is simply that the composer just liked the sound at that particular spot.

Creating a Pentatonic Song

An easy way to start improvising is by playing only the black keys on the piano. (If you have a set of melody bells, it may substitute for the piano.) Create a songlike melody no more than an octave in range and from eight to sixteen measures long. When the melody is completed to your satisfaction, create a contrasting figure or line. The contrasting line should differ generally from the melody. For example, when the melody has long note values, the contrasting line can move more quickly, and vice versa. When the melody ascends, the contrasting line can descend, and so on. When both the main and contrasting melodies are completed, play them on instruments with another person, or sing the lines on a neutral syllable.

In chapter 8 you created a rondo. Repeat the assignment, but this time put the music in a pentatonic framework. The contrasting sections can be composed or improvised.

Create a pentatonic song in the style of American Indian music.

Exercises

1. Play these phrases on the recorder or piano.

2. Identify and play these modes.

Review Questions

1. Write a pentatonic scale on D.

Write a pentatonic scale on G♭.

2. Write the dorian mode on G.

Write the mixolydian mode on C.

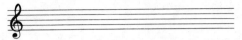

3. How many different pitches are in a pentatonic scale?

4. The dorian mode can be played on the piano by sounding the white keys consecutively from ___ to ___.

5. Atonal music has no

    a) variation in dynamic level

    b) vocal text

    c) designated voice or instrument

    d) key center or tonic

    e) form

6. If simultaneous pitches create the effect of tension, the sound is described as:

    a) dissonant

    b) consonant

    c) atonal

    d) modal

    e) asymmetrical

14 *Learning a New Song*

Since the purpose of vocal music is to convey verbal as well as musical ideas, consideration of the text is basic to understanding a song and interpreting it correctly. The text is also the easiest element for the beginning musician to assess, so it is presented first in the following checklist of learning steps. The next steps are the elements of rhythm: determining the meter, tempo, and note values; and interpreting any unusual rhythmic factors in the song. Features of pitch and key need to be performed accurately for musically satisfying results. Finally, elements of dynamics, timbre, and form must be considered for effective interpretation of a song.

The steps outlined below will help you focus your attention in a systematic manner on the important features of the song you wish to learn.

1. *Read the text* to determine whether the song is narrative, religious, or recreational, or whether it is a work song, lullaby, love song. Decide what style of singing will best convey the spirit of the text.

2. *Determine the meter* of the song, both the number of beats per measure and the note value that lasts for one beat. Decide whether the meter is compound or simple. Scan the music to see if the meter changes.

3. *See if a suggested tempo is marked* at the upper left-hand corner of the song. If there is none, decide what tempo would be appropriate by speaking the text in the rhythm specified by the notation. Normally the tempo should be one that can be conducted comfortably, although some popular music styles favor a very rapid beat. The final decision on the tempo depends on the mood of the music, its style (waltz, march, etc.), and any tempo marking such as those provided in Appendix B.

4. *Scan the song for borrowed patterns and syncopation.* Tap out the rhythms of the entire song or read it with rhythmic syllables at the tempo you feel is best.

5. *Determine the key signature* and find out whether the song is in a major or minor key by scanning the music and deciding which of the two possible keynotes is prevalent. The keynote is often the last note of the melody. Check to see whether the key changes during the course of the song.

6. *Find the starting pitch* by sounding the first note on a pitch pipe, recorder, bells, or piano. If the first note of the song is not the tonic as indicated by the key signature, play or sing from the first note to the nearest tonic, moving by scale steps either upward or downward until you reach it. To find the second note of a wide interval, mentally sing up or down the intervening scale steps to determine the proper distance.

7. *Listen to see if the song sounds typically major or minor* as you sing it. If it does not, check the whole and half steps in the music to see if the sound is supposed to be modal, pentatonic, or atonal. Notice and identify any accidentals within the piece and sing it slowly, if necessary, until you can sing all the pitches accurately.

8. *Look for indicated dynamic levels.* If there are none, decide what dynamics would be appropriate for the song text and produce them as you sing, maintaining a good tone quality at both loud and soft levels.

9. *Observe where the phrases occur* and make a slight break or breath lift at the end of each.
10. *Notice the form* of the music and decide what implications it has for variations in tone quality, dynamic level, and overall interpretation.

Try the recommended steps as you teach yourself the following song. When you have learned the round, ask a friend to sing it with you.

From High Above

Transl. Alice Firgau   German Round

From high a-bove The rain/snow keeps fall-ing, fall-ing down,

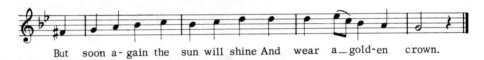

But soon a-gain the sun will shine And wear a—gold-en crown.

From *Making Music Your Own.* © 1971 General Learning Corporation. Used by permission.

"Chester" was written by William Billings during the Revolutionary War. Billings was originally a tanner, but he gave up that career and became the first native American to make a profession of composing music. Notice that the words of "Chester" are intensely patriotic and religious. (At the long slurs, a solid horizontal line means that a word is sustained; a dotted horizontal line means that the word is incomplete and only a syllable of it is sustained.)

Teach yourself "Chester" as best you can by following the suggestions presented earlier in this chapter. Then compare your version with the recording.

Chester (*Recorded*)

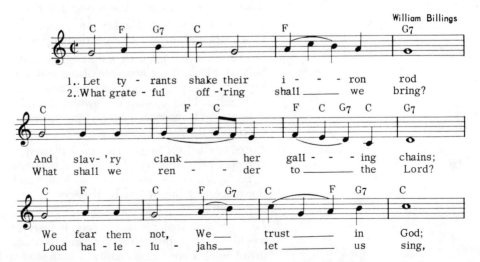

New___ Eng - land's God _____ for ev - - - er reigns.
And _praise His name_____ on ev - - -'ry chord.

"Chester" and two other songs by Billings have been incorporated into a larger orchestral work by the contemporary composer William Schuman. Schuman's three-part composition, *New England Triptych*, suggests the rugged and vigorous nature of Billings' original music.

The second movement of *New England Triptych* is the round "When Jesus Wept." Again, teach yourself the song in the step-by-step manner outlined above, then sing it as a round with three other people.

When Jesus Wept

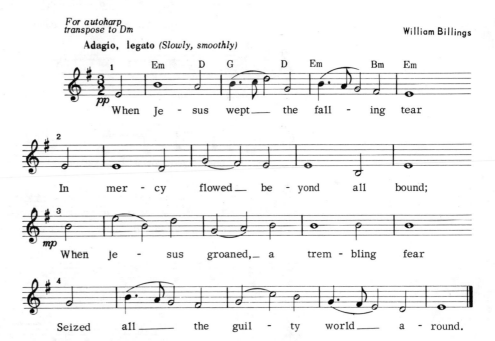

When you are familiar with both of the Billings songs, listen to a recording of Schuman's *New England Triptych* and try to follow the melody of each song as you hear it.

"Havah Nagilah" features an unusual interval that is characteristic of Israeli music. It is a very wide second, wider even than a whole step, and it occurs first in measure 1, between the F♯ and E♭. The same interval occurs nine more times in the song. Mark the ten appearances of the wide second and then play the two notes on the piano, bells, or recorder until you can duplicate the pitches exactly with your voice. Practice singing the interval until your ear and voice become accustomed to its sound and you can sing it accurately in the context of the music. The song is recorded to help you sing it accurately.

Havah Nagilah (*Recorded*)

For autoharp
transpose to Am

Israeli Folk Song

Out in the mead-ow mu - sic is play - ing;

Peo - ple are danc - ing, They cir - cle a - bout.

Arms linked with one an - oth - er, They dance the

ho - ra And while they dance mer - ri - ly shout:

"Come, do the ho - ra now, Watch, and we'll show you how;

Step, hop, and once a - gain. See how it is done.

Hear how we keep the beat Step - ping and live - ly feet;

Come, join our cir - cle now; Come, dance with your friends!

Now that we're to - geth - er, Ev-'ry one steps a lit-tle fast - er,

Ev - 'ry one hops a lit - tle fast - er;

See how the cir - cle's turn - ing fast - er,

See how the cir - cle's turn - ing fast - er!

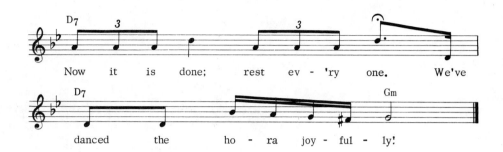

Now it is done; rest ev - 'ry one. We've

danced the ho - ra joy - ful - ly!

The *hora* mentioned in the song is an Israeli folk dance in which the dancers form a circle, lock arms, and dance to the left or right with small steps and hops. When you have learned "Havah Nagilah" thoroughly and can sing it easily, try the dance as you sing. Children enjoy this kind of movement, and it is an excellent form of enrichment for their musical experience.

The Hora

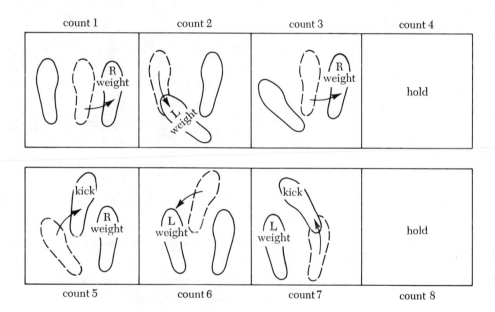

These hints may help you with the dance:

1. Think "Step step step hold, kick step kick hold," with all eight counts occurring evenly.
2. Take small steps to maintain balance.
3. When each person can do this individually, form a group circle and put your hands on the shoulders of the dancers on either side of you.
4. Stay closer than arm's length to your neighbors, so the circle won't break.
5. Proceed with the circle moving to the right, as in the diagram, or to the left.
6. *Always* follow the beat of the music.

The "Galway Piper" also adapts well to simple dance steps.

Galway Piper

When you have learned the song, try this dance. The partners stand in a double circle, facing but remaining several steps away from each other:

1. Take three steps forward and bow or curtsy.
2. Take three steps backward and bow or curtsy.
3. Take four skips forward to partner's right and do-si-do (French *dos à dos*, meaning *back to back*).
4. Skip backward to place.
5. Facing partner, join both hands and move two steps sideways, counterclockwise.
6. Move two steps clockwise.
7. Link right arms and take four skips around partner.
8. Take three steps backward to place, facing partner again.

Look for other songs that suggest dances and devise your own steps. Pay special attention to the style of music and the form of the song.

As with any skill, the more adept you become at reading, performing, and creating music, the more you will enjoy it, and your efforts at sharing the art with children will be more successful.

Review Questions

1. Why should you carefully consider the words to a song when you are deciding on its interpretation?

2. Which is suggested for earlier consideration, rhythm or pitch?

3. How many measures in "Havah Nagilah" contain borrowed units?

4. Name two aspects of notation or words that provide clues as to where phrases begin and end.

5. What are some ways to find the correct starting pitch of a song?

6. What aspects of a song determine the best dynamic levels for the music?

Appendixes

**Appendix A
Glossary**

Accent — Making one sound louder than other sounds near it, or making the start of a sound louder than its conclusion.

Accompaniment instruments — Instruments that are generally used for song accompaniment because they can produce several notes simultaneously.

Alla breve — Notation in which the half note represents the beat.

Alto — The lower part for women's or unchanged voices.

Art song — A composed song that consists of an expressive unity of text and music.

Asymmetrical meter — A meter that is not divided into equal portions by the stressed beats; for example, 1 2 3 4 5.

Atonal music — Music with little or no feeling of key center.

Autoharp — An instrument with metal strings stretched across a frame and strummed to produce a group of sounds determined by a pushbutton mechanism.

Bar — Another term for *measure*.

Barlines — The vertical lines indicating measures.

Bass — (BASE) The lower part for men's voices.

Beam — The thick line or lines connecting two or more stems that would otherwise have flags attached.

Beat — The recurrent throb or pulse in music.

Block chords — Chords containing only one simultaneous sounding of the chord members.

Blue notes — The optional lowering of the third, fifth, or seventh steps in a major scale while performing in the blues style. The blue notes are harmonized with the unaltered major chords.

Borrowed patterns — The presence of a rhythmic figure from one type of meter in a piece with a different type of meter.

Canon — A musical work in which one part is imitated strictly in another part a few beats or measures later. The imitation may be at the same or a different pitch level.

Castanets — Two small, hollow, wooden cup-shaped pieces attached to a handle and sounded by a quick motion of the player's hand. They can also be struck together or against part of the body.

Chorale — A straightforward melody sung in many Protestant churches; especially associated with Martin Luther.

Chord — The simultaneous sounding of three or more pitches.

Chord members — Notes in a chord.

Chromatic — A succession of half steps indicated by flats and/or sharps in the notation.

Claves — (CLAH•vays) Two thick wooden sticks that are struck against each other. Used often in Latin American music.

Clef — A sign placed on the staff to indicate the exact pitches of the notes.

Coconut shells — Two hollowed half-spheres that are struck together on the open ends, hit singly on a flat surface, or struck on the outside with a mallet.

Coda — A distinct concluding portion of a musical work.

Common time — A metrical pattern of four beats per measure, with a quarter note representing the beat. The meter is indicated by $\frac{4}{4}$ or by a sign that looks like a large C.

Composing — The development and writing of a musical work over a period of time.

Compound meter — Meter in which the beat subdivides into three background pulses.

Conductor's beat — Standardized arm motions which indicate the tempo and metrical pattern of the music.

Consonance — The impression of agreement between pitches sounded together.

Countersubject — The contrasting theme in a fugue.

Crescendo (Cresc.) — A directive telling the performer to get gradually louder.

Curwen-Kodály hand signals — A system of hand signals that indicate the sol-fa syllables.

Cut time — A meter in which there are two beats to the measure and a half note represents the beat. It is indicated by $\frac{2}{2}$ or by the symbol ₵.

Cymbals — Large metal discs struck together or suspended singly and hit with a mallet or brush.

Decrescendo (Decresc.) — A directive telling the performer to get gradually softer.

Descant — A separate melody that complements the main melody. It is usually higher than the main melody.

Diminuendo (Dim.) — A directive telling the performer to get gradually softer.

Dissonance — The impression of tension or disagreement between pitches sounded together.

Dominant chord — The chord built on the fifth step of the scale. It is often designated by the Roman numeral V.

Dominant seventh chord — A seventh chord built on the fifth step of the scale.

Dorian mode — A scale resembling minor with a raised sixth step. It can be produced on the white keys of the piano by playing from D to D.

Dotted note — A note with one dot to the right of the note head. The dot increases the value of the note by one half.

Double dotted note — A note with two dots to the right of the head. The first dot adds half the value of the note, and the second dot adds half the value of the first dot.

Downbeat — The first beat of a measure. When conducted, it is indicated by a downward motion.

Drum — Instrument having a stretched skin or membrane that is struck with the fingers, a beater, or sticks.

D.S. al Fine — A directive to the performer to return to the sign (𝄋) and go on to the end or *Fine.*

Duple meter — A metrical pattern of two beats in each measure, the first one stressed and the other not stressed.

Dynamics — The varying levels of loudness and softness.

Eighth note — A note with a solid head and a stem with one flag. It is half the value of a quarter note.

Eighth rest — A rest indicated by this symbol 𝄾 .

Exposition — The opening section of a fugue. It is the section in which the subject and countersubject are presented.

Fermata — A sign (𝄐) telling the performer to hold the note or the rest until he feels the music should resume its regular tempo.

Final — The note around which a pentatonic or modal piece of music seems to center.

Fine — (FEE•nay) The end of a piece of music, occurring after an interior portion of the music has been repeated.

Finger cymbals — Small metal discs struck against one another on their edges.

Flag — The curved line attached to the stem of eighth and sixteenth notes.

Flat — A symbol (♭) indicating that a pitch should be lowered one half step.

Form — The overall design on which a musical work is constructed.

Forte — (FOR•tay) A loud dynamic level. The word is often indicated by its first letter, *f*.

Frets — The crosswise ridges against which the strings are pressed on a guitar or ukulele.

Fugue — A contrapuntal instrumental work for two or more parts that follow one another as in a round.

Grand staff — Two staffs connected, one with a treble clef and one with a bass clef. Piano music is written on a grand staff.

Gregorian chant — Sacred vocal music consisting of one melodic line with neither accompaniment nor strong metric accents.

Guiro — (WEE•roh) A notched gourd scraped across the notches by a stick and heard often in Latin American music.

Guitar — An instrument with six strings stretched over a hollow wooden body. They are plucked or strummed with the fingers.

Half note — A note with a hollow head and a stem, but no flag. It is twice the value of a quarter note.

Half rest — A rest that looks like this: ▬ .

Half step — The smallest pitch distance possible on a keyboard instrument.

Harmonizing — The creation of an accompanying part to a melody.

Harmony — The effect created when pitches are sounded at the same time.

Head — The egg-shaped portion of a note.

Hold — See *Fermata*.

Hora — An Israeli folk dance.

Huapango — (Wah•PANG•go) A lively dance from the Caribbean in which the meter alternates between $\frac{6}{8}$ and $\frac{3}{4}$, with the speed of the eighth notes remaining constant.

Improvising — The process of making up music at the moment.

Interval — The distance from one pitch to another.

Inverted chord — A chord in which the root is not the lowest pitch.

Key — The effect created when pitches are related to a tonal center.

Keyboard — A repeated arrangement of five black and seven white keys that produce a wide range of pitches, as on a piano and organ.

Keynote — See *Tonal center*.

Key signature — The group of flats or sharps at the left of each staff in a musical work. The key signature indicates which notes are consistently raised or lowered by one half step.

Leger lines — Short horizontal lines on which notes too high or too low for the regular staff are placed.

Lydian mode — A scale resembling major with a raised fourth step. It can be produced on the white keys of the piano by playing from F to F.

Major scale — A seven-note scale with a half step between 3-4 and 7-8.

Major triad — A triad with a wide third on the bottom and a narrow third on the top.

Maracas — Rattles, often in pairs, that are shaken to produce the sound of moving pellets.

Measure — The area between two barlines. It represents one unit of the prevailing metrical pattern.

Melody bells — Metal strips arranged in keyboard fashion and struck with a mallet.

Melody instruments — Instruments that produce definite pitches and are especially well suited for playing melodies.

Meter signature — The two numbers or the symbol that indicates the metrical pattern and the type of note representing the beat.

Middle C — The C nearest the middle of the piano keyboard and in the middle of the grand staff.

Minor scale — A seven-note scale that in its natural form has half steps between 2-3 and 5-6.

Minor triad — A triad with a narrow third on the bottom and a wide third on the top.

Mixed meter — Several changes of meter in a piece.

Mixolydian mode — A scale resembling major with a lowered seventh step. It can be played on the white keys of the piano by going from G to G.

Mode — A seven-note scale that is neither major nor minor.

Movement — A sizable independent section of a musical work.

Natural — A symbol (♮) that cancels a previous sharp or flat.

Natural minor scale — See *Minor scale*.

Nonmetrical music — Music that has no regular metrical patterns.

Note — The letter name assigned to a pitch. Also a symbol composed of a head, often with a stem attached, that indicates the pitch and rhythmic value of a musical sound.

Octave — The pitch distance between a note and the nearest pitch with the same letter name.

Open string — A string that is not fingered.

Opus (Op.) — Latin for *work*. Composers often assign opus numbers to their compositions, generally in chronological order.

Ostinato — A persistent melodic or rhythmic pattern that is repeated several times in succession.

Parallel keys — Any two keys that have the same tonal center but different key signatures; for example, C major and C minor.

Part song — A song with one or more voice parts in addition to the melody.

Pentatonic — A five-note scale containing no half steps and no interval larger than a step and a half.

Phrase — A group of notes that belong together as a musical idea, like a phrase in language.

Phrygian mode — A scale resembling minor with a lowered second step. It can be duplicated on the white keys of the piano by playing from E to E.

Picardy third — The raising of the third step of a minor scale in the final chord of a piece.

Piano — 1) A keyboard instrument capable of producing eighty-eight pitches. 2) A directive to the performer to perform the music softly. The word is usually shortened to its first letter, *p*.

Pickup — An unstressed note that begins a musical phrase.

Pitch — The highness or lowness of a sound.

Plainsong — See *Gregorian chant*.

Polyphonic music — Musical works made up of two or more equally important lines or parts.

Preparatory beat — The silent beat given by a conductor to indicate tempo and to help the performers begin together.

Primary chords — The tonic or I, subdominant or IV, and dominant or V chords in a major or minor key.

Quadruple meter — A metrical pattern of four beats, with the first beat stressed.

Quarter note — A note with a solid head and a stem with no flag. It is frequently used to represent the beat.

Quarter rest — A rest that looks like this: ⅞ .

Recorder — A wind instrument whose holes are covered to alter the length of the air column and thereby change the pitch.

Relative keys — Any two keys that have the same key signature but different tonal centers.

Repeat sign — A sign (:‖) indicating the immediate repetition of a section of music.

Rest — Measured silence in music.

Rhythm — The progression of music in terms of time.

Rhythm instrument — Any instrument that produces no specific pitches.

Rhythm sticks — Two rods that are hit against one another.

Rhythmic syllables — Syllables that indicate the relative rhythmic value of notes.

Rondo — A piece of music in which one melody returns several times, with other melodies interspersed between its various appearances.

Root — The note on which a chord is built.

Round — A song in which the same music is performed at the same pitch level but at different times in a "follow-the-leader" fashion.

Sandblocks — Sandpaper stretched over wooden blocks to produce a raspy effect when they are rubbed together.

Scale — A series of pitches ascending and descending in a prescribed pattern of intervals.

Semitone — See *Half step.*

Sequence — The immediate repeating of a short melodic figure at different pitch levels.

Seventh chord — A chord with four pitches, each a third apart.

Sharp — A symbol (♯) indicating that a pitch should be raised one half step.

Sightreading — The performance of unfamiliar music without rehearsing or studying it beforehand.

Simple meter — Meter in which the beat subdivides into two background pulses.

Sixteenth note — A note consisting of a solid head and a stem with two flags. It is one-fourth the value of a quarter note.

Sleigh bells — Small spherical bells attached to a strap or frame and shaken for a light jingling effect.

Slur — A curved line between two or more notes of different pitch, indicating that there should be no separation between the notes.

Sol-fa syllables — Syllables that indicate the relative position of pitches in a scale.

Soprano — The highest pitched part in a choral group. It is sung by women or unchanged voices.

Staff — The five lines and four spaces on which notes are placed.

Stem — The vertical line attached to the head of certain kinds of notes.

Subdominant chord — The chord built on the fourth step of the scale. It is often designated by the Roman numeral IV.

Subject — The main theme of a fugue.

Syncopation — The removal of an accent or stress where it is expected and/or the addition of one where it is not expected.

Tablature — A system of notation that pictures finger placement on instruments such as guitar and ukulele.

Tambourine — An instrument that has a skin or membrane stretched across a wood hoop with discs around its edge. The player may shake the hoop or strike the head.

Temple blocks — Hollow wooden blocks that are struck with a mallet.

Tempo — The rate of speed of the beats.

Tenor — The higher part for men's voices.

Terraced dynamics — Distinct planes or levels of loudness and softness.

Theme — The central melody of a musical work.

Theme and variation — A composition in which a theme is treated in a variety of ways.

Through-composed — A musical work with no repetition of phrases.

Tie — A curved line connecting two notes of identical pitch to indicate that the duration of the two notes should be combined into one continuous sound.

Timbre — (TAM·ber) The tone quality of a voice or instrument.

Time signature — See *Meter signature*.

Tonal center — The pitch on which a scale is built and toward which the music tends to gravitate.

Tonic — See *Tonal center*.

Tonic chord — The chord built on the first step of the scale. It is often designated by the Roman numeral I.

Transposition — Writing or performing notes at a pitch level different from the original.

Treble clef — The clef on which G above middle C is the second line. Also called the G clef. It looks like 𝄞 .

Triad — A chord containing three pitches, each a third apart.

Triangle — A three-sided suspended metal frame struck with a beater.

Triple meter — A metrical pattern of three beats, the first one stressed and the other two not stressed.

Triplet — A group of three equal notes to be performed in place of more or fewer notes of the same value.

Two-part song — A song with two vocal parts that are performed together.

Upbeat — A one-beat note at the beginning of a musical phrase. It is an unstressed beat — the last one in the preceding measure.

Ukulele — An instrument with four strings stretched over a hollow wooden body. It is played by plucking or strumming with the hand.

Value — The indicated duration of a note.

Whole note — A note with a hollow head and no stem. It has four times the value of a quarter note.

Whole rest — A rest (▬) which hangs from the fourth line of the staff.

Whole step — A pitch distance equaling two half steps.

Appendix B
Tempo Markings

Here are some of the Italian words most commonly used to indicate tempo.

Italian Term	Meaning
Largo	Very slow, broad
Grave	Very slow, heavy
Adagio	Slow, leisurely
Andante	"Walking," moderate tempo, unhurried
Moderato	Moderate speed
Allegretto	"Little allegro," moving easily
Allegro	Moderately fast, moving briskly
Allegro molto	"Much allegro," very brisk
Vivace	Lively
Presto	Very fast
Prestissimo	As fast as possible

Composers often couple other directives with the tempo marking. Usually the additions have more to do with style than with speed (such as *con fuoco*, "with fire or force"; *sostenuto*, "smooth, sustained"). Within the broad framework of a specific tempo there may be indications of lesser tempo changes: *meno*, "less" (as in *meno allegro*); *piu*, "more"; *poco*, "a little"; *rit.* or *ritard*, "gradually slower"; *accel.* or *accelerando*, "gradually faster."

***Appendix C
Phonetic
Pronunciation for
Foreign Language
Songs***

Frère Jacques (page 4) French

Freh-reh Jhah-keh, dor-may voo?
Soh-neh leh mah-tee-neh, din din dawn.

Es Regnet (page 30) German

Es rayg-net, es rayg-net, dee Air-deh veert nahs,
Dee Air-deh, dee zoh der-shtik ist,
Dee ee-ren Durst noon balt fair-gist.
Es rayg-net, es rayg-net, dee Air-deh veert nahs.

Die Musici (page 43) German

Him-mel oont Air-deh moos-sen fair-gayn;
Ah-bair dee Moo-zee-chee, ah-bair dee Moo-zee-chee,
Ah-bair dee Moo-zee-chee bly-ben be-shtayn.

Dona Nobis Pacem (page 44) Latin

Doh-nah noh-bees pah-chem.

Die Forelle (page 72) German

1. In eye-nem beck-line hel-leh, Da shoss in fro-er ile
   Dee lah-ni-sheh for-el-leh For-ee-ber vee ine file.
   Ick shtahnd ahn dame ge-shtah-deh Oont sah in soo-ser roo
   Des moon-tern fish-lines bah-deh Im klah-ren beck-line tsoo!
2. Ine fish-er mit dair roo-teh Voll ahn dame oo-fer shtahnd,
   Oont sahs mit kal-tem bloo-teh, Vee zick dahs fish-line vahnd.
   Zo lahng dame vas-ser hel-leh, Zo dahkt ick, nikt ge-brikt,
   Zo fengt air dee for-el-leh Mit zeye-ner ahn-gel nikt.
3. Doke end-lick vard dame dee-beh Die Tsite tsoo lahng.
   Air mahkt dahs beck-line too-kish troo-beh, Oont ay ick es ge-dahkt
   Zo tsook-teh zeye-nek roo-teh Dahs fish-line tzap-pelt drahn,
   Oont ick mit ray-gem bloo-teh Zah dee be-trohg-neh ahn.

Veni, Veni Emmanuel (page 92) Latin

Vay-nee, vay-nee Em-mah-nyoo-el, Cahp-tee-voom sol-vay Is-rah-el,
Kwee geh-meet in ex-ee-lee-oh, Pree-vah-toos Day-ee fee-lee-oh.
Gaw-day, gaw-day, Em-mah-nyoo-el Nahs-kay-toor pro tay, Is-rah-el!

Pat-a-Pan (page 94) French

1. Gee-yohm prahn tohn tahm-boo-ran, Twah, prahn tah floo-teh, Roh-ban;
   Oh sohn deh sez een-stroo-mahn . . . Zheh dih-ray No-eh gay-mahn.
2. Say-tay lah mohd oh-treh-fwah Deh loo-ay leh Rwah day rwah,
   Oh sohn deh sez een-stroo-mahn . . . Eel noo ahn foh fair oh-tahn.
3. Lohm ay Dyoo sohn ploo dah-cor Keh la floo-teh ay leh tahm-boor.
   Oh sohn deh sez een-stroo-mahn . . . Shan-tohn, dahn-sohn, soh-tohn-sahn.

A la nanita nana (page 95) Spanish

Ah lah nah-nee-tah nah-nah,
Nah-nee-tah ay-ah, nah-nee-tah ay-ah.

Nun Ruhen Alle Wälder (page 99) German

Noon roo-en ahl-leh Veld-er,
Fee, Men-shen, Staht' oont Feld-er,
Es shleft dee gahn-tseh Velt;
Eer ah-bair, my-neh Zin-nen,
Auf! auf! eer zolt be-gin-nen,
Vahs oy-rem Shup-fer vohl-geh-felt.

The Virgin's Cradle Hymn (page 100) Latin

Dor-mee, Yay-soo! Mah-tair ree-det
Kwy tahm dool-chem som-noom vee-det,
Dor-mee, Yay-soo! blahn-doo-lay!
See nohn dor-mees, mah-tair ploh-raht
In-tair feel-ah cahn-tahns oh-raht,
Blahn-day, vayn-ee, som-noo-lay.

Lovely Evening (page 120) German

Oh vee vohl ist meer ahm ah-bend, Ven tsoor roo dee glock-en loy-ten.

Joseph Dearest, Joseph Mild (page 122) German

Yoh-sef lee-bair, Yoh-sef mine,
Hilf meer veeg'n mine Kin-deh-line,
Gawt dair vill dine Loh-nair zein
Im Him-mel-rike,
Dair yoong-frou Zohn Mah-ree-ah.

Sakura (page 129) Japanese

Sah-koo-rah, sah-koo-rah, Yah-yoh-ee noh soh-rah-wah.
Mee-wah-tah-soo kah-gee-ree Kah-soo-mee kah koo-moh-kah
Nee-oh-ee zoh ee-zoo-roo Ee-zahyah Ee-zahyah
Mee-nee yoo-kah-oon.

Navajo Happy Song (page 145) Navajo

Hai yoh, hai yoh ip see nai yo!
Hay nah yay nah yoh.

Noel Nouvelet (page 147) French

No-el noo-veh-lay, No-el shahn-tohn ee-see,
Day-voh-tay jhahn, kree-ohns ah Dyew mair-see!
Shahn-tohn No-el poor leh Rwah noo-veh-lay, No-el!
Shahn-tohn No-el poor leh Rwah noo-veh-lay,
No-el noo-veh-lay, No-el shahn-tohns ee-see!

Appendix D
Recorder Fingering Charts

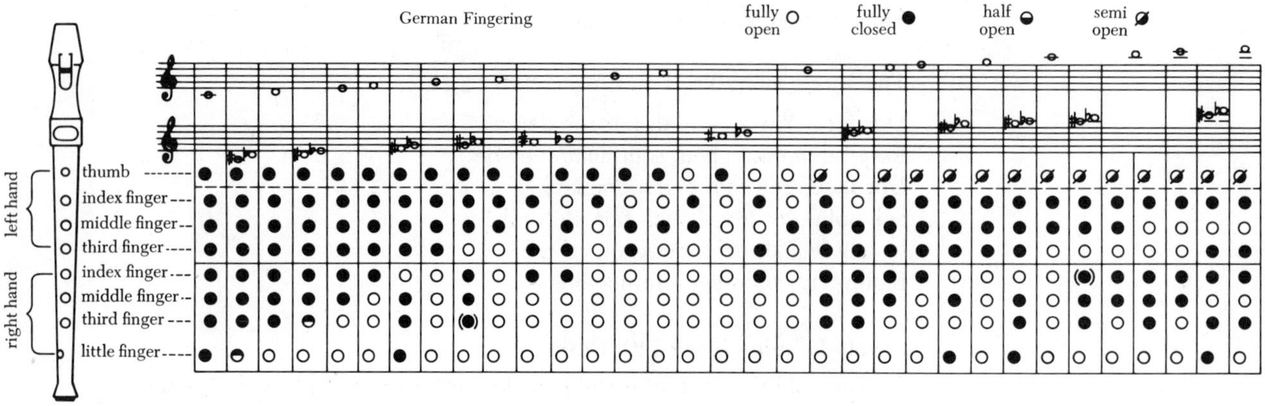

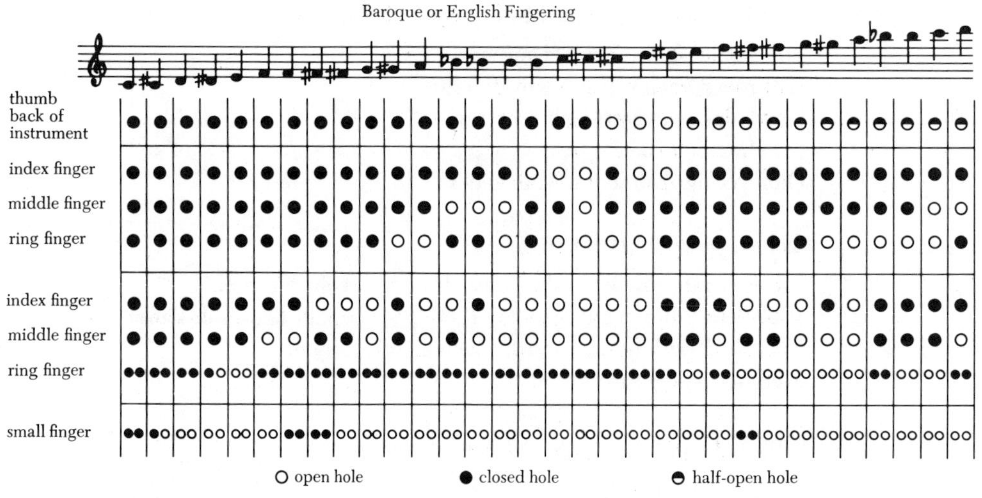

the "C" soprano recorder sounds one octave higher than written

Appendix E
Curwen Kodály
Hand Signs

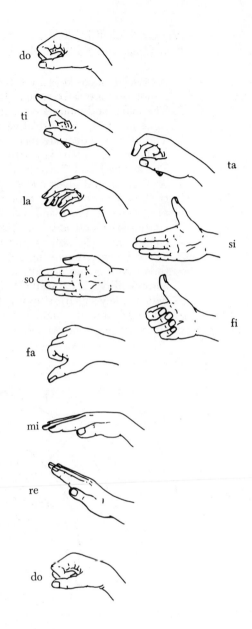

do
ti
ta
la
si
so
fi
fa
mi
re
do

The syllables *fi*, *si*, and *ta* are chromatic alterations that sometimes occur in a key. They are indicated by accidentals in the music, because they represent a departure from the prevailing key signature.

There are 12 different half steps between one *do* and the next. In ascending order the syllables for these chromatic variations are *do, di, re, ri, mi, fa, fi, sol, si, la, li, ti, do*. In descending order the syllables are *do, ti, te, la, le, sol, se, fa, mi, me, re, rah, do*.

Appendix F
Circle of Fifths

The circle of fifths illustrates the way in which key centers change according to their signatures. Notice in the diagram below:

1. All twelve major keys are listed around the outside in capital letters. All twelve minor keys are listed around the inside in small letters.
2. The major and minor keys paired in each pie-shaped wedge share the same key signature, so they are relative keys.
3. The twelve wedges are placed like numbers on a clock. The key with one sharp is at one o'clock; the key with one flat is horizontally across from it at 11 o'clock. The key with two sharps is at two o'clock; the key with two flats is at ten o'clock.
4. At five, six, and seven o'clock you see two sets of signatures and two sets of key centers. The double key centers are really the same sound, as you can tell if you play them on the piano: C♯ = D♭, F♯ = G♭, and B = C♭. The minor key centers are identical sounds also: a♯ = b♭, d♯ = e♭, and g♯ = a♭. Such pairs are *enharmonic*. The notes sound the same but are spelled differently.
5. The key center moves up a fifth with each additional sharp because the sharps themselves go up by fifths. The key center moves *down* a fifth with each additional flat because the flats themselves go down by fifths. The sharps and flats in a key signature appear to be written at random because they have to be squeezed onto the staff, but they really progress by fifths. Check this by the charts on pages 82–83 and 90.

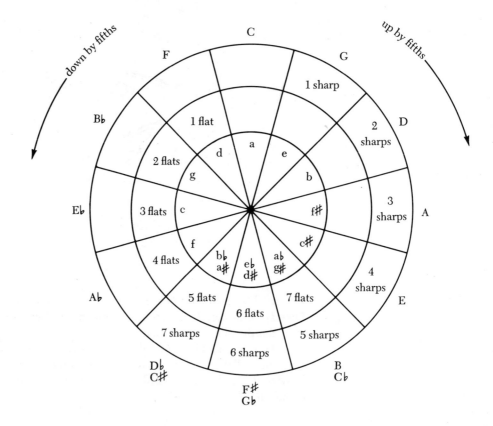

Appendix G
Guitar Chord
Diagrams

The chords are listed in alphabetical order. The (o) indicates an open string which should be sounded along with the other fingered strings. The (x) indicates that the string should not be sounded. The curved line indicates that the first finger should depress all of the strings indicated. The letter m indicates a minor chord.

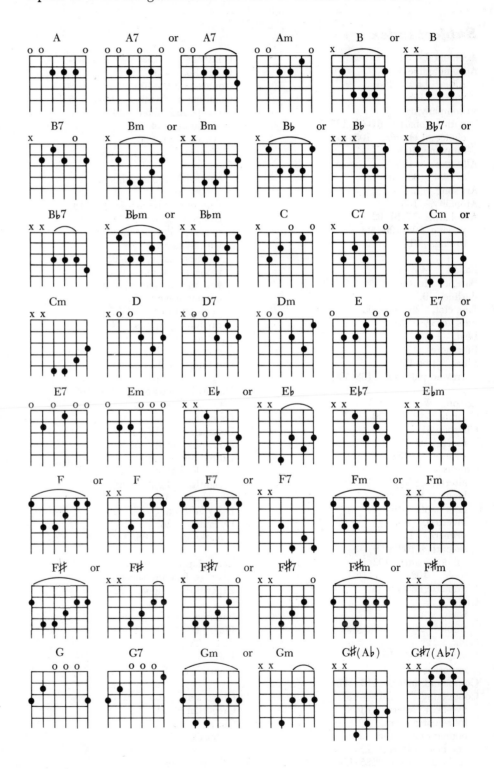

Indexes

Alphabetical Index of Songs

Classified Index of Songs

Index of Appropriate Harmonizations

Songs That Can Be Harmonized with Three Primary Chords (I, IV, and V)

Songs Involving Primary and Other Diatonic Chords — Chords without Accidentals

Songs Involving Altered Chords — Chords with Accidentals

Eb
Maj.

D
Maj.

F 7
Sev.

Gm
Min.

Bb
Maj.

A7
Sev.

C7
Sev.

Dm
Min.

F
Maj.

E7
Sev.

G7
Sev.

Am
Min.

C
Maj.

D7
Sev.

G
Maj.

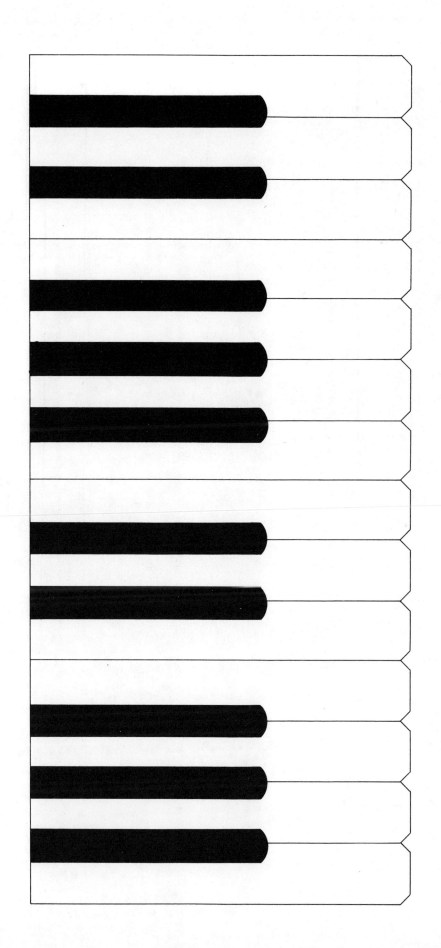

DATE DUE

COMPUTING FUNDAMENTALS

COMPUTING FUNDAMENTALS

Marjorie Leeson

GLENCOE

Macmillan/McGraw-Hill

New York, New York
Columbus, Ohio
Mission Hills, California
Peoria, Illinois

Library of Congress Cataloguing in Publication Data

Leeson, Marjorie
    Computing fundamentals / by Marjorie Leeson.
      p.   cm.
    Includes index.
    ISBN 0-02-800330-6 (text).—ISBN 0-02-800345-4 (IMK)
    1. Electronic data processing.   I. Title.
QA76.L422   1993
004—dc20   92-7213
                                        CIP

Imprint 1994

Send all inquiries to:
Glencoe Division, Macmillan/McGraw-Hill
936 Eastwind Drive
Westerville, OH 43081

Order Information:
ISBN 0-02-800330-6

  3 4 5 6 7 8 9 10 11 12 13 14 15   RRW   00 99 98 97 96 95 94

Copyright acknowledgments are on page 292.
Trademark listings are on page 293.

PREFACE

To the Reader

It seems that not a day goes by without some type of announcement about an improvement in microcomputers. We are told that each new change will make our lives easier and more fulfilling. Strangely enough, the claims are not far off.

Already it is difficult to imagine a world without microcomputers. Their impact on our daily lives has been enormous. Such routine activities as purchasing merchandise or paying a bill are, as often as not, conducted using a microcomputer. At school or on the job, you, too, will probably use a microcomputer with increasing frequency. In fact, microcomputers have become so pervasive that people in all walks of life, people who never dreamed of owning a microcomputer a year ago, are now purchasing their own microcomputer systems. We are, indeed, living in the midst of a revolution—a microcomputer revolution.

No one text can tell you everything about computer systems—the hardware and software that work together to process your data. Besides, few people want to learn everything. Each person has different reasons for learning about computers. A detail that is important to you may not be important to another individual. That is why this book is designed to provide you with the critical information about computer systems—both hardware and software—that you will need to use computers effectively.

This text provides coverage of computer topics, but its real focus is microcomputer topics. It will help you to understand the microcomputers that you will be using more and more frequently. It will also help you to communicate effectively with computer professionals.

Most of you have already communicated with a computer. You may have used a terminal to register for a class or at the bank to withdraw or deposit funds. This text is designed to take you beyond the "button pushing stage" and provide a basic understanding of microcomputer technology. Ultimately, it will help you to join the microcomputer revolution.

As you examine this book, look at the following features that make it a valuable resource to you:

- **In-depth coverage of hardware.** The basic components of microcomputer systems—the system unit, input devices, secondary storage, and output devices—are *fully* covered. The focus is on information that will be *useful* to you as you use computers, primarily microcomputers, in the future.

- **Comprehensive coverage of software.** In the future, it will not be enough to know one type of software application, or one "name-brand" software package. To use computers effectively, you will need a comprehensive knowledge of software applications. This book covers the six basic types of software applications. It discusses, and often compares, specific "name-brand" software packages, for both IBM-compatible and Macintosh computers.

- **Introduction to the application development process.** You will not always use "off-the-shelf" software packages, particularly in the business world. An awareness of how software applications are developed will help you participate more fully in the development process.

- **System solutions.** How do you use your knowledge of hardware and software to address real-world business requirements? Chapter 14, the final chapter, discusses how computer systems, a combination of hardware and software, are used to meet specific business objectives.

- **Current issues/hot topics.** The world of computers is changing so rapidly, it is hard to keep up. That is why each chapter contains two summaries of current articles about new technology or current issues related to the chapter. Additionally, each chapter ends with a section on "Future Trends."

- **Advice about computer selection.** Each chapter contains a section entitled "You and Your Personal Microcomputer" that summarizes the information in the chapter that is most relevant to an individual who is selecting a personal computer or who already owns a microcomputer system.

- **Time line.** It is easy to forget just how short a period it has been since the first microcomputer was introduced. The time line in Chapter 1 relates important events in microcomputer technology to other significant events that have affected our lives.

- **Hundreds of full-color illustrations.** Photographs, drawings, and other illustrations are used to present concepts clearly and effectively. Photographs of actual screens from a wide variety of software programs show exactly what the software looks like.

- **Topics for research and discussion.** Every chapter includes thought-provoking questions for in-class discussions and research. Some of these questions ask you to think about the implications of technology that you might otherwise have taken for granted. Other questions are "mini-case studies," describing a situation and asking you to determine a course of action. As you can imagine, these questions rarely have "correct" answers.

- **Objectives and review questions.** Each chapter opens with a list of objectives and ends with review questions to help you determine if you have met those objectives.

- **Glossary.** Many computer terms may be new to you. The glossary ensures that you will be able to look up the meaning of any word you may have forgotten from one chapter to the next. Key words in the chapter are highlighted, and an easy-to-understand definition of the term is given in the glossary.

It is my hope that this book will serve you as more than a textbook. I hope it becomes a handbook, helping you become more knowledgeable about microcomputers and, ultimately, helping you use microcomputers in ways that are both fulfilling and enjoyable.

Marjorie Leeson

PREFACE

To the Instructor

This book is designed for students enrolled in a one-quarter or one-semester first course on computers. It has a definite microcomputer focus. There are no course prerequisites. The book is intended as a handbook that will remain useful to students as they continue in school or as they enter the work force.

As a faculty member teaching a computer course you may have been searching for a comprehensive text that:

- provides in-depth coverage of microcomputer hardware and software.

- covers only relevant, timely information pertaining to microcomputers and microcomputer applications.

- includes actual descriptions and illustrations of software.

- will serve as a reference when the student is required to make decisions regarding the use of microcomputer technology.

All of the individuals who have worked long and hard on this text believe that it will "end your search." After using this text your students will have an in-depth understanding of microcomputer hardware, system software, major software packages, specialized software, data communications, and connectivity.

To assist you in teaching this course, an *Instructor's Manual and Key* offers a teaching outline, student objectives, lecture notes, and an answer key for each chapter. Additionally, applicable artwork from the text is provided in a format designed for making transparencies.

Other support materials include:

- **Test bank.** The test bank contains 1500 multiple choice, true-false, short-answer, and short-essay questions. The test bank is available in a computer-generated software format.

- **Texts for specific software applications.** Investigate Glencoe's *Increasing Your Productivity* series, as well as Glencoe/Osborne's *Mastering* series. Both series provide hands-on experience with the most popular word-processing, spreadsheet, database, and system software.

This book has taken a practical, microcomputer-oriented approach that we believe will help students long after they leave the course. We hope that this approach has created a book that will make teaching enjoyable, one that will help you touch your students' lives directly.

Marjorie Leeson

CONTENTS

PART TWO   ■   SOFTWARE   97

CHAPTER 12 COMMUNICATIONS AND CONNECTIVITY 218

CHAPTER 13 SPECIALIZED SOFTWARE 239

PART ONE

HARDWARE

When you think about a computer,
you probably picture *computer hardware,*
the physical components of a computer system.
That's what this section focuses on. You'll be
introduced to the *system unit,* which contains the
electronic circuitry that performs the actual processing
work of the computer and controls the operation of all
the other components. You'll see how *input devices,*
such as a keyboard or a mouse, translate human communication into a form that the computer understands.
Then you'll learn about the various types of *secondary
storage devices* used to store information so it can be
used by the computer. Finally, you'll take a look at *output devices,* such as monitors and printers, that display
or print information you have processed using the
computer or stored on a secondary storage device.

CHAPTER 1

WORKING WITH MICROCOMPUTERS

OBJECTIVES

The information in this chapter will enable you to

- Describe the impact that microcomputers have had, especially on the business world.
- Outline the most important events in the development of microcomputer technology.
- Explain what a computer is, and distinguish between hardware and software.
- Explain how modern computers are classified and why these classifications are blurring.
- Discuss the role computers are likely to play in your career and what you will need to know about them.

Microcomputers, also known as *personal computers,* are the smallest and least powerful computers. Microcomputers are everywhere. You encounter them every day, and perhaps you use them daily, too. If you look, you will find them in classrooms as well as in offices (Figure 1-1). You have also seen them at work in retail stores. For example, the store where you rent videotapes probably uses a microcomputer to keep track of its tapes. You are likely to encounter microcomputers in many other places, such as your physician's or dentist's office. If you have a job, you may use a microcomputer in your work. You might even have one at home.

Many people take microcomputers for granted. These devices have become so familiar that it seems as if we have always had them. But, they have not been around long at all. This chapter describes the microcomputer's emergence and its ever-expanding role in our day-to-day lives.

A Revolution in Your Lifetime

The Microcomputer Has Brought Vast Changes, Especially to the Business World, in a Very Short Time.

You have been part of a revolution, although you may not be aware of it. Our world has been changed irreversibly by a series of events that began when many of you were children. That revolution is still going on today, and it may continue for many years, but the generation that is coming of age today has been part of it from the start.

The first commercially available microcomputer, the Altair 8800, was sold in 1975. Before then, few people knew much about computers except for the technically trained specialists who worked with them. Only large organizations could afford computers, which cost hundreds of thousands of

FIGURE 1-1

Computers are now used in classrooms for students of all ages.

dollars or more. Computers were kept in special rooms, where the temperature and humidity had to be controlled carefully so the computers would not break down. Only the specialists had access to these rooms—and to the power of computing. The Altair helped to change all that.

Except for its size and price, the Altair had little in common with today's microcomputers. To do anything with the Altair, you needed a lot of technical know-how. Slow and clumsy, it had only a small fraction of the information processing speed and power of modern microcomputers. But the development of the Altair was among the first in a fast-moving series of events that made computer power available to virtually everyone. These events have followed one another at a rapid pace, so fast that they seem to blend into one another, like the frames of a movie.

The same year the Altair was introduced, two young men named Bill Gates and Paul Allen adapted the BASIC programming language for use with microcomputers. This innovation became the first product of the Microsoft Corporation, now one of the most prosperous companies in America. Gates, the chairman of Microsoft, has become a multibillionaire (see Figure 1-2).

Microsoft is at the forefront of an entire industry that has sprung up around microcomputers. This new industry ranges from giants like Microsoft to thousands of smaller companies and home-based businesses. It has created hundreds of thousands of jobs for people with a wide range of skills (Figure 1-3). The industry employs not just technicians and programmers but also factory workers, salespeople, writers, and business managers.

The microcomputer revolution has also spurred the development of such technologies as robotics, which allow microcomputers to control the tedious routine work so common on assembly lines. While this has meant that some jobs were lost when repetitive jobs were automated by computers, the microcomputer revolution has created many jobs, not just in the computer industry but throughout the business world. Most offices no longer employ typists; instead, they employ people who can use computers for word processing, desktop publishing, invoicing, analyzing data, and a variety of other tasks.

Microcomputers have become indispensable in the business world in a remarkably short time. Whatever career you pursue, you will probably encounter microcomputers in your day-to-day work. Many homes are

FIGURE 1-2

In 1975 Microsoft chairman Bill Gates, with Paul Allen, introduced a version of the BASIC programming language for use with microcomputers. Gates had just dropped out of Harvard to go into business.

FIGURE 1-3

The microcomputer has created jobs in factories, offices, stores, repair shops, and classrooms.

equipped with microcomputers, too. These devices may soon become as much a part of the American household as television.

Imagine how different our world was when television was not part of everyday life. Most people had far less information than they do now about what was going on outside their immediate neighborhoods. Companies relied on magazines, newspapers, and radio to tell people about their products and services. State and national election campaigns depended on meet-the-candidate rallies and radio broadcasts. Almost overnight, television changed the way we view the world, the way we make purchasing and voting decisions, and the way we spend our leisure time. For people born after television became commonplace, it may be difficult to imagine a world without it. Your parents or grandparents, though, may remember when television first came into their homes.

Similarly, you can probably recall a time when you could not use the power of a computer for doing your office work or your homework, exchanging messages with other computer users far away, or playing video games. The microcomputer revolution is still young and many people are just now joining in. For the next generation, though, a world without microcomputers will seem just as unlikely as the pre-TV world does to you.

What Is a Computer?

Computers Are Electronic Devices for Processing Many Kinds of Information Automatically.

A *computer* is an electronic device that can follow instructions to process information automatically. The processing may involve retrieving records, sorting, arithmetic calculations, or other kinds of manipulation. Computers can display information electronically, print it, or produce it in other forms.

You can better understand the usefulness of computers if you think about the difference between data and information. *Data* consists of raw facts. These facts can take the form of words, numbers, or codes that include both letters and numerals. *Information* consists of data that has been processed and made useful (Figure 1-4). For example, a person's name is a piece of data. Addresses are also data.

Many businesses store customers' names and addresses in a form their computer can read, along with other data about customers and their purchases. The computer can manipulate this data to produce many kinds of information. For example, someone in the company's sales office may want a list of all customers who live in Ohio. Someone in the billing department will use the data to produce invoices. The customer list and the invoices are two of the many kinds of information the computer can produce from the same data. A computer makes many employees' jobs easier because it stores data so that it can be retrieved and manipulated for many purposes.

A *computer system* includes all the equipment and instructions needed for entering data into the computer and producing information from it. The system includes both hardware and software. ＋ *an operator*

The term *hardware* refers to the computer system's physical components (Figure 1-5). A computer's electrical circuitry, screen, keyboard, cables, and so forth, are all part of the system's hardware.

The instructions you give a computer are called *software*, or *programs*. Without software, the hardware is useless. Software is written in *programming languages* by people called *programmers*. There are hundreds of programming languages that are used for different purposes. Perhaps you have heard of some programming languages, such as BASIC, COBOL, or C.

Less than 20 years ago, only people who knew how to write programs could use computers. Fortunately, that is no longer true. Ready-made software is now available for most tasks you want to perform with a computer.

Popular Drafting Machines
Highest quality, with features that will make your work easier and more precise.
• Vertical braking system
• Micrometer adjustment
• Full view protractor
• 10 year warranty

Size	List Price	Our Special Price
32" × 42"	$579.00	**$425.99**
38" × 50"	$589.00	**$435.99**
38" × 60"	$609.00	**$445.99**
38" × 72"	$623.00	**$456.99**

FIGURE 1-4

This price list is a form of information. A computer created it by processing many pieces of data, such as product names, product descriptions, and individual prices.

FIGURE 1-5

The video screen, keyboard, electrical circuitry, and all other physical parts of a computer are referred to as hardware.

THE MICROCOMPUTING REVOLUTION

Pre-1975

In 1969 Ted Hoff, an Intel employee, designs the first microprocessor (a single chip containing the elements of a microcomputer), the Intel 4004, with its 2,300 miniature circuits. It's first sold in 1971.

In 1972 Intel introduces a second microprocessor, the 8008.

Atari releases *Pong*, the first video game.

In 1973 Intel introduces the 8080 microprocessor. Scelbi Computer Consulting makes the first microcomputer: the 8008-based Scelbi 8-H.

1975

MITS develops the Altair 8800 microcomputer. It has an Intel 8080 microprocessor, but no keyboard, monitor, or software. Programmed by flipping switches and reading lights on the front panel, the kit is priced at $395 ($495 assembled). It needs up to $2,000 worth of extras. About 2,000 units are shipped in the first year.

Bill Gates and Paul Allen write the first program allowing Intel microprocessors to use the BASIC programming language. They license "Microsoft BASIC" to MITS, and found today's largest microcomputer software company: Microsoft Corporation.

Motorola introduces the 6800 microprocessor.

1976

Steve Wozniak and Steve Jobs build the first Apple (named after a summer job in an apple orchard) in their garage. Based on MOS Technology's 6502 microprocessor, it sells quickly at a local retail store. Soon, churning out their microcomputers by the dozens, they decide to form Apple Computer.

Seven hundred microcomputer enthusiasts gather in Albuquerque, New Mexico, for the World Altair Computer Conference, the first microcomputer conference.

Michael Shrayer writes the first software for word processing: *Electric Pencil.*

United States evacuates civilians from Saigon as communist forces complete takeover of South Vietnam.

FBI agents capture newspaper heiress Patty Hearst, who took part in a bank robbery after being kidnapped by terrorists.

Muhammad Ali retains his heavyweight boxing title with a 15-round decision over Jimmy Young.

The United States celebrates its 200th birthday.

Jimmy Carter of Georgia is elected the 39th president of the United States.

1977

Apple introduces the Apple II at the first West Coast Computer Fair in April (cost: $1,298). It comes fully assembled with case, keyboard, TV screen connection, BASIC interpreter, and color-capable graphics/text display.

Commodore Business Machines moves from calculators to computers with its introduction of PET (Personal Electronic Transactor) for $595. It features 4K (4,000 characters) of RAM (random access memory), a built-in monitor (screen), keyboard, and cassette tape drive, and graphics characters available at the press of a key.

Tandy Radio Shack plunges into the market with its first microcomputer, the TRS-80, for $600.

1978

Epson America introduces the first inexpensive dot-matrix printer, the MX-80.

MicroPro International Corporation announces *WordMaster* software. It is the precursor to *WordStar*, one of the best-selling word processing packages of all time.

Harvard Business School student Dan Bricklin and programmer Bob Frankston amaze the business world with the first electronic spreadsheet program, *Visi-Calc*. They design it for use with Apple II, and executives rush to buy Apples just to use the software. *VisiCalc* is marketed by Personal Software, later called VisiCorp.

Both Apple and Radio Shack introduce 5¼-inch floppy disk drives.

1979

Wayne Ratliff develops the *Vulcan* database program, which allows users to store data in files and to produce reports containing the data. The program eventually lives long and prospers as *dBASE II.*

Intel introduces the 8088, a faster microprocessor that later will be used in the IBM PC.

Hayes Microcomputer Products presents the Micromodem 100, the first modem specifically designed for microcomputers (cost: $399).

Magic Wand becomes *WordStar*'s first serious competitor in the war of the word processors.

Video games such as *Space Invaders* blast off, and *Pac Man* gobbles up the market.

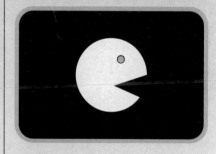

Star Wars dazzles audiences and becomes the film of the decade.

The State Department proposes the emergency admission into the United States of 10,000 additional boat people fleeing from Vietnam.

John Travolta launches the disco craze with *Saturday Night Fever,* and the Bee Gees garner a hit album.

The House Select Committee on Assassinations, investigating the killings of President Kennedy and Martin Luther King, Jr., concludes that conspiracies were likely in both cases, but finds no hard evidence to support further prosecutions.

Chrysler Corporation, with losses of $207 million in the second quarter, asks the federal government for a $1 billion loan.

Star Trek: The Motion Picture voyages into U.S. theaters.

1980

Sinclair Research produces the ZX80, the first microcomputer for under $200. Its successor, the ZX81, is later sold by Timex for less than $100.

The microcomputer industry has its first million seller: the Commodore VIC-20. It sells to the mass market through chain stores like Toys R Us, Montgomery Ward, and K Mart. It uses the 6502A microprocessor, offers a color display, and costs only $299.

Personal Software releases the popular adventure game *Zork, the Underground Empire*.

Apple announces the Apple III for the business market. The $3,495 microcomputer fails due to design errors and faulty components.

Satellite Software International (later WordPerfect Corporation) announces *WordPerfect*, a word processing program designed for Data General computers. It soon becomes the program of choice for office and professional word processing.

1981

The microcomputer revolution is legitimized: IBM introduces the IBM PC. It has an 8088 microprocessor, 64K of RAM, a single 5 1/4-inch floppy disk drive, and a price tag of $3,005. IBM projects sales of 250,000 PCs in five years. It soon sells that many in a month.

Microsoft releases the operating system MS-DOS Version 1.0 just for the IBM PC.

Hayes introduces what will become the PC industry's standard for modems: the Smartmodem 300.

Epson America introduces the notebook-size HX-20, considered the first laptop microcomputer. Weighing less than 3 pounds, with a standard-size keyboard and a 4-line display, it runs on batteries.

The big hits of the Christmas season are Intellivision video games developed by Atari and Mattel.

1982

Commodore presents the Commodore 64 microcomputer. For $595, it includes 64K bytes of RAM, 20K bytes of ROM (Read Only Memory, which is dedicated to a specific use), a custom sound chip, and color graphics. Later, the price drops to $200.

Non-Linear Systems (later called Kaypro) successfully challenges Osborne with its first portable, the Kaycomp II. It has a 9-inch screen and software, and retails for $1,795.

Radio Shack introduces the TRS-80 Model 16. The $4,999 microcomputer has an 8-inch floppy disk drive.

The first IBM PC clone—the MPC—appears from Columbia Data Products. It features easy expansion for multiusers. Later, Compaq and Corona also offer clones, and Compaq takes the lead.

Lotus Development unveils *Lotus 1-2-3*. The integrated software system has three attractions: an electronic spreadsheet, database functions, and graphics. It quickly replaces *VisiCalc* as king of the PC spreadsheets.

President Carter announces that the United States will boycott the Moscow Olympics to protest the Soviet intervention in Afghanistan.

The Polish government recognizes the newly formed Solidarity party's right to strike. Lech Walesa leads workers back to work after a 17-day strike.

Ronald Reagan wins a landslide victory over Jimmy Carter.

Iran releases 52 American hostages minutes after Ronald Reagan is inaugurated.

Prince Charles and Lady Diana are wed in royal splendor.

Poland declares martial law after Solidarity labor leaders call for a vote on the future of the government.

Argentina invades the Falkland Islands.

Delighted moviegoers think *E.T.* is out of this world.

Michael Jackson dances his way to a top-selling album with "Thriller."

1983

IBM introduces the PC XT in March for $5,000. Its main attraction is a built-in hard disk with 10MB (80 million characters) of storage. Eager buyers have to be put on waiting lists.

Radio Shack announces the 4-pound TRS-80 Model 100, the first portable with a standard-size keyboard, a relatively large display, and 20 hours of power on four AA batteries. It fits into a briefcase with room left over.

IBM introduces the PC Jr, its first microcomputer aimed at the home market. Featuring a "Chicklet" keyboard, it has a price tag of $699, but few buyers.

Apple presents Lisa, the first microcomputer for under $10,000 that features a mouse, windows (for displaying more than one file within a program), and icons (pictures instead of words) to indicate functions. It also simulates a desk environment with built-in notepads, file folders, a calculator, and other office tools. Priced at $4,495, it is a sales disaster.

1984

Apple introduces the user-friendly Macintosh for $2,495. It features a mouse, windows, and icons, and takes only a few hours to learn to use. By the end of the year, almost 500 software programs are available for the Macintosh, and Apple is a Fortune 500 company.

IBM announces the PC AT—the first microcomputer to employ an Intel 80286 microprocessor—with four times the processing speed of the IBM PC XT (cost: $5,469).

WordPerfect is introduced for the IBM PC, Victor 9000, DEC Rainbow, Zenith Z-100, and Tandy 2000.

Hewlett-Packard unveils the LaserJet, the first popular laser printer. It soon boasts the largest share of the laser printer market.

Apple introduces the Apple IIc, its first portable. For $1,823, it includes a built-in disk drive and 128K of RAM. It weighs 11 pounds without the monitor.

IBM announces its Portable PC, marking its first entry into portable computers. At 34 pounds, it finds few takers.

1985

Intel announces the swift and potent 32-bit Intel 80386. It gets the nickname "386," and becomes the new industry standard for microprocessors.

Microsoft Corporation produces *Windows*, the operating environment that allows separate software programs to run simultaneously in different windows on an IBM PC-compatible microcomputer's screen.

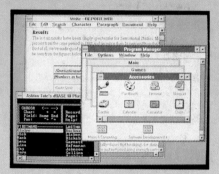

Aldus Corporation introduces *PageMaker*, a desktop publishing program with multicolumn formatting and text/graphics combinations. It is designed for use on a Mac with 512K of RAM.

Commodore introduces the Commodore Amiga 1000, the first multimedia personal computer, for $1,295. It features a multitasking, windowing operating system.

President Reagan denounces the Soviet Union as "the focus of evil in the modern world" and rejects a call for a nuclear freeze without additional Soviet arms reductions.

Physicist Sally Ride blasts off in *Challenger* and becomes the first American female astronaut to travel in space.

A Soviet fighter shoots down Korean Air Lines Flight 007, killing 269 people.

The Supreme Court rules it's legal for consumers to use video recorders to tape television programs for their own use. Television networks and motion picture companies vow to fight the decision.

Geraldine Ferraro is the first woman to run for vice president on a major party ticket. Ronald Reagan is reelected in a landslide.

Konstantin Chernenko dies and Mikhail Gorbachev is named the new Soviet leader.

In response to consumer protests against the new Coke, Coca-Cola reintroduces the original as Coca-Cola Classic.

Ronald Reagan signs the Gramm-Rudman bill, which mandates slicing the federal budget deficit to zero by 1991.

1986

The first microcomputer using Intel's 80386 microprocessor is announced by little known Advanced Logic Research. The computer is dubbed the Access 386.

Apple introduces the Apple IIgs microcomputer, with improved graphics, sound, and speed, targeted at the home and educational market.

Motorola announces the 68030 microprocessor, another powerful version of the 68000.

IBM brings out the PC Convertible, its second unsuccessful portable. It uses a 3 1/2-inch disk drive.

1987

In April, IBM introduces the Personal System/2 (PS/2) line and the OS/2 operating system by launching the PS/2 Model 80, based on the 386 microprocessor. PS/2 is IBM's second generation of small computers. It offers more built-in features, expansion capabilities, and a Video Graphics Array (VGA) display.

Apple introduces the Mac II for $5,000, and the Mac SE for $2,600.

Lotus files a lawsuit against Paperback Software and Mosaic Software, charging they have copied the "look and feel" of *Lotus 1-2-3*.

Microsoft announces *Excel* for the PC, a spreadsheet program designed to take full advantage of the *Windows* environment.

Compaq becomes one of the first manufacturers to introduce a 386-based portable, the Portable III.

1988

NEC's 4.4-pound UltraLite portable computer is well received.

Compaq produces the SLT/286 portable, the first VGA laptop widely distributed in the United States.

Apple presents the Mac IIx, 10% to 15% speedier than the Mac II.

Steve Jobs, pushed out of Apple in a power struggle, unveils the Next workstation. The Motorola 68030-based multimedia workstation runs on the Unix operating system (price range: $7,000 to $10,000).

Apple Computer sues Microsoft and Hewlett-Packard, charging that the overlapping windows and icon manipulation screen features in their products (*Windows* and *New Wave*, respectively) violate Apple's copyrights.

The *Challenger* Space Shuttle explodes 73 seconds after lift-off, killing all seven crew members.

The 100-year-old Statue of Liberty, newly refurbished from torch to toe, gets a birthday party.

The Iran-contra scandal begins to unravel in Washington.

Soviet General Secretary Gorbachev signals a new era of *glasnost* ("openness"), proposing economic and social reforms.

The public hearings by the Senate and House committees investigating the Iran-contra affair begin; in the process, Lt. Col. Oliver North becomes a media sensation.

Wall Street crashes, plummeting a record 508 points—22.6%—in one day.

With the United States suffering the worst drought in more than 50 years, one-half of the nation's agricultural areas are declared disaster areas. James Hansen, a NASA scientist, says that a "greenhouse effect" is taking place.

George Bush is elected 41st president of the United States.

1989

Apple presents the Macintosh SE/30. It has a 68030 microprocessor and costs $4,369. It also introduces the powerful, compact Macintosh IIcx, which proves an instant success.

Apple unveils the Mac Portable, which has a built-in trackball and can go 12 hours between battery charges. It's heavy, at 16 pounds, and pricey, with a nearly $6,000 price tag. It is not a hit.

Poqet Computer Corporation announces a real lightweight—its 1-pound DOS PC for $1,995.

Lotus presents the 3-D spreadsheet: *Lotus 1-2-3, Release 3.0.*

GRiDPad Systems unveils the GRiDPad, which recognizes handwriting.

1990

The long-awaited *Microsoft Windows 3.0* appears. Enormously successful, it spurs the development of many new *Windows*-based software products.

Apple's Mac IIfx is unveiled. Sporting a 40-MHz Motorola 68030 microprocessor and a 40-MHz Motorola 68882 math coprocessor, it is Apple's most powerful microcomputer.

IBM introduces the RS/6000 family to the workstation market. The workstations use RISC technology and the Unix operating system.

Apple introduces three low-end Macintosh models—the Mac Classic, the Mac LC, and the Mac IIsi—and faces off with the increasingly popular IBM compatibles.

For the home and home office PC market, IBM presents the PS/1. The complete system, including 512K of RAM, one 1.44MB floppy, a black and white VGA display, an internal modem, and a two-button mouse sells for $999.

1991

Apple Computer and IBM announce an alliance that includes the formation of two new joint-venture companies. Their goal is to develop a common operating system so programs can be used on Macintoshes or IBM PC compatible computers.

Borland (which owns *Paradox,* a database management system that has just emerged as the market leader) purchases Ashton-Tate (which owns the *dBASE IV,* the displaced market leader) for $440 million. Borland vows to support both programs.

Lotus releases its long-awaited *Lotus 1-2-3 for Windows.*

NCR introduces a 386 pen-based portable microcomputer that weighs less than 4 pounds.

The long-anticipated revision of DOS (DOS 5.0) is released. *Disk Operating System*

Apple releases System 7.0, the Macintosh's operating system.

The tanker *Exxon Valdez* strikes Alaska's Bligh Reef and causes the largest oil spill in U.S. history.

Chinese students demonstrate in the Tiananmen Square uprising.

Thousands celebrate New Year's Day at the recently reopened Brandenburg Gate, rejoicing that the Berlin Wall has finally come down.

Iraq invades Kuwait.

Operation Desert Shield becomes Operation Desert Storm as the United States and its allies begin forcing Iraq to withdraw from Kuwait.

A coup led by the Soviet Old Guard fails and the Soviet Union begins its dramatic reformation.

The Senate confirms the appointment of Clarence Thomas, a federal judge from Georgia, to the U.S. Supreme Court by a hair-thin margin.

FIGURE 1-6

This retail store is part of a national chain that sells software to consumers. It is one small component of a vast industry that has arisen from the microcomputer revolution.

For just a few hundred dollars—or less, in some cases—you can buy a program that may have taken thousands of hours to write. Retail software stores today are nearly as common as bookstores (Figure 1-6).

THE INCREDIBLE SHRINKING GIANT

The first true electronic computers were developed about a half century ago. Ever since, computers have been constantly shrinking in size and growing in power. The first general-purpose electronic computer actually put to work was called ENIAC (which stood for *E*nhanced *N*umerical *I*ntegrator *a*nd *C*alculator). ENIAC ran from February 1946 to October 2, 1955, when it was retired to the Smithsonian. ENIAC weighed 20 tons and filled a room the size of a house (Figure 1-7).

ENIAC's electrical circuitry depended on vacuum tubes, devices that worked much like transistors and resembled light bulbs full of fine wires

FIGURE 1-7

ENIAC, one of the earliest computers, was as big as a house. Programmers gave ENIAC its instructions by plugging electrical wires into different sockets on a panel. ENIAC was a wonder in its day, but it had less speed and power than today's inexpensive hand-held scientific calculators. What's left of this behemoth is on display in the Smithsonian.

(Figure 1-8). Televisions and radios used vacuum tubes before the days of transistors and printed circuits. An early television had only a dozen vacuum tubes, but ENIAC used 18,000 of them! About every 10 minutes, a tube would burn out, and the colossal computer would shut down until the dead tube was found and replaced. Not all of today's computers are small enough to fit on desktops, but even the most powerful modern computers take up no more space than a closet, and even the cheapest desktop microcomputer available today is far more powerful—and reliable—than ENIAC.

CLASSIFYING MODERN COMPUTERS

Computers are classified according to how fast they can process the multitude of instructions that make up a computer program and how much data they can store. The three major computer classifications are mainframes, minicomputers, and microcomputers. However, the lines between the categories are blurring as more power is packed into smaller devices.

Mainframes

The largest modern computers are called *mainframes* because building one of them once involved placing various components on a chassis, or "main frame." A mainframe is generally used as the central computer for a very large organization.

The processing speed of a mainframe is measured in *MIPS*, which stands for *M*illions of *I*nstructions *P*er *S*econd. Big companies began using mainframes in the 1950s to handle accounting and other large-scale information processing.

A mainframe can have more than a thousand *terminals*, or *workstations*, which generally include keyboards and video screens. A mainframe can be the center of an elaborate *network* that includes not only terminals but also several smaller computers.

The fastest and most powerful mainframes are called supercomputers. These computers process information so fast that their power is measured in *BIPS*, or *B*illions of *I*nstructions *P*er *S*econd. They are used for tasks that involve analyzing vast amounts of data, such as weather forecasting and nuclear research. Nearly half of the supercomputers in existence are used by the military, companies in the defense industry, or large research organizations.

Minicomputers

A *minicomputer* (Figure 1-9) is powerful enough to handle the information processing needs of a small company or a department within a big one. Minicomputers usually have terminals, like mainframes, but not as many. A typical minicomputer has between 4 and 100 terminals, although some have more. Minicomputers are far less expensive than mainframes.

Microcomputers

Microcomputers, as we have seen, are the smallest and least powerful computers. Even so, many microcomputers are considerably more powerful than mainframes were a decade ago.

Whereas a mainframe is most often used for processing a big company's data and a minicomputer for departmental needs, a microcomputer typically is used by just one person. That is why microcomputers are also known as *personal computers.*

FIGURE 1-8

The earliest computers used thousands of vacuum tubes like this one as part of their electrical circuitry. This is one reason for their immense size. When the computers were running, the vacuum tubes generated a great deal of heat, which caused the computers to fail frequently. The tubes themselves also burned out often.

FIGURE 1-9

This VAX minicomputer, made by the Digital Equipment Corporation, can handle the information processing needs of a large department or a small company.

Increasingly, however, organizations are linking their microcomputers with each other and with larger computers, as shown in Figure 1-10. A microcomputer that is part of such a network can be used as a *stand-alone* system, independent of other computers, or as the terminal of a minicomputer or mainframe.

Many different companies make microcomputers, and their designs are varied. A microcomputer can be large enough to take up most of a desktop or small enough to fit neatly inside a briefcase. But microcomputers of all types and sizes generally include these components:

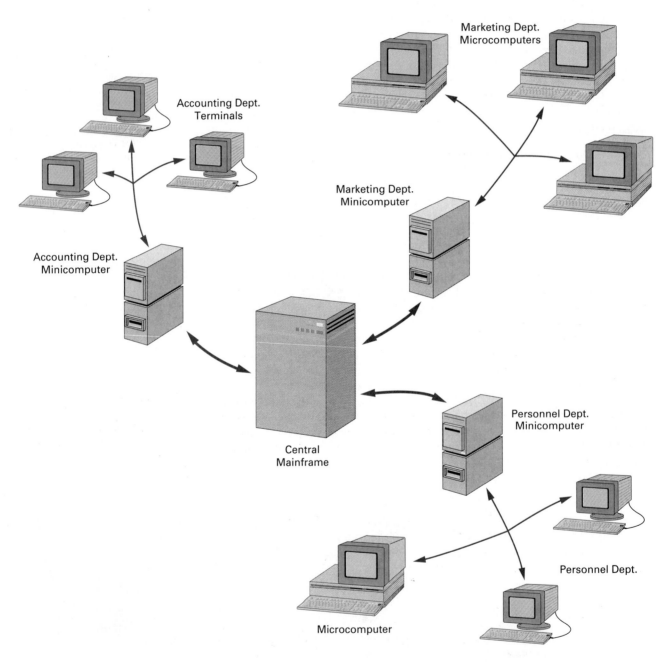

FIGURE 1-10

In big organizations today, mainframes are at the center of computer networks. These networks typically include minicomputers that handle data for individual departments. They also include microcomputers, which can be used as stand-alone computers or as terminals of the larger units.

- A system unit. This component houses the circuitry that does the computing. Chapter 2 focuses on the system unit.
- A keyboard. This is the device most often used for entering data. The keyboard and other input devices are the subject of Chapter 3.
- Disk drives. These house the magnetic disks that store software and data. Chapter 4 discusses disks and other forms of storage media in detail.
- A monitor. This is where the computer displays the data you enter as well as the results of its processing. Monitors and other output devices are the subject of Chapter 5.
- A printer. This device transfers information to paper from the computer's internal memory or storage device. Printers are discussed in Chapter 5.

Although many kinds of microcomputers are available today, most of those used in offices are one of two types:

- *IBM-compatible,* or modeled after microcomputers made by the International Business Machines Corporation.
- *Macintosh,* made by Apple Computer, Inc.

Since this book deals with microcomputers mainly in the context of business and careers, we focus on these two types.

IBM-COMPATIBLE MICROCOMPUTERS

IBM was by no means the first company to make microcomputers, and many critics say its products are far from being the best, although they are among the most expensive. Even so, because its computers were so dominant in the business world, the IBM Personal Computer immediately set the standard for microcomputers when it appeared in 1981 (Figure 1-11).

IBM intentionally revealed the internal design of its first microcomputers. It did this so that people would quickly be able to develop software and add-on devices that would work with IBM products and help them to catch on. IBM's strategy worked, up to a point. Programmers all over the country began writing software that would run on the IBM PC, as opposed to microcomputers made by other manufacturers. However, other hardware manufacturers began producing microcomputers that use the same internal design as the IBM. These machines are called *IBM compatibles,* or *clones.* They can run the same software as IBM microcomputers, and most of them cost far less or offer improved performance.

FIGURE 1-11

The original IBM Personal Computer, which IBM no longer makes, looked much like today's models, but its capabilities were primitive by comparison.

Because of the clones' success, IBM has been more guarded about the design of its later microcomputer models. However, software that runs on the clones will also run on these models.

THE MACINTOSH

Apple began making microcomputers several years before IBM. In fact, the Apple II was the first microcomputer to catch on among businesspeople, who used it with a software product called *VisiCalc* for developing financial infor-

IBM PC'S FIRST 10 YEARS

The year 1991 marked the 10th birthday of the IBM PC, the desktop personal computer that changed forever the way business is conducted. Back in 1981, new brands of desktop computers kept appearing, each significantly different from the next. If you bought one, it would not work with any other. Who could have guessed, in 1981, that two companies, IBM and Apple, would emerge from the pack and set the standards by which microcomputers were judged for the next decade?

Although the IBM PC (and its many imitators) now dominates the office desktop computer arena, in 1981 it was not so obvious that this would happen. After all, the IBM PC was not the first personal computer. And the first IBM PCs—although faster than much of the competition (IBM introduced the first 16-bit PCs)—were plodders by today's standards. Expandable memory of up to 512K also gave IBM an edge. But several of IBM's competitors, such as Tandy, Apple, Kaypro, and Xerox, were friendlier or cheaper. In theory, any of these computers could have set the standard for office desktop computers.

What gave IBM its edge was its distribution channels. More than any other computer manufacturer, IBM realized that the key to success was a marketing and distribution program aimed at business users. IBM's sales force outdid the competition, hitting both its business customers and the major computer stores, such as ComputerLand, with aggressive and knowledgeable marketing. Giant IBM, with its corporate muscle, created an irresistible bandwagon effect and everybody jumped aboard. Apple Computer, still aiming its marketing at users in schools and homes, was quickly left behind in the race for office desk space.

Several years later, after the dust had settled, Apple emerged as the number-two desktop computer manufacturer on the strength of its user friendliness and its graphics capabilities.

Today, IBM and Apple dominate the personal computer business. In fact, today's decision to purchase desktop computers comes down to buying an IBM, or a brand that runs like an IBM PC but costs less (called a PC compatible or clone), or an Apple Macintosh.

Now, just when you think you know who's who in the computer world, the two leaders are getting married (sort of). Driven by fear that consumer electronics powerhouses such as Sony and Nintendo will infiltrate the PC market, IBM and Apple are working together on joint ventures, breaching corporate barriers that only yesterday seemed as permanent as the Berlin Wall once seemed.

After 10 years, the IBM PC revolution is over. The two computer superpowers have joined forces. Together, they are planning to change the face of modern computing once again.

The IBM PC—which changed forever the way business is conducted—celebrated its 10th birthday in 1991. Many think that if IBM and Apple Computer successfully join forces, another revolution is in the offing.

Sources: "The Tenth Anniversary of the IBM PC," by John Dvorak, *PC Magazine*, July 1991, p. 83. "Home Electronics Giants Bring IBM, Apple, Together," by Kristi Coale, *InfoWorld*, July 1 1991, p. 1.

FIGURE 1-12

From the beginning the Macintosh featured superior graphics capabilities that made it an immediate favorite with designers.

mation. However, in the business world the IBM PC, and the superior software developed to run with it, quickly eclipsed both the Apple II and *VisiCalc*.

In 1984, though, Apple introduced the Macintosh (Figure 1-12), which has gained a stronger foothold in the business world than the Apple II. The reason for the Macintosh's growing popularity is that most people find it easier to use than IBM-style micros. Instead of requiring you to enter commands with a keyboard, the Macintosh allows you to enter them by selecting icons (pictures) from the monitor. Unlike IBM, Apple did not disclose its design secrets, so there are no Macintosh compatibles.

The difference between the Macintosh (Mac) and the IBM is not as distinct as it once was. IBM micros can now use software that makes them work much like a Macintosh; the Mac can now use software that makes it function more like an IBM. Furthermore, IBM and Apple Computer have begun working together to develop products that should blur the difference between their microcomputers even more.

Computers and Your Career

Knowing How to Use Computers Is Becoming Essential to Success in Many Occupational Fields.

Understanding computers can help you in your career, regardless of the occupation you choose. For more and more occupations, a basic understanding of computers has become one of the minimum requirements (Figure 1-13). Designers and engineers who once worked primarily with pencils and paper are now using microcomputers to create more precise drawings in less time. Lawyers are using microcomputers to research legal issues faster and more thoroughly than they could in the past. In countless other fields, too, people are using computers to do their jobs better and more efficiently.

Chances are that you already have some knowledge of microcomputers. You may have used one in school, on a job, or at home. If you already have experience with microcomputers, you may be wondering why you should read this book. The answer is that it will broaden your understanding of how microcomputers work, how they are used in various types of office settings, and how you will be able to use them in the future.

Whatever your experience with computers has been so far, you probably have only a partial picture of what they can do. Using computers to do schoolwork or play games gives you only a hint of the power that has made

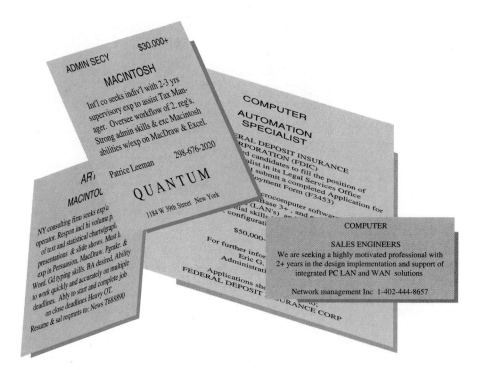

FIGURE 1-13

A look at the want ads in today's newspapers shows that many jobs require familiarity with computers.

these machines indispensable in business. By focusing on their usefulness in business, this book will expand on what you already know about microcomputers and prepare you to use them in a variety of jobs.

This book will increase your understanding of how computers work. For example, if you have ever used a computer, you undoubtedly used a keyboard to enter data. You may also have used a mouse. But Chapter 3 of this book will introduce you to many additional means of inputting data, such as touch screens, image scanners, and other devices used in business.

In short, this book tells you what you need to know about computers to work in today's business world, and it will help you to see what you will need to know in the future. It will also give you a vocabulary to talk about computers and to continue learning about them.

YOU AND YOUR PERSONAL MICROCOMPUTER

The early users of personal computers were mathematicians, engineers, or hobbyists who built their own computers. Once a typical hobbyist built a computer, it was seldom used. Even people who bought the preassembled Altair computer in 1975 made little use of its computing power.

Why? In 1975 low-cost, efficient input and output devices, good programming languages, and reliable programs to process data were not available. Many of the individuals who developed the early software had little knowledge of software applications or how software should be developed and tested. For example, an Altair user who bought home security system software programmed it so when the front door was opened, the message "DOOR IS OPEN" displayed on the television screen used as the system's output device. The system did not provide for security late at night when the television set had been turned off or when no one was watching it.

Also in 1975 input and output devices were expensive or nonexistent. Printers used for minicomputer systems cost anywhere from $20,000 to $50,000. Data could not be randomly retrieved from the storage devices available for use with microcomputers.

Today a wide range of input and output devices and excellent software are available at a reasonable cost. Also, microcomputers are "user friendly" and can be used by almost anyone—not just engineers or mathematicians. As you progress through this text, you will find that you will have a better understanding of computer systems and will be able to make more informed decisions regarding your microcomputing needs.

UNDERSTANDING COMPUTER TERMINOLOGY

People with technical backgrounds in computing have their own jargon, or specialized terminology. It includes terms that can get a point across quickly to another specialist but that have little or no meaning to others. Many computer terms are acronyms, which means they are made up from initials or syllables of several other words (Table 1-1).

Table 1-1: Computer Industry Acronyms		
Acronym	**Represents**	**Definition**
ASCII	*A*merican *S*tandard *C*ode for *I*nformation *I*nterchange	A universal code for storing data so it can be used with different kinds of software.
Bit	*Bi*nary digi*t*	The smallest unit of information in computing.
CPU	*C*entral *p*rocessing *u*nit	The part of the computer that executes instructions and processes data.
MIPS	*M*illions of *i*nstructions *p*er *s*econd	A measure of how fast a computer can process data.
RAM	*R*andom *a*ccess *m*emory	The part of the computer where instructions, input, and the results of processing data are stored temporarily.
ROM	*R*ead *o*nly *m*emory	A part of the computer's memory containing built-in instructions that cannot be altered.

In having its own jargon, computing is no different from many other fields. Physicians use specialized terms, too, and so do lawyers, newspaper editors, theater people, accountants, and workers in many other occupations. What is different about computer jargon is that, as more and more people use computers, this terminology is becoming part of our common language. Just think how often you hear the word *input*. It's a computer word that's been around for a long time, but before the microcomputer revolution, hardly anyone but computer specialists used it.

Computer terminology, like any other jargon, can be intimidating, like a secret code known only to members of a club. It can make computers seem more mysterious and more difficult to understand than they really are. This book will help you to understand the most important computer terms so that you, too, can join this ever-expanding club.

LEARNING TO USE SOFTWARE PACKAGES

Throughout your career, you will probably use microcomputers for many kinds of tasks that will require different kinds of software. In many occupations, for example, you will use one program to maintain data about sales or other items, another to write letters and reports, and a third to retrieve data from computers at remote locations. You will also need a basic understanding of the *systems software* that enables the computer to run these different programs.

In addition to using software packages yourself, you will work with people who use other packages for different purposes. These people will include not only co-workers within your organization but also outsiders whose services you use. A general understanding of the major kinds of software and their capabilities will enable you to work with these people more productively. Suppose, for example, that you are revising a procedures handbook, and your company's publications staff will design and print it. Knowing something about the publications staff's software will help you to understand your writing options, such as what kinds of illustrations you can include.

Part Two of this book focuses on software. It includes a separate chapter for each major category of software. From these chapters, you will learn about the capabilities of different software products for IBM-compatible microcomputers and the Macintosh. Any one of these chapters provides a solid foundation for learning to use a specific software product. Taken together, these chapters will give you a basic understanding of all the categories of software you are likely to encounter on the job.

MAKING PURCHASING DECISIONS

In your work, you may need to make purchasing decisions about microcomputer hardware or software. This book tells you what is involved in selecting and using computer components as well as software for different

ALAN KAY: PHILOSOPHER OF THE COMPUTER AGE

Are you ready for the throwaway computer? It's quite a leap to think of computers as being disposable, like pens and pads. But that's just the kind of "what if?" thinking that Alan Kay has been doing for more than 20 years—philosophizing about the computer and taking giant speculative leaps into the future.

Back in 1968, 10 years before the first personal computers were built, the word *computer* brought Cadillac-sized mainframe computers to mind. Kay, though, was already imagining a machine about the size of an 8½ x 11-inch notebook. He predicted that in the late 1970s or early 1980s, as manufacturers learned to make smaller and smaller parts, his notebook-sized computer would become a reality. Amazingly, he was only off by a few years (notebook-sized computers became a reality in the late 1980s).

Kay built a cardboard model of his computer, which he called the *Dynabook*. The reason for its name? First, he didn't want to use the term *computer.* But, more important, Kay believed that computers were basically a *communications medium,* like writing, printing, and broadcasting. Basically, he thought, a computer is like a book. And computers, he predicted, would change our world as profoundly as the books and the printing press had transformed Europe during the Renaissance.

Today Kay meditates on the nature of computers at a think tank sponsored by Apple Computer. More a philosopher of technology than a "techie," Kay believes that computers, like books, will become more personal. People will be able to use them anywhere—and everyone will use them. In fact, computers will become so commonplace that people will buy them in stationery or variety stores. When you buy a computer, Kay thinks you might pay a deposit on it. Then, since computers will be all one piece and there won't be anything to fix, the computer will be recycled and melted down when it doesn't work anymore.

The computers that Kay envisions will be more than personal. They'll be *intimate*—able to learn from an individual user. They'll know what you want without having to be directly programmed. You will ask it to do something and it will do it, in exactly the way that you like it done.

Throwaway intimate computers are still a few years down the road, but that's where visionary philosophers like Alan Kay have always preferred to gaze.

Alan Kay has been dreaming about compact, disposable computers since 1969. Technology is rapidly catching up with him.

Source: "Dynabook Revisited with Alan Kay," BYTE, February 1991, p. 203.

FIGURE 1-14

A wide array of software products is available for almost every
business task.

tasks (Figure 1-14). Unlike most textbooks on computers, this one names many of the products you might consider and makes comparisons among them. It doesn't tell you what to buy, but it will give you a solid basis for making your own decisions.

SETTING UP COMPUTER SYSTEMS

Sooner or later, you will work in an organization that computerizes a task for the first time, or switches to a new computer system. You may even be involved in decisions about how to set up a new system. The more you understand about the systems approach to business problems, the easier such changes will be. Chapter 14 explains the systems approach. It discusses how businesses decide what tasks to automate, what procedures to put in place, and what hardware and software to use for them, along with other factors they must consider.

PREPARING FOR THE FUTURE

The microcomputer revolution is far from over. Hardware and software companies are continually introducing products based on ever-changing technologies. You need to know about today's computers and software, but what will you need to know next year or even next week? For example, consider the *Windows* software environment, which Chapter 6 discusses. Windows enables you to run several different programs at once. In 1989 and 1990, it began a rapid sweep through the business world. Suddenly, people who had been using one software package for years had to learn a new package—or at least a new version of their old software that would run with Windows.

This book prepares you for the future as well as the present. While telling you what you need to know about hardware and software today, it also discusses the products and technologies being developed for tomorrow. It will leave you ready for the ongoing excitement and challenges of the microcomputer revolution.

REVIEW QUESTIONS

1. What is a computer?
2. What is the difference between data and information? Give an example.

3. What is computer hardware? What is software?

4. What are the three major classifications of modern computers? Which one is the most powerful?

5. When were mainframes first used? Who used them, and for what purposes?

6. Why are microcomputers also called personal computers?

7. Name the basic components of a microcomputer, and tell what each one does.

8. What two types of microcomputer are most often used in businesses?

9. What was the first microcomputer to become popular among businesspeople? When was it introduced? How was it used?

10. Why do you need to understand how computer systems are set up?

TOPICS FOR RESEARCH AND DISCUSSION

1. While few people would deny that computers have had a tremendous effect on the world, there are wide differences of opinion about how positive the changes have been. How would your own life—now and in the foreseeable future—be different if the microcomputer had not been invented? What benefits do you believe the microcomputer has brought to you, to the business world, and to society in general? What negative effects do you see? On the whole, do you regard microcomputing as a positive or negative development?

2. In the library, locate magazine articles about one of these past or present-day microcomputers:

   • Apple III
   • The first IBM PC
   • Compaq Portable
   • IBM PC Jr.
   • The first Macintosh
   • IBM PS/2
   • IBM AT
   • Poqet computer
   • NCR's pen-based computer

   Find out if the microcomputer is/was popular. Which features do you think contributed to its success or failure?

3. Think about what you would like to be doing in 10 years—where you would like to live, how you would like to make a living, what you might do with your leisure time. Write an essay of 5 to 10 paragraphs about the uses you could make of computers in your future home, career, and spare time pursuits. You need not limit your discussions to tasks already performed with computers; you can include uses of the computer that you wish were possible in addition to those that are already available. For example, perhaps you would want a computer in your car that determines the quickest route to any destination and enables you to avoid traffic jams. After you write your essay, you might want to do some research to learn which of the computer uses you have mentioned are possible or probable in 10 years.

THE SYSTEM UNIT

OBJECTIVES

The information in this chapter will enable you to

- Understand the relationship among bits, bytes, and words.
- Describe the components of the central processing unit and their functions.
- Explain the importance of computer processing speed.
- Explain the function of the system data bus.
- Describe the features of RAM and ROM memory.
- Describe serial, parallel, and SCSI ports.

What Is the System Unit?

The Processing Power of the Microcomputer Is Found in the System Unit.

If you have ever watched a microcomputer being set up, you probably noticed that it is made up of several components. These components are linked with *cables*—one or more electrical wires sealed in insulating plastic. There is a keyboard to send information into the computer and a *monitor* to send information out. There may be other components as well, such as a

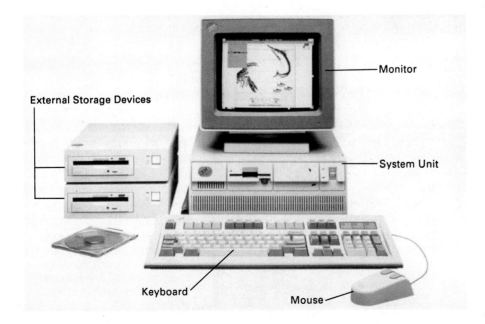

External Storage Devices

Monitor

System Unit

Keyboard

Mouse

FIGURE 2-1

Laptop microcomputers (above) pack most of their components into one case; desktop microcomputer systems like this IBM PS/2 (left) usually consist of several components.

Power Supply

Data Storage Device

Motherboard

FIGURE 2-2

Only a few items are found in the system unit, but they are the "brain" of the microcomputer.

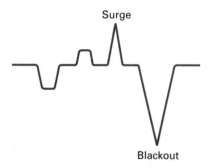

Surge

Blackout

FIGURE 2-3

Disturbances in the flow of electricity into the microcomputer can cause damage or loss of data.

storage device to store programs and data, a *modem* to transmit information to other computers, and a printer. Sometimes two or more of the components are housed together. For instance, some models of the Macintosh computer have built-in monitors, and most *laptop* microcomputers pack all of their components into one small case. But more often you find separate components for specific functions, as in the IBM PS/2 series of microcomputers (see Figure 2-1).

Whether housed separately or together, all the microcomputer's components are connected to one central component called the *system unit*. The system unit contains the electronic circuitry that performs the actual processing work of the computer and controls the operation of all other microcomputer components. Through a network of internal and external connectors and cables, the system unit runs all parts of the microcomputer system.

The most important item inside the system unit is called the *motherboard*. The motherboard (see Figure 2-2) holds the processing components that give the microcomputer its ability to accept, store, locate, and act on information. In a sense the motherboard contains the computer.

Also inside the system unit is a small box, usually marked with a voltage warning label. This is the power supply, which provides low-voltage electrical power for the system.

A constant supply of electrical current is needed to run the microcomputer. Disturbances in the flow of electrical current may cause damage to the microcomputer's hardware or loss of data. The two most common types of disturbances are *surges* and *blackouts*. A *surge* is a sudden rush of electrical current to the power supply that can damage the microcomputer. A *blackout* is a complete loss of power to the microcomputer that can result in loss of data (see Figure 2-3). A device called a *surge protector* guards against sudden increases in electrical current. (see Figure 2-4).

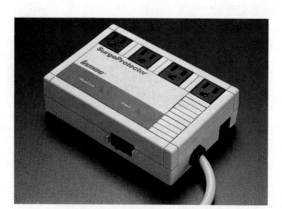

FIGURE 2-4

Many microcomputer users have surge protectors connected to their machines to protect internal components from sudden rises in electrical power.

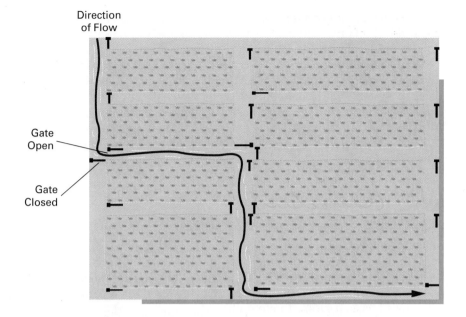

Direction
of Flow

Gate
Open

Gate
Closed

FIGURE 2-5

The flow of electricity in a circuit is controlled by open and closed switches just as the flow of water in an irrigation system is controlled by open and shut gates.

For complete protection against disturbances, including surges and blackouts, a device called a *Universal Power Supply,* or *UPS,* can be connected to the microcomputer. A UPS provides battery power when blackouts occur and filters out surges before they reach the microcomputer.

The system unit may also contain data storage devices, such as disk drives, for long-term data storage (see Chapter 4).

Computer Basics

Bits, Bytes, and Words Make Up the Internal Language of the Microcomputer.

A microcomputer may seem amazing in its ability to process information. But the only thing the microcomputer really understands is the simple language of electronics, in which only two states are possible: power on and power off.

One example of a system that works like the *binary* (two-state) system of microcomputer circuitry is a farm irrigation system. A farm can have several fields, each watered according to a different schedule, as Figure 2-5 shows. A system of gates is used to control the order in which the fields are watered. Some gates are opened to let water flow into the fields that require water. Other gates are closed to keep water from flowing into fields that do not need it.

Similarly, the computer's circuitry is made up of tiny electrical switches that regulate the flow of electricity through different parts of the circuit. Each independent switch can be on (open) to let electricity flow through a circuit, or off (closed) to keep electricity out. The computer sets some switches on and others off, and then sends electrical signals through the paths created by the switch settings. In this way, electricity is directed to different locations in the system to move, store, and process information.

BITS

People who work with microcomputers need a concrete way to communicate with each other about the internal workings of the microcomputer.

Because the microcomputer is a binary system with only two possible states (on and off), binary mathematical notation is used to describe the information processing function of the microcomputer.

Binary notation consists of two digits: 1 and zero. These are the only two digits in the binary, or *base-2,* system of mathematics, unlike the familiar decimal system, which has the 10 digits zero through 9. When discussing information flow through the microcomputer, computer people talk about **binary digits**, or *bits* for short. A bit is the smallest storage unit in the computer. It is represented by a 1 or zero and indicates one of the two electrical states of on or off.

BYTES (*Characters*)

Computer processing involves setting many switches at a time to direct electricity through different circuit paths. For this reason, a single bit seldom has meaning to the microcomputer. A bit needs to be surrounded by other bits to form instructions that the computer understands and can use. A string of bits is called a *byte*. A byte ("bite") is a series of bits that work together as a group to store characters or digits. Bytes are usually 8 bits long. *8 bits = 1 character*

As a computer user, you communicate in bytes. For example, when you enter the letter "F" at the microcomputer keyboard, the computer recognizes the following byte: 0100 0110, which tells it that you have entered an "F." A standard code called *ASCII* ("as-key"), for American Standard Character Information Interchange, determines the relationship between the keys on the keyboard and computer bytes (see Table 2-1). When ASCII is used, the computer has the ability to store 256 different characters. The letter "A" has a different binary value from the letter "F." An uppercase "F" has a different binary

Table 2-1: ASCII and Binary Notation (for Uppercase Letters Only)			
ASCII Character	Binary Notation	ASCII Character	Binary Notation
A	0100 0001	S	0101 0011
B	0100 0010	T	0101 0100
C	0100 0011	U	0101 0101
D	0100 0100	V	0101 0110
E	0100 0101	W	0101 0111
F	0100 0110	X	0101 1000
G	0100 0111	Y	0101 1001
H	0100 1000	Z	0101 1010
I	0100 1001	0	0011 0000
J	0100 1010	1	0011 0001
K	1000 1011	2	0011 0010
L	0100 1100	3	0011 0011
M	0100 1101	4	0011 0100
N	0100 1110	5	0011 0101
O	0100 1111	6	0011 0110
P	0100 0000	7	0011 0111
Q	0101 0001	8	0011 1000
R	0101 0010	9	0011 1001

value from a lowercase "f." There are ASCII codes for characters that may not appear on every keyboard. Although other codes also are used for storing data, ASCII is the most widely used coding system for microcomputers.

The first microcomputers made in the 1970s could accept only one byte of information for processing at a time. Since then the technology has improved greatly. Some microcomputers now can accept as many as 32 bits, or 4 bytes of information, at once. These strings of bytes are called *words* (see Figure 2-6). The data processed by a computer is made up of bytes.

If each letter or number is represented by one byte, a microcomputer needs the capacity to store many bytes to keep even a few pages of information in its memory. In fact, a typical microcomputer's memory contains much larger units:

- **Kilobytes,** abbreviated to **K.** A kilobyte (1K) is 1,024 bytes, which is roughly equivalent to 1,000 letters or numbers.

- **Megabytes,** abbreviated to **MB.** One megabyte is about 1 million bytes. Current long-term storage devices (such as hard disks) can hold anywhere from 10MB to 100MB or more.

The Motherboard

The Motherboard Is the Base for Expansion of the Microcomputer's Power.

The motherboard, also called the *system board,* is a *printed circuit board.* A printed circuit board, or *p.c. board,* is a thin sheet of plastic on which metallic electrical circuits are printed and electronic devices are mounted. You see plastic p.c. boards everywhere these days. For example, you may have noticed one when you replaced a battery in a radio or a television remote control.

The microcomputer's motherboard is printed with a pattern of electrical circuits that make up the basic processing pathways within the microcomputer. Sockets and soldered connections on the motherboard link these circuits to the microprocessor, the memory chips, and the expansion slots. These items are described in detail later in this chapter; however, a brief description of chips is helpful at this point.

A *computer chip* is a small square of silicon on which circuits containing thousands of miniature electrical switches have been etched (see Figure 2-7).

FIGURE 2-6

Bits, bytes, and words form instructions the microprocessor can understand.

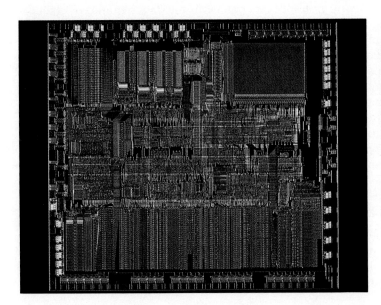

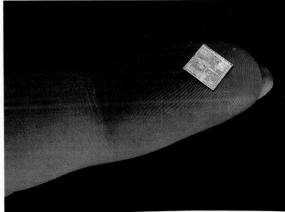

FIGURE 2-7

A lot of processing power is contained in a tiny chip of silicon.

Because the circuits are within the chip, computer chips are often called *solid state devices* or *integrated circuits.*

Computer chips are manufactured with different etched patterns, depending on their functions. One chip may be designed to run a video game; another may control the colors on your television set. Some computer chips are mounted to connectors that plug into sockets on a p.c. board; others are mounted directly on the p.c. board.

Microprocessors (*chips*)(*microcomputer chips*)

A Microprocessor Provides a Division of Labor for Efficient Processing.

When a computer chip is etched with the circuitry needed to process data, it is called a *microprocessor chip* or just *microprocessor.* Another name for this powerful kind of chip is *microcomputer chip,* which better defines its importance to the microcomputer system. A microprocessor is divided into different areas by function.

THE CENTRAL PROCESSING UNIT (CPU)

The area that schedules and directs the activities of the microcomputer is called the *central processing unit,* or *CPU.* The CPU stores and executes one instruction at a time. It also controls the data required to execute the instructions. Within the CPU are two basic functional components: the control unit and the arithmetic-logic unit.

- **Control unit.** The control unit manages the activity within the CPU by keeping track of all instructions that are being processed. It directs data into and out of other parts of the CPU and to other components of the microcomputer.
- **ALU.** The *Arithmetic-Logic Unit,* or *ALU,* performs numerical operations, such as adding two numbers, and logical operations, such as comparing two numbers.

REGISTERS

The areas on a microprocessor that contain all the data required by the current processing instruction are called *registers.* Each register holds one piece of data—a number, a letter, or an instruction. Because data is continually moving in and out of these registers as instructions come in, for quick access the registers need to be on the same microprocessor chip as the CPU.

Special function registers contain specific types of data. For example, an instruction register holds the part of a program indicating the process to be performed; an address register holds the portion of a program that indicates where a piece of data is located. Storage registers hold pieces of data being used by the program instruction. Figure 2-8 illustrates the functional areas of a microprocessor.

THE PROCESSING CYCLE

The steps involved in processing one instruction are known as a *processing cycle.* A computer program may contain thousands or even millions of instructions, which are all processed using the same cycle. Generally, the control unit gets an instruction, decodes it, and performs the operation. If

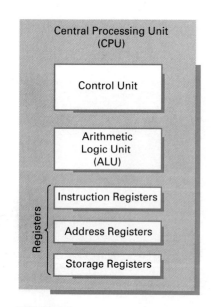

FIGURE 2-8

The components of the CPU move and process data.

Table 2-2: Families of Microprocessors

Word Size	Manufacturer	Chip Number	Personal Computers Using Chips
16-bit	Intel	8088	IBM Personal Computer
	Motorola	8086	AT&T Personal Computer 6300
		80286	IBM PC/AT, Compaq Portable II
32-bit		68000	Apple Macintosh
		68010	AT&T Personal Computer 7300
		68020	Apple Macintosh II
			Apple Macintosh IIcx
		68030	NeXT Computer
		68040	Hewlett-Packard Workstations
			IBM Personal System/2 Model 80
	Intel	80386	Compaq Deskpro 386
		80486	IBM PS/2 Model 70

the instruction involves a numerical operation, the control unit directs the instruction to the ALU. After the instruction is processed, the result goes to an internal location for storage.

FAMILIES OF MICROPROCESSORS

Presently, there are two dominant groups of related microprocessors, or microprocessor families: the Motorola 68000 family of microprocessors, found in the Apple Macintosh, and the Intel 80000 family of processors, found in IBM PCs, PS/2s, and compatibles. The microprocessors in these families can be differentiated in terms of performance and capacity by looking at the size of an instruction they can process in one processing cycle.

Early IBM PCs based on the Intel 8088 microprocessor could execute 16-bit (2-byte word) instructions, but would receive only 8 bits at a time, causing these machines to go through two processing cycles to process one instruction.

The later IBM PC/AT with an Intel 80286 microprocessor could *receive* and execute 16-bit (2-byte word) instructions, making it a faster machine because it used only one processing cycle to process a 16-bit instruction.

The further evolution of microprocessor technology to the current 32-bit (4-byte word) instructions has brought much greater performance. The Motorola 68000, the Intel 80386, and the Intel 80486 microprocessors are examples of 32-bit processors. They receive and process 4 bytes at a time. Table 2-2 summarizes these microcomputer families.

Math Coprocessors

Math Coprocessors Increase a Microcomputer's Ability to Perform Mathematical Calculations with Precision and Speed.

The microprocessors used in early microcomputers had only limited mathematical abilities because they were designed for general-purpose information processing. For users wanting to perform complex mathematics, a spe-

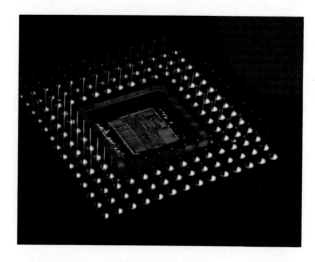

FIGURE 2-9

A math coprocessor allows the microcomputer to perform calculations that otherwise might be impossible or very slow.

cial math coprocessor was recommended. Most IBM-compatible microcomputers have a socket on the motherboard next to the microprocessor. This socket is reserved for a plug-in math coprocessor.

As Figure 2-9 shows, the math coprocessor looks much like a microprocessor, but was designed for a different purpose: to perform math calculations with precision and speed. Today, other processors, such as the Weitek math processor, provide greater precision than the coprocessors originally available. Also, for many applications where highly complex mathematical processing is required, specific products used with the microcomputer have their own math processing abilities to compensate for the limitations of the original microprocessor.

The System Clock

The System Clock Sets CPU Timing.

Because the operations in a microcomputer happen at tremendous speed, they must be carefully synchronized. The *system clock* provides this timing function to tell the CPU when to perform an operation. Based on a quartz crystal that vibrates at a certain rate — the same technology used in quartz watches — the system clock sends out electronic signals at specific intervals, allowing the CPU to synchronize the computer's activities. The CPU listens for timing information or electronic pulses coming through its circuitry. Each time it receives a pulse, it performs the next operation (see Figure 2-10).

Microprocessor speed is based on the system clock speed, which in turn is based on how fast the clock's quartz crystal vibrates. The vibration is so fast that it is measured in millions of vibration cycles per second, or *megahertz (MHz)* ("mega-hurts"). For example, a 20 MHz 80386 processor is capable of executing 20 million instructions per second; a 33 MHz 80386 can execute 33 million instructions per second. Some new processors boast even faster clock speeds.

FIGURE 2-10

Regular pulses from the system clock synchronize CPU operations.

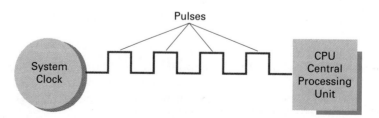

Architecture (System Data Bus)

The System Data Bus Transfers Data between the CPU and Other Components of the System.

To move information from one location to another within the microcomputer, a set of electrical connections is provided on the motherboard. These connections form a data pathway known as the *system data bus,* an electronics term meaning interconnected path. The system data bus brings in data from devices outside the microcomputer, such as the keyboard, moves data between the CPU and other components within the microcomputer for processing, and sends data out to devices outside the microcomputer, such as the monitor (see Figure 2-11).

The number of data bits that can be transmitted on the system data bus at one time is indicated by the system data bus size. The original IBM PC was designed with an 8-bit system data bus, which could transmit 1 byte (8 bits) of data at a time. Since the microprocessor in this machine could process 16 bits at a time, the system data bus was actually holding back the processing power of the microcomputer.

This problem was corrected in the IBM PC AT, which had a 16-bit system data bus to match its 16-bit microprocessor (80286). The latest PC compatibles and Apple Macintosh microcomputers are based on 32-bit microprocessors and also have 32-bit system data buses.

In addition to providing links for data traffic, the system data bus also provides paths for electrical power and control signals to the various components of the microcomputer. To enhance the functions of microcomputers, computer manufacturers and other vendors produce *add-on* products, designed to work with the basic system. Printers are the most common type of add-on. Some add-on products such as coprocessors are placed inside the system unit. Other add-on products, such as printers and monitors, are outside the system unit and connected to it by cables.

Microcomputer manufacturers establish a set of rules for the design of add-on products, contained in the system data bus specification document. These rules ensure that add-on products will be compatible with the operation of the microcomputer. In other words, add-on products must be able to communicate with the microcomputer over the system data bus. The system

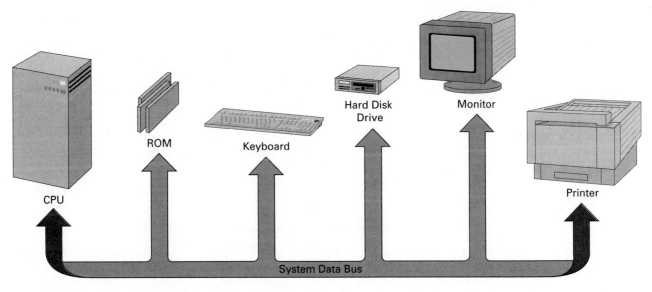

FIGURE 2-11

All data to and from the microprocessor travel along the system data bus.

AN ANGLE AND AN ATTITUDE: AST RESEARCH, INC.

In the fiercely competitive world of personal computer manufacturers, AST Research, Inc. is a master at finding small market niches overlooked by industry giants, such as IBM and Compaq. Now the third largest builder of IBM compatible PCs, AST was founded in 1979 by three immigrants to the United States: Thomas Yuen, the son of a Hong Kong chauffeur, and his friends, Albert Wong and Safi Qureshey.

To start a computer company, you need energy, inspiration, and lots of cash. AST's three founders had lots of energy and inspiration, but just a meager $2,000 in capital. So they needed an angle. Perceiving that customers would want an inexpensive way to add options such as extra memory to PCs, they decided to sell low-priced memory add-on boards. Although the check from their first sale bounced, the company had found its first niche in the computer hardware market.

As it grew, AST continued to maneuver between the computer giants, seeking its ever-changing market niche. AST now builds PCs of every size, from small notebook PCs to PCs that can drive huge networks.

Besides consistently lower prices, another niche mined by AST is speed: not just faster PCs, but faster production and marketing. For example, when the Intel Corporation's top-of-the-line 80486 microcomputer chip was first developed, AST was one of the first PC makers to ship PCs based on this new chip.

A recent AST inspiration is the idea of "upgradable PCs"—PCs which allow owners to update their machines easily when new chips come along. To make it work, AST mounts components that are likely to become obsolete, such as the microprocessor and memory chips, on a separate circuit board that can be replaced by the machine's owner. Buyers don't have to worry that their computers will be outdated in six months (a reason buyers often delay new purchases). Corporations can extend their depreciation periods beyond the normal two years, a significant cost reduction.

AST founder Thomas Yuen's approach to finding a productive angle, whatever the circumstances, is exemplified by his courageous and canny attitude toward the three days a week of kidney dialysis he undergoes: "What other executive," he says, "gets 15 hours a week of uninterrupted time to think about the business?"

With this kind of attitude, it's no wonder AST has flourished despite the odds.

With an upgradable computer you can update your microcomputer without having to buy an entirely new system.

Source: "This 12-Year-Old Has Come of Age," *Business Week,* May 6, 1991, p. 122.

data bus specification defines many items related to data transfer over the system data bus, including the speed of data transfer, the number of bits that can be transferred at one time, and the instructions used to govern data transfer. Because the specifications differ, add-on products that are compatible with one system data bus are not compatible with another.

As microcomputers have evolved, the requirements for the system data bus have expanded. Currently, there are three major microcomputer system data bus specifications for IBM PCs and compatibles and a separate specification for the Apple Macintosh.

INDUSTRY STANDARD ARCHITECTURE (ISA)

The original 8-bit IBM PC system data bus design, which was later enhanced to handle the PC AT's 16-bit traffic, has come to be known as the *Industry Standard Architecture,* or *ISA.* This system data bus provides both 8-bit and 16-bit data transfer, so that most add-on products that worked with the PC will work with the AT.

MICRO CHANNEL ARCHITECTURE (MCA)

The standard ISA could not handle the data traffic of 32-bit microprocessors. Rather than add to the ISA, IBM developed a completely new system data bus specification, based on its experience with mainframe computers. This new system data bus architecture, the *Micro Channel Architecture,* or *MCA,* was incorporated into many add-ons for the PS/2 line of personal computers. MCA add-ons can be used only with microcomputers using the Micro Channel Architecture.

EXTENDED INDUSTRY STANDARD ARCHITECTURE (EISA)

A consortium of seven microcomputer manufacturers led by Compaq Computer and AST, known as the "Gang of 7," provided an alternative to the Micro Channel system bus architecture by extending the ISA to accommodate 32-bit processors. This *Extended Industry Standard Architecture,* or *EISA,* allows the use of 8-bit, 16-bit, and 32-bit add-on products, ensuring compatibility among all generations of microcomputers.

NUBUS

With the introduction of the Macintosh II family of microcomputers in 1987, Apple Computer produced its version of the 32-bit system bus architecture, which it called the *NuBus.* Add-ons for the Macintosh are compatible only with the NuBus specifications, and cannot be used with computers from other manufacturers.

Random Access Memory (RAM)

Temporary Data Storage Is Provided in RAM.

Random Access Memory, shortened to *RAM* ("ram"), is composed of silicon chips designed to hold data temporarily during processing (see Figure 2-12). Sometimes RAM is called *user memory,* because the user has control over its contents, which may be program instructions, user input, computation

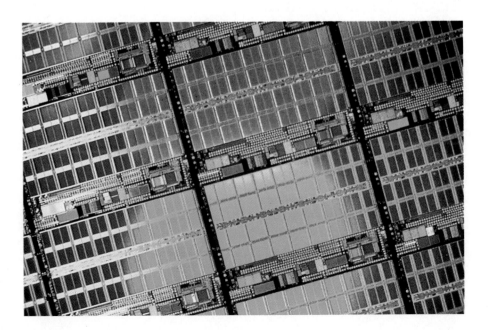

FIGURE 2-12

RAM chips increase a microcomputer's memory. Shown here is a detail of a chip.

results, or other data. The personal computers available in the early 1980s had only 16K of RAM; today's microcomputers can be loaded with several megabytes of RAM.

One troublesome aspect of RAM is that any information stored in it can be erased by interrupting power to the microcomputer. Simply turning the microcomputer off without saving work in progress can mean having to redo everything. Power failures have the same destructive results. Therefore, it is a good habit to save your work frequently to avoid having to duplicate it.

An important consideration when working on a microcomputer is the quantity of RAM available in the system. Most IBM PC-type microcomputers are limited to 640K RAM. Early software programs worked comfortably within this limit, but contemporary software often requires more.

Computer owners can buy more RAM chips and plug them into the motherboard to upgrade a microcomputer system. Today, 1MB and 4MB RAM chips are readily available. In addition, 16MB chips are in production, and 64 megabyte chips are being developed in research laboratories.

Another way to upgrade RAM is to buy groups of RAM chips on small p.c. boards made to plug into special slots in the computer. These *Single In-line Memory Modules, or* SIMMs ("Simms"), have become the standard for microcomputer memory because of their compact size and ease of installation.

Read Only Memory (ROM)

ROM Is the Microcomputer's Memory.

Read Only Memory, or *ROM* ("romm"), is made up of computer chips that have been encoded with the instructions the microcomputer needs to operate. The microcomputer can read these instructions but cannot alter or erase them. When a microcomputer is first turned on, the system's ROM takes control and performs the operations needed to start the system.

A familiar example of a device that uses ROM chips is a video game cartridge. The plastic case holds one or more ROM chips containing the particular video game program. The program instructions are executed as the game is played, but the player cannot access or change the program itself.

Expansion Slots and Cards

P.C. Boards in Expansion Slots Add Functions to the Microcomputer.

Most microcomputers can accommodate new hardware features that were not provided with the original purchase. New features or options are easily added to the microcomputer by inserting specialized p.c. boards, called *expansion cards,* into the system data bus connections provided on the motherboard. These plug-in bus connections on the motherboard into which the cards fit are called *expansion slots* (see Figure 2-13). Each system data bus connection has an opening at the rear of the microcomputer that allows the expansion card to be connected to an external add-on device.

Some features that can be added to the microcomputer through expansion cards are as follows:

- Video cards which expand the range of monitors that can be used with the microcomputer (see Figure 2-14).
- Modems that allow for data transfer between computers over the telephone lines.

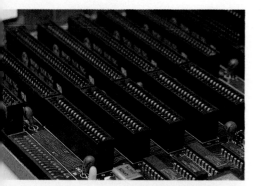
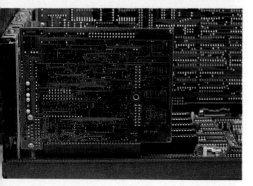

FIGURE 2-13

Many users feel comfortable installing expansion cards themselves.

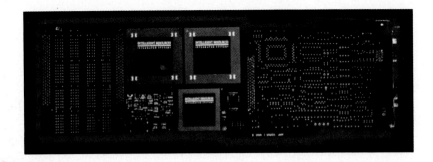

FIGURE 2-14

Video cards are available for many monitors. They allow the microcomputer to communicate with the monitor.

- Network interface cards that attach the microcomputer to other computers in a network.
- RAM cards that hold additional RAM memory (see Figure 2-15).

Ports (Interfaces)

Ports Connect the Microcomputer System to External Devices.

Ports are physical connectors used to attach external add-on devices to the microcomputer system unit. For instance, the keyboard and monitor are attached by cables and plugs to ports on the back of the system unit. An external modem is attached to the system unit through a port connection as well.

General-purpose ports on the back of the system unit provide connection points for devices such as printers and external modems. These ports are typically described by the type of information transfer they provide, either parallel or serial.

FIGURE 2-15

One way to boost the performance of an older microcomputer is by adding RAM memory.

PARALLEL PORTS

Parallel ports transfer information by sending electrical signals across multiple wires simultaneously. An entire 8-bit byte (or ASCII character) is sent in a single transmission across eight separate wires, one for each bit.

Parallel ports are most often used for print functions. Most popular printers for microcomputers come equipped with a parallel interface, which is connected to a parallel port on the system unit.

SERIAL PORTS

Serial ports send signals one after another across a single wire. An 8-bit byte would require eight separate transmissions, one for each bit. Serial ports are most often used for modem communications, although early laser printers required them. Many scientific devices that can be connected to a microcomputer also employ serial ports. Figure 2-16 shows parallel and serial ports on an IBM-compatible computer.

SCSI PORTS

A fairly recent development in microcomputer interfaces is the *Small Computer Systems Interface,* or *SCSI* ("scuzy") port. The Apple Macintosh was the first microcomputer to use this type of port. SCSI ports provide high-speed data transfer and allow multiple SCSI devices to share a single port on the microcomputer.

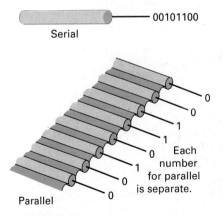

FIGURE 2-16

A parallel port sends an entire 8-bit byte in a single transmission. A serial port sends the byte one bit at a time.

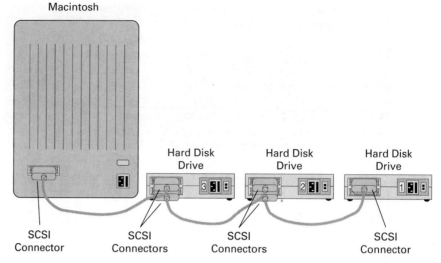

Macintosh

SCSI
Connector

Hard Disk
Drive

SCSI
Connectors

Hard Disk
Drive

SCSI
Connectors

Hard Disk
Drive

SCSI
Connector

FIGURE 2-17

The daisy chain arrangement of SCSI devices adds flexibility to the Macintosh system.

Each SCSI add-on device has two SCSI interfaces. Using both interfaces (one to and one from each device), up to seven SCSI devices may be connected to one another in a chain. The chain begins at the microcomputer's SCSI port and ends at the last device in line (Figure. 2-17).

Future Trends

The Future of Microcomputers: More Speed, Greater Affordability, and Enhanced Features.

Microprocessor technology is advancing so quickly that microcomputing power will soon rival that of mainframe computers. Since 1984, microprocessors have doubled in speed and capacity about every 18 months, while at the same time system cost was being cut roughly in half.

Presently, 50 MHz 80486 microprocessors are being incorporated into new microcomputer models. Intel's new 80586 processor will take microcomputers one step closer to their larger relatives. The processing speed and power once available in systems priced in the tens of thousands will soon be accessible to users with far smaller budgets.

MULTIPLE PROCESSORS

Some complex computing tasks, such as three-dimensional graphics, require more computing power than is available from a single microprocessor. Microcomputer manufacturers are responding to this requirement by incorporating multiple microprocessors in the system unit. Compaq Computer, for instance, offers multiprocessors as an option for its SystemPro microcomputer.

In a typical multiprocessor arrangement, one microprocessor is devoted to a single task such as managing access to a storage device. This frees the second microprocessor to handle computational tasks.

Expansion cards with additional microprocessors are often used to upgrade older microcomputers, thereby extending their lives. The original microprocessor is relegated to some simple task such as printing; all other functions are controlled by the new, faster microprocessor.

ENHANCED MICROPROCESSORS AND MOTHERBOARDS

As microcomputer manufacturing techniques are refined, more and more functions are being added directly to the microprocessor and the motherboard. Processing power that took up over 20 computer chips on the original IBM PC is today contained on a single chip. The result is a single component that takes up less space, uses less power, and costs a fraction of the original components it replaces.

Today serial, parallel, input, and storage device ports are being combined with the system data bus on the motherboard. This advancement limits the requirement for expansion slots. For the original IBM XT, introduced in March of 1983, to match a stripped-down modern microcomputer for features, nearly all of its eight expansion slots would have to be filled with expansion cards.

THE INCREDIBLE SHRINKING COMPUTER

Do you remember the movie about the incredible shrinking man? There's a point in the film when the man is small enough to fit in the palm of a person's hand, and you wonder, nervously, just how small he can get.

Something like that has happened to the computer. Yesterday's huge, hulking mainframes, accessible only by computer wizards, have shrunk down to today's desktop microcomputers, which just about everyone can use. More recently, two even smaller types of computers have become commonplace: the lightweight, portable laptops, which run on batteries and can be carried like a briefcase almost anywhere; and notebook computers, slightly smaller than laptops, that fit easily into a briefcase.

Now we have the incredible palmtop computers, which can fit, like that incredible shrinking man, on your palm, in your jacket pocket, or even in your shirt pocket. The key to their tiny size is the newest development in storage devices—credit card-sized RAM and ROM cards.

These marvels of engineering— like the Poqet PC, which weighs less

than a pound, and the similarly downsized Hewlett-Packard 95LX Palmtop PC—can run sophisticated spreadsheet and word processing software. They are changing the shape (and size) of what we thought possible.

Where once laptops were mere peripherals to desktop computers, palmtops are now considered peripherals to both desktops and laptops. They are useful when you're on the run, when even a 5 pound computer may be too heavy, or you don't have room in your briefcase (or you don't even have a briefcase).

These first-generation palmtops are especially useful for "personal information management," which means you can use them to update your address book, your schedule, or your "to-do" list while you're on the road. When you return to the office, your palmtop can be easily connected to a desktop computer. You can also use your palmtop to send FAX transmissions.

Will computers keep shrinking? Not likely, because there are limits imposed by users. Computer screens and keyboards can only get so small before we aren't able to see the

screen or type on the keyboard (unless of course, we find a way to shrink people . . .).

Powerful computers such as this Poqet PC are small enough to fit in the palm of your hand.

Source: "Palmtop PCs: Power by the Ounce," by Jonathan Matzkin, *PC Magazine*, July 1991.

When selecting a microcomputer system for your personal use, one of the most important considerations is the microprocessor used by the system unit. Another important consideration is the amount of RAM included with the system unit when you purchase it and the amount of additional RAM that can be added to the system unit. The add-on products supported by the system and the software products available for the system are also of vital importance.

Before you can determine what system unit you should obtain, you should learn more about how you can effectively use the input and output devices that are available for your system. These are discussed in the next two chapters.

FIGURE 2-18

RISC-based microcomputers are fast because they use a minimum of instructions.

RISC VERSUS CISC — A NEW LANGUAGE

A further enhancement to microcomputer technology is occurring at the instruction processing level. Current *machine language,* the language of binary numbers, contains hundreds of instructions that the microcomputer must understand.

Researchers have found that by developing a new machine language with a minimum of instructions, a microprocessor can process much faster. A microprocessor that can understand this new machine language is known as a *Reduced Instruction Set Computer,* or *RISC* ("risk") processor. Processors that understand the current machine language are known as *Complex Instruction Set Computers,* or *CISC.* Fortunately, microcomputer users and programmers do not need to know RISC. Programs are written in high-level languages and translated into RISC.

RISC-based microcomputers, from such companies as Sun Microsystems (Figure 2-18), are popular now as high-end microcomputers used for applications that require a lot of mathematical calculations and for multiuser systems. However, the computing power of RISC may someday replace the familiar CISC used in microcomputers, making microcomputers even faster and more powerful machines.

REVIEW QUESTIONS

1. What is the system unit?
2. Name two items you may find inside the system unit.
3. What is a surge?
4. What is a blackout?
5. Name two things a Universal Power Supply does to protect the microcomputer from electrical disturbances.
6. What is a bit and what does it indicate?
7. What is a byte?
8. What is the relationship between ASCII code and binary notation?
9. In relation to bytes, what is a word?
10. What is a kilobyte? A megabyte?
11. What does the CPU's control unit do?
12. Name three types of registers and describe their contents.
13. What is a processing cycle?
14. What is a math coprocessor and when is it used?

15. How does the system clock influence the operation of the microprocessor?

16. What is the system data bus?

17. What are the four standard system architectures and how do they differ?

18. Why is it important to know what system architecture your microcomputer uses?

19. How do RAM and ROM differ?

20. Why is it a good idea to save your work before turning off the microcomputer?

21. When are expansion slots used? Where on the microcomputer do you find them?

22. Describe how parallel and serial ports transmit data.

23. Give three reasons why an enhanced microprocessor is an improvement over older microprocessors.

24. What does RISC stand for and why is it an important trend?

TOPICS FOR RESEARCH AND DISCUSSION

1. Computers seem to get smaller and smaller. Do you think there's a limit to how small a computer can get—and still be useful?

2. Over the last several years continuous technological improvements have made microprocessors faster and smarter. Some businesses buy the latest, fastest, smartest computers. Others put off their decisions until "next year"—year after year—hoping things will "settle down." What are the advantages of a "buy today" strategy? Of a "wait until next year" strategy?

3. Some computer companies have made their computers upgradable. Others do nothing to assist customers in upgrading old machines. As new computers come on the market, what do you think computer companies should do about those customers who bought their previous computers? Research what computer companies are doing about upgrading customers.

INPUT DEVICES

OBJECTIVES

The information in this chapter will enable you to

- Explain the purpose of input devices.
- Describe the features of the keyboard and explain the functions of the various types of keys.
- Describe the different varieties of pointing devices.
- Describe the different varieties of touch-sensitive devices.
- Explain how optical scanning works and describe the three types of optical scanning devices commonly used with microcomputers.
- Describe OCR, MICR, and OMR processes.
- Describe the two main types of voice processing.

What Do Input Devices Do?

Input Devices Translate Real World Sounds, Pictures, and Sensations into Data for the Microcomputer.

To get a microcomputer to work for us, we need a link between human methods of communication and the machine. This link is established by *input devices* that translate human communications into combinations of bits the microcomputer can process. Input devices translate real world sounds, pictures, and sensations into binary (on or off) electrical signals and transfer these signals to the microcomputer system unit. Input devices are separate components, usually connected to the system unit with cables. The process of transferring information into a microcomputer is often referred to as *inputting* (see Figure 3-1).

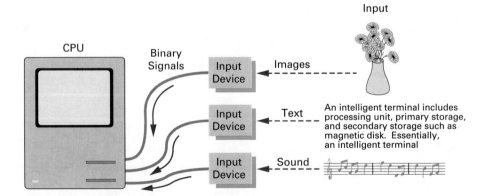

FIGURE 3-1

Input devices translate words, images, and sounds into binary electrical signals (on and off) and transfer these signals to the microcomputer system unit.

The need for more efficient and flexible input devices increased as microcomputers became more popular and more technically advanced. Since the introduction of the microcomputer, input devices have increased in variety and decreased in cost.

As you learned in Chapter 2, the microcomputer processes information in the form of bits, or binary digits, consisting of 1's and 0's that represent the electrical states of power on and power off. Besides microcomputers, other machines process information as bits, including stereos, calculators, machines used in industry, and many home appliances. *Digital* is the term used to define this type of information processing.

Through a process called *digitizing,* input devices convert nondigital communications into digital form. This chapter covers many input devices available for use with the microcomputer.

The Keyboard

A Keyboard Is Used to Type Instructions and Data.

The most commonly used input device for microcomputers is the *keyboard.* Similar to a typewriter, it contains typewriter keys (letters, numbers, and special typing symbols) and some extra keys you do not find on typewriters, as you can see in Figure 3-2. The keyboard is used by secretaries to enter letters and memos, by customer service personnel to input sales orders, mailing lists, and customer complaints, by managers to retrieve information, and by computer programmers and engineers to enter computer programs. Because the keyboard is still the most common way to input data to the system, manufacturers of microcomputers usually include keyboards with their computers.

Some microcomputer users have to spend hours at a time working at a keyboard, which can cause a strain on their hands and wrists. To reduce such strains and make keyboards easy to use, manufacturers have designed certain features into keyboards. Some of these features are the following:

- Adjustable slanted keyboards that allow you to choose the most natural position for your hands.
- Keyboards, keyboard wrist rests, and keyboard drawers with ledges for resting your hands to reduce the strain on your wrists.

FIGURE 3-2

Keyboards for use with different makes and models of computers have different arrangements of keys.

FIGURE 3-3

The extended keyboard provides extra keys to help the user be more productive when inputting.

• *Extended* keyboards, which have extra groups of keys arranged by functions for quick access and to reduce the amount of hand movement (see Figure 3-3).

Some manufacturers have found niches in the microcomputer market by providing specialized keyboards, such as Braille keyboards for the blind and keyboards with limited sets of special keys that are used with foreign languages and specific computer programs.

Most keyboards available for use with microcomputers include the following five types of keys:

• Alphabetic keys
• Numeric keys
• Function keys
• Arrow keys
• Special-purpose keys

ALPHABETIC KEYS

Alphabetic keys (often called *alpha* keys) are similar to the keys on a typewriter. They are used to enter program instructions, reports, names and addresses, and other written data into the microcomputer (see Figure 3-4).

FIGURE 3-4

The alpha key typewriterlike arrangement eases the transition for some users from the typewriter to the microcomputer.

Typewriter Area

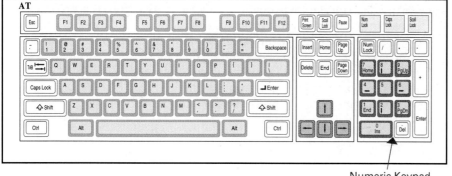

Numeric Keypad

FIGURE 3-5

The numeric keypad is used to input lots of numbers quickly.

NUMERIC KEYS

Most keyboards have keys for the numbers 0 through 9 along the upper edge of the alpha key area. Extended keyboards contain another section of keys, usually to the right of the alpha keys, called the numeric keypad, which is shown in Figure 3-5. A *numeric keypad* is a separate group of number keys arranged like a calculator for inputting numbers quickly. The numeric keypad is an important keyboard feature for accountants, bookkeepers, and others who regularly input numbers.

FUNCTION KEYS

Many programs have built-in shortcuts for commonly used commands assigned to a special group of keys called *function keys,* or *F keys,* which are labeled F1, F2, and so on (see Figure 3-6). The functions assigned to these keys are determined by the program in use and are different for each

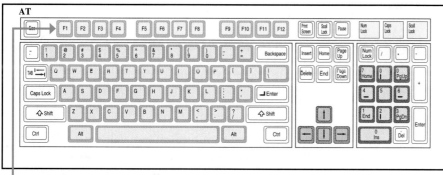

Function Keys

Function Keys

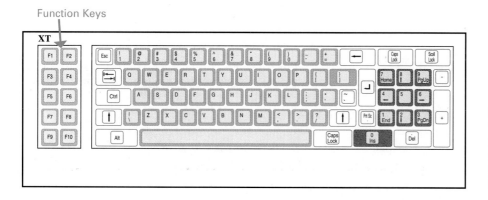

FIGURE 3-6

The function keys on the early IBM PC XT-style keyboard were arranged differently from those on the later IBM PC AT-style keyboard.

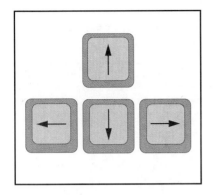

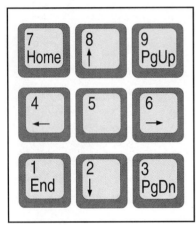

FIGURE 3-7

Arrow keys can be combined with the numeric keypad or grouped separately.

program. For example, one program uses F7 to exit from the program and F2 to search for a word. Some programs use a lot of function key shortcuts; others do not. Function keys are arranged in either of two ways: across the upper edge of the keyboard above the alpha and number keys or in a separate group at the left of the keyboard. For example, in the IBM XT style of keyboard the function keys are found to the left; the IBM AT style of keyboard groups the function keys above the other keys.

ARROW KEYS

Arrow keys let you change your place in a document or program. Each time you press an arrow key, you move one place in the direction of the key: left, right, up, or down. Some keyboards group the arrow keys with the numeric keypad. Others provide a separate group of arrow keys for easy access, as shown in Figure 3-7.

SPECIAL-PURPOSE KEYS

Keyboards contain extra keys that perform specific operations. Some resemble keys on a typewriter, such as the *Return,* or *Enter,* key, which is similar to the Carriage Return key on a typewriter, and the *Caps Lock* key, which works like a typewriter's Shift Lock key. Other special-purpose keys perform operations that don't exist on a typewriter. Some of these keys are *Delete (DEL), Escape (ESC), Clear, Home,* and *End.* The operations performed by these keys are determined by the program in use. Table 3-1 lists and describes some common special-purpose keys.

Some keys are used in combination with other keys to perform special functions. For example, some word processing programs combine the Control (often labeled "Ctrl" on the keyboard) and Alternate (often labeled "Alt" on the keyboard) keys with numbers or letters to complete a function. Pressing the Control key together with the letter "P" is the print command in some word processing programs.

Table 3-1: IBM-Compatible Special-Purpose Keys	
Key Name	**Description**
Backspace	Deletes the character to the left of your current location on the screen.
Caps Lock	Locks the keyboard so you can type only capital letters.
Delete (DEL)	Deletes the character to the right of your current location on the screen.
End	Takes you to the end (bottom) of the current page, document, or screen.
Enter or Return	Sends the current input data to the microcomputer and advances you to the next line on the screen.
Escape (ESC)	Cancels your current operation or program.
Insert (INS)	Locks the keyboard so that each character you type is inserted in your current location on the screen without overtyping other characters already on the screen.
Home	Takes you to the beginning of the page, document, or screen.
Page Up (PgUp)	Takes you to the previous page or screen.
Page Down (PgDn)	Takes you to the next page or screen.

Since you use a keyboard to enter most new data into a personal computer system, a keyboard is usually included in the base price of a microcomputer system. If you type slowly or inaccurately, you may want to brush up on your keyboarding skills. Software programs are available that can help you improve your skill.

A mouse may also be included as part of your basic microcomputer configuration. How much a mouse will be used to select choices and enter data depends on your software. So, before buying your system, check to see if the software you expect to use most will support a mouse.

Because entering data using a keyboard is relatively slow, many businesses strive to reduce the amount of data that must be keyed in. They use scanning or voice recognition devices. A system designed primarily to meet the personal needs of an individual will rarely include this type of device.

Pointing Devices

Pointing Devices Select Items on the Monitor by Pointing to Them.

The Macintosh computer introduced a new way to work with computers. Rather than typing in commands, you moved on the screen to a picture that represented a command. This approach to working with a computer is called a *graphical user interface (GUI)*. (You'll learn more about GUIs in Chapter 6.) Graphical user interfaces make the standard keyboard an awkward method of input. They require a different type of input device with greater flexibility than keyboards can provide.

The most popular input device for use with GUIs is the mouse. With so many companies changing to graphical user interfaces, the mouse has become the standard input device of many microcomputer systems. It has not replaced the keyboard, but is a common supplement to it.

THE MOUSE

The *mouse* is a small box with buttons on top that is usually attached to the microcomputer by a cable. It gets its name from its mouselike size and shape and its cable "tail." Moving the mouse across the desktop moves an on-screen pointer in a document or program. The mouse controls the direction and speed of the pointer's movements. You select items by moving the pointer to them and pressing a button on the mouse.

Three types of mouses are currently used with microcomputer systems: the mechanical mouse, the optical mouse, and the cordless mouse. Although they work slightly differently, they are interchangeable.

The Mechanical Mouse

The *mechanical mouse* rolls on a small rubber ball, which you can see if you turn the mouse upside down (see Figure 3-8). Sensors located behind the ball sense the location and movement of the mouse as you roll it around on your desk or on a flat rubber pad called a *mouse pad*. The mouse's location coordinates (its horizontal and vertical positions) are sent through the cable to the microcomputer, which moves the pointer in the document or program in the direction indicated by the mouse. The mechanical mouse is the most commonly used mouse and is often included in the purchase of a microcomputer system. Its chief disadvantage is that its mechanical parts wear out with time and use.

FIGURE 3-8

The mechanical mouse rolls on a rubber ball.

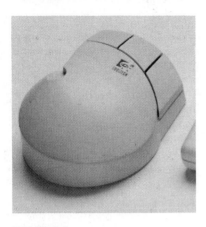

FIGURE 3-9

A cordless mouse works just like an optical mouse, but uses battery power and infrared signals rather than a cable.

The Optical Mouse

An *optical mouse* uses a light sensor, or optical sensor, combined with a mouse pad containing a grid. As the optical sensor underneath the mouse passes over points on the grid, it generates electrical location coordinates that are sent to the microcomputer.

The optical mouse is used for the same applications as the mechanical mouse and may be chosen as an alternative to it. The main advantages of the optical mouse are greater precision in location and movement and fewer mechanical parts to wear out. The disadvantage is that it must be used with a grid mouse pad.

The Cordless Mouse

A *cordless mouse* has no cable; it uses infrared light to communicate with the microcomputer. It is battery powered and uses an optical sensor to determine location and movement just like the optical mouse. The main advantage of this mouse is that there is no cord to hinder movement (see Figure 3-9). The disadvantages are that it can be misplaced and that the batteries run down and must be replaced, which is an added expense.

THE TRACKBALL *used c̄ laptops a lot*

Manufacturers developed a stationary input device called a *trackball* by turning a mechanical mouse upside down so the ball is on top. Many types of trackballs are available, from small models that attach to the side of the keyboard to large models with several extra buttons providing additional functions (see Figure 3-10).

To operate a trackball, you move the ball around with your thumb or finger; the trackball box remains stationary. The trackball is useful for people whose work demands precise movement, such as artists and designers. The advantage of this device is that your hand stays in one place while very small finger movements direct the activity of the pointer. The disadvantage is that this same sensitivity can cause you to overshoot your targets. Trackballs also contain mechanical parts that wear out eventually.

FIGURE 3-10

The trackball is widely used by people in the graphic arts.

Touch-Sensitive Devices

Touch-Sensitive Devices Convert the Touch of a Finger or Pen into Microcomputer-Understandable Input.

Touch-sensitive devices let you input information by pointing with your finger or a pen. These devices contain two layers of wires that form a grid under a flat pliable surface. When you touch the surface, the wires make contact and signal the location of your finger (see Figure 3-11). Four types of touch-sensitive devices are currently being used with microcomputers.

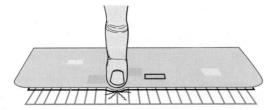

FIGURE 3-11

When you press a touch-sensitive device, your finger causes two layers of wires to come in contact and generate a location signal.

THE TOUCH SCREEN

A *touch screen* is a computer monitor with a soft overlay that you touch to select items on the screen (see Figure 3-12). Touch screens are available for microcomputers and are used with special programs designed to work with this technology. For example, touch screens are used to place orders in fast-food restaurants because—unlike keyboards—they are waterproof. Libraries and grocery stores have also developed touch-screen systems for locating books and grocery items. Automatic teller machines (ATMs) at banks are yet another form of touch screen.

THE TOUCH PAD

Touch pads are small touch-sensitive input pads. There are two types of touch pads. One type of touch pad is located on the keyboard. These touch pads are a popular option on laptop microcomputers because they eliminate the need for a separate mouse and cable. The other type of touch pad is attached to the computer by a cable.

HANDWRITING RECOGNITION TABLETS

Handwriting recognition tablets, also known as *pen-based* input devices, let you print letters on a touch-sensitive pad for automatic transfer into the microcomputer. Some can use a regular pen; others require a pen designed specifically for the tablet. The type of microcomputer now using this technology is called a *notebook* microcomputer. The notebook microcomputer is a battery-operated portable microcomputer the size of a clipboard, as you can see in Figure 3-13. It has no keyboard or mouse, just a large touch-sensitive surface on which you can write just as you would on a notepad. Pen-based devices are used by corporations for taking orders and filling out forms away from the office. United Parcel Service uses a small pen-based tablet to record customer approvals of deliveries.

There are many advantages of pen-based devices:

- Quiet, so they can be brought into meetings and seminars where noisy keyboards would be a distraction.
- Easily used by people who can't use a keyboard efficiently.
- Portable and light enough to be carried by field service personnel, insurance claims adjusters, and other people who work outside of the office.
- Helpful in reducing or eliminating paperwork.
- Appealing to high-level executives and others who balk at using keyboards.
- Useful for sketching.

The main disadvantage of current pen-based devices is that they can recognize only very neatly printed letters.

GRAPHICS TABLETS

Artists use graphics tablets to input their original designs and to trace existing pieces of art into the microcomputer. A *graphics tablet* is a pad, similar to a mouse pad, used with a pointing device. There are two types of pointing devices used with graphics tablets: the cursor and the stylus (Figure 3-14). The *cursor* is a small mouse that is designed for precise tracing and drawing. The *stylus* is an inkless pen that is useful for freehand art such as drawing. This system of stylus or cursor and pad combines the functions of pointing

FIGURE 3-12

ATM banking has become popular in part because the touch screen input device is so easy to use.

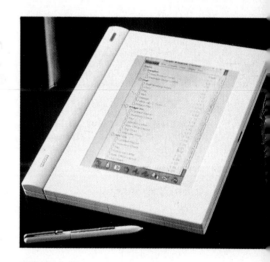

FIGURE 3-13

The notebook microcomputer from NCR uses handwriting recognition.

FIGURE 3-14

A graphics tablet, which looks something like a sophisticated artist's tablet, works with a cursor or stylus.

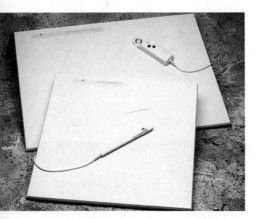

FIGURE 3-15

This specialized tablet contains many functions right on the drawing surface.

and touch-sensitive input devices to provide the most natural means of input for the artist.

Graphics tablets with a cursor and those with a stylus each have advantages. Because of the flat, solid shape of the cursor, it is better for doing accurate traces of existing art. But the stylus has a more natural feel for the artist who wants to create original art.

Many graphics tablets are designed for specific activities, like publishing, graphic design, presentations, drafting, and technical drawings (see Figure 3-15).

The features of graphics tablets vary somewhat depending on the intended use, but their defining characteristics can be summarized as follows:

- **Size**. Graphics tablets come in various sizes from mouse pad size to 4 by 5 feet. The larger sizes allow much more detailed drawing than the small sizes, and are also used for tracing large pictures. The size and accuracy of large graphics tablets makes them ideal for an architect preparing blueprints. However, they take up too much space for the average desktop and are more expensive than the small tablets.

- **Touch sensitivity**. Not all graphics tablets have this feature. One tablet currently available allows you to adjust the width of the line by increasing or decreasing the pressure you exert on the tip of the stylus as you draw. The pressure sensitivity of the pen can also be used to vary colors, brush widths, and image density. These features are useful for artists.

- **Corded or cordless stylus**. When using a stylus attached to the microcomputer by a cable, an artist's hand movements are restricted. The cordless stylus eliminates this problem, but, as with regular pens, a cordless stylus is apt to be misplaced.

Optical Scanning Devices

Optical Scanning Devices Capture Printed Images and Text in Digital Form.

An *optical scanning device* uses optical means to record images, letters, or numbers in digital form for computer processing. The three types of optical scanning devices most commonly used with microcomputers are image scanners, FAX machines, and bar code readers.

"PENPOINT'S" THE WAY

Pen-based personal computers have arrived. Don't throw out your keyboard or mouse just yet, but a new generation of personal computers will let you write information directly onto the computer's screen with an electronic pen.

In California's fabled Silicon Valley, where scores of computer and software companies work at the cutting edge of computer science, a small start-up company called Go Corporation is developing software they call the *PenPoint* operating system, which allows computers to accept input from a specially designed electronic pen.

The Go Corporation has built a prototype, pen-based, notebook sized computer with all the computing power of a desktop personal computer. Pen-based computers can understand such things as writing an X to delete a word and simple printing. (Understanding cursive writing is still down the road.) Drawings, sketches, and diagrams also can be made directly on the screen and stored in the computer.

Developers foresee countless uses for pen-based computing. One target audience is fast-moving corporate executives, who delegate most tasks and almost never use computers. On the road, they need a communications tool that's as light and handy as a notepad. And there are still millions of computer-phobic people whose blood runs cold at the thought of working with a keyboard or even a mouse, but who certainly can write on a pad. There are also countless jobs where keyboard and mouse-driven computers are just not practical.

For example, Norman Vincent, the data processing vice president for State Farm Insurance, has steadfastly resisted supplying his employees in the field with laptop computers. Laptops, he contends, are too heavy and unwieldy for the dangerous and inaccessible places that adjusters have to inspect, such as disaster sites. Employees, he adds, can't hold a PC and operate it at the same time, because keyboards take two hands. Furthermore, claim forms are too difficult to fill out at a keyboard, nor can they be easily illustrated with accident or damage diagrams. And there's no way to rig laptops to accept signatures.

But a State Farm insurance adjuster, using a pen-based, notebook-sized computer to assess a damaged car in a garage, could use the electronic pen to call up an exploded-view diagram of the damaged auto and mark the parts that need to be replaced. The computer could calculate damages on the spot and record the assessment for transmission to State Farm's central computers at the end of the day. It could even accept signatures—so all the necessary forms could be filled out on screen. Says Vincent, "I've been in this job for 20 years, and this is honestly the most exciting technology I've ever seen. I could easily come up with 25,000 people who could use these things at State Farm."

Say good-bye to messy clipboards and notepads. Notebook-sized, pen-based computers allow you to enter data by writing directly onto the computer's screen.

Sources: "Hot New PCs That Read Your Writing," by Brenton R. Schlender, *Fortune*, February 11, 1991, p. 113. "PenPoint Puts It in Writing," by Richard Landry, *PC World*, March 1991, p. 83.

IMAGE SCANNERS

Image scanners are optical scanning devices that scan printed artwork, black and white photographs, and color photographs. They are used to add artwork and photographs to documents and presentations on the microcomputer. The three types of image scanners are flatbed, sheet fed, and hand held:

- **Flatbed.** Like a copy machine, a flatbed scanner has a cover that opens and a glass area where you place the image to be scanned, as shown in Figure 3-16. The advantage of the flatbed scanner is that the image scanned does not have to be perfectly flat. For example, an open book can be scanned. Flatbed scanners are relatively fast and come in different sizes to accept a variety of image sizes. Available in a wide price

49 at bottom right

FIGURE 3-16

A flatbed scanner scans one piece of art at a time.

range, they are good general office scanners. The main disadvantage of flatbed scanners is that they accept only one image at a time for scanning. You have to place and remove each image in turn.

- **Sheet fed.** Like sheet-fed copiers, sheet-fed scanners allow you to stack many sheets of paper at a time for automatic feeding. These scanners are the best choice for scanning many pages of loose-leaf documents. They cannot be used to scan individual images printed on anything other than standard size sheets of paper. Some flatbed scanners come with sheet feeder attachments. *(Half-page scanner)*
- **Hand held.** Hand-held scanners are small and portable. A hand-held scanner is restricted by the length of its cable. However, it allows you to scan any printed image you can reach. Hand-held scanners are less expensive than the stationary models. Their main disadvantage is that they cannot scan a page-sized image all at once. They have to take two or more scanning passes across different parts of the image. Unless you have a very steady hand, you can get distorted scans on large images. Therefore, hand-held scanners are best suited to scanning small images like logos and small pieces of art (Figure 3-17).

FIGURE 3-17

Hand-held scanners take two or more passes to scan a standard 8-by 11-inch page.

FAX MACHINES

Facsimile machines (*FAX machines*) are widely used in offices to transmit printed material over telephone lines. A FAX machine works like a scanner by illuminating and scanning a document and converting it to digital form. FAX technology has been incorporated into microcomputers through add-on products. To send or receive FAX input, the microcomputer is attached to a telephone line and the document or image is sent in digital form over the line. *(Comb. of copier and modem)*

BAR CODE READERS

A *bar code reader* is an optical scanning device that reads the black and white stripes called *bar codes* found on most product containers. You may have watched bar code readers at work at the grocery store checkout counter. The bar code found on products, known as the UPC or Universal Product Code, is one type of bar code. Another is the POSTNET code found on the lower left edge of many preprinted envelopes, which is used by the U.S. Postal Service to read ZIP codes. These two types of bar codes are shown in Figure 3-18.

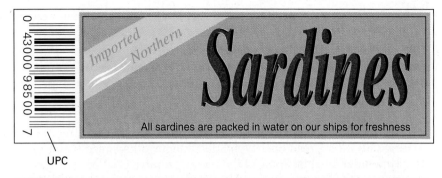

UPC

POSTNET

FIGURE 3-18

UPC codes are used on grocery store products; POSTNET codes are used on envelopes.

How Optical Scanning Works

Optical Scanning Is the Process of Separating Out Differing Degrees of Reflected Light to Read Images or Letters.

All printed images, letters, and numbers have dark and light areas that distinguish them from the background on which they are printed. *Optical scanning* senses the varying amounts of light reflected by these dark and light areas. The scanner illuminates the printed image or text and then reads, or *scans,* the light reflected from it. Wherever a change occurs in the amount of light reflected, the scanner records these differences in digital form to recreate the image, words, or numbers for input into the microcomputer.

OPTICAL CHARACTER RECOGNITION (OCR)

Optical character recognition, or *OCR,* is the process that optical scanners use to read the characters (letters, numbers, and special symbols) in typed or printed documents. All types of optical image scanners, including flatbed, sheet fed, and hand held, can scan characters. However, special computer programs are required to allow image scanners to interpret text, rather than just recording the entire page as a picture.

OCR programs are great time-savers for any business that transfers text from printed documents into the microcomputer because they eliminate the need to retype the text. Although OCR is a continually improving technology, current OCR programs have some limitations:

- **Character recognition.** Variations in the darkness and thickness of letters, numbers, and special symbols can cause an OCR program to miss some of the text in an original document. The result can be either words with letters missing or special symbols, called *wildcard* characters, that are automatically placed wherever the OCR program can't read a character. Some OCR programs have better character recognition than others, but none is perfect.

- **Type recognition.** The type used in a document may have unusually heavy, thick characters or thin, delicate characters. OCR products are designed to recognize some of the most commonly used type designs and may have trouble recognizing less familiar type. Also, most OCR programs have trouble recognizing light type.
- **Quality of originals.** OCR programs can be picky about the quality of originals. Some read only typed documents; others read both typed and printed documents. Some of the more complete OCR programs can read originals that have been typed, printed, or sent through a FAX machine.

OPTICAL MARK RECOGNITION (OMR)

Optical Mark Recognition, or *OMR,* is the process of scanning handwritten marks on cards or forms. The cards are coded with pencil or pen strokes to represent numbers or letters. A scanner reads the marks and translates them into characters.

The two most common uses of OMR programs are in state lotteries and on standard tests:

- State lottery cards. You select your numbers by placing pencil or pen marks next to the appropriate numbers, as shown in Figure 3-19.
- Standardized tests. You select your answers by filling in the adjacent circles.

Magnetic Scanning

Magnetic Scanners Read Numbers and Letters Printed with Magnetic Ink.

Magnetic scanners work with text that has been printed using a special magnetic ink. These scanners capture the magnetically printed text (usually numbers) in digital form. The two most familiar types of magnetic scanning devices are wand readers and magnetic ink character recognition (MICR) readers.

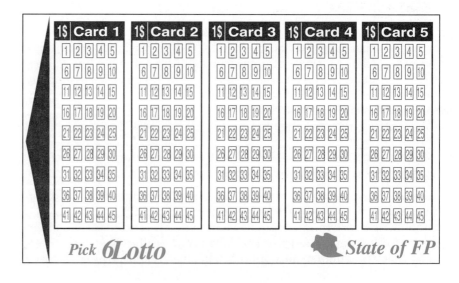

FIGURE 3-19

Lotto cards use pencil marks to indicate selections.

FIGURE 3-20

Wand readers are used to scan shipping labels and price tags.

WAND READERS

A *wand reader* is a magnetic scanning device that reads data from a magnetically coded price tag. This type of scanner, shown in Figure 3-20, is commonly used in shipping departments and department stores. When a shipping label or a price tag is scanned, the microcomputer records the item identification and price, which are then printed on the sales slip. The item identification number may be used to retrieve the item's record, update the quantity on hand, and rewrite the updated record.

MAGNETIC INK CHARACTER RECOGNITION (MICR) READERS

Magnetic ink character recognition, or *MICR,* is the process of reading characters that have been printed with magnetic ink. This system is most commonly used in banks to process checks.

Preprinted checks are coded on the lower left edge with the branch and customer account number in magnetic ink, as shown in Figure 3-21. At the bank, the checks pass through MICR readers that read the codes and direct the checks for processing. This type of coding is used on checks to minimize errors and automate processing.

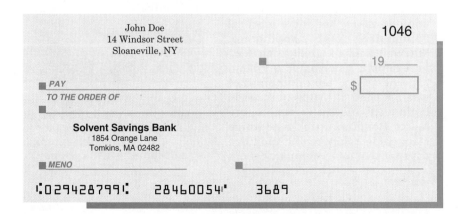

FIGURE 3-21

Your checks are identified and properly sorted at the bank because they are printed with this magnetic ink code.

Magnetic ink character recognition is seldom used with microcomputer systems.

Digital Sound Processing

Digital Sound Processing Started in the Music Industry.

Natural sounds and music can be input and played back from properly equipped microcomputers through a process called *digital sound processing*. Digital sound processing involves taking a sample of a natural sound or music with a microphone, converting it to digital data, and inputting it into the microcomputer. Digital music is familiar to all of us because of the popularity of digital compact discs (CDs). The same process used to convert music to digital form for CDs is used to input sounds and music into microcomputers.

IT'S HARD TO WRECK
A NICE BEACH

Lalit Bahl has been working since 1972 to design a computer that can understand human speech. Bahl, who works at IBM's Thomas Watson Research Center, thought he would reach his goal years ago. But progress has been slow, and today's computers can understand only a limited range of human speech.

That's the bad news. The good news is that even this small capacity to understand speech has powerfully affected many lives. Handicapped attorney David Bristol, for example, is certainly not complaining. Bristol, who has cerebral palsy and cannot use a keyboard, dictates his legal briefs and other documents directly into his computer system, thanks to *DragonDictate*, a voice recognition system designed by Dragon Systems, Inc.

Today, based on the research done at IBM's Watson Research Center and similar work done at AT&T Bell Labs, specialized computers such as the one used by David Bristol *can* understand human speech, but with major limitations.

The biggest problem is that computers can understand only discrete words, such as "yes" or "no," which act like commands. They are baffled by continuous speech, where words are uttered rapidly, in a particular sequence, as in a conversation between two people. For example, the sentence "It's hard to recognize speech" sounds almost the same as "It's hard to wreck a nice beach." We can make such distinctions based on our knowledge of the speaker and the context, but computers aren't that smart.

One way around this problem is to design systems that *specialize* in one subject, such as making airline reservations or trading stocks. The *DragonDictate* system, which attorney David Bristol uses, is one of the most ambitious systems to date, recognizing 30,000 words.

Permitting handicapped people to pursue their careers is reason enough to welcome voice recognition systems, even in their relatively primitive state. And more practical applications keep popping up. Kurzweil Applied Intelligence, Inc., for example, has created a system for emergency room doctors that was installed at Mercy Hospital in Springfield, Massachusetts. Before Mercy Hospital introduced voice recognition computers, it took five days to generate emergency room reports, largely because secretaries had to transcribe doctors' scribbled notes. Now a printed report takes *five minutes*.

So, while researchers like Lalit Bahl may fret about not reaching their lifelong goal of a computer that recognizes continuous speech, what they have accomplished has already transformed many lives.

Attorney David Bristol has cerebral palsy and can't use a keyboard. But with *DragonDictate's* voice recognition system, he can *dictate* complex legal documents to his computer.

Source: "A Computer That Recognizes Its Master's Voice?" by Evan I. Schwartz, *Business Week*, June 3, 1991, p. 130.

The first microcomputer to use digital sound technology was the Apple II. Since then, sound capability has evolved through a variety of microcomputer systems. Current Macintosh IIsi and LC computers come equipped with microphones so you can record sample sounds. The ability to use the microcomputer to record and play back sound is useful for businesspeople delivering presentations and for composers creating songs.

Voice Recognition Devices

Voice Recognition Devices Let You Give Spoken Commands to Your Microcomputer.

Voice recognition devices record spoken language and translate it into commands and data for the microcomputer. The human voice is extremely complex, containing multiple tones and resonances that are as individual as fingerprints. Capturing a person's voice requires the ability to separate out and recognize all its elements. Thus voice recognition devices for microcomputers have lagged behind other input devices.

Two types of voice recognition, or *voice-activated* systems, are currently available. They don't always work well, as the technology is still developing.

- **Speaker dependent.** Only one speaker can use a speaker-dependent system. The system is trained word by word to respond to one voice only. Using a microphone connected to the microcomputer, the speaker repeats commands while the microcomputer takes samples of the speaker's voice. The microcomputer then uses the samples as a reference to compare to the actual voice when the speaker uses the microcomputer. Speaker-dependent systems are the easiest to implement.

- **Speaker independent.** Speaker-independent systems identify key words and commands spoken by many different voices. These systems require a much larger voice sample for the microcomputer to use for reference. To make speaker-independent systems work, the vocabulary recognized by the microcomputer is limited to simple commands.

Specialized Input Devices

Science, Industry, and the Military Use Specialized Devices to Create Input for Microcomputers.

The special requirements of the research sciences, medicine, industry, and the military demand input from sources other than those found in most offices. Some of these special input devices and their uses are as follows:

- **Digital image input.** Digital image input consists of photographs that are digitized for use in a computer or for transmission to a remote location. These photographs are taken with a camera similar to a standard 35mm camera that is specially designed for use in outer space. The most famous examples of digital images are the photographs of other planets sent back from the Voyager spacecraft. The pictures Voyager took with its special cameras were digitally stored and sent back to earth on command.

- **Surveillance cameras.** Photographs and videos taken by surveillance cameras can be used as input for microcomputers. These cameras use a heat-sensitive scanning technology to create digital portraits of terrain and objects for analysis by the military (see Figure 3-22).

- *Video digitizers.* Video images are converted to digital form using video

FIGURE 3-22

The sensitivity of surveillance cameras allows them to see people and objects in the dark by sensing the heat they generate.

cameras connected to digital input devices. Video digitizing is available on microcomputer systems and is often used for presentations and sales demonstrations.

- *Medical devices.* Medical diagnostic and test devices provide digital input for analysis on microcomputers. Photographs taken by electron microscope, medical image scanners, and X-ray equipment can be digitized. Digital sampling of a three-dimensional object, like the brain, creates a two-dimensional "slice" of the area that is used for medical analysis.

- *Engineering test devices.* Many engineers use digital technology to analyze test results. They connect their test equipment to a digital converter that changes the test signals to digital form. Then the digital signals are sent to a microcomputer, where special programs are used to analyze the test data.

- *Weather input from satellites.* When we see the radar weather map on the nightly news, we are looking at the results of a digitizing process. Weather satellites constantly scan the sky and ground using a long horizontal array of specialized optical scanners. These scanned images are transmitted to powerful computers to be manipulated into the images we see on television.

Future Trends

Input Devices Will Continue to Become Easier to Use and More Convenient.

The future of input devices lies in two areas that are currently being developed. Because input devices are our link to microcomputers, future developments in each of the three input areas may soon change the way we work with computers.

THE FUTURE OF VOICE RECOGNITION

Voice recognition could easily become the most popular input device in the future. Once it is fully developed, it will make working with the microcomputer as easy as talking to the person in the next office. Speaker-independent systems, able to cope with continuous speech, are currently in development. They will allow near-normal speech interaction with the microcomputer.

One day, you will be able to dictate to your microcomputer and see what you've said immediately on the monitor. Speed, accuracy, and convenience will make microcomputer dictation a favorite form of input in the future.

MOVEMENT AND TOUCH-BASED SYSTEMS

Microcomputer input devices that recognize touch and movement will continue to develop. Systems currently used by the military and by researchers working with the handicapped record eye movement commands, thereby eliminating the need to interact physically with the microcomputer. Other systems that make use of touch, such as handwriting recognition systems, will find a niche. Future systems will be able to learn to read your handwriting, no matter how poor it is.

REVIEW QUESTIONS

1. What is an input device?
2. What is digitizing?
3. Name the five types of keys on the keyboard and describe their functions.
4. What are the three types of mice?
5. How does a mechanical mouse work? How does an optical mouse work?
6. How do you operate a trackball?
7. How do touch-sensitive devices work?
8. Name three places where you might use a touch screen.
9. List three advantages of handwriting recognition tablets.
10. When is a stylus used with a graphics tablet? When is a cursor used?
11. Name one specific use for large graphics tablets.
12. Name the three types of optical image scanners.
13. When would you use a flatbed scanner, a sheet-fed scanner, a hand-held scanner?
14. Where would you expect to see a UPC code? A POSTNET code?
15. How do optical scanners work?
16. What types of input devices are used for OCR?
17. Name three limitations of optical character recognition.
18. Name one common use of a wand reader.
19. What is magnetic ink character recognition (MICR)?
20. How is magnetic ink character recognition used in banks?
21. How does digital sound processing work?
22. Why is voice recognition difficult to achieve?
23. What is the main difference between speaker-dependent and speaker-independent voice recognition systems?
24. What is a digital image?
25. Why is voice recognition one of the most promising input devices for the future?

TOPICS FOR RESEARCH AND DISCUSSION

1. Voice recognition is one of the most promising areas of current research. What advantages do you think voice recognition would offer? What disadvantages? Make sure to consider such issues as ease of use, naturalness, usefulness, the ability to be used in a variety of situations, appropriateness for certain tasks, current work styles, and ease of learning.

2. Visit a local computer store and find out which input devices an architect might purchase. List and describe these devices, give a summary of the types of programs to be run, and list the cost of each input device. Indicate which input devices would be mandatory and which ones would be optional.

3. One type of input device that is increasingly used for both business and personal activities is the touch-sensitive device. Some of the benefits of these devices are discussed in this chapter. Locate a touch-sensitive device used in your area and talk to the people using it. What do they say are the biggest advantages? The biggest disadvantages? What would you predict will happen to touch-sensitive devices in the future? Will they be used more or less? How will they differ from the ones currently in use? As a follow-up to your interviews, research what news and computer magazines have written about touch-sensitive devices.

CHAPTER 4

SECONDARY STORAGE

OBJECTIVES

The information in this chapter will enable you to

- Explain the purpose of secondary storage on microcomputers.
- Describe the two basic types of storage technology and how they work.
- List all the commonly used secondary storage devices utilized by modern microcomputers, along with their advantages and disadvantages.
- Explain the proper care of magnetic disks.
- Describe the evolution of secondary storage devices.
- Describe some probable future developments in microcomputer storage.

When you type a letter, create a financial spreadsheet, or build a database, your information is stored in the computer's main memory, also called *random access memory* (RAM). Main memory is also known as *volatile* memory—and for good reason. Turn off the computer and everything in main memory is lost forever. Main memory is like a blackboard where you can enter and manipulate data, but you cannot store information there for later use (Figure 4-1).

One of the most important features of a computer is its ability to retain information permanently, for repeated use. All computers have some form of *permanent* storage, or *nonvolatile* memory, which retains information after the computer is turned off. It's this permanent storage capability that lets you perform financial analysis on data entered months ago or search for information entered years ago.

Permanent storage of data files and software programs requires *secondary storage devices*, also called *auxiliary* or *mass* storage devices ("mass" storage refers to the large quantities of information they can store).

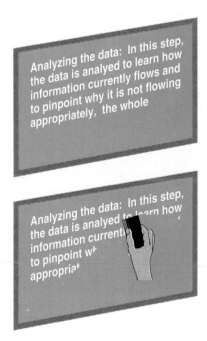

FIGURE 4-1

Main memory (RAM) is like a blackboard: You can enter data, but when the computer is turned off, the data is erased.

Types of Secondary Storage Devices

There Are Three Types of Secondary Storage Devices.

There are three types of secondary storage devices in common use:

- Magnetic disks (both floppy disks and hard disks)
- Optical disks
- Magnetic tape cartridges

Magnetic disks are the most common form of secondary storage for microcomputers. Optical disks use laser technology and are becoming popular for certain applications. Magnetic tape is used primarily for backup purposes.

59

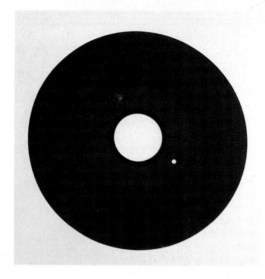

FIGURE 4-3

A floppy disk is the same type material as an audiotape.

Magnetic Disks (Floppy and Hard Disks)

Magnetic Disks Are the Most Common Permanent Storage for Microcomputers.

The *magnetic disk* has been the permanent storage device of choice for microcomputers ever since they were introduced. There are two general types. The floppy disk (Figure 4-2), which comes in a protective jacket, can be removed from the computer and stores relatively small quantities of data. The hard disk, often built into the system unit, stores large amounts of data. Both types of disks use the same technology to store data.

Both sides of magnetic disks have a smooth, shiny coating like that on an audio- or videotape (see Figure 4-3). The coating contains a metal oxide that can store electromagnetic charges permanently.

How Data Is Stored on a Magnetic Disk

Data Is Often Stored on Disks in Bytes—Groups of Electromagnetic Charges That Are Turned On or Off.

When you consider how much data a disk can store, it's hard to imagine that the only thing a disk can save is simple *on* or *off* electromagnetic charges on its surface. But as we saw in Chapter 2, computers store every kind of information in bits.

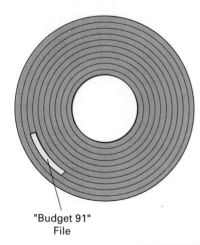

"Budget 91"
File

FIGURE 4-4

A file is a specific collection of bytes stored on a disk and identified by a specific name.

BITS, BYTES, AND FILES

Usually a character is saved on a disk is saved as a byte, or sequence of eight bits (eight 1's and zero's). A specific collection of bytes, called a *file*, is identified by a file name (see Figure 4-4). For example, when you save a file you've named "Budget91," you are instructing the computer to place that entire collection of bytes on a disk for permanent storage under that file name. As the word *file* suggests, computer files are the electronic equivalent of paper files that used to be stuffed into filing cabinets. But you can retrieve computer files in a matter of seconds. Try that with a filing cabinet!

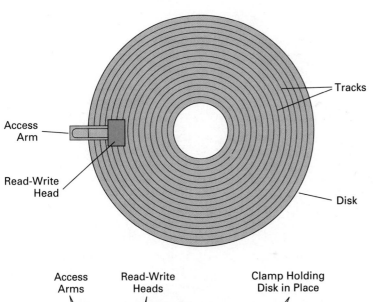

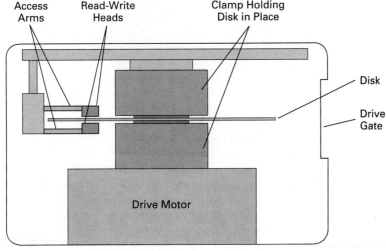

FIGURE 4-5

A floppy disk drive is the most common type of secondary storage device.

TRACKS

A file is saved on the tracks of a disk. These *tracks* are individual concentric rings. The tracks are not visible because they are composed of electromagnetic charges instead of physical grooves. The disk sits in a *disk drive* (shown in Figure 4-5). The drive has a motor that spins the disk at a constant speed and *read/write heads* that can read information from the spinning tracks or write new information on them. The read/write heads ride only a few thousandths of an inch above the disk surface.

The number of tracks across a disk is measured in *tracks per inch (tpi)*. The amount of data a disk can store depends on the size of the disk, the number of tracks per inch, and the closeness of the bits to each other on the track, called *linear density*, which is measured in *bits per inch (bpi)*.

A file is stored on as many tracks as are needed to hold the entire file. As Figure 4-6 illustrates, these tracks may not be next to each other. The pieces of a file can be scattered throughout a disk and found on portions of many tracks. The computer *operating system* software program, which manages all computer operations, can retrieve all parts of a file either randomly or sequentially. (You will learn more about the operating system in Chapter 6.) Each track is identified with a number, with the outermost track being *zero*.

SECTORS

The disk is also divided into *sectors,* which, as you can see from Figure 4-7, look like slices of a pie. Older computers used *hard-sectored* disks, which

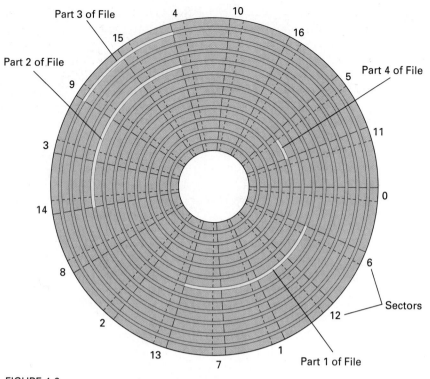

FIGURE 4-6

Parts of a file can be scattered all over the disk.

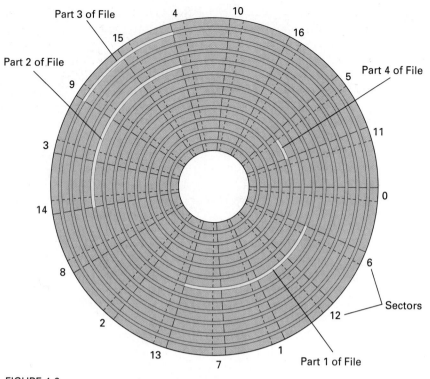

FIGURE 4-7

A floppy disk's sectors are like slices of a pie.

meant the sectors were identified by small holes around the perimeter of the center hole. Newer computers use *soft-sectored* disks: the operating system creates and identifies the sectors along with the tracks. The operating system uses both the track and sector numbers to locate a file.

FORMATTING

Because tracks and sectors do not exist when a disk is new, they must be created. Both floppy and hard disks must be *formatted,* or *initialized,* before use. A *format command,* which is part of the operating system, establishes where the tracks and sectors are placed on the disk. Although all 5 1/4-inch disks, for example, look alike, they may be formatted differently to meet the requirements of various computers.

Floppy Disks

Microcomputers Typically Use Two Sizes of Floppy Disks: 5 1/4 Inch and 3 1/2 Inch.

Floppy disks were introduced by IBM in the early 1970s as removable storage media for mainframe computers. The first microcomputers used only floppy disks for secondary storage; hard disks weren't yet available. Floppy disks, also called *floppies* and *floppy diskettes,* are removable platters that slide into the disk drive through a *drive door,* also called a *drive gate.* A typical drive motor spins the disk at about 360 revolutions per minute (rpm). The disk drive *access arm* moves the read/write heads across the disk to access files and write new ones on it.

Microcomputers use either 5 1/4-inch or 3 1/2-inch diameter floppy disks, or both. Mainframes and a few older computers used an 8-inch diameter floppy, which today is considered obsolete. Floppy disk drives are often

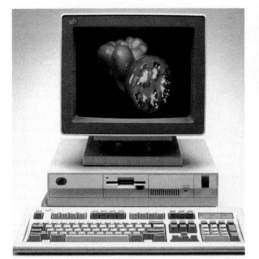
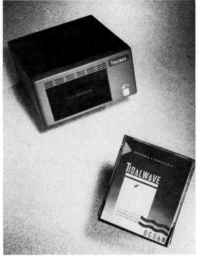

FIGURE 4-8

Floppy disk drives can be built into the system unit, like this 5 1/4 inch disk drive (left) or a stand-alone unit connected to the system unit by a cable, like this 3 1/2-inch disk drive (right.

built into the system unit, but they also can be purchased as external units (Figure 4-8).

To manipulate files, the operating system identifies each disk drive in a computer with a letter or a number. This enables the computer user to indicate the location of the file to be created, accessed, copied, or deleted. If a computer has one floppy drive, it is designated as the A, or 1, drive. If it has two floppy drives, one is the A, or 1, drive, and the other is the B, or 2, drive.

ADVANTAGES AND DISADVANTAGES OF FLOPPY DISKS

The major advantage of floppy disks is that they are removable. Files can be physically transferred from one computer to another or mailed. Floppies are routinely used to backup copies of files in case the hard disk, which stores the originals, is damaged.

The big disadvantage of floppies is their relatively low capacity. Floppy disks can store only a few hundred pages of text, which is low compared with hard disks (discussed later). Another disadvantage is their relatively slow *access time*, which is how long it takes to move information from a disk to internal memory. Floppy disk access time is about 10 times slower than that of a hard disk.

5 1/4-INCH FLOPPY DISKS

The *5 1/4-inch floppy disk,* or diskette, is a thin and flexible plastic platter, coated on both sides with metal oxide. The platter has a center hole about an inch in diameter to accept the drive spindle, which spins it. The platter is barely visible; it is stored in a square protective cardboard or plastic cover. The cover has an opening for the center hole and a cutout window, called the *access window,* where the read/write head reads data or writes it onto the disk surface as it spins. There is also a small *index hole* near the center hole, which enables the disk controller to locate disk sectors (see Figure 4-9).

The square notch in the corner of the disk is called the *write-protect* notch. If this notch is covered with an adhesive tab (supplied with the disks), the disk can be read, but nothing can be written on it. This prevents someone from writing over or erasing important information. If the notch is not covered, the disk can be written on and files can be erased.

The 5 1/4-inch floppy comes in both *high density* and *low density* versions. The low density 5 1/4-inch floppy holds approximately 360K (360 kilobytes or 360,000 bytes) of information. This translates to approximately 200 pages of text. Low density disks are also called *double-sided, double density* disks, commonly abbreviated *DS, DD.*

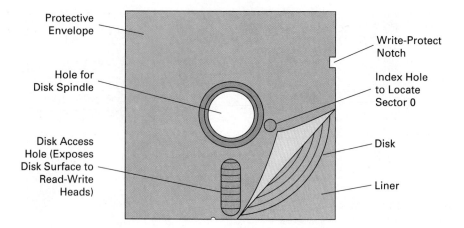

FIGURE 4-9

The 5 1/4-inch floppy disk was one of the first types of floppy disks. It has become less popular recently.

They are called double-sided because the first floppies used only one side of the disk for storage. The double density portion of the name comes from disk technology improvements that have doubled the amount of data which can be stored on each side of the disk.

These double-sided, double density disks store 48 tracks per inch and have a linear density of 2,800 bits per inch. Both read/write heads move back and forth together, so only one side is used at a time.

Further technological advances produced the high density 5 1/4-inch disks that hold about three times as much information as DS, DD disks. With a capacity of 1.2MB (1.2 million bytes), these disks store 96 tracks per inch and up to 600 pages of text. They are called *DS, HD* for *double-sided, high density*.

3 1/2-INCH FLOPPY DISKS

In the early 1980s, a 3 1/2-inch diameter disk, often called a *micro disk* or *micro diskette*, was introduced. Using the same technology as its larger counterpart, a 3 1/2-inch disk can store more data despite its smaller size. These disks have a hard plastic protective casing and no exposed access window, as Figure 4-10 shows. Instead, a retractable cover remains closed until the disk is put into the disk drive. This reduces the chance of accidentally touching the disk surface. Instead of a center hole, there is a hub on the back of the disk that the drive spindle engages to spin the disk. The write-protect notch is a plastic switch, eliminating the need for adhesive tabs.

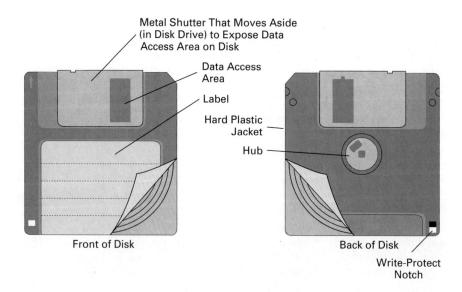

FIGURE 4-10

The 3 1/2-inch floppy disk is much more durable than its 5 1/4-inch counterpart.

Table 4-1: Types of Floppy Disks			
Physical Size	**Density**	**Referred to as**	**Capacity**
5 1/4 inch	Low	Double-sided, Double density (DS, DD)	360K
	High	Double-sided, High density (DS, HD)	1.2MB
3 1/2 inch	Low	Double-sided, Double density (DS, DD)	720K (800K on the Macintosh)
	High	Double-sided, High density (DS, HD)	1.44MB

All 3 1/2-inch disk drives have dual heads, so all of these disks are double-sided and designated DS. However, 3 1/2-inch disks also come in a high and a low density. The low density disk holds about 720K (800K on the Apple Macintosh) of information and is designated as DS, DD; the high density holds about 1.44MB (1.44 million bytes) and is designated as DS, HD. Both high and low density disks store 135 tracks per inch and look identical. But high density disks squeeze more data onto a disk with increased linear density (bits per inch).

Many manufacturers label their 3 1/2-inch disks as 1MB and 2MB for low and high density disks, respectively. They are referring to the total capacity—unformatted. Once the disks are formatted they will either be 720K or 1.44MB (see Table 4-1).

COMPATIBILITY OF FLOPPY DISKS AND DRIVES

Obviously, you must use a 5 1/4-inch disk in a 5 1/4-inch drive and a 3 1/2-inch disk in a 3 1/2-inch drive. However, in addition to the physical size of the disk matching the drive, the density of the disk must be compatible with the type of drive. There are high and low density drives, as well as high and low density disks. Using a high density disk in a low density drive, or vice versa, may result in some disk functions not working properly.

A drive performs three functions on a disk if they are totally compatible. It formats the disk, writes information to the disk, and reads information from it. High density drives can perform all three functions with high density disks, and low density drives can perform all three functions on low density disks.

A high density drive can format a low density disk, but requires a special format command to do so properly. A low density drive can format a high density disk with a special format command, but only as a low density disk. This means you are wasting most of the disk capacity you paid for. A low density drive cannot read or write to a high density disk that has been formatted as a high density disk.

A basic rule is always to match the density of the disk with that of the drive (Figure 4-11).

CARE OF FLOPPY DISKS

The 5 1/4-inch disks are the most vulnerable to damage because they are flexible and have an exposed access window. Considering the density with which the information is stored on disks, it doesn't take much to destroy an entire file. Remember these precautions:

- Keep fingers off the access window.
- Store disks in a protective jacket, with the exposed window in the jacket.
- Don't bend the disk or put anything heavy on it.

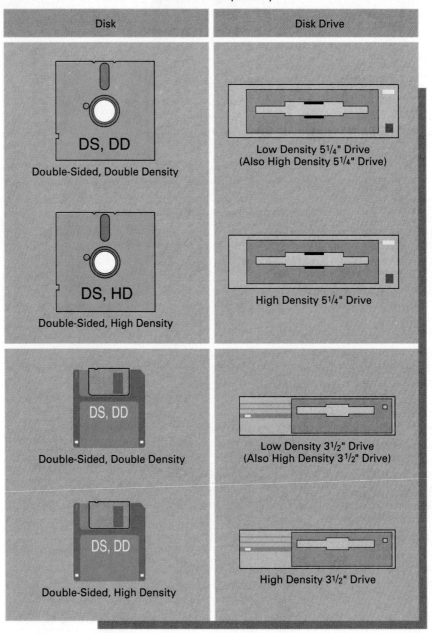

Disk	Disk Drive
DS, DD Double-Sided, Double Density	Low Density 5¼" Drive (Also High Density 5¼" Drive)
DS, HD Double-Sided, High Density	High Density 5¼" Drive
DS, DD Double-Sided, Double Density	Low Density 3½" Drive (Also High Density 3½" Drive)
DS, DD Double-Sided, High Density	High Density 3½" Drive

FIGURE 4-11

Generally, the best advice is match the density of the disk with that of the drive.

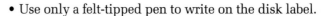

- Use only a felt-tipped pen to write on the disk label.
- Don't expose disks to extreme heat or cold, which may warp or crack them.
- Don't use paper clips or rubber bands on a disk.
- Keep disks away from electric motors, phones, and magnets; magnetism can destroy data (see Figure 4-12).
- Store disks upright in a dustproof case.
- Be sure each file stored on a disk has a unique name and is labeled.

Although 3 1/2-inch disks are less vulnerable than 5 1/4-inch disks, they, too, must be handled with care. Even though they have no exposed recording surfaces and cannot bend, the warnings we listed for 5 1/4-inch disks also apply to 3 1/2-inch disks. In addition, never open the retractable

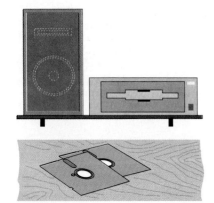

FIGURE 4-12

A magnetic object (such as a stereo speaker or telephone) can damage your magnetic data.

cover to expose the disk surface, and don't handle the disk roughly; you can jam the disk within its case.

A WORD ABOUT VIRUSES

Recently, microcomputer users have faced a new problem—computer *viruses*. These are programs created for the sole purpose of disrupting computer operations. Virus programs can destroy information in any type of software, usually by erasing or scrambling it.

These programs can be spread if a floppy disk containing the virus is placed in your computer or if your computer communicates over telephone lines with another computer. If your computer does not use telephone lines to access information, floppies are the only thing to worry about.

To prevent your computer from becoming contaminated, never use a floppy disk of unknown origin in your computer. If someone put a virus program on this disk, it can infect and damage the files on your hard disk. If you often use floppy disks provided by others, consider getting a virus protection program that automatically checks all floppies before you use them and warns you if they are infected (see Chapters 6 and 14).

Hard Disks

Hard Disks Have Greater Storage Capabilities Than Floppy Disks.

Storage capacity limitations became obvious only a few years after floppy disks were introduced. New programs required more disk space than floppies could handle, and users found they needed more and more room for larger data files. IBM introduced the aptly named *hard*, or *fixed*, disk for microcomputers to resolve these problems (the terms are used interchangeably). The disk is called hard because the platter, made of metal, is rigid and heavy. The term *fixed* is used because the disk is often fixed in place within the system unit. Almost all hard disk drives are now *Winchester* drives, in which the disk, the drive, and the read/write heads are all sealed in a single box to protect them against dust, smoke, and dirt.

Except for the obvious difference between a plastic platter and a metal one, a hard disk platter looks much like a floppy platter, as Figure 4-13 shows. The diameter of the hard disk depends on the manufacturer, although most are the same diameter as floppy disks so they can fit into existing system unit cases.

FIGURE 4-13

The airtight lid of this Winchester drive has been removed to show that the hard disk looks very much like a floppy disk.

STORAGE CAPACITY AND ACCESS TIME OF HARD DISKS

The storage capacity of microcomputers skyrocketed with the advent of hard disks. The earliest hard disks held 5 to 10MB (5 to 10 million bytes) of data, or roughly 2,500 to 5,000 pages of text. Most hard disks today range from 20MB to 100MB. The most common fixed disks in microcomputers today have a capacity of 20MB to 40MB.

There are two reasons for this high storage capacity. First, the track density of hard disks is much greater than floppy disks—usually over 300 tracks per inch. Second, the larger capacity hard disks consist of multiple platters stacked up like plates, as Figure 4-14 shows.

A typical microcomputer hard disk has four stacked platters, resulting in six available sides for data storage. (The top and bottom surfaces of the stack are not used for storage.) Each side must have a read/write head, so a four-platter hard disk has six read/write heads. Like the floppy disk drive read/write heads, these all move back and forth across the disk together, as a single unit. Thus, only one track on one surface can be accessed at a time.

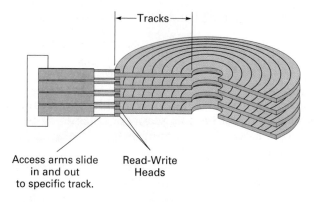

FIGURE 4-14

A hard disk has multiple disks and multiple read/write heads (shown in cutaway).

Nonetheless, most hard disks have access times 10 to 20 times faster than floppies, because they spin at about 3,500 revolutions per minute—10 times faster than floppy disk drives.

CYLINDERS

Like floppies, each platter on a hard disk has tracks. However, each track number occurs multiple times. For example, on a four-platter hard disk there are six number 5 tracks—one for each available surface (see Figure 4-15). All the tracks with the same number on a hard disk with multiple platters are referred to collectively as *cylinders*, which describes the appearance of the stacked tracks.

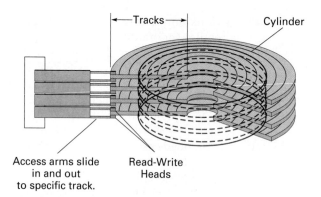

FIGURE 4-15

A cylinder is the same track on all the used sides of the disks in a hard disk drive.

Hard disks are divided into sectors, as are floppies, but a sector refers to all the platters in the stack (see Figure 4-16). Hard disks also have soft sectors, which are created when the disk is first formatted.

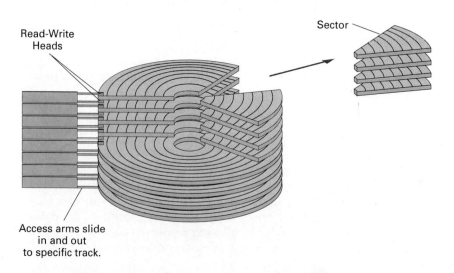

FIGURE 4-16

On a hard disk, sectors are like slices of a layer cake.

DRIVE SPECIFICATIONS AND PARTITIONS

Each disk drive is assigned a drive specification to differentiate it from others. Most microcomputers have one hard disk. Since floppy disk drives are identified as A and B, the hard disk is often called the C drive. This is done even if there is no B floppy drive, to make sure that the A and B drives always pertain to floppies.

A hard disk with a large storage capacity can pose two problems. First, it is difficult to keep track of files on a disk that can hold hundreds of megabytes of data. Second, some types of computers are incapable of formatting and accessing more than a certain number of megabytes on one disk. For example, some IBM-compatible personal computers, because of the operating system they use, can format and access only 32MB of data on one disk. A 40MB hard disk would have 8MB of storage capacity unused.

Both problems can be solved by *partitioning* the hard disk, or making a single physical disk act like multiple disks. These multiple disks are called *logical* disks, since they do not physically exist. Partitioning a disk is done when the disk is formatted. For example, a 40MB hard disk can be partitioned to act like a 32MB C drive and an 8 MB D drive.

CARE OF HARD DISKS

Because hard disks cannot be handled, they are less likely to be abused. However, users must treat them with care. A damaged hard disk can result in losing years of information.

The primary concern is to prevent a *head crash* that occurs when the read/write heads, which hover above the spinning disk on a thin cushion of air, come in contact with the disk surface. This crash scrapes off the surface material and your files along with it. Usually the contents of the entire disk are lost when this happens. A head crash can occur when smoke or dust particles interfere with the path of the head, as Figure 4-17 shows. Dropping or jarring the computer also can cause head crashes.

FIGURE 4-17

Minimal disk head clearance makes for faster access time, but increases the risk of a head crash.

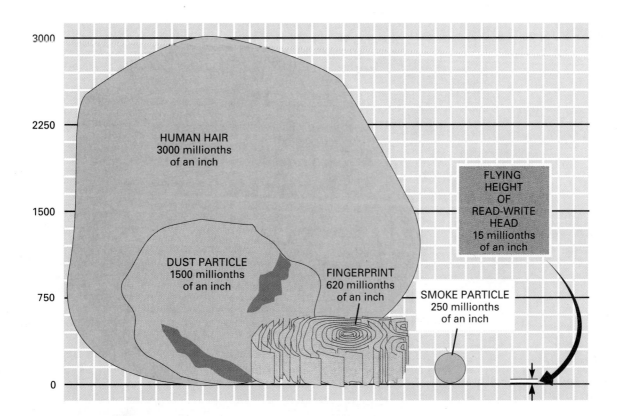

Follow these precautions to prevent damage to the hard disk:

- Keep smoke, dirt, dust, and food away from the system unit.
- Avoid static electricity by using antistatic spray, mats, and a humidifier if necessary.
- On older microcomputers, be sure to park the drive heads with a utility program provided with the computer. (Most new computers do this automatically when the computer is turned off.)
- When moving the system unit, avoid jarring motions.
- Avoid high heat, which can damage the disk and the entire system.

Typical Microcomputer Configurations

Newer Microcomputers Have Both Floppy and Hard Disk Drives.

Many older microcomputers have only floppy disk drives. These computers have extremely limited capabilities, since most computer programs today require a hard disk. Computers with only one floppy drive require constant swapping of disks to run most programs and also make you keep your data files on the same disk as the program files. Microcomputers with two floppy drives allow you to keep data files on one disk and the program on another.

The vast majority of microcomputers found in business today have a hard disk and one or more floppy drives. The floppy drive is used to load programs and data files onto the hard disk and to make copies of files from the hard disk. The hard disk enables the user to store large volumes of information and large program files.

Because a hard disk can read and write data more than 10 times faster than a floppy, it is always more efficient to do your work directly on the hard disk.

Alternative Hard Disks

Hard Disk Cards and Hard Disk Cartridges Are Alternatives to Hard Disks.

Many microcomputers come with built-in hard disks, but other types of hard disks are available. Most of these are considered add-on products, since they are usually purchased after the computer and added on later. These add-ons include hard disk cards and hard disk cartridges.

HARD DISK CARDS

Factory-installed hard disks fit into the system unit in an area specifically designed for disk drives. The number of drives that can be installed depends on the manufacturer and model of computer. But most microcomputers can incorporate at least two disks or drives and some can handle four or more.

If an additional hard disk is needed, but there is no room for it, a hard disk card may solve the problem. A *hard disk card* is a hard disk mounted on an expansion card that fits into a slot on the motherboard. There must be a slot available for the hard disk card, but most computers come with at least one or two spare slots.

Hard disk cards are easier to install than a regular hard disk, but usually cost more. Access times of hard disk cards are as quick as those of regular hard disks. Hard cards range from 10MB to 80MB and more. Most need only one slot, but the larger capacity cards can require two or more slots because they are so wide.

MAGNETIC CARTRIDGE DRIVES

Magnetic cartridge drives, such as the one shown in Figure 4-18, combine the large storage capacity of the hard disk with the "removability" of floppy disks. This type of storage is used when the application demands unlimited disk storage in a microcomputer. It consists of an external disk drive with a large door, which accepts a disk cartridge that is like a hard disk in a box. The disk cartridge is accessed by being inserted into the drive like a floppy disk. The disk cartridge drive, connected to a special card placed into the system unit, is assigned a drive name, such as drive D. Disk cartridges come in sizes up to 90MB per drive.

Optical Disks

Optical Disks Use Laser Light to Read and Write Data.

Although almost all microcomputers use magnetic disks, a new and different technology for secondary storage was introduced in 1986. *Optical disks* use laser light to read and write data, instead of electromagnetic charges.

There are three types of optical disks:

- CD ROM
- WORM
- Erasable Optical Disk

Optical disks can store enormous quantities of information in a small package, ranging from about 600MB up to many *gigabytes* (1,000 million). = *billion* However, optical disks have much slower access times than hard disks and cost much more than comparable capacity hard disks. Most important, CD ROM disks can only be read, not written to, and WORM disks can be written to only once.

Only the CD ROM has gained popularity so far. The WORM may soon be pushed aside by the erasable optical disk, which gives users more flexibility than a WORM.

HOW OPTICAL DISKS WORK

All three types of optical disks use similar technology. They use disks (often spelled *discs* to differentiate them from electromagnetic disks) that range from about 4 1/2 inches to 14 inches in diameter. A CD ROM looks identical to an audio CD; WORM and erasable disks are usually larger.

Data is physically stored on the disk as tiny depressions called *pits* and flat areas called *lands*. These act like the magnetic 1's and zero's on magnetic disks. The pits and lands also form tracks around the disk, like a magnetic disk. However, the optical disk stores tracks at a much greater density than magnetic disks—over 15,000 tracks per inch.

The disk is made of a hard clear plastic, like the material used in bulletproof windows. The pits are burned into the surface of the disk with a powerful laser (Figure 4-19). The disk is then covered with a metallic layer and lacquerlike layer, making the data almost indestructible.

The data is read from the disk when the drive focuses a low-power laser beam onto the track. If the beam strikes a land, a specific amount of light is

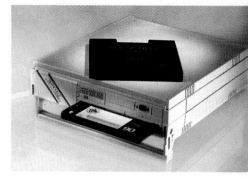

FIGURE 4-18

This Bernoulli drive gives you all the advantages of a hard disk and is removable.

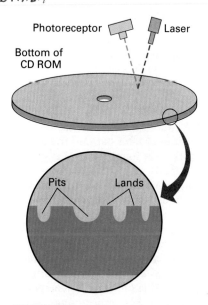

FIGURE 4-19

An optical disk drive focuses a low-power laser on the track. The specific amount of light reflected by the beam indicates pits or lands. Pits and lands correspond to bits.

reflected into the drive's photoreceptor. If the beam reads a pit, a different amount of light is reflected. In this way, digital signals are read off the disk. As the data is read, a decoder in the drive translates the disk's code, which is in 14-bit blocks, into the standard microcomputer's 8-bit bytes.

The optical disk drive can be internal or external to the system unit. Microcomputers that come with an optical disk as original equipment usually have an internal drive; add-on optical drives are usually external. External drives are connected to the system unit with a controller or interface card.

Because optical disk drives are not standard equipment on most microcomputers, additional software is needed to access them.

CD ROM DISKS

As you can see in Figure 4-20, a CD ROM disk looks and works just like your audio CD, but stores data instead of music. A single CD ROM disk can hold about 600MB of data or the equivalent of about 300,000 pages of text.

COMPACT DISKS THAT PLAY MORE THAN MUSIC

The compact disk is dramatically expanding what we can expect from desktop computers, and it may also help save the world's forests. It all has to do with the use of compact disks to store vast amounts of computer data.

Those same compact disks (or CDs) that have transformed the music and recording industry can store enormous amounts of audio and visual information. A single CD can hold about 680MB of data—666 million characters, or *a quarter of a million pages of text!* A computer printout of that amount of text would create a 72-foot-high pile of paper. If you think of paper in terms of trees, then one CD can save the equivalent of 16 trees.

The technological advance that made this possible is the development of a disk drive, no larger than a floppy disk drive, called a CD ROM (Compact Disk-Read Only Memory). A CD ROM has one major limitation: you can't add to or alter data on the disk, as you can with a floppy disk or a hard drive. But its vast and flexible storage capacity opens up many new possibilities for storing huge amounts of information, such as sophisticated financial data, dictionaries, and encyclopedias.

Perhaps the most dramatic advantage of CD ROM is its ability to store and quickly retrieve audio and visual information such as photos, slides, film, and video. National Geographic's *Mammals: A Multimedia Encyclopedia* is a good example of what can be done with CD ROM. This program, developed in cooperation with IBM, employs live action video and synchronized sound as well as text and graphics. It fits easily on one compact disk, yet it contains more than 700 color photographs, 600 pages of text, 155 animal vocalizations, and 45 video clips of mammals in motion. Watching *Mammals* is like seeing an encyclopedia come to full-color life. It's an example of how CD ROMs can almost magically transform the process of education, and, perhaps, save some forests in the process.

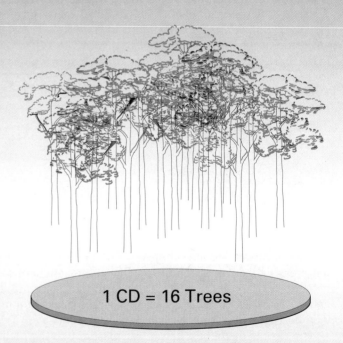

1 CD = 16 Trees

One compact disk can store 250,000 pages of text. It would take 16 trees to create that amount of paper.

Sources: "After Hours: National Geographic and IBM Team Up to Capture Mammals on CD-ROM," by Don Trivette, *PC Magazine*, June 25, 1991. "Peripherals: Time to Make Way for CD-ROM?" by L. R. Shannon, *New York Times*, June 18, 1991. "Buyers' Guide: CD ROM Drives," by Robert Luhn, *PC World*, April 1991.

Once all this information is put on the disk, it can be read by the optical disk drive, but not erased or edited, hence the name CD ROM—*compact disk, read only memory.*

Since the disks can be inexpensively mass produced, CD ROM provides an alternative to printed publications. CD ROM disks are used to replace large printed publications, such as encyclopedias and directories. Vast databases of information, normally available only on large mainframe computer storage devices, can be placed on a CD ROM disk and used on a microcomputer.

Since all CD ROM drive manufacturers have accepted a standardized format called High Sierra, any company's disk can be read on any company's drive.

WORM DISKS *highest of all storage capacities*

A WORM disk can hold as much as three gigabytes (3,000 million) of data on a single disk. Unlike the CD ROM, data can be written to a WORM disk, but only once—hence its name, *Write Once, Read Many,* or *WORM* ("worm"). Producing WORM disks is more costly than making CD ROMs, since the data is written to it instead of stamped on it. The WORM drive is plugged into the microcomputer with a special controller or interface card.

A typical application for a WORM drive is continually adding records to a large database that will not require changes once entered. Hospital records and tax information are two examples.

No standards have yet been accepted by the manufacturers of WORM drives, which means the drive and the disks must be from the same company. Both drives and disks are expensive, further limiting their popularity.

ERASABLE OPTICAL DISKS

Erasable optical disks use both optical and magnetic technologies to store data. Instead of using a laser beam to permanently change the structure of the disk (as with CD ROM disks), the laser beam is used to trigger the application of a magnetic field. This allows erasable optical disks and their accompanying drives to store, edit, and erase data just like hard disks. These devices can store about 500MB to a gigabyte of data. Although they fulfill the same functions as hard disks, they have access times almost 20 times slower, which makes them desirable only when the application requires more capacity than speed.

Both the disks and the drives are more expensive than comparable hard disks. Universally accepted format standards do not yet exist, so you must use the disks supplied with the drive and cannot use them on any other vendor's drives. These drives require special controller or interface cards so they can be plugged into the microcomputer.

Magnetic Tape Cartridges

Standard operating procedures in many organizations require that every electronic file have a duplicate copy. On a computer with one floppy drive and one hard disk, the standard procedure is to keep the original file on the hard disk, where it is created, and make a duplicate with the operating system's copy or backup commands to a floppy disk.

This procedure can become a nuisance if large amounts of information must be transferred, as it can take many floppy disks and considerable time to complete. A *magnetic tape cartridge* can perform the copy or backup process much more efficiently and conveniently.

FIGURE 4-20

CD ROMs can contain a staggering amount of data.

Table 4-2: Summary of Secondary Storage Usage

Secondary Storage Device	Application	Ability to Change Information
Floppy Disk	Loading Programs	Can Be Edited and Erased
	Storing Copies of Data Files	
Hard Disk	Storing Programs	Can Be Edited and Erased
	Storing Data Files	
CD ROM	Reading Published Information	Cannot Be Edited or Erased
WORM	Permanently Storing Large Data Files	Cannot Be Edited or Erased
		Can Be Appended to
Erasable Optical Disk	Storing Large Data Files	Can Be Edited and Erased
Tape Cartridge	Making Copies of Programs and Data Files from a Hard Disk	Cannot Be Edited; Can Be Erased

These tape drives copy information from the hard disk onto a tape cartridge in a fraction of the time it would take to copy files to floppies. In addition, a single cartridge that looks like an audiocassette can hold the equivalent of 20 to 80 or more megabytes of data. Magnetic tape stores data at about 6,000 bits per inch, which is far greater than hard disks. A 20MB hard disk can be backed up onto a single cassette-size tape in a few minutes instead of taking hours and possibly 40 or more floppies.

This combination of high density and speed makes magnetic tape a perfect backup device for a microcomputer hard disk. Tape cartridge drives may be built directly into the system, or an external drive can be plugged into the system using an adapter card.

Magnetic tape is used on microcomputers only for backup, because it accesses data *sequentially* instead of directly or *randomly*, like a hard disk. This means it locates data by starting at the beginning of the tape and reading all the information until it finds what it is searching for. Disks, on the other hand, access data randomly, meaning the read/write head jumps to any position on the disk and accesses data. Since random access takes a fraction of a second compared to sequential access that can take minutes, magnetic tape is not practical for secondary storage where speed is critical.

These magnetic tape drives come with their own software, which reads information from the disk to the tape and restores the information to the disk if necessary.

Table 4-2 summarizes the applications and features of the most common secondary storage devices.

The Future of Data Storage

Higher capacity and faster access of data are the primary needs of microcomputer users. Floppy and hard disks with higher densities, resulting in greater storage capacity and faster access times, are continually being developed. Just as single-sided, single density floppies are considered antiques today, so too will 20MB hard disks in the not-too-distant future. Magnetic disks with one gigabyte (1,000 million bytes) of storage capacity will be readily available within the next few years.

Optical disks hold enormous potential. CD ROM disks will store volumes of information now available only in print. Libraries will have larger collections of CD ROM disks and smaller collections of reference books.

Erasable optical disks have the advantages of hard disks, but can hold far greater amounts of data. Their access times will improve as the technology

FIGURE 4-21

An erasable optical disk and its drive—they represent the shape of things to come.

advances, and the costs will drop once universal standards are accepted. Smaller erasable optical disks with faster access times have already appeared (Figure 4-21). Look for erasable optical disks to first begin replacing magnetic hard disks in laptop computers, where size and weight are most important.

Another area showing great promise is *multimedia,* which combines the storage of data, images, and sound (Figure 4-22). All three can be combined

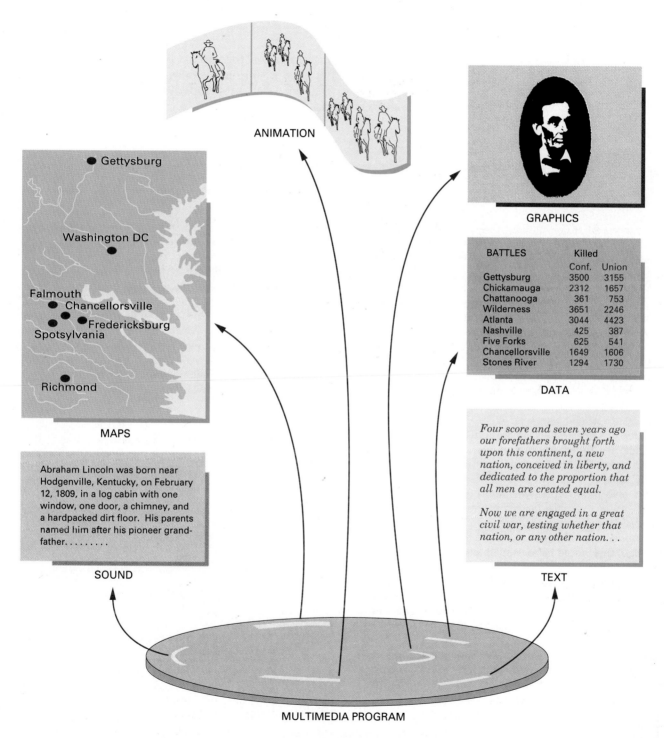

FIGURE 4-22

Multimedia storage devices store all types of data, images, and sound.

on a single optical disk for play on a microcomputer or other type of display. Multimedia programs surround you with moving images and realistic sounds—and involve you by responding to your input. These disks are already becoming popular for instructional purposes where they are used for such divergent tasks as learning how to fly a plane and locating stores in a shopping mall.

Multimedia disks are usually larger in diameter than CD ROM disks because they must store more information. Currently they require special drives, but in the future they may use a standardized CD ROM type of disk drive. Today's microcomputers already have excellent video capabilities, but look for vastly improved speaker systems to use multimedia's sound capabilities.

Before the year 2000, a typical microcomputer configuration may include a 1 gigabyte erasable optical disk for mass storage of data and programs; a CD ROM drive for checking your encyclopedia, dictionary, and other databases; and a multimedia disk drive for education and entertainment.

ARE YOU A "POWER USER?"

In the world of computers, some people are known as "power users." How can you spot them? You can't always tell by the number of hours people spend at their computers or by the number of software packages on their shelves. It's the data storage capacity of their computers' hard disks that reveals the power users among us.

In the past few years, the data storage capacity of computer hard disks has grown dramatically, and that growth has brought smiles to the faces of America's power users. Back in 1983, a 10MB hard disk provided more than enough data storage capacity. Today, power users expect their desktop computers to have as much as a 100MB capacity—a tenfold increase.

What do power users do with all that data storage capacity? It's not just a case of more is better. Rather, we have learned to ask our computers to do new and more varied tasks. The first desktop computers were used primarily to work with text and numbers, but today's computers also must work with and store *graphic images.* These images require far more memory storage space than text and numbers. Storing just three or four images can consume as much as *20MB* of hard disk space. Not long ago, this would have used up all the space on a hard disk.

The growth in storage capacity has made many new business, scientific, and educational applications possible. These new applications typically require a much larger data storage capacity because they make more use of graphic images.

Many power users also work with database programs, and the more data—whether in the form of text, numbers, or graphic images—that a hard disk can store, the better.

Another trend that's bringing smiles to the faces of power users is the development of portable computers with ever-larger hard drive capacities. Increasingly, power users expect their portables to be able to run the same programs as their desktop computers. Because portables were limited until recently to a maximum 40MB hard disk size, power users couldn't run their favorite programs when they traveled. But even that barrier is breaking down. Portables with 60 to 100MB have now appeared on the market, and major companies like the Coors Brewing Company and the New York Life Insurance Company are outfitting their thousands of sales reps with these new high-capacity portables. Before long, it seems, we may all be power users.

Storing images like the one on this screen takes up several megabtyes of space on a computer's hard disk. Many new software programs require hard disks that can store 60 or more megabytes of data.

Sources: "Desktop Capacities Packed into Laptop Disks," by Michael Fitzgerald, *ComputerWorld,* March 18, 1991, p. 37. "Smaller, Cheaper Still the Rule," by Michael Fitzgerald, *ComputerWorld,* September 16, 1991.

Is it a microcomputer's speed that allows computers to save businesses money and make workers more productive? Is it a micro's ability to execute a program over and over without becoming tired or making errors?

Both a micro computer's speed and its ability to execute programs repetitively contribute to its cost effectiveness. However, one of the major advantages of obtaining a computer system is that once records are created and stored in a file, the data can be retrieved, updated, and used to produce reports.

Often you will find that the majority of data you need is stored in your files. This means that very little new data needs to be entered. Also, information stored on a hard disk or diskettes can be retrieved, displayed, and updated faster than when conventional paper-and manila-folder files are used.

Until microcomputer floppy disks and hard disks were available, microcomputers were used for very few personal or business applications. A quantum leap in utilization was achieved when random storage of information was available—and at an affordable price.

Depending on how you will use your computer, and the price you want to pay, you will probably select a system that has a built-in hard disk and one or more diskette drives. The hard disk will be used to store your operating system, frequently used programs, and some of your files. Diskettes will be used to backup your hard disk and to store less frequently used software and files.

REVIEW QUESTIONS

1. What is the difference in function between random access memory and secondary storage?

2. What are the three categories of secondary storage devices?

3. What form of secondary storage is used primarily for backup purposes?

4. What is a file?

5. Are the following statements true or false? (a) If you started at the outer track of a disk and followed it around, you would end up on the inner track. (b) The disk drive read/write head reads and writes data by touching the surface of the disk. (c) The tracks of a disk are not visible to the naked eye. (d) A single file can be scattered on many tracks.

6. What is measured in terms of tracks per inch (tpi)? What is linear density and how is it measured?

7. What does formatting a disk mean?

8. What are the advantages and disadvantages of floppy disks?

9. What is the purpose of the write-protect notch?

10. What does DS, DD on a 5 1/4-inch disk label mean? What does DS, HD mean?

11. What are the major advantages of the 3 1/2-inch disk compared to the 5 1/4-inch disk?

12. Name five precautions to take when using 5 1/4-inch floppies.

13. Why is a hard disk also called a fixed disk?

14. What are the advantages and disadvantages of hard disks when compared with floppy disks?

15. What is the storage capacity range of hard disks in use today?

16. What is a cylinder?

17. What is a head crash and what causes it to occur?

18. What are the two main reasons for having a floppy disk drive on a microcomputer with a hard disk drive?

19. What is the advantage of a hard card compared with a hard disk?

20. What is the advantage of a hard disk cartridge?

21. How do optical disks store bits on the disk platter?
22. What is the primary advantage and disadvantage of CD ROM?
23. WORM stands for "write once, read many." What does this mean?
24. Erasable optical disks hold great promise for the future but have many disadvantages today. Name three of these disadvantages.
25. Why are magnetic tape cartridges useful for disk backup but not secondary storage?
26. What is multimedia?

TOPICS FOR RESEARCH AND DISCUSSION

1. CD ROMs can hold a staggering amount of data. One disk could contain an entire encyclopedia, a collection of reference books (automobile repair manuals, cookbooks, or travel guides, for instance), or the entire works of an author.

   Would you use a CD ROM that contained an encyclopedia? A collection of reference books? All your favorite author's novels?

2. Imagine you work in the library of a large business-oriented magazine. It is considering the purchase of a CD ROM player. The CD ROM player would be used with CD ROMs that contain financial information about businesses. When reporters need background information about companies, they will be able to search for the information on the CD ROM. The library currently is using a PC-compatible microcomputer.

   Investigate the cost and features of CD ROM players. Which CD ROM player would you recommend?

3. Assume your office has microcomputers that use all four types of diskettes. (Some of the microcomputers have hard disks and some don't.) Everyone must share disks, but people are continually finding that their disks won't work on another employee's computer.

   What short-term solutions that don't involve purchasing hardware would you recommend? What solutions would you recommend that would involve purchasing hardware, but no new computers? (For this solution, research the relative costs of each type of floppy disk drive.)

CHAPTER 5

OUTPUT
DEVICES

OBJECTIVES

The information in this chapter will enable you to

- Describe the types of technology used in a monitor's display.
- Understand the relation among pixels, display resolution, and the sharpness of an image.
- Explain the advantages and disadvantages of monochrome monitors and of CGA, EGA, VGA, and super VGA color monitors.
- Describe the features and advantages of dot-matrix, daisy-wheel, ink-jet, bubble-jet, and laser printers.
- Describe the two types of plotters.
- Explain what voice output devices do.

Chapter 3 discussed how you enter information into the computer, and Chapter 4 explained how the computer stores information. But information is useless if it's hidden inside the computer system. That's why computers include output devices as well as input and storage devices. Most computer systems have at least two output devices: a monitor and a printer. Some systems have other output devices as well.

Monitors

Monitors Display Computer Output. They Vary in Their Image Sharpness and Color Capabilities. Desktop Computer Monitors Have Cathode-Ray Tubes; Laptop Models Have Flat Panel Displays.

The most common computer output device is a *monitor*. Monitors are also known as *video display terminals,* or *VDTs.* The text and pictures displayed on a computer monitor are sometimes called *soft copy* because you can make changes in them as you are viewing them.

Monitors vary in the quality of the images they display. Some monitors can display images in many colors; others can display only a few shades of one color. Aside from the use of color, monitors also vary in the sharpness of their images.

PIXELS AND RESOLUTION

An image on the screen of a monitor, whether it consists of text or pictures, is made up of thousands of dots called *pixels.* As Figure 5-1 shows, pixels are arranged in columns and rows. Responding to the software instructions,

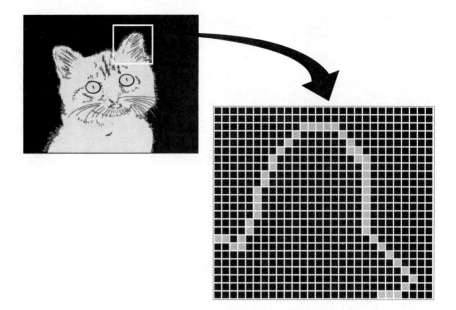

FIGURE 5-1

Images on computer monitors are made up of dots called pixels. Software tells the computer how to create the images by turning pixels on or off, assigning colors to them, or adjusting their brightness.

a computer can turn each pixel on or off. The computer can also change the brightness of each pixel, and a color system can change the color.

A monitor's *resolution,* which is the sharpness and clarity of the images it displays, is measured by the number of pixels in its columns and rows. The more dots a monitor uses, the higher its resolution and the clearer the image. For example, a monitor with a resolution of 800 by 600 pixels has a total of 480,000 dots, arranged in 800 columns and 600 rows. Its displays are much sharper than a monitor with a lower resolution of, say, 640 by 350 pixels—with a total of 224,000 dots.

Computers used for design and other tasks that involve high-quality pictures require monitors with high resolution, or large numbers of pixels. For people who work with text rather than graphics, monitors with lower resolution are usually sharp enough.

MONOCHROME MONITORS

A *monochrome monitor* can display letters, numbers, and graphic images in only one color against a background. Many monochrome monitors display green or amber characters against a black background. Others, such as a monochrome Macintosh, display black characters on a white background.

Monochrome monitors can display different shades of their image color by varying the brightness. For example, a green-on-black monitor highlights bold text by displaying it in a brighter shade of green than other text. Figure 5-2 shows how highlighted text appears on a monochrome monitor.

Typical monochrome monitors have a resolution of 640 by 350 pixels, which makes numbers and letters easy to read. In the early 1980s, most businesses used monochrome monitors for tasks that did not require color graphics. In those days, characters looked blurry on color monitors. On today's color monitors, letters and numbers usually appear just as clear as on monochrome monitors. Still, many users select monochrome monitors because they usually cost less than color monitors.

You can display graphics on a monochrome monitor only if the computer is equipped with a circuit board called a *graphics adapter card.* This name is often shortened to *graphics adapter* or *graphics card.* The graphics adapter for a monochrome monitor is called a monochrome graphics adapter. A graphics adapter plugs into an expansion slot in the system unit.

The Hercules brand of monochrome graphics adapters, often called

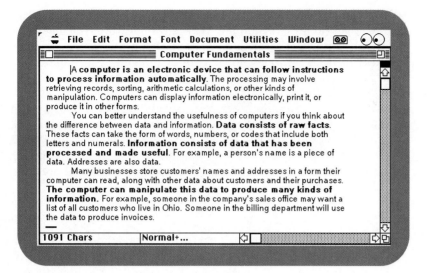

FIGURE 5-2

A monochrome monitor displays only one color against a background, but it can use increased brightness to highlight text.

simply *Hercules cards*, became a standard throughout the industry. The best-selling monochrome graphics adapters still use the technology developed by Hercules, even though many are made by other companies.

COLOR MONITORS

Although you can display graphics on monochrome monitors with adapter cards, color graphics are often easier to read and are more attractive. For example, if you create a line graph of sales for Regions 1, 2, and 3, you can use a different color for each region's line. The different colors make it easier to follow each line.

Today's color monitors can display sharp images of letters and numbers as well as graphics. Many businesses use color monitors for working with text and numbers because even letters and numbers are more attractive, and sometimes easier to read, in color.

Like monochrome monitors used for graphics, color monitors require graphics adapter cards. Color monitors today work with at least one of the four types of graphics cards: CGA, EGA, VGA, and Super VGA.

Often when a microcomputer is obtained, the basic configuration includes a color monitor and the required graphics cards. The user is required only to attach cables from the display to the system unit.

CGA

The earliest color monitors used *CGA*, or *color graphics adapter*, circuit boards, which were first sold by IBM. A CGA card provides a resolution of only 320 by 200 pixels—far less than that of a monochrome monitor—but it provides for four colors. CGA cards and monitors are still in use, but most color monitors sold today offer much higher resolution and more colors. CGA monitors are not suitable for people who work primarily with text, because text is difficult to read at low resolution. To make text easier to read, many monitors can be tilted to the best viewing position, as shown by Figure 5-3.

EGA

Monitors built for *EGA*, or *enhanced graphics adapters*, have a resolution of 640 by 350 pixels, the same as monochrome monitors. That makes them

FIGURE 5-3

You can set a monitor on a stand enabling you to tilt it to an angle that you can view comfortably.

suitable for displaying text as well as color graphics, and the graphics are sharper than on a CGA monitor. With most software designed for use with EGA, you can select the colors that appear on the screen. For example, if you use an EGA computer to prepare documents, you might select a blue background with regular text in white and bold text in red.

EGA monitors provide for 16 colors, or four times as many as a CGA monitor. With most EGA monitors, you can use software and circuit boards designed for CGA, but the reverse is not true. You cannot use an EGA card with a CGA monitor, so you cannot run software that requires an EGA card on a system with a CGA monitor. Monitors with more colors and higher resolution are now available, but EGA monitors cost less and are adequate for most business needs.

VGA

A *VGA,* or *video graphics array,* monitor provides sharper resolution than monochrome, CGA, or EGA displays. For graphics displays, VGA monitors offer a trade-off between high resolution and a wide range of colors.

If you set up your computer to display only text, VGA provides a resolution of 720 by 400 pixels with 16 colors. You can display both text and graphics in 16 colors at a resolution of 640 by 480 pixels, still higher than that of monochrome, CGA, and EGA monitors. If you are using the computer for work in which range of colors is more important than high resolution, you can set it up to display 256 colors at a resolution of 320 by 200 pixels. With this setup, it can display 16 times as many colors as an EGA monitor, but at a resolution equal only to that of CGA. Table 5-1 lists the options available with a VGA monitor.

Table 5-1: VGA Monitor Options		
Setting	**Resolution**	**Colors**
Text only	740 x 400	16
Text and graphics	640 x 480	16
Graphics only	320 x 200	256

FIGURE 5-4

The Toshiba 3200 SCX was one of the first portable computers with a VGA graphics card and a monitor that displays color.

Laptop computers generally have monochrome monitors. However, many laptops are equipped with VGA adapter cards. You can attach these laptops to desktop VGA monitors to display images in color. On the laptops' built-in monitors, the adapter cards enable you to display high-resolution graphics in shades of one color, such as gray.

The Toshiba 3200 SXC, shown in Figure 5-4, is a portable computer with a VGA monitor. This model—weighing 17 pounds and much heavier than most laptops—is about twice as expensive as monochrome laptops.

Super VGA

With *Super VGA,* monitors and adapter cards provide a resolution of at least 800 by 600 pixels and as much as 1,024 by 768 pixels. This means that Super VGA displays are much sharper than those provided by ordinary VGA.

You can display 256 colors with Super VGA, the same as with VGA, but you can select them from among 262,144 colors. This selection allows for subtle shadings of color, perhaps even more than if you were mixing paints or watercolors by hand.

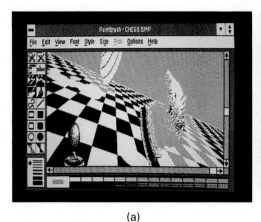
(a)

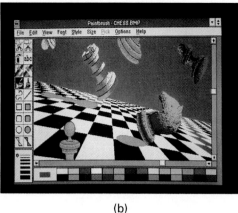
(b)

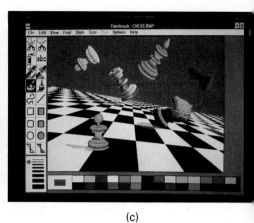
(c)

Switching to Super VGA from CGA, EGA, or VGA requires a new graphics card and software as well as a new monitor. This makes the change expensive. Therefore, although Super VGA has been available since 1988, most businesses do not use it unless they require extremely high-quality graphics output.

Figure 5-5 shows a comparison of the various types of IBM-compatible monitors.

FIGURE 5-5

CGA (a) and EGA (b) monitors have the lowest resolution of all IBM-compatible monitors, and Super VGA (c) monitors have the highest. The higher the resolution, the sharper the image.

Macintosh Graphics

Apple's Macintosh computers were designed from the outset to communicate with users by means of graphic images. For example, a picture of a trash can is used to indicate that a document you are viewing on screen may be discarded. IBM computer users must generally type commands to communicate with their computers (although recent innovations in the IBM world are stressing graphics communication).

Graphics output from the Macintosh has long been considered superior to that of IBM-compatible microcomputers (see Figure 5-6), even though the early Macintosh models could not display color. With the development of Super VGA displays and software that uses graphics commands, the IBM world has begun to catch up to the Macintosh.

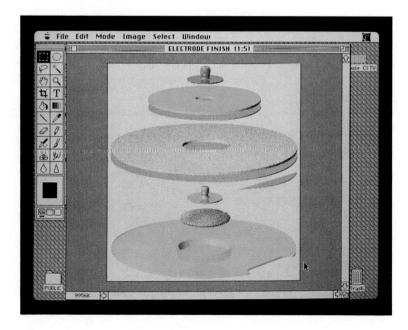

FIGURE 5-6

The graphic images displayed on Macintosh computers have long been regarded as superior to those displayed on IBM computers and their look-alikes.

Because of its superior graphics capabilities, a greater variety of software for creating and displaying graphics is available for the Macintosh than for IBM-compatible models. That is because programmers have been writing software for the Macintosh for years. Now that IBM and its look-alikes are emphasizing high-quality graphics, programmers are writing more graphics software for IBM-compatible computers.

CATHODE-RAY TUBES

Most monitors for desktop computers are built with *cathode-ray tubes,* often called *CRTs,* which use the same technology as television picture tubes.

FLAT PANEL DISPLAYS

Laptop computers use a different kind of monitor, the *flat panel display,* because cathode-ray tubes are too bulky. Computer companies use several different technologies to make flat panel displays.

Liquid Crystal Displays (LCDs)

Some laptop computers have *liquid crystal displays,* or *LCDs,* like those in digital wristwatches. The LCD was one of the earliest technologies for portable monitors. In an LCD monitor, an electrical charge causes liquid crystals in the monitor to reflect light while others that aren't charged don't reflect any light. The big problem is: Where does the light come from?

The earliest LCD monitors had no light source of their own. Instead, a mirror behind the layer of liquid crystals *reflected* room light back through them. These monitors were often hard to read, especially in sunlight or brightly lit rooms. Some newer LCD monitors are *backlit,* which means they have their own light sources behind the crystals, or *sidelit,* which means they have light sources alongside the crystals. Backlit and sidelit LCDs provide brighter images with more contrast, making them easier to see than LCDs without their own light sources. Figure 5-7 shows some laptop computers using liquid crystal displays.

Reflected light

Backlit

Sidelit

FIGURE 5-7

The quality of the images displayed on LCD monitors depends on their light source. Those that rely on reflected light can be difficult to read. On LCD monitors with built-in light sources, images have more brightness and contrast.

Electroluminescent Displays (ELs)

Portable computers made by Hewlett-Packard and some other companies use *electroluminescent displays,* or *EL,* monitors. An electrical charge causes these flat panel displays to give out light of their own. Generally ELs are easier to read than LCDs.

Gas-Plasma Displays

The most readable laptop monitors are those with *gas-plasma displays.* The gas these monitors contain emits light when the electrical current is turned on, like the gas in a neon light tube. But gas-plasma monitors use more power than other flat panel displays, which can be a problem for battery-powered laptop computers.

Printers

Dot-Matrix, Daisy-Wheel, Ink-Jet, Bubble-Jet, and Laser Printers Vary in Price, Speed, Noise Levels, and Quality of Output.

In addition to the soft-copy output that appears on monitors, microcomputers can produce *hard copy,* which is printed output. With some printers, you can print not only on paper but also on acetate sheets, to create overhead transparencies for use in presentations.

Several types of printers are available. They differ in price, versatility, and the quality of the hard copy they print. Their prices range from a few hundred to several thousand dollars. What printer you select for a computer system depends on the kinds of documents and the quality of the documents you need to produce and how fast you need to print them.

DOT-MATRIX PRINTERS

A *dot-matrix printer* forms images by striking a printing element with pins in it against a ribbon and paper. The printer arranges the pins so that their ends form individual characters or graphic images, as shown in Figure 5-8. A dot-matrix printer can produce a hard copy of any image that appears on the screen, not just letters and numbers.

A typical dot-matrix printer can produce about six pages a minute. Most dot-matrix printers are bidirectional, which means they can print from right to left as well as from left to right. This enables them to print faster than printers that are not bidirectional.

Printers that strike their print elements against the paper are known as *impact printers.* Like other impact printers, a dot-matrix printer can print on carbon paper sets or NCR (short for "no carbon required") copy sets to print several copies of a document at one time. Nonimpact printers cannot do this.

Dot-matrix printers are relatively inexpensive, reliable, and vary widely in the quality of the hard copy produced. Many dot-matrix printers can print either letter-quality or draft mode. Although printing in draft mode is much faster, the quality of the printing is acceptable only for rough drafts and other working documents.

Using colored ribbons, some models can print documents in several colors. Fijitsu Systems makes one model, the DL3600, that can print seven colors. Figure 5-9 shows output from this printer.

The clarity, or resolution, of a dot-matrix printer's output depends primarily on the number of pins in its printing element. It can have 9, 12, or

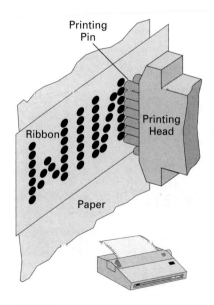

FIGURE 5-8

A dot-matrix printer arranges the pins in its print head to form images, then strikes the print head against a ribbon and paper. Because of the impact, a dot-matrix printer can be noisier than some other kinds of printers.

FIGURE 5-9

This image was produced with a Fujitsu Systems DL3600 dot-matrix printer. Unlike most dot-matrix printers, this model can print up to seven colors.

24 pins. The more pins it has, the more dots it can use to form a character, and the sharper the character appears. Figure 5-10 shows the output quality of 9-pin and 24-pin printers.

With some 24-pin printers, you can vary the speed and quality of the output by selecting settings that use different numbers of pins. For example, some printers have a draft-quality setting that uses only 9 pins to produce rough drafts very quickly and a near-letter-quality setting that prints more slowly, using 18 pins. For output that looks almost as if it came from a typewriter, you select the letter-quality setting, which uses all 24 pins and is the slowest.

(a)
```
123456789:;<=>?@ABCDEFGHIJKLMNOPQRSTUVWXYZ[\]^_`
23456789:;<=>?@ABCDEFGHIJKLMNOPQRSTUVWXYZ[\]^_`a
3456789:;<=>?@ABCDEFGHIJKLMNOPQRSTUVWXYZ[\]^_`ab
456789:;<=>?@ABCDEFGHIJKLMNOPQRSTUVWXYZ[\]^_`abc
56789:;<=>?@ABCDEFGHIJKLMNOPQRSTUVWXYZ[\]^_`abcd
6789:;<=>?@ABCDEFGHIJKLMNOPQRSTUVWXYZ[\]^_`abcde
789:;<=>?@ABCDEFGHIJKLMNOPQRSTUVWXYZ[\]^_`abcdef
89:;<=>?@ABCDEFGHIJKLMNOPQRSTUVWXYZ[\]^_`abcdefg
9:;<=>?@ABCDEFGHIJKLMNOPQRSTUVWXYZ[\]^_`abcdefgh
```

(b)
```
fghijklmnopqrstuvwxyz{|}~´àç£`µ°▼†§®©¼¾½¶¥ÄÖÜ¢~
ghijklmnopqrstuvwxyz{|}~´àç£`µ°▼†§®©¼¾½¶¥ÄÖÜ¢~ä
hijklmnopqrstuvwxyz{|}~´àç£`µ°▼†§®©¼¾½¶¥ÄÖÜ¢~äö
ijklmnopqrstuvwxyz{|}~´àç£`µ°▼†§®©¼¾½¶¥ÄÖÜ¢~äöü
jklmnopqrstuvwxyz{|}~´àç£`µ°▼†§®©¼¾½¶¥ÄÖÜ¢~äöüß
klmnopqrstuvwxyz{|}~´àç£`µ°▼†§®©¼¾½¶¥ÄÖÜ¢~äöüß™
lmnopqrstuvwxyz{|}~´àç£`µ°▼†§®©¼¾½¶¥ÄÖÜ¢~äöüß™é
mnopqrstuvwxyz{|}~´àç£`µ°▼†§®©¼¾½¶¥ÄÖÜ¢~äöüß™éù
nopqrstuvwxyz{|}~´àç£`µ°▼†§®©¼¾½¶¥ÄÖÜ¢~äöüß™éùè
```

FIGURE 5-10

Output from a 9-pin printer (a) is not as sharp or clear as the output from a 24-pin printer (b), because fewer dots are used to form the characters.

With a dot-matrix printer, you can use a *tractor-feed attachment,* which enables you to print on continuous-form paper rather than on individual sheets. Sheets of *continuous-form paper* have rows of holes on their long sides. The holes fit over pins on the tractor, which guides the paper through the printer (Figure 5-11). The sheets are connected to each other, and the rows of holes are connected to the sheets, with perforations. You can separate the sheets from each other and from the rows of holes to create individual sheets.

With some dot-matrix printers, you can also use a *sheet feeder,* which is an attachment that feeds individual sheets of paper into the printer automatically.

Other dot-matrix printers, such as the IBM PS/1, permit you to put continuous forms on "park" and allow individual sheets, forms, and envelopes to be inserted and printed. With these printers it isn't necessary to remove the continuous form feed and replace it with a single-sheet feeder.

DAISY-WHEEL PRINTERS

The printing element on a *daisy-wheel printer* consists of spokes arranged around a hub. At the end of each spoke is a character cast in metal or plastic (Figure 5-12). The printing element, which snaps in and out, contains an entire set of characters in a specific type style. Thus, you can use one daisy wheel for printing regular characters, a second wheel to print a section in italics, and so forth.

As Figure 5-13 shows, the daisy wheel's function is similar to that of the type bars or type element on a typewriter. When you press the "A" key, for example, the printer rotates the wheel to position the spoke with the "A" at its end over the paper. Then it strikes the end of the spoke against a ribbon and the paper to print the "A." Because daisy-wheel printers are impact printers, you can use carbon sets or NCR sets with them to print multiple copies.

The more expensive daisy-wheel printers are bidirectional, so they are faster than less expensive, right-to-left printers or typewriters. Even so, a daisy-wheel printer can produce only about one page a minute.

Some printers have removable print elements that function in the same way as a daisy wheel but are shaped differently. For example, the NEC Spin-Writer uses a thimble-shaped print element containing cast characters, as shown in Figure 5-14.

Daisy-wheel printers are generally slower, noisier, and more expensive than dot-matrix printers. Moreover, they can print only letters, numbers,

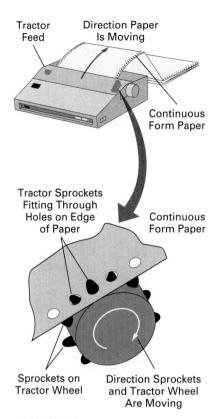

FIGURE 5-11

A tractor-feed attachment lets you use continuous-form paper on a dot-matrix or daisy-wheel printer.

FIGURE 5-12

A daisy wheel contains a full set of letters, numbers, and punctuation marks in a specific type style. The characters are cast in metal or plastic at the ends of the wheel's spokes. You can use different daisy wheels with the same printer to print characters in different type styles.

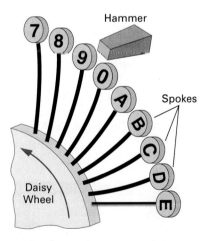

FIGURE 5-13

Software tells a printer what character to print next. If the next character to be printed is an "A," a daisy-wheel printer rotates the daisy wheel to position the "A" over the paper. Then it uses a tiny hammer to strike the "A" against a ribbon and paper and print the character.

FIGURE 5-14

The NEC SpinWriter, like a daisy-wheel printer, has a removable type element with characters arranged at the ends of spokes.

```
'Twas brillig, and the slithy toves
  Did gyre and gimble in the wabe;
All mimsy were the borogoves,
  And the mome raths outgrabe.

"Beware the Jabberwock, my son!
  The jaws that bite, the claws that catch!
Beware the Jubjub bird, and shun
  The frumious Bandersnatch!"
```

FIGURE 5-15

Daisy-wheel printers were popular because their print quality is virtually identical to that of a high-quality business typewriter. However, they cannot print graphics.

and punctuation marks—not graphics. As illustrated in Figure 5-15, however, their quality of output is very high. A daisy-wheel printer can produce form letters that look as if they were typed individually on a top-of-the-line business typewriter.

Like dot-matrix printers, daisy-wheel printers can be used with tractor-feed attachments and continuous-form paper. You can also feed individual sheets of paper into a daisy-wheel printer. With some daisy-wheel printers, you can attach a sheet feeder to feed in a stack of single sheets automatically.

In the early 1980s, the daisy-wheel printer was the most popular means of producing high-quality text from a computer. Their sales have been declining since 1984 and today few businesses buy them. Instead, they are buying high-quality dot-matrix printers, laser printers, and ink-jet printers.

INK-JET PRINTERS

An *ink-jet printer* forms characters and graphic images by spraying dots of ink onto paper from its print element (Figure 5-16). Ink-jet printers can print at a resolution of 300 dots per inch, which means the quality of their output can equal that of a more expensive laser printer.

Ink-jet printers are more versatile than dot-matrix or daisy-wheel printers. Unlike daisy-wheel printers, ink-jet printers can produce graphics as well as text. They can print in more colors than either dot-matrix or daisy-wheel models.

Ink-jet printers are also much quieter than dot-matrix and daisy-wheel printers because a print element isn't hammered against the paper. However, you cannot use carbon sets or NCR sets with ink-jet printers or other nonimpact printers.

One problem of ink-jet printers is that they may leave ink smudges on the paper, although some manufacturers have found ways to overcome this drawback. For example, Hewlett-Packard's DeskJet 500 model, shown in Figure 5-17, comes with water-resistant ink cartridges that prevent this problem.

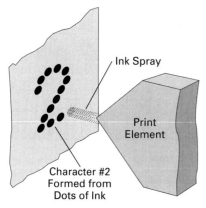

FIGURE 5-16

Ink-jet printers spray tiny dots of ink to form images on paper. Because this process does not involve impact, carbon sets cannot be used with these printers.

FIGURE 5-17

The Hewlett-Packard DeskJet 500 is a popular ink-jet printer. It is slower than a laser printer, but the quality of its output is similar.

Ink-jet printers are *page printers*. They print on one page at a time, not continuous forms. Sheets of paper are placed in a tray and feed into the printer automatically. Ink-jet printers are often used for making hard copies of charts and other graphics created with computer software.

BUBBLE-JET PRINTERS

Bubble-jet printers were designed for use with laptop computers. They are small, lightweight, and battery powered, which makes them easily portable. Among the first bubble-jet printers is the Canon BJ-10e, shown in Figure 5-18, which weighs only 4.6 pounds.

A bubble-jet printer is a type of ink-jet printer. It forms images by spraying dots of ink onto paper. However, bubble-jet printers can print 360 dots per inch. That means the resolution of their output is higher than other ink-jet printers and even most laser printers. Bubble-jet printers print only on individual pages, not on continuous forms.

Before bubble-jet printers became available in 1990, lightweight dot-matrix printers were the ones most often used with laptop printers. Bubble-jet printers, which cost about the same and produce higher-quality copies, are replacing dot-matrix printers for use with laptops.

FIGURE 5-18

The lightweight Canon BJ-10e bubble-jet printer runs on batteries and is used primarily with laptop computers.

LASER PRINTERS

A *laser printer* uses a laser to focus light in an intense, thin beam that forms images on a drum. Next, it applies *toner,* which is a powder made up of plastic, iron, and coloring agents, to the images on the drum. Then it rolls paper or acetate sheets along the drum to transfer the images. The transfer process uses heat to make the toner—and the images—stick to the paper or acetate. This process, pictured in Figure 5-19, is virtually the same as the one used by photocopiers, FAX machines, and devices for scanning input documents.

Ozone, a gas that can irritate human eyes and skin, is a by-product of the laser printing process. Most people who work in offices with laser printers suffer no ill effects from exposure to this gas, although some people are very sensitive to its smell. Employers can minimize the chances of overexposure to ozone by placing their laser printers in well-ventilated rooms and by not using several laser printers in one room. They should also place the laser printers so their exhaust vents are not directed at anyone's face. The printer's laser beam is completely enclosed in protective housing, so it does not pose a hazard to users.

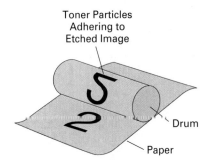

Toner Particles
Adhering to
Etched Image

Drum

Paper

FIGURE 5-19

A laser printer uses a laser beam to form images on a drum. Next, it applies magnetized toner powder, which sticks to those images. Then the printer rolls paper over the drum to transfer the images, using heat to affix them to the paper.

THE CHINA
P A L A C E

FIGURE 5-20

Laser printers print graphics and text equally well. Most laser printers use 300 dots per inch to form images, but some use more dots for even sharper images. Output from the best laser printers looks as if it were produced with typesetting equipment.

of Napier was
ilboats manned by
er Yachtclub was
of peewee regatta.
ri girl in a little fishing boat came out to greet
ister. Lydia always managed to come up with a
e guided us into the marina where a crowd of rela-
and waving; Lydia had really outdone herself this time.

The images produced by a laser printer are made up of dots, like those from a dot-matrix printer. However, a laser printer's output is sharper because it uses more dots. Most laser printers use 300 dots per inch, but some can use as many as 1,200. At 1,200 dots per inch (d.p.i.), the output from a laser printer looks as sharp as the fine typesetting used to produce books and magazines. It can reproduce photographs as well as other kinds of graphics and text. Figure 5-20 shows some examples of laser printer output.

Most laser printers can print only with black toner. Some of the more expensive models, however, can print in several colors.

Like ink-jet printers, laser printers are usually much quieter and faster than dot-matrix and daisy-wheel printers. Table 5-2 gives the noise levels, measured in decibels, of a laser printer, a typical dot-matrix printer, and other sounds.

Table 5-2: Printer Noise Levels			
Source	**Decibels**	**Source**	**Decibels**
Dot-matrix printer	55	Car horn	120
Laser printer	41	Hair dryer	80
		Air conditioner	60

Laser printers, which are page printers, are generally faster than other kinds of printers. One popular model, the Hewlett-Packard LaserJet, can produce about eight pages a minute, and some are even faster. Table 5-3 compares the speed of a typical laser printer with the speeds of other printer types.

Table 5-3: Printer Speed		
Printer	**Type**	**Pages per Minute**
HP LaserJet III	Laser	8
HP DeskJet 500	Ink-jet	2
Canon BJ-10e	Bubble-jet	2
NEC P5300	Dot-matrix	6
C. Itoh F-10	Daisy-wheel	1

Although their cost is decreasing, laser printers generally cost more than other kinds of microcomputer printers. Among the least expensive is the HP LaserJet IIIP. This model has many of the same features as other LaserJet models but can print only four pages a minute.

Plotters

Flatbed Plotters and Drum Plotters Draw Slowly with Pens and Colors to Produce High-Quality Hard Copy.

A *plotter* uses pens and a wide range of colors to draw images directly on paper. Software directs the movement of the pens as they draw. Plotters are used for producing multicolored hard copies of drawings, maps, architects' drawings, and other graphics.

The quality of a plotter's output is even higher than that of a laser printer because a plotter does not form images from dots. Instead, it draws the images with fine pens, using and combining as many as 16 different colors. Some plotters can also produce much larger copies than a printer.

Compared to printers, plotters are very slow; some people who use them jokingly call them "plodders." Producing a large complex drawing with a plotter can take more than an hour.

Two types of plotters are available: flatbed plotters and drum plotters. They differ in the way they handle the paper on which they draw images.

FLATBED PLOTTER

A *flatbed plotter* holds paper flat and steady while the plotter's pens move across it to draw images. Flatbed plotters, also called *table plotters*, can produce architects' drawings and other documents too large for a regular printer.

DRUM PLOTTER

A *drum plotter* (Figure 5-21) holds paper on a cylindrical drum that rotates as the plotter's pens move around on it. Drum plotters cannot produce copies as large as those from a big flatbed plotter.

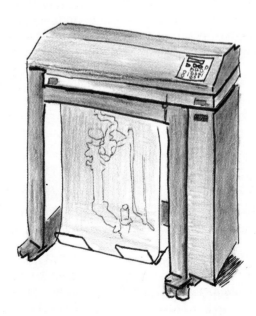

FIGURE 5-21

Plotters are used for drawings, maps, architects' drawings, and other highly detailed graphics.

FIGURE 5-22

With *Voice It* software, users can add voice output to their documents by speaking into telephone handsets.

Voice Output

You Can Use Voice Output Devices with Computers to Imitate Human Speech.

Voice output is the use of a computer to make sounds that resemble human speech. For example, you may have ridden in a car with an electronic voice that says, "Your key is in the ignition" if you open the driver's door before you remove the key. That voice was produced by a computer. You also hear computerized voice output when you ask a telephone company's directory assistance operator for a phone number.

A computer can imitate the human voice by combining individual sounds that have been recorded on a disk, then playing them back through a speaker. The sounds are recorded by using special-purpose software and hardware. To produce high-quality voice output, a microcomputer must be equipped with a circuit board called a *digitizer.* This device converts the human voice to *digital signals,* which are binary on/off signals that computers can recognize, record, and play back.

Most software for creating voice output requires large amounts of disk storage space. One software product that enables you to record voice and other sounds is called *Arkay Multimedia Extensions.* You can use it to add human speech or computer-generated speech to computer graphics presentations. With another product, called *Voice It,* you can add voice and other sounds to computerized financial worksheets. For example, you can record a message that the computer plays back whenever a specific number or column is highlighted. To record messages with *Voice It,* you use a telephone-style handset (Figure 5-22).

Future Trends

Manufacturers Are Making Monitors That Emit Less Radiation, Printers That Are More Versatile, and More Applications Software with Voice Output.

We'll look at future trends for the two most common output devices—monitors and printers—and then discuss one of the most promising new output technologies—voice output.

Computer monitors, like television sets, emit electromagnetic radiation when they are turned on. Concerns have emerged about whether this radiation can cause miscarriages and eye problems. So far, researchers have found no proof that radiation from computer monitors harms people. Even so, manufacturers have responded to the concerns by introducing low-emission models. Since low-emission monitors do not cost much more to make than other models, they could become standard even if the emissions are never proven harmful.

COMPUTER MONITORS: FRIEND OR FOE?

The computer monitor has become a commonplace and familiar object in both offices and homes. But some researchers are suggesting that commonplace and familiar does not necessarily mean *safe.*

Computer monitors emit a steady stream of electromagnetic radiation. Millions of office workers, professionals, and students sit in front of monitors, often for eight or more hours a day, absorbing some of that radiation. Does this make the ubiquitous computer monitor something of a Trojan Horse, entering our lives under the guise of a useful tool, only to emit invisible but destructive radiation?

Research studies have produced contradictory results. A 1988 study of environmental hazards in Oakland, California, found that women who used video display terminals (VDTs) had a higher rate of miscarriages. However, follow-up studies failed to duplicate those findings. In fact, some scientists argue that *stress* is the culprit, not radiation. It seems that people who work at VDTs all day usually have high stress jobs, and the miscarriages could be stress related.

Another issue which makes it difficult to reach a conclusion is that monitors emit two kinds of electromagnetic radiation, very low frequency (VLF) and extremely low frequency (ELF). So far, researchers have investigated only the effects of VLF radiation. ELF radiation has already been found to cause problems for people who live near power lines (and, possibly, for people who use electric blankets). But researchers have not studied the effects of ELF radiation on computer users. And to complicate matters further, ELF radiation is emitted from the *back* of computer monitors.

If you're confused about how seriously to take all this, you're not alone. Nobody really knows yet whether a problem even exists. Still, operating on the assumption that it's better to be safe than sorry, manufacturers are taking the initiative and building a new generation of low-emission monitors. Their low-emission levels meet safety standards developed in Sweden in 1986. Keep in mind, though, that these "Swedish standards" are not based on

any conclusive medical evidence that monitors are dangerous. Rather, they are based on the premise that "the less radiation, the better."

Meanwhile, the *University of California at Berkeley Wellness Letter* recommends the following precautions: Sit at least an arm's length from your computer screen; sit at least 4 feet from your co-workers' monitors and turn your monitor off when you are not using it—don't just dim it.

Finally, if you're about to buy a monitor, there's some good news—you won't have to pay extra; low-emission monitors cost the same as their "high"-emission counterparts.

Scientists don't know for sure if the rays emitted by computer monitors are harmful.

Source: "Monitor Emissions: Should You Worry?" by Winn L. Rosch, *PC Magazine,* July 1991, p. 106.

PRINTERS

Printer makers are designing models that can also serve as FAX machines, photocopiers, and image-scanning input devices. This is possible because FAX machines, copiers, scanners, and laser printers use many of the same parts, such as lasers and drum-based scanning systems.

A single machine that prints, copies, scans images for input, and sends facsimiles will take up less space and cost less than separate machines. On the other hand, a breakdown leaves a business without several functions, not just one, until the machine is repaired. If these combination models become popular, the prices of regular laser printers, FAX machines, scanners, and photocopiers could decrease.

Printer companies are also adding features to their products that give users more control over their output. For example, more printers are now set up with *scalable fonts,* which enable you to scale printed characters up or down to any size. A *font* is a type size and style, such as 32-point Times Roman or 12-point Courier. Before scalable fonts were available, most printers were built to print characters in only a few fonts in standard sizes, although you could use software to print characters in additional styles and sizes. A printer with scalable fonts allows you to select a standard or nonstandard size for any type style your software or printer can create. This gives you much more flexibility in designing documents.

HAVE OFFICE, WILL TRAVEL

Can you imagine taking all your essential office equipment along with you on a business trip? Only a few years ago this idea might have seemed a science fiction fantasy—but with today's cordless cellular phones and pocket-sized computers, you can actually pack much of your office equipment in your briefcase.

You're probably familiar with cordless phones (maybe you already own one), and you may have seen or read about those amazing pocket-sized and notebook-sized computers. But, you may be wondering, what about printers? What if you're traveling and your boss or client wants you to print a quality document, ASAP (as soon as possible, in business jargon)?

Well, now you can pack along a lightweight, compact portable printer. For example, the Mannesmann Tally MT 735 portable printer,

at 8¾ by 11½ by 2½ inches and just over 8 pounds, is not much larger or heavier than a notebook-sized com-

The Mannesmann Tally MT 735 is one of a new generation of lightweight, silent, portable printers that provide near-laser-quality text.

puter. Although it is a dot-matrix printer, it prints high-quality text, like a laser printer. It also operates much like an office laser printer, silently and rapidly printing whole pages.

If your briefcase is a bit heavy and you require an even *lighter* printer, the Seikosha LT-20 weighs in at under 6 pounds, and measures 14.6 by 11.3 by 2 inches. Print quality doesn't match laser quality (the Seikosha offers dot-matrix near-letter-quality text), but it's small, light, cheap, and will definitely fit into your briefcase. If your briefcase is too full, you can always move your pocket-sized PC into your jacket pocket.

So, whether you're on your way to Topeka, Toronto, or Taipei, don't forget to pack your telephone, your computer, your printer—and your toothbrush.

Sources: "Tiny Laser-Like Printer Ups Ante on Totables," by Peggy Wallace, *PC Computing,* May 1991, p. 38. "Trim Dot Matrix Hits the Road for Just $500," by Chris Shipley, *PC Computing,* May 1991, p. 39.

Most individuals today find their output needs include a monitor and a printer. If you plan to use your microcomputer for educational software, games, or graphics, you should select an EGA or VGA color monitor.

Most people's personal uses for a microcomputer include such things as budgeting, tax applications, household records, and correspondence. In these cases, a dot-matrix printer, an ink-jet printer, or a personal laser printer will probably meet your needs. If you choose a dot-matrix printer, you will probably want one with variable pitch and both letter-quality and draft mode.

Unless your system will be used to prepare a variety of graphic materials, a high-speed laser printer or a printer with the ability to print multicolored output won't be required.

Plotters and voice output devices are used infrequently by the typical microcomputer system user.

VOICE OUTPUT

Software companies are introducing more products that programmers can use to add sound to software applications. As a result, applications with voice output will probably become more common. Some of these applications might enable people to present reports, sales presentations, and other information in a livelier and more efficient way.

Suppose you create financial worksheets that show sales figures for your company. You might soon be able to do this with software that allows you to add a spoken explanation for each number in a worksheet. Then, if the January sales figure for Region 1 is unusually low, you can add a spoken message explaining that a major customer in Region 1 went out of business in December. The computer will play back the explanation whenever someone viewing the worksheet highlights the Region 1 figure for January. This could save you the time required to write a report that explains the figures. It would also save time for the viewer, who would not have to look up the information in a separate report.

Voice output from computers could also help people who do not see well, or people who cannot read. For example, computers with voice output could be used to teach arithmetic to children even before they learn to read. The continuing development of voice output will help to make computers even more useful to greater numbers of people.

REVIEW QUESTIONS

1. What is soft copy?
2. Describe how a monitor's resolution is measured.
3. Which produces sharper images, a high-resolution monitor or one with low resolution? Why?
4. What is the resolution of a typical monochrome monitor? A CGA monitor? An EGA monitor? A VGA monitor?
5. Which type of computer has traditionally been regarded as the best for graphics output: the Macintosh or IBM compatibles?
6. What household device uses the same technology as cathode-ray tubes for desktop computer monitors?
7. What computers use flat panel displays? Name and describe three kinds of flat panel displays.
8. What is hard copy?

9. How does a dot-matrix printer form images on paper? How does this differ from the way a daisy-wheel printer forms images?

10. What is a tractor-feed attachment? Which kinds of printers use it?

11. Why is an ink-jet printer quieter than a dot-matrix or daisy-wheel printer?

12. How are bubble-jet printers different from other ink-jet printers? For what kinds of computers were they designed?

13. Describe how a laser printer forms images on paper.

14. Which type of printer is fastest? Which is slowest?

15. How does a plotter form images on paper?

16. How does a printer's output differ from a plotter's output? Who uses plotters?

17. Name and describe two types of plotters.

18. Give an everyday example of voice output.

19. What device must a computer have to convert voice signals to computer form?

20. What kinds of signals must the human voice be converted to so that computers can recognize, record, and play it back?

21. How are manufacturers responding to health concerns about computer monitors?

22. What other office machines use the same technology as laser printers?

TOPICS FOR RESEARCH AND DISCUSSION

1. People often picture the office of the future with one all-purpose machine that will print, copy, scan images for input, and send facsimiles. This all-purpose machine would be much cheaper than the combined costs of all the single-purpose machines. As the text noted, one potential problem with such a machine is that a breakdown leaves a business without several functions, not just one, until the machine is repaired. If you were a business owner, would you consider such a machine? Explain your answer. If you wish, research the latest developments in this area.

2. You work in a medium-sized company that supplies dairy farmers in the Midwest. You are shopping for a laptop computer that you and your co-workers will use for writing reports and working with statistical information outside the office. Some people might be using the computers outdoors and carrying them on airplanes. Some might also need to print drafts of their documents. What kind of display might you want, and what kind of printer would you want to purchase with the computer? Visit a computer store, or look at advertisements in computer magazines or newspapers to see what specific models of computers and printers are available with the features you want. How much do they weigh? What are their prices? What would you recommend? Explain your choice.

3. To this point, researchers have not found proof that radiation from computer monitors harms people. However, low-emission monitors do not cost much more than other models. Investigate the latest findings of researchers, the levels of radiation in current computer monitors (both traditional monitors and low-emission ones), and the monitors' prices. Based on your research, is it worth the price for a company to buy low-emission monitors or to replace current monitors with low-emission monitors? (Both of these actions could mean hundreds of monitors for large companies.)

PART TWO

SOFTWARE

This section focuses on *software,* the instructions that tell computers what to do. First, you'll be introduced to *system software.* It's the most basic type of software and controls the computer's operation. Then, you'll see how two types of software, *wordprocessing* and *desktop publishing* software, let you work with words and documents. You'll take a look at other types of software: *spreadsheets,* electronic versions of accounting worksheets; *database management systems,* used to store, manipulate, and retrieve data; and software used to create *computer graphics.* You'll also learn about *data communications,* which lets computers access data from other locations, and *connectivity,* which lets computers work together. After a description of specialized software and a look at *programming,* the section concludes with a discussion of how to match the appropriate hardware and software to real-world problems.

SYSTEM SOFTWARE AND UTILITIES

OBJECTIVES

The information in this chapter will enable you to

- Identify the components of system software.
- Describe the role of the operating system.
- Describe the three types of user interfaces and explain their advantages and disadvantages.
- Describe the historical development of operating system products.
- Discuss the advantages and disadvantages of DOS, OS/2, and UNIX.
- Describe the most common system utility programs.

What Is System Software?

System Software Tells the Microcomputer How to Interact with Users and with Other Programs.

As you learned in Chapter 1, the many kinds of programs used to operate a microcomputer are known as *software.* The two main categories of software are *application software* and *system software.* Application software includes all of the programs you use for work or entertainment, such as accounting programs and computer games. System software refers to the programs that allow your application software to work on your microcomputer. System software unlocks the resources of the microcomputer, so that you and your applications can use them.

System software is responsible for the following:

- Controls the microcomputer's operation from the time it is first turned on.
- Controls how the microcomputer reacts to input from a user or an application program.
- Allows application programs to run on the microcomputer.

As you can see in Figure 6-1, system software governs all activity between the microcomputer, the user, and other programs.

System software was first developed as a labor-saving device by computer programmers, who knew that every computer program had certain instructions in common. Rather than write these instructions line by line in all their programs, programmers created a group of standard commands to perform common tasks. They would then incorporate these instructions into their programs. Collections of standard instructions formed the basis for system software. Today some of the system software for microcomputers is contained in the system unit's microprocessor chips. Because these instructions

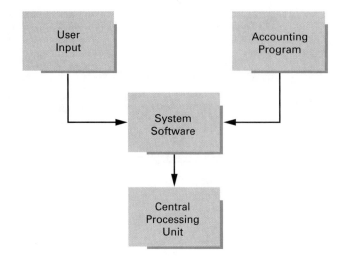

FIGURE 6-1

System software processes all input from users and application programs.

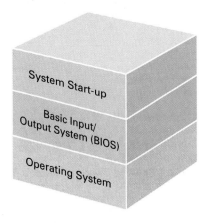

FIGURE 6-2

System software is divided into three functional areas.

are part of the microcomputer's hardware, they form a category of programs known as *firmware*.

System software can be divided into three functional areas, as shown in Figure 6-2:

- System start-up
- Basic input/output system (BIOS)
- Operating system

System Start-up

When a Microcomputer Is Turned On, System Start-up Software Prepares It for Use.

When you turn on a microcomputer, it goes through a series of automatic operations. Often you see lights on the front of the system unit blinking, and sometimes you can hear the microcomputer beep and the disk drive whirl. During these first few seconds of operation, you cannot interact with the microcomputer because it is busy with preoperation activities. System software is going through the process of checking the microcomputer's resources. This process is known as *system start-up*. After a few seconds, a message from system software lets you know the microcomputer is ready for use.

System start-up includes the following two functions:

- **Bootstrap loader.** The first set of program instructions the microcomputer follows when it is turned on is called the *bootstrap loader*. This small program is stored in read only memory (ROM), the permanent computer memory contained in a chip in the microcomputer. It tells the microcomputer how to start. The bootstrap loader prepares the microcomputer to perform diagnostic tests of its components.

- **Diagnostics.** After the bootstrap loader is finished, a diagnostic program tests the microcomputer's memory, the central processing unit (CPU), and the other hardware components to make sure they are working correctly. If any are not, system software lets you know which component has failed the diagnostic tests. For example, if a storage device such as a hard disk drive fails its diagnostic test, the system software displays a message on the computer screen to let you know you have a problem with your hard disk.

Basic Input/Output System (BIOS)

BIOS Controls Activity between the System Unit and Other Components.

The *Basic Input/Output System (BIOS)* ("bye-oss") is a set of programs that governs all activity to and from the components attached to the system unit (see Figure 6-3). Components are attached to the system unit by cables to send data in (input) and out (output) of the system unit. BIOS programs direct input and output activities. Much of BIOS is contained in ROM chips in the system unit.

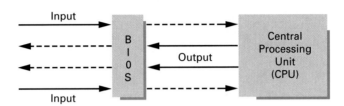

FIGURE 6-3

Everything that goes in or out of your microcomputer passes through BIOS.

The Operating System

The Operating System Accepts User Requests and Manages Microcomputer Processing.

The *operating system* is the single most important part of system software for the microcomputer user. It gives the user access to the microcomputer's internal resources. The operating system takes over after system start-up and accepts, interprets, and runs all the other programs used by the computer (see Figure 6-4).

There are four basic components in all microcomputer operating systems:

- The kernel program
- The command interpreter
- The operating system utilities
- The user interface

Let's take a brief look at the first three components and then examine user interfaces in detail.

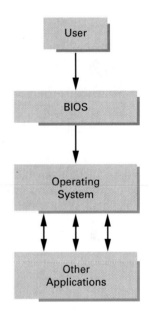

FIGURE 6-4

Input goes through BIOS to reach the operating system. The operating system directs these requests to other programs.

THE KERNEL PROGRAM

The *kernel* program acts as an interface between BIOS and the central processing unit (CPU). The kernel program is made up of a *command processor*, which gets input ready for processing in the CPU, and *core programs*, built-in programs that handle the most basic tasks. For example, the operating system program that makes copies of files is a core program.

THE COMMAND INTERPRETER

The *command interpreter* reviews all input that comes into the microcomputer from any input source. Its job is to determine whether input is valid. A valid command, for example, is one the microcomputer can execute. The command interpreter weeds out erroneous or invalid input.

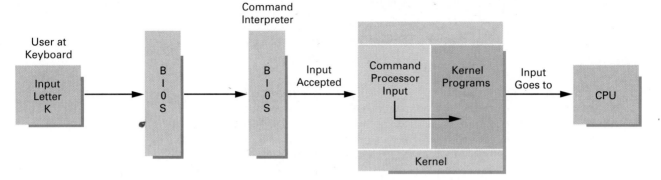

FIGURE 6-5

The components of the operating system work together to process input quickly and efficiently.

OPERATING SYSTEM UTILITIES

Like the kernel program, *operating system utilities* are programs that carry out routine tasks. However, rather than being added to the kernel program, they are kept separate. This keeps the kernel program small, fast, and efficient. Only the most basic tasks are in the kernel. Operating system utilities provide additional functions that aren't provided by the kernel programs. For example, disk formatting is not part of the kernel, but is considered an operating system utility.

Figure 6-5 shows how input travels through the operating system.

The User Interface

The User Interface Is the Part of a Program That Lets You Communicate with the Computer.

When you use a program on a microcomputer, you use a keyboard or mouse to enter or select input. You use a monitor or printer to display the resulting output. Each time you enter input or receive output, you are working with that program's user interface. *User interface* is the part of a program that lets you communicate with the computer. The results of these communications appear on the monitor.

Operating systems use three types of user interfaces: command line, menu, and graphical.

COMMAND LINE INTERFACE

One of the earliest user interfaces is the *command line,* which accepts input in the form of commands, or instructions, entered from the keyboard, as shown in Figure 6-6. The command TYPE, for instance, directs the microcomputer to display the contents of a file on the screen.

Command line interfaces are the fastest and most efficient to use—once you have learned the commands. But they can be frustrating for a new computer user because both the keyboard and the commands must be mastered. Until you gain some experience by working with the operating system, these interfaces will slow you down. People who do not keyboard well are also hampered by command line interfaces.

MENU INTERFACE

A *menu* interface provides a shorthand method of entering commands at the keyboard. Instead of entering the complete command, the user selects a command or responds to a question. The menu interface then converts the user's choice to the command just as if the user had entered it. The most common types of menu interfaces are *yes-and-no, pull-down,* and *item selection.*

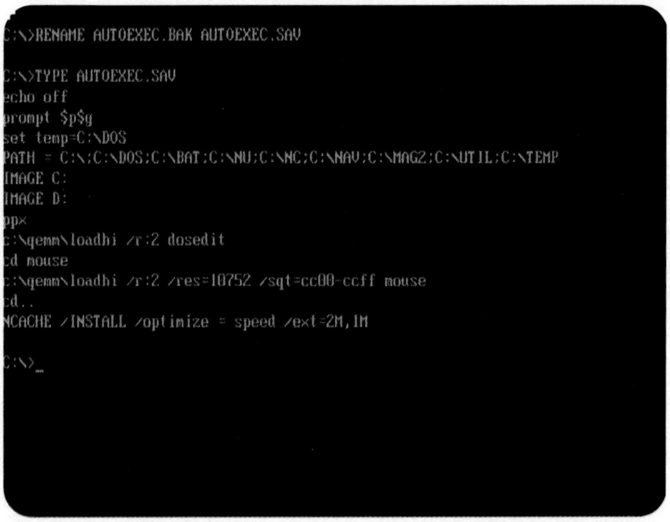

FIGURE 6-6

A command line interface offers experienced users fast access to the operating system.

Yes-and-No Menu

A yes-and-no menu presents choices in the form of questions (see Figure 6-7). The user usually enters the letter "Y" for yes or "N" for no to make a choice. After making a choice, the user may be presented with another question, or the microcomputer may perform a task based on the user's answer to the question.

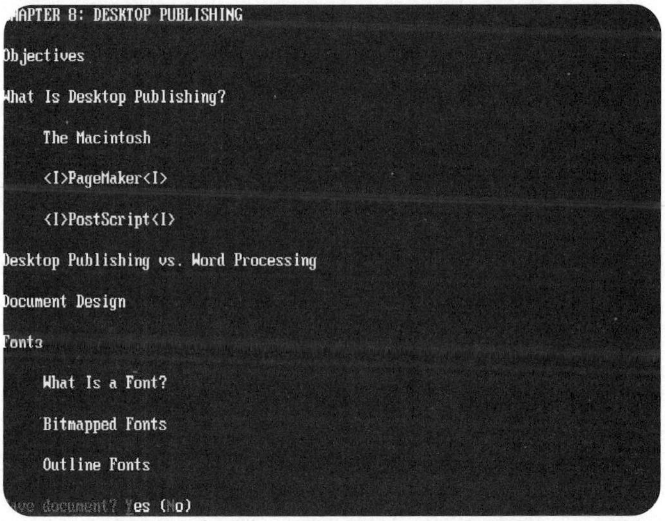

FIGURE 6-7

The prompts in a yes-and-no menu direct the user from option to option.

Pull-Down Menu

A pull-down menu contains a list of command options. To see the list the user must pull down (or open) the menu, which is hidden behind its title. Once the menu is open, the user can select an option from the list, as shown in Figure 6-8.

Item Selection Menu

The options in an item selection menu appear in a list, in which each item is usually numbered or designated by a different letter. The user selects an item from the list by typing its corresponding number or letter designation.

Menu interfaces allow a new user to learn the operating system quickly by limiting the knowledge of commands and the keyboarding skill required. However, to remain current, menu interfaces must be updated for each new

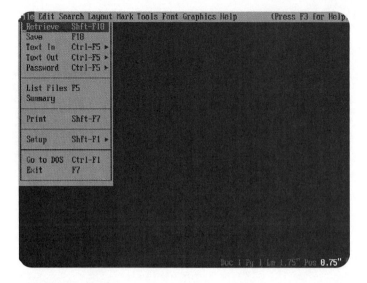

FIGURE 6-8

A pull-down menu appears only when you activate it. Otherwise it stays behind its title and out of your way.

function added to the operating system. This can require many revisions of the menu. Also, once users become familiar with the operating system, they often want to use advanced operating system functions that don't appear on the menu, such as the operating system function to establish communications with another computer.

GRAPHICAL USER INTERFACE (GUI)

The *Graphical User Interface,* or *GUI,* first appeared in the mass market on the Apple Macintosh microcomputer in the mid-1980s. The GUI uses pictures called *icons* to represent operating system commands on the monitor and a mouse to select from among the icons. Figure 6-9 shows a GUI and explains what the icons mean. See how many meanings you can guess before you read the explanation.

Because they are so easy to use, GUIs are becoming the most popular interface on today's microcomputers.

GUIs allow users with little or no training to easily figure out which icon represents which command. While new users often like GUIs, some long-time microcomputer users don't like them because they separate the user from direct access to operating system commands. Microcomputer users who have worked with command line interfaces sometimes have trouble adjusting to the mouse and icons.

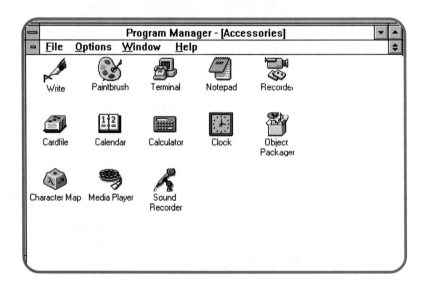

FIGURE 6-9

Graphical user interfaces (GUIs) are easy to use once you learn what the icons are.

The Operating Environment

The Operating Environment Enhances the Functionality of the Operating System.

Users of early microcomputers entered commands to direct their microcomputers to perform tasks. Today, many users take advantage of a more sophisticated approach to human/computer interaction known as the *operating environment*. The operating environment is a system software program that sits between the user and the operating system. It provides easy access to the operating system and does not require knowledge of operating system commands. It also supplies functions that enhance the operating system's ability to interact with users and application programs. For example, an operating environment makes it easy to locate, open, save, and close files without knowing the operating system commands.

The Apple Macintosh *Finder* can be thought of as the first operating environment available on a microcomputer. Microsoft Corporation's *Windows* provides a similar operating environment on the IBM and compatible microcomputers. These are some of the features of Windows and the Macintosh Finder:

- A graphical user interface containing pull-down menus and *windows*. A window is an on-screen frame through which you can view the contents of your applications files.

- The ability to change the size and style of type.

- *Desk accessories.* Programs that perform small tasks such as displaying an on-screen clock, calculator, and calendar.

- *Clipboard.* A temporary memory storage area used for storing text and graphics when moving them from one application program to another.

The Development of Microcomputer Operating Systems

The Constantly Changing Microcomputer Market Demands Up-to-Date Operating Systems, and Manufacturers Compete to Provide Them.

Since the introduction of the first microcomputers in the 1970s, vast improvements in hardware and technology have prompted many changes in operating systems. Today's microprocessors demand a level of speed and efficiency from an operating system that was not dreamed of when the first microcomputer operating systems were written. The widespread use of microcomputers in businesses and homes has also prompted changes in user interfaces to make it easier for nonprogrammers

The first microcomputer operating systems were developed for computer programmers and hobbyists. These systems used command line interfaces and had strict rules governing input. Over time these operating systems were modified to make them friendlier, and new operating systems were developed. Here's a brief review of microcomputer operating systems so you can see how much they've changed in two decades.

CP/M

The first commercially available operating system for microcomputers was *CP/M,* or *Control Program for Microcomputers.* This operating system, originally developed in 1974 by Digital Research Inc., was designed for use with Intel Corporation's first general-purpose microprocessor, the 8080.

Because it was the first of its kind, CP/M was the building block for all later microcomputer operating systems. It included programs for system start-up, input and output control, and command processing. CP/M enjoyed a useful life until the early 1980s, when it was pushed aside by DOS.

DOS

When IBM entered the microcomputer business in 1980 with its personal computer, the IBM PC, it chose Microsoft Corporation to provide the operating system, which became *Disk Operating System,* or *DOS* ("doss") for short. This operating system was written by programmers at Seattle Computer Products for microcomputers based on the Intel 8086 microprocessor. The IBM PC was an 8086 machine. Microsoft bought the rights to DOS and renamed it MS-DOS, short for Microsoft Disk Operating System. DOS quickly became the new standard for microcomputer operating systems. But the value of CP/M as a model should not be dismissed. Table 6-1 shows a few of the CP/M commands that DOS incorporated.

Table 6-1: CP/M Commands Incorporated in DOS

CP/M	DOS	Description
DIR	DIR	Displays a list of files
ED	EDLIN	Edits a file
ERA	ERASE	Erases a file
REN	REN	Renames a file

DOS has gone through several revisions in the last decade (see Table 6-2). The current version is DOS 5.0 Until version 5.0, DOS had a command line user interface, but the Windows operating environment from Microsoft Corporation gave DOS a graphical user interface.

DOS remains the most widely used microcomputer operating system. According to the July 1991 issue of *PC Magazine,* 50 million users are working with DOS versions 2, 3, or 4. Most microcomputers in the workplace use DOS, and most of today's popular microcomputer programs were originally written to work with DOS.

Because DOS is so widespread, new users can find a lot of help when

Table 6-2: Revisions of DOS

Version Number	Features
1.0	Limited memory support. Did not support hard disk drives.
2.0	Developed for IBM XT. Hard disk drive support added.
3.0	High density floppy disk drives supported; 3.5-inch floppy diskettes supported.
4.0	Large (greater than 32MB) hard drives supported directly. Menu interface options added.
5.0	Smaller RAM requirements. Better memory management. Graphical user interface, much like Windows.

learning DOS. Some fellow employees probably know it, many books have been written about it, and courses in DOS are available. Finally, DOS is inexpensive and will run on all generations of IBM microcomputers and compatibles, from the original IBM PC to the newest IBM PS/2 series. DOS does not require major investments in expensive new hardware.

DOS has two glaring disadvantages: its limited random access memory (RAM) and its single-task design. DOS was designed to provide only 640K of RAM. In 1980, no one imagined that microcomputers would ever need more. Today, 640K is insufficient RAM for many programs used on microcomputers, but because of its internal design, DOS cannot be expanded. Another limitation of DOS is that it is a *single-task* operating system, meaning that it can run only one program at a time. Again, the DOS developers never thought that a microcomputer would be able to run more than one program at a time.

OS/2

To enable microcomputer users to move beyond the limitations of DOS, IBM and Microsoft designed *OS/2,* short for *Operating System 2.* OS/2 uses a graphical user interface called *Presentation Manager* that allows the user access to the complex operating system. OS/2 also eliminates the RAM limitations of DOS by allowing programs to access many megabytes of RAM.

OS/2 offers a more powerful file system than DOS. Files can be larger, there can be more of them, and they can be accessed faster. It also provides a compatibility feature that lets you run a DOS program from within OS/2.

OS/2 has not been well received as a replacement for DOS because it is costly to implement. The basic OS/2 operating system is much more expensive than DOS. Also, OS/2 does not work on older microcomputers like the IBM PC and the IBM XT. Microcomputers based on the Intel 80286 processor, like the IBM AT, are barely capable of using OS/2. For a microcomputer to make full use of OS/2, it needs an Intel 80386 microprocessor, 4MB of RAM, and an 80MB hard disk. Such a system can cost several thousand dollars.

The biggest current disadvantage to OS/2 is that there are few application programs on the market written for it, although many have been promised.

Table 6-3 summarizes the advantages and disadvantages of the DOS and OS/2 operating systems.

Table 6-3: Advantages and Disadvantages of DOS and OS/2

Advantages	Disadvantages
DOS	DOS
Most popular programs work with DOS.	Limited RAM (640K).
Help is readily available.	Single-task design.
Many books and courses are available.	
Inexpensive.	
Runs on all generations of IBM microcomputers and compatibles.	
OS/2	OS/2
Access to many megabytes of RAM.	Expensive to implement.
Multitask design.	Does not work on older microcomputers.
Powerful system.	Few applications written for OS/2.

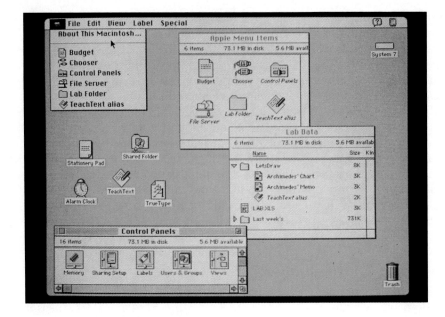

FIGURE 6-10

The Macintosh has its own set of icons.

APPLE MACINTOSH SYSTEM

The Apple Macintosh operating system, called simply the *System,* was designed to be easy to learn and to use. Because the operating system and the microcomputer were designed concurrently, they are particularly well integrated and give the new user few problems. The System is designed to work with Apple's operating environment called the *Finder,* shown in Figure 6-10.

Over the years as new versions of Macintosh microcomputers have become available, the System and Finder have been revised often. The newest version is called System 7.0. Because they work so closely together, you must use the correct Revision System with its corresponding Finder (see Table 6-4).

Table 6-4: Apple System and Finder Versions and Recommended Macintosh Models		
System	**Finder**	**Macintosh**
3.2	5.3	512K, 512Ke
6.02 or later	6.1 or later	Plus, SE, II
6.03 or later	6.1 or later	SE/30, IIx, IIcx
6.04 or later	6.1 or later	IIci, Portable
6.05 or later	6.1 or later	IIfx

APPLE II PRODOS

The Apple II microcomputers, found mainly in homes and schools, use an operating system called *ProDOS.* Because it is somewhat like DOS, knowledge of ProDOS makes working with DOS microcomputers an easy transition. However, Apple II applications programs typically include menu interfaces that make them very easy to use.

UNIX

The *UNIX* operating system was originally developed for minicomputers by AT&T's Bell Laboratories. At first, UNIX was too big and powerful to adapt to microcomputers. But today's microcomputers have the processing power needed to run UNIX effectively. A company called Santa Cruz Operation, or SCO, has enjoyed success with its UNIX operating system tailored for microcomputers.

Apple Computer also has developed a version of UNIX, *A/UX,* to work on the Macintosh family of computers, and Microsoft has a version called *XENIX* that is used with IBM-compatible microcomputers.

One advantage of UNIX is that it has been implemented on many different microcomputers and minicomputers. Applications written for one version of UNIX usually require little effort to convert to other versions. Another strength is its ability to have many application programs open and running at once, a process known as *multitasking.*

The main disadvantage of UNIX is the small number of standard business programs that currently work with it. Most of the available programs for UNIX are focused on science and engineering applications. Also, there is currently no graphical user interface for the Microsoft version of UNIX that runs on IBM and compatible microcomputers.

BILL GATES: TOO MUCH OF A GOOD THING?

Back in 1980, IBM asked a small company with the funny name of Microsoft to provide system software to run its first personal computers. This was a turning point in the history of personal computers—and in the life of Bill Gates, who had dropped out of Harvard five years earlier, at the age of 19, to found Microsoft.

The computer became the IBM PC. The software was christened MS-DOS, for "Microsoft Disk Operating System." MS-DOS quickly became the industry standard for the IBM PC and PC compatibles. It made Microsoft a powerful competitor in the computer software industry throughout the 1980s.

In the 1990s, though, it seems everyone wants to cut Bill Gates and Microsoft down to size. Even former rivals IBM and Apple are getting together, looking for ways to break Microsoft's stranglehold on the personal computer market.

Is it just competitive zeal, laced with a bit of envy, that's driving them together? Is it because Gates himself is such an aggressive and successful competitor? (His share of Microsoft is worth about $4 billion.) What is their complaint, and why is the Federal Trade Commission also "mad" at Bill Gates?

The "problem" everyone seems to have with Gates and Microsoft is that Microsoft not only makes system software but also application software: word processing programs, such as *Microsoft Word,* and spreadsheet programs, such as *Microsoft Excel.* Many argue that when the company which provides the operating system also makes applications software to run on that operating system, that company has an unfair competitive advantage over other software companies.

Will we witness the day when Microsoft, like AT&T in the early 1980s, is divided by government decree into smaller companies, one devoted to operating systems and another to applications software? Or is Bill Gates guilty only of being consistently smart and successful in an industry he helped create?

Bill Gates and his company Microsoft not only make the system software for IBM-compatible microcomputers, but also develop application software.

Source: "The Whiz They Love to Hate," by Michael Rogers, *Newsweek,* June 24, 1991, p. 38.

System Utility Programs

System Utility Programs Fill in Gaps in the Operating System.

While the microcomputer's operating system handles all of the basic functions, many people use additional programs called *System Utility Programs* which provide features that are unavailable in their operating system. These system utility programs allow you to add on to an operating system, so that it handles routine and specialized tasks more quickly and efficiently. System utility programs are available to provide just about any operating system enhancement you might want. For example, a utility called *Double DOS* from Digital Research allows you to run two programs at the same time on an IBM or compatible microcomputer.

MS-DOS 5.0: DOS MADE EASY

Before you stop by your local software store to purchase DOS 5.0, the newest version of Microsoft's venerable operating system, ask yourself this: Have you, or anyone you know, ever bought Microsoft DOS before at a software retail outlet? The answer is no. DOS 5.0 marks the first time that DOS has been available to individual consumers at software retail stores.

When DOS was first released in 1981, PCs came without DOS as standard equipment. Buyers had to ask their computer dealer to order DOS. For most of the 1980s, though, DOS came as standard equipment on all IBM PCs and compatibles. Microsoft licensed DOS directly to computer companies, who included the cost in the price of a system. Microsoft was then paid a royalty on each computer sold. This system worked until you wanted to upgrade your computer with the newest version of DOS. In that case, you had to buy it from your dealer.

DOS 5.0's easier availability is only part of the good news. This new version of DOS, according to many experts, is the most important DOS update since the release of DOS 2.0

in 1983. While Microsoft's Windows 3.0 has been garnering all the attention, many users have complained that the operating system itself (DOS 3.3 and 4.0) was increasingly antiquated. Complaints ranged from DOS's difficult user interface to its lack of new features. DOS 4.0, in particular, with its many bugs, was considered a major failure.

So, what does DOS 5.0 offer to make computing easier? For one, commands are easier to understand and to enter. And you can enter commands by using a mouse or the more traditional keyboard. DOS 5.0 also features easy to access, easy to understand HELP functions.

In addition, DOS 5.0 includes many features to help solve everyday computing problems, such as retrieving deleted data. Before DOS 5.0, users had to buy separate software programs, called DOS utilities, to perform these tasks. DOS 5.0 is also the first version of DOS that can take full advantage of the fast new computers—the 286, 386, and 486 generations.

Easy to use, easy to buy, DOS 5.0, the granddaddy of personal micro-

computer operating systems, suddenly looks quite nimble and spry as it enters the 1990s.

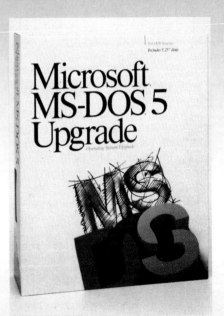

The newest version of DOS, 5.0 is both easy to use and easy to buy. It's the first new version of DOS to be sold at software retail stores.

Sources: "Everything DOS Should Have Been," by Ray Duncan, *PC Magazine*, July 1991, p. 35. "After Ten Years, DOS Becomes a Retail Product," by Gus Venditto and Robin Raskin, *PC Magazine*, July 1991, p. 37.

System utility programs require little memory and are relatively inexpensive. Since several companies offer similar programs within a wide price range, it pays to compare prices and features.

Many system utility programs are available at little or no cost through computer clubs and electronic data distribution services. Some programmers actually give away their programs. The name for this category of programs is *freeware*. Other programmers request a small fee for their programs. Such programs are called *shareware*. Many useful system utility programs are available as either freeware or shareware.

TSRs/DESK ACCESSORIES

Some system utility programs should be available at all times. One example is a program that provides an on-screen calculator whenever you press a certain combination of keys. You may want to use the calculator often while writing a report or working with financial data. This program lets you calculate without disrupting your main task. When used with IBM and compatible microcomputers, this type of program is called a *TSR*, short for *Terminate and Stay Resident*. A terminate and stay resident program can be loaded into RAM where it will wait to be activated by the microcomputer or user. This same type of program when used on an Apple Macintosh or in the Windows operating environment is known as a *desk accessory*.

FILE MANAGEMENT UTILITY PROGRAMS

As you know from Chapter 4, the data you create and the programs you use are stored in files. Files are simply collections of information that are organized so the microcomputer can retrieve them. *File management utility programs,* such as *Norton Commander* from Symantec Corporation, help you locate and keep track of where your files are stored in the microcomputer.

MEMORY MANAGEMENT UTILITY PROGRAMS

Memory management utility programs are available for the DOS operating system to make more RAM available than the 640K the operating system allows. These programs work by removing programs from RAM and placing them in other unused memory locations. Memory managers allow the programs they have moved to be used as though they were still in their original RAM location.

Products such as *386 MAX* from Qualitas Trading Corporation let you allocate parts of RAM memory to speed up your microcomputer's operation. Some products such as Microsoft's Windows include a memory management utility to help you work with larger programs or more programs at one time.

Only microcomputers that have an 80286, 80386, or 80486 microprocessor can take advantage of most memory management utility programs.

FILE RECOVERY UTILITY PROGRAMS

Occasionally, even the most experienced microcomputer users make mistakes. When the error causes the microcomputer to permanently delete, or erase, a file, *file recovery utility programs* can often bring the file back. File recovery utility programs are also useful when files are lost because of a malfunction within the microcomputer. Although these programs are seldom needed, they are among the most important because of the time and effort they save in duplicating files. One of the most popular file recovery

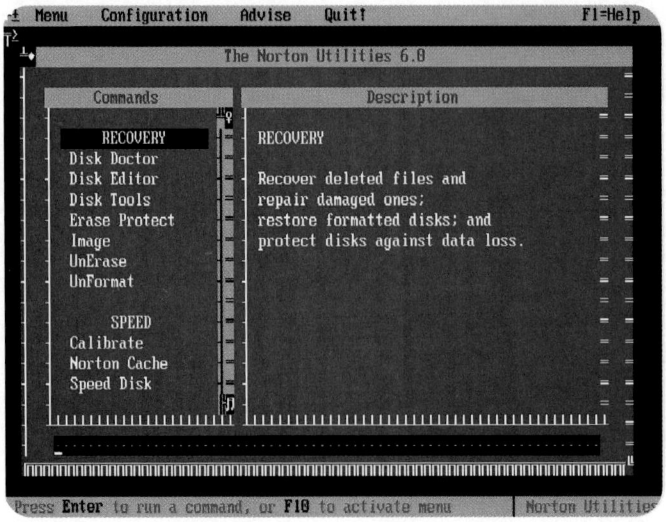

FIGURE 6-11

File recovery utilities let you "unerase" your lost files.

utility programs is *Norton Utilities* from Symantec Corporation, which runs on the IBM and compatibles and the Macintosh. Figure 6-11 shows a sample screen from *Norton Utilities.* Another widely used file recovery utility for the IBM and compatibles is *P.C. Tools Deluxe* from Central Point Software, Inc.

BACKUP UTILITY PROGRAMS

How long do you think it would take to copy all the files on a large hard disk that was full, one containing 80MB, for example? Using high density IBM diskettes, which can hold 1.44MB, it would take 56 diskettes! That could take an hour or more. Yet, experts urge you to make a copy of your hard disk regularly. If you suffer a hard disk crash you can use the copy.

That's where backup utility programs come in. *Backup utility programs* quickly make a copy of a hard disk on floppies or on a tape cartridge. Many backup utility programs also compress files so they take up less space (and you use fewer disks). That alone would make backup utility programs valuable. Most of these programs have many additional features. For example, they can make copies of only those files that have changed since the last copy was made. They can back up your hard disk automatically at a preset time every day or week. That way your hard disk can be backed up during the middle of the night, when no one is using the computer. One backup utility program available for use with IBM and compatible microcomputers is *Fastback Plus* from Fifth Generation Systems, Inc. *DiskFit* from SuperMac Technology is a common backup utility for Macintosh microcomputers.

FILE CONVERSION UTILITY PROGRAMS

When data is stored in a file, the data usually can be accessed again only by the program being used when the file was created. If you need to access the data while using a different program, *file conversion utility programs* let you do this.

File conversion utility programs are available to convert files containing pictures, or *graphics files;* files containing text, or *text files;* and files containing other business data, from one program to another. Some file conversion utility programs, such as *MacLink Plus/PC,* from DataViz, Inc., let you convert text, graphics, or business data files back and forth from programs that work only on the Macintosh to programs that work only on IBM microcomputers or compatibles. *MacLink Plus* is available for use with Macintosh systems. A graphics file conversion utility program for IBM systems is *HiJaak* from InSet Systems, Inc.

FILE COMPRESSION UTILITY PROGRAMS

Data is stored in secondary storage devices, such as hard disks and diskettes. As you create more files, they take up more room on these devices. *File compression utility programs* make files smaller by removing repetitive parts and reorganizing the data so that they take up less room on your hard disk or diskette. These programs do not change the content of the files. An example of a file compression utility program for use with IBM and compatible microcomputers is *ARC Plus* from System Enhancement Associates, Inc. *StuffIt Deluxe* from Aladdin Systems is a file compression utility available for Macintosh systems.

VIRUS PROTECTION UTILITY PROGRAMS

A *virus* is a computer program that interrupts your ability to work on your microcomputer by corrupting the data or programs you have stored on a hard disk or diskette, or by introducing destructive programs into your microcomputer. Viruses can get into your microcomputer in two ways:

- An *infected* disk, a disk containing a virus, can be inserted into your diskette drive.
- An infected file can be brought into your system from an online source via your modem.

Virus protection utility programs can help to remove a virus from an infected microcomputer. More important, they can prevent a virus from ever getting into the microcomputer by examining diskettes placed in a disk drive for hidden programs that may prove dangerous to the computer system and by alerting you to the danger. Here are some steps you can take to prevent a virus from entering your system:

- Do not allow other people to use your microcomputer.
- Do not download programs from online services that are not protected from viruses.
- Install virus protection that scans disks for viruses.

Virus protection utility programs are available for IBM and compatible

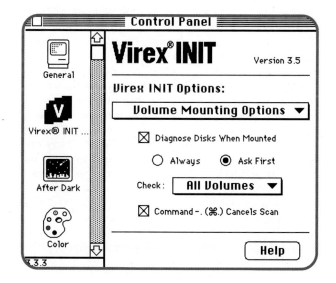

FIGURE 6-12

Because viruses are invisible and potentially damaging, everyone should have a virus protection utility program.

and Macintosh microcomputers. *Certus* from Foundation Ware is a virus protection utility program for use with IBM and compatible microcomputers, and *Virex* from Microcom, Inc. is available for Macintosh microcomputers. Figure 6-12 shows a virus protection program.

SECURITY UTILITY PROGRAMS

Because contemporary office layouts favor partitions rather than walls, many microcomputers are within easy reach of anyone. To prevent unintended users from gaining access to your data and programs, you can install a *security utility program*. For example, a security utility program available for IBM and compatible microcomputers is *Watchdog* from Fischer International Systems; one for use with Macintosh microcomputers is *Nightwatch* from Kent Marsh Ltd. These utility programs feature a password system that denies access after one or more unsuccessful tries. These systems are similar to those used in automatic teller machines at banks. Some security utility programs allow you to specify which files are off limits to others, and some provide different levels of access for different users of the same microcomputer. Many will also notify you that an unauthorized attempt at access was made and refused.

MACRO UTILITY PROGRAMS

Macro utility programs let you record a sequence of commands and give them an identifier, like a name or abbreviation. Once you record the sequence, you can repeat it simply by keying in the identifier.

For example, suppose that every week you make copies of all the files on your hard disk. This could involve many steps. But with a macro utility program all of your steps are remembered. You might decide to call the file containing all those steps "WKLYCPY." The following week, you run the file "WKLYCPY," and the macro utility program makes copies of all the files. Macro utility programs are time-savers for repetitive tasks. Borland International manufactures the macro utility program *SuperKey* for IBM and compatible microcomputers, and Affinity Microsystems, Inc. produces the macro utility program *Tempo* for Macintosh microcomputers.

YOU AND YOUR PERSONAL MICROCOMPUTER

When you select your personal microcomputer system you will probably find that the operating system is included in the base price. However, make sure you receive a manual that fully describes your operating system.

Although a small portion of the operating system resides in RAM, the major portion of the software is stored on the hard disk or on diskettes.

If the operating system runs into any problems, it will usually generate a message telling you what the problem is. Your operating system manual will usually list these messages and describe how to remedy the problem. Don't worry—although operating system software is complex, most users do not need to be aware of all the tasks it performs.

After you purchase a microcomputer system, you should learn to use the operating system and any other utilities that may have come with the microcomputer. Often "help screens" or tutorial programs are available. Additional help is available from users clubs and your vendor's "hot line." Many bookstores also have a wide selection of books that will help you understand operating systems and other software.

In selecting additional utilities and software you may need to know your system's microprocessor and the version number of your operating system.

MENU SHELL UTILITY PROGRAMS

For people who prefer working with a menu interface, *menu shell utility programs* are available to add menus to either a command line interface or a graphical interface. The purpose of these utility programs is to speed up operations that work best as menu selections. One example of a menu shell utility program for IBM and compatible microcomputers is *The Norton Commander* from Symantec Corporation. A comparable menu shell utility program for Macintosh microcomputers is *XTree* from XTree Company.

SCREEN SAVER UTILITY PROGRAMS

If you leave your microcomputer on for long periods of time, the image on the monitor can be burned permanently into the coating on the inside of your monitor screen. A *screen saver utility program* either blanks out the image entirely or changes the image constantly to prevent any one image from remaining on the monitor too long.

Two popular screen savers for the Macintosh or IBM-compatible microcomputers are *Pyro!* from Fifth Generation Systems, Inc., and *After Dark* from Berkeley Systems. These programs put entertaining moving images on the screen, as Figure 6-13 shows.

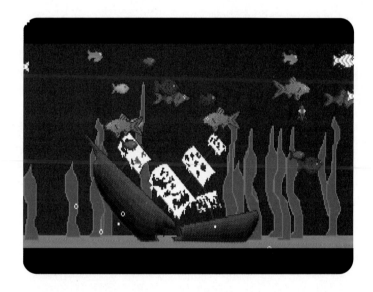

FIGURE 6-13

Screen saver programs can be entertaining as well as useful.

Table 6-5 lists some of the examples of the various types of systems utilities discussed in this chapter.

Future Trends

Operating Systems Will Become Transparent to the User and Add Built-in Features.

Imagine when you will use a microcomputer made by IBM, Apple, or another manufacturer and run any application software you like without even thinking about the operating system. Imagine when the operating system will look and act the same on all microcomputers, and you will not notice it is there—as if it were transparent. The idea of a transparent operating system may not be so far in the future.

The first big step in this direction was made by Microsoft with its Win-

Table 6-5: System Utility Programs

Type	Examples	Manufacturer	Computer
File Management Utilities	*P.C. Tools Deluxe*	Central Point Software	IBM Personal Computer and Apple Macintosh
	Norton Commander	Symantec Corporation	IBM Personal Computer
	XTree	XTree	Apple Macintosh
Memory Management Utilities	*386 MAX*	Qualitas Trading Corporation	IBM Personal Computer
	Above Disc	Above Software	IBM Personal Computer
	Virtual	Connectix Corporation	Apple Macintosh
Disk Recovery Utilities	*Norton Utilities*	Symantec Corporation	IBM Personal Computer and Apple Macintosh
	P.C. Tools Deluxe	Central Point Software	IBM Personal Computer
	P.C. Tools for the Macintosh	Central Point Software	Apple Macintosh
Backup Utilities	*Fastback Plus*	Fifth Generation Systems, Inc.	IBM Personal Computer
	COREfast	CORE International	IBM Personal Computer
	Fastback II	Fifth Generation Systems, Inc.	Apple Macintosh
File Conversion Utilities	*HiJaak*	InSet Systems, Inc.	IBM Personal Computer
	MacLink Plus	DataViz, Inc.	Apple Macintosh
File Compression Utilities	*ARC Plus*	System Enhancement Associates, Inc.	IBM Personal Computer
	Stacker	Stac Electronics	IBM Personal Computer
	StuffIt Deluxe	Aladdin Systems	Apple Macintosh
Virus Protection	*Certus*	Foundation Ware	IBM Personal Computer
	SAM	Symantec Corporation	Apple Macintosh
	VIREX	Microcom Software Division	Apple Macintosh
Security Utilities	*Watchdog*	Fischer International Systems	IBM Personal Computer
	Protec	Sophco, Inc.	IBM Personal Computer
	Nightwatch	Kent Marsh, Ltd.	Apple Macintosh
Macro Utilities	*SuperKey*	Borland International	IBM Personal Computer
	Tempo	Affinity Microsystems, Inc.	Apple Macintosh
Menu Shell Utilities	*Norton Commander*	Symantec Corporation	IBM Personal Computer
	Direct Access	Delta Technology	IBM Personal Computer
	XTree	XTree Company	Apple Macintosh
Screen Saver Utilities	*After Dark*	Berkeley Systems	IBM Personal Computer and Apple Macintosh
	Pyro	Fifth Generation Systems, Inc.	Apple Macintosh

dows operating environment. For the first time, an application program run on an IBM or compatible microcomputer looked similar and had an analogous user interface to the application program run on a Macintosh. The trend in the future may be to bring the two environments even closer together. Apple Computer and IBM have plans to develop a microcomputer system together with an operating environment that will run on both machines. The need of users to share data and programs with other users has started another trend in operating systems.

For users to share data and programs, their microcomputers must be connected. The process of connecting computers to share data and programs is called *networking*. A group of connected computers forms a *network*. Often business microcomputer users find themselves working on networks, and this trend will become more prevalent in the next few years. With IBM, Apple, and other computers routinely sharing data and application programs over networks, incompatible operating systems on the different types of machines only get in the way. Operating systems currently being developed for use on computers in networks may replace current operating systems like DOS and OS/2. One such product is *Solaris* from SunSoft, which allows a powerful version of UNIX to run on microcomputers from several manufacturers, including IBM.

Microcomputer users can expect to throw away many of their system utility programs as future operating systems and environments build in more of these features and more powerful microcomputer systems make them obsolete. For example, memory management utility programs will not be needed as newer versions of operating systems, such as DOS 5.0, remove the RAM memory limitations of earlier versions. The Apple Macintosh System 7.0 also incorporates many new features, including ones that were formerly available only in system utility programs.

REVIEW QUESTIONS

1. What are the three main functions of system software?
2. What is firmware?
3. What two functions are included in system start-up?
4. What does the BIOS do?
5. What does an operating system do?
6. What are the three basic components of a microcomputer operating system?
7. What do operating system utilities do?
8. What is a user interface?
9. Name the three types of user interface. Describe each type.
10. What are the two main disadvantages of command line user interfaces?
11. What are three types of menu interface?
12. Why are graphical user interfaces becoming so popular?
13. What does an operating environment do?
14. List three advantages of DOS.
15. Why was the OS/2 operating system developed?
16. What are two disadvantages of OS/2?
17. What are the two key design aspects of Apple Computer's System and Finder?
18. What are the names of the versions of UNIX developed for the Apple and IBM and compatible microcomputers?
19. What is the main disadvantage of UNIX?
20. What do system utility programs provide?
21. What are freeware and shareware?
22. What are TSRs and desk accessories?
23. Why have memory management programs been developed for microcomputers using DOS?
24. Why are file recovery utility programs so important?

25. What is a computer virus, and how can your microcomputer become infected?
26. What is the purpose of a screen saver utility?

TOPICS FOR RESEARCH AND DISCUSSION

1. Virus protection utilities are becoming increasingly important in business today. Computer viruses are a major issue in microcomputing because of the huge problems they can cause.

   What do you think about computer viruses? Do you make a distinction between viruses that are meant to do harm and those that aren't?

2. Imagine you are responsible for a small office that uses IBM AT microcomputers with Microsoft's DOS operating system. You have been asked to review system utility programs to increase office productivity and to decide what type of system utility programs the office needs. From the highest priority to the lowest priority, make a list of the types of system utility programs you would buy. If you need to obtain more information about any system utility programs, look at some recent issues of computer magazines such as *BYTE* or *PC Magazine* for descriptions and reviews of these programs. Write a brief explanation of your choices.

3. Research recent articles in computer magazines about the future trends in operating systems and environments. Look for developments from IBM, Apple, and Microsoft, and for changes to UNIX, DOS, OS/2, and the Macintosh System and Finder. Write a description of the trends you find and your thoughts on what they mean for microcomputer users in the future.

CHAPTER 7

WORD PROCESSORS

OBJECTIVES

The information in this chapter will enable you to

- Understand what a word processor is and the advantages of using a word processor rather than a typewriter.
- Explain the basic and advanced functions of word processors.
- Discuss, in general terms, word processors for IBM-compatible and Macintosh computers.
- Name and discuss three popular word processors for IBM-compatible computers and three for Macintosh.
- List and describe at least four kinds of utility software you can use with word processors.
- Discuss the future of word processing.

System software performs housekeeping tasks for a computer system. For managing projects and for business tasks such as preparing budgets, reports, and correspondence, application software is used. One kind of application software found in almost all businesses is a word processor. Most office workers need to use word processors occasionally or regularly.

What Is a Word Processor?

A Word Processor Automates Typing and Other Tasks Involved in Preparing Documents.

A *word processor* is software for producing documents that consist mainly of text, such as letters, memos, and reports. You may have heard of some popular word processing programs, such as *WordPerfect, Microsoft Word, WordStar,* or *MacWrite.* However, many other word processors are available for business and home use.

Before desktop computers became commonplace, word processing was done on *dedicated word processors,* which are computers with no other purpose. Today, most businesses do their word processing on microcomputers they can also use for other tasks, such as accounting and project management.

To people who have switched to word processors from typewriters, word processing is a miraculous advance. Word processing greatly reduces the amount of repetitive work you must do and vastly simplifies the process of correcting and revising text.

For example, suppose you are writing a report. You are on page 3 when you realize that the paragraph you just typed should be on page 1. How much trouble is it to move the paragraph? With a typewriter, you must retype everything you have written so far. But with a word processor, a few keystrokes will relocate the paragraph.

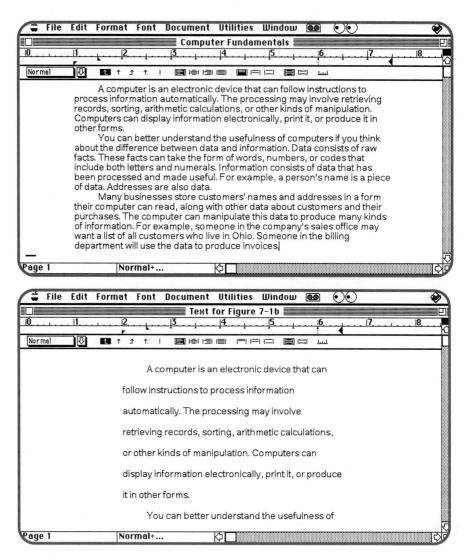

FIGURE 7-1

Using simple commands with a word processor, you can experiment with a document's margins and line spacing until it looks the way you want it to look. Changing the margins or spacing takes only seconds.

A word processor also enables you to use the same text in many documents without keying it. In a matter of seconds, you can change a document's margins or spacing (Figure 7-1). You can also use the word processor to find and correct spelling mistakes. Because of these and other advantages, word processors have almost replaced typewriters in the business world.

Basic Functions

Using Only the Basic Functions of a Word Processor, You Can Enter, Insert, and Delete Text; Move Blocks of Text; Search for a Specific Phrase and Replace It Automatically; and Format, Store, and Print Documents.

Word processors vary in the additional features they offer, but virtually all have the same basic functions for entering text and editing, formatting, and printing documents.

TEXT ENTRY

When you use a word processor, text appears on the computer screen as you use the keyboard. A spot of light called a *cursor* marks your working position on the screen. The cursor may appear as an underline, a square, or a rectangle. The shape of the cursor, and whether it flashes so you can spot it quickly, depends on the software you are using. With some word processors, you can choose the cursor's shape and whether it flashes.

As you key in data, text appears on the screen and enters the computer's random access memory (RAM). That is why keying in text with a word processor is often called *text entry*. Text entry resembles typing so much that if you can type, you can quickly learn to enter text. However, there are a few differences.

Word Wrap

A feature called *word wrap* is one reason word processors are much more efficient than typewriters. With a typewriter, you must use the Carriage Return key to go from the end of one line to the beginning of the next. A word processor does this automatically. If the word you are entering cannot fit on the line, the word processor moves it to the next line.

The word wrap feature also adjusts line lengths when you make changes. Suppose you delete several words from the second line of a long paragraph. Instantly the word processor pulls up as many words as necessary from the next line to even out the line length. Then it does the same thing to the rest of the lines in the paragraph, as shown in Figure 7-2.

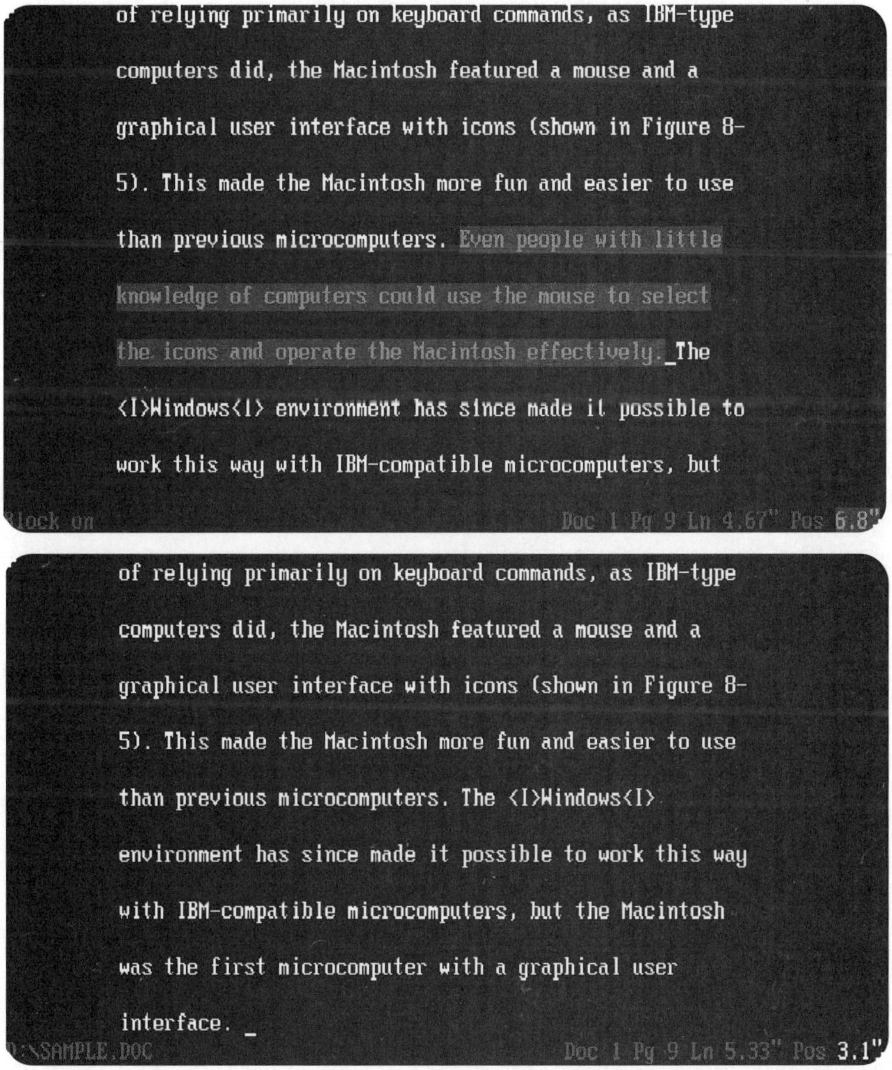

```
of relying primarily on keyboard commands, as IBM-type

computers did, the Macintosh featured a mouse and a

graphical user interface with icons (shown in Figure 8-

5). This made the Macintosh more fun and easier to use

than previous microcomputers. Even people with little

knowledge of computers could use the mouse to select

the icons and operate the Macintosh effectively. _The

<I>Windows<I> environment has since made it possible to

work this way with IBM-compatible microcomputers, but

Block on                          Doc 1 Pg 9 Ln 4.67" Pos 6.8"
```

```
of relying primarily on keyboard commands, as IBM-type

computers did, the Macintosh featured a mouse and a

graphical user interface with icons (shown in Figure 8-

5). This made the Macintosh more fun and easier to use

than previous microcomputers. The <I>Windows<I>

environment has since made it possible to work this way

with IBM-compatible microcomputers, but the Macintosh

was the first microcomputer with a graphical user

interface. _

C:\SAMPLE.DOC                     Doc 1 Pg 9 Ln 5.33" Pos 3.1"
```

FIGURE 7-2

When the text highlighted on the screen at top is deleted, the word processor automatically adjusts the document's line lengths to accommodate the change. The screen at the bottom shows the result.

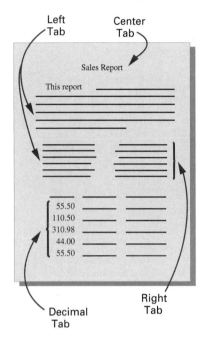

FIGURE 7-3

This document contains sections of text aligned at four kinds of tab settings: left, center, right, and decimal tabs. Setting tabs with a word processor is faster than with a typewriter.

Scrolling

With a word processor, text appears on the computer screen as you enter it. What do you do when you have filled the screen but there's still more text to enter? You just keep right on entering it. The text at the top moves off the screen to make room for the next line you enter, but it stays in the computer's random access memory. This is called *scrolling.* If a sentence you want to read no longer appears on the screen, you can scroll to it by pressing the appropriate key.

Enter (Return) Key

Most computer keyboards have an *Enter* or *Return* key, which moves the cursor to the beginning of the next line. Because of word wrap, you don't press the Enter key at the end of each line. But you do need to press it at the end of each paragraph, to start your next paragraph at the left margin. You also press the Enter key to create a blank line after a heading or between paragraphs. Some word processors also use the Enter key for carrying out other commands.

Tabs

Computers have *Tab keys*; hit the Tab key and the cursor moves a preset distance. Most word processors allow you to set several kinds of tabs. In addition to tabs for aligning indented text on the left, like the tabs on a typewriter, you can set tabs for centering text, aligning it on the right, or aligning it around a decimal point. Figure 7-3 illustrates left, center, right, and decimal tabs.

Suppose you are preparing a document that includes a table with several columns of numbers. You want to align the decimal points in the columns so the table is easier to read. You can set tabs at the decimal points with a typewriter or a word processor. With the typewriter, it's a lot of work. A word processor lines up the decimal points automatically, so there's no need to backspace. This can save a lot of time if you are entering a large statistical table.

INSERTING AND DELETING TEXT

Have you ever typed a letter on a typewriter and then discovered that you left out a word? If so, you know how frustrating it is to retype an entire letter just to insert one word. But with a word processor, inserting a word—or any amount of text—requires only these few steps:

- Position the cursor where you want to insert the text.
- Press the Insert (Ins) key if the computer's insert feature is not already turned on.
- Enter the text you want to insert.

The word processor, using its word wrap feature, adjusts the remainder of the document to accommodate the text you inserted.

Deleting text is just as easy. You can do it in any of these ways:

- Move the cursor to the text you want to delete; then press the Delete (Del) key until the text is deleted.
- Move to the character or space immediately after the text you want to delete; then press the Backspace key until the text is deleted.
- Move the cursor to the text you wish to delete and press the appropriate key, which will delete either the rest of the sentence or the rest of the page.

If only a few words are deleted, the word processor adjusts the line lengths in the rest of the paragraph. Most word processors also adjust the page lengths in the rest of the document if necessary. With many word processors, you can restore deleted text if you change your mind.

BLOCK MOVES

What if you want to move a couple of paragraphs of text to another place in the document? With a word processor, that's easy too, using a procedure that's called a *block move* or *cut and paste*. First, you highlight the block of text you want to move. Then you move the cursor to where you want to put the highlighted text, and you press another key or a key combination. The word processor "cuts" the highlighted text from its first location and "pastes" it in the new location (Figure 7-4).

You use a similar procedure to copy text from one location to another, so that the text appears in both places. With many word processors, you can display two documents on the screen at once, and you can move or copy text from one document into the other. For example, suppose document 1 and document 2 are both on the screen. Document 1 contains a paragraph that you want to add to document 2. Mark the paragraph in document 1, move the cursor to the point where you want it to appear in document 2, and press the key for copying the marked paragraph. The word processor adds the paragraph to the second document without deleting it from the first.

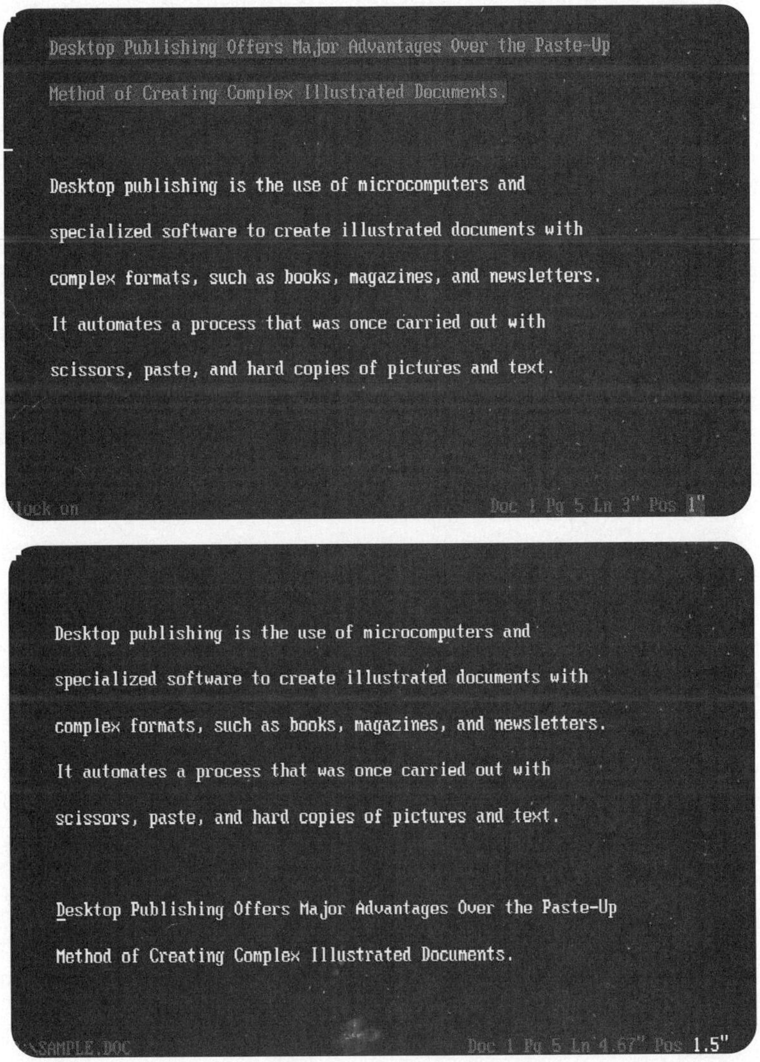

FIGURE 7-4

With a word processor, you can highlight a block of text, as shown at the top, and then move it to a new location in the document (bottom).

SEARCH AND REPLACE

Suppose you use the name "McNeil" throughout a long document and then you discover that the correct spelling is "MacNeil." You must read every page carefully to find each misspelling, right? Not if you're using a word processor. Word processors have a feature called *search and replace.* If you specify the misspelling and the correct spelling, the word processor replaces every instance of the misspelling with the correct spelling. You can confirm each replacement, if you want to, or you can allow the word processor to make all the changes automatically.

You can also search for words, names, or phrases without replacing them. Let's say you want to check a paragraph that contains the phrase "size 10D shoes," but you don't remember the paragraph's location in the document. When you specify the phrase using the search feature, the word processor moves the cursor instantly to the first place where the phrase appears. If that's not the right paragraph, you can press a key to find the next place where the phrase appears.

FORMATTING

A word processor allows you to experiment with a document's format without rekeying. For example, suppose you've used double-spacing and you want to see how the document looks single-spaced. With a word processor, you can switch to single-spacing with a keystroke or two. If you don't like the way the document looks, you can switch back to double-spacing. You can change the margin settings and tab settings, too. You can also experiment with justifying lines, which spaces the words so that all lines (except the final lines of paragraphs) are the same length.

Formatting features vary from one word processor to the next, but these additional options are found in most popular word processors.

- Preventing widows and orphans. A *widow* is the last line of a paragraph that appears at the beginning of a page, separated from the rest of the paragraph. Similarly, an *orphan* is the first line of a paragraph that appears at the end of a page. Figure 7-5 shows a widow and an orphan.

- Using headers and footers. A *header* is text that appears at the top of every page. A *footer* is text that appears at the bottom of every page. For example, you might write a header or footer that includes a report's title and date. Headers and footers are shown in Figure 7-6.

FIGURE 7-5

This document starts with a widow and ends with an orphan. A widow is the last line of a paragraph that appears alone, and an orphan is the first line of a paragraph that appears alone.

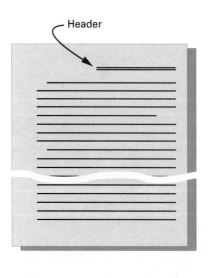
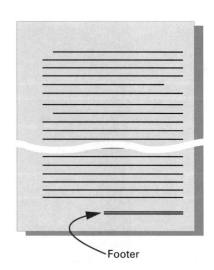

FIGURE 7-6

A header appears at the top of a page. A footer appears at the bottom of a page. Headers and footers usually contain information that identifies documents, such as titles, descriptions, and dates.

- Numbering pages. You can set word processors to number pages automatically or omit page numbers. With some word processors, you can use Roman numerals or regular numbers.

SAVING DOCUMENTS

When you create a document with a word processor, you may save your work on a disk. You can then retrieve the document at any time to edit it, print it, or send it through electronic mail.

With a word processor, you should save your work at regular intervals, such as every five minutes, not just when you finish it. This is also true of many other applications. If the computer is turned off by accident or if you lose power, you won't lose the work you've saved.

You can also save different versions of a document under different names. For example, if you want to change a document without destroying the original version, you can save the original version and the experimental version under different names.

PRINTING

With a word processor, you don't have to print a document until you're satisfied with its content and appearance. You can usually specify the number of copies you want to print. You can print the whole document or specific pages. If your computer system includes several printers, you can tell the word processor which printer to use.

Word processors give you control over the printer. For example, you can cancel printing or interrupt it temporarily if the printer is needed urgently for another document. A word processor generally prints documents in the order that you specify them. However, most word processors allow you to change the priority of a document, so that, for example, the printer produces the seventh document on its job list before it prints the second one.

Advanced Features

With a Word Processor's Advanced Features, You Can Reuse Document Formats and Text, Automate Mass Mailings and Other Repetitive Tasks, and Do Arithmetic.

Even if you use only their basic features, word processors offer much greater efficiency and versatility than typewriters. However, most word processors used in business have sophisticated features that provide still more advantages.

STYLE SHEETS

Suppose you produce monthly sales reports that all have the same complicated format, with tables that break down sales totals by product, region, and salesperson. With a word processor, you can set up the format once and save the format as a *style sheet*. You can then reuse it every month. There's no need to repeat the lengthy procedure of setting the margins and tabs, creating headers and footers, and specifying other format options each time.

You can create style sheets for parts of documents, too. Let's say you use tables of regional sales totals for various product lines. The tables are identical in format, but they have different product headings. You can create a single style sheet and use it for all of these tables, simply by inserting new product headings and sales figures.

MAIL MERGE

Business word processors have *mail merge* features that automate mass mailings of form letters. The procedure depends on the word processor you are using, but usually it includes these steps:

1. Create a shell document that includes the body of the form letter and spaces for names, addresses, greetings, and other individual elements.
2. Create a mailing list that includes all the individual information for each addressee.
3. Merge the shell document with the mailing list. Figure 7-7 illustrates the process.

You can create any number of shell documents and any number of mailing lists, and you can reuse them. For example, you can use the same mailing list for each edition of a newsletter. Or you can send a form letter to people on one mailing list this month, people on another mailing list next month, and so forth.

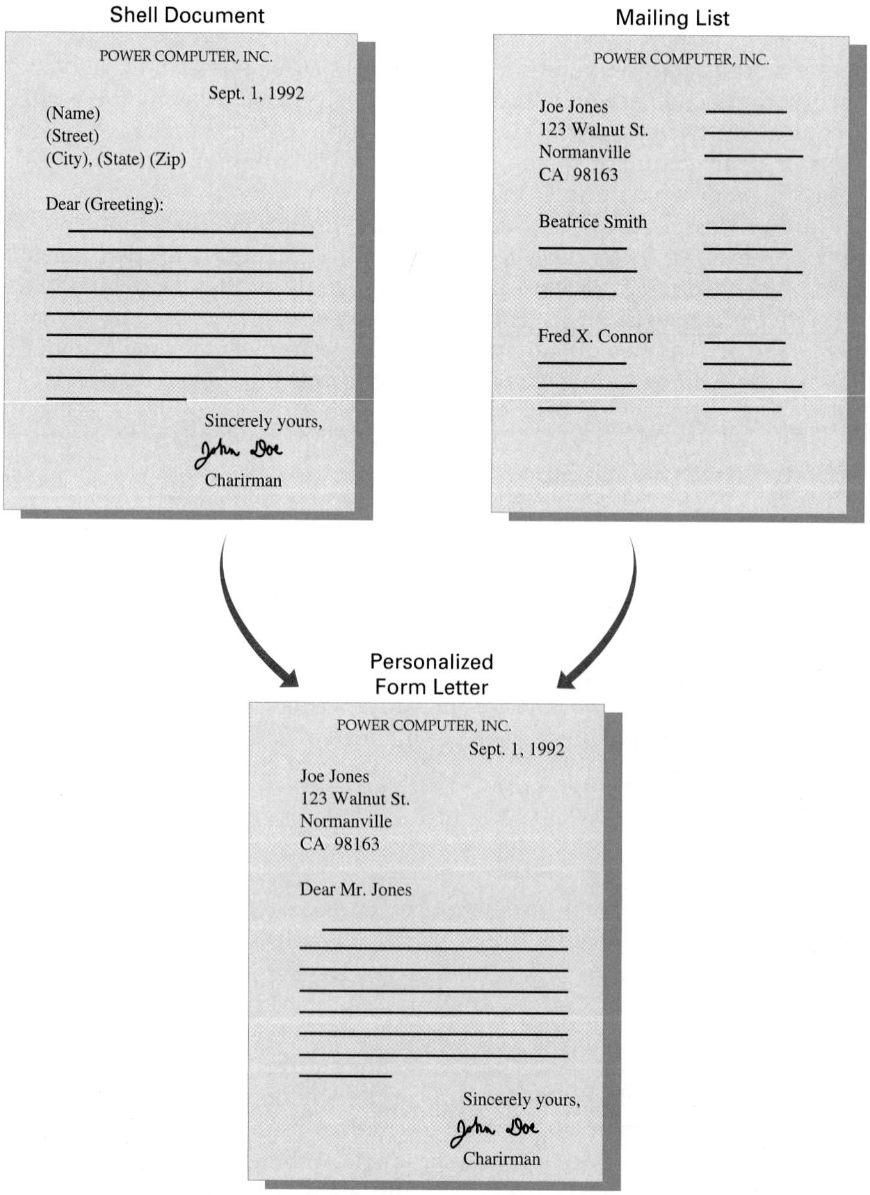

FIGURE 7-7

To produce a mass mailing with a document, you create a shell document with blanks for individual information. Then you create a mailing list that contains the individual information. Finally, you merge the shell and the mailing list to produce personalized letters.

LIBRARIES

With any word processor, you can maintain libraries of text that you can use in many documents. Suppose your company includes a standard description of its business in all news releases. Saving this description in a library enables you to retrieve it whenever you prepare a news release.

You can also include entire documents in a library and then customize them as needed. Many law firms, for instance, maintain libraries of forms for routine legal documents, such as leases and different kinds of affidavits. Suppose a secretary at one of these firms is preparing a lease for a client. The secretary uses a word processor to retrieve the lease form from the library, then adds the client's name, the start and end dates, and other information to customize the lease. The secretary saves the customized lease under a different name from the form's name so that the form remains unchanged. Keeping the form in the library does away with the need for repeatedly entering the pages of routine text, called *boilerplate*, that appear in all leases.

MACROS

A *macro* is a series of keystrokes that you record and play back to simplify a repetitive task. A macro may include dozens of keystrokes, but playing back a macro generally requires only a few. You can create macros with most word processors used in business. Many people record macros for operations such as these:

- Entering names or phrases used in many documents
- Adding a routine closing to letters
- Saving and printing documents
- Retrieving forms from a library and customizing them

For example, suppose you have a memo form in your library. With a typical word processor, you might retrieve the form by pressing a command key sequence, entering the form's name—including the directory where it is stored—and then pressing the Enter key. While this procedure is much faster than typing the same heading for every memo you write, it can still involve two dozen keystrokes. However, you can record these keystrokes in a macro.

Depending on the word processor you use, you might name the macro or assign it a key combination. The key combination might include the Alt key, which is used only in combination with other keys to give them additional functions. Pressing the M key by itself just enters the letter "M," and pressing the Alt key by itself has no effect with most word processors. But if you assign the Alt-M key combination to a macro, you can press the Alt and M keys together to replay the macro. If you have assigned the macro a name rather than a key combination, you can replay it by pressing a command key and then specifying the name.

MATH FUNCTIONS

Word processors used in business generally include math features. You can, for example, use the math feature in *WordPerfect* to total or average a column or row of numbers in a table, and you can enter formulas for making calculations that include multiplication and other math operations. With *WordStar* and some other word processors, you can display and use a calculator on the screen while working with a document. The *WordStar* calculator can find square roots and perform other sophisticated math operations.

Word Processors

Many Powerful Word Processors Are Available for Both IBM-Compatible and Macintosh Computers.

In the early 1980s, when desktop computing was just catching on, few word processors were available. Today, you can choose from dozens of word processors. These products differ in their features, ease of use, and the computers on which they run. Various word processors are available for both IBM-compatible and Macintosh computers.

IBM-COMPATIBLE WORD PROCESSORS

Until recently, nearly all businesses that used desktop computers for word processing used IBM-compatible machines with the DOS operating system. But since the Windows graphical user interface for these computers caught on in 1990, more and more word processors for Windows have been appearing on the market. Even non-Windows word processors now feature graphical user interfaces that make them resemble Windows and Macintosh products.

With a Windows word processor, you can run other applications, such as accounting or project management programs, at the same time. This gives you capabilities you don't have in a non-Windows environment. For example, you can use an accounting program to experiment with budget figures and use the word processor to write a report on them at the same time.

There is one important difference between DOS and Windows word processors: with most DOS word processors, you use a keyboard to enter commands as well as text. With Windows word processors, you still use the keyboard for text entry, but you use the mouse to make selections from lists of options. You also use the mouse for other tasks, such as highlighting, moving, and copying blocks of text.

WordPerfect

No single word processor dominated the business world until the mid-1980s. Then *WordPerfect* became the leader and has held that position for several years.

WordPerfect was developed for use with DOS and the keyboard. In 1989, its developers released versions 5.0 and 5.1, which can also be used with a mouse. A Windows version of *WordPerfect* appeared in 1991.

Microsoft Word

The first several versions of *Microsoft Word* were designed to work with DOS, which wasn't surprising. Microsoft, the company that sells the word processor, also sells DOS. In 1990, Microsoft introduced *Word for Windows*. For more than a year, it was the only major word processor designed for Microsoft's popular new Windows. Figures 7-8 and 7-9 show editing screens from *Word* for DOS and *Word for Windows*.

WordStar

In 1981, soon after the IBM Personal Computer (PC) came on the market, the MicroPro Corporation introduced a version of *WordStar* word processor to run on it. *WordStar* was originally designed for the Apple II microcomputer,

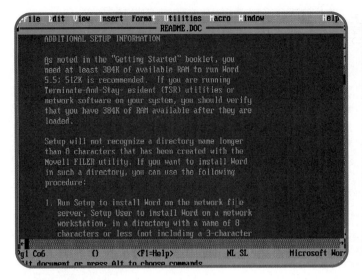

FIGURE 7-8

Word for DOS is different from *Word for Windows,* shown in Figure 7-9. Among other things, *Word* for DOS does not assume that you are using a mouse.

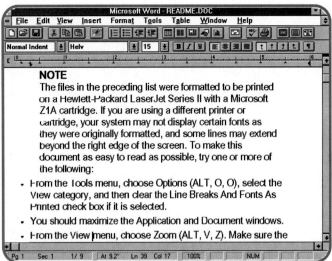

FIGURE 7-9

Word for Windows editing screens contains graphic objects, such as scroll bars and menu items, that you select with a mouse.

introduced in 1979. At first, *WordStar* was the only major commercial word processor available for the IBM PC. Perhaps because it was the first widely used word processor, it remained popular through the early 1980s.

In the mid-1980s, *WordStar* began losing ground to other word processors that most people found easier to use. The newer word processors include *Word* and *WordPerfect.* However, more recent versions of *WordStar* are easier to use, and many people still prefer it.

MACINTOSH WORD PROCESSORS

The success of the Macintosh computer is based primarily on its graphics capabilities. Artists, designers, desktop publishers, and others concerned primarily with graphics have long preferred Macintosh to IBM-compatible computers. As Macintosh computers have spread throughout the business world, however, Macintosh versions of several popular word processors have become available.

Microsoft Word

Microsoft originally developed its *Word* software for IBM-compatible computers, but in the mid-1980s it created a Macintosh version of this software. Like the Windows-based word processors that came after it, *Word* for the Macintosh is designed for use with a mouse as well as a keyboard.

MacWrite

Most major word processors that run on the Macintosh were originally written for IBM-compatible machines and then adapted for the Macintosh. One word processor designed solely for the Macintosh is *MacWrite.* As with other word processors for the Macintosh and IBM Windows, a *MacWrite* user enters text with the keyboard but uses the mouse for tasks such as selecting options. Figure 7-10 shows a *MacWrite* editing screen.

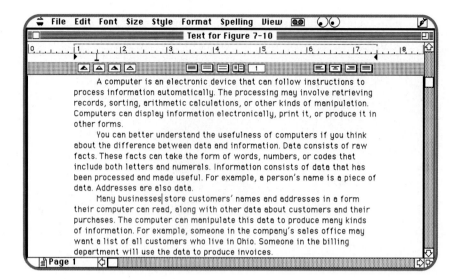

File Edit Font Size Style Format Spelling View

Text for Figure 7-10

A computer is an electronic device that can follow instructions to process information automatically. The processing may involve retrieving records, sorting, arithmetic calculations, or other kinds of manipulation. Computers can display information electronically, print it, or produce it in other forms.

You can better understand the usefulness of computers if you think about the difference between data and information. Data consists of raw facts. These facts can take the form of words, numbers, or codes that include both letters and numerals. Information consists of data that has been processed and made useful. For example, a person's name is a piece of data. Addresses are also data.

Many businesses store customers' names and addresses in a form their computer can read, along with other data about customers and their purchases. The computer can manipulate this data to produce many kinds of information. For example, someone in the company's sales office may want a list of all customers who live in Ohio. Someone in the billing department will use the data to produce invoices.

Page 1

FIGURE 7-10

This editing screen is from *MacWrite,* which was the first word processor designed exclusively for use with the Macintosh computer.

WordPerfect

When *WordPerfect 2.0* for the Macintosh became available in 1991, it immediately caught the attention of businesses that use the Macintosh. (The WordPerfect Corporation assigns different version numbers to its Macintosh and IBM-compatible word processors. *WordPerfect 2.0* for the Macintosh was released after *WordPerfect 5.1* for IBM-compatible computers.) According to reviewers, *WordPerfect 2.0* has more powerful formatting and style sheet features than other Macintosh word processors, including the previous version of *WordPerfect.*

One reason for the immediate interest in *WordPerfect 2.0* is its compatibility with *WordPerfect* for IBM-type computers. Many businesses that use Macintosh computers for some tasks use *WordPerfect* on IBM-compatible machines as their standard word processor. With the introduction of *WordPerfect 2.0,* they can now work with the same document on both computers.

Special-Purpose Utilities

You Can Use Utilities That Work with Word Processors to Enhance the Quality of Your Documents.

All major word processors include utilities that you can use to check documents for spelling errors. Other utilities are also available for word processors.

DICTIONARIES

A word processor's spelling-check utility checks the words in a document against a dictionary stored on a disk. The spelling checker points out each spelling it does not find in the dictionary. With most word processors, you can then correct the spelling, add the spelling to the dictionary, or ignore the word and go on to the next one, as shown in Figure 7-11.

Spelling checkers are useful tools for proofreading documents. However, it is also important to proofread them yourself, because most spelling checkers highlight only words that are not in the dictionary. They do not highlight words that appear in the dictionary but are used incorrectly in the document. For example, if you enter "their" when you mean to enter "there," a spelling checker will not catch the error.

```
illustrated documents ready for printing. This need led to

the development of publishing from your dask, called desktop

publishing. Desktop publishing software programs, like word

processors, are offering more features and power all the

                              Doc 1 Pg 7 Ln 5.33" Pos 5.5"
{   ▲   ▲   ▲   ▲   ▲   ▲   ▲   ▲   ▲   ▲   }

  A. dank          B. dark          C. dash
  D. desk          E. disk          F. dusk
  G. ask           H. desks         I. disc
  J. discs         K. disks         L. dusks




 ot Found: 1 Skip Once; 2 Skip; 3 Add; 4 Edit; 5 Look Up; 6 Ignore Numbers: 0
```

FIGURE 7-11

Dask is not in the *WordPerfect* dictionary, so the software's spelling checker highlights it as an error and lists words that might be the correct spelling. If you press the D key to select *desk* from the list, the program automatically substitutes the correct spelling in the document.

Spelling checkers also highlight correctly spelled words and names that are not in its dictionary. You can save time during spelling checks if you add to the dictionary all words and names that you use often in documents, such as technical terms or proper names that you use frequently.

While each major word processor has a main dictionary built in, you can also buy or build other dictionaries. For example, *WordPerfect* offers dictionaries in French, Catalonian, Dutch, Icelandic, Norwegian, German, Spanish, and Swedish as well as American English.

GRAMMAR CHECKERS

While most spelling checkers don't point out correctly spelled words that might be misused, many grammar checkers do. These utilities also spot other mistakes, such as singular verbs used with plural subjects. They'll even point out ways to make writing more readable. For example, most grammar checkers highlight unusually long sentences and uses of the passive voice, both of which can make writing hard to read.

Like spelling checkers, grammar checkers often highlight text that doesn't need to be changed. As with spelling checkers, you can make corrections or ignore the highlighted words and go on to the next possible problem.

One popular grammar checker is *Grammatik;* another is *RightWriter.*

YOU AND YOUR PERSONAL MICROCOMPUTER

Word processing software is one of the basic requirements of most personal computer users. However, many people do not learn to take advantage of the many features available in their word processing software. They also may not learn how to use their word processing software most effectively. Spend some time with your software to make sure you are making the most of all that it offers.

When selecting your personal computer you should determine what software is included as part of the basic configuration. For example, *Microsoft Works*, which comes with some IBM personal systems, includes word processing, spreadsheet, and database management software. The word processing software includes such features as a spelling checker, thesaurus, and many of the other features described in this chapter.

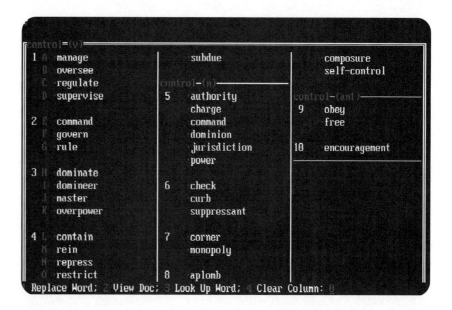

FIGURE 7-12

This display appears on the screen if you use *WordPerfect*'s thesaurus utility to find a synonym for *control.*

THESAURUSES

If you want to use a synonym for the word *control* in a letter you are writing, do you need to pause and pull a reference book off the shelf? Not if your word processor has a thesaurus.

One word processor that has its own thesaurus is *WordPerfect*. To use it, you press a combination of keys and then enter the word you want to look up. Figure 7-12 shows what appears on the screen when you look up the word *control.*

You can buy inexpensive thesaurus programs to use with many word processors. For example, a utility called *Thesaur Plus,* which costs about $20, works with most word processors.

OTHER UTILITIES

In addition to spelling checkers, grammar checkers, and thesauruses, several other utilities can enhance the documents you create with a word processor. Among them are indexing programs and software for converting documents from one word processor to another.

Indexing Programs

One way to index a report is to read it carefully, noting the page number of every appearance of each item you want to include in the index, and then using the word processor to create the text of the index. But what if you add a few paragraphs to the front of the report after you index it? The page numbers will change, and you'll need to find each new location for the terms in the index. With indexing software, you can specify the terms you want to index and let the software find them for you. If the page numbers change, you can run the utility again with the same list of terms and it will correct the page numbers.

Conversion Programs

One problem with word processors has been that each one has its own way of creating documents, and different brands are not compatible with each other. For example, you cannot use *WordPerfect* to edit a *WordStar* document. Conversion utilities can solve this problem.

Some word processors come with built-in conversion utilities. *Word for Windows*, for example, can convert documents to and from *WordPerfect*, *WordStar*, and a number of other word processors. Suppose you create a document with *Word for Windows*, and someone who uses *WordStar* needs to edit your document. Using *Word for Windows*, you can save it on a disk as a *WordStar* document. The *WordStar* user can then retrieve your document and edit it. If you receive a *WordStar* version of the edited document, you can use *Word for Windows* to reconvert the document from *WordStar* so you can·work with it again.

Some major word processors, however, can't convert documents. This accounts for the success of software products that do only conversions.

SOFTWARE PIRATES BEWARE

Did your company pay for the word processing software you work with daily? Sometimes entire companies use unlicensed copies, for which no money was paid. Using unlicensed or "pirated" software is a crime because it violates federal copyright laws. Software companies often spend several years and millions of dollars on research and development before releasing a new program. Software pirates, like their predecessors who plundered ships at sea, deprive software companies of legitimate returns on their investments of time and money.

The job of enforcing software copyright laws has fallen to an arm of the *Software Publishers Association (SPA),* an industry association of major computer software companies. The mission of the "software police," formed in 1979, is to locate companies which, in the words of SPA Executive Director Ken Wasch, "willfully and wantonly use pirated software." Wasch says the SPA is not interested in isolated, individual copying, only in large-scale violations of the software copyright laws. "We reserve hardball tactics for those people who deserve it," says Wasch.

One company that the SPA thought deserved it was the National Business Academy, a software training school in California. An SPA raid found 600 allegedly pirated copies of

software such as *Wordperfect,* worth $250,000, at just one site. The unannounced raid (which was accompanied by a court order), can force a company to close down its operations for several, very expensive days; it is one of the SPA's most extreme weapons. Usually, though, the threat of a lawsuit and possible fines (which can range up to $100,000) is enough.

The SPA learns about possible violations through an 800 hot line number, receiving as many as 20 calls a day. According to Wasch, the SPA investigates all accusations very carefully before proceeding. But two recent disputes have raised serious ethical issues. The SPA failed to win its lawsuits against both Computer Dynamics, Inc. and Snap-On Tools Corporation The CEO of Computer Dynamics, Robert Starer, charged that the SPA had gone too far: "This is a very clear case that an employee gave false information to someone and cost us a lot of money. CDI spent $110,000 to $120,000 to prove its innocence," he charged.

Most callers to the SPA hot line are disgruntled employees or former employees, and that's where the problem lies. What will stop an angry employee, for example, from making a false accusation that results in an expensive investigation and lawsuit? Even more troubling, what if an

angry employee copies software and plants it on a company's computer network? In addition, some employees will illegally copy software despite the best efforts of their company to prevent such abuses.

Although these complex legal and ethical issues are not easily solved, one thing is certain: the rights of software companies and the rights of their customers must both be protected.

The Software Publishers Association is very serious about enforcing the software copyright laws.

Sources: "SPA Set to Raid Business Site," by Michael Fitzgerald, *Computerworld,* November 12, 1990, p. 1. "User Charges SPA Excess," by Kim Nash, *Computerworld,* August 19, 1991, p. 8.

THE MEDIUM AND THE MESSAGE

Does the computer on which you write affect the quality of your writing? A provocative study from the University of Delaware suggests that it just might.

Professor Marcia Halio noticed something odd about the essays that freshman composition students were writing on their computers. There were dramatic differences in the quality of their writing based on what kind of computer they used. Prof. Halio surveyed her colleagues and found that they all reported the same phenomenon: students using Macintosh word processing software (on Macintosh computers) produced essays that "looked good" but were inferior in content, style, and grammar, compared to essays written by students using IBM-based software.

Statistical analysis confirmed her conclusion. Students writing on the Mac made many more grammatical and spelling mistakes, relied more heavily on slang, and wrote in brief paragraphs and short, choppy sentences, which reflected simpler, undeveloped thoughts. Furthermore, students chose strikingly different subjects to write about. Given the task of writing about some social phenomenon, Mac users wrote about "light" subjects, such as fast food, dating, and sports. IBM users wrote about "serious" subjects, such as nuclear war, capital punishment, and drunk driving.

Prof. Halio offers several reasons for this phenomenon. Mac software allows students much more freedom to play with the "look" of the written page. Students can change the type they use easily and see those changes displayed on the screen just as they will appear on the printed page. Prof. Halio argues that the power to make your writing "look good" is important, but it can easily distract writers from what they are writing.

In addition, Prof. Halio thinks that the user-friendly Mac, with its playful mouse, wide margins, cute icons, and large screen print, reminds students of the computer games they played at home. In other words, it reminds them of a toy. She also observed that Macs in the writing lab were nicknamed Happy, Doc, Dopey, Grumpy, and Bashful. IBM users, on the other hand, seem to associate writing on the more intimidating, "computerlike" IBM machines with seriousness of purpose and adult activities.

However, the distinctions Prof. Halio noted are quickly changing. IBM software and hardware is rapidly becoming just as user friendly as the Macintosh's. As all computers become more Maclike, will the quality of writing decline, even as it looks better and better?

Does the computer you use affect your writing?

Source: "Student Writing: Can the Machine Maim the Message?" by Marcia Peoples Halio, *Academic Computing,* January 1990, p.16.

Future Trends

Word Processors Are Becoming More Powerful and Easier to Use with Other Software Applications.

Word processing, once completely separate from other computing tasks, is being integrated with other applications. For instance, more word processors are now including hypertext and desktop publishing features.

HYPERTEXT FEATURES

Hypertext is a software feature that links documents so you can browse through them on the computer screen to find information on a variety of related subjects. For example, say you are reading an article on the New York Mets and decide that you want to read about Dwight Gooden's career with the team. While reading the article about Gooden, you decide you want to see a list of statistics for pitchers in the Baseball Hall of Fame. That may lead you to a diagram illustrating the physics of the curveball or an article on the history of baseball. Hypertext delivers all of these related articles on screen at your request.

Several new word processors include hypertext features that enable you to create the links while you are writing the documents. One of these products, called *TransText 90*, allows you to link text with graphics as well as other text. Another product, *Hyper-Word*, allows text links only.

DESKTOP PUBLISHING FEATURES

Desktop publishing allows microcomputers to develop complex document formats for newsletters, books, and brochures. Software especially designed for desktop publishing has been on the market since 1985. As a rule, people use desktop publishing software to design formats for documents created with word processors. But more word processors are including desktop publishing features.

 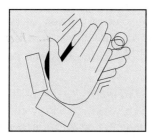  

FIGURE 7-13

WordPerfect comes with dozens of graphics, including these, that you can incorporate into your documents. You can also use graphics from other sources.

With the most recent versions of *WordPerfect*, for example, you can create documents with newspaper-style columns that can wrap around other text or parallel columns that occupy the full length of a page. You can also include pictures in documents. *WordPerfect* even comes with a set of pictures you can use, including those in Figure 7-13.

With most business word processors, you can assign different sizes and styles of type to different parts of a document. You can assign inch-high bold letters for a report's title page, half-inch italic letters for its section headings, and regular letters for its main text. Figure 7-14 shows a document containing these three different type sizes.

Businesses are now using word processors for simple desktop publishing tasks, such as producing newsletters and announcements (Figure 7-15). However, the most sophisticated desktop publishing continues to be done by people using the special-purpose software that is discussed in Chapter 8.

FIGURE 7-14

You can use some word processors to produce documents with different type sizes, like this one.

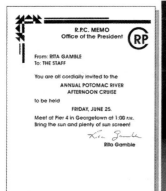 

FIGURE 7-15

You can use a word processor's desktop publishing features to create documents with graphics in relatively simple formats, like the announcement at left. More sophisticated documents, like the brochure on the right, require full-featured desktop publishing software.

REVIEW QUESTIONS

1. What is a word processor?

2. Name three kinds of documents you can produce with a word processor.

3. What is a dedicated word processor?

4. Give three examples of how word processing is more efficient than using a typewriter.

5. What kind of noncomputer work closely resembles text entry?

6. What happens to text when you enter it with a word processor?

7. Describe what word wrap does.

8. What do you do when you have entered enough text to fill the screen but you still have more to enter?

9. When text scrolls off the screen, do you lose your work? Explain your answer. *No*

10. With a word processor, do you press the Enter key at the end of each line? At the end of each paragraph? *L-No P-Yes*

11. How do you create a blank line between paragraphs with a word processor?

12. What kinds of tabs can you set with a word processor that you cannot set with a typewriter?

13. Suppose you enter a sentence and discover that you have left out a word. How do you insert the word with a word processor?

14. Describe two methods of deleting a word with a word processor.

15. What is the difference between moving a block of text and copying a block of text?

16. Give four examples of format changes you can make with a word processor without retyping a document.

17. In word processing, what are headers and footers?

18. What two page-numbering options are available with most word processors?

19. Why should you save your work from time to time as you create a document with a word processor?

20. What is a style sheet? When is it useful?

21. Explain the three basic steps involved in using a word processor to produce a mass mailing of a form letter.

22. What is a word processing library? Give an example of how a library can be useful.

23. What is a macro? Give an example of a macro's usefulness.

24. If you enter *discrete* when you meant to enter *discreet,* will a word processor's spelling checker point out the error? Explain. *No.*

TOPICS FOR RESEARCH AND DISCUSSION

1. How do you think computers and word processors have affected the writing skills of the people who use them? Are people likely to edit and polish their writing more because it is less trouble than with a typewriter? What are the positive and negative effects of utilities such as thesauruses, spelling checkers, and grammar checkers?

2. Suppose you work for a manufacturing company's office that has been using *Word* for word processing. The company has just purchased Windows for all its microcomputers, and you are in charge of recom-

mending a word processor that can run in the Windows environment. In this chapter, you read about some word processors designed to run with Windows. Look in computer magazines to find out about more about these and other Windows-based word processors. Which one would you recommend, and why?

3. Suppose you earn your living by doing word processing in your home using *WordPerfect.* Most of your clients are students, for whom you process term papers, and law firms, for which you process long legal documents. The chapter discussed utilities you can use with word processors, such as grammar checkers and indexers. Go to a software store or check magazine and newspaper advertisements to find out more about these and other kinds of word processing utilities. What are some of the specific products available, and what do they do? What are the differences between some products used for the same purpose, such as one indexing utility and another? What do the utilities cost? Which ones would you buy for your work, and why? What kinds of utilities would you decide not to buy, and why?

CHAPTER 8

DESKTOP PUBLISHING

OBJECTIVES

The information in this chapter will enable you to

- Describe how desktop publishing developed and how it differs from word processing.
- Explain what fonts are and how they are used in desktop publishing.
- Explain the basic desktop publishing process.
- Explain and compare two methods of page composition.
- Name and compare several popular desktop publishing programs for IBM-compatible and Macintosh microcomputers.
- Discuss the points to consider when choosing desktop publishing software.

Word processing software made the process of creating letters and business reports far simpler and more efficient. But what about books, magazines, and other documents with complex formats and illustrations? With a different kind of computer program, called *desktop publishing* software, you can now use a microcomputer to blend text and pictures into high-quality illustrated documents.

What Is Desktop Publishing?

Desktop Publishing Offers Major Advantages Over the Pasteup Method of Creating Complex Illustrated Documents.

Desktop publishing is the use of microcomputers and specialized software to create illustrated documents with complex formats, such as books, magazines, and newsletters. It automates a process that was once carried out with scissors, paste, and hard copies of pictures and text.

Compare a page in a book with a page of a typical business document produced with a word processor (Figure 8-1). As you can see, the book page has a more refined look than the word processor output. In addition to print type, a book has more sophisticated illustrations than those you can produce with a word processor. A book also has a more complex format than most word processor output.

The type in books and magazines looks better than that in most letters and memos because it is *typeset*, which means it is produced by specialized *typesetting machines.* (The operators using typesetting machines are called *compositors.*) These machines can produce hard copy of very high resolution—usually 1270 dots per inch or more—much finer than most laser printers used with microcomputers. A resolution of 1270 dots per inch is four times the resolution of a typical laser printer's output (Figure 8-2).

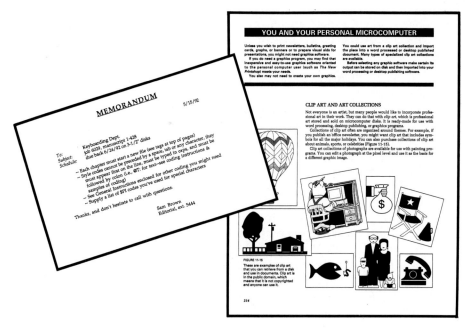

FIGURE 8-1

All documents have formats, but documents you create entirely with a word processor, like the memo at left, usually have simple formats. Book pages, like the one shown on the right, often have photographs or other illustrations as well as several styles of text.

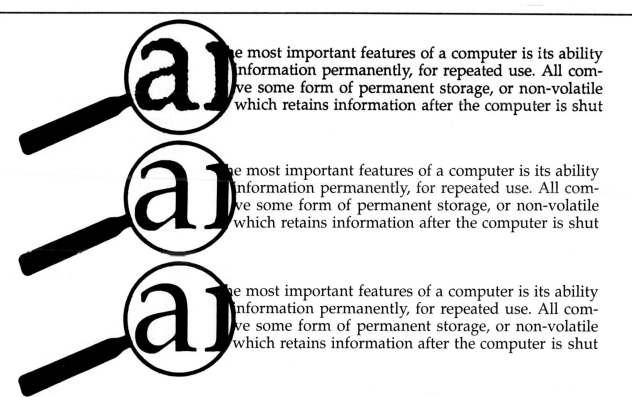

FIGURE 8-2

Output from a typesetting machine can have a resolution of 1270 dots per inch, like the sample in the center, 2540 dots per inch (bottom), or higher. It is much sharper than output from a typical laser printer (top), which has a resolution of 300 dots per inch.

Until a few years ago, creating pages for a book or magazine was a slow, expensive process. The manual pasteup process involved the following steps:

1. A designer determined where the text, headings, and pictures would go on each page.
2. Artists and photographers created the graphics and pictures.
3. Typesetters generated a hard copy of the text.
4. Another specialist, following the designer's plan, cut out the pictures and the text and pasted them onto cardboard to create a model of each

page, called a *mechanical.* The mechanicals were photographed and the negatives used to create metal plates for printing the pages.

Even if the text had been written with a word processor, the typesetter had to enter it, character by character, into the typesetting machine. Corrections to typeset text were time consuming and expensive. Deleting a word near the beginning of a paragraph meant that the typesetter would have to adjust every line in the paragraph by hand. If the deletion reduced the number of lines in the paragraph, the mechanical for the whole page (and perhaps additional pages) might need to be taken apart and pasted together again. A change that shortened or lengthened a paragraph by more than a couple of lines might require adjustments in the mechanicals for a whole chapter or section. Making a change in an illustration could be even more complicated. Last minute revisions could easily keep businesses from meeting their deadlines or staying within their publication budgets.

To offset costs and shorten production cycles, businesses had to find a faster, easier, and cheaper way to get illustrated documents ready for printing. This need led to the development of desktop publishing. Desktop publishing software programs, like word processors, are offering more features and power all the time. From the beginning, however, desktop publishing provided these enormous advantages over the old-fashioned pasteup method of laying out pages:

- It saves time and gives more control over the publishing schedule. You don't have to wait for hard copy from a typesetting shop before you begin combining text and graphics on pages.

- Laying out pages electronically gives you much more flexibility than pasting illustrations and text onto a board. For example, you can move an illustration, change its size, or make the text flow around it, all on the screen. Similarly, you can change the size or look of a headline or any other element on the page.

- You can see a document as you create and revise it. Because you can make changes on the screen without waiting for hard copies, there's no need for repetitive printing or typesetting.

- Desktop publishing software enables one person to do work that once required specialists in typesetting, illustration, and page layout as well as word processing.

- After laying out pages, you can print them in seconds with a laser printer or typesetting machine. As Figure 8-3 shows, these pages can be just as attractive as pages laid out with the pasteup method.

Desktop publishing arrived on the scene in the mid-1980s, with three groundbreaking products: the Apple Macintosh microcomputer, Aldus *PageMaker* software, and the *PostScript* page description language.

FIGURE 8-3

A typeset document laid out with desktop publishing software (left) is of the same high quality as one pasted up by hand (right). It may even be superior because it is less likely to contain misaligned text or smudges.

Unlike IBM-compatible microcomputers, the Macintosh's design is based on graphics rather than text. Instead of relying primarily on keyboard commands, as IBM-type computers did, the Macintosh featured a mouse and a graphical user interface with icons (shown in Figure 8-4). This made the Macintosh more fun and easier to use than previous microcomputers. Even people with little knowledge of computers could use the mouse to select the icons and operate the Macintosh effectively. The Windows environment has since made it possible to work this way with IBM-compatible microcomputers, but the Macintosh was the first microcomputer with a graphical user interface.

Besides being easier to use, the Macintosh could display on its monitor an accurate view of how text and graphics would look together on paper. The Macintosh was one of the first microcomputers to feature WYSIWYG (wiz-ee-wig), which stands for "What You See Is What You Get."

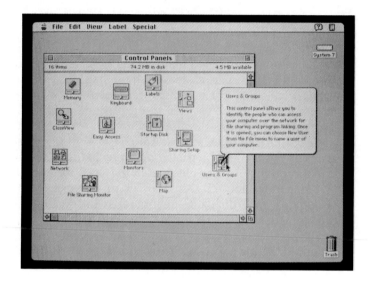

FIGURE 8-4

The Macintosh was the first microcomputer with a graphical user interface, which is well suited to desktop publishing. IBM-compatible computers can also be set up with graphical user interfaces today.

PAGEMAKER

To take advantage of the Macintosh's features, the Aldus Corporation developed a software program called *PageMaker.* With *PageMaker,* you can design a typeset-quality format that combines computerized graphics and text, and you can revise the format quickly. You can make as many revisions as necessary, and you don't have to print hard copies of the text or pages until the document design is final. *PageMaker* was the first widely used desktop publishing software, and at first it could run only on the Macintosh. Today, many desktop publishing programs are available for use on IBM-compatible computers as well as the Macintosh.

POSTSCRIPT

A special type of programming language called *PostScript,* which the Adobe Corporation created, enabled desktop publishing software to communicate efficiently with printers. *PostScript* is a *page description language,* which means that it tells the printer to reproduce a page exactly as it appears on the screen. (For this reason, page description languages are sometimes called *printer languages.*) Without a page description language, a printer uses one format for text and another for illustrations. This limits your ability to use text and graphics on a page. But *PostScript* treats the entire page as a single

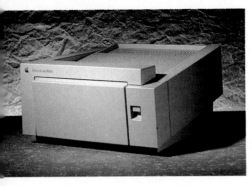

picture. You can refine the "picture" on the screen in minute detail, then print it as displayed.

The Apple LaserWriter (Figure 8-5) was the first *PostScript* printer, and it could not work with an IBM-compatible computer. But *PostScript* was soon available for many printers and typesetting devices. Now, nearly all desktop publishing programs can create instructions in *PostScript*. As a result, *PostScript* has become a sort of universal language for communication among many kinds of publishing software and hardware, including typesetting machines that produce the highest quality output. Now other companies have also developed page description languages. For example, Hewlett-Packard's Printer Command Language (PCL) is used by all the popular LaserJet printers.

Desktop Publishing versus Word Processing

Word Processors Now Offer Some Desktop Publishing Features, But Desktop Publishing Programs Have More Formatting Power.

Word processing automated many of the steps required to format relatively simple documents such as letters, term papers, and business proposals. However, for laying out an illustrated document with a complex format, such as a booklet or newsletter, word processing offered little help before desktop publishing was developed. Just like typewritten text, a word processor's output had to be entered into a typesetting machine to create hard typeset copy that could be pasted onto mechanicals.

Desktop publishing has eliminated the need for entering the text repeatedly. Using a desktop publishing program, you can retrieve a word processor's output from a disk and combine it with illustrations to create a complex document.

Some word processors now include many features once found only in desktop publishing software. With both *WordPerfect* and *Word,* for example, you can view text and graphics together on the screen as they will look on the printed page. Many companies use only word processors and laser printers to produce documents with a few simple illustrations, such as procedural manuals, departmental reports, and flyers (Figure 8-6).

FIGURE 8-6

Each of these pages was written and laid out using only a word processor.

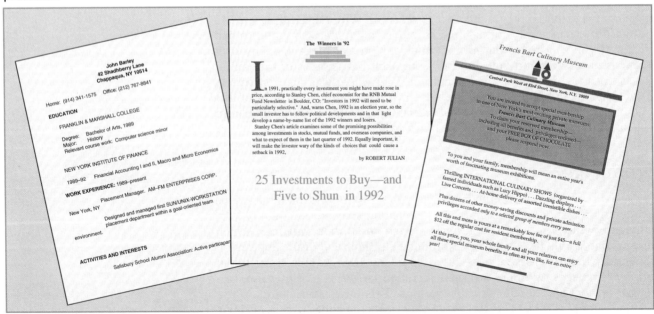

Meanwhile desktop publishing programs have acquired features once found only in expensive typesetting systems. Today's full-featured desktop publishing programs offer far more power than any word processor for manipulating document formats.

The difference between desktop publishers and word processors has narrowed, but these two kinds of software have different primary purposes. You use a word processor to enter and edit text and format simple documents. To combine the text with graphics and make it look as good as possible, you use desktop publishing software. For laying out documents with many illustrations or sophisticated graphic designs, such as brochures, customer newsletters, investor reports, or magazines, you need the extra power of a desktop publishing program. In short, the choice of word processing or desktop publishing software for laying out pages depends on the kind of material you create.

Document Design

Desktop Publishing Requires the Same Design Skills as Traditional Publishing.

Desktop publishing has made it possible for almost anyone with a microcomputer to publish complex documents quickly and inexpensively. However, desktop publishing has automated only the physical process of laying out pages, not the mental process of designing a document. While anyone can produce a document with a desktop publishing program, producing an attractive document requires careful thought about its design.

A good design is appropriate to the purpose of the publication. The style of type you use can help to give the document a casual look or a more formal feeling. In a flyer announcing an office party, you might use large bold headlines in an informal type style. But for a financial report to your company's shareholders, you would use a much more formal approach.

You also need to consider the kinds of information the document will include. A three-column format might be best for a newsletter with several short articles and small illustrations. If it has just one major article and a number of news briefs, however, a format using two columns of different sizes might be better. The design should clearly separate the items from each other and show which ones are most important (Figure 8-7).

FIGURE 8-7

You can use varying headline sizes to show the relative importance of the different pieces of information in a document.

Fonts

With Desktop Publishing Software, You Can Use a Variety of Type Designs from Different Sources.

Desktop publishing software allows you to use a wide variety of type designs. This frees you to create some striking effects as you lay out documents. For example, you can use one style of type for headlines, another for regular text, and a third for captions. Figure 8-8 shows a document with several styles of type on a single page.

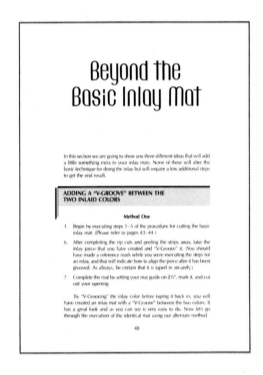

FIGURE 8-8

A variety of type styles can make a page interesting. Too many, however, can make it difficult to read.

WHAT IS A FONT?

A set of characters of a specific design and size is called a *font*. The characters include the letters of the alphabet in upper- and lowercase. They also include numerals, punctuation marks, and other symbols such as dollar signs.

Printed characters are usually measured in points. A *point* is a printer's unit of measurement (Figure 8-9). There are 72 points to an inch.

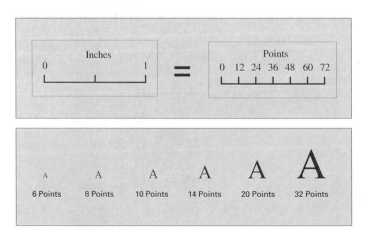

FIGURE 8-9

Printers and typesetting specialists measure type with rulers calibrated in points. A point equals 1/72 inch.

FIGURE 8-10

The typeface on the left is a serif font; the one on the right is a sans serif font.

FIGURE 8-11

The character on the left is printed in Univers; the one on the right is printed in Avant Garde. Both fonts are sans serif, but the characters have different shapes.

FIGURE 8-12

Serif typefaces such as New Century Schoolbook (left) and Palatino (right) use different ornamental details.

The design of a font is called a *typeface.* Although each typeface is unique, typefaces fall into two general categories: *serif* and *sans serif.* Characters in serif typefaces have decorative details; sans serif characters are plainer (Figure 8-10).

Sans serif typefaces differ from each other in their general shape, width, and line thickness. Figure 8-11 gives examples of different sans serif typefaces.

Serif typefaces differ from each other in their decorative details as well as in their shape and dimensions. Figure 8-12 gives examples of different serif typefaces.

Traditionally, a font has been designated by both a point size and the name of its typeface. For example, Figure 8-13 shows a complete 12-point Times Roman font. This terminology is a holdover from before the mid-1960s, when type was generally cast in lead rather than formed on pages with photographic processes. At that time, the person designing a document had to decide in advance on both the typefaces and type sizes for all text in the document. If the design called for 36-point Times Roman headings and 12-point Times Roman text, the typesetter had to set up the equipment differently to produce each size of the design.

A B C D E F G H I J K L M N
O P Q R S T U V W X Y Z

a b c d e f g h i j k l m n
o p q r s t u v w x y z

1 2 3 4 5 6 7 8 9 10

! @ # $ % ^ & * ( ) _ - + =
{ } [ ] | \ : ; " ' < > ? / , .

FIGURE 8-13

A complete font includes all the letters of the alphabet in upper- and lowercase as well as numbers, punctuation marks, and other symbols. This font is 12-point Times Roman.

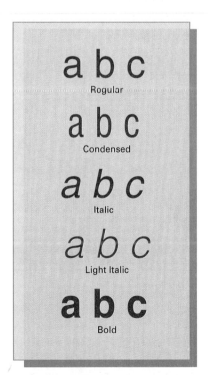

FIGURE 8-14

These are a few of the variations in the Helvetica font family.

With desktop publishing, you can print some typefaces in any size you want. Thus the term *font* is often used in much the same way as *typeface,* to refer to a type design but not necessarily to a specific size.

A *font family* includes all variations on a single font, such as bold, italic, bold-italic, and condensed type. Some font families have more variations than others. Figure 8-14 shows some of the many variations on the Helvetica font.

BITMAPPED FONTS

A *bitmapped font* is one that must be mapped out, one pixel at a time by the monitor and one dot at a time by a printer. A bitmapped font is typically limited to a single size. You must use a different font to print each size of a typeface. For example, you use one font for 14-point Helvetica characters and another font for 24-point Helvetica.

OUTLINE FONTS

Some software and printers today have *outline fonts*, which are not limited to any one size. With an outline font, the outline for a character is stored in the computer's memory and can be enlarged or reduced as needed. For example, you can use an outline Helvetica font to print Helvetica-style characters in 8 point, 24 point, 36 point, or any other size (Figure 8-15).

All outline fonts are *scalable,* that is, characters can be printed in any size. Although some software can enlarge or reduce bitmapped fonts, the results are often unsatisfactory—particularly when the bitmapped type is enlarged. Because of this, many people use the terms *outline fonts* and *scalable fonts* interchangeably.

FIGURE 8-15

You can print a type style in a standard size, such as 36 points (top), or an odd size, such as 15 points (bottom), from a single scalable font. This font is called Helvetica.

Helvetica 36 points

Helvetica 15 points

WHERE ARE FONTS LOCATED?

A desktop publishing program can use fonts from three different sources: resident fonts, cartridge fonts, and soft fonts. Table 8-1 compares fonts based on their location.

Resident Fonts

Resident fonts are built into a printer. They take up little space in the computer's memory, and the printer reproduces them very quickly. Resident

Table 8-1: Font Location

Font Type	Location	Advantages	Disadvantages
Resident Font	Built into printer	Fast; easy to use; conserves printer memory	Limited number available
Cartridge Font	Microchip in a removable printer cartridge	Fast; conveniently grouped with other fonts in families; conserves printer memory	Limited number available
Soft Font	Hard disk	Varied; flexible	Slow; uses lots of printer memory

fonts are typically the easiest to use. However, most printers come with only a few of the most commonly used fonts built in.

Cartridge Fonts

Cartridge fonts are fonts contained on microchips in cartridges that plug into a printer (Figure 8-16). Like resident fonts, they print quickly, and they don't require any of the computer's memory. Installing cartridge fonts is a convenient way to add variety to the resident fonts. Font cartridges often contain families of fonts.

Soft Fonts

Soft fonts are stored on a floppy or hard computer disk and loaded from the disk drive to the printer as needed. This transfer process is sometimes called *downloading,* so soft fonts are sometimes called *downloadable fonts.* Soft fonts provide for a much greater variety of type styles and sizes because many more can be stored on a disk than in a cartridge or printer. However, the downloading process slows down printing.

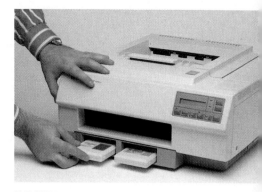

FIGURE 8-16

You can expand the printing capabilities of most laser printers by plugging in font cartridges that contain microchips where font families are stored.

The Desktop Publishing Process

The Desktop Publishing Process Involves Creating a Grid and Adding Text and Pictures to It.

Desktop publishing programs differ in their features and in their approaches to page layout, but they all use a similar process. This process involves creating a grid on the screen that represents the page, then adding text and pictures to the grid.

DESIGNING A GRID

To lay out a document with any desktop publishing program, you begin by designing the document's *grid,* which is the underlying structure of a page in the document. A grid appears on the screen as a set of horizontal and vertical lines that divide the page into areas (Figure 8-17). The lines do not appear when you print the document or preview the printed version on the screen.

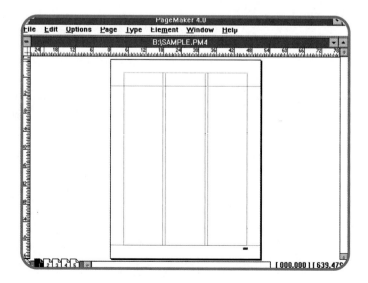

FIGURE 8-17

This grid shows the positions of page numbers and headers. It also indicates the page size for the entire document and the number of columns per page. This grid serves as the unifying design for the document, although each page will have additional formatting details.

Each page of a document will have different text and pictures. The grid shows the placement of design elements that apply to all of its pages. This gives the document a consistent look and feel. For example, imagine a document where page numbers appear at the bottom center of some pages, the top center of others, and the bottom left of still others. You wouldn't know where to look for the page numbers, and the document would be difficult to use. On a grid, you can designate a consistent page number position. You also specify the following unifying elements of the document's design on a grid:

- The page size
- The number of columns per page
- The amount of blank space between lines, paragraphs, and columns
- The margin widths
- The placement of *headers*, which are lines of text to be printed near the top of every page
- The placement of *footers*, which are lines of text to be printed near the bottom of every page

Figure 8-18 shows how a grid applies to different pages of a document.

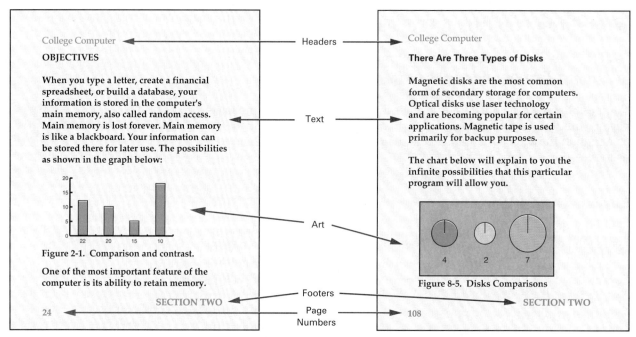

FIGURE 8-18

These pages of the same document have different text and pictures, but they use the same page number positions, page size, and footer. This gives the document a unified look.

USING GRID TEMPLATES

To save time, you can set up grids of the page layouts you use often, then save these grids as *templates*, or *master pages*. For example, you would probably use the same grid for every issue of a newsletter. You can think of a template as a reusable mold. It allows you to use the same document setup many times without repeating the work of creating the grid.

IMPORTING TEXT

Although it's possible to enter and revise text directly on the screen with a desktop publishing program, text entry is faster with a word processor. After saving text on a disk with a word processor, you can *import* the text, or

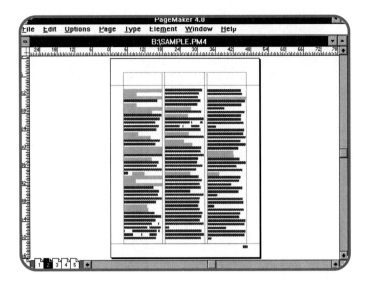

FIGURE 8-19

If a grid calls for three columns per page, imported text fills the columns as it flows onto the page.

transfer it electronically, from the disk to the document you are laying out. Text is generally added to a desktop publishing program by importing it after it is created on a word processor. With most desktop publishing programs, you can import text from several different word processors.

You import the text onto pages after you set up their grid. Like Jell-O taking the shape of its mold, the text flows onto the pages, taking the shape of the grid into which it is poured (Figure 8-19).

IMPORTING GRAPHICS

You can import illustrations into documents from disks in much the same way that you import text. The illustrations can come from various sources. For example, you can import charts or drawings created with graphics software. You can also use photographs or hand-drawn pictures that have been digitized, or converted to a format the computer can read, and stored on disks.

DOCUMENT FILES

You can import text and illustrations into a document from many different word processing and graphics files. The desktop publishing software creates a separate document file that includes all of the text and illustrations.

Full-featured programs also establish links with the original source files, so that any changes you make in the document file are transferred to the source files. For example, if you delete a paragraph of text from a page layout, the desktop publishing software deletes the paragraph from the word processor version of the text that you imported.

LAYING OUT INDIVIDUAL PAGES

You lay out individual pages by placing the imported text and pictures on the pages and assigning specific characteristics to the text and pictures. For example, you assign fonts to the headings and the text, and you specify the size of each illustration. If you don't like the way the page looks, you can easily and quickly change its appearance by assigning different characteristics to the text and graphics or by changing their positions. For example, you can reduce or enlarge the size of an illustration or change the font of a heading

Suppose you want to print only one area of a photograph because the rest of it includes details unrelated to the information you are trying to convey.

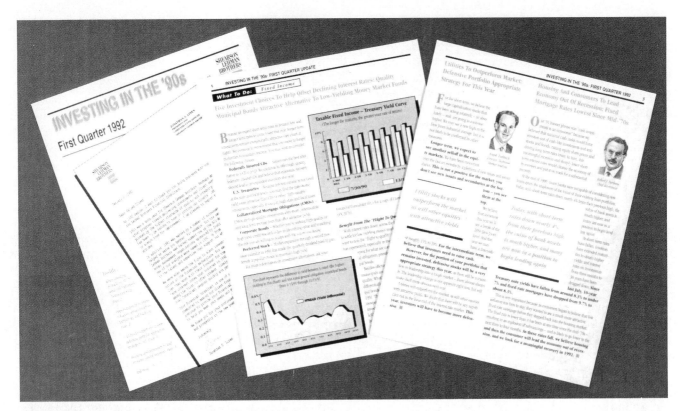

FIGURE 8-20

Instead of occupying rigid columns, text and pictures can flow together.

You can trim off part of the photo, which is called *cropping*. You can even position a graphic so that text flows around it, as shown in Figure 8-20.

This ability to customize a page layout on the fly is one of the greatest advantages of desktop publishing. It gives you the freedom to experiment with a page until you get it just the way you want it, with no need to make hard copies until then.

Page Composition Methods

Desktop Publishing Programs Differ in Their Approaches to Page Composition.

The process of laying out pages is often referred to as *page composition,* or *page makeup.* Most desktop publishing programs take one of two approaches to page composition: direct page makeup or the use of a style sheet (Table 8-2). Some use a combination of both.

Table 8-2: Page Composition Methods	
Software	**Method**
PageMaker	Direct Page Makeup
Ventura Publisher	Style Sheet
QuarkXPress	Combination
Letraset DesignStudio	Combination
Do-It	Direct Page Makeup
Front Page	Direct Page Makeup

PageMaker and some other desktop publishing programs use the *direct page makeup* approach. With these programs, you position the text and illustrations on the page and assign characteristics to them directly. For example, you assign a font to each heading and each piece of text, and you assign dimensions to each piece of art.

The direct page makeup approach resembles the manual paste-up process more closely than the style sheet approach does. Because of this similarity, page makeup programs are usually easier to learn for people experienced at using hard copy, scissors, and paste to create mechanicals.

LEARNING DESKTOP PUBLISHING

Desktop publishing is taking over the publishing industry, according to industry consultants Howard Cohen and Steven Moonitz. Magazines especially are investing heavily in state-of-the-art hardware and software. But, although desktop publishing can be faster and cheaper than traditional publishing methods, it's not easy to get the most out of this costly investment.

Training publishing staff on the latest software presents formidable problems. But if the artists, designers, production personnel, and editors who create a magazine are not well trained, projects face problems and delays. While solutions abound, it's becoming clear that no one solution can solve all problems.

At *Entertainment Weekly,* for example, technology manager Chris Kronish began by sending her designers to Businessland (a retail computer store), which teaches an introductory course in the Macintosh. For more in-depth training in desktop publishing software, she sent them to the Wheeler-Hawkins training center in New York, where they took separate two-day classes in *Adobe Illustrator* and *QuarkXpress.*

Classroom instruction helped, says Kronish, but it was not enough. She hired a consultant, who worked with her staff for a full year, providing individualized, on-site training and support. Finally, prior to the magazine's first issue in 1990, the

staff "published" four dummy issues to test the new system.

At *Sports Illustrated for Kids,* Karen Meneghin, director of editorial operations, took a different approach. She began by sending her staff for classroom instruction in *Adobe Illustrator* and *QuarkXpress,* and quickly concluded that, because the instruction is not customized, "the two-day blitz of training offered in the schools is just not effective."

Meneghin switched to the more costly approach of hiring consultants, who worked intensively with her staff at their offices over an eight-week period. In addition, because the magazine was already up and running, she made the transition to desktop publishing over the course of a year, beginning with 10 pages and adding more pages to each new issue.

At Surfer Publications, home of *Surfer Style* and *Beach Culture,* art director and former university professor Jeff Girad took a very different approach. "I've developed a lab environment," he says, "where all of our art and production staffers are encouraged to talk to each other and experiment. We encourage a cross-pollination of ideas." Although Girad thinks there's a place for formal classroom training, his staffers return from the classroom saying they've learned very little. "Often," says Girad, "we can learn more by setting aside a day to go skiing. You'd be

surprised at the ideas that can be traded and the frustrations that can be vented during the two-hour drive to the slopes."

Clearly, the transition to desktop publishing presents many challenging problems. As consultants Cohen and Moonitz quip, "You can lead a horse to water, but you can't make him water-ski."

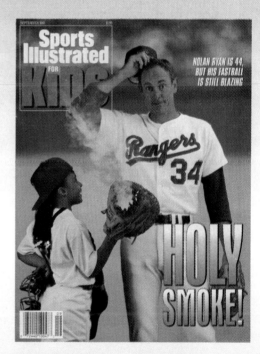

Desktop publishing is revolutionizing magazine production. Although it can lower costs and increase productivity, workers must be adequately trained to use the latest software.

Source: "Desktop Training: Getting the Right Mix," by Howard Cohen and Steven Moonitz. *Folio Magazine,* March 1991, p. 74.

USE OF A STYLE SHEET

Products such as *Ventura Publisher* use the *style sheet* approach to desktop publishing. With these products, instead of placing text and pictures directly on a page, you first position rectangular frames on the page. A *frame* marks the position of a picture or a block of text on a page. Then you import text and pictures into the frames. Instead of assigning fonts directly to text, you create *tags*, which are codes that represent the fonts, and assign the tags to the text. Creating frames and tags requires extra steps at first, but in the long run it eliminates a lot of repetitive work.

Frames

After you place the frames on a page, and before you import text or graphics into them, you can save the page as a template. When you use this template to create another page, the frames are already in position. Thus you can import text and pictures into the frames without repeating the work of positioning them. Figure 8-21 shows two different pages created from the same page template with a desktop publishing program that uses the style sheet approach.

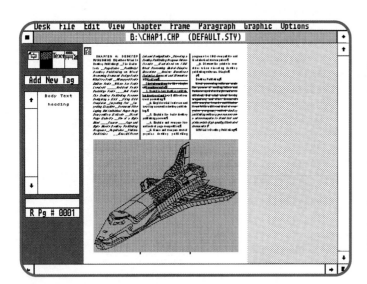 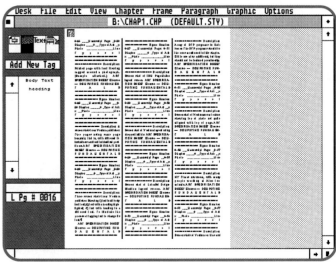

FIGURE 8-21

With *Ventura Publisher,* you position frames on a page's grid, then import text and pictures into the frames. You can move the frames or change their sizes at any time.

Tags and Style Sheets

With the style sheet approach, you create a *style sheet* that is a list of all the fonts used in the document. For example, suppose you publish a newsletter every month that uses the Helvetica Bold typeface in 14-point, 24-point, and 36-point sizes for headings and 10-point Times Roman for the body text. The first time you publish the newsletter, you might create a style sheet that includes these tags:

- "H1" to specify 36-point Helvetica Bold
- "H2" to specify 24-point Helvetica Bold Italic
- "H3" to specify 14-point Helvetica Bold
- "Body" to specify 10-point Times Roman

When you import text into a frame, the software automatically assigns the body text tag to all of it and displays it as 10-point Times Roman. If you highlight a paragraph and select a different tag from the style sheet, the software reformats the paragraph in the specified font. Figure 8-22 illustrates this step, which you would repeat for each heading.

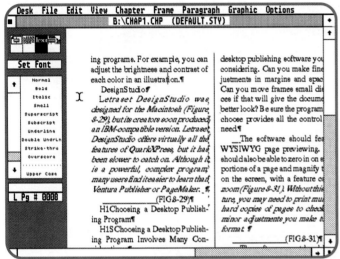

(1)

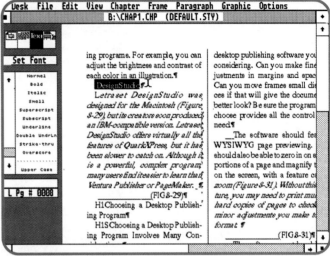

(2)

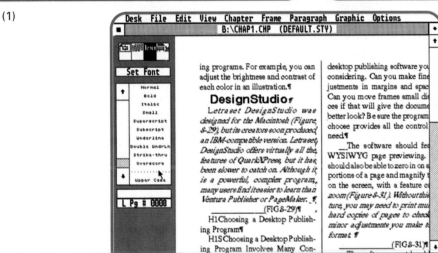

(3)

FIGURE 8-22

(1) *Ventura* assigns the body text font to all imported text without a tag. (2) To change a tag, first highlight the text you want to change. Then give it a new tag. (3) The text will display and print in the new font.

When you publish the next issue of the newsletter, you can use the same style sheet. There's no need to create the tags again. In addition to saving steps, using the same style sheet for each issue gives the newsletter a consistent look, or *style,* that ties the issues together.

Desktop Publishing Programs

Several Powerful Desktop Publishing Programs Are Available for Macintosh and IBM-Compatible Computers.

PageMaker, which helped to start the desktop publishing revolution in the mid-1980s, is still one of the most popular products for this purpose. Since then, however, many others have come on the market for both Macintosh and IBM-compatible microcomputers. Other widely used programs include *Ventura Publisher* and *QuarkXPress*.

PAGEMAKER

PageMaker was the first professional-quality page-layout software for microcomputers. Originally designed for the Macintosh, *PageMaker* is also available in an IBM-compatible version running in the Microsoft Windows environment (Figure 8-23). It is still one of the most powerful programs, and therefore

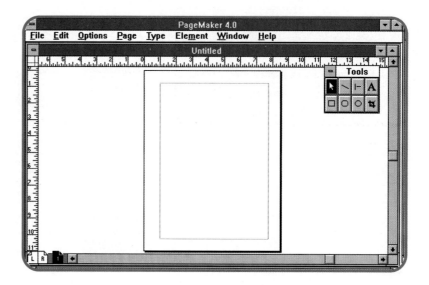

FIGURE 8-23

With *PageMaker,* you position text and graphics directly on pages. *PageMaker* was the first desktop publishing program, and it is still one of the most widely used.

one of the most complicated. Nonetheless, most users find *PageMaker* easy to learn. This program uses direct page makeup, which automates fewer steps than some programs but can also allow for more control over a page layout.

PageMaker has more powerful word processing features built into it than most other desktop publishing products. Therefore, making extensive text revisions efficiently doesn't necessarily require that you switch from the *PageMaker* document file to a word processor file. *PageMaker* also has other advanced features, such as creating the color separations needed to reproduce color photographs in print.

VENTURA PUBLISHER

The Xerox Corporation originally developed *Ventura Publisher* for IBM-compatible, DOS-based computers. Xerox has also created a version of this powerful product that runs in the Windows environment. A Macintosh version of *Ventura Publisher* is also available. This program has features that most of its competitors lack, such as the ability to number illustrations automatically.

Ventura Publisher was the first desktop publishing program to offer control over the finer points of typesetting, such as the spacing between and within words. Some of its typesetting features, such as automatic drop initials, are still not available with most other programs (Figure 8-24).

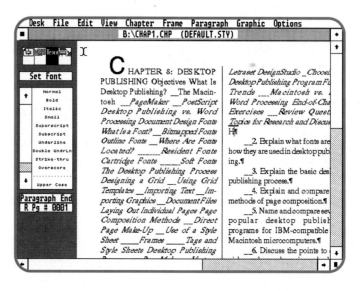

FIGURE 8-24

With *Ventura Publisher,* you can use special typographic effects such as these dropped initials to add visual appeal to documents.

QuarkXPress, designed for the Macintosh, combines the page makeup program and style sheet approaches to page composition. Like style sheet programs, it uses frames where you can import text or graphics. However, like page makeup programs, it allows you to store text and graphics outside the page borders. This enables you to change the contents of the boxes very quickly. *QuarkXPress* also has a library feature that lets you store combinations of text and graphic frames and use them repeatedly. It was the first major desktop publishing program with a spelling checker built in.

This program was also among the first that could be linked with the advanced electronic publishing systems used to produce big newspapers and magazines. It also offers more control over color than most competing programs. For example, you can adjust the brightness and contrast of each color in an illustration.

ONE MAN'S BRIGHT IDEA

In the computer business, sometimes putting two and two together—particularly the right software for the right computer—can add up to a billion-dollar industry. That's what Paul Brainerd discovered in 1984 when he founded the Aldus Corporation to produce *PageMaker,* now the best-selling desktop publishing software program in the United States.

Back in 1984, Brainerd was an ex-newspaperman with an idea. He knew that Apple Computer's new desktop computer, the Macintosh, could produce high-quality print graphics with relative ease. Although few in the computer software industry were quick to take a chance on the quirky new Mac, Brainerd, with his newspaper background, had the vision to see the Mac's potential in publishing.

In 1984, creating professional-looking documents such as newsletters, brochures, and pamphlets was an expensive and time-consuming business performed by specialists. Brainerd realized that if the user-friendly graphics capability of the Macintosh could be harnessed to produce low-cost, professional-looking publications, the possibilities were endless. All that was needed was the right kind of software, and anybody who could afford a Mac and

a laser printer could become "a desktop publisher." *PageMaker* became that program. Five years later, desktop publishing software had become a $3.6 billion industry.

Although Brainerd's Aldus Corporation may have "created" the desktop publishing industry, it has lots of competition today, particularly from the second most popular software program, Xerox Corporation's *Ventura Publisher* (which was originally published for IBM-compatible computers).

Now, both *PageMaker* and *Ventura Publisher* are available in Macintosh and IBM-compatible versions. In addition, many word processing programs, such as *WordPerfect* and *Microsoft Word,* have added desktop publishing features to their programs.

Desktop publishing has also evolved to meet the needs of large corporations. For example, Microsoft's *PowerPoint* program produces slides and transparencies for business meetings, and Quark, Inc.'s *QuarkXpress* produces the kind of graphics required by corporate electronic publishing departments. Aldus, which for several years seemed to rest on its success with *PageMaker,* has been forced to take on its competition. In the process, the company has grown larger, and Brainerd has had to learn to give up doing every-

thing himself. "Originally," he recalls, "four engineers and I did everything—including emptying the wastebaskets." As he has begun to delegate more authority over day-to-day operations, he's learned that vital lesson of any start-up entrepreneur who's become a big success: "It's really important to let go."

Paul Brainerd founded Aldus in 1984 with the idea of capitalizing on the Macintosh's graphics capability. This was the beginning of desktop publishing.

Source: "For Aldus, Being No. 1 Isn't Enough Anymore," *Business Week,* June 11, 1990, p. 76.

Unless you plan to develop newsletters, brochures, or flyers that use both text and graphics, you probably do not need desktop publishing software.

If you plan to purchase desktop publishing software, make sure to determine the program's requirements in terms of: microcomputer, RAM, operating system, fixed-disk storage, and printer (most desktop publishing requires a laser printer).

Usually, it is easier to write using a word processing program, so you should also determine that the desktop publishing program is compatible with the word processing program you plan to use to generate documents.

If you plan to use graphics with the desktop publishing program, you will also need to purchase graphics software to generate the graphics. Again, the graphics program must be compatible with the desktop publishing program you are considering. Chapter 11 contains more information about graphics programs.

Choosing a Desktop Publishing Program

Choosing a Desktop Publishing Program Involves Many Considerations.

Desktop publishing involves a considerable investment in time, money, and equipment, so make your choice of a desktop publishing program carefully. Any program you select should enable you to carry out these steps automatically:

- Position headers and footers
- Number pages, footnotes, sections, and chapters
- Create an index with at least two levels of topics
- Create a table of contents

Another important consideration is how easy it is to import illustrations and text. Different graphics programs and word processors create files in many different formats. The desktop publishing software you buy must accept the file formats you are most likely to use. For example, if you plan to create documents using text entered with *WordStar*, you should look for a program that accepts text in the *WordStar* format. Otherwise, you will have to convert the text to another format before you import it, which can waste a lot of time.

Another question to ask is how precisely you can place text, illustrations, and tables on the page with the desktop publishing software you are considering. Can you make fine adjustments in margins and spacing? Can you move frames small distances if that will give the document a better look? Be sure the program you choose provides all the control you need.

The software should feature WYSIWYG page previewing. You should also be able to zero in on small portions of a page and magnify them on the screen, with a feature called *zoom*. Without this feature, you may need to print multiple hard copies of pages to check out minor adjustments you make to the format.

The software must be able to send output directly to a laser printer or a typesetting machine using a standard page description language such as *PostScript*. This provides for compatibility with many kinds of reproduction equipment as well as for better-looking documents.

Make sure that the desktop publishing program you choose is fully compatible with your operating system and environment. Several programs, including *Ventura Publisher* and *PageMaker*, are available in both IBM-compatible and Macintosh versions, but some programs are not. Some programs that are available in an IBM-compatible version require a particular environment (such as Windows).

Desktop publishing programs can require a substantial amount of memory. As a rule, the more memory your computer has, the more efficiently it can run a desktop publishing program. If your system doesn't have enough memory for the desktop publishing program you want, you might be able to add more.

Find out how much hard disk space the desktop publishing program requires. The more features the software has, the more disk space it takes up. You also need disk space for the documents you publish, and those with lots of graphics can take up a lot of space. What matters is not just the size of your hard disk but the amount of space available on it. For example, suppose you have a 40MB hard disk, but the software and documents already on the disk have taken up 34MB To use a desktop publishing program that requires 7MB, you will have to remove some of the existing programs or documents or add more hard disk space to your system.

Future Trends

Desktop Publishing Will Become More Widespread as Its Software and Hardware Improve.

Desktop publishing programs resemble the minicomputer-based electronic publishing systems most big magazines and newspapers have used since the early 1980s (Figure 8-25). These huge systems, which cost millions of dollars, can coordinate hundreds of text and graphics files from many sources—something microcomputer desktop publishing programs cannot do. However, the desktop publishing programs for microcomputers offer more design flexibility than the larger systems. The companies that produce the larger systems are attempting to create links with several popular desktop publishing programs. This will allow the publishing companies to combine the file-handling power of their bigger systems with the flexibility of the smaller programs.

At the same time, software companies are working to improve the file management power of the desktop publishing programs. Before long, even your local daily newspaper may be produced with a desktop publishing program.

FIGURE 8-25

In the *Atex* electronic publishing system used by *The New York Times*, minicomputers are used to manage and format stories, photographs, and advertisements from employees working at hundreds of terminals.

MACINTOSH VERSUS IBM

At one time the Macintosh was the preferred microcomputer for desktop publishing, but the difference between it and IBM is narrowing fast. With graphical user interfaces on IBM-type computers, using desktop publishing programs has become much the same as working on a Macintosh (Figure 8-26).

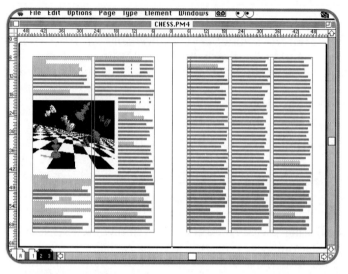

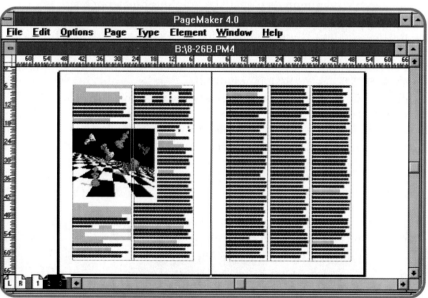

FIGURE 8-26

PageMaker running under Windows on an IBM microcomputer resembles its counterpart on the Macintosh.

REVIEW QUESTIONS

1. What is desktop publishing?
2. Why does the text in books and magazines look better than that in a memo?
3. Before desktop publishing, what steps were involved in creating pages for a book or magazine?
4. What advantages does desktop publishing have over manual pasteup?
5. What three products brought about desktop publishing with microcomputers? Explain what each of them did to make desktop publishing possible.
6. What is the primary purpose of desktop publishing software? Compare it with the primary purpose of a word processor.

7. What factors should you consider when designing a document?

8. What is a font? A font family?

9. Name and describe three locations for fonts you can use in desktop publishing.

10. What basic steps does desktop publishing involve?

11. What is a grid? What information does it include?

12. How do you generally add text to a grid?

13. How do you develop a layout for an individual page? Once you have created a layout, is it difficult to change?

14. What two approaches to page composition do desktop publishing programs use? Describe each.

15. What is a frame? A tag? A style sheet? How can they save you time?

16. Name two desktop publishing programs that are available for both IBM-compatible and Macintosh computers.

17. What tasks should be carried out automatically by any desktop publishing software you purchase?

18. How does desktop publishing software compare with the electronic publishing systems used by big magazine and book publishers?

19. Is desktop publishing on an IBM-compatible microcomputer like working on a Macintosh? Explain.

TOPICS FOR RESEARCH AND DISCUSSION

1. When you write with a word processor, how much do you think about the document's appearance? Do you decide on the details of a document's appearance before you finish writing it or afterward? If you knew that the document was going to be imported into a desktop publishing program, would it affect your concern for its appearance? Discuss the implications of your answers.

2. Imagine you work for a small travel agency that uses *WordPerfect* and IBM microcomputers. You want to publish a flashy monthly newsletter to inform customers about vacation bargains. Each issue will have eight pages, and you want to include maps and photographs of attractive resorts and cruise ships.

   Would you use *WordPerfect* to publish the newsletter, or would you purchase a desktop publishing program? Why? If you use a desktop publishing program, which one might you select, and why? Use the library or visit software stores to find out more about *WordPerfect* and desktop publishing programs.

3. Graphic design experts say that different typefaces make different psychological impressions on readers. We associate typefaces with specific kinds of information. For example, Corona fonts remind many people of newspapers and convey a sense of urgency. Elaborate fonts that resemble calligraphy create a sense of formality.

   Collect examples of advertisements, books, newsletters, and other publications that use different fonts. Describe your reactions to the type used in the publications. Do you think your reaction was intended by the person who designed the publication?

   Look at a book of typefaces (available from the library or local typesetters or desktop publishers) and try to identify the type used in the publications.

SPREADSHEETS

OBJECTIVES

The information in this chapter will enable you to

- Describe the functions and advantages of a spreadsheet.
- Describe the elements that make up a spreadsheet.
- Explain how to move through a spreadsheet using the keyboard or a mouse.
- Describe the purpose of labels, values, and formulas.
- Explain what a range is and how it is used.
- Explain what a macro is and what it is used for.
- Explain how different spreadsheets use multiple spreadsheets simultaneously.
- Describe various spreadsheet utilities and explain their functions.

If you have ever worked on your personal or business finances using a sheet of paper with rows and columns of numbers, you have used a worksheet. Figure 9-1 shows a worksheet for a small business. The horizontal

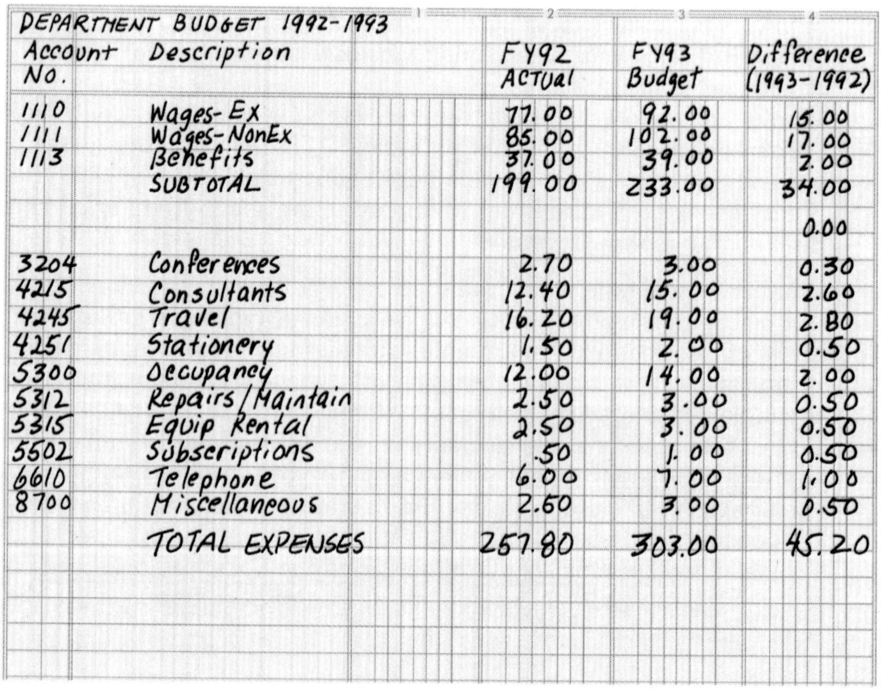

DEPARTMENT BUDGET 1992-1993				
Account No.	Description	FY92 ACTUAL	FY93 Budget	Difference (1993-1992)
1110	Wages-Ex	77.00	92.00	15.00
1111	Wages-NonEx	85.00	102.00	17.00
1113	Benefits	37.00	39.00	2.00
	SUBTOTAL	199.00	233.00	34.00
				0.00
3204	Conferences	2.70	3.00	0.30
4215	Consultants	12.40	15.00	2.60
4245	Travel	16.20	19.00	2.80
4251	Stationery	1.50	2.00	0.50
5300	Occupancy	12.00	14.00	2.00
5312	Repairs/Maintain	2.50	3.00	0.50
5315	Equip Rental	2.50	3.00	0.50
5502	Subscriptions	.50	1.00	0.50
6610	Telephone	6.00	7.00	1.00
8700	Miscellaneous	2.60	3.00	0.50
	TOTAL EXPENSES	257.80	303.00	45.20

FIGURE 9-1

Worksheets with rows and columns are used by virtually every business. With a manual worksheet, all the values must be added across the rows and down the columns.

rows list various types of expenses; the vertical columns show budgeted and actual expenses. After writing in all the figures, you add up each column of expenses. Then you write the expense totals on the bottom line.

If you want to change some of the values, say to account for a 5% pay raise in July, you must erase the budgeted wage totals, rework your calculations, and then write in the new figures. The electronic version of a worksheet is called a *spreadsheet*. A spreadsheet program on a computer performs these tasks quickly and easily.

Some typical applications for spreadsheets include budgeting, profit and loss statements, sales estimates, financial projections, and cash flow management. Most of these applications involve tracking money over a period of time. A spreadsheet provides you the ability to project the financial future, based on your results to date.

A word of caution is necessary. Projecting the financial future, like performing any mathematical operation in a spreadsheet, is based on the data you entered. The old adage "garbage in, garbage out" certainly applies to spreadsheets. You must be sure the information you put into the spreadsheet is accurate if the output is to be accurate. Your estimate of future income and outflow must be realistic or your projections will be misleading.

History

Early Spreadsheets Revolutionized Microcomputing.

On May 11, 1979, *VisiCalc,* the first commercial spreadsheet program, was introduced. Running on an Apple II computer, which had been introduced two years earlier, *VisiCalc* revolutionized microcomputing.

What took accountants, managers, and analysts hours to figure out with a pencil and pad could be done in a matter of minutes. Instead of recalculating numerous formulas manually to see what would happen if sales rose or dipped, or how a change in the interest rates might affect your finances, *VisiCalc* recalculated the numbers automatically—in seconds. The ability to ask "What if this happens?" or "How will these changes affect my calculations?" made owning a microcomputer a necessity. Many people considered it the first compelling reason to purchase a microcomputer.

The popularity of *VisiCalc* led to a flood of similar programs. *Lotus 1-2-3,* running on the new IBM PC, soon became the standard of the industry. Today, *Lotus 1-2-3* is still the market leader, with versions that run on practically all computers, including IBM compatibles, Apple products, Unix, VAX, and even mainframes. Many other spreadsheet programs have also become popular, among them Microsoft's *Excel,* Borland's *Quattro Pro, Lucid 3-D, PlanPerfect,* and *SuperCalc5.*

What Is a Spreadsheet?

Spreadsheets Are Similar to Worksheets in Many Ways.

Compare Figure 9-1 with Figure 9-2. Note that Figure 9-2, a computer printout of a spreadsheet, looks much like the manual worksheet. Both have columns, rows, headings, values, subtotals, and totals. The major difference between the two is that the subtotals and totals in the spreadsheet itself don't really contain values. Instead, they each contain a formula that calculates the value. Figure 9-3 illustrates what is really entered into the spreadsheet shown in Figure 9-2.

```
DEPARTMENT BUDGET  1992-1993
Account     Description          FY 92     FY 93      Difference
No.                              Actual    Budget     (1993-1992)
================================================================
 1110       Wages-Ex              77.00     92.00       15.00
 1111       Wages-NonEx           85.00    102.00       17.00
 1113       Benefits              37.00     39.00        2.00
            SUBTOTAL             199.00    233.00       34.00
                                                        0.00
 3204       Conferences            2.70      3.00        0.30
 4215       Consultants           12.40     15.00        2.60
 4245       Travel                16.20     19.00        2.80
 4251       Stationery             1.50      2.00        0.50
 5300       Occupancy             12.00     14.00        2.00
 5312       Repairs/Maintain       2.50      3.00        0.50
 5315       Equip Rental           2.50      3.00        0.50
 5502       Subscriptions          0.50      1.00        0.50
 6610       Telephone              6.00      7.00        1.00
 8700       Miscellaneous          2.50      3.00        0.50
            TOTAL EXPENSES       257.80    303.00       45.20
```

FIGURE 9-2

A computer spreadsheet adds all the values automatically and also calculates the differences.

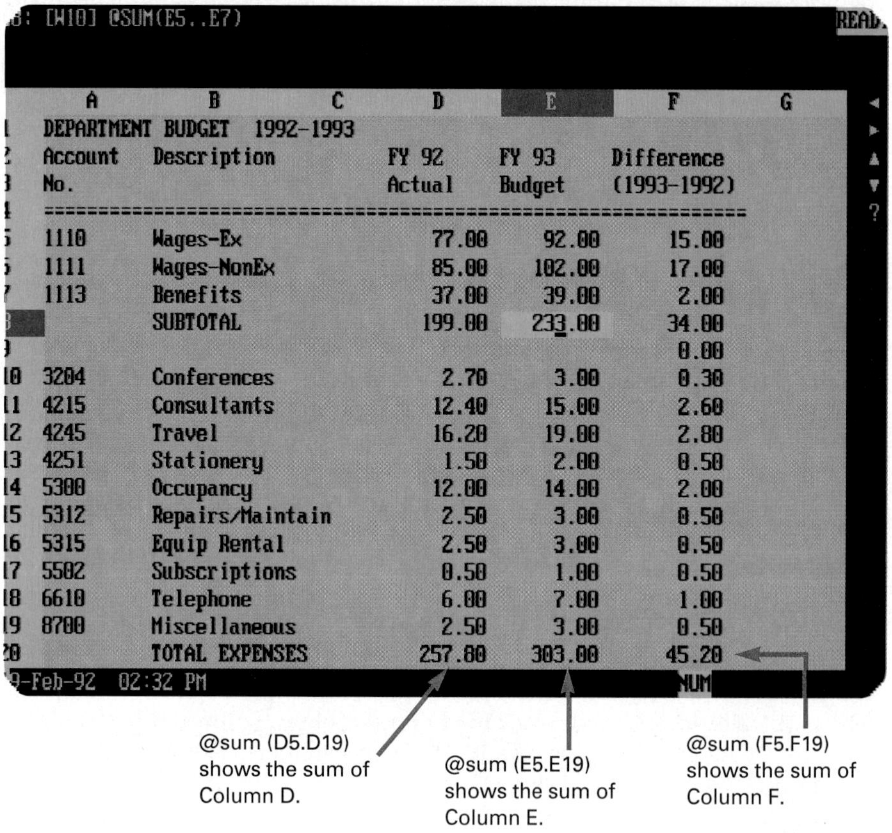

FIGURE 9-3

The real power of a spreadsheet is that the values can be changed and the totals will be automatically recalculated.

@sum (D5.D19) shows the sum of Column D.

@sum (E5.E19) shows the sum of Column E.

@sum (F5.F19) shows the sum of Column F.

The Parts of a Spreadsheet

A Spreadsheet Consists of Rows, Usually Identified with Numbers, and Columns Identified with Letters.

Lotus 1-2-3 can handle up to 8,192 rows; Microsoft's *Excel* can have 16,384 rows. Both have 256 columns labeled A to IV (the letter I and the letter V). (When they run through the alphabet, they use two letters to identify a column, such as AA, AB, etc.)

The intersection of a row and a column is called a *cell*. Each cell is identified by the column letter, followed by the row number, such as E5 or AR3090. This identification is called the *cell address*. So "E5" is the cell address for the cell at the intersection of column E and row 5.

The *active cell* is the cell where the cursor is currently located. Some programs call the cursor a "cell pointer" or "highlight bar." The cursor is moved around the spreadsheet with various keys or a mouse.

The top three or four lines of the screen, above the spreadsheet, are often called the *control panel*. In *Lotus 1-2-3,* the left corner of the top line shows the active cell address and its contents. In *Excel,* the active cell indicator is on the fourth line from the top. Figure 9-4 shows both the *Lotus 1-2-3* and Microsoft *Excel* screens for comparison.

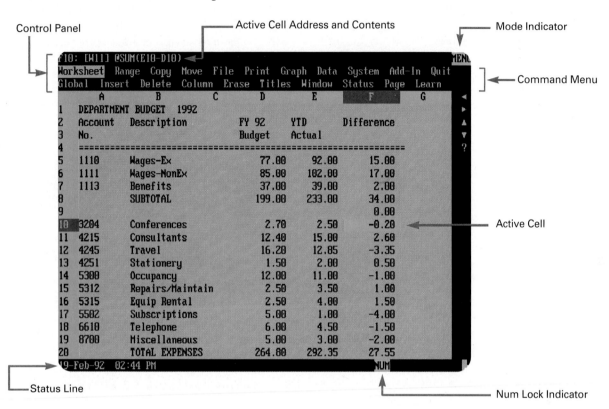

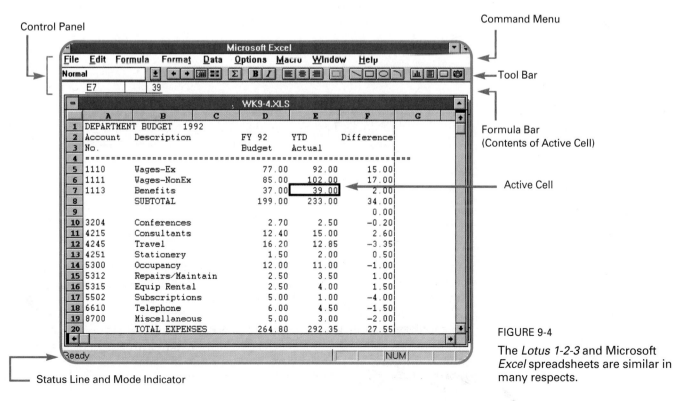

FIGURE 9-4

The *Lotus 1-2-3* and Microsoft *Excel* spreadsheets are similar in many respects.

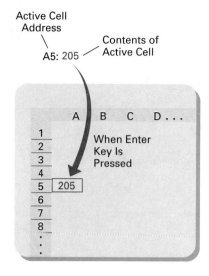

Active Cell
Address

A5: 205

Contents of
Active Cell

FIGURE 9-5

Data you enter first appears in the contents of the active cell area on the control panel. If you press the Enter key, the data is entered in the active cell on the spreadsheet.

As you key in information for the spreadsheet, it first appears in the control panel. (*Excel* calls this area the *formula bar*.) When you press the Enter key, the information is put into the active cell (see Figure 9-5).

The control panel includes the *command area*. In some versions of *Lotus 1-2-3*, the command menu appears only when the Slash key (/) is pressed. In other versions, you can request the commands with the mouse. In *Excel*, a command menu appears at all times.

Lotus 1-2-3's control panel also contains a *mode indicator* in the upper right corner of the screen, which gives the current *operating mode*. For example, "Ready" means *Lotus 1-2-3* is waiting for you to perform some action, "Error" indicates a problem exists, and "Wait" means *Lotus 1-2-3* is processing data. The mode indicator appears at the bottom of *Excel*'s screen.

Excel uses a *tool bar*, also located in the control panel area. This bar exploits the program's graphical capabilities by using icons to make changes in the appearance of a spreadsheet. For example, there are bold and italic icons to let you change the appearance of the type in the spreadsheet and drawing icons to let you draw lines and boxes around areas of the spreadsheet.

The bottom of the screen has a *status line* that displays information such as error messages and keyboard status. For instance, "CAPS" displayed on the right side of the status line in *Lotus 1-2-3* means the Caps Lock key is turned on.

Basic Functions

Creating a Simple Spreadsheet Involves a Few Basic Functions.

The basic spreadsheet functions include

- Moving from cell to cell within the spreadsheet.
- Entering information in the spreadsheet, including values, labels, and formulas.
- Issuing commands to perform such tasks as formatting values as currency and saving and printing a file.

MOVING AROUND THE SPREADSHEET

A computer monitor can show only a small portion of an entire spreadsheet—usually only about 7 of the 256 possible columns and about 20 of the many thousand possible rows (see Figure 9-6). Think of your monitor as a small magnifying glass that must be moved around above a large sheet of paper, allowing you to read different portions of the sheet. This process is called *scrolling* across and down the spreadsheet.

Scrolling is accomplished either with directional keys on the keyboard or with a mouse. A mouse is used on programs that use a graphical user interface such as *Excel* (which uses Windows), *Quattro Pro* (which uses a custom interface), or *Lotus 1-2-3/Graphical* (which uses OS/2 or Presentation Manager).

A mouse makes moving around a spreadsheet easier than using keys. But with the many spreadsheets that weren't designed for a mouse, you must use the directional keys.

For programs using directional keys, the Right and Left Arrow keys move the cursor one column at a time; the Up and Down Arrow keys move one row at a time. For large spreadsheets, moving about with these keys gets tedious, so shortcuts are provided. For example, in *Lotus 1-2-3*, the PgUp and PgDn keys move up and down a full screen at a time, the Tab key moves

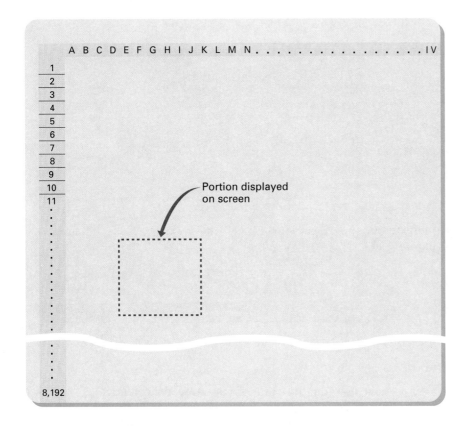

A B C D E F G H I J K L M N IV

Portion displayed
on screen

FIGURE 9-6

A spreadsheet can be huge. You can see only a small portion of it at a time.

one full screen to the right, and holding down the Shift key and pressing the Tab key moves one full screen to the left.

In *Lotus 1-2-3*, if you ever lose your bearings and want to return to the upper left corner of the spreadsheet, you can press the Home key to return to cell A1, which is also known as the *home* position. In *Excel* you can return to the home position by holding down the Ctrl key and pressing the Home key.

Spreadsheet programs use *function keys* for various shortcuts. The F5 key is called the *GoTo* key in *Lotus 1-2-3*. When F5 is pressed, you are asked to enter the cell address to which you wish to move.

If you are using a mouse to move about the spreadsheet, you move the cursor to the cell you want to make active and click. If the cell is not on the screen, you must use scroll bars first to make the cell visible.

ENTERING INFORMATION INTO THE SPREADSHEET

Once you learn to move about in a spreadsheet, you can begin to build the spreadsheet by entering information into it.

The directional keys are used to select the active cell that will receive the new information. When you key in information, it appears in the data entry portion of the control panel, not the active cell. When you press the Enter key or move the cursor to another cell, the information is placed into the active cell. The contents of the cell can be seen in the status line when the cell is active—that is, when the cursor is highlighting it.

Four types of information can be entered into a spreadsheet:

- Labels
- Values
- Formulas
- Macros

The first three will be covered now; macros will be covered later in this chapter.

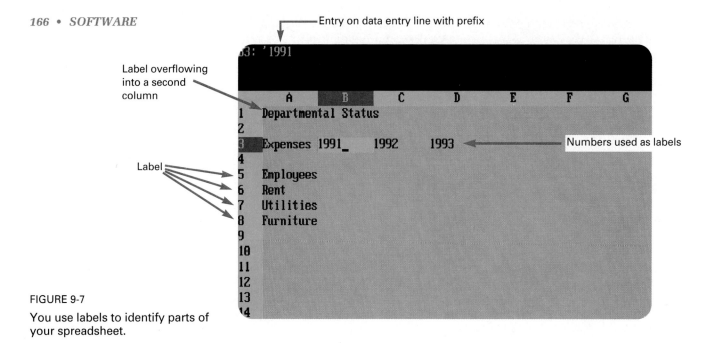

FIGURE 9-7

You use labels to identify parts of your spreadsheet.

Labels

Labels are text that identify parts of your spreadsheet, such as column and row headings. Figure 9-7 shows labels across row 3, the column headings, and down column A, the row headings. Labels can be aligned in various ways to enhance the spreadsheet's appearance.

In *Lotus 1-2-3,* a *label prefix* indicates the text entered is a label and determines its alignment. The apostrophe (') prefix left aligns the label; the double quote (") right aligns the label, and the caret (^) centers the label. While entering a label, the mode indicator reads "label." These label prefixes are shown in Table 9-1.

Table 9-1: Summary of Label Prefixes	
Label	**Positioning in Column**
' (Apostrophe)	Left Aligned (Default Setting)
" (Double Quote)	Right Aligned
^ (Caret)	Centered

The label prefix does not appear in the spreadsheet, but is visible in the status line if the cell is active. The main advantage of entering information as a label is that the text can be aligned and balanced.

If you enter label text into a cell without a label prefix, the program will put one in, called the *default prefix.* This is usually the left-aligned prefix (').

Labels need not be letters. Column headings that contain numbers, such as 1992, can be used as labels. However, labels cannot be used in a mathematical operation. For example, you can't enter a series of numbers down a column as centered labels to make them look good and then try to calculate their sum.

A label can extend beyond the width of a column into the next column. In Figure 9-7 the label on line 1 ("Departmental Study") is entered into column A, but extends into column B. This works only if there is nothing in the adjacent cell. For example, if you entered something into cell B1 in Figure 9-7, the label in cell A1 would be cut off at the right edge of column A. To solve such a problem, the width of a column can be increased using the appropriate commands.

Values

Once headings are entered, the spreadsheet can be filled in with data, or *values*. Values have no prefixes and are always right aligned in a column. While entering a value, the mode indicator reads "value." Values are never entered with dollar signs, commas, or percentage signs; these are handled with formatting commands.

Since spreadsheets contain many values, the quickest method of entry is to key in a value and press the down or right arrow key, so that you can enter a column or row of values at a time. This eliminates using the Enter key repeatedly or going back and forth between the mouse and the keyboard.

If a value is entered and a series of asterisks appear in the cell, the column is not wide enough to accommodate the value. The column width must be increased to include the entire value.

Formulas

The real power of a spreadsheet is its ability to perform "what if" calculations quickly and easily. This can be done because formulas are entered into the spreadsheet rather than the resulting values. Whenever a value in a cell changes, the formula recalculates that cell and any others affected by the change.

Formulas begin with a prefix, as do labels. In *Lotus 1-2-3* a plus sign (+) is typically used; *Excel* uses an equals sign (=). (Prefixes are required only if the formula begins with a cell address, but are optional if they begin with a value.)

A formula contains values and/or cell addresses and arithmetic operators such as "+" for addition, "–" for subtraction, "*" for multiplication, "/" for division, and "^" for exponentiation (see Table 9-2). For example, the *Lotus 1-2-3* formula "+A5+30" entered into cell B1 will add the contents of cell A5 to the value 30 and place the result in cell B1. The first plus is a prefix to indicate this is a formula. If the content of cell A5 changes, the value stored in B1 changes.

There is an order of precedence when building formulas. For example, the formula "+B7+A4*100" does *not* add the contents of B7 to A4 and then multiply the resulting value times 100 because multiplication takes precedence over addition. This formula will first multiply the contents of cell A4 by 100 and then add the content of cell B7.

Table 9-2: Arithmetic Operators Used in *Lotus 1-2-3* and Microsoft *Excel*	
Operation	**Operator (Symbol)**
Addition	+ (Plus Sign)
Subtraction	- (Hyphen or Minus Sign)
Multiplication	* (Asterisk)
Division	/ (Slash)
Exponentiation	^ (Caret)

Since parenthetical statements have the highest order of precedence, you can force a formula to be calculated in a certain way by inserting parentheses. If we modified our example to read "+(B7+A4)*100," B7 would be added to A4 first, and the result would then be multiplied by 100.

This type of formula can become cumbersome if many cells are involved. For example, if you wish to add 50 values, the formula would be extremely long. Spreadsheet programs offer an easier way to add values, as you will see later in this chapter.

ISSUING COMMANDS

So far, we have only discussed entering information into the spreadsheet. The spreadsheet and its contents must also be modified and saved before it is completed. For example, you may need to adjust the width of columns and format some values for currency and others for percentages, among other things.

These functions, and many others, are accomplished by issuing commands. To show commands most programs use a horizontal menu across the top of the screen in the control panel. *Excel's* command menu is always visible, and selections are made by clicking on your menu choice with the mouse. *Lotus 1-2-3's* command menu must be requested with the Slash key (/). Selections can then be made either by using the Right and Left Arrow keys to highlight the menu choice and then pressing the Enter key or by keying in the first letter of your choice. When a choice is highlighted, the line below the main menu shows the submenu (see Figure 9-8).

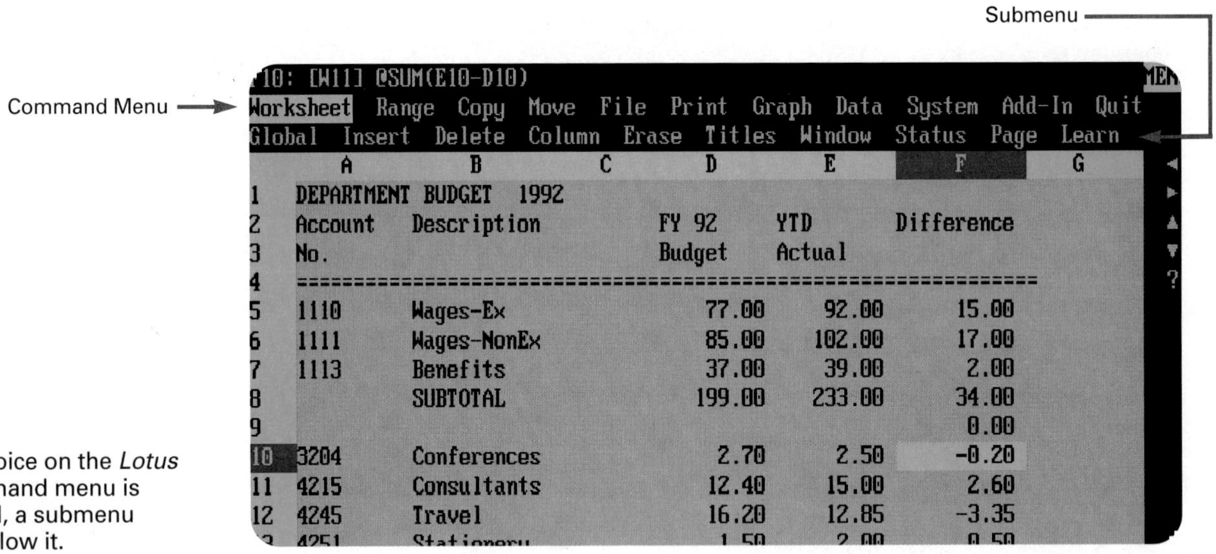

Submenu ──────

Command Menu ──────➤

FIGURE 9-8

When a choice on the *Lotus 1-2-3* command menu is highlighted, a submenu appears below it.

In *Lotus 1-2-3,* making a selection from the main menu brings up a submenu, from which you make another selection. This procedure continues until the action you are requesting finally occurs. In many instances, *Lotus 1-2-3* prompts you for information before the action occurs. For example, to format all the values in a spreadsheet as currency, you do the following:

1. Press the Slash key ("/") to bring up the main command menu.
2. Select "File," which brings up a submenu.
3. Select "Global" from the submenu.
4. Select "Format" from the next submenu.
5. Select "Currency" from the next submenu.

6. At this point, you are prompted to enter the number of decimal places. Two is the default. You can either press the Enter key to select the default value of 2 or change it.

After this sequence of commands, all the values in the spreadsheet appear with dollar signs, commas, and two decimals. *Lotus 1-2-3* users often represent the sequence of commands used to accomplish a task as a slash followed by the actual commands. For example, the preceding sequence would be represented as "/" File, Format, Global, Currency, 2 Decimals.

In *Excel,* making a selection from the menu bar brings up a submenu panel or a dialogue box. This box has selections and empty boxes that you must fill in with the required information.

Earlier we discussed increasing the width of columns to accommodate large values. In *Lotus 1-2-3,* this command sequence is "/" File, Column, Width, followed by the required width. We also discussed saving your spreadsheet to disk. In *Lotus 1-2-3,* this command is "/" File, Save, followed by entering the name of the spreadsheet.

Other commands are used to insert or delete rows or columns in an existing spreadsheet. For example, if you built a spreadsheet with data in columns A through H, but you must now add a new column between column D and E, you don't have to redo the entire spreadsheet. Simply position the cursor on column E (where you need a new column) and issue the "/" File, Insert, Column command. A new column will be inserted after column D. It will become the new column E. The other columns will be relabeled (the old column E becomes column F, and so on).

Advanced Features

Once You Understand the Basics, You Can Begin to Use More Powerful Features of Spreadsheet Programs.

Advanced features include

- Using ranges
- Formulas with functions
- Macros
- Customizing a spreadsheet

Many additional commands are available to let you change the appearance of the spreadsheet and perform a number of tasks.

UNDERSTANDING RANGES

Sometimes you want to change only a portion of the spreadsheet. For instance, you want to change the format of one column of values to percentages. Commands that change the entire spreadsheet are *global* commands; those that change only a portion of the spreadsheet are called *range* commands.

All the cells in a range must be next to one another and in the shape of a rectangle; Figure 9-9 shows examples. In *Lotus 1-2-3,* a range of cells is identified by the cell address of the upper left cell, followed by a period, followed by the cell address of the cell in the lower right portion of the range. Once again, see Figure 9-9. The command "/" Range, Format, Currency, 2 Decimals, and entering A1.C5 when prompted for the range would format all the cells between A1 and C5 (cells in columns A, B, and C and rows between 1 and 5) as currency with two decimals.

You can also designate a range by highlighting the range. Before issuing

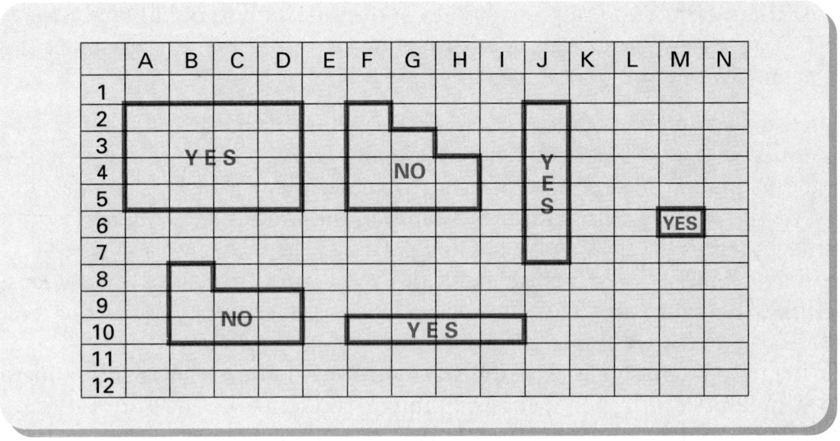

FIGURE 9-9

The cells in a range must be next to each other and in the shape of a rectangle. A single cell is considered a range.

the command with the "/", position the cursor in the upper left corner of the range, it need not be entered. Then issue the command. When prompted for the range, it need not be entered. The first address will already be in the data entry line since you already placed the cursor there. The cursor is anchored into position by depressing a period. Then use arrow keys to move to the right and down to the lower right corner of the range. As you do this, the range is highlighted and the cell address is entered in the data entry line. This accomplishes the same task as if you keyed in the range yourself. The advantage is that you don't have to know what the range is before issuing the command.

In a graphical spreadsheet such as *Excel,* you indicate the range before issuing the command by clicking on the upper left corner cell and dragging the cursor to the lower right corner cell. Then you use the command bar to issue a command that will affect only the highlighted range.

Range commands perform many functions. You can copy or move a range of cells from one area of the spreadsheet to another. First you identify the range to be copied or moved and then you specify where to copy or move the cell or range.

The contents of cells can be removed by erasing a range of cells. For example, if you want to remove the contents of cells F10 through F20, the command is "/" Range, Erase, F10..F20. If you want to erase the contents of a single cell, you must use the range command. To erase the contents of cell BR500, the range to be erased is BR500..BR500.

You also use a range of cells when printing a spreadsheet. If the entire spreadsheet is to be printed, you must specify the range—in this case, the entire spreadsheet.

NAMING RANGES

A range can be assigned a name. The "/" Range, Name, Create command in *Lotus 1-2-3* prompts you to enter a range and its name. Once a range has been named, whenever a prompt appears to enter the range, you can simply enter the name. For example, if you name each of the columns by the month it represents, you can enter the name of the month when prompted for the range.

Named ranges can also be used in formulas. For example, if you name the cell that contains the January revenue total "JANREV" and the cell that contains the January expense total "JANEXP," you can build a formula to subtract expenses from revenues, "+Janrev-Janexp."

You can print out only certain ranges of a spreadsheet by using an easily recognized name. Instead of remembering that the March numbers are in the range C3.C50, you can name it "March." When prompted for the range, you can enter March instead of the actual range.

FORMULAS WITH FUNCTIONS

Using the arithmetic operators in a formula can be tedious if the formula contains many cells, such as totaling an entire column of values (+A1+A2+A3+A4...), or for complex formulas, such as figuring out the monthly payment on a loan at various interest rates. All the popular spreadsheet packages have *functions*, which are predefined formulas. In *Lotus 1-2-3,* functions are identified by an "@" sign, such as @sum, @avg, and @pmt; *Excel* simply uses the name. (If the *Excel* function is at the beginning of a formula, it must have the equals sign prefix, like all *Excel* formulas.) Functions have two advantages over simple formulas—they save space and time.

Functions have two basic parts: the function's name and a parenthetical statement containing the *arguments,* or variables, required. If multiple arguments are needed, they are separated with commas. *Lotus's* @sum function simply sums a range of cells. The only argument needed in the parentheses is the range to be summed.

For example, @sum(B5..B15) would sum all 10 cells in the range B5..B15. The formula @avg(B5..B15) would not only sum the values but also calculate the average (see Figure 9-10). A named range can be used with a function. If B5..B15 had been named "Estimate," the formula just cited could read @avg(Estimate). In *Excel,* functions work in the same way, but you indicate the range before you select the function.

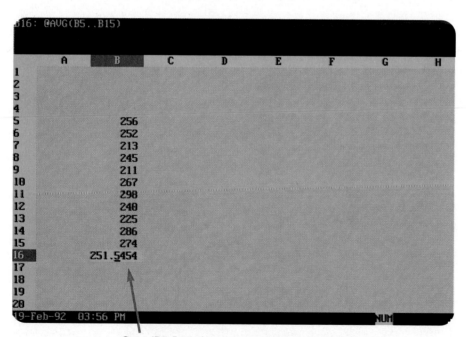

@avg (B5..B15) shows the average of cells B5 to B15

FIGURE 9-10

The @avg ("average") function in *Lotus 1-2-3* automatically calculates the average of a range of cells.

A more complex example is the *@pmt* function, which calculates the payment due on a loan. The function name is followed by three arguments: the *principal* (amount of the loan), the *interest rate*, and the *term* (length of the loan). For example, @pmt(10000,.1,4) would calculate the repayment on a $10,000 loan at 10% interest over four years.

Formulas can use cell addresses as well as values. This is also true with formulas containing functions. Our loan payment example can be written as @pmt(A1, A2, A3), where A1 contains the principal, A2 contains the inter-

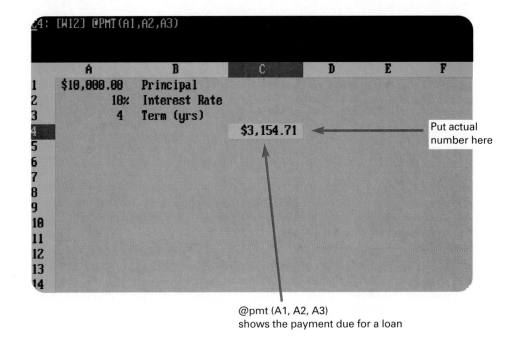

FIGURE 9-11

The @pmt ("payment") function uses cell addresses, rather than values, to calculate the payment due on a loan.

est rate, and A3 contains the term. Figure 9-11 shows how this looks on screen. You can change the contents of these cells and watch the formula automatically recalculate, allowing you to "what if" at will.

RELATIVE CELL ADDRESSES

Since most spreadsheets contain numerous formulas, a great deal of time can be saved by copying formulas throughout a spreadsheet. If you copy the formula @sum(B5.B50) from cell B51 to cell C51, you might think the sum of column B would end up in column C. But spreadsheet programs are smarter than that.

Formulas can contain *relative* cell addresses, which means when copied

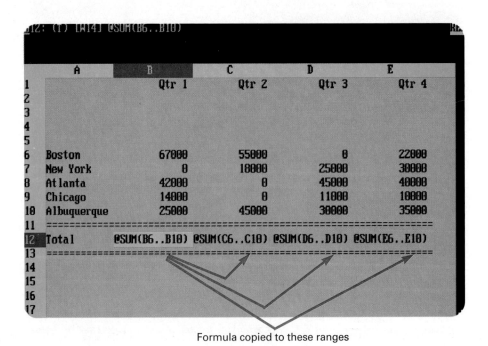

FIGURE 9-12

When a formula that contains cell addresses is copied to another range, *Lotus 1-2-3* adjusts the formula based on its relative position.

the spreadsheet program adjusts the formula based on its relative position. For example, if you copied the formula @sum(B5.B50) to cell C51, the program will adjust the formula so that it becomes @sum(C5.C50). Instead of getting the sum of column B you get the sum of column C.

You can copy formulas across a range, and the program will adjust the formula for each column. Figure 9-12 shows the result of copying a formula containing relative cell addresses from column B to columns C through E.

Cell addresses in a formula can be forced to remain constant, or *absolute*, if necessary. In *Lotus 1-2-3*, this means placing the dollar sign ($) before the row and the column that must remain constant when copied. For example, a formula containing the range B5 will remain the same, regardless of where it is copied in the spreadsheet.

EXCEL 3.0 ISN'T JUST ANOTHER PRETTY FACE

The newest trend in software development is applications that are both friendly *and* smart.

What makes a software application both friendly and smart? Well, *user-friendly* software applications are those that make it easy to learn and execute commands. For example, Macintosh applications and IBM systems that use the Windows operating environment are considered the friendliest. You can click your mouse on a picture, or "icon," on the screen (such as a garbage can or a file cabinet), as opposed to entering a keyboard command—such as pressing the Alt key and the F10 key simultaneously—that has no significance to the user.

A *smart* application, though, involves more than just a friendly visual display. A smart application is one that seems to *understand* how users think and how they actually work. *Excel 3.0*, a spreadsheet program designed for a Windows environment, is a good example of this trend. The developers of *Excel 3.0* watched people working with spreadsheet programs. They noted what commands were made most frequently and what commands most often led to mistakes. They also asked users what underlying assumptions they made at each point.

In addition to their own research, the *Excel 3.0* designers relied on a study conducted at Rice University, which found that 5% of commands typically get 85% of the use. Specifically, 70% of spreadsheet formulas are sums.

This told software designers that they should make the calculation of *sums* easy to execute at any point in the program. For example, *Excel 3.0* includes an "Autosum" button that guesses which numbers in a column you probably will not want to include in a sum. (It excludes cells with subtotals, for instance.)

Functions like Autosum are examples of software *anticipating* what the user is trying to do by making reasonable "guesses."

Here's another example of this kind of flexibility: say a column is too narrow for the numbers you want to put into it. Double-click the mouse button and the program will guess what width the column should be, accommodating your numbers.

The feature that may be the "smartest" and "friendliest," though, is one which recognizes that many of its users were trained on the *Lotus 1-2-3* spreadsheet. If you type in a *Lotus 1-2-3* command, *Excel 3.0* shows you how to restate the command for *Excel 3.0.*

At long last, it seems, a new era may have dawned in the often stormy relationship between workers and their software—software that actually tries to help the users do their jobs.

Smart software anticipates what the user will need. This makes spreadsheet programs like *Excel 3.0* much easier to use.

Source: "Microsoft's Spreadsheet, on Its Third Try, Excels," by Esther Dyson, *Forbes*, April 1, 1991, p. 118.

MACROS

Most spreadsheet programs provide for *macros,* a series of commands and/or keystrokes that can be saved and then retrieved whenever you want to execute the commands or enter the keystrokes. Each series of commands or keystrokes is given a one-letter name, which you enter instead of entering all of the commands or keystrokes.

A simple macro can be a sequence of a few keystrokes to save time performing a repetitive procedure. For example, to format a range of cells requires the series of commands "/" Range, Format, Cell, and pressing the Enter key. The keystrokes required for this task are "/rfc~". The Enter key is represented by a tilde (~). The macro is then given a name and saved. In *Lotus 1-2-3,* a macro name must begin with a backslash ("\"), followed by a single letter or number, such as "\F".

When you want to execute the macro, you press the Alt key in combination with the name of the macro. In this case, the macro you created to format a range of cells would be executed by holding down the Alt key and pressing the letter "F."

Macros can be much more sophisticated than simply repeating keystrokes. Some programs have a macro language that can perform basic programming functions.

Some spreadsheets let you create your own command menus. The custom menu options each have an accompanying macro. When you make a selection from the custom menu, that particular macro is executed. Users can create highly customized spreadsheet applications to match their special needs.

Working with Multiple Spreadsheets

Many Applications Require Multiple Spreadsheets.

In many business situations, individual spreadsheets must be consolidated into a single spreadsheet that shows the totals for all the individual spreadsheets. For example, branch offices of a business each will have an individual spreadsheet. The company headquarters will want to consolidate all the individual spreadsheets into a master spreadsheet that shows how the entire company is doing.

There are two ways that multiple spreadsheets can be used in conjunction with one another—dynamic, or "hot," links and three-dimensional spreadsheets. A *dynamic link* means a cell in one spreadsheet has a formula that accesses data from a cell in another spreadsheet. It is called dynamic because a change in the data of one spreadsheet will automatically be reflected in the other spreadsheet. A *three-dimensional spreadsheet* not only has rows and columns, but also has pages of spreadsheets. A change on one spreadsheet could be reflected not only horizontally and vertically on one spreadsheet, but on other pages as well.

DYNAMIC LINKS

Almost all the popular spreadsheet packages today can link multiple spreadsheets with a formula in one spreadsheet, can access data from others, and can reflect changes made in the other spreadsheets. For example, changes made in any departmental spreadsheet are automatically reflected in a master consolidation spreadsheet. (Figure 9-13 shows how this works.)

Besides simplifying consolidation, dynamic links make it easier to produce sophisticated yet easy-to-use spreadsheets by separating into individual spreadsheets the data entry functions, formulas, reports, and macros.

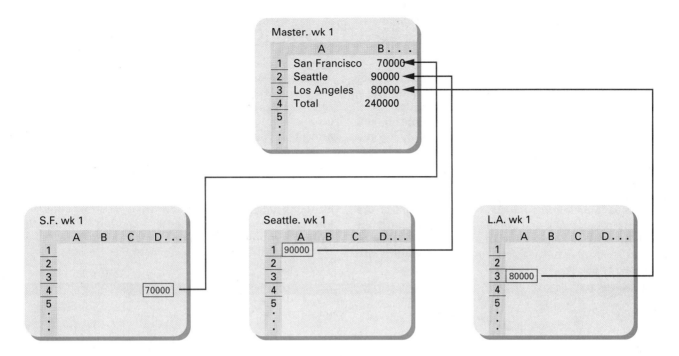

In *Lotus 1-2-3,* the *linking* formula, +<East.WK1>A4, in a spreadsheet named Master.WK1 uses data in cell A4 from another spreadsheet named East.WK1. Cell A4 in East.WK1 can be a value, but it is more likely a formula. If the values in the spreadsheet East.WK1 change, and these changes affect cell A4, the cell containing the linking formula in the spreadsheet Master.WK1 will be updated. In this way, a master consolidation file can be continually updated by changes made in files it is linked to.

Some programs let you view multiple files in linked spreadsheets at the same time, using a "windowing" environment. *Excel* using *Windows* calls this using a *workspace. Quattro Pro* and *Lucid 3-D* use their own windowing environments to view multiple files simultaneously. Handling multiple files in a windowing environment usually requires a great deal of computer memory.

THREE-DIMENSIONAL SPREADSHEETS

Some programs, such as the newer versions of *Lotus 1-2-3,* use three-dimensional spreadsheets that contain multiple layers or pages. You can move not only up and down in a spreadsheet but also from the top layer to deeper layers. Formulas can access data found in any layer, and commands can be used that affect several layers. For example, you can copy a range that includes not only columns and rows but also multiple layers.

Three-dimensional spreadsheets simplify analyzing and graphing the data to be consolidated. They let you view in cross-section the data that would otherwise be difficult to envision. They also make it easy to manipulate data and make changes to the spreadsheets, since range commands can encompass all the pages of the spreadsheet—something that cannot be done with dynamic linking.

The cell addresses in a three-dimensional spreadsheet identify the column, row, and page. The cursor can be moved to any page of the spreadsheet just as it is moved to cell addresses in a two-dimensional spreadsheet. The location of the cursor determines the active page that is displayed on the screen.

Many people use spreadsheets on their personal microcomputers. How do they use spreadsheets? Good financial management is easier when you use a spreadsheet. For example, once your basic budget is determined, you can ask "What if" questions such as: What if my income increases by 5%? What impact will a 6% increase in federal income tax have on the money I spend or save?

You can also use spreadsheet software to determine the real cost of your home. Once your formula is entered and the variable information such as the amount of the loan, interest rate, and amount of your monthly payment is determined, you can see the interest rates, the amount of your loan, or whether your monthly payments are increased or decreased.

Your results will be accurate *if the formulas you enter are accurate and the data keyed in or imported is accurate.* A basic rule to follow is: "Never assume your formulas and input are correct!" Use all available resources to prove that your formulas and input are valid.

Just as with a word processing application, you may want to consider a program that includes an integrated collection of software tools such as Microsoft *Works,* which contains word processing, database, and communications software, in addition to spreadsheet software. Information can be imported or exported between the various tools.

Graphics

Most Spreadsheet Programs Have Built-in Graphics Capabilities.

Although the graphing capabilities of spreadsheets don't match those of many graphics programs, spreadsheet graphics are good enough for many people's needs. *Excel,* with its graphical interface, can produce many types of charts.

The data in most programs are dynamically linked to graphs, which means that graphs continually reflect any changes made to the data in the spreadsheet. In some programs, such as *Excel,* graphs can be viewed at the same time as the spreadsheet. In other spreadsheet programs only the graph or the spreadsheet can be viewed at a time.

Importing and Exporting

The Data in a Spreadsheet May Be Needed for a Report and Therefore Must Be Entered into a Word Processing or a Graphics Program.

Data transferred to another program is said to be *exported*; data transferred into a program is *imported*.

Since different programs use their own internal formats, transferring data means not only physically moving it from one program to another but also converting it from the original program's internal format into the new program's format. The most common internal format for spreadsheets is the *Lotus 1-2-3* format, which is denoted by a file extension of .WK1. Since many spreadsheet and nonspreadsheet programs can import from, or export to, the .WK1 format, it is easy to get spreadsheet data in and out of other programs.

When a spreadsheet is exported to another program such as a word processing package, there is no dynamic link. A picture of the spreadsheet is placed into the word processing document. If changes are made to the spreadsheet, the file must once again be exported if the numbers are to be updated.

Some programs, however, have *warm links* in which the data in the spreadsheet is exported into a word processing program but a link remains. Therefore, changes in the spreadsheet are reflected in the word processing document.

Early Versions of Spreadsheets Did Only Number Crunching, So Add-in Utilities Were Created to Make Them More Flexible.

The first spreadsheets performed the basic mathematical operations and little else. They could not audit or debug a spreadsheet and left it up to you to find mistakes. Another weak area was their print capabilities. The early spreadsheet printouts were designed only to be functional.

5-6-7-8 INNOVATE DON'T LITIGATE!

When software guru Richard Stallman was awarded the $240,000 MacArthur grant (popularly known as the "genius" award because it is given to people in all fields who show great potential), few thought he would use the money to organize a street demonstration. But that's exactly what he did.

Stallman, a maverick software developer, founded the *League for Programming Freedom*, which put up picket lines outside the Cambridge, Massachusetts, offices of the Lotus Development Corporation in the summer of 1990. Angry computer programmers carried picket signs and chanted (with a sly reference to the hexadecimal counting scheme that is a basic tool of their trade):

1-2-3-4 kick the lawsuits out the door!
5-6-7-8 innovate don't litigate!
9-A-B-C interfaces should be free!
D-E-F-0 look and feel has got to go!

Why is Stallman so mad at Lotus, which makes the number-one spreadsheet program, *Lotus 1-2-3?* Stallman and friends are angry about Lotus's "look and feel" lawsuit against three other software companies that make competing spreadsheet programs—Paperback Software International, which makes *VP Planner;* Mosaic Software, maker of *Twin;* and Borland International, which makes *Quattro Plus.* All three are low-cost programs that, according to Lotus, copy the graphics, menus, and command structure of *Lotus 1-2-3.* That is, they copy the "look and feel" of *Lotus 1-2-3.* Lotus claims that this amounts to copyright infringement.

Stallman worries that if Lotus wins its case against these smaller companies (and in 1990 Lotus did win its case against Paperback), software innovation in the United States will be stifled, leaving an open field for the Japanese and the Europeans.

It's a complex issue. Some argue, using Microsoft's *Excel* spreadsheet program as an example, that it is not so difficult to create programs that duplicate *Lotus 1-2-3's* features without blatantly copying the "look and feel" of

Lotus. One software developer, in fact, is confident that strict copyright protection will *help* software development, arguing that "developers will be encouraged at the thought that their original achievements can be safeguarded and not just picked off at will."

What's more, Lotus's critics claim that Lotus itself borrowed heavily from one of the most popular earlier spreadsheet programs, *VisiCalc.* Mitch Kapor, one of *Lotus 1-2-3's* creators and now head of ON Technology, contends that programmers have always borrowed ideas. "Nobody does anything from scratch," says Kapor.

In the short run, users will suffer if Lotus's court victories result in higher prices. But will strict ownership of a program's "look and feel" ultimately squelch innovation or encourage it? The software industry is still too new to predict its future with any certainty. Still, it's likely that any action that discourages software innovation won't be good for users or for the U.S. software industry.

Many software developers fear that if computer companies can copyright the "look and feel" of a software program, such as *Lotus 1-2-3*, it will stifle innovation.

Sources: "Computing the Cost of Copyright," by John Schwartz and Debra Rosenberg, *Newsweek,* August 27, 1990, p. 52. "Lotus Scores Copyright Win," by Nell Margolis, *ComputerWorld,* July 2, 1990, p. 1.

These shortcomings prompted the creation of an entirely new type of software product, and companies were formed to make these products. These companies developed *add-in* software utilities that filled the gaps in the early spreadsheet packages. Add-in utilities are designed to run in conjunction with the spreadsheet and provide features not included in the original program.

AUDITING UTILITIES

A few years ago it was necessary to use add-in programs such as the *Cambridge Spreadsheet Analyst* to perform a series of logical tests that probed the integrity of the spreadsheet. They looked for formulas that referenced empty cells, cells with data that were not referenced by any formula, and problems with logic, such as trying to add the contents of a cell to itself. Then they generated an audit report.

Today, most spreadsheets have built-in audit procedures. But many people assume that a spreadsheet will work properly and use it without a thorough audit, which is a serious mistake. Spreadsheet audit procedures should be used before putting any spreadsheet on the job.

SPREADSHEET PUBLISHING

At first the only type of output you could get from a spreadsheet program was one that looked as if it had come right off an adding machine, with the closest thing to artwork being a series of "====". Then, in 1989, Funk Software produced *Allways* as a *Lotus 1-2-3* add-on that changed the way spreadsheets would be printed.

Allways converts the character-based spreadsheet into a graphical image on the screen and lets you enhance the appearance of the spreadsheet dramatically before you print it. *Allways* lets you use a variety of different styles and sizes of type, add boxes and line drawings, and use shading. This package was so successful that Lotus bought the technology and now includes it in some versions of *1-2-3*. *Lotus's* WYSIWYG mode now lets you create very attractive spreadsheets (see Figure 9-14). ("WYSIWYG" stands for "What You See Is What You Get.")

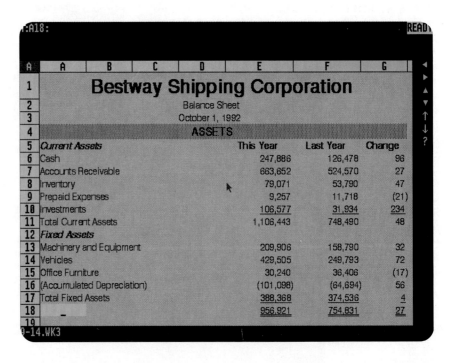

FIGURE 9-14

Lotus's WYSIWYG mode lets you enhance the appearance of a *Lotus 1-2-3* spreadsheet.

A program called *Impress,* by PC Publishing, was released as a *1-2-3* add-on a year after *Allways. Impress* lets you use the features that enhance the appearance of the spreadsheet while still in the spreadsheet mode. In *Allways* you must switch between the graphic mode and the spreadsheet character-based mode. Lotus also bought the rights to *Impress* and includes it with some versions of *1-2-3.*

Spreadsheet programs with built-in graphical capabilities, such as *Excel,* produce attractive spreadsheet output more readily than add-ons. Spreadsheet publishing features now have become highly competitive selling points for all the spreadsheet manufacturers.

Future Trends

Graphical User Interfaces, Publishing Features, Data Sharing, and Connectivity Will Be Important Aspects of Future Spreadsheet Programs.

Spreadsheets that take advantage of existing graphical user interfaces (such as Windows, Presentation Manager, or OS/2) will dominate the spreadsheet market in the years to come. The older character-based spreadsheet programs will probably fade in popularity, except for people who demand speed over all other features. Even these people will switch to graphics-based spreadsheets as the hardware becomes faster.

Spreadsheet publishing will continue to evolve. More and more publishing features will be incorporated into spreadsheets. You will be able to make spreadsheets very attractive and use a wide variety of graphics.

Data sharing will be the driving force. The ability to use data found in one application, such as a spreadsheet, directly and dynamically in another application, such as a word processing program, will probably determine which spreadsheet will dominate the market.

As an example of data sharing, the Dynamic Data Interchange (DDI) is a Microsoft Windows protocol that allows applications to exchange information in a computer's memory without user intervention. In other words, your word processing document can include a table of figures directly accessed from your spreadsheet, and it will dynamically update itself whenever the spreadsheet is updated.

Finally, *connectivity* to database information will be a powerful new tool. The ability to perform queries and extract data directly from a database while in your spreadsheet will become an increasingly common feature of spreadsheet programs.

REVIEW QUESTIONS

1. List three ways a business might use a spreadsheet. *Profit/loss stmt, sales estimates, cash flow mgmt.*
2. What does the phrase "What if?" have to do with spreadsheets?
3. What is currently the most popular spreadsheet program? List three other spreadsheet programs. *Lotus 1-2-3 (b) PlanPerfect, Excel, and Quattro Pro*
4. How are the columns of a spreadsheet identified? *alphabet letters*
5. What is a cell? What is a cell address? *(a) intersection of row & column*
6. Name two things found in the control panel. *active cell address & contents*
7. How is *Excel's* tool bar used? *uses program's graphical abilities & icons to change appearance of a spreadsheet*
8. What does scrolling mean?
9. What is the home position in spreadsheet terminology? *cell A1*

★ scrolling — moving monitor across and down, to read different parts of a sheet.

10. What is a label? *text that ID's parts of spreadsheet (rows, columns)*

11. In *Lotus 1-2-3*, how do you establish the alignment of a label? *^ = l. align,*
    " = r. align, ^ centers label

12. What is a value? *data c̄ no prefix, always r. aligned*

13. What does a series of asterisks mean in a cell? What must be done to solve the problem? *column not wide enough to accomodate value*

14. What must be entered into *Excel* to indicate you are about to enter a formula? What is typically used in *Lotus 1-2-3*? *(a) = sign (b) + sign*

15. Formulas can contain which of the following: (a) arithmetic operators, (b) cell addresses, (c) values, (d) a prefix, (e) only a and c, or (f) all of the above. *f*

16. What is a range? *rectangular portion of spreadsheet; cells must be next to each other and rectangular*

17. What does the phrase "highlighting a range" mean? *Before issuing command to the /, position cursor in upper l corner of range, need not enter;*

18. What is a named range? Why would you use a named range? *formulas, can enter name only c̄ range*

19. What are functions in a spreadsheet? Name two advantages of using them. *(a) predefined formulas (b) save space + time*

20. What is the advantage of using cell addresses in a formula instead of values? *When*

21. What is the advantage of using a formula that contains a relative cell address? *When copied, the spreadsheet program adjusts formula based on its relative position.*

22. What is a macro? Why are macros used? *(a) series of commands or keystrokes you can save/retrieve whenever (b) save time doing repetitious work*
    (M = .1 letter name)

23. Explain the difference between a spreadsheet with dynamic links and a three-dimensional spreadsheet. *When copied, the spreadsheet program adjusts*

24. Why have add-in programs been developed to work with spreadsheets? Give examples. *Make more flexible (audit, publish)*

Dynamic link - cell in 1 spreadsheet has formula to access data from cell in another spreadsheet
3 dimensional — has rows + columns, but also pages of spreadsheets changes can reflect hor., vert., & other pages as well

TOPICS FOR RESEARCH AND DISCUSSION

1. Most businesses now rely on computer spreadsheets instead of manual worksheets. The advantages of using these programs are obvious, but what are the possible disadvantages or dangers? What do you think businesses should do about these potential problems?

2. You work in a small plumbing supplies company. Your boss wants you to do some financial projections using a spreadsheet. Currently, the office is using an older model IBM-compatible computer that runs slowly (at 12 MHz) with a monochrome monitor. The company is not using Windows. Some of the financial projections look as though they might be pretty complicated, and you have not used a spreadsheet program before. So you are a bit worried. However, your boss has assured you that "it doesn't matter what the projections look like, just so I can read them." Research your options. Look in computer magazines and visit your local software store. What would you recommend to your boss?

3. Your company is about to standardize on a spreadsheet program. It is concerned about producing attractive financial reports that will be sent directly to customers. The reports must include many graphs. The company uses both Macintosh and IBM computers. Investigate the available spreadsheets to see which would be best suited to the task. Focus on the spreadsheet's publishing and graphics capabilities. Based on your research, make a recommendation for each type of computer. Give the reasons for your choice, the cost of the software, and if applicable, other software packages with which it can interface.

CHAPTER 10

DATABASE MANAGEMENT

OBJECTIVES

The information in this chapter will enable you to

- Explain the structure of a database.
- Explain the different tasks for which database management systems are used, and discuss who carries them out.
- Distinguish between flat-file and relational database management systems.
- Explain the functions of data dictionaries, indexes, and query languages.
- Describe the ways in which you can use an existing database.
- Explain the usefulness of commercial databases.
- Outline the process of building a database.
- Describe how issues of privacy and security affect the use of information in databases.

The computer's ability to store, organize, and retrieve data is at the heart of electronic information processing. This chapter focuses on software used for managing data—not only numbers, but facts of all kinds about people, places, and things.

What Are Database Management Systems?

Database Management Systems Store Data So That Computer Users Can Retrieve It for Many Purposes.

A *database management system,* or *DBMS,* is a set of programs used to store data in files and to retrieve and manipulate that data for various purposes. For example, many merchants use database management systems to maintain information about their sales transactions, inventories, employees, and payrolls. Merchants use such information to plan their finances, prepare paychecks and income tax reports, avoid running out of popular items, and decide which items to continue selling and which employees deserve promotions.

Using its DBMS, a retail business can create a record for each item it keeps in stock, each sales transaction, each employee, and each paycheck. A *record* is a collection of information about a specific person, place, or thing (Figure 10-1). This person, place, or thing is called an *entity*. An employee is an entity, and so is a sales transaction or an item in a store's inventory.

Records are made up of *fields,* which contain separate facts about an entity. An employee record typically includes a field for the employee's last name, another field for the employee's first name, and additional fields for the employee's address, social security number, hiring date, and so forth.

FIGURE 10-1

A card in a phone file (top) is a simple example of a record. Each card contains information about one person or organization. The same information can be stored in a record in a database (bottom).

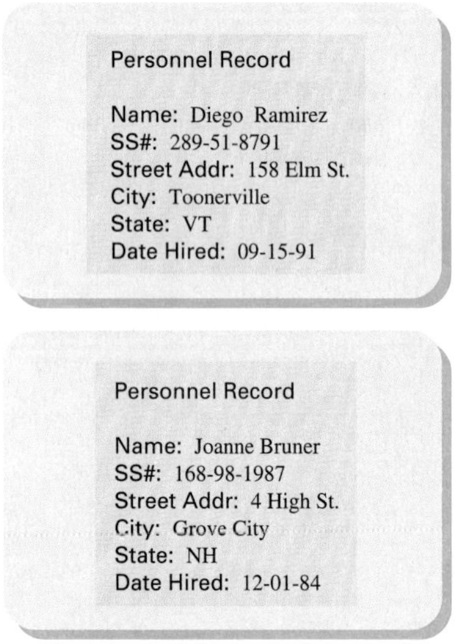

Personnel Record

Name: Diego Ramirez
SS#: 289-51-8791
Street Addr: 158 Elm St.
City: Toonerville
State: VT
Date Hired: 09-15-91

Personnel Record

Name: Joanne Bruner
SS#: 168-98-1987
Street Addr: 4 High St.
City: Grove City
State: NH
Date Hired: 12-01-84

FIGURE 10-2

These personnel records have identical fields, but the information in the fields is different for each employee. All of a company's personnel records together make up its personnel file.

A set of records containing the same kinds of data about different entities is called a *file* (Figure 10-2). A retail store's employee file, for example, includes a record for each of its sales clerks and other employees, and its inventory file includes all of its inventory records. All the employee records have the same fields, although the information in the fields is different for each record. Likewise, all the inventory records contain the same kinds of data about different items in the inventory.

A set of files is called a *database.* A store's database might include its employee file, its sales transaction file, and its inventory file. These files might have some fields in common, although each one also has fields that the others do not have. For example, a payroll record, a sales transaction record, and an employee record might all have fields for an employee's social security number. However, only a payroll record would have a field that contains a paycheck amount.

Figure 10-3 illustrates how fields, records, and files serve as the building blocks of a database.

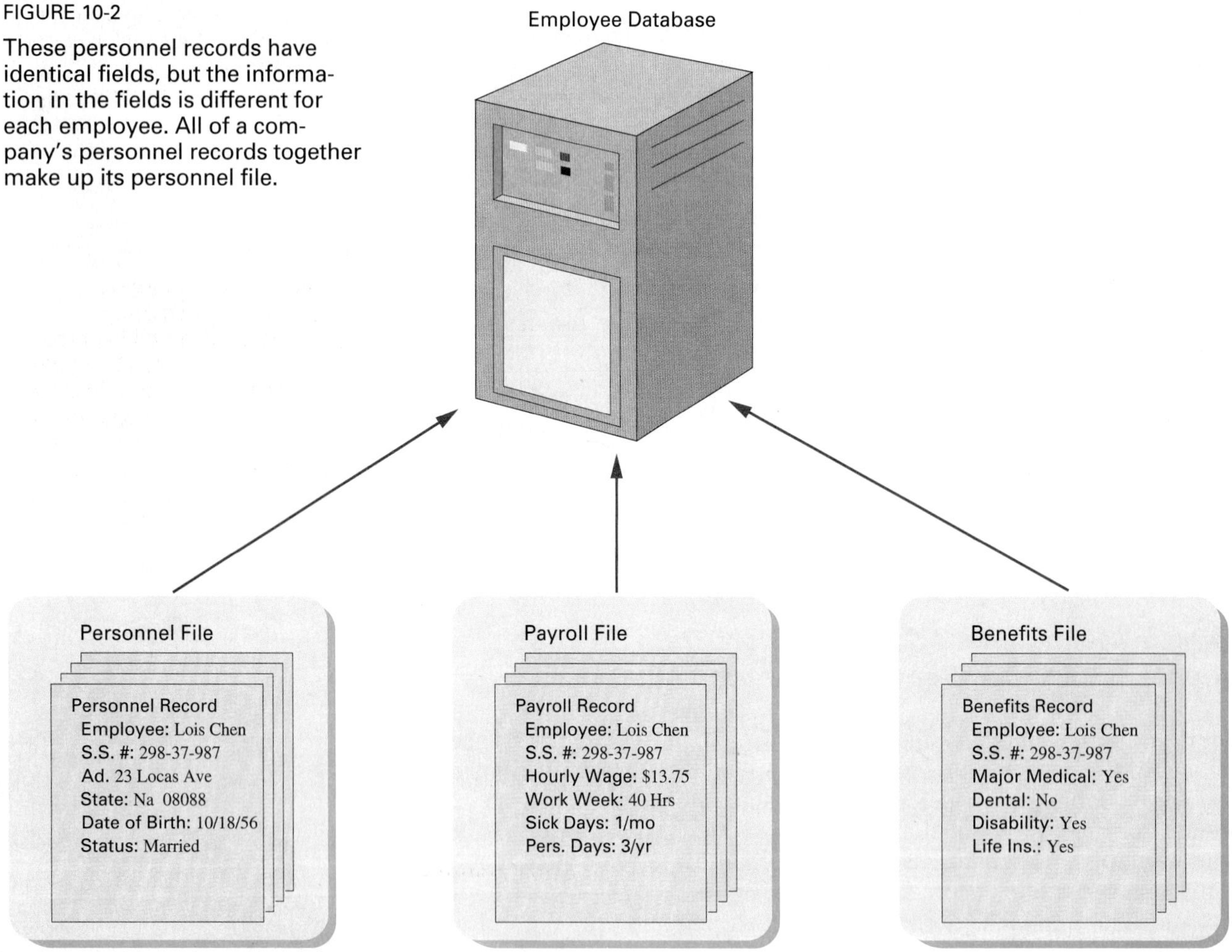

Employee Database

Personnel File

Personnel Record
Employee: Lois Chen
S.S. #: 298-37-987
Ad. 23 Locas Ave
State: Na 08088
Date of Birth: 10/18/56
Status: Married

Payroll File

Payroll Record
Employee: Lois Chen
S.S. #: 298-37-987
Hourly Wage: $13.75
Work Week: 40 Hrs
Sick Days: 1/mo
Pers. Days: 3/yr

Benefits File

Benefits Record
Employee: Lois Chen
S.S. #: 298-37-987
Major Medical: Yes
Dental: No
Disability: Yes
Life Ins.: Yes

FIGURE 10-3

A company's personnel records make up its personnel file, payroll records make up its payroll file, and benefits records make up its benefits file. The company's employee database includes all of these files.

THE HISTORY OF MICROCOMPUTER DATABASE MANAGEMENT SYSTEMS

The first database management systems were created in the early 1960s, for use with mainframe computers. Microcomputer DBMS products first appeared in the early 1980s, soon after microcomputers were introduced.

The early database management systems on big computers required computer specialists to set up databases, files, and records. Clerical workers could add, modify, delete, or look up individual records, but only the specialists could retrieve information based on data from many different records or files. Today, a microcomputer DBMS enables anyone to set up a database and retrieve information based on data from many records. A set of information based on data from several records is called a *report.* Figure 10-4 shows an example of a report from a database.

Small organizations today are likely to manage all of their information with microcomputers. Only very large organizations still maintain their databases primarily on storage devices accessed by main frames.

Some organizations use *distributed databases,* which include files stored in different computers (Figure 10-5). For example, a microcomputer might contain a company's project and client files; a larger computer contains its payroll and employee files. The computers that access the files must be linked so they can exchange information.

Abbet E.53 Cox Av Whtng NJ 07980
Bartlow Les D Jama. Blvd Q. NY
Coates A Cobain Rd Jcks CA 38596
Dunne P M 39 Main St FL 19206
Fetch J 9 Ocean La MA 86741
Gray H 343 River Av Key West FL 22435
Heck John 17 Clark St Alba NY 96143
Kaufman T 8 Linden Dr Bklyn NY 68790
Lynch Y 49 6th Ave Man. NY 67922
Martin Clair Tampa Rd Atl.Ct NY 41140
Otto M 34 S. John Pl Na TN 30718
Possta V 1025 E.13th St Chgo Ill 83883
Reyes M 21-2 Neil Av T.R. NJ 49827
Scala J.K.91 16th St NH 12321 . . . . . .
. . . .

FIGURE 10-4

This mailing list is a simple example of a report produced with a DBMS. To produce such a report, you specify which records and fields you want to include in it.

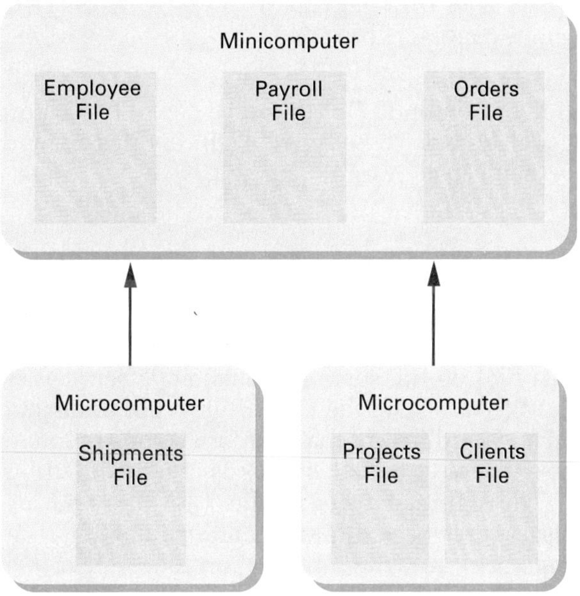

FIGURE 10-5

In this distributed database, a manufacturing company's employee and payroll files are stored in a minicomputer at company headquarters, but its project and client files are on microcomputers at its branch offices, and its shipments file is in a microcomputer at its warehouse. The computers are linked so they can exchange data.

WHO USES A DBMS?

All kinds of organizations use DBMS software to manage many kinds of data. Hospitals use database management systems to keep track of data about patients and medical supplies. Governments use them to manage data about tax collections, drivers' licenses, vehicle registrations, and welfare payments. Businesses use them to keep information about customers, inventories, and employees up to date. Any organization that maintains data about many people, places, or things needs a DBMS for storing, maintaining, and retrieving data.

Database management actually involves three categories of tasks:

- Creating and controlling databases
- Keeping data up to date
- Retrieving information

A typical DBMS is used for all of these tasks. In a small office with only a few employees, one person may use the database management system to create and control databases as well as to enter and retrieve information. In a larger organization, people with different responsibilities use the DBMS in

Table 10-1: DBMS Users	
Employees	**DBMS Tasks**
Computer professionals	Creating and controlling databases
Managers	Retrieving information
Clerical workers	Keeping data up to date

different ways. For example, computer specialists may create databases using the DBMS; clerical workers use it to enter and modify data, and managers use it to retrieve information (Table 10-1).

Types of Database Management Systems

Files Are Integrated in a Relational DBMS But Not in a Flat-File DBMS.

A microcomputer DBMS can be one of two types: a flat-file system or a relational system. These types of DBMS differ in the way they organize data and in their capabilities.

FLAT-FILE SYSTEMS

A flat-file DBMS creates files that are completely independent of each other. In fact, you can think of each file in a flat-file system as a separate database. The files do not share information. When you enter data into a record in a flat-file database, the DBMS does not automatically add that data to any other record. All of the data in a record is entered directly into that record, not retrieved from other records in other files (Figure 10-6).

The simplicity of a flat-file DBMS is both its biggest advantage and its biggest drawback. Building and maintaining a flat-file database is very easy, and so is retrieving information. But a flat-file system cannot use the data you enter in one file to update another file automatically, as a relational system can. With the more advanced flat-file systems, such as Buttonware's *PC-File,* you can retrieve information based on data from several files. However, no flat-file system has reporting features as powerful as those found in a relational DBMS.

With a flat-file DBMS, you can assign passwords that users must enter to view or sort a file or to add, delete, or modify records. With some flat-file systems, including Symantec's *Q&A,* you can even limit access to individual records or fields. At best, though, the security features of a flat-file DBMS do not equal those of a relational DBMS.

Flat-file systems are so much less powerful than relational systems that many experts do not regard them as true DBMSs. Instead, they reserve that term for relational systems and refer to flat-file systems as file managers.

Despite their limitations, flat-file systems are ideal for many relatively simple data management tasks. For example, a small company's sales office might use a flat-file system to manage information about prospective customers—their names, addresses, telephone numbers, when they were last called, and so forth. At home, you might use a flat-file DBMS to manage information about a collection of books, baseball cards, compact disks, or other items.

Q&A and *PC-File* are among the most popular flat-file DBMS packages for IBM-compatible microcomputers. Both of these products have some features

FIGURE 10-6

If a flat-file database includes a payroll file and a personnel file, information about employees must be entered manually in both files. That is because the files are not integrated, so they cannot share information.

usually associated with relational database managers. For example, you can use either of these products to retrieve information from some relational database management systems.

For the Macintosh, Claris's *FileMaker* is one of the best-selling flat-file systems. Other DBMS packages for the Macintosh include ProVue Development's *Panorama* and *Microsoft File*.

RELATIONAL SYSTEMS

In a *relational DBMS,* files can be linked so that they share data, as shown in Figure 10-7. This linkage is called *file integration.* Integrated files can be set up so that when you enter data in one record, the DBMS automatically uses that entry to update records in other files. Integrating files helps to ensure that records in different files do not contain conflicting information. It also saves data entry time by eliminating the need to enter the same data about an entity in several records.

Personnel File

S/S#: 231-23-1329
Last Name: Chen
First Name: Lois MI D

Payroll Rec.
S/S# 231-23-1329

FIGURE 10-7

Files in a relational DBMS can be integrated so that they share data. In this example, the payroll and personnel files both use social security numbers to identify employees. If you change an employee's payroll record, the DBMS automatically enters this new information in the employee's personnel file.

Relational systems are much more expensive than flat-file systems, and they use far more RAM and disk space. Because they are so much more complex, they are also harder to learn. With a relational DBMS, you need to use a special-purpose language to obtain many kinds of information. However, a relational DBMS offers much more flexibility than a flat-file system, and it offers much better control over access to data. You can store data about an entity in several different files and control access to each file separately. For any organization that needs to maintain a complex database, a relational DBMS is a necessity.

Popular relational DBMS packages for IBM-compatible microcomputers include *dBASE,* created by Ashton-Tate, Microrim's *R:base,* and Borland International's *Paradox.* Among the many choices for the Macintosh are ACIUS Inc.'s *4th Dimension* and Odesta Corporation's *Double Helix.* Fox Software makes two popular relational DBMS packages: *FoxBASE+,* which is available for the Macintosh as well as IBM compatibles, and *FoxPro,* a faster system for IBM compatibles.

PARTS OF A DBMS

A DBMS has several components that usually include a data dictionary, indexes, and a query language.

Data Dictionaries

A *data dictionary* spells out the rules for using a database and controls access to data. It lists all the fields in the database and specifies what kinds of data can be entered in them. For example, if the data dictionary specifies that the Lastname field can contain only letters, you cannot enter numbers in that field.

The data dictionary can also include rules governing which users are allowed to see, add, change, or delete records. On a network, the data dictionary allows only one user at a time to make changes in a record. Many users, however, may view the record at the same time.

In a relational DBMS, the data dictionary may also specify that some fields in a record are *protected fields*. You cannot change the data in those fields, although you might be able to change them on another record. For example, the address field on a payroll record might be protected. If an employee moves, you cannot change the address in the payroll record. However, if you change the address on the employee's personnel record, where the address field is not protected, the system will make the change in the payroll record automatically. All files will have the same address for the employee, which helps to prevent mistakes and confusion.

In a large organization, the person who sets up and maintains the data dictionary is usually called the *database administrator*. When a new employee joins the organization, the database administrator assigns that employee a password and specifies what tasks that employee may carry out with the database. For example, the database administrator may give an employee the right to view the personnel file but not the payroll file, or to view data but not to change it. The database administrator is responsible for *data security,* the confidentiality and safety of the organization's data. The database administrator is also responsible for *data integrity,* which means making sure that records do not contain conflicting information. The database administrator also determines what data should be stored in online databases.

Indexes

A database *index* tells the DBMS where records are located on the computer's storage disk. The DBMS uses the index to find specific records, just as you can use the index of this book to find specific information.

In a database, each record has at least one *key field,* which contains entries that can be indexed in a logical order. For example, personnel records can be indexed on social security numbers, names, or employee numbers, and the fields containing these three entries can be key fields. The person who creates a database selects the key fields for files.

You can use any key field to find a record. If a key field might contain the same entry for two different entities, you can use a combination of key fields to narrow the search. For example, a company may have several customers with the same name, but they will probably have different addresses. To find a record for one of those customers, you can enter both the customer's name and address.

In a relational system, primary key fields can be used to integrate files. A *primary key field* contains a piece of data that distinguishes an entity from all other entities in a file. A social security number can be a primary key because no two people have the same social security number. Names are not good primary keys because an organization may maintain records about several people with the same name.

A database index contains a database's primary key field entries and the disk addresses for those entries, as shown in Figure 10-8. The data may be positioned at random in the file and on the disk, but the primary key field entries are listed in order in the index. A DBMS can find a record quickly by scanning the index for the primary key field entry. For example, by scanning the index for an employee's social security number, a DBMS can determine where to find the employee's personnel record.

Primary Key Field	Disk Address
432-18-1985	Track 6, Sector
159-19-1897	Track 17, Sector 7
298-65-6987	Track 41, Sector 9
166-86-6598	Track 2, Sector 6
761-69-1986	Track 9, Sector 12

FIGURE 10-8

A DBMS has an index for each file. The index lists the primary key field for each record, along with the record's disk address.

Query Languages

You use a DBMS's *query language* to produce reports. If a DBMS did not have a query language, you would have to use a programming language for this task. Unlike some programming languages, query languages use English-like commands. A simple command in a query language does the work of many lines of programming language.

Many DBMS products have a *proprietary* query language that is used only in that product. *Paradox,* for example, has a query language that cannot be used with *dBASE, R:base,* or other DBMS products. But many proprietary query languages resemble *Query by Example,* or *QBE,* a query language IBM developed for mainframe systems. A QBE-type language lets you produce reports without having to learn the language. Instead of writing command lines, you simply specify what information goes in a report by filling in blank fields on a screen that lists all the fields in the database, as shown in Figure 10-9.

FIGURE 10-9

With a query language modeled on QBE, you tell the DBMS what records to include in a report by entering criteria for different fields. This query, for example, tells the DBMS to include all records where the Style field contains the word *Sneakers,* the Color field contains the word *Red,* the Size field contains the number 7, and the entry in the Price field is less than $75.

ITEM 3	BRAND	STYLE	COLOR	SIZE	PRICE	LOCATION
		Sneakers	Red	7	<75	

Query languages that are used with many products include *Query Language,* also known as *QUEL* ("quell"), and *Structured Query Language,* also known as *SQL* ("sequel"). *SQL* has become a standard language for producing reports with many DBMS products. *R:base, dBASE,* and some other DBMSs with proprietary query languages now include *SQL* components as well (Table 10-2). *SQL* was developed by IBM.

Table 10-2: Query Languages	
DBMS	**Query Language**
PC-File	Proprietary
Ingres	QUEL
Oracle	SQL
Paradox	Proprietary
R:base	Proprietary, SQL
Q&A	Proprietary, SQL
dBASE	Proprietary, SQL

Using Databases

You Can Use Databases to Look Up Existing Records, Enter or Modify Data in Them, Delete Records, and Produce Reports.

Once a database is set up, users can search it for specific records and enter or modify data in records. They can also produce reports that contain information drawn from many records. Carrying out these tasks does not require much experience with a DBMS. Many people who use databases use them only for some of these purposes.

SEARCHING A DATABASE

Suppose a customer calls a store to ask if it has a certain item in stock. Using a DBMS, a clerk can answer the question in seconds, without going into the stockroom and looking on shelves. To find the answer to the customer's question, the clerk uses the DBMS's "search" feature to locate the record for that item in the inventory file. In some DBMS packages, the search features have different names, such as "view" or "find."

The search feature is used to look up a record without making changes in it. Although each DBMS package has its own search procedure, most of them work in the same way. You start by selecting a file, then you select the search option to display a record form. A *record form* is a record in which the fields have not been filled in (Figure 10-10). Record forms are created by the person who sets up the database.

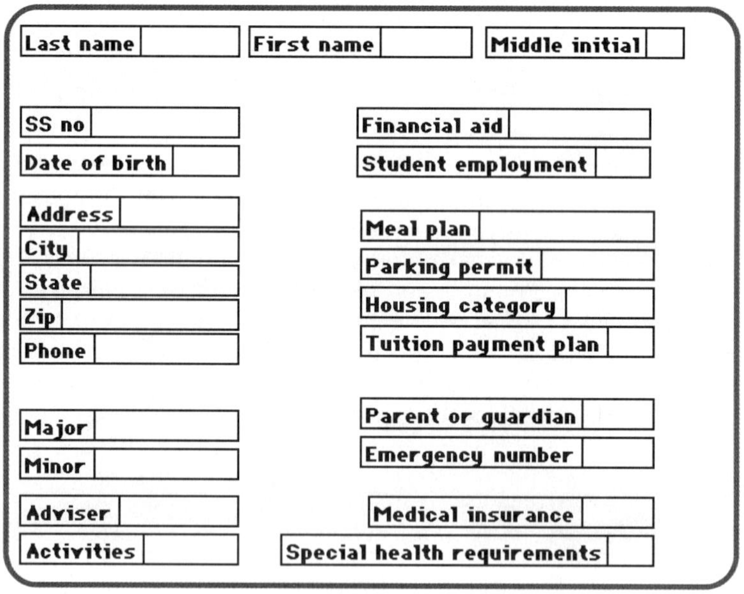

FIGURE 10-10

A record form looks just like a record, except that its fields are not filled in. You use record forms to search databases, by filling in one or more fields to specify what records you want to see. You add records to a database by filling in the fields and storing your entries.

On the record form, you fill in one or more fields to identify the record you want to look up. The DBMS displays the first record with entries that match what you filled in. For example, if you fill in the name Lois Chen in the name field on a form, the DBMS displays the first record in the file with that name in the name field. If the file contains several records for people named Lois Chen, you can view the first one, then press a key to go on to the next one, and so forth. If you know that the file includes records for several Lois Chens and you want to look up only one of them, you can fill in more fields to specify which one you want. You might fill in an address or a telephone number, since the other Lois Chens would probably have different addresses and telephone numbers. The DBMS displays only the records with field entries that match all the information you fill in.

You can look up a record even if you know only part of the data that appears in one of its fields. For example, you can look up a record by someone's last name, even if you don't know the person's first name. If you filled in the name Moore in the name field, the DBMS might display records for several people named Moore. You could look at the records individually to determine which one you need. With some DBMS products, you can even find records for people when you are not sure how to spell their names. *PC-File,* for example, has a search feature called "soundex" that identifies field entries by how they sound. If you use this feature to look up the name Nilsen, the software might display records for people named Nelson and Neilson as well as Nilsen.

Displaying Files as Tables

Most DBMS packages give you the option of displaying a table that shows all the records in a file, with all the fields. Displaying the file as a table, rather than displaying records one at a time, allows you to scan the file at random. It also enables you to sort the records in different ways.

Sorting Files

You can sort a file on any indexed field. For example, suppose you are working with a customer file in which the name, amount purchased, and ZIP code fields are all indexed. You could sort the file to list records in any of these ways:

- In alphabetical order of customers' names
- By ZIP code, so that all customers with the same ZIP code are grouped together
- According to the amounts they have purchased

You can sort records in *ascending* or *descending* order. If you sort the customer records in descending order by the amounts the customers have purchased, the record for the customer who purchased the most would appear first, and the record for the customer who purchased the least would appear last. An ascending alphabetical list would start with Z and work up to A.

What if you sort the file by customers' names and several customers have the same name? You can use a *secondary sort field* to distinguish between them. If you use amount purchased as the secondary field for a descending sort, the Lois Chen who purchased the greatest amount would be listed before anyone else with that name. You can designate other sorting fields as well, in case two people with the same name purchased the same amount.

ENTERING AND MODIFYING DATA

Suppose a construction firm maintains a database that includes a client file and a project file. When the firm acquires a new client, it must add a record for the client to the client file. For each project the firm handles for the client, it must add a record in the project file. If the client's telephone number changes, the firm needs to change the phone number entry in the client file. Similarly, as a project progresses, the firm must make changes in the project record to keep it up to date. All of these tasks come under the category of *data entry,* which involves entering and modifying data in databases to keep them up to date.

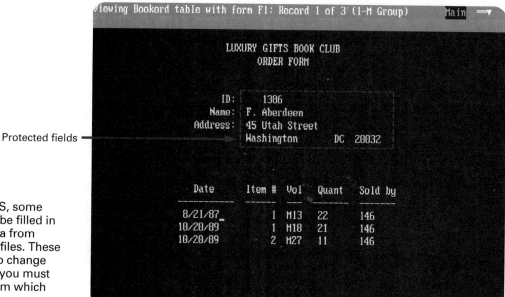

Viewing Bookord table with form F1: Record 1 of 3 (1-M Group)   Main ▼

FIGURE 10-11

With a relational DBMS, some fields in a record may be filled in automatically with data from other records in other files. These fields are protected. To change the data they contain, you must modify the records from which the data was retrieved.

Protected fields ——

Data entry, like searching a database, generally starts with selecting a file. Next, you select the DBMS feature for adding or modifying a record.

To add a record, you fill in the fields on a record form. Some fields may be filled in automatically if you are using a relational DBMS, as shown in Figure 10-11. When you save your entries, the DBMS stores them in the database on the computer's disk. It also adds them to the database index so you can retrieve the record later.

To modify a record, you must fill in enough information in the record form to identify the record you want to change. When the DBMS finds and displays that record, you move the cursor to the field where you want to make the change and you fill in the new data. Remember that some fields may be protected, so that you cannot make changes in them. When you save your work, the DBMS makes the changes in the database and revises the database index.

DELETING RECORDS

You may also need to delete records from time to time to keep a database up to date. For example, suppose you provide word processing services to companies in your town, and you maintain a database of prospective clients. If a company in your database goes out of business, you need to delete the record from the file. Otherwise, if you use the database to create mailing lists, you would continue to waste time and money sending mail to a company that no longer exists.

All DBMS packages have commands for deleting records, but the procedures for using them are varied. Typically, you select a file, select the delete option, and then identify the record you want to delete. The DBMS displays the record and asks you to confirm that you want to delete it. If you confirm, the system deletes the record from the database and the index.

PRODUCING REPORTS

Suppose you want a list of all the sales representatives in your company who sold more than $10,000 worth of products last month, with their home addresses. The database does not include individual records that show how much each representative sold, but it does include a record of each sale, with the name of the representative who made the sale. But the sales representatives' addresses do not appear on the sales records. Can your company's DBMS produce the list you want? It can if it is a relational system. The list is typical of the kinds of reports you can produce with a DBMS.

To produce a report, you must specify what information you want it to include. You must also define a format for the report, which determines how it will look on the screen or on the printed page. How you specify the contents of a report and define its format depends on the DBMS software you are using and on its query language.

With some DBMS packages, you define the contents of a report by filling in fields to indicate what the report should include. With others, including those that use *SQL,* you write a list of commands that define the report's contents. You create the list free form, using the syntax of the query language, as shown in Figure 10-12.

```
SELECT  brand, price
FROM  inventory
WHERE  size = 7,  price <$75,
              color = red
ORDER BY  price
```

FIGURE 10-12

This SQL query tells the DBMS to produce a report from the inventory file listing all the brands and models of size 7 red sneakers that are priced under $75.

USING COMMERCIAL DATABASES

Many organizations maintain large collections of data that they make available to subscribers or to the general public. These are called *commercial databases.* A commercial database contains information on a specific subject of interest to a large number of organizations or individuals. For example, the *Lexis* commercial database contains federal court cases. Lawyers can search the *Lexis* database to find out how courts have ruled in cases similar to the ones they are handling for their clients. They can get this information much faster through *Lexis* than by searching manually through court records. Although law firms must pay a fee for each *Lexis* search, using *Lexis* costs far less than the firms would spend to maintain this enormous amount of information in their own computer systems.

Some commercial databases are run by nonprofit organizations, such as the U.S. Census Bureau, which makes its population data available to outsiders. *Lexis,* which is run by *Mead Data Central,* is an example of a profit-making commercial database. Other profit-making commercial database services include *Dow Jones News/Retrieval*, which offers databases with news and information of interest to investors; *Prodigy*, which offers databases of news, shopping services, travel information, and games; and *Disclosure*, a service for investors. Several commercial database services also offer the *Official Airline Guide,* which lists departure and arrival places and times as well as other data about scheduled flights.

The procedures for using a commercial database depend on the database. However, one guideline applies to all commercial databases: it pays to be as precise as possible when you request information. Take *Lexis* as an example. If an attorney searches this database for cases that use the word *fraud, Lexis* will produce thousands of cases. The search will cost a great deal, and the attorney will have to sort through these cases manually to find the relevant ones. A search for cases using the words *insurance fraud* will produce many fewer cases and cost far less. A search for cases using those words along with the word *automobile* and the name of a specific insurance company would produce still fewer. In summary, the more information you provide for narrowing down the search, the more efficient the search will be.

Building Databases

To Build a Database, You Develop a Plan, Then Create a Structure, Then Add Data.

Building a database is something like building a house. Before you start, you determine how many rooms you need and how you want to use each room. Then you create the structure of the house: its roof, its walls, and so forth. Once the structure is in place, you can add furnishings.

You also need to think about what files to include and what those files will contain. You also need to think about who will have access to each of the files, records, and fields. Then you build the structure of the database according to the plan. Once you have created the structure for the database, you can begin storing data in it.

DEVELOPING A PLAN

Developing a plan for a database can begin with a pencil and paper. You start by listing the entities for which you want to keep records. Then you list the data items you want to store about each entity. For example, you might want to keep an employee's social security number, name, home address, and phone number.

Next, determine the relationships among the entities you have listed. If you want to save the same data for several entities, those entities are related. For example, suppose you listed inventory items and sales as entities. For each inventory item, one of the data items you want to keep is its name. For each sale, you also want to record the names of the items sold. Thus, the inventory items and sales entities are related. You can map out such relationships as part of your plan (Figure 10-13).

The next step is to determine what data items you can use as primary keys to identify and link entities. For example, you can assign a unique item number to each inventory item and use that number as a primary key. You can also assign customer numbers and sale numbers. For salespeople and other employees, you can use social security numbers as primary keys.

FIGURE 10-13

When you store the same pieces of data for different entities, those entities are related. In this database plan for a videotape rental business, the tape and customer files are both related to the rental file. A map showing how entities are related should be part of your plan.

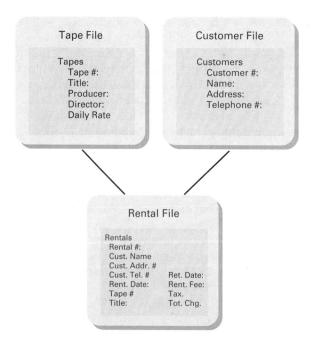

Finally, you determine how many characters are needed for each data item, and what kinds of characters they will be. Let's say you are recording the state and city where each employee lives. City names can be quite long, so you might want to allow as many as 20 characters. For states, however, you can use the Postal Service's two-character codes. State codes and city names are both alphabetic, but some data items, such as ZIP codes, are numeric. Others, such as customer numbers, can contain both letters and numbers.

CREATING A STRUCTURE

To create the structure of the database, you use the DBMS. If you have made your plan carefully and thoroughly, creating the structure is easy. As you create the structure of a database, you are also creating its data dictionary.

The procedure for creating the database structure depends on which DBMS you are using, but in a typical DBMS the first step is to select an option from a menu (Figure 10-14). You then enter a name for the database. The name must be one that is not assigned to any other DBMS in the computer system. Next, you refer to your plan and create a file for each entity you have listed. To create a file, you define a record form. The record form must include a field for each data item you want to store about the entity. When defining a field, you specify how many characters, and what kinds of characters, it can contain.

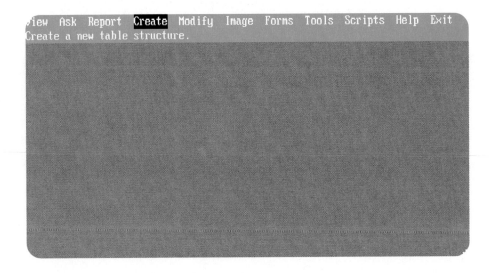

View Ask Report **Create** Modify Image Forms Tools Scripts Help Exit
Create a new table structure.

FIGURE 10-14

A DBMS typically includes a menu of tasks you can perform with it, including a listing that you select to create a new database.

With a relational DBMS, you can include *pointers* in some fields to indicate that the data for those fields comes from other files. For example, the Employee name field in a payroll file might point to the personnel file.

You can also include other information in field definitions. For example, when defining a field that contains dates, you need to define a format for entering and displaying dates (Table 10-3).

Table 10-3: Date Formats	
Format	**Entry and Display**
MM/DD/YY	03/13/49
MM-DD-YY	03-16-49
MM/DD/YYYY	03/16/1949
Month DD, YYYY	March 16, 1949

AUTHORIZING USERS

Most organizations will need to specify who is authorized to use the database and what kinds of tasks each user can perform. This usually means assigning a password and an authority level to each user. Typically, only users at a certain authority level are allowed access to certain sensitive fields.

As your organization changes, you must update the user list regularly. You need to add new employees to the list of authorized users and remove those who leave the organization. You may also need to change employees' authority levels when they are given new assignments. But once you have created the structure and authorized people to use the system, they can begin adding data to it and using it to process information.

DATABASE APPLICATIONS

Years ago all applications software was written in programming languages such as Fortran, BASIC, C, and Pascal. Many microcomputer applications are still written this way, but others are now written with DBMS packages. These are called *database applications.*

A database application is simply a database that is tailored for a specific organization or industry. For example, a database for a medical practice would include records for patients, invoices, supplies, employees, and payroll. Using a DBMS, a software developer could build an application for this practice that includes all of the record forms it needs. Employees of the medical practice, which might not have any computer professionals on staff, could then use the DBMS to add data to the database, keep it up to date, and retrieve information from it. One employee might also be responsible for keeping the list of authorized users up to date.

Since most medical practices keep similar kinds of records, a developer might be able to sell the application to many practices. Each practice could use the same application to maintain its own database. Database applications written for whole categories of businesses, such as a database that can be used by any medical practice, are called *vertical market applications. Custom applications*, on the other hand, are written for one organization only.

Some DBMSs make it so easy to build a database that nonprogrammers in large organizations can create their own applications instead of requesting them from the computer specialists. This possibility has aroused considerable controversy in many organizations. Department managers tend to view the microcomputer DBMS as a means of getting applications immediately

YOU AND YOUR PERSONAL MICROCOMPUTER

If you intend to use your microcomputer for applications such as developing and maintaining a household inventory, keeping track of investments, collecting data for federal and state tax returns, or maintaining an address file, you will need database software.

Although it takes time to analyze your informational needs and to determine the contents of the records to be stored in your databases, your efforts will be rewarded. Once a file is created, your software provides for adding, deleting, updating records, and generating reports.

If you defined your needs carefully, you will be able to use the data stored in the records in many ways and to generate a variety of reports. Multiple use of the data is your reward for careful planning.

When you are selecting database software, make certain the functions described in this chapter are included, the instructions are well written and easy to follow, and a "hot line" is available that can be used if a problem occurs. Also, make certain you can import data from your database into your word processing and spreadsheet programs.

Whenever changes have been made to your database, back up the file. Loss of a database due to an error, a disk crash, or a track on your disk becoming defective can be a disaster. There may be no way to obtain all the information that was stored in the database.

DATABASE PUTS BUSINESS ON FAST TRACK

In 1986, Donald Douglass was a race car driver looking for a new career. Today, Douglass mastery of a simple database software program, *Professional File*, has put him at the helm of his own million-dollar travel company, Torque Trip, Inc.

As a professional race car driver and official on the International Motor Sports Association (IMSA) circuit, Douglass was all too aware of the chaos surrounding major racing events such as Watkins Glen in upstate New York, particularly around booking hotel rooms. His idea was simple: someone with an insider's perspective, such as himself, would become the booking agent, coordinating hotel rooms, airline tickets, and car rentals.

The problem, initially, was that Douglass had limited capital (he was operating out of his home) and little knowledge of computers. He required a database system that could juggle information about races, hotels, teams, credit card numbers, contacts, number and types of hotels booked, and payments owed to hotels. This database program also had to be inexpensive, easily learned by a novice, and able to run on inexpensive hardware.

Douglass found he could do almost every task he required with *Professional File,* using two IBM-compatible 386 computers, a modem, and a FAX machine. To book airline tickets, he connected his system with the airline computer system, SABRE.

Douglass created a series of files to store information about hotels, drivers, and events. These files had to be integrated, so that while he worked in one file, he could pull information from any other file. This is crucial to his business, because race car drivers are always changing their reservations. Although more expensive relational databases usually are required for such tasks, Douglass figured out how to use the "look-up" function of *Professional File* to get the job done.

Douglass knows that his system can't do everything. Eventually, he realizes, he'll have to invest in more expensive software and hardware. But, for now, he's mighty happy having shaped a million-dollar business using such relatively simple tools.

Former race car driver Donald Douglass's mastery of a simple database program helped him to build a million-dollar travel company.

Source: "Make Your Business Succeed by Taking Control of Data," by Lisa Kleinholz, *Home-Office Computing,* July 1991, p. 32.

rather than waiting weeks or months to get them from the programming staff. But computer professionals argue that they must control database applications to maintain data integrity and confidentiality.

DBMS Utilities

External Utilities Are Available That Make Some DBMS Tasks Easier.

All DBMS packages have utilities built in for creating record forms, producing reports, and building applications. However, enterprising software developers have created many external utilities for use with popular DBMS packages to make these tasks easier.

FORM GENERATORS

Although all DBMS packages have built-in utilities for creating record forms, formatting the forms can be tricky. This is especially true if the forms will be printed, then filled in manually before being turned over to data entry workers.

Several utilities are available that make the job easier. These include Bloc Publishing's *Form Tool* (Figure 10-15), FormWorx Corporation's *Form Publisher,* JetForm Corporation's *JetForm Design,* and Ventura Software, Inc.'s *FormBase.* These utilities combine "what you see is what you get" desktop publishing tools with other features that facilitate computerized entry.

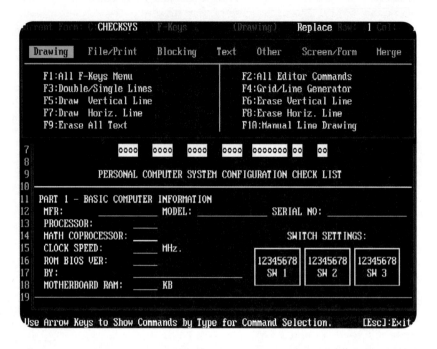

FIGURE 10-15

Form Tool is a DOS-based utility that makes it easier to create record forms for data entry.

REPORT GENERATORS

All DBMS packages also come with built-in report generators, but many products are available that make it easier to produce reports. These report generators are popular among applications developers, who use them to create report templates that help them to work faster. Clarion Software Corporation's *Report Writer* is a report generator for the Macintosh (Figure 10-16). IBM-compatible report generators include Concentric Data Systems, Inc.'s *R&R Report Writer,* Data Access Corporation's *FlexQL,* and Quadbase, Inc.'s *dQUERY.*

FIGURE 10-16

Report Writer is a utility you can use to define the contents and formats of reports and create report templates on Macintosh computers.

File Edit Format Font Document Utilities Window

Immigration Report

Immigration to U.S. by Country of Origin

Countries	1988	1971-80	1961-70	1951-60	1941-50	1931-40
Albania	82	329	98	59	85	2,040
Austria	514	9,478	20,621	67,106	24,860	3,563
Belgium	581	5,329	9,192	18,575	12,189	4,817
Bulgaria	217	1,188	619	104	375	938
Denmark	558	4,439	9,201	10,984	5,393	2,559
Estonia	11	91	163	185	212	506
Finland	390	2,868	4,192	4,925	2,503	2,146
France	2,524	25,069	45,237	51,121	38,809	12,623
Great Britain						
..England	13,228	137,374	174,452	156,171	112,252	21,756
..Scotland	--	--	29,849	32,854	16,131	6,887
..Wales	--	--	3,675	3,884	--	--
Greece	2,458	92,369	85,969	47,608	8,973	9,119
Hungary	1,227	6,550	∞,401	36,637	3,469	7,861
Ireland	5,058	11,490	37,461	57,332	29,967	13,167
Italy	2,949	129,368	214,111	185,491	57,661	68,028
Latvia	31	207	510	352	361	1,192

Page 1   Normal+...

Another product, FirstMark Technologies, Ltd.'s *KnowledgeSeeker,* includes artificial intelligence features to help users decide what data to include in reports. This utility can scan files to spot trends and patterns in the data. For example, a charitable organization might use it to determine which donors are likely to respond to a plea for emergency funds. Although a person could examine the data to make the same determination, *KnowledgeSeeker* can often do the job faster and more accurately.

Future Trends

As Database Management Systems Increase in Number, Power, and Ease of Use, So Will Concerns about Privacy and Data Accuracy.

DBMS software is becoming easier to use. DBMS developers, like other software producers, are creating products with graphical user interfaces that call for making selections with a mouse rather than entering complex commands with a keyboard. DBMS developers are also simplifying their query languages, which will make it easier to obtain reports from databases.

COMPUTERS CALL THE SHOTS IN THE NBA

Selecting players for the National Basketball Association (NBA) is a headache for everybody involved—particularly for the people who represent the team at the annual NBA player draft. Not only must they juggle information from their team's scouts and coaches, but, because they don't know which players will be selected before their turn comes around, they must come prepared for any and all possibilities. It's not that they don't have access to a database, it's just that their database exists in their heads. It makes for a sometimes effective, but not very efficient system.

Recently, one NBA team, the Indiana Pacers, brought along some extra help. In the process, they may have changed the face of professional sports. The Pacers showed up at the 1990 NBA player draft with a pocket-sized personal computer, the Poqet PC, connected to a sophisticated database. The computer-database link was the brainchild of the Pacers' computer analyst, Michael Mullen.

Here's how it works: coaches input information about prospective players into a program called *PC File,* a file manager with relational reporting abilities. Mullen then loads the files into the *dBase IV* database program. The Pacers, after watching all the top choices selected by the clubs ahead of them in the 1990 draft, used Mullin's database network to pull a winner out of the remaining pool when they selected Kenny Williams. Because Williams had not played basketball in a year and had attended a junior college, little was known about his potential. Despite all the second-guessing of the fans and players, Williams made the team and played well.

The Pacers are also using computers to make play selections from the bench. The club uses computer systems to analyze what the other teams will do in certain situations with particular players on the floor. Although Mullin is still developing programs that coaches can use during the game, he may soon be sitting on the bench himself, advising coaches.

Whether it's calling plays during a game or drafting players, people ultimately make the decisions. But it surely doesn't hurt to have *all* the information you need on tap from that computer in your pocket.

The Indiana Pacers of the National Basketball Association use a computerized database to help draft players at the NBA's annual draft and to make play selections during games.

Source: "Indiana Team Sets Pace for Game Preparation," by Michael Fitzgerald, *Computerworld,* April 29, 1991, p. 45.

As microcomputer DBMS packages become cheaper, more powerful, and easier to use, bigger and bigger databases are being developed with them. Also, more people are using these packages to retrieve information from mainframe database files. The collection of more and more data, and its availability to greater numbers of people and organizations, inevitably raises questions about privacy, data integrity, and the ethics of using this data. DBMS developers and database administrators clearly must find better ways of restricting access to credit files, medical records, and other sensitive data.

REVIEW QUESTIONS

1. What is a database management system? Give a general example of how a business might use one.
2. What is a record? An entity? A field? A file? A database?
3. When did the first microcomputer DBMS products begin appearing?
4. What is a distributed database?
5. What three types of activities are involved in database management? In a large organization, who is most likely to perform each of these tasks?
6. What are the two major types of DBMSs for microcomputers? What is the main difference between them?
7. Which type of microcomputer DBMS has more powerful reporting and security features?
8. What is file integration? Give an example of file integration.
9. What are two benefits of file integration?
10. Which type of microcomputer DBMS is easier to learn?
11. What is a data dictionary?
12. What is a protected field? Give an example.
13. What is a database administrator?
14. What is the purpose of a database index?
15. What is a key field? A primary key field? What purposes do they serve?
16. What is a query language? A proprietary query language? What is *SQL*?
17. What tasks can you perform with an existing database?
18. Suppose a file is indexed on the customer number and amount purchased to date fields. The customer number field contains a unique number for each customer, and the amount purchased to date field shows the customer's total purchases. In what ways could you sort the records in this file?
19. How do you add a record to a file in an existing database?
20. In general, how do you define a report using *SQL*?
21. What is a commercial database?
22. What decisions must you make when planning a database?
23. What is a database application?
24. What are two categories of external utilities for use with DBMS software?

TOPICS FOR RESEARCH AND DISCUSSION

1. Government agencies, insurance companies, and other organizations store a great deal of data about individuals in their databases. Some people are alarmed about violations of privacy that could result from

organizations sharing their data about individuals. Do you think this concern is well founded? Should organizations be held responsible if they release data that damages a person's reputation? What if this data helps others to avoid business dealings with an individual who is dishonest or unreliable? What if the data is incorrect? In the library, you might find newspaper or magazine articles about this controversy, including stories about laws that have been proposed or adopted to protect privacy. These stories could be the basis of a written report on databases and privacy.

2. Suppose you are opening a videotape rental store. You have an IBM-compatible computer, and you need a DBMS to store data about the store's videotapes and its customers. From the database, you want to be able to find out if a copy of a particular tape is available, or if all copies are rented out. When a customer rents a videotape, you want to know if that customer still has other tapes that are overdue.

   What other information might you want to retrieve from the database? Would you select a flat-file DBMS or a relational DBMS for the store? Why? You might also read recent reviews in computer magazines and select a specific product. If you do, explain why you selected the product.

3. Develop a plan for a database that would be useful to your school. For example, it might include a personnel file and a student file. What other files might it include? Specify the fields in each file, including the numbers and types of characters that can be entered in each field. Would you need to integrate the files? If so, specify how the files would be related and how you would link the files.

GRAPHICS

OBJECTIVES·

The information in this chapter will enable you to

- Define computer graphics and graphics software.
- Discuss the usefulness of computer graphics.
- Distinguish between drawing programs and painting programs.
- Describe CAD programs, presentation graphics software, and several other kinds of specialized programs.
- Describe several graphics utility programs and explain their usefulness.
- Discuss the future of computer graphics.

Earlier chapters discussed desktop publishing, which you use to incorporate graphics with text in documents, as well as monitors that enable you to display graphics. This chapter deals with the different kinds of software you can use to create and edit graphics.

What Are Computer Graphics?

Computer Graphics Software Allows Us to Draw and Change Images on the Computer Screen.

Computer graphics are pictures that you create, modify, or view on the computer screen. To create, edit, or display computer graphics requires *graphics software*. You can reproduce computer graphics with a printer or plotters, and you can transfer them to word processors or desktop publishing programs.

Computer graphics include many kinds of drawings, with or without color, that can be created on the screen. They also include photographs or images that are created on paper but then scanned and converted to a digital format that computers can read. Figure 11-1 shows some examples of computer graphics.

THE HISTORY OF MICROCOMPUTER GRAPHICS

Computer graphics have been around since the early 1950s, and graphics software was available for some of the first microcomputers. For example, you could create simple charts and graphs on early Apple and IBM models. However, it was only when Apple introduced the Macintosh computer in 1984 that microcomputer graphics really caught on. The Macintosh was designed to work with graphics, and its monitor could display them more

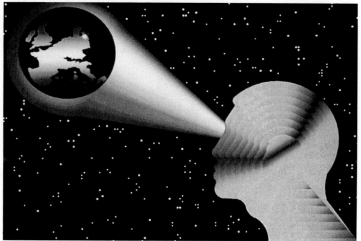

FIGURE 11-1

Computer graphics can range from simple drawings to precise technical drawings, from artistic paintings to photographic images.

clearly than any other microcomputer monitor at that time. Creating graphics was also easier with the Macintosh than with earlier microcomputers.

Each Macintosh originally came packaged with a graphics program, called *MacPaint*, that revolutionized the computer graphics world. *MacPaint* was so simple that anyone could quickly learn to use it, yet it was powerful enough to make highly detailed illustrations.

From the beginning, you could hook up a Macintosh to an Apple *ImageWriter,* which was one of the first microcomputer printers that could reproduce graphics. But microcomputer graphics took a giant step in 1985 when Apple introduced the *LaserWriter.* This printer was equipped with the *PostScript* page description language discussed in Chapter 8. *PostScript* enables a printer to reproduce exactly what appears on the computer's monitor. The Macintosh, with its graphics software and the LaserWriter, offered a fast and easy way to produce graphics of very high quality.

Since then, other laser printers with *PostScript* and other page description languages have become available for IBM-compatible computers as well as the Macintosh. High-quality graphics monitors have also been developed for IBM compatibles. As these hardware products have become more popular, they have also become more affordable. These developments have helped to make the use of computer graphics widespread in the business and art worlds. The increasing popularity of graphics also has encouraged software companies to develop more products. Scores of powerful, versatile graphics programs are now available for both IBM-compatible and Macintosh computers.

USES OF GRAPHICS

Graphics software is now widely used to create illustrations for many kinds of documents (Figure 11-2). Because these programs can create dramatic images, they have become essential tools for preparing marketing and advertising brochures as well as business reports for investors and managers. Computer graphics are enlivening desktop published documents, from simple school newsletters to technical manuals. In addition to illustrating printed materials, you can create slides and overhead transparencies for sales presentations, workshops, and seminars with graphics software.

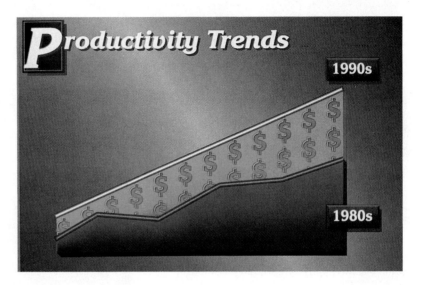

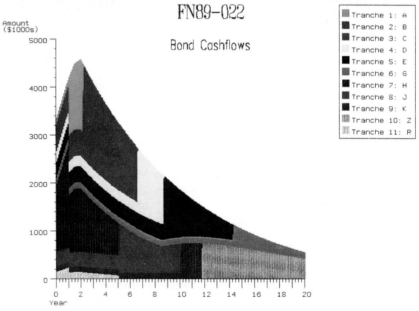

FIGURE 11-2

Graphics are an important part of many printed documents.

TYPES OF GRAPHICS PROGRAMS

There are two basic types of graphics programs: drawing programs and painting programs. They differ in how the computer handles the work you do with them and in the kinds of graphics you can create. Increasingly, though, graphics software products are being developed with features of both kinds of programs.

Drawing Programs

Drawing Programs Build Shapes by Combining Line Segments, and They Treat Each Shape as a Separate Object.

With *drawing programs*, you create images by combining line segments. For example, to a drawing program, a circle is a single curved line, and a box is four line segments. To draw a box, you draw line segments so that the end point of each segment is the starting point for the next.

The shapes you draw appear as outlines. You can fill the outlines with patterns, or you can insert text in them (Figure 11-3). You can also move them around on the screen, enlarge them, or make them smaller.

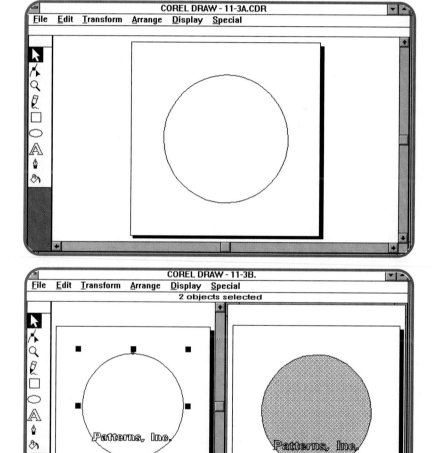

FIGURE 11-3

With a drawing program, you can create the outline of a shape, then fill it with patterns. You can also add text.

A drawing program uses mathematical formulas to tell the computer how to display or print each line segment. Thus, each shape you draw is actually a series of formulas. This allows the computer to treat the images as separate objects, each with its own formulas. Because of this, you can draw many shapes and manipulate them independently of each other. For example, if you create a box, a circle, a triangle, and an oval on the same screen, the computer treats each shape as a separate object. Even if they overlap each other, you can easily move any of them without disturbing the others. You can also reduce or enlarge each shape separately, change their colors or shading, or modify them in other ways.

Because they treat shapes as objects, drawing programs let you work in layers. A square might be on top of a circle, and under the circle there might be a triangle. Since each of these shapes is an object, you can move the square and the circle to get to the triangle if you want to change it.

Drawing programs can create much more than simple shapes. You can create elaborate images by combining line segments in complex ways, then filling the resulting shapes with a variety of patterns (Figure 11-4).

Drawing programs have one other significant advantage. Since all the graphics in a drawing program are represented as math formulas by the computer, they take up little storage space on a disk, and the program can draw them quickly on the screen or on paper. This can be a very important consideration if you produce documents with many diagrams.

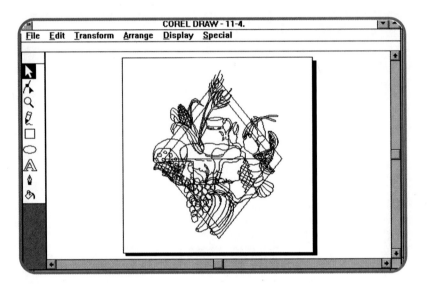

FIGURE 11-4

This elaborate image was created with a drawing program. It consists of a series of individual shapes that were filled with different patterns.

USING A DRAWING PROGRAM

All this discussion about formulas may suggest that you must use a lot of math to use a drawing program. Not so. It's only the computer that regards the graphics as formulas. You just draw on the screen by using a mouse to move the cursor.

Figure 11-5 shows a screen from a typical drawing program before a

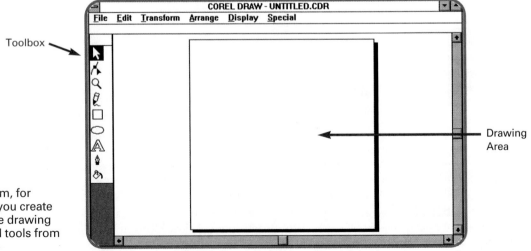

FIGURE 11-5

With a drawing program, for example, *Corel Draw*, you create and edit graphics in the drawing area, using shapes and tools from the toolbox.

drawing has been added to it. The large blank area is the *drawing area* where you actually draw your graphic. The area on the left is called the *tool-box*. It contains geometric shapes, such as rectangles and circles, and lines of different thicknesses that you can select and use in a graphic. The toolbox also contains icons of drawing tools, such as a pencil and an eraser. In addition to the toolbox and the drawing area, a drawing program displays an assortment of patterns and colors you can use to outline or fill in shapes. Various type styles for labeling graphics may also be displayed.

Using the *ruler line* along the top edge of the drawing area, you can draw a graphic to precise measurements. The dotted *grid lines* also act as drawing guides. You can change the units of measurement shown on the ruler line and the grid line to inches, centimeters, and picas. (The pica is a unit that typesetters and publishers use. It equals about one-sixth of an inch.)

Once a figure is drawn, you can use commands to alter its appearance. Most drawing programs list their commands in *pull-down menus* along the top of the screen (Figure 11-6). When you select pull-down menus with the mouse or keyboard, they pull down like a window shade.

Some of the most common commands—cut, copy, paste, and undo—don't need explanations. They do exactly what you would expect. Most drawing programs also have *zoom* commands that work like a zoom lens on a camera to magnify your view of a small area. This makes detailed editing much easier. Then, when you want the big picture, you can turn off the zoom command.

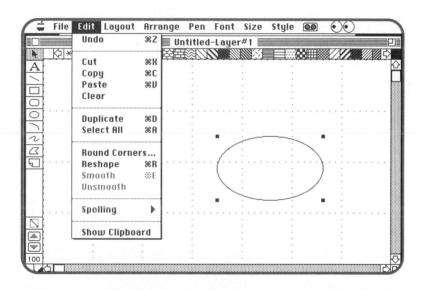

FIGURE 11-6

The pull-down Edit menu from *MacDraw*.

DRAWING PROGRAM PRODUCTS

Many drawing programs are available for Macintosh and IBM compatible computers. One of the most powerful is Adobe's *Illustrator*, produced by the same company that created *PostScript*. *Illustrator*, which is also one of the most complex microcomputer graphics programs to use, is available for both Macintosh and IBM compatibles. Aldus has created a drawing program called *Freehand* that is similar to *Illustrator*. *Freehand* graphics can be used easily with *PageMaker*, the desktop publishing software also created by Aldus.

Another drawing program, *Corel Draw*, was designed for use on IBM compatibles with the Windows environment. Graphics created with *Corel Draw* can easily be used with the Windows version of *Ventura Publisher*, which is one of the most popular desktop publishing packages.

MacDraw, which was the first drawing program for microcomputers, is still one of the most widely used programs for the Macintosh. This program is compatible with the *Word* word processor, which means that it's easy to use *MacDraw* graphics for illustrating documents created with *Word*. *MacDraw* has become the standard graphics software for newspaper illustrations.

Painting Programs

Painting Programs Build Graphics Dot by Dot.

Painting programs create graphics dot by dot. As you learned in Chapter 5, dots on a computer screen are called pixels. So a painting program creates graphics on the screen pixel by pixel.

Pixels are arranged in grids, and a Super VGA monitor can display a grid with as many as 1,024 by 768 pixels. A painting program creates an image on the grid by turning pixels on and off. At its most basic level, the painting program assigns each pixel to a bit in the computer's memory. This process of assigning pixels to bits is called *bitmapping*. Bitmapped graphics are similar to bitmapped fonts, discussed in Chapter 8.

Images stored in this way can take up a great deal of space in the computer's RAM and on a disk. To deal with this problem, many graphics programs have built-in means of condensing bitmapped images. Still, images created with painting programs take up more space than those created with drawing programs. The computer also takes more time to display or print images created with painting programs.

Unlike drawing programs, a painting program treats whatever is on the screen as a single image, not as a group of separate objects. Thus, you cannot manipulate the individual shapes that make up an image the way you can with a drawing program, even though images created with drawing and painting programs can look the same on the screen.

One advantage a painting program offers over drawing programs is that it allows you to magnify portions of an image to show the individual pixels (see Figure 11-7). That means you can edit an image, including its colors and shading, at the most detailed level possible.

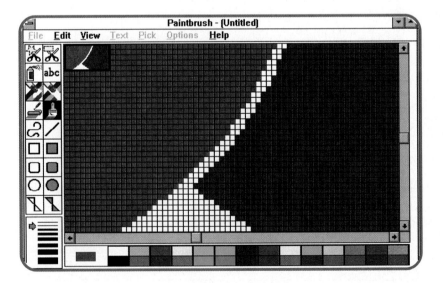

FIGURE 11-7

With a painting program, you can control the color and shading of each individual pixel. This allows for the most detailed editing possible.

Painting programs are often used to modify images that have been scanned into a computer system. As you learned in Chapter 3, a scanner converts images into digital files that the computer can read, store, display, and print. A scanned file has a bitmapped format—the same format as an image created by a painting program. This means you can use a painting

FIGURE 11-8

With a painting program, you can display a scanned image on the screen (top) and then edit it to change the image.

program to display the scanned image on the screen, edit it, and store the edited image (Figure 11-8). Drawing programs cannot be used for working with bitmapped images.

Table 11-1 summarizes how drawing and painting programs meet different needs for users.

Table 11-1: Drawing and Painting Programs	
To . . .	**You need a . . .**
Edit images in fine detail	Painting program
Use as little disk space as possible for storing images	Drawing program
Edit scanned images	Painting program
Print or display images as quickly as possible	Drawing program
Edit individual shapes that make up an image	Drawing program

USING A PAINTING PROGRAM

A screen for a painting program looks much like a screen for a drawing program. Like a drawing program, it has a drawing area and a toolbox containing geometric shapes, lines, and patterns. A painting program has some additional tools represented by icons. For example, a typical painting program has an icon for a spray can. When you select this icon, you can "spray" color on screen just as if you were using a real can of spray paint.

Painting programs use many of the same commands as drawing programs, but there are some differences in how the commands work. For example, the zoom command in a painting program shows the pixels that make up an image, and a drawing program's zoom command does not. Showing the pixels allows for finer editing.

PAINTING PROGRAM PRODUCTS

PaintBrush, which comes with the Windows environment, is one of the most popular paint programs for IBM-compatible microcomputers. It is also one of the simplest paint programs to use. A more powerful painting program, *ColorRIX,* includes specialized tools such as an airbrush and makes full use of the range of colors available on high-end monitors.

MacPaint, the first painting program for the Macintosh, is still among the most popular and easiest to learn. *MacPaint* is compatible with the word processor *Word.* Another painting program for the Macintosh, *Studio 32,* specializes in sophisticated color work. *Adobe Photoshop* and *Letraset ColorStudio* are designed especially for working with photographs and other scanned images on the Macintosh.

Specialized Graphics Programs

As Computer Users' Graphics Needs Have Become More Specialized, Programs Have Been Developed to Meet These Needs.

At first, graphics software consisted entirely of general purpose drawing and painting programs. However, as graphics software caught on, a demand for more specialized programs developed quickly. For example, business managers needed programs for creating simple charts from numerical data, but engineers needed a different kind of software for creating highly detailed three-dimensional drawings. As a result, many programs are now available for specific uses.

COMPUTER ASSISTED DESIGN (CAD) PROGRAMS

Computer Assisted Design programs, called *CAD* ("cad") programs for short, are drawing programs used by engineers, designers, and architects to produce detailed technical drawings. With CAD programs, you can create three-dimensional images.

A three-dimensional image created with a CAD program can serve as an on-screen model of an object you are designing. You can then move or rotate the model on the screen to view it from different angles. You can even slice through the model on the screen to view a cross section of it. For example, an airplane designer might create a model of a new airplane on the screen, then slice through the plane's body to be sure it is wide enough to accommodate a given number of passengers.

A screen from a CAD program doesn't look much different from a standard drawing program (Figure 11-9). However, a CAD screen can display images in much more precise detail than a standard drawing program. This is possible because a CAD program has a wider variety of tools.

Many CAD programs allow you to add variable shading to images, which

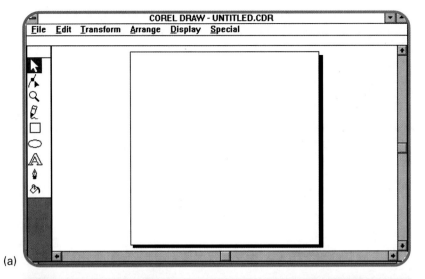

(a)

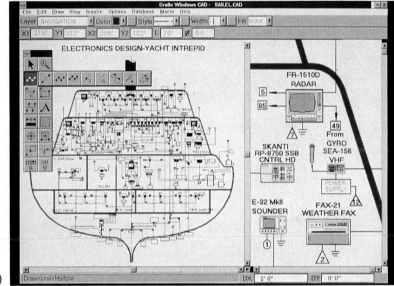

(b)

FIGURE 11-9

A CAD program's work area, such as that shown (b) from *Drafix Windows CAD,* resembles that of a drawing program (a), but its toolbox has more tools. You can use these tools to create extremely precise drawings.

helps to create three-dimensional effects. With some CAD programs, you can even move the "light source" to adjust the shading automatically.

One of the most powerful CAD programs is *AutoCAD,* which is available for IBM-compatible and Macintosh computers. *Drafix Windows CAD,* for IBM-compatible computers, can produce very precise engineering drawings. *Design CAD*, for IBM compatibles, lets you view a shape from the inside out.

PRESENTATION GRAPHICS PROGRAMS

Presentation graphics programs are drawing programs used to produce graphics for sales presentations, seminars, and other kinds of meetings. These programs help you create images that communicate clearly when seen from a distance. You can print the images on acetate sheets for use with an overhead projector, or you can use them to create slides for use with a slide projector.

Presentation graphics programs are designed to create sharp but simple images that get a point across quickly (Figure 11-10). Presentation graphics are typically business-oriented charts, diagrams, and graphs, such as pie charts, bar charts, and line graphs.

Harvard Graphics is one of the most popular IBM compatible presenta-

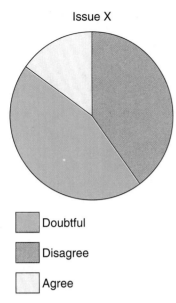

Issue X

Doubtful

Disagree

Agree

FIGURE 11-10

This image, created with a presentation graphics program, conveys its message quickly even to people viewing it from a distance.

FIGURE 11-11

This graph shows sales figures by month for several products. You can see at a glance which product sold the most and which product sold the least in any given month.

tion graphics programs. Others include *Applause, Chart-Master, Microsoft Chart,* and *PowerPoint. Persuasion* and *Cricket Presents* are popular Macintosh presentation programs.

GRAPHING PROGRAMS

Graphing programs are drawing programs for creating graphs, which show relationships between two or more sets of variables (Figure 11-11). Many graphing programs can use data from a variety of spreadsheet programs. Some graphing programs automatically choose the type of graph that best shows the relationship between variables.

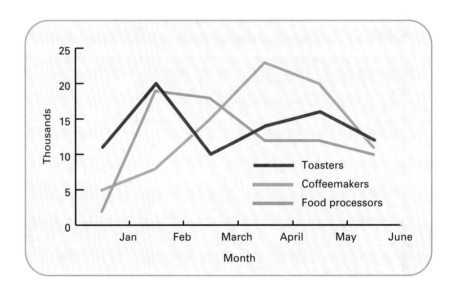

Since presentation programs are used primarily to create charts and graphs, there is a lot of overlap between presentation programs and graphing programs. But there are two major features that all graphing programs must have. They must be able to do the following:

- Use data directly from spreadsheets (which some presentation programs can also do).
- Create sophisticated graphs using complex math calculations.

    Which kind of program you should use to create a graph depends on how the graph will be used. To graph the output of a simple spreadsheet for a report, you can probably use the spreadsheet software's graphing feature. To dress up a graph for a presentation, you can use a presentation program to add color, text in a variety of fonts, and so forth. But to graph the results of a complex scientific experiment so you can look for relationships among large numbers of variables, you would use a graphing program.

    Graphwriter is a graph program for IBM-compatible microcomputers that comes with a wide variety of standard graphing formats. *Exec*U*Stat, Statgraphics,* and *Samna Decision Graphics* are sophisticated graphing programs especially suited to statistical analysis on IBM compatibles. *Energraphics,* also for IBM compatibles, lets you create three-dimensional graphs. *MacGraphX* is a math-oriented graphing program for the Macintosh that has 50 math functions to help you produce graphs from formulas.

ORGANIZATION CHART PROGRAMS

An *organization chart* is a graphic that shows the formal structure of a business, using boxes to represent management levels and lines to connect the boxes (Figure 11-12). You can create them with standard drawing programs, but an *organization chart program* makes this task easier. With a general-purpose drawing program, you would have to add all the boxes and lines to the chart individually. With an organization chart program, you can specify the number of levels in an organization, then specify the number of positions on each level and let the software do the drawing for you. One of the most popular organization chart programs is *Org Plus,* which runs on IBM-compatible microcomputers.

FIGURE 11-12

This chart shows an organization with three vice presidents in charge of different business areas. The lines in the chart show that all of the vice presidents report to the company president.

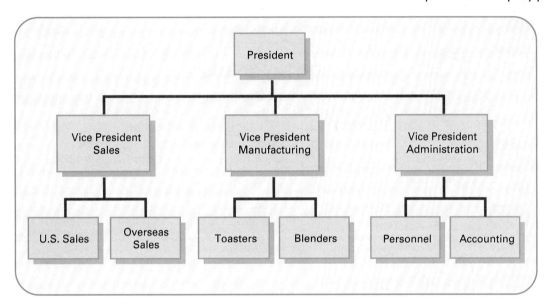

FLOWCHART PROGRAMS

Flowcharts illustrate processes, using standard shapes to represent different steps or phases (Figure 11-13). *Flowchart programs* are drawing programs designed especially for creating flowcharts. The standard shapes used in flowcharts are built into these specialized programs, so you don't have to draw them individually. Popular flowchart programs include *ABC*

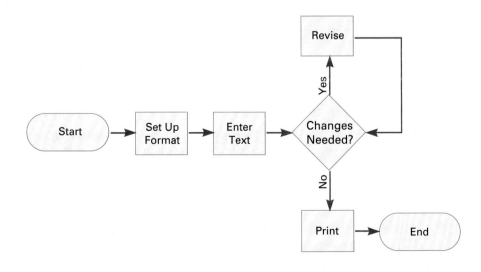

FIGURE 11-13

This simple flowchart depicts the process of creating a document with a word processor. The standard flowchart shapes it uses are ovals to depict the start and end of the process, rectangles to represent individual steps, and a diamond to represent a decision point.

Flowcharter and EZ-Flow for IBM-compatible microcomputers and Flow Master for the Macintosh.

MAPPING PROGRAMS

Just think how difficult it would be to draw a map of Idaho, Wisconsin, or Delaware, even on a computer. A *mapping program* can save you the trouble. Mapping programs generally come with built-in maps, which you can modify for different purposes. For example, you can use the state outlines built into a mapping program to create maps of sales territories. You can group the state maps to create maps of regions, and you can add color, text, and other enhancements. Popular mapping programs include *MapMaster* (for IBM-compatible microcomputers) and *MapMaker* (available for both IBM-compatible and Macintosh computers).

ANIMATION PROGRAMS

Animation programs allow you to create graphics that move. You can display these graphics on a computer monitor or record them on videotape and play them back on a television or projection screen. Some animation programs are drawing programs; some are painting programs.

Any animated image, like a cartoon or a movie, actually consists of a series of slightly different images displayed in quick succession (Figure 11-14). Graphics software lends itself to creating animated images because it allows you to copy a figure, edit it, store the new figure, copy and edit the new figure, and so on. *Pictor* and *Autodesk Animator* are animation programs for IBM-compatible microcomputers, and *HyperAnimator* is an animation program for the Macintosh.

Graphics Utilities

With Utilities and Add-On Products, You Can Enhance the Output from Graphics Programs.

Since microcomputer graphics took off in 1984, there has been a flood of graphics-related programs and add-on hardware for a wide range of business and artistic endeavors.

FIGURE 11-14

These still images are part of a series of hundreds of images that make up a cartoon. Each image in the series is slightly different from the one before it. Displaying the individual images in quick succession conveys a sense of movement.

YOU CAN'T ALWAYS BELIEVE WHAT YOU SEE

The actual scanned image (left) was edited to produce an altered image (right).

Photographs never lie. Or do they? Image-editing software, such as *Adobe Photoshop* and *Digital Darkroom,* are rapidly undermining this piece of conventional wisdom.

Skilled artisans have been retouching photos for a long time. But theirs was a tedious art, and few could do a convincing job. Image-editing software, though, has changed all that.

The change began with image-scanning technology, a process by which photographs were "scanned" into a computer file and the image displayed on a screen or printed. Magazine and advertising art directors were the first to take advantage of image scanning, using it to simplify the process of laying out text and graphics on the page. But they soon realized that once a photographic image was turned into computer bits and bytes, it could be manipulated like any other computer graphic image. Software developers quickly provided the tools needed to accomplish this task.

Travel brochures provide a relatively harmless example of retouched art. Do they ever show power lines looming over your vacation vista? Of course not, because they've been edited out. This may seem innocent enough, but imagine the consequences if an unscrupulous real estate developer used misleading photos to sell retirement homes near a Florida swamp or Arizona highway to retirees in Pennsylvania? The photos might look realistic to naive buyers, who might learn about the offending highway or swamp only when it was too late.

And what if you found out that your newspaper or magazine was doing the same thing with newsphotos? What if a picture was *created* that convincingly put a politician in a "compromising" situation? And what if a newspaper printed that photo (innocently or deliberately) and ruined someone's career? As more and more magazines and newspapers rely on image-scanning/editing technology, sinister examples such as this become a very real possibility.

How can you tell when a photographic image is real, partly real, or completely made up? In the past these were easy questions to answer. They aren't now, though, with the advent of image-scanning software. Now, each time you see a photograph reproduced in a newspaper or magazine, ask yourself: "Is it real?"

Source: "The Right Graphics Tool for the Job," by G. Armour Van Horn, *BYTE*, July 1991, p. 123.

Unless you wish to print newsletters, bulletins, greeting cards, graphs, or banners or to prepare your own visual aids for presentations, you might not need graphics software.

If you do need a graphics program, you may find that inexpensive and easy-to-use graphics software oriented to the personal computer user (such as *The New Printshop*) meets your needs.

You also may not need to create your own graphics. You could use art from a clip art collection and import the piece into a word processed or desktop published document. Many types of specialized clip art collections are available.

Before selecting any graphic software make certain its output can be stored on disk and then imported into your word processing or desktop publishing software.

CLIP ART AND ART COLLECTIONS

Not everyone is an artist, but many people would like to incorporate professional art in their work. They can do that with *clip art,* which is professional art stored and sold on microcomputer disks. It is ready-made for use with word processing, desktop publishing, or graphics programs.

Collections of clip art often are organized around themes. For example, if you publish an office newsletter, you might want clip art that includes symbols for all the major holidays. You can also purchase collections of clip art about animals, sports, or celebrities (Figure 11-15).

Clip art collections of photographs are available for use with painting programs. You can edit a photograph at the pixel level and use it as the basis for a different graphic image.

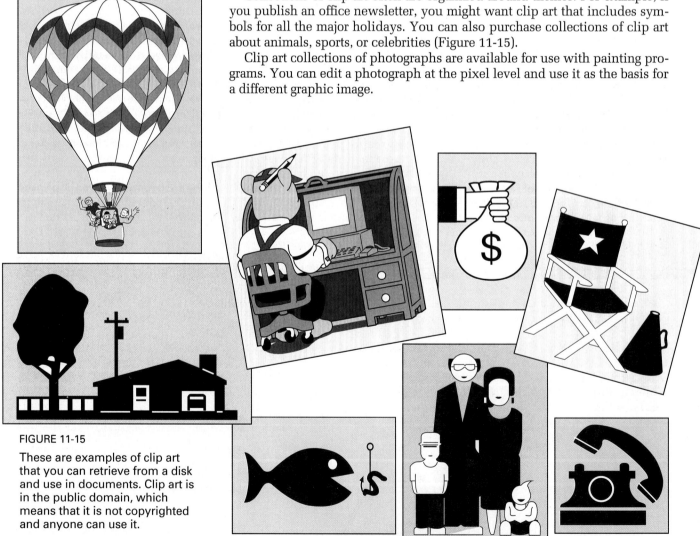

FIGURE 11-15

These are examples of clip art that you can retrieve from a disk and use in documents. Clip art is in the public domain, which means that it is not copyrighted and anyone can use it.

Don't remove discs when drive light is <u>on</u>

Don't use reset button if you haven't saved
your work

Write enabled – covered write protect opening – can't see
thru opening

When using a presentation graphics program to create graphics for a meeting, you'll often want to create transparencies for use with an overhead projector or slides for use with a slide projector. Some laser printers can print on acetate. To give variety to a presentation, you can use colored transparencies. Many office copy centers and commercial copying services can photocopy graphics onto acetate.

Creating 35 millimeter slides for use in a slide projector requires either a camera to take a picture of the graphic on the monitor (often with less than satisfactory results) or a specialized device such as the Polaroid Palette. Attached to an IBM-compatible microcomputer and containing a 35 millimeter camera, the Polaroid Palette electronically transfers full-color graphics from the computer to film. The film can then be developed with Polaroid's Instant Slide System, which is included as part of Polaroid Palette.

VIRTUAL REALITY?

Imagine learning about computers by taking a trip inside one. Begin your trip by strapping on a futuristic helmet, which lets you "see" inside the computer. Next, slip on a pair of high-tech gloves, which let you "pick up" and "manipulate" objects inside your computer. Now, "walk" along your computer's circuits to see where they lead. If you see something that you don't understand, pick it up and examine it. Want to take a closer look at your computer's memory card? You can walk up to it and around it, examining it from all sides.

Does this all sound farfetched? Well, given the incredible sophistication of today's computer graphics, from increased resolution to image scanning to 3-D images, it was only natural that scientists, engineers, and designers would want to touch and manipulate those images.

This new technology, called "Virtual Reality," is actually a way to see and enter into a three-dimensional world via computer. It includes a variety of tools, called virtual tools, that can be used to manipulate virtual objects. The ability to manipulate virtual objects allows users to work with what designers call prototypes. Thus, if you want to design or modify a piece of furniture, a molecule, or a nozzle for a rocket engine, you can work with a computer model long before you actually touch the real thing.

Is Virtual Reality just around the corner? Microsoft's announcement that it will use Silicon Graphics' 3-D software in a future operating system for personal computers suggests that Microsoft is already preparing for a 3-D future. And Virtual Reality is the next step, technologically, after 3-D graphics. Three-dimensional graphics are already taken for granted by designers who work with CAD—

Computer Assisted Design—systems, and by their kids, at home with their Nintendo and Sega computerized games.

So, whether you use funny-looking headgear like that designed by NASA's Ames Research Center, which allows you to enter a virtual world and walk around in it, or virtual that will let you manipulate virtual objects with your hand, such as the *DataGlove* from VPL Research, or the SimGraphics Engineering's *Flying Mouse*, you too may soon enter into a 3-D world from your desktop computer.

Virtual Reality, provided by this helmet, lets you see an image so lifelike that it seems real.

Sources: "Living in a Virtual World," by Scott Fisher and Jane Tazelaar, *BYTE,* July 1990. "Telltale Gestures," by Paul McAvinney, *BYTE,* July 1990. "Is Silicon Graphics Busting Out of Its Niche?" by Robert Hof, *Business Week,* April 22, 1991, p. 100.

Future Trends

Microcomputer Graphics Programs Are Becoming More Sophisticated, Better Able to Share Files, and More Specialized.

While most graphics software can display richly colored output on a high-resolution monitor, high-quality hard copy of color graphics has posed problems. However, graphics and desktop publishing software are becoming better able to transfer color output to paper. Color laser printers will contribute to this trend.

It will also become easier to convert graphics from one format to another. Software companies are unlikely to standardize on just a few formats, but increasingly powerful conversion utilities will enable the use of different programs to work with the same graphic.

More programs for creating three-dimensional art will also be developed. At the same time, animation programs will become easier to use, and their output will be more lifelike. This could pave the way for something right out of *Roger Rabbit*, videos with computer-generated people—not cartoons, but realistic, lifelike characters.

REVIEW QUESTIONS

1. What are computer graphics?

2. What kind of microcomputer helped computer graphics gain popularity, and why?

3. What are the two basic types of graphics programs?

4. What elements do you combine to create graphics with a drawing program? What role do mathematical formulas play in this process?

5. Name two advantages that drawing programs have over painting programs.

6. What does a toolbox in a graphics program contain?

7. How does a painting program create an image on the screen?

8. Compare a drawing program and a painting program in terms of the amount of space required to store an image.

9. What advantage does working at the pixel level offer?

10. Can you edit scanned images with a painting program? Can you edit them with a drawing program? Explain.

11. How do zoom commands differ in painting and drawing programs?

12. What does the abbreviation CAD stand for, and what are CAD programs used for?

13. What are presentation graphics programs, and what are they used for?

14. What are graphing programs, and what are they used for?

15. When would you draw a graph with a graphing program rather than a spreadsheet program's graphing feature or a presentation graphics program?

16. What is an organization chart? How can organization chart software help you to create one?

17. What is a flowchart? How does a flowchart program help you to create one?

18. When would you use a mapping program instead of a general-purpose drawing program?

19. What can you use to play back graphics created with an animation program?
20. What is clip art?
21. How are 35 millimeter slides of graphic images created?
22. What do graphics conversion programs do?

TOPICS FOR RESEARCH AND DISCUSSION

1. Graphics programs use many different formats for storing graphics on disks. Does anyone benefit from the existence of so many formats? Do you think companies will ever adopt a standard format for storing graphic images? Why?

   To find out more about the various graphics formats, go to the library and find out as much as possible about several different graphics formats from computer books and magazines. What are some of the different formats, and how do they differ from each other? What are the primary uses of the different formats?

2. Suppose you want to start a company that provides charts, graphs, cartoons, and other graphics to illustrate seminars and other spoken presentations. You already have an IBM-compatible microcomputer with a Super VGA graphics card and monitor. What types of general and specialized graphics software would you need? For example, would you want to purchase a painting program, a drawing program, or both? Would you need a graphing program? A presentation graphics program? Explain your answers.

   Once you have decided on the types of software you need, look in recent issues of computer magazines for reviews of specific products. Which ones would you purchase for your new business. Why?

3. Using graphics software, you can alter photographs after scanning them into a microcomputer. The altered images still look like photographs, but the alterations change the messages they convey. For example, you can combine a photo of a man with a photo of a place so that the man appears to be in a place where he has never been. Or, in an image that includes a clock, you can change the time on the clock.

   How might this technique be used, or misused, in advertising, news reporting, and other fields? In the library, you might be able to find newspaper and magazine articles about controversies involving altered photographs.

COMMUNICATIONS AND CONNECTIVITY

OBJECTIVES

The information in this chapter will enable you to

- Explain the main concepts of data communications.
- Give examples of how microcomputer users benefit from data communications.
- Explain the uses of networks and connectivity.
- Give examples of how networks improve productivity.
- Describe the advantages and trade-offs of connectivity solutions in an organization.
- Give examples of the exciting future developments promised by connectivity technology.

In this chapter, we explore two important capabilities of microcomputers: *data communications*, which lets your computer access data and services at remote locations; and *connectivity*, which lets multiple computers work together and share resources. These concepts are related, but the terms normally refer to different technologies.

Data Communications

Microcomputers Use Modems to Access Remote Data and On-Line Services.

Communications technology has grown rapidly along with the rest of the computer industry. Facsimile (FAX) machines, cellular telephones, voice response systems (*". . . Press '1' to obtain your account balance. Press '2' to speak to a representative . . . "*), and the computerized point-of-sale (POS) cash registers used by many stores have all brought high-tech communications into our daily lives (Figure 12-1).

WHAT IS DATA COMMUNICATIONS?

In its broadest sense, *data communications* (or *telecommunications*) refers to any electronic transfer of information starting from or ending at a computer. This includes transactions from automatic bank teller machines, police officers checking car registrations using hand-held computer terminals, and retail purchases from point-of-sale terminals. These and many other devices transmit data electronically to computers.

When talking about microcomputers, we're interested in a particular kind of data communications. In this book, *data communications* means the

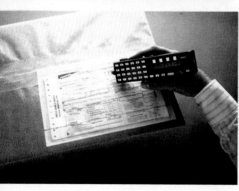

FIGURE 12-1

High-technology communications devices are a part of our everyday life.

transmission or exchange of messages between a microcomputer and a remote device, such as another microcomputer, a mainframe computer, an office telephone system, or a facsimile machine. The messages are usually transmitted over telephone lines, as Figure 12-2 shows.

TELEPHONES AND MODEMS

Microcomputers communicate over telephone lines using a device called a *modem*, shown in Figure 12-3. Modems let two computers exchange data over a telephone line. Modems dial telephone numbers, transform computer data into sounds, send messages, transform sounds received back into computer data, and control the telephone connection. *Communications software* tells a modem what to do.

For most machines, a modem is either installed inside the computer, as an option in an expansion slot (an *internal modem*), or it is located outside the computer and connected to it using a serial or parallel port (an *external modem*).

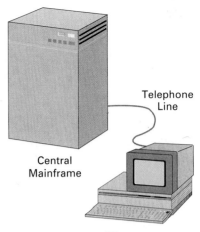

Telephone Line

Central Mainframe

Microcomputer

FIGURE 12-2

Data communications means the exchange of messages between a microcomputer and a remote device such as a mainframe computer. The message is usually transmitted over telephone lines.

FIGURE 12-3

An internal modem (left) doesn't require any room on the desk; you can see the lights on an external modem (right) as it works.

How do modems work? To answer that question, we need to get a bit more technical.

Digital Messages

Microcomputers use *digital* data—precise sequences of bits and bytes that represent numbers, characters, and images. A file on a floppy disk is just a sequence of bits. If you make a copy of that file, it is an *exact* copy—the same number of bits, appearing "on" or "off" in exactly the same positions. This is the advantage of digital data: it can be copied precisely and verified.

This advantage is important. Consider the major audio technology breakthrough of the last decade: compact disks. Because CDs store sound as digital data, they have a clearer, cleaner sound than a record or tape. Every copy of a CD is exactly the same as every other, and this can be verified electronically. A record or cassette tape is an *approximate* copy of the studio's master recording. A CD is *identical* to the master digital recording.

Computers, like CDs, use precise digital data. Telephones, however, use *analog* data—they send and receive complex sounds, changing constantly in pitch, volume, and tone. Such changes are essential to our understanding of speech and to our enjoyment of music. However, they aren't best for computers. Figure 12-4 shows the difference between digital and analog signals. Analog signals are transformed into digital data by converting these complex sounds into a series of "on/off" pulses. Your CD player can transform these digital signals back into the analog signals, recreating the original voices and music.

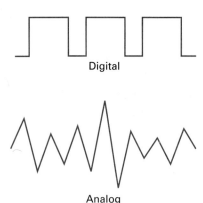

Digital

Analog

FIGURE 12-4

Digital signals are simple on/off pulses. Analog signals (such as those in speech) are much more complex.

FIGURE 12-5

The telephone's analog signal is modulated by a modem, transmitted over the telephone lines as a digital signal representing data, and demodulated by a modem on the other end, converting the signal to data that can be used by a microcomputer.

In a similar way, a modem transforms digital data—words, numbers, word processing files, or spreadsheets—into analog signals that can be transmitted over a telephone line. Telephone lines are designed to reproduce the human voice, which uses just a narrow range of sound. The modem creates sounds in that same range to represent the digital bits being transmitted. If you've ever dialed a telephone number connected to a modem (or a FAX machine), you've heard the high-pitched *carrier signal*—the tone that modems use to send data.

"Modem" is short for "MOdulator/DEModulator." When sending a message, a modem's carrier signal is *modulated*—raised and lowered in pitch—based on the sequence of bits being transmitted. Then, at the receiving end of the telephone line, another modem *demodulates* the sound to recover the original sequence of bits. This process is shown in Figure 12-5.

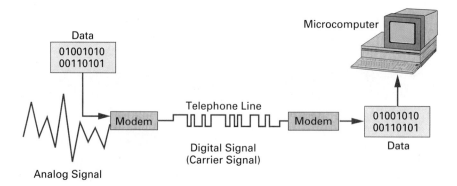

Communication Speeds and Protocols

Modems vary in many technical details. The most important difference is the speed at which they operate. Modem speed is measured in *baud*—the number of bits transmitted per second. Twenty years ago, most modems operated at only 300 baud—around 30 characters per second. This is faster than a good typist, but much slower than a modern printer or FAX machine. Today, most modems are much faster. Typical modem speeds for microcomputer use today are 1,200, 2,400, 9,600, and sometimes 19,200 baud.

Modems also vary in other technical ways. Some only send and receive data; some can also dial telephone numbers; some verify data for accuracy and retransmit messages that aren't correct; some use special codes to control the communications process.

COMMUNICATIONS SOFTWARE

Like any other computer device, the modem only does what a piece of software tells it to do. Standard communications software programs let a microcomputer control a modem and use it to send messages and access remote data.

MODEM CONTROL

Early modems just did the basic digital-to-analog-to-digital conversions needed for transferring characters. Modern modems do much more, such as dialing telephone numbers, answering incoming calls, detecting other modems, and controlling the data communications process.

Communications software takes advantage of these modem capabilities.

For example, most software lets you maintain a list of telephone numbers, access codes, and other data that you would normally enter as digits on a telephone's touch-tone keypad. Figure 12-6 shows a telephone list in use— you just highlight the desired number on your list, and tell the software to dial the number by choosing the "dial" option.

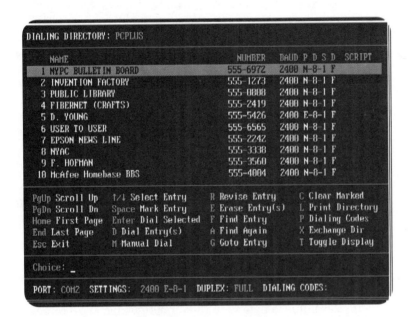

FIGURE 12-6

You can use a communications software program to make calls.

TERMINAL EMULATION/REMOTE ACCESS

The most common use of data communications is *terminal emulation*, where a microcomputer simulates a traditional computer terminal. A computer terminal is an input/output device used with mainframes and minicomputers. It is essentially just a keyboard and a monitor, both connected to a modem. Anything entered on the keyboard is sent to the *host computer* (the mainframe or minicomputer being accessed by the terminal) as input. The computer's responses are then displayed on the monitor.

Terminal emulation uses the microcomputer's own keyboard and monitor as if they were a terminal. All input is sent through the modem to the remote system; all output from the modem is displayed on the monitor.

Terminal emulation is part of most data communications tasks. It lets microcomputers access the traditional world of business computing, plus a wide range of new communications-driven services such as *bulletin boards* and *public network services*, which we discuss later.

FILE TRANSFER

We've described how terminal emulation lets us access remote computers. Another major use of data communications is *file transfers*, where files are moved from one computer to another. This is the advantage of using a microcomputer instead of a traditional computer terminal. Traditional terminals only let you enter and display messages. A microcomputer can also store whatever is received.

File transfers use a number of different strategies:

- *Raw data capture* is a "passive" operation, which means that the remote system doesn't know about it. During terminal emulation, the microcomputer simply makes a log of the output received through the modem. The file that is created can be used later. The data can be imported to a word processor, for example, or printed.

• *Verified file transfer* is the most common operation. It uses a *file transfer protocol* to check the accuracy of the data being sent. A protocol specifies rules for detecting and correcting errors. Many different transfer protocols are in common use, including XMODEM, YMODEM, KERMIT, and SEALINK. These standard protocols let different communications software talk to one another, using the same "language," even though the programs come from different vendors. Although file transfer protocols are sometimes called *modem protocols*, this term properly refers to low-level communication rules used by the modems themselves. These protocols have alphabet-soup names like "CCITT V.42 bis," "MNP Level 4," and "SNA/SDLC."

• *Data compression* squeezes more characters per second into each data transfer by eliminating redundancies. For example, instead of sending a line of hyphens as 80 "-" characters, a short sequence like "@80-" might be used. Some of these techniques are incorporated in the standard file transfer and modem protocols just discussed; others are added "on top of" the basic protocols by communication software.

• *Data transformation* (or *data translation*) converts data from one format to another as it is being transferred. Such operations are needed when moving files between different kinds of computer systems—such as Macintosh to PC, or PC to DEC mainframe. Individual characters or words are replaced, according to certain rules. For example, most mainframes use a character set called *EBCDIC* ("EBB-see-dick"), which is quite different from the ASCII characters found on microcomputers. (For example, a byte with the numeric value of 78 represents an "N" in ASCII, but it represents a plus sign ("+") in EBCDIC. Data transformation programs let mainframes and microcomputers communicate by automatically translating from EBCDIC to ASCII or vice versa.

SCRIPTS

People who use communications software to access a mainframe, submit a transaction, check a balance, or transfer a file often must carry out a long dialogue with a remote computer system. Entering the same exact sequence of data each time, day after day, gets tedious. To simplify such repetitive tasks, most communications software lets you record a *script*—a stored

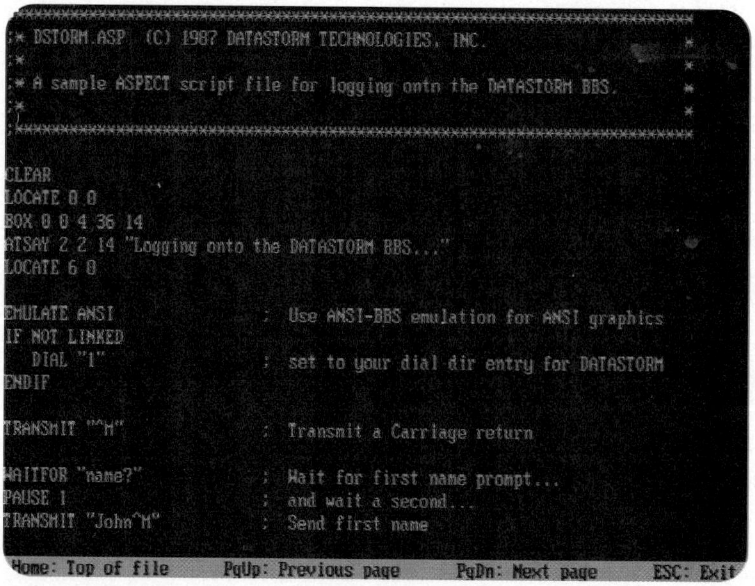

FIGURE 12-7

A script, a stored sequence of communications commands, makes accessing this bulletin board very simple. The script can be used over and over.

sequence of communications commands, including telephone and modem controls, keystrokes, and other communications operations. Scripts can be "played back," like a macro for a word processor or a spreadsheet. Figure 12-7 shows a script being used to access a bulletin board.

POPULAR COMMUNICATIONS SOFTWARE AND DEVICES

Many communications software programs are in common use, as are some specialized communications devices.

- **General communications.** The largest group of communications software programs provides integrated, general-purpose communications, including telephone dialing, basic terminal emulation, and file transfer using several different protocols. Common PC programs include *CrossTalk*, *ProComm*, *BLAST/PC*, *DynaComm*, *Smartcom*, *Telix*, and *Windows Terminal* (which comes with Windows). Common Macintosh programs include *Smartcom*, *MicroPhone*, and *Red Rider*.

- **Specialized terminal emulators.** Many mainframe applications are tailored for a particular brand and model of terminal, and only that kind will work. To use such applications, a microcomputer requires a *specialized terminal emulator*—a device that imitates a specific terminal model. *Reflection Series* and *IRMA* are two specialized terminal emulation devices available for both the PC and the Macintosh.

  This brings up a technical matter that you may encounter. In organizations in which microcomputers must communicate with IBM mainframes, a *3270 board* is commonly used in place of (or in addition to) a modem. A 3270 board is basically just a more expensive, more complex kind of modem. It requires different software and has different capabilities, but it performs the same basic functions as a modem. It simulates the behavior of a large family of IBM terminals collectively called "3270s." The most popular 3270 board is the "IRMA" board, but many other brands exist. Figure 12-8 shows a 3270 in action.

FIGURE 12-8

IBM 3270 terminals are common in large businesses.

- **Facsimile Machines**. In the last few years, price cuts have transformed the facsimile machine from a gadget in a few offices into a basic fixture as common as an office copier. Virtually every office, sales organization, and hotel has a FAX. In many cities, office workers use FAX machines to send their lunch orders to local restaurants!

  What does this have to do with data communications,—other than the computer chips inside a FAX that make it smart and cheap? *A microcomputer can now talk to a FAX machine,* either by using a low-cost internal *FAX board* or an external *FAX interface* that connects to a computer port. A FAX board or FAX interface lets a computer exchange data with a FAX machine via a telephone line. Sending output directly to a FAX is easier and faster than printing a document and then FAXing it by hand. As you can see in Figure 12-9, many FAXes have excellent output quality. Like a normal facsimile machine, a FAX board can receive calls. Data received this way is stored in a file and can either be printed or viewed on line.

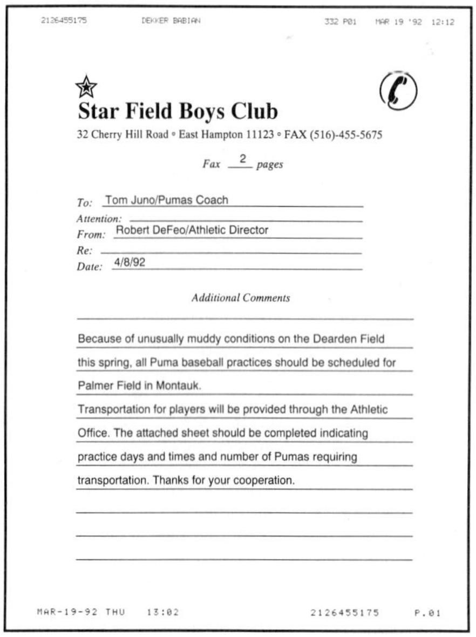

2126455175 DEKKER BABIAN 332 P01 MAR 19 '92 12:12

Star Field Boys Club

32 Cherry Hill Road • East Hampton 11123 • FAX (516)-455-5675

Fax 2 *pages*

To: Tom Juno/Pumas Coach
Attention:
From: Robert DeFeo/Athletic Director
Re:
Date: 4/8/92

Additional Comments

Because of unusually muddy conditions on the Dearden Field this spring, all Puma baseball practices should be scheduled for Palmer Field in Montauk.
Transportation for players will be provided through the Athletic Office. The attached sheet should be completed indicating practice days and times and number of Pumas requiring transportation. Thanks for your cooperation.

MAR-19-92 THU 13:02 2126455175 P.01

FIGURE 12-9

A FAX from a FAX board in a microcomputer is often of higher quality than a FAX from a FAX machine.

Using Data Communications

Microcomputer Users Can Access Many External Services by Using Data Communications Software.

Communications software gives microcomputer users access to remote network services, bulletin boards, electronic mailboxes, and databases, as well as various transaction services.

NETWORK SERVICES

Probably the most visible use of data communications is to access *public networks* such as Prodigy, CompuServe, Dow Jones, GEnie, or MCI Mail. Accessing them often costs little more than a local telephone call. An example of some of the services offered by Prodigy is shown in Table 12-1.

The many public network services fall into four basic categories:

- *Electronic mail* can be sent from one microcomputer user to another. The "mail" is sent as a text file—a letter or memo created with a word processor. Mail can be sent to you even if you are not currently using the network. Messages are held until the next time you *log on* (or *sign on*) by connecting to the network and identifying yourself. MCI Mail, for instance, is becoming an "electronic answering service" for many businesses.

Table 12-1: Services Offered by Prodigy

Type of Service	Examples of Service
Communication	Electronic Mail, FAX, On-Line Group or One-to-One Conversations
News	Associated Press, UPI US and World, Weather Reports and Forecasts, AP Sports Wire
Forums (On-line Special Interest Groups)	Types of Personal Computers (IBM, Macintosh, etc.), Types of Software Programs, Various Hobbies, Various Topics of Interest, Games, Financial and Investment Topics, Travel, Professional and Industry Interests
Travel	Airline Reservation System, Airline Guide, Hotel Guide
Shopping	Clothes, Food, Compact Disks, Books, Florist, Toiletries, Cars, Consumer Reports, Classified Ads
Investing and Personal Finance	Current Stock Quotes, Standard & Poor's, Mutual Funds, Market and Industry Index Lookup, On-Line Brokerage Services, U.S. Government Publications, TRW Business Credit
Reference	Academic American Encyclopedia, Books in Print, Census Bureau Data, Marquis Who's Who, Neighborhood Demographics, Peterson's College Guides
Games and Entertainment	Multiplayer Games, Hollywood Information, Soap Opera Summaries

- *Bulletin boards and forums* are like electronic conferences. Users who "join" a special-interest group can access the group's bulletin board at any time and read messages "posted" there by other members. Bulletin boards range from professional organizations and standards committees to hobbies, games, and clubs. Figure 12-10 shows some typical listings.

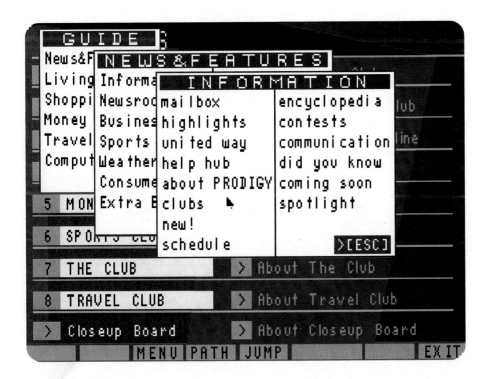

FIGURE 12-10

There are many forums and bulletin boards for special interest groups on Prodigy.

- *Databases*, which can be examined on-line, include such popular topics as up-to-the-minute stock market quotes, airline schedules, census data, magazine articles, and financial information about U.S. companies. Hundreds of such databases are available.
- *Transactions* can be generated from your microcomputer, such as paying bills, making airline reservations, or checking your bank account status.

Users of these services normally pay a membership fee, plus access charges, when they use the network. There are additional charges for specific activities, such as paying a bill or accessing a credit report. Considering the range of services available, the costs are very low.

OTHER SERVICES

Networks like CompuServe and Prodigy offer services to the general public. Similar services are available from smaller organizations to address specific needs.

- Bulletin boards are often used to provide technical support for a company's products.
- Many companies offer customers automated banking and other transaction services, using their own mainframe computer systems instead of connecting to a public network.
- Specialty firms offer on-line databases on many subjects. Such databases range from computer hardware to auto parts, from scientific articles to legal briefs.

Connectivity

Connectivity Lets Microcomputers Work Together and Share Resources.

Data communications lets a microcomputer reach out through telephone lines to access other systems and services. *Connectivity* is another form of data communications; it links different computer systems together, to let them share data and resources.

WHAT IS CONNECTIVITY?

Connectivity and data communications have the same two goals: sending messages and transferring data between systems. However, as Figure 12-11 shows, the approach is different.

- Data communications provides temporary connections between a microcomputer and external services. Remote services are presented to the user through terminal emulation.
- Connectivity creates a network of interacting systems that work together. It presents remote services *transparently*. This means that remote services don't "seem" remote, but instead appear to be present in the microcomputer itself.

This section explores some of the benefits of connectivity services, and shows some of the technical issues you might face in a network environment.

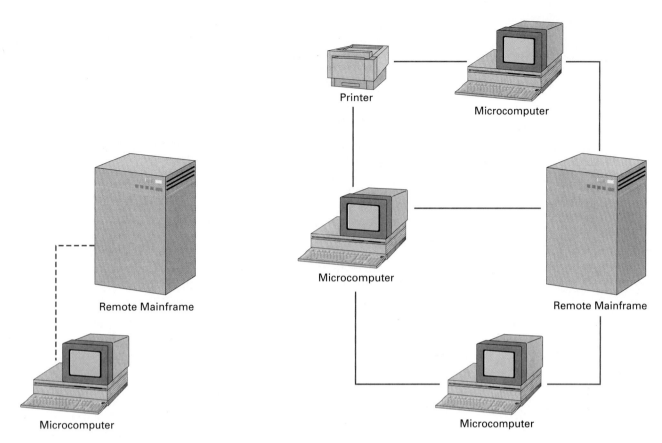

Printer

Microcomputer

Remote Mainframe

Microcomputer

Remote Mainframe

Microcomputer

Microcomputer

FIGURE 12-11

Data communications (right) provide only temporary connections between a microcomputer and external service. Connectivity (left) creates a network of systems that work together.

LOCAL-AREA NETWORKS

Many microcomputers are used as *stand-alone* systems—they aren't connected to any shared devices (except perhaps via a telephone line or modem). On a stand-alone system, accessories such as printers and hard disk drives are *dedicated devices*, controlled by that microcomputer alone.

However, many organizations are linking their microcomputers, printers, mainframes, and other devices to form a *local-area network,* or *LAN.* A LAN is a high-speed pathway for exchanging messages and data, a technology that is having a major impact on the computer industry.

- A LAN shares the cost of expensive equipment such as laser printers and high-capacity disk drives among many different users.

- Unlike a mainframe or a minicomputer, a LAN still leaves each user with a private microcomputer system. Each system can have the best set of software and hardware for a particular job. If one system malfunctions, it doesn't affect anyone else.

Printer Sharing

Consider an office with 10 microcomputers. Instead of buying 10 $600 printers, one for each system, it makes more sense to put a single $3,000 laser printer on a network. This gives better, faster output, at half the cost. Printer sharing is a simple concept, but it is probably the most heavily used network application.

A network printer is used just as if it were your own printer. Standard commands and operations work normally. The system automatically sends printer output through the network.

Network printing is very cost effective. Offices that can't justify the cost of a "real" LAN often install a low-cost *printer network*. These systems let many users share a printer, resolving access conflicts automatically, yet avoid the high cost of a complete LAN.

File Servers and File Sharing

Most LANs have one or more *file servers*—high-speed microcomputers with large disk drives. File servers provide disk storage that can be accessed and shared by all network users.

Each user accesses the file server as if it were a "local" disk drive. For example, the file server might be seen as the "E:" drive on a PC or as a hard disk icon on a Macintosh. Files on the server are accessed using the same software and the same techniques used for any "local" files.

There is one big difference between files on a local disk and files on a server: more than one user can access a given file stored on the server. Sharing data on a file server is much easier than carrying a floppy disk from office to office. File servers also offer security controls for private data and can resolve conflicts when multiple users try to access the same data at the same time.

File servers offer three advantages over hard disk storage on an individual microcomputer:

- **Shared data access** is often very important. Some data, such as desktop publishing style sheets, spreadsheet templates, and customer lists, need to be standardized within an organization. Everyone should use the same version of such files. Most database systems are designed to work with file servers, so they allow many users to access shared data easily and efficiently.

- **High-capacity storage** is cheaper. The bigger the disk, the lower the cost per byte. Suppose six systems are on a network. For the cost of installing an extra 40MB disk drive on each system, you could put an extra 600MB on the file server, which all users can share.

- **Reliability** is usually better. Most file servers are high-end microcomputers, with higher quality, more rugged components than individual desktop microcomputers. Data reliability is also enhanced because the files are centralized. One person can monitor a file server and back up its files on a regular schedule, instead of requiring each individual user to make back ups.

Figure 12-12 shows a typical file server. Because they are large, fast, and rugged, file servers are fairly expensive—ranging from $10,000 to $25,000, including the necessary network software.

LAN Technology

Many different technologies and strategies are used to implement LANs. Options range from simple low-cost components for low-volume needs to rugged high-speed systems for heavy use.

There are three main implementation issues that network users need to know about:

- How fast is the network? How quickly can data be moved from one system to another? Most LANs transfer data at speeds between 2 and 20 million bits per second (megabits per second). This means that a file containing 100,000 characters (a 25 to 30 page document) can be transferred in less than a second.

FIGURE 12-12

File servers are high-end microcomputers, with higher-quality, more rugged components than individual desktop microcomputers.

Table 12-2: Network Terminology

Term	Description	Use
Node	A device connected to a network, by a network card (in an expansion slot), by an external interface (through a parallel port), or by a built-in option (as on the Macintosh).	Microcomputers, printers, and file servers are all nodes on a network.
Topology	How the basic network is organized: ring (nodes connected to a loop or circle of network cable); bus (nodes connected to a network cable with two "ends"—not a loop); star (nodes all connected to a single device); or hierarchy (a network built up from more than one network topology—two rings connected to a bus, for example).	A network's topology is interesting from a technical standpoint—it affects the cost of components, for example—but has little impact on use.
Bridge	A high-speed link between two networks; a "remote bridge" connects networks at different locations, often using telephone lines.	Bridges create hierarchical networks. Users normally don't have to be aware of where the bridges are and what they connect—there's just one big logical network.
Gateway	An interface between a network and a different environment, such as a mainframe or an incompatible network; network users can access the other environment through the gateway.	Gateways are most commonly used to permit modem-style data communications through a network. Network users can access mainframes or other resources through terminal emulation and other services.
Diskless Workstation	A microcomputer that has no disk drives; instead, it uses a file server on the network for all data management.	If a network is fast and reliable enough, the cost per microcomputer can be brought down dramatically by eliminating its disk storage.

- What shared devices are connected to the network? Such devices often include file servers, printers, mainframes, FAX machines, and modems.

- What network-related services are available on each microcomputer? Network software often lets users send and receive electronic mail, share databases, and transmit FAXes.

Technicians are very concerned with the details. A wide range of network hardware and software components offer many distinct advantages and disadvantages. Table 12-2 lists some of the terminology and concepts you may encounter in a network environment.

WIDE-AREA NETWORKS (WANS)

Many large organizations have set up *wide-area networks,* or *WANs.* These networks cover an area too large for a LAN, which is limited to roughly a mile or two. A WAN usually incorporates a number of different network technologies: several different LANs, at different locations, are connected using *bridges* and *gateways.*

- A network *bridge* connects two LANs. A high-speed connection is used to transfer messages from one network to the other. Many different technologies can be used to bridge networks, including microwave (radio) transmissions, satellite links, and special high-speed telephone lines.

- A network *gateway* lets network users access an incompatible environment, such as a mainframe or a different kind of network.

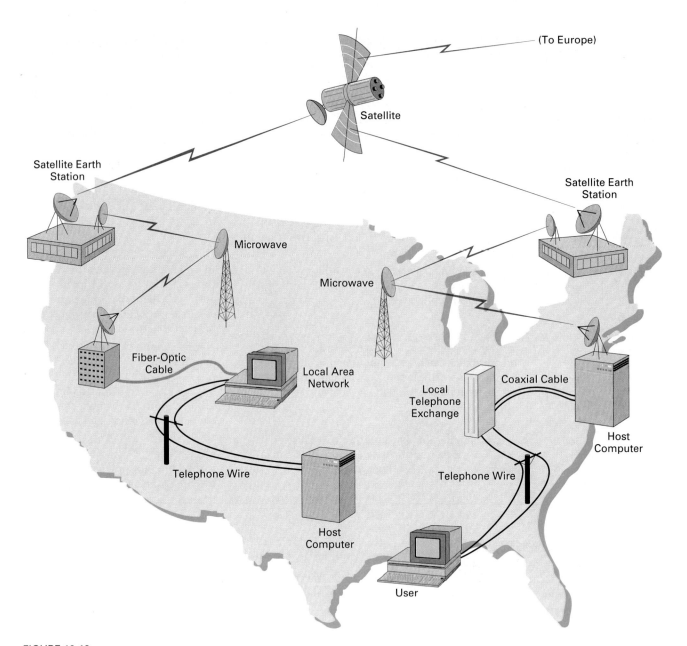

Satellite

(To Europe)

Satellite Earth
Station

Satellite Earth
Station

Microwave

Microwave

Fiber-Optic
Cable

Local Area
Network

Coaxial Cable

Local
Telephone
Exchange

Host
Computer

Telephone Wire

Telephone Wire

Host
Computer

User

FIGURE 12-13

A wide-area network (WAN) from
a large organization can employ
many network technologies

From a user's standpoint, a WAN is no different from a LAN. You access
a file server or printer in another city just as if it were in the next room.

Most WANs use a high-speed *network backbone*—a set of network
bridges that carry most of the long-distance traffic. The WAN backbone
defines the basic shape and coverage of the network. It often connects an
organization's mainframes that are located in different cities. LANs in each
city are also connected to the "backbone." Figure 12-13 shows a typical
WAN, employing a variety of network technologies.

OTHER CONNECTIVITY OPTIONS

Non-LAN Star Networks

LANs (and WANs) are the most popular forms of connectivity. However, some
organizations don't use a LAN; instead, microcomputers are connected to a
mainframe or minicomputer, as shown in Figure 12-14. This is called a *star*
configuration—the "host computer" is at the center of a star, with the microcomputers at the points. Unlike LAN services, these environments aren't stan-

Today many microcomputers have built-in modems. A modem is necessary if you wish to use information services such as Prodigy or CompuServe. By subscribing to this type of information service, you can obtain a wealth of information—from up-to-the minute news to weather reports to information on investing and finance. Friends can also communicate with each other either in an on-line group or in one-to-one conversations. Some users regularly use these services to shop, select gift items, and make travel arrangements.

Modems also may allow you to do such things as communicate with a local user's group or use your computer as a terminal so you can exchange data with another computer.

dardized. Instead, each star network is tailored to a particular environment. Sometimes, just basic data communications services—terminal emulation and file transfer—are available to the microcomputers. Other star systems also provide electronic mail, printer access, and other LAN-type services.

A star configuration is dependent on a central computer. If that machine becomes overloaded or unavailable, every user is affected. With a LAN, each microcomputer acts independently. As LAN technology becomes more widespread, the star approach will be used less often. Instead, most central mainframes will be connected to LANs.

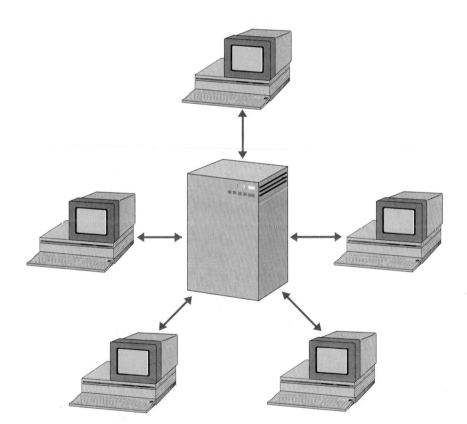

FIGURE 12-14

A mainframe computer can be used as the hub of a non-LAN star network.

Non-Network Connectivity

For file transfer or other operations, two or more systems are often connected by specialized high-speed links. For example, by using their serial or parallel ports, users might connect two PCs, or a PC and a Macintosh. Figure 12-15 shows the software program *LapLink* being used to transfer files from one system to the other.

FIGURE 12-15

Programs like *LapLink*, which allow files to be transferred directly from one system to another, are low-cost alternatives to file transfers in a network.

This approach is a low-cost alternative to a network. Although the services are limited, data transfers occur much faster than when using modems. Users of laptop computers are especially fond of such software programs. In a few minutes, an entire diskful of data can be moved from one system to another.

Using Networks

Networks Provide High-Speed Access to Shared Resources.

LAN users share printers and file servers "transparently"—with the same techniques they use to access local printers and local files. However, LANs offer many other services as well.

NETWORK-AWARE APPLICATIONS

Many software programs take advantage of network services, and especially of LAN-based file sharing. These software applications are referred to as *network-aware applications.*

- Desktop publishing systems, such as *Ventura* and *PageMaker*, have special network services to simplify the use of shared files. This ensures that common files, such as style sheets, are kept consistent.

- Spreadsheets, such as *Excel* and *Lotus 1-2-3*, often include network tools to help access shared data or templates.

- Database management systems, such as *Paradox* and *Progress*, let many LAN users access the same shared database. These systems today offer many services that were once only available on mainframes, including powerful tools for integrating data from different systems, sophisticated multiuser security controls, mechanisms that preserve data integrity even when two users try to change the same data, and advanced tools to protect against data loss even after a hardware failure.

Some systems offer all of these services in the basic program; in others, network support is an added-cost option. Programs with advanced network versions often include major new features beyond those in the standard version. In addition, network-based versions are often substantially easier to administer, and many have a lower "cost-per-seat" than buying separate copies for each microcomputer.

Figure 12-16 shows a network user accessing shared data.

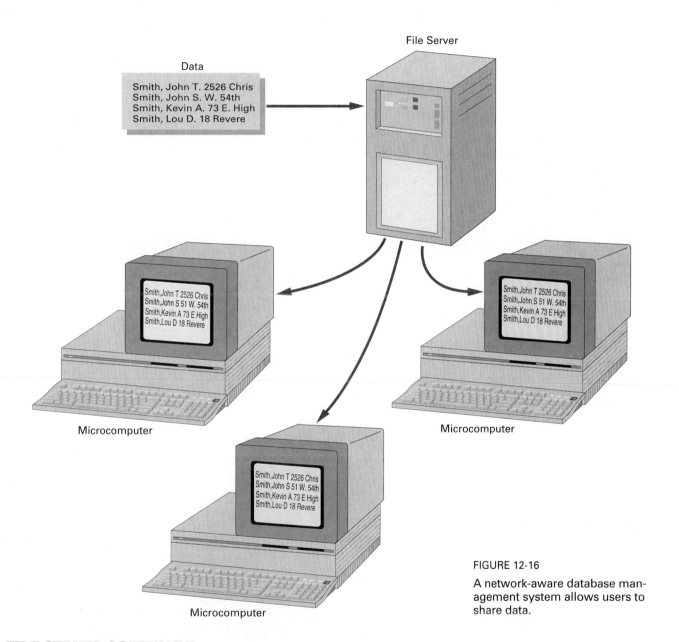

FIGURE 12-16

A network-aware database management system allows users to share data.

FILE SERVER SOFTWARE

LAN file servers have sophisticated *network operating systems* that manage shared disk files and perform other services. As file servers grow more powerful, their capabilities are also expanding. Today, most file servers support the following services, in addition to basic "disk housekeeping":

- *Electronic mail*, which provides message handling for all users of the LAN. This is like the electronic mail capabilities described for network services such as CompuServe and MCI Mail.

- *Print spooling* provides automatic management of network printers. This service avoids problems when multiple users try to print at the same time. Output is queued (like a movie-ticket line), scheduled, and printed in order.
- *Security* protects private data, requiring users to enter a password before they can access it.
- *File administration* provides tools to manage the many files and directories stored on a file server.

Future Trends

Connectivity Is the Way of the Future.

If you walked into the headquarters of 10 large U.S. firms and asked their vice presidents in charge of technology to predict the future, you would probably get 10 versions of the same answer: "Connectivity, cooperative process-

FREEDOM OF (COMPUTER) SPEECH

Not long ago, the term *utilities* described companies that provided essential public services such as electricity, gas, and water, delivered through wires and pipes. Telephone service, which began as a luxury, quickly became an essential public service, too. Today, many people consider cable TV, now found in millions of homes, an essential public service.

In today's information age, companies such as Prodigy, CompuServe, and GEnie are creating what may become yet another new kind of utility. This newest utility delivers a different kind of service—information, the "fuel" that drives today's world.

These new utility companies, which already have 2 million paying customers, are on-line information services connected via phone lines to a computer in your home or office. Although not all companies deliver all services, most transmit the latest in news, financial, and sports reports. With Prodigy's extremely popular computer baseball league, "Baseball Manager," you can even play ball.

Two of the most popular features are also the most controversial: computer bulletin boards, which allow users to post messages to each other, and chat channels, which connect people from all over the country who wish to discuss a particular subject on screen. Because the chat channels and the bulletin boards include some topics that are "adult" in language and content, the new utility companies must decide whether they are neutral conveyors of information, or active editors of the information they transmit. CompuServe, for example, takes a hands-off stance toward its freewheeling, uncensored, and enormously popular Adult and Alternative Lifestyles channels.

But rival Prodigy closely controls content and will not post bulletin board messages that it thinks are obscene or irrelevant. Prodigy says it's just exercising the same kind of editorial choice a newspaper or magazine would make.

Are these services impersonal utilities like a telephone company that simply provide connections? Or are they media in their own right, like magazines, TV, and radio? Is computer speech protected by the First Amendment? Regardless of which way these issues are decided, on-line information services are likely to become another essential part of our lives.

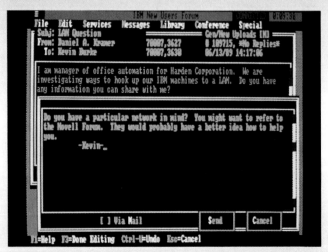

On-line information services, such as CompuServe, Prodigy, and GEnie, connect you to their other customers. Should these companies censor what you say?

Sources: "Adventures in the On-Line Universe," by Evan Schwartz, *Business Week*, June 17, 1991, p. 112. "How Long Will Prodigy Be a Problem Child?" by Jeffrey Rothfeder and Mark Lewyn, *Business Week*, September 10, 1990, p. 75.

ing, and distributed computing." As computer costs continue to decline and technology improves, every organization is taking advantage of connectivity.

- *Cooperative processing* lets different computer systems work together, sharing data and exchanging messages as they work.

- *Distributed computing* takes advantage of the computer systems throughout an organization. Each piece of data is entered, processed, and accessed on the machine where it can do the most good.

The growth of LANs, and of microcomputers in general, is a clear sign of where we're going. Industry will steadily increase the use of microcomputers and connectivity.

One important way that connectivity is improving involves a kind of software called *groupware*. Some programs, like those mentioned earlier, use networks "passively." For example, most word processors, spreadsheets, and other traditional applications use networks only to share files. *Groupware* does more; it uses a network "actively" by helping users work together and by exchanging data between systems. Perhaps the most well-known program is *Lotus Notes,* which lets many users interact using a common pool of shared data. Other groupware applications include the following:

- Planning agendas and scheduling meetings for an entire group. The groupware system accesses each person's schedule, and automatically finds the first available time when a particular set of people can meet (Figure 12-17).

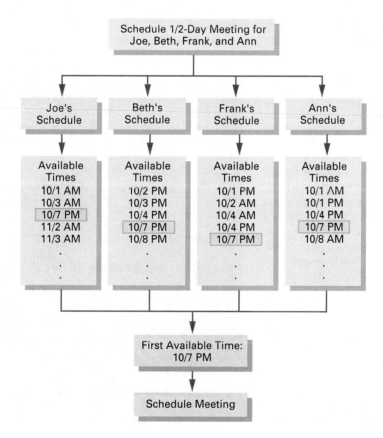

FIGURE 12-17

A groupware scheduling system examines each person's schedule, automatically finds the first available time when all the people can meet, and schedules the meeting.

- Time reporting and management. The system reviews each person's activities and helps managers make assignments, forecast delays, and determine productivity.

- Map making. The system maintains an electronic map for a city or some other area. Individual users can "check out" sections of the map to update.

These are the kinds of applications that usually run on mainframes and minicomputers. LAN technology makes it possible to move such applications to microcomputers.

Current groupware programs for specialized purposes, such as map making, are discussed in Chapter 13. Other groupware programs take limited advantage of the network environment, but are moving in the direction of generalized workgroup computing. Many more groupware programs will appear in coming years.

GROUPWARE: A NEW WAY TO WORK TOGETHER

Groupware is the name for a type of networking software that allows users to work together, exchanging data between systems.

For example, assume you are a project manager with a bank that has operations in North America, Europe, and Asia. Using input from managers and systems experts in New York, Chicago, Los Angeles, Paris, London, Tokyo, and Hong Kong, you're putting together a report that will propose a major international reorganization of computer operations. The report is due in two days and the bank's president has just asked for major changes.

This time, conference calls, FAX transmissions, and overnight delivery won't make it. You need a face-to-face meeting where each manager can contribute essential facts and ideas and respond immediately to the president's changes.

With groupware, your managers won't actually be face to face, but they can work together, simultaneously, to edit and revise your proposal from wherever they are in the world.

One current example of groupware is Group Technologies' *Aspects* software program, designed for the Macintosh. *Aspects* makes it possible for up to 16 people to work on the same document simultaneously. Each signs on as a participant and picks a distinctive icon to use as a pointer. "Meetings" can be unstructured, with every participant working on a document at once. *Aspects* also provides rules for structured meetings, which require people to take turns or to get permission to make changes from a designated "master of ceremonies."

One of the first groupware programs was Lotus's *Notes* software program. *Notes* enabled the Manufacturers Hanover Trust Company to tap into the power of its new local-area networks (LANs). With *Notes*, the bank could organize customer data and track client contacts automatically. This gave salespeople and account managers information for analyzing markets and preparing tailor-made sales pitches.

IBM has invested heavily in another example of groupware, the "electronic meeting." At an electronic meeting, up to 50 people sit around a table at microcomputers and type their comments. With their anonymity preserved, people seem to lose their shyness and sometimes become brutally honest. Electronic meetings seem especially useful for bringing together people who have traditionally fought and argued with each other.

Still, groupware is finding its place slowly. Dereck Naef, who was a college sophomore when he helped develop *Aspects,* acknowledges that "Changing the way people work takes time." But businesses must improve productivity to survive. People must work together more efficiently. Groupware may just be the right productivity tool at the right time.

One popular example of groupware is the electronic meeting. Because comments displayed on screen are anonymous, participants are often more honest and direct than they would be face to face.

Sources: "Plugging the Gap between E-Mail and Video Conferencing," by Edmund Andrews, *New York Times,* Business Section, June 23, 1991, p.9. "How Lotus Wove a Web That Won over Manny Hanny," by Deidre Depke, *Business Week,* June 4, 1990, p. 105. "At These Shouting Matches, No One Says a Word," by Jim Bartimo, *Business Week,* June 11, 1990, p. 78.

Data communications and connectivity are transforming the consumer market. Millions of people with home computers already use public networks such as CompuServe or Prodigy. New network services are springing up every month. As home computers become more common, this trend will increase. Computerized "smart telephones" are also starting to appear. These devices, in the $100 to $500 price range, will let consumers access network services without buying a computer. Our options will expand considerably once that happens. Figure 12-18 shows AT&T's SmartPhone.

Despite amazing growth in the last few years, communications and connectivity are still in their infancy. New industry standards, better software, and declining hardware costs promise more exciting developments in the near future.

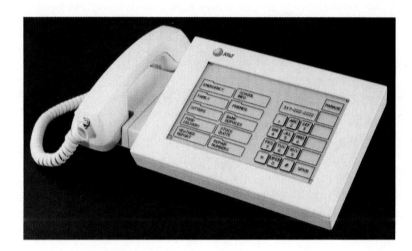

FIGURE 12-18

"Smart telephones," like AT&T's SmartPhone, let consumers access network services without buying a computer.

REVIEW QUESTIONS

1. When talking about microcomputers, what is the difference between the terms *data communications* and *connectivity*?

2. What does a modem do?

3. What does communications software do?

4. What is the difference between an internal modem and an external modem?

5. What is the difference between digital data and analog data? Where is each used?

6. What is a modem's carrier signal?

7. *Modem* stand for "MOdulator/DEModulator." What is modulating and demodulating?

8. Modem speed is measured in *baud*. What does the modem speed 1,200 baud mean?

9. What is terminal emulation? What is a computer terminal?

10. What does *host computer* mean?

11. What is a file transfer? Name at least two file transfer strategies.

12. What is a file transfer protocol (such as XMODEM or KERMIT) used for? Are they the same as *modem protocols*?

13. What is a data transformation (or data translation) as used during file transfers? Give an example.

14. What is a data communications script?

15. What is a specialized terminal emulator?

16. What is a 3270 board, such as an IRMA board?

17. What is a FAX board?

18. What kinds of services can a microcomputer access via a public network such as CompuServe?

19. Can electronic mail be sent to you when you're not using your microcomputer?

20. What does the term *log on* (or *sign on*) mean?

21. What are some of the databases that can be accessed using network services?

22. What are some of the transactions that can be generated from a microcomputer?

23. What does it mean to say that connectivity services are accessed *transparently*?

24. What is a LAN? What does it do?

25. Can LAN users share a printer? What is a *printer network*?

26. What is a file server?

27. What is the normal speed range of a LAN?

28. What is a WAN?

29. What is a *non-LAN star network*?

30. What is a network-aware application? Give an example.

31. What are some of the services offered by file server software, other than basic file sharing?

32. What is groupware?

TOPICS FOR RESEARCH AND DISCUSSION

1. What security problems do you think would result from the widespread use of data communications in a large company? Would some organizations need to put restrictions on access to their computers and data? How could an organization protect itself against computer criminals trying to get inside information or to change company records? How will this situation change as portable computers become more common?

2. Network services offer many benefits to an organization, but they have real costs. A small network might run $25,000 to $35,000, including network installation, microcomputer connections, and a file server.

   Suppose you worked in a small architecture firm with a dozen microcomputer users. If you were asked to evaluate the benefits of installing a network, what issues would you focus on? What kinds of benefits would an organization need to see to justify this kind of expenditure? What cost savings would help pay for the network?

3. Services like CompuServe and Prodigy are extremely popular today, both in business and with home computer users. Obtain literature on these or similar network services, and evaluate the costs and benefits involved. What services are available? How would they help a small business? A large business? A home user? Which services simply save time or money (such as airline reservations, which you could make by telephone)? Which activities couldn't be done at all without a computer (such as up-to-the-minute stock quotes)? If possible, get access to one of these services and evaluate the capabilities available.

CHAPTER 13

SPECIALIZED SOFTWARE

OBJECTIVES

The information in this chapter will enable you to

- Describe the difference between specialized application programs and standard tools like spreadsheets and word processors.
- Describe the difference between off-the-shelf programs and custom programs.
- List the steps in the application development process.
- List the participants in a development project.
- Describe programming languages and several other development tools.

This chapter discusses *application software*—software designed for the special requirements of a particular business or activity. Spreadsheets and word processors can help in nearly any job, from clerical tasks to executive decision making. Computers also help in more specialized ways—from catalog order processing at a department store, to checking statements printed by your bank, to point-of-sale terminals at a fast-food restaurant.

It's easy to forget bread-and-butter computer applications when talking about microcomputers. Such practical applications aren't exciting to read about. They aren't featured in periodicals like *PC Magazine* and *Macworld*. Specialized programs are just that—*specialized*. Each one fits only one or two specific situations. But it's often a specific application that can justify the cost of purchasing a computer for a business.

At the heart of most specialized applications is a database, containing details about business operations or record keeping, such as customer records, work orders, and employee records (Figure 13-1 shows an example). The application provides ways to maintain and utilize that database. *The presence of a business-specific database is the major difference between specialized software applications and the general-purpose software discussed earlier.*

When Do Businesses Need Specialized Software?

Special-Purpose Software Automates a Particular Business Function, and Is Often Tailored to a Single Organization's Needs.

Businesses use specialized software for a variety of reasons. Two of the most common are automating certain repetitive business functions, and structuring business procedures so the procedure is always performed in the same way. Some businesses even use computers to perform technical or mechanical services that, until a few years ago, would have been performed by specialists.

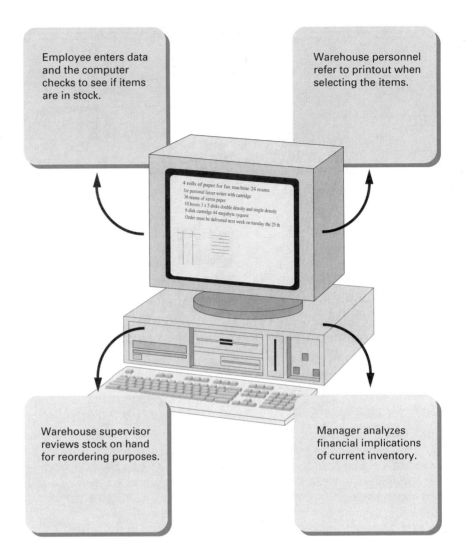

FIGURE 13-1

At the heart of a specialized applications is a database. An inventory database is used to take orders from customers, fill the order, review stock on hand, and assess the company's financial condition.

Employee enters data and the computer checks to see if items are in stock.

Warehouse personnel refer to printout when selecting the items.

Warehouse supervisor reviews stock on hand for reordering purposes.

Manager analyzes financial implications of current inventory.

AUTOMATING BUSINESS FUNCTIONS

Computers can reduce paperwork and increase accuracy by taking over most of the repetitive detail work in a business. Thirty years ago, this kind of automation was usually handled by *keypunching* data onto *punch cards*, as Figure 13-2 shows. Today, a punch card is a rarity. Instead, computer users use a keyboard to enter information into the computer.

FIGURE 13-2

Keypunching data on punch cards was the main automation strategy for the 1950s and 1960s.

Computers can automate clerical operations such as the following:

- A *customer order system*, like that shown in Figure 13-3, is used to process orders and create the invoices, statements, and shipping orders needed.
- An *inventory control system*, which records orders and shipments and automatically adjusts inventory levels.
- A *telemarketing system*, which helps give fast, efficient service to customers over the telephone.

STRUCTURING BUSINESS PROCEDURES

Most specialized applications do more than automate paperwork. They also provide a structure for how work gets done. Office procedures make the difference between a smooth-running system and chaos. Think about a big organization, like an airline. Getting reservations, tickets, seat assignments, or boarding passes requires a dialogue with a computer. Airline employees seldom have to decide what to do—there's a standard operating procedure, established and maintained by computer.

Specialized applications help make many kinds of work efficient, predictable, and consistent. For example, an *accounting system* helps businesses keep their records by the book, following federal, state, and local laws, and standard U.S. accounting practices. A *records management system* is needed in many regulated industries—from construction to nuclear power plants—where strict rules dictate what records have to be kept, for how long, and at what level of detail.

PERFORMING TECHNICAL AND MECHANICAL SERVICES

Many specialized applications rely on the microcomputer's advanced control capabilities. Some control systems are designed for specialists, such as machinists or architects. Others reduce the need for technical knowledge, transforming an unusual expertise (such as drafting or typesetting) into a normal office skill.

Engineering and mapping systems are like the general-purpose graphics programs discussed in Chapter 11, but offer special services for a particular industry. Tools are designed around a particular technical problem, such as sewer design, injection molding, or hazardous waste management.

Process control systems are used to operate milling machines, lathes, heating systems, security systems, and a wide range of other machinery (see Figure 13-4).

FIGURE 13-3

Automating clerical functions is an important use of special-purpose software. It can speed data entry and increase accuracy.

FIGURE 13-4

Robots, machinery, and control applications have transformed industry.

Types of Specialized Software

Off-the-Shelf Applications Meet Common Needs; Custom Applications Meet Unique Needs.

In any organization, you will find specialized applications like those just described. These applications will run on mainframes, minicomputers, local-area networks, or desktop microcomputers. The choice of where they run and what they actually do depends on several factors, the most important being who builds the application. *Off-the-shelf programs* are sold by software companies. *Custom applications* are created when an organization's needs don't fit a standard off-the-shelf program.

OFF-THE-SHELF APPLICATION PROGRAMS

Specialized off-the-shelf applications are software programs used for specific nonentertainment purposes by a limited number of users. Because they are tailored for such narrowly specialized groups of users (often a single profession), off-the-shelf applications are sometimes called *vertical market software.* You might be surprised at how many there are, especially when you consider that most off-the-shelf applications aren't sold through retail stores (see Figure 13-5).

FIGURE 13-5

Specialized software programs are available for virtually every profession.

What Is Off-the-Shelf Software?

An *off-the-shelf program* is a piece of software that you can buy, install, and run to perform a specific function. It may sell only 10 copies, or it may sell 10,000.

"Ten copies?" you say. Believe it or not, many off-the-shelf programs have just a few users. For example, there are many off-the-shelf billing systems, but a dentist can't use a florist's billing system. Their databases, their billing procedures, even their vocabularies are different. Every business has its own set of billing needs. To build an off-the-shelf application program, a vendor must have detailed knowledge of the particular business being served.

The quality of off-the-shelf software varies. If you order software at random from a catalog, you may get a rugged, shrink-wrapped program from a major vendor, with high-quality manuals; a locally developed, poorly documented program with only a few users; an obsolete, poor-quality program that remains popular just because it's cheap; or an unknown system with few users that is beautifully designed and documented. This variability makes it hard to generalize about standard application programs—and makes it *essential* to evaluate such programs carefully.

Advantages and Disadvantages

Most organizations prefer to use off-the-shelf microcomputer software because the cost of development is spread over a large group. (A standard product that retails for $500 might cost $50,000 to build if it were a custom program.) Even more important, a standard program is *already designed and built.* Many off-the-shelf program publishers provide a hot line for customers who have problems and an extensive user's manual that explains how to use the program. Organizations can test many programs, select the one best suited to their needs and practices, and start using it immediately.

However, off-the-shelf programs impose several important restrictions. Using an off-the-shelf program means accepting that program's view of your needs. Your work procedures may have to change to fit the program. Also, many programs are *closed*; the only way to access data is to use the program's own services. If any function is missing, there's no way to add it on. The more common the problem, the more likely that a good off-the-shelf solution exists.

Modifying Standard Software

Most application programs need to be *configured* before use. Sometimes this is just for technical details, such as defining the brand of printer. But more often, application programs require a tailoring step, to specify such things as the name of the organization, the layout of invoices, and the size of the checks. This tailoring is done in four basic ways:

- **Set-up procedures.** The software's installation procedure may ask configuration questions ("Enter your name . . ."), as shown in Figure 13-6. This is the simplest case.

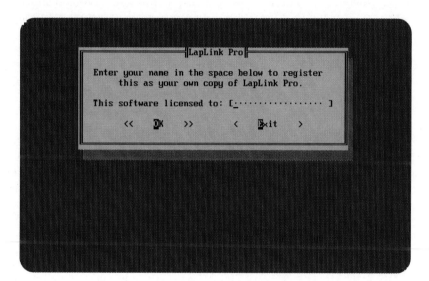

FIGURE 13-6

Some specialized programs offer you the ability to configure your system easily and quickly using its set-up procedures.

- **Table-driven configuration.** Many programs use tables to control some of their processing. For example, an invoicing program might come with two standard customer codes: "ACTIVE" and "INACTIVE." You might be able to add other codes to draw attention to special customers ("BAD CREDIT," "VICE PRESIDENT'S BROTHER"). *Table-driven configuration* is handy; it lets users change the behavior of a program as easily as changing screen colors, simply by entering new values.
- **Report customization.** Some applications let users control report layout—column headings, sort order, titles, and other details—or even to specify new reports from scratch.
- **Customization by an expert.** Many application programs need to be customized by an expert—usually the organization that sells the program. Recall that most application programs are not sold over the counter. Instead, a dealer or consultant sells the software as part of a complete program including installation and training services (see Figure 13-7).

CUSTOM APPLICATIONS

Sometimes, an off-the-shelf program just won't do the job—because of missing functions, unusual company-specific needs, incompatible hardware, or connectivity requirements. In such situations, many organizations use their

FIGURE 13-7

Some specialized programs need to be installed and configured by an expert.

technical staff to create custom applications. These specialists can draw on a wide range of options and approaches. They can weigh the available standard solutions against the cost of creating a custom system.

Programming: How Applications Get Built

Software Is Created by Technicians Who Write Programs.

Generations of bad science fiction have made programming sound mysterious, even magical. In fact, programming involves less magic and more plain hard work than you might expect. Computers do precisely what they're told; and they're told what to do by *software programs* containing extremely simple commands.

You may be wondering why this book should describe how software is created. Its focus is on *using* microcomputer software, not about *writing* software programs. But most organizations have custom software and, sooner or later, you'll use a custom system. As a user of that system, you may have a role in changing, replacing, or evaluating it. Furthermore, as software products get more powerful and easier to use, they rely less on professional programmers and more on users. So the more you understand about software development, the better prepared you'll be for evaluating and using software.

Programmers are technicians who create software. They use a variety of tools and techniques to do this. Many people think that microcomputer programming must be simpler than mainframe programming. If it takes a year to build a *mainframe* billing system, then a *microcomputer* billing system logically should take only a few weeks. Unfortunately, that's not how things work. Programming is essentially the same task for large systems or small ones. The same kinds of tools are used. The same kinds of problems occur. Of course, mainframe applications usually tackle bigger problems, and their cost can be spread over more users. But the same development process is used in both environments.

The System Life Cycle

Software Has a Life Cycle—from Planning and Design to Implementation and Use.

There are two basic strategies for building application software. *Little projects* use limited time and resources, but often produce only temporary solutions. *Big projects* use a large team and substantial effort, but can take months or even years. We'll look at a typical project—the kind where you might be asked to help. As you'll see, building quality software is expensive and time consuming.

THE SOFTWARE DEVELOPMENT PROCESS

Before we dive into the specific life cycle steps, let's look at the overall structure of the software development process (Figure 13-8).

- **Planning.** Before any specific technology steps are taken, an organization must identify a problem and develop plans for solving that problem.
- **Design.** Once a problem has been identified and alternative plans have been considered, a general solution is selected and then designed in some detail.
- **Implementation.** Software that can fulfill the design goals is then created and tested.

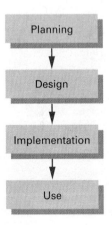

FIGURE 13-8

The same basic application life cycle fits most software development needs.

- **Use.** Finally, the new application is installed, users are trained, results are evaluated, and improvements begin.

Although each organization follows its own specific steps, this basic structure is common to most projects.

PLANNING

Planning is the most variable component in the system life cycle. In a large corporation, with thousands of employees, entire departments are dedicated to technology planning. In a little project, planning might consist of 10 minutes spent sketching diagrams on the back of an envelope. On a big project the work might be straightforward, but it might be assigned to a 50-member project team. Then, every tiny decision takes study.

- *Needs analysis* identifies ways that new applications can improve work. Most planning begins with a general problem: "There are too many mistakes in our orders." Before starting to build a solution, needs analysis is used to form a clearer picture of the problem.

- *Information modeling* is another planning activity used in large organizations. It creates an "information road map" that shows every important scrap of data and every business procedure. Why do this? Because in many giant organizations, nobody really understands how the business works. Nobody sets out to design a wasteful bureaucracy; it just grows up over the years, like a tangle of vines. Information modeling is a way to find wasteful procedures and bottlenecks and plan strategies for preventing them. Figure 13-9 shows a typical information modeling diagram.

Planning helps organizations make key technical decisions. Needs for custom software and mainframe applications are identified to support *mission-critical systems*—systems that run the business and must be reliable, uniform, and centrally controlled.

FIGURE 13-9

Information Resource Modeling is used by many large organizations.

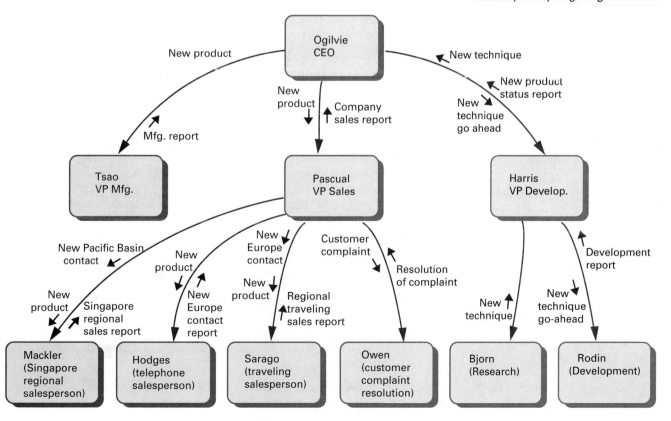

DESIGN

The *design* process creates *external specifications* for a system, spelling out what it will do, based on a defined set of needs. Depending on the size of the problem, design efforts can range from formal technical studies to quick and dirty brainstorming sessions.

- Defining *system requirements* is the first design task—specifying what the system will do in enough detail to know what to build. The easiest method is to list each major function supported, such as placing an order, adding a new customer, or paying taxes. Then, for each activity, define the *outputs* (what results must be created) and the *inputs* (what information is obtained from the user). It's easier to start with the output—tangible results like invoices, forms, and reports—and then decide what input is needed to create that output. It's a repetitive process: each output creates the need for new input, and each input enables new output. Figure 13-10 diagrams this process.

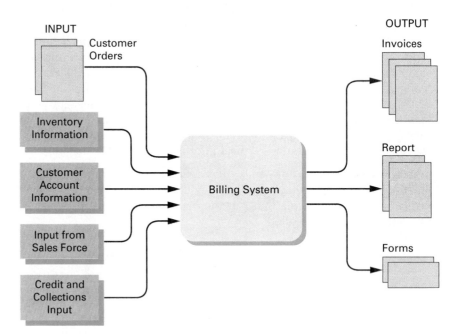

FIGURE 13-10

System requirements reflect what the system will do, in enough detail to know what to build.

- A related activity is defining *user requirements.* A given system capability (such as tracking orders) can have different meanings, depending on who will use the system. A system that manages billing records can provide basic bookkeeping services for a clerk, or a financial modeling system for a company president (see Figure 13-11). Any specialized application can be designed to meet the needs of specific users.
- *Interface design* matches users' requirements with system requirements. Applications use different strategies for presenting their underlying data, based on how the data will be used. *Transaction processing systems* (like automated grocery checkout counters) use a structured, "event-driven" user interface for high-volume processing of sales "events." *Analysis tools,* such as *decision support systems* and *executive information systems,* allow senior staff to evaluate many alternative ways of using the same basic data. Those sales events at the checkout counter may be used to improve a grocery chain's inventory or distribution systems, for example.

A major goal of the design process is to resolve the *make-versus-buy* decision. Each system function depends on a piece of software. But any problem

-- ACCOUNTS RECEIVABLE --
as of January 31, 1992

Account: **Rightway Publishing Co., Inc.**

Our Job No.	Customer P.O. No.	Job type/ TITLE	Invoice Date	Amount Due
5766	D39742	Design/HEROES	9/4/91	385.00
5824	D07503	Maps/IROQUOIS	9/20/91	115.00
5883	D40963	Reprint Patches	10/17/91	90.00
5885	D40967	Design/SEASHORE	11/1/91	400.00
5968	A23112	Frontmatter/LIVES	11/18/91	288.50
5990A	D46557	Covers/COOKBOOK	11/25/91	375.00
6002	A23113	Typesetting/GAMES	11/25/91	995.75
5942A	D47503	Editing/FAMILY	12/18/91	728.50
5969	A23166	Illustrations/STORIES	12/21/91	425.00
5978	A23168	Full Service/BASIC	1/6/92	1,877.50
6002A	A23210	Pagination/HUNT	1/10/92	865.00
6041	D49372	Design/CHILDREN	1/15/92	535.00

(a)

-- ACCOUNTS RECEIVABLE OVER 60 DAYS --
as of January 31, 1992

Our Job No.	Customer P.O. No.	Job type/ TITLE	Invoice Date	Amount Due
Account:	**Better Books, Ltd.**			
5842A	1503	Editing/LIGHT	10/24/91	728.50
5923	2166	Illustrations/SQUARE	11/8/91	425.00
5957	2168	Full Service/PEACE	11/14/91	1,877.50
5975A	2210	Pagination/KING	11/21/91	865.00
5994	2372	Design/CHRONICLES	11/26/91	535.00
Account:	**Rightway Publishing Co., Inc.**			
5766	D39742	Design/HEROES	9/4/91	385.00
5824	D07503	Maps/IROQUOIS	9/20/91	115.00
5883	D40963	Reprint Patches	10/17/91	90.00
5885	D40967	Design/SEASHORE	11/1/91	400.00
5968	A23112	Frontmatter/LIVES	11/18/91	288.50

(b)

-- ANNUAL BILLING SUMMARY --
as of December 27, 1991

Account Name	1991	1990	% Change
Alto Publishing Company	631.96	608.50	+ 4%
Answer Group Member Services	1,877.50	544.78	+245%
Better Books, Ltd.	9,378.96	8,773.21	+ 7%
Christina Designs	345.37	422.80	(18%)
Faraway Travel, Inc.	5,909.00	5,195.00	+ 12%
Green Castle Press	2,809.50	1,963.25	+ 43%
Gummacher International	16,303.95	9,587.39	+ 70%
Hess Educational Books	2,012.25	2,989.00	(33%)
Humphrey Graphics	694.35	572.20	+ 21%
Kennedy & Nelson	7,989.50	4,693.45	+ 70%
Mystery Writers Assoc.	12,033.30	8,445.60	+ 42%
Oxford News Group	3,266.79	1,034.24	+216%
Rightway Publishing Co., Inc.	8,677.05	9,539.88	(9%)
Rockford Community College	3,199.00	1,266.75	+153%
Theatre Productions	1,302.75	1,052.25	+ 24%

(c)

FIGURE 13-11

Different users have different requirements when using the same data. A clerk needs to be able to confirm the billing amount for a customer over the phone (a). The clerk's supervisor needs to check the current status of all the overdue accounts (b). An executive needs to check the current billings against last year's (c).

can be tackled in dozens of ways, ranging from high-cost custom software solutions to inexpensive but limited off-the-shelf programs. To pick a strategy, we must weigh the costs and benefits of each solution. Figure 13-12 illustrates this cost-benefit question in graphic form.

Suppose you need to create a system for tracking periodic maintenance on company equipment, such as copiers and printers. This means tracking each piece of equipment's make and model, who sold it, who services it, how old it is, and the history of past service calls. How can you do this?

- *Off-the-shelf.* The simplest solution, if available, is an off-the-shelf program.
- *Custom.* A programmer can design a custom software application. The finished system will maintain precisely the data you want, using precisely the input and output techniques you need.
- *Database.* You can create an inventory database, using a standard database management program like *dBase*, *Paradox*, or *r:Base*. You would then have to design simple screens and reports using the tools that come with the program.
- *Spreadsheet.* You could create an inventory list in a spreadsheet, such as *Lotus 1-2-3*, *Quattro Pro*, or *Excel*. You would use the many data management and display tools provided by that software to simplify administration.

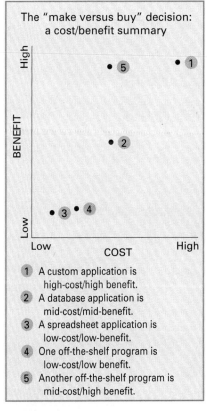

The "make versus buy" decision: a cost/benefit summary

1 A custom application is high-cost/high benefit.
2 A database application is mid-cost/mid-benefit.
3 A spreadsheet application is low-cost/low-benefit.
4 One off-the-shelf program is low-cost/low benefit.
5 Another off-the-shelf program is mid-cost/high benefit.

FIGURE 13-12

Make-versus-buy decisions usually trade functionality for cost.

These four solutions cover a broad range of costs and benefits. There are two little project solutions—using an off-the-shelf program or spreadsheet (which is usually much less work to use than a database management system)—and two big project solutions—using a database management system or a programming language. Programming from scratch is the most work, but offers the most options. Although a spreadsheet doesn't take much work, it doesn't provide much in the way of specialized functions.

IMPLEMENTATION

Let's assume that the easy solutions have been ruled out—a spreadsheet won't do the job. It's time to implement a solution. What's next?

- An *internal design* (*system design, implementation plan*) is created to specify each program. Internal design is similar to the requirements definition. While requirements focus on what the *users see*, the internal design focuses on what the *programs do*. There are many different design strategies. The most common is called *top-down design*, which uses a process called functional decomposition. Each function performed by the system is described by breaking it into smaller pieces. The goal is to define the whole system as the sum of its parts.

- *Programming* creates software that implements the internal design. A programmer does this by using a programming language—discussed later in this chapter—plus other tools and techniques.

- *Testing* is an integral part of development—the detection and removal of errors. Errors typically don't reveal themselves until long after they are created. Thus, it takes a major investment of testing time to root out the bugs. Many software vendors spend 70% to 80% of their development time on testing and quality control. If it takes them three months to plan, design, and build a system, it may take a year to find and fix the errors.

The normal implementation and testing process is based on quality management procedures to meet two essential needs: *quality control,* which discovers, diagnoses, and corrects defects, and *quality assurance,* which creates methods to avoid the accidental creation of defects in the first place.

USE

The final phase of the application life cycle brings software to its users.

- *Installation* takes place once a system's basic testing is complete. Users are trained, and production use begins. Most systems are phased in gradually, in either a *pilot project* with a small number of users, or a

FIGURE 13-13

An important aspect of installing a new system is training the new users how to use the software.

parallel test with simultaneous use of both the new software and the old system it is replacing (Figure 13-13).

- *Maintenance* efforts keep the application running. Despite the expense of creating a new application, most organizations spend around 80% of their technical resources just operating, maintaining, and enhancing existing applications. The maintenance phase of the life cycle can continue for many years.

Roles on the Development Team

Many People Typically Contribute to a Development Project.

A development project can involve a large group or a single person, depending on the complexity of the problem, the number of users, and other parameters (see Figure 13-14).

- In many projects, a senior technician is designated as *system architect* or *system designer.*
- *Analysts* (and *programmer/analysts*) do planning and design tasks—they evaluate current practices, define system requirements, and create specifications.
- *Programmers* create software to match specifications.
- Applications are designed to support the needs of *end users*, ranging from clerks to executives. End users must make their needs clear to developers.
- A special group of end users is called *knowledge workers.* These are people whose jobs revolve around computer data, such as financial analysts (who help corporations make financial decisions) and planners (who create long-term business strategies). Knowledge workers often become very sophisticated computer users.

FIGURE 13-14

Many people often participate in software development, each with special skills.

Software Development

Software Is Created Using a Variety of Tools.

We've discussed many aspects of application development. We're now going to the heart of the matter: how software actually gets created.

PROGRAMMING LANGUAGES

Software is written using a *programming language.* Programming languages are quite different from the languages familiar to us, such as English or Spanish. They are highly structured, simplified frameworks for expressing computations. Many programming languages used today were developed in the 1960s and 1970s.

Microcomputer software generally is written using the languages C, BASIC, or Pascal. Most mainframe software, by contrast, is written in COBOL, with FORTRAN a distant second.

Programming involves incredible detail. To give you a sense of scale, consider this: a typical program for updating an inventory file may require 3,000 lines of Pascal *source code*—statements written in a programming language. Experienced programmers in large organizations, working at peak efficiency, average in the range of 35 to 120 *lines of fully tested code per day.* (depending on the complexity of the program).

BASIC

BASIC was designed as a language that would be easy to use. It is deliberately simple, to minimize learning time and let beginners create small programs easily. Program lines are numbered, and the computer runs the program line by line in the order specified by the line numbers. (Figure 13-15 shows a typical BASIC source code.)

```
Ok
10      REM      BASIC PROGRAMMING IS EASY TO LEARN
20      LET      PRIN    = 10000            'AMOUNT OF LOAN
30      LET      RATE    = .9               'RATE OF INTEREST
40      REM      INTEREST = INTEREST FOR 30 DAYS
50      LET      INTEREST = PRIN * RATE * 30 / 360
60      PRINT    "IINTEREST = "; INTEREST

RUN
INTEREST =          75
Ok


1LIST   2RUN   3LOAD"   4SAVE"   5CONT   6,"LPT1   7TRON   8TROFF9KEY   0SCREEN
```

FIGURE 13-15

BASIC is good for beginners, and helps address simple needs.

Pascal

Pascal was created as a language for teaching programming concepts. It became popular during the 1970s because it fit the computer science curriculum. Students learn a great deal about programming in a semester of Pascal.

```
program frequency

    const
    size = 80;

    var
    s: string[size];
    i: integer;
    c: char;
    f: array[1..26] of integer;
    k: integer;

    begin
    writeln('enter line');
    readln(s)
    for i :=1 to 26 do
        f[i] := 0;

    for i := 1 to size do
        begin
        c := asLowerCase(s)[i]);
        if isLetter(c) then
            begin
            k := ord(c) - ord ('a') + 1;
            f[k] := f[k] + 1;
            end
        end;

    for i := 1 to 26 do
        write (f[i],' ')
    end
```

FIGURE 13-16

Pascal is structured, making it easy to read and maintain.

Just as there are specialized off-the-shelf software programs for business, there are specialized off-the-shelf programs for personal use.

For example, there are specialized databases for coin and stamp collectors. There are specialized databases for wine collectors. Another specialized database contains the calorie count for every type of food.

Specialized spreadsheet programs are available for home budgets and personal finance. There are specialized tax programs and programs that let you plan for your retirement. Specialized graphics programs help create family trees and genealogies.

If you are interested in using your microcomputer for a hobby or a specialized personal use, visit your local software or computer dealer. They often have information about specialized software programs, even if they don't carry the particular software. You could also look in a magazine devoted to your interest.

Today there is a vast array of specialized software for your personal use. Although it can be fun to develop your own, keep in mind the steps that are required to develop, test, debug, and document quality software. Your personal computer should be used to enhance your life and to make you more productive. Don't get bogged down in attempting to do tasks that should be done by a professional.

Pascal, unlike BASIC, is a *block-structured language.* This means that Pascal programs are broken visually into *blocks*, as you can see in Figure 13-16. The behavior of the program is reflected in its visual organization. This structured approach, also found in C, is one of the key components of a modern programming language.

C Language

C has become one of the most popular languages for microcomputer development. Many microcomputer software products are implemented using C, including many major products, such as those designed for the Microsoft Windows environment. C is a powerful language, in an industrial-strength program.

C is not as easy to learn or read as Pascal or BASIC. It was designed to maximize the effectiveness of an expert, rather than reduce the learning time for a beginner. Nevertheless, look at the number of books on C in the computer section of a bookstore—C is everywhere. For an experienced programmer, C code is easy to write, and it is ideal for large-scale applications.

C is a *tools-oriented language.* C programs draw on libraries of prewritten tools for such needs as graphics, statistics, and data management. The C programmer can thus use off-the-shelf components as part of an application. As a result, C is ideal for complex development needs, such as the Windows environment.

C++ and Object-Oriented Programming

You may have heard about C++, or seen the term *object-oriented* in an advertisement or product description. Object-oriented technology was a narrow, highly technical specialty for 20 years. But since it burst into prominence a few years ago, it's become one of the hottest buzz words in computing. We won't explore this technology—it's complex. Instead, let's look at its *uses*:

- The graphical user interfaces in both the Macintosh and Windows— with their icons, mouses, pop-up menus, and scroll bars—were borrowed from Smalltalk, a revolutionary object-oriented system developed in the early 1970s by Xerox.

- Object-oriented technology lets developers create better software, faster. A system that would take a month to build using C or Pascal might take only a few days with a language like C++ or Smalltalk, and it probably would do more.

- Traditional programming technology focuses on programs. Object-oriented technology is concerned with *data*. Developers describe what they want the data to do, and the system figures out how to give the data that behavior.

AMERICAN AIRLINES FLIES MULTIMEDIA INTO THE FUTURE

Imagine sitting at your travel agent's desk planning that dream trip to Florence, Italy. You've heard from friends about ruined vacations spent in "romantic villas" that turned out to be dank hovels miles from nowhere. Now, your agent recommends a romantic hotel near the best museums, and with a gorgeous view. Can you believe the agent?

Not so long ago, you'd have had to take the travel agent's word for everything. Now, thanks to American Airlines's new *SABREvision*, you can see full-color pictures and maps that enable you to preview your trip in advance.

SABREvision, which was installed in more than a thousand travel agents' offices in the fall of 1990, is just one of many customized multimedia applications pioneered by American Airlines.

Other programs have been devel-oped to help train employees. American Airlines has an enormously varied staff, with wide-ranging training needs. Pilots, ground crews, flight attendants, security staff, cargo handlers, ticket agents, and caterers all require training on new technology.

The American Airlines Learning Center in Fort Worth, Texas, has developed many customized multimedia training programs. For example, one helped to familiarize a generation of American Airlines pilots with the new digital display panels.

Some of these customized applications were created in house with *Authorware Professional* software, and others by outside companies, such as WICAT Systems, which developed a course for new flight attendants.

Although some programs require a laser videodisk player, many, such as a new program that shows caterers and flight attendants how to prepare in-flight food, were developed for microcomputers equipped with CD-ROM drives.

Developing customized software for a business can be expensive, especially on the scale undertaken by American. So, while it continues to save time and money by training employees more efficiently with multimedia applications, American Airlines is thinking of selling some of these programs to other airlines. It may start selling them slowly—as a "pilot" program.

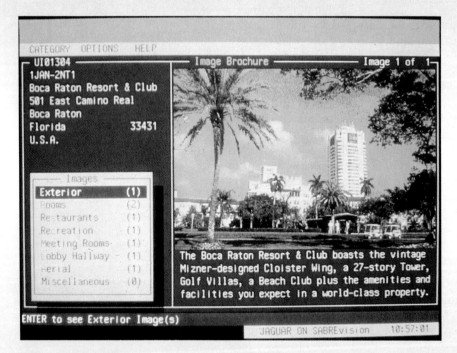

With American Airlines' *SABREvision* you can research your vacation from your travel agent's office.

Source: "American Pilots Multimedia into the Airline Industry," by Daniel Todd, *New Media Age,* June 1991.

SOFTWARE DEVELOPMENT TOOLS

We've talked briefly about the programming languages that are used to create software; but there's more to development than writing lines of Pascal or C code.

Traditional Development

Most programmers create programs using a handful of simple tools. Developers use a *text editor*—a simple word processor for programming—to create source code files. A *compiler* is then used to translate source code into *object code,* the instructions that the CPU understands. A *linker* creates an *executable file* from one or more object files. A *debugger* is used to test the finished program.

Integrated Tools

Many new development tools streamline the traditional development process. *Incremental compilers* let programmers change source code while it is being debugged. *Smart text editors* check source code for errors while it is being entered. *Integrated development environments* provide tools that work together, often tailored to a particular language, database, or windowing environment.

Computer Assisted Software Engineering (CASE)

Integrated tools are examples of *CASE tools*—automated techniques to make development easier. (CASE stands for Computer Assisted Software Engineering and is pronounced "case.") Most CASE tools fit in two categories: *upper-CASE tools,* which support the "upper" or "front" part of development (planning and design); and *lower-CASE tools,* which support the "lower" or "back" part of development (implementation and use). One of the most important uses of CASE is for *prototyping*—creating mock-ups of system functions for users to try (see Figure 13-17). CASE tools are reducing the cost of software development and increasing the quality of new applications.

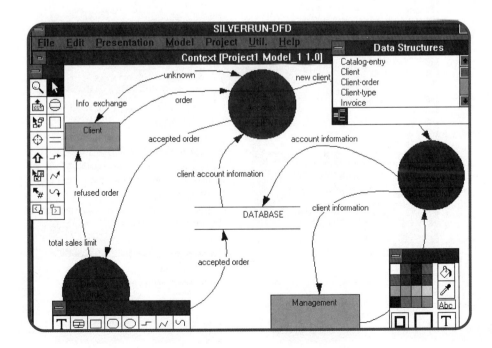

FIGURE 13-17

CASE (Computer Assisted Software Engineering) tools, such as this example created from SILVERRUN, speed the development process.

Hypermedia

Hypermedia applications let users mix different kinds of data. Some hypermedia capabilities can be seen in the new word processing and desktop publishing systems, which combine text and graphics in the same document. Other tools go even further, such as *HyperCard* on the Macintosh, or *ToolBook* (from Asymmetrix) and *IconAuthor* (from AimTech), both of which operate in the Windows environment. These new tools let users, not programmers, create sophisticated multimedia environments for presentations, training, or information management.

Specialized Environments

We've been focusing on application development with BASIC, Pascal, and C, with a nod to the integrated tool sets from database and hypermedia sys-

CONDUCTING BUSINESS

Conventional systems, with their varied and often proprietary approaches to computing, have created islands of information that separate departments and impede workflow within an organization. NCR COOPERATION integrates these islands into a powerful network that lets people share information and ideas—across workgroups, departments, and the entire company.

COOPERATION is a suite of software blending users, information, and applications. Its enterprise-wide environment helps people navigate easily through the information resources of complex organizations. Users do not have to be concerned with where information is located or the details of how to get it, whether that information resides down the hall or across the world. Opening an electronic file, for example, is as easy as activating the "file drawer" icon.

In addition to integrating computing resources, COOPERATION offers services that make communication remarkably efficient. Electronic mail and facsimile technology let people transmit messages—as well as documents incorporating combinations of text, images, data, and graphics—across an enterprise.

The COOPERATION Group Calendar/Scheduler helps users manage time and resources by maintaining calendars for individuals, work groups, and projects.

Workflow Automation, an enhancement added in 1992, will manage the flow of work from person to person, automatically routing electronic forms to appropriate individuals, confirming the successful completion of tasks, and flagging any delays.

COOPERATION gives virtually everyone in an organization access to data stored in diverse systems, breaking down the invisible walls that have traditionally isolated workgroups and departments.

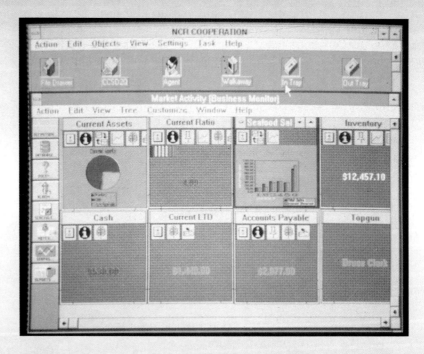

NCR's COOPERATION facilitates team work among employees.

Source: NCR Corporation.

tems. However, a specialized application can be created *without programming*—by using standard tools such as spreadsheets.

How can we call a spreadsheet—for payroll, say—a specialized application? It all depends on how much work you put into designing and implementing the spreadsheet. As you know, spreadsheet programs come with powerful capabilities, such as forms, graphics, and macros. If you take full advantage of these facilities, the result can be just as powerful as an application created by a professional programmer.

In fact, many off-the-shelf application programs are not created by traditional programming. Some are database applications, using systems like *dBase* or *Progress*; others are based on spreadsheet macros and templates, using systems like *Lotus 1-2-3* or *Excel*. If you get serious about using the more advanced features of a standard program, and plan what you do carefully, then you too can be an application developer.

Future Trends

New Tools and New Techniques Are Changing the Scope of Specialized Applications.

Specialized applications are at the forefront of expanding technology. Today, most specialized programs are built by professional programmers. But as we have seen, an increasing number of specialized needs can be met directly by end users working with spreadsheets, database managers, hypermedia systems, and other new tools. This trend is important. As the tools get better, users will have less need for specialists.

- Off-the-shelf programs will get less rigid; they will permit more customization to be done without programming.
- GUIs will continue to grow in popularity. You will see windows and icons everywhere.
- The traditional lines between mainframe computers and microcomputers will blur. Centralized data will reside on the mainframe, but local processing and decision making will reside in each department and on each desk.
- Programmers will spend more time on business analysis and planning. End users will spend more time using technology and getting value from computerized data. As the tools get better, everyone will worry less about the automation *process* and more about the information *results*.

The computer world is changing rapidly. Ten years ago, the technology change was frightening; if you didn't keep up, you got left behind. Today each change makes it easier, not harder. You still need to watch for change, but not to keep from being left behind. Instead, we all watch for easier methods and better tools that let us do a better job.

REVIEW QUESTIONS

1. What is the major difference between specialized software applications and general-purpose software?
2. Name two reasons businesses use specialized software.
3. What is the difference between off-the-shelf software and custom software? What are the advantages of using off-the-shelf software?
4. What does it mean for a specialized application to be a *closed system?*

5. Describe four ways in which specialized programs are configured before use.

6. Give three reasons why an off-the-shelf program might be unsatisfactory.

7. In terms of building application software, what are *little projects*? What are *big projects*?

8. What are the four steps in the software development process?

9. What is the purpose of needs analysis?

10. What are *mission-critical systems*?

11. What do you do when you define system requirements?

12. What does the interface design do?

13. Why is an internal design created? What does an internal design focus on?

14. How much of their development time do many vendors spend on testing and quality control? (a) 10%–20%, (b) 30%–40%, (c) 50%–60%, (d) 70%–80%, (e) nearly 100%.

15. What is the difference between quality control and quality assurance?

16. What is the difference between an analyst and a programmer?

17. What is a programming language? Name three common microcomputer programming languages.

18. Name three software development tools other than programming languages.

19. What is prototyping?

20. What do hypermedia applications allow users to do?

21. When can using a spreadsheet be considered a specialized application?

TOPICS FOR RESEARCH AND DISCUSSION

1. Should end users be able to define what applications do, or should professional programmers always be responsible for making sure that all the technical details are addressed? Do you think that there might be aspects of your job that you would understand better than an outside computer expert? How would you feel if you were told how to do your job by an outside computer expert? If you were the computer expert, how would you feel about having an end user telling you how to design a program?

2. Locate three specialized off-the-shelf application programs. Describe what the program does, what system requirements the program has, and the program's cost. For information on off-the-shelf programs, look through magazines or journals for professional associations. The "Marketplace" in *PC Magazine* also contains many specialized off-the-shelf programs.

3. This chapter describes the make-versus-buy decision. From reading this chapter and from your own experience, what factors can you think of that might affect a make-versus-buy decision about software to manage your school's class registration? What factors would influence you either to create a custom software program or to use a specialized off-the-shelf program?

SYSTEM SOLUTIONS

OBJECTIVES

The information in this chapter will enable you to

- Explain the relationship between business needs and computer technology.
- Describe how business computer requirements are analyzed.
- Describe how microcomputer systems get evaluated and selected.
- Explain important issues in installing and configuring a system.
- Describe system management techniques.
- Identify practical needs for data security and integrity.

In this book, we've discussed many roles that microcomputers play in the workplace—from word processing to specialized company-specific applications. In this final chapter, we step back and look at the overall microcomputer environment. Because computers can do so many different things, people often view them from a narrowly technical perspective—as spreadsheet tools or as database machines. But this view is one-sided. It's much more important to understand the day-to-day business goals that computers address.

In your career, you will often face situations where technology is expected to solve a given problem. You may be asked to evaluate a piece of hardware or software; you may help select new products; or you may need to use a particular tool in a new way. This chapter moves from the technical details of hardware and software to the business requirements that computers serve.

Solving Real-World Problems

Computers Are Purchased to Meet Practical Needs.

Computer systems, like other business tools, are purchased to meet specific objectives. A given piece of hardware or software is eventually judged by the results produced, not by technical details of training or use.

REAL PROBLEMS NEED REAL SOLUTIONS

Think about the business needs that could justify a computer purchase. They can be broken into two basic groups:

- **Employee productivity.** Word processing, desktop publishing, spreadsheet creation, and database administration all play important roles in most organizations and help employees be more productive (Figure 14-1).

FIGURE 14-1

Microcomputers improve employee productivity in many ways. By reducing errors and expanding options, computers let office workers do more high-quality work in less time.

- **Task automation.** Order processing, accounting, inventory management, and many other business tasks are generally administered by computer systems. The computer becomes an integral part of many day-to-day operations, as shown in Figure 14-2.

In each kind of use, the computer must pay its way, that is, the benefits of using the system must repay the time and cost of purchase, installation, training, maintenance, and operation.

HIGH-TECH ISN'T ALWAYS THE ANSWER

In today's climate of rapid technical change, it's easy to forget this basic truth: newer isn't always better. A given piece of technology only has value in the context of a particular need. A $20,000 workstation might be perfect for an architect, but terrible for a secretary. It's essential to find the right tool for the job.

How do you pick the right tool? *Understand the job it has to do.* Technical experts can get so wrapped up in details that they lose sight of their business objectives. The most valuable lesson you can learn from this book is to keep practical goals in mind.

WHY SOME SYSTEMS FAIL

Technology can fail for many reasons. Like most systems, computers tend to break down at their weakest link: a failure in one component can make the entire system useless. A word processor that doesn't work with your printer, a spreadsheet that can't perform a critical calculation, a network that can't access a mainframe database—a single incompatibility or defect can ruin an otherwise perfect solution. This may be surprising. How could a reputable manufacturer sell a product that doesn't work? But technical defects are often subtle. A product can work in most setups, yet still contain an undetected flaw.

A computer system that looks fine on paper can still fail in practice; a system that gives trouble during its first days of use may still turn out to be excellent, after the operational kinks have been smoothed out.

Creating Technology Solutions

Picking the Right Technology Takes Analysis.

Suppose you were asked to select and install a computer system for a new secretary about to be hired. Or suppose you wanted to request a computer system for your own use, to make you more productive. How would you go about it? What strategy would you use to select a particular set of hardware and software components? The following strategy is normally used for acquiring new technology (Figure 14-3 shows it in diagram form):

1. **Analyze the requirements.** Start by reviewing how the computer system will be used.
2. **Identify alternatives.** Create a list of technology options for meeting those needs, and evaluate the costs and benefits of the different approaches.
3. **Implement the system.** Specify the exact system configuration to be purchased; acquire and install it; then configure it for use.

Let's examine these steps in more detail.

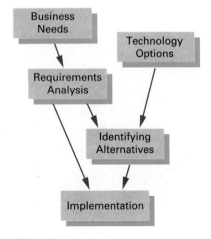

There are many ways that a computer system can fail, even if the technology works perfectly. To avoid such problems, technical purchases should always start with a formal and deliberate analysis of needs. The result should be a written set of answers to questions like those shown in Figure 14-4.

Questions to ask when analyzing requirements:

* Who will use the system?

* What will it be used to do?

* What problems will it address?

* How can system usefulness be measured?

* What are the minimum requirements?

* How would such a system change current practices?

* What other needs or problems might be created?

FIGURE 14-4

Requirements analysis focuses on needs rather than technology; not what equipment is available or where to buy it, but what problems need to be solved.

As an example, suppose you work for a small import/export company and are evaluating the need for a microcomputer to streamline office operations. Figure 14-5 shows how you might answer these questions. This analysis shows that a fairly simple technology purchase—a microcomputer for word processing and simple administration—can have a major positive impact on this business.

Of course, a five-minute analysis like this is rarely enough to support real business decisions. It's easy to say, "There must be a better way," but it's not

---

Acme Trading Company—new computer requirements

Who will use the system?

Office manager / administrator

What will it be used to do?

Write letters, send invoices, record payments, track shipments

What problems will it address?

Now takes 2-3 days to send an invoice, missing shipments are sometimes lost

How can system usefulness be measured?

Get letters and invoices out faster, notice late shipments

What are the minimum requirements?

Edit and print letters; edit and print invoices; record shipments in transit

How would such a system change current practices?

Reduce paperwork, faster order turn-around, eliminate one typewriter and desk

What other needs or problems might be created?

More computer training for staff, better inventory control as orders increase

---

FIGURE 14-5

Requirements for an import/export business. The questions from Figure 14-4 have been answered, at a general level.

always clear what needs improvement. If you were studying a real business need, you'd go through a longer process, interviewing people, reading magazine articles, observing current practices, and looking for potential bottlenecks and opportunities. This process might be spread out over days, weeks, or even months.

IDENTIFYING ALTERNATIVES

Once the general requirements are understood, it's time to start considering solutions. As with any complex problem, the best starting point is often "the back of an envelope." Start with your overall goals, not with details. Make a list of the main options available—preferably not more than four or five. Figure 14-6 shows five options for your import/export business to consider.

FIGURE 14-6

Five automation options for the example in Figure 14-5. The best starting place is always the big picture.

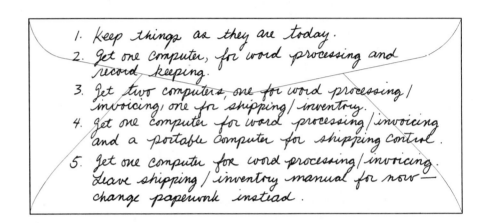

1. Keep things as they are today.
2. Get one computer, for word processing and record keeping.
3. Get two computers, one for word processing / invoicing, one for shipping / inventory.
4. Get one computer for word processing / invoicing and a portable computer for shipping control.
5. Get one computer for word processing / invoicing. Leave shipping / inventory manual for now—change paperwork instead.

Once you have a list of general options, what do you do next? You can't make a choice without more information about what those options mean. To get that information, you need to look at specific technical alternatives. This is the time when you might visit a computer store, call a software company for information, or watch product demonstrations.

Information Sources

As you move from requirements to technology, it's important to get accurate, objective information. It's helpful if a salesperson recommends a particular package, and the personal experience of a co-worker provides useful background information. Such input can clarify your options and suggest products you haven't considered. However, it can also lead you up a blind alley.

Fortunately, there are several good sources of technical information that can help you make informed decisions. Perhaps the best source is computer magazines. Many excellent ones are available in libraries, bookstores, and supermarkets. *PC Magazine, Byte,* and *Macworld* are three popular publications, all of which offer product reviews and other data.

Other useful sources include mail-order houses, which frequently have technical support staff and toll-free 800 numbers, computer stores, hardware and software vendors, and books. Before buying books, look for a current publication date.

It's easy to get overwhelmed with information. Always remember to link what you learn back to your original needs, requirements, and options. Set aside the bells and whistles that don't really matter, and focus on your core problems. Also, remember to keep an open mind.

You can never get every answer before you select a particular system configuration. There will always be some unknowns. To make effective use of your time, it's important to break the decision into manageable units. Here's a good strategy:

1. For each of the general options identified, make a list of the technical components needed to do the job—not specific products, but classes of products. Table 14-1 shows a list of components needed to implement Option 5 from our earlier example—a computer system to support word processing and invoicing.

Table 14-1: Configuration Example—Word Processing/Invoicing					
Computer	**Disk**	**Monitor**	**Printer**	**Word Processing**	**Invoicing**
PC (80286)	20MB	Monochrome	Dot Matrix	Basic (Character)	Via Word Processor
PC (80386)	40MB	Color VGA	Laser (Non-Postscript)	Advanced (Graphic)	Via Spreadsheet
PC (80486)	80MB	High Resolution	Laser (PostScript)	Desktop Publishing	Via Billing Application
Macintosh	100MB	High Resolution	Laser (PostScript)	Desktop Publishing	Via Spreadsheet

2. For each component in this list, identify the approximate costs and other implications. Then, design three or four system configurations: a minimum system, using only the lowest cost components; an ultimate system, with the best and most advanced options; and one or two mid-range systems. Table 14-2 shows four such configurations.

Table 14-2: Four Basic Configurations for a Word Processing/Invoicing System						
Configuration Number	**Computer**	**Disk**	**Monitor**	**Printer**	**Word Processing**	**Invoicing**
1. Minimum	PC (80286)	20MB	Monochrome	Dot Matrix	Basic (Character)	Via Word Processor
2. Mid-Low	PC (80386)	80MB	Color VGA	Laser (Non-Postscript)	Advanced (Graphic)	Via Spreadsheet
3. Mid-High	Macintosh	80MB	High Resolution	Laser (PostScript)	Advanced (Graphic)	Via Spreadsheet
4. Ultimate	PC (80486)	100MB	High Resolution	Laser (PostScript)	Desktop Publishing	Via Billing Application

3. Identify specific hardware and software components for each configuration. You can't consider every vendor and every model, so pick representative offerings. Later on, you can take a more thorough look at the top contenders.

4. Revise your basic configurations with data about specific models, and compute the cost of each solution. You may need to expand your list of configurations, but try to keep the number small. Table 14-3 shows this next stage.

Table 14-3: Four Detailed Configurations for a Word Processing/Invoicing System (Actual prices may vary from those shown.)

Configuration Number	Computer*	Disk	Monitor
1. Minimum	Dell 210 ($1,499)	20MB	Monochrome
2. Mid-Low	CompuAdd 320sc ($2,515)	80MB	Color VGA
3. Mid-High	MAC IIsi ($3,049)	80MB	High Resolution
4. Ultimate	Dell 433P ($4,999)	100MB	High Resolution

* Includes cost of disk drive and monitor.

5. You now have enough information to start asking serious technical questions. You need to understand how the different components will work together, what benefits you get from each approach, how well they fit your requirements, and exactly what the resulting systems would cost.

By developing a list of possible configurations, you'll have a focus for asking questions. You can take a list like this to a computer dealer, a consultant, or your company's computer department. Instead of asking, "What kind of computer system should I get?" you can say, "I need something like *this.*" Then, the expert can make realistic suggestions in the context of your technical needs.

Learning Curve Considerations

Every technical product requires a *learning curve*—a period when users are still gaining familiarity with new concepts and techniques and haven't yet reached full proficiency. The term comes from graphs like that shown in Figure 14-7, measuring skill development over time. A product that helps beginners achieve useful results quickly is referred to as having a short learning curve, as opposed to one demanding more time and effort.

Why would anyone buy a product that's hard to learn? As usual, it depends on the particular business requirements being addressed. As Figure 14-8 shows, easy-to-use products are often limited in scope; they are easy because they offer few options. A flexible product with many capabilities often requires a longer learning curve, simply because it does more.

Of course, some products really *are* hard to use. But, when evaluating a product, you must bear in mind that you're getting only a first impression. Your evaluation will be colored by the window dressing of the product, and not necessarily by those capabilities most important in daily use.

There's no substitute for practical experience. If possible, talk to people in your organization about specific products, training needs, problems, and hidden benefits. If there are no experienced users in your organization, ask prospective vendors for names of users you can talk to.

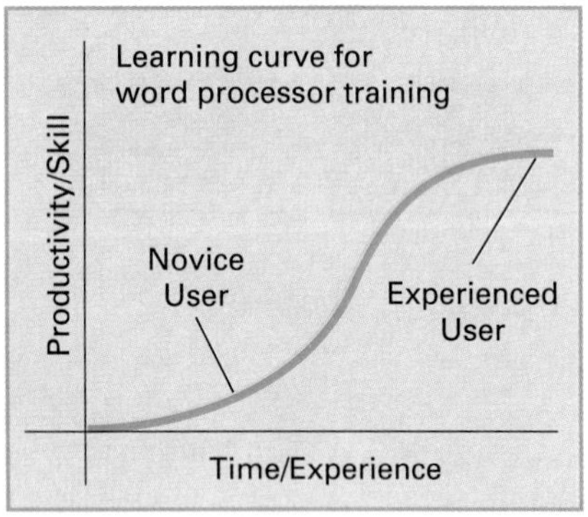

FIGURE 14-7

The learning curve measures user productivity versus user experience. Most learning begins with a slow period, when a novice can't accomplish much of value. Then, as the user starts getting the hang of it, results emerge more quickly.

Testing and Evaluating Choices

Use a product before buying it, either on another user's machine or on a demo system at a computer store. Remember that learning curve issues can make it hard to assess a product until it's been in use for weeks or months. Ask about guarantees. Satisfaction guarantees are sometimes made by manufacturers, computer stores, and mail-order houses, letting you return an

Table 14-3: *(Continued)*

Printer	Word Processing	Invoicing	Total
Epson LQ510 ($245)	*WordPerfect* ($249)	(Via *WordPerfect*)	$1,993
HP IIP ($899)	*Word for Windows* ($319)	*Excel* ($299)	$4,032
NEC SW90 ($1,659)	*Word* ($250)	*Excel* ($250)	$5,208
NEC SW90 (1,659)	*Word* + *PageMaker* ($319 + $495)	*Accounting by Design* ($695)	$8,167

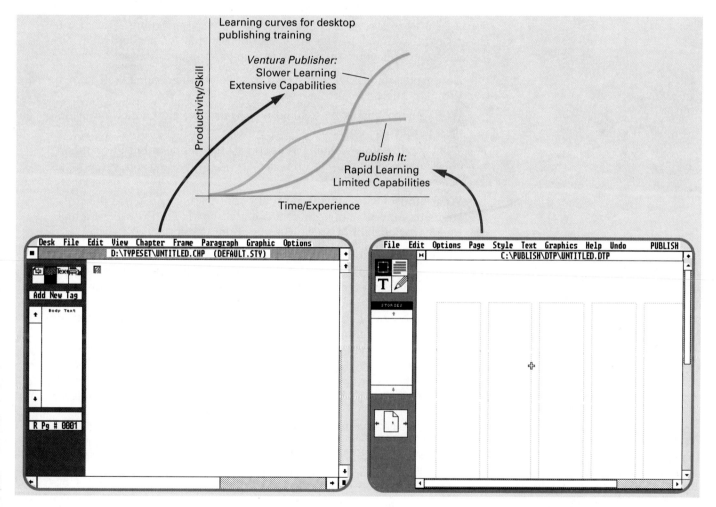

FIGURE 14-8

Products often have very different learning curves. Here, two desktop publishing systems are compared. One is easy to learn but has limited capabilities; the other can do much more, but its added sophistication takes more time to learn.

unacceptable product for a refund within a period, such as 30 days. Many software products also have limited demo versions, available free or for a small charge (typically $5 to $15). It's always worth asking to evaluate a product before purchase.

Unlike test-driving a car, your computer evaluation needs to be carefully structured. Since each product will have distinct strengths and weaknesses, it will be easy to lose sight of your real priorities. Often, the "best" (or most advanced) product isn't the right one for your particular needs. To avoid getting lost in technical details, be sure that you have a clear list of requirements and a definite set of product alternatives. Then, as you learn about the different products you are considering, score them with respect to your goals.

An important element of many technology purchases is a *benchmark*—a structured test showing system performance. Normally, several different products are put through the same benchmark to show their relative capabilities. Comprehensive benchmarks are performed by magazines and laboratories. Individual buyers, choosing between products, often conduct limited benchmarks based on their own needs—such as simply measuring how long it takes to open a file or print a page.

Selecting Vendors

You have many places to obtain technical information, guidance, sales, and support, including computer stores, manufacturers, distributors, mail-order houses, software stores, and consultants. As with any other kind of purchase, not all vendors are the same. As you consider your alternatives, use the same standards you would apply to a noncomputer purchase:

- How well established is the organization? Is their name well known? Will they still be in business next year?
- Will your purchases be covered by a warranty? How much protection does it offer?
- What services are available? Will you get telephone or hot line support? Can you get on-site support if necessary? Are qualified support or repair personnel available?
- What kind of sales organization are you dealing with? Are the prices competitive? Are many different products available? Do you get a high-pressure sales pitch? Can you ask questions comfortably?

Each type of vendor has its own advantages and disadvantages. Mail-order houses usually have low prices, return policies, and good telephone support. A local computer dealer or software store will often provide better service if problems arise. Some manufacturers have excellent reputations for dealing directly with consumers; others rely on dealers and distributors for customer contact. Again, the key to vendor selection is understanding your own goals and requirements.

IMPLEMENTING A SOLUTION

Your evaluation process finally produces a handful of technical choices, along with specific costs, benefits, and other details that emerged as important. Now you need to pick a solution. Most technology purchasers use a process called *cost-benefit analysis*—weighing the costs of each proposed solution against the benefits they will provide. The best solution is the one that offers the highest value for the lowest cost. This analysis is easiest if you can identify a cash value that offsets the system cost, for example, a savings in postage costs, or avoiding the need to hire additional or temporary staff, or reducing errors. Figure 14-9 shows a typical cost-benefit analysis.

Cost-benefit analysis is harder if the benefits can't be linked to specific dollar amounts. Then you have to weigh the various options based on intangible factors, as shown in Figure 14-10.

After the system components have been chosen, ordered, and delivered, another technical process begins: somebody needs to make it work! Unless a vendor or other technical expert does it for you, this will be your problem. Here are some practical guidelines for installing hardware or software components yourself.

Richards Manufacturing—cost/benefit analysis for proposed desktop publishing system

Goal: Reduce spending on outside services, improve quality, reduce errors, reduce delays

Solution: Create the monthly newsletter ourselves

Costs for us to create the monthly newsletter in-house for two years:

  Computer equipment: $5200

  Desktop publishing software: $495

  Training: $800

  Supplies: $450

  Staff salary cost (20 hours/month): $4800

Total: $11,745

Benefits from producing newsletter in-house:

  Current fees from design agency saved ($350/month): $8400

  Current fees from typesetter saved ($100/month): $2400

  Current extra printing costs due to errors saved ($500/year): $1000

Other benefits:

  Authors can review drafts more easily and make changes until the last minute.

  Other projects can be done using this equipment.

FIGURE 14-9

A cost-benefit analysis is used to justify a purchase. It only makes sense to buy a computer if it can pay for itself.

City of Morrisville—cost/benefit analysis for proposed word processing system

Goal: Improve current secretarial services

Solution: Replace a typewriter with a word processor

Costs to get a word processor:

  Computer equipment: $1800

  Word processing software: $295

  Training: $400

  Supplies: $250

Total: $2,745

Benefits from word processing:

  Reduced delays: expect to cut average wait from 12 hours to 4 hours

  Improved productivity: expect to complete twice as many letters per week

  Improved accuracy: expect to cut number of errors in half

  Improved quality: better print quality, no white-out, more time for proofreading

Evaluation: Spending $2745 will produce a major improvement in quality and output.

FIGURE 14-10

Cost-benefit analysis is more difficult if there are no measurable cash benefits. How much is better quality worth? This example summarizes a cashless trade-off.

- **Read the instructions.** It seems so obvious, but most people don't bother. Even if it's boring or confusing, it helps.

- **Document everything.** At many points during installation, you will make technical decisions. Each time, write down exactly what choices you make. If you have technical problems, you'll need to describe your exact configuration when you call the vendor for help.

- **Look for** README **files.** Most distribution disks include text files with valuable information about installation and setup. These files usually have names like "README," "README.TXT," "READ.ME," or "README.DOC" and can be viewed using standard facilities, such as the DOS **TYPE** command. Often, technical changes or problems are reported in these files that don't appear in the documentation.

- **Keep it simple.** Whenever possible, use default names, default options, and standard functions. If you want to make special modifications, defer them until you are sure that the standard system works.

- **Watch your operating system configuration.** Virtually every hardware and software component is affected by your system configuration. Under DOS, this means your **CONFIG.SYS** and **AUTOEXEC.BAT** files. Under Windows, it also includes your **WIN.INI** file. In the Macintosh environment, it means your System Folder. Print out the contents of these files periodically, and observe the changes that occur as new products are installed. You may not understand all the technical details they contain, but most compatibility problems stem from problems in these files. When calling a vendor for technical support, you will often be asked for these details.

System Operations

Systems Must Be Managed and Data Must Be Preserved.

Most computer systems are used at random. People create and delete files, run software programs, and perform other tasks, without thinking about the system as a whole. Yet computers are not pocket calculators. The real value of most computers is in the data they access, not in what their hardware or software does. If a hard disk crashes, the risk is not the loss of *WordPerfect* or *Paradox*. Such products can be reloaded from the distribution disks. The risk is that vital organizational data will be lost, including documents, inventory files, invoices, and customer records.

This section discusses several aspects of effective system operations: system management, backup procedures, and data security and integrity.

SYSTEM MANAGEMENT

To get the most value out of a computer system, it's necessary to keep a big picture of its data, and to manage how that data gets created, used, and removed.

Organizing Disk Storage

One of the most important aspects of system management is organizing the hard disk. When a new computer is first installed, it has a large, nearly empty hard disk. Gradually, the hard disk fills. Then, one day, there isn't enough room to create a new file or to add a new software product. From then on, every time a new file is created, old ones have to be deleted. Experienced users know that this process leads to serious problems; critical files get deleted or misplaced.

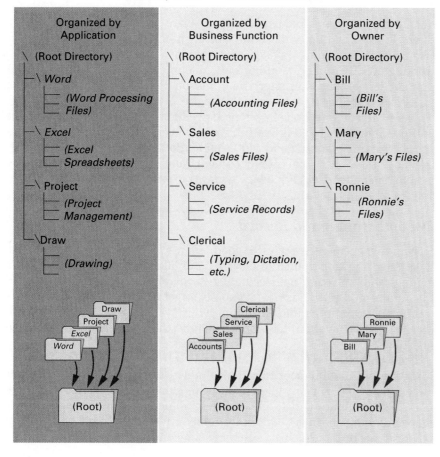

FIGURE 14-11

Your hard disk's directory structure is a powerful tool for organizing data. Files grouped in directories (folders) are easier to manage. Here, three different approaches are used for grouping files: by application, by business function, and by owner (the person who creates them).

It's important to use the computer's directory structure to group related data. Doing so takes some planning. You must choose an organizing strategy based on your work requirements. There are many strategies for organizing disk and directory storage. Examples are shown in Figure 14-11: by application, such as all word processing files together; by topic, such as all sales files together; by date, such as all September files together; or by owner, on a system used by several people.

Many other strategies are also possible. The important thing is to choose and maintain a strategy. On a weekly or monthly basis, review both the directory structure and your activities. Does the structure still match your work patterns? Should you create a new directory and combine files from several different existing directories? Are some directories obsolete?

It's vital to identify obsolete files and remove them. This task is easy when done on a regular basis, but becomes huge if put off for too long.

Rules for Naming Files

Choosing file names is another important system management activity. "BOB.LET" and "SALES2.XLS" may seem perfectly clear the day you create them, but after six months you may have no idea what they are. It's important to develop consistent rules for naming your files and to make sure these rules fit your work patterns.

Naming rules become critical if some files are preserved for long periods of time. If a file is not kept beyond a few days, you can safely delete a file even if you can't remember what it is. However, as we rely more on computers for long-term data storage, naming rules become as important as the file cabinet filing systems of the past.

FIGURE 14-12

File sharing is often done using "sneaker-net"—carrying diskettes from one office to another. This method has its problems: it's easy to lose changes, and it's hard to keep track of the most current version of a file.

Workgroup Planning

Microcomputer users frequently need to share data. Whether a network file server is used or floppy disks are carried from office to office, it's easy to lose control of the data. In such environments, two or three people may be working on different parts of the same document at the same time. Eventually, as files get passed from person to person, it's easy for one set of changes to get lost. See Figure 14-12.

There are some technical options for reducing these problems, and there will be more such tools in the future. However, the best approach remains simple: careful planning and old-fashioned attention to details. If multiple users need to collaborate on a document, such as a report or a manual, it's vital to decide *who* will see *which sections* in *what order*.

Documentation and Records

System management is easiest if good records are preserved. We've already mentioned the importance of clear records during system installation and configuration. System management records are even more important. As the months and years pass, even experts forget technical details. If you have a problem 18 months after installing your system, you'll be lucky to find the installation manual, let alone remember how you answered the setup questions!

Each computer system should have its own library—a set of manuals, diskettes, installation records, technical notes, and other materials that affect system use. Like so many good habits, this step is often overlooked. A complete system library is helpful when upgrading a system component, when reporting or diagnosing a technical problem, when training a new user, and when selling or transferring a system to someone else.

Licenses and Ethics

Software products are frequently copied from system to system, in the same way that people copy videotapes and music cassettes. Most people know that software licenses usually prohibit this. Each user is supposed to buy a separate copy, with its own license agreement. Yet many people ignore this requirement, even though unauthorized copying is legally considered a form of theft.

Consider the following:

- Unlike videotapes and records, few software products are sold in the hundreds of thousands or millions of copies. Many software vendors are actually very small companies—sometimes just a few people. Most vendors have only one or two products. Each software license fee makes a direct difference to these vendors.

- Software products are extremely expensive to build. Developing a moderately complex product can easily cost a million dollars or more. Yet that same product may be sold for only a few hundred dollars. The only way a developer's costs can be recovered is by selling many copies.

- When you buy a software product and send in the warranty card, you get real benefits, such as a complete set of documentation, access to the vendor's technical support staff by telephone, notification of new releases of the software, and usually a discount on purchasing upgrades.

Software may *seem* expensive because it seems intangible; it's hard to see why a product is worth $300 if it can be copied for $3. Yet the value of a computer is more dependent on the quality of the software than on its hardware.

You may work for an organization where people freely transfer software from system to system, buying only one official copy per office. However, violators are getting caught by software vendors and industry groups, and they receive heavy fines and other penalties.

Illegal copying causes a dilemma for many workers. You need to use the software, but don't feel right about using an illegal copy. If placed in this situation, try to get the matter out in the open. Remind other workers that this really *is* theft. Although some software vendors seem like big faceless bureaucracies, many are struggling little companies that can't afford lost sales. More important, remind them that many giant corporations get into big trouble for allowing this to continue. Widespread software piracy invites strict management controls over office computer use, which is something that benefits nobody.

BACKUP PROCEDURES

The real value of most computer systems is in the data stored on their hard disks. Broken machines can be replaced or repaired, but lost data can be disastrous. For that reason, the most important system management activity is making regular *backups*—copying data off the hard disk onto removable media such as floppy disks or tape cassettes.

Disk failures used to be common. Ten years ago, you could almost rely on having a hard disk failure every year or two. Backups were a matter of survival. Today, the apparent reliability of computer hardware can make backups seem unnecessary. But hardware still wears out as it ages, and disk crashes still happen—catastrophic failures where every file on the drive is lost. At the end of each day, *assume* that your system won't come up tomorrow. Be sure that your critical data can be loaded onto another machine, if necessary.

Like other system management tasks, it takes time and effort to maintain good backups. But that time and effort are well spent, even if your disk never falters. A well-managed system will give you confidence in your data. You'll know exactly what files are stored on the disk, how they are related, and how to recover them in the event of troubles.

Backup Software

Several different techniques are used to create backups.

- **Copy.** The simplest approach is to use the operating system's normal COPY function to create floppy disk copies, just as you would copy files from one directory (folder) to another. This is fine if a single file or directory is important, and you just want a safe copy. However, copying files is not a good general backup technique, for two reasons: it is subject to certain undetected data errors, and it normally works only if all the data will fit on a single floppy disk.

- **BACKUP utility.** Most operating systems have built-in services for creating backups, such as BACKUP under DOS. Using these tools, individual files, one or more directories, or even an entire hard disk drive can be backed up onto floppy disks. If problems occur later, these files can be reloaded onto the disk. These services are widely used, but they have three problems: they take a long time to create backups, they require many floppy disks (20 high-density diskettes for a 20MB drive), and they may let undetected data errors slip in.

- **Backup products.** Many popular software packages streamline the backup process, as shown in Figure 14-13. These tools are similar to the built-in operating system backup services, but add important capabili-

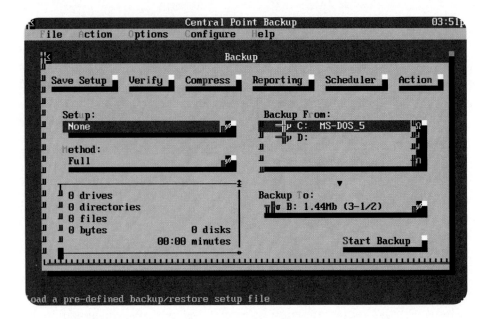

FIGURE 14-13

Backup utilities offer sophisticated services.

ties. Some use high-volume cassette tapes instead of floppy disks. Most work much faster, and they compress data, reducing the number of diskettes or tapes required. They help automate the backup process, letting you predefine which data get backed up together. And they use advanced techniques to ensure data accuracy, so that files can be recovered even if parts of the backup copy become unreadable.

Most users find a backup utility, such as *Fastback,* well worth the cost. A simple menu-driven interface lets you complete the backup process in a matter of minutes.

Each backup mechanism provides an equivalent technique to *restore* data—to reload files from the backup copy. For example, DOS offers the RESTORE command to recover BACKUP files. Most restore services let you choose whether to restore an entire disk, a directory tree, a directory, a set of files, or just a single file.

Backup Cycles

To be useful, backups must be made regularly. You need to be confident that, after a failure, you'll be able to find the most recent backup, restore the data, and resume work quickly. To simplify this process, most users follow a *backup cycle*, or regular series of backup operations.

YOU AND YOUR PERSONAL MICROCOMPUTER

Even if you are purchasing a system for your personal use only, you still need to analyze your requirements and identify the alternatives available.

It is essential that you consider the support provided by the hardware and software vendors. For example, is a hot line available that can be used to solve a hardware or software problem?

Organizing disk storage, using predetermined rules for naming files, backing up system and data files, and documenting all procedures are as important for an individual user as they are for a business.

As an individual you should also keep current in regard to technological changes in both hardware and software. In considering updating your system, the advantages in terms of benefits provided should be weighed against the increase in cost.

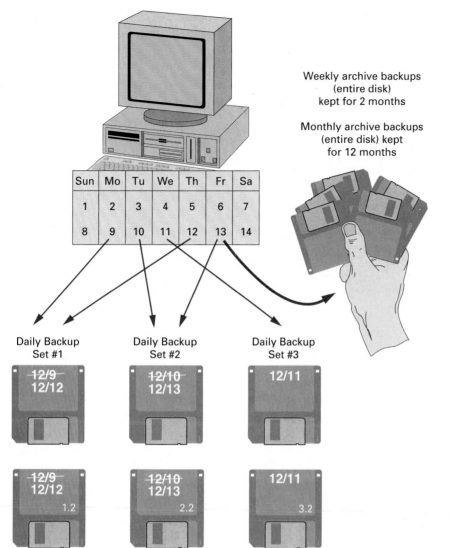

Daily Backups (Working Files Only)

FIGURE 14-14

This daily/weekly/monthly backup cycle creates working backups every day, plus archive backups at weekly and monthly intervals. This approach ensures that files can be restored after a problem, and also retains long-term backup copies.

Figure 14-14 shows a common backup cycle. This basic approach can be adjusted to meet the needs of any organization. The monthly full-system backup might be shifted to a quarterly cycle; or it might be done weekly or even daily, depending on the frequency of change, the amount of disk storage, and the value of the data.

Archiving Data

Backup copies are more likely to be needed after a *user* error than a *system* failure. Sooner or later, nearly everyone deletes or overwrites the wrong file by accident. That's when you'll be glad you keep regular backups! Regular backups give you confidence that you're protected from careless errors. As a result, you don't have to worry about typing the wrong command—the worst that can happen is having to reload the backup copy. Backup files should not be kept in the same location as the original files.

Copies of historical records can also be useful. For example, to save space in an invoicing system, you may periodically delete invoices paid more than 90 days ago. Yet that payment history is potentially valuable when planning a budget, evaluating credit history, or tracking an error. To preserve these values, simply create an archive copy each month before deleting the old invoices. By saving 12 sets of diskettes, you can keep a year of invoice data without consuming on-line disk space.

Two particular archives deserve special mention:

- Be sure to have a backup system disk, so that if your hard disk crashes you can reboot your computer from a floppy disk.
- Keep a backup copy of your system configuration files, including a printed listing. This routine will help identify problems during software installation and make it easier to get technical support by telephone.

DATA SECURITY AND INTEGRITY

Given the high value of computer data, some additional system management steps are often required to safeguard data from accidental or deliberate invasion and damage. The amount of effort you expend on security should reflect your worry level. How much damage could occur if your files were viewed or vandalized without your knowledge? For some files, security is essential (see Figure 14-15). Consider the following:

- **Sensitive data.** Many computers hold data that should be viewed only by certain people, such as salary data, credit history, medical records, and trade secrets.
- **Critical data.** Some data must be kept completely accurate and up to date. Major problems would result if even a small data error occurred in files containing financial records, stock purchases, or inventory data.
- **Malicious threats.** Not all potential users are friendly—a competitor, a customer, a disgruntled employee, or some nosy passerby could commit what amounts to computer vandalism if able to access your machine. There are many *computer hackers,* people who enjoy getting past computer security systems. Some hackers just like to beat the system; others are destructive, and some are computer thieves.

FIGURE 14-15

Security risks exist in most environments. If your system has sensitive or critical data, you must take steps to limit casual access.

When considering security on the job, assess your data. Does it represent enough real value or temptation for someone to invest time trying to access or change it? Is it critical enough that an accidentally deleted file might cause a disaster? If so, your system management efforts must address your security concerns.

Physical Access to Computers

Despite extensive research and development on high-tech security, the single best security measure remains the obvious one: keep the machine locked up and out of sight. A machine with sensitive or critical data should be physically isolated from normal traffic. If it can't be put in a private office, it should be in a locking desk. Even removing the keyboard, the power cable, or the monitor can help deter malicious use when the machine must be left unattended.

Passwords

Many software products help enforce security measures by using *passwords*—secret code words that must be entered before you can access data or services. Most passwords are linked to a particular *user name* or *user ID*, a short identifier that is assigned to each valid computer user. Normally, you pick the user name and password yourself.

Passwords are effective, but not perfect. Much computer crime relies on the fact that people have trouble remembering their passwords. As a result, people use obvious passwords, such as their initials, or they write down their passwords in plain sight near the computer (see Figure 14-16).

FIGURE 14-16

Bad password practices are common. A password is effective only if it's secret!

Computer Viruses

The computer virus is a widely publicized computer security threat. Computer viruses are software programs that attach themselves to normal programs and replicate themselves. They move through networks from system to system via floppy disks, and especially through data communications with bulletin boards. Figure 14-17 shows how viruses spread. Viruses are written by hackers, normally as a joke but often as a malicious one. Some viruses just print a message, but others erase data, corrupt files, and worse.

Unlike real viruses, computer viruses don't evolve or adapt to their surroundings. A virus programmer thinks up ways for the virus program to hide, such as by writing itself to the end of an operating system program on the hard disk. Then, whenever that program is run, the virus activates and tries to copy itself onto other disks. The virus has precisely the behavior given to it by the programmer. However, since there are many different programmers writing viruses, there are many different viruses.

There are many antivirus software packages available. These programs search through your disk, looking for telltale signs of certain viruses. How-

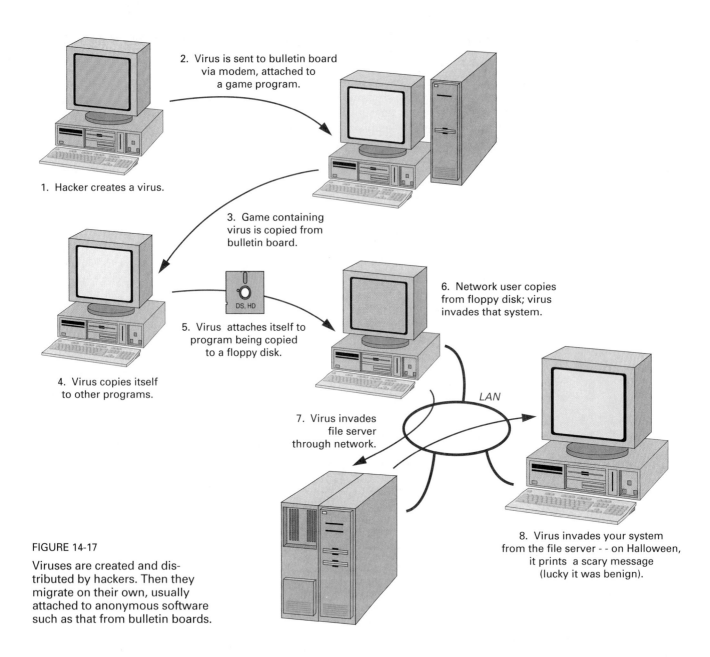

2. Virus is sent to bulletin board via modem, attached to a game program.

1. Hacker creates a virus.

3. Game containing virus is copied from bulletin board.

DS, HD

5. Virus attaches itself to program being copied to a floppy disk.

6. Network user copies from floppy disk; virus invades that system.

4. Virus copies itself to other programs.

7. Virus invades file server through network.

LAN

8. Virus invades your system from the file server - - on Halloween, it prints a scary message (lucky it was benign).

FIGURE 14-17

Viruses are created and distributed by hackers. Then they migrate on their own, usually attached to anonymous software such as that from bulletin boards.

ever, these programs can find only viruses they already know about. Although software from a reputable vendor is virtually guaranteed to be virus-free, programs you get from bulletin boards or from friends may be infected. If a new virus appears, a virus checker will not find it. Viruses are another good reason to maintain effective backups of your programs and data.

TROUBLESHOOTING

As you start taking system management seriously, you'll find that you become more sensitive to small changes in the computer environment. If you observe problems developing, or if you have trouble making a new piece of hardware or software work, you need to analyze the situation and diagnose the trouble. Most computer errors can be traced to a handful of basic problems, listed in Table 14-4.

If you observe strange behavior, don't ignore it. Assume that the last system change you made—new software, new hardware, new options—is having an unexpected side effect. Try to get the problem to repeat. Intermittent problems are difficult to track down; but if the problem is repeatable, you

Table 14-4: Troubleshooting: Common Problems and Their Causes

Problem	Description
No power	This is the most common problem! Either the power cord falls out, the surge protector is turned off, or the power outlet goes dead.
Loose cable	Cable problems are common with printers, monitors, mouses, and keyboards—they get loosened, cut, or damaged. Check all cables from end to end, and be sure that the screws are tight.
Wrong port	Most printers, modems, and other external devices are connected to serial or parallel ports. The ports are not interchangeable! Check your setup options, and see which port is specified (COM1:, COM2:, or LPT1: on a PC), or try moving the cable from one connector to another.
Not enough disk space	If your disk is full, strange behavior can occur. If you don't have a megabyte or two of free disk space, free up some space and try again.
Wrong configuration	Many software packages and hardware products require changes in operating system configuration. If you run into problems or if an existing package stops working, check manuals and README files for information about system configuration, and compare your current configuration to your backup copies.
Incompatible products or versions	Many products or product versions simply can't work together. If you can't track the problem down, call for technical assistance. Vendors often know work-around solutions for incompatibilities.
Corrupt disk data	If output looks garbled, or if system messages tell you about disk problems, you may need to use a disk utility to diagnose and repair the errors. Many hard disk utilities can assist in this process.

can probably isolate it. Once you know exactly how to make the problem occur, you can decide who can help solve it—a hardware vendor, a software vendor, a technical expert, or maybe yourself.

Planning for the Future

Today's Technology Is Already Old.

We've seen how different hardware and software components fit together, creating systems that meet business needs. As you work with these systems, it's important to keep looking ahead. Remember that every piece of software will soon have a newer, better version. Every piece of hardware will have a faster, lower cost replacement. If you think about computers just in terms of the specific products available today, you'll quickly fall behind. Instead, think about computers as families of problem-solving systems, getting steadily smarter and better integrated.

Businesses like to make purchases on a predictable cycle. After a desk, a lamp, or a copier is purchased, its value is expected to decline steadily over its useful life. A desk bought for $500 in 1989 might thus be worth $200 to $300 in 1991. Because computer costs keep decreasing so quickly, computers are a problem.

Suppose a computer is bought in 1989 for $5,000, and the same or a better machine can be bought in 1991 for $2,500. What is the 1989 computer worth in 1991? If it were like a desk, it should be worth $2,000 to $3,000, but in reality it's probably worth only $1,500. From a depreciation standpoint, most computer hardware is *old* after two years and nearly *obsolete* after three. Most of its resale value has already disappeared.

Moreover, most computer software products have new versions released every year or two. Most businesses must upgrade their software regularly to take advantage of the new features, to keep different products compatible, and to ensure that staff skills and training remain up to date. Yet software upgrades cost money, and they are unpredictable.

Because of rapid change and unpredictable maintenance costs, computers don't fit the traditional long-life view of office equipment.

INDUSTRY TRENDS

Several trends are causing important changes in the computer industry. These changes will affect the future options available and the value of today's investments.

- **Open systems.** Ten years ago, most vendors worked hard to keep their products "closed." They made it difficult for other vendors to access their data or use their services. Today, most vendors sell *open systems*. They publish specifications for their interfaces to help products work

THE LEGION OF DOOM

Katie Hogue didn't take her "Flu Shot" in 1990 and did she ever pay the price. No, Katie didn't get sick, but her company's computers did. And the "Flu Shot" she missed is not a medical vaccine, but, rather, one of many new software programs designed to either prevent or eliminate computer viruses.

Hogue, president of Media Markets, Inc. in Alexandria, Virginia, found that two of her firm's PCs were disabled by a virus after they had been upgraded at a local computer store. "All of my disks were infected," she lamented, "and because I never made backup copies of my masters, we lost all of our programs."

Computer viruses—which are often given exotic names, such as the Jerusalem B virus, named after the city where it was first spotted—are a painful and expensive plague to their victims. They are trouble enough when they infect small businesses such as Hogue's. But viruses that infect large and complex computer networks—networks that today run much of our country's communications and transportation systems—are far more than a nuisance. Such viruses amount to *computer terrorism*. Computer terrorists create virus programs that can infect and destroy anything from the files on one computer to an entire system.

One of the first viruses to achieve notoriety was the virus that Cornell University graduate student Robert Morris, Jr. unleashed on a government research network. Although Morris may have been engaging in a student prank that got wildly and destructively out of hand, more recent cases are clearly malicious. The Legion of Doom, for example, is a group of two dozen computer hackers who used illegally obtained data from the BellSouth Corporation to disrupt the 911 emergency phone service in nine states. When lives are at stake, a virus is not a prank.

The battle against computer terrorism is advancing on several fronts. Powerful antiviral software, such as Software Concept Design's *Flu Shot* and Interpath's *Viruscan*, can help diagnose, treat, and in some cases prevent an

infection. Industry, government, and university associations—such as the Computer Virus Industry Association, the National Computer Security Association, and the Computer Emergency Response Team—are studying the problem and planning prevention and treatment strategies.

However, viruses may be a permanent problem. Designers of computer viruses create ever more sophisticated programs, and thereby stay one step ahead of the computer industry's defense forces. The virus that infected Katie Hogue's PC, for example, is one of a new generation of viruses called "Stealth" viruses, which can spread quickly and change like chameleons to avoid detection. Still, according to some experts, the probability of getting a virus in a business setting is very low. Most damage, it seems, is caused not by viruses but by computer users trying to rid their infected PCs of viruses.

Computer viruses can wreak havoc with small businesses, as well as vital national computer networks.

Sources: "Preventing the Dreaded 'Call' to Virus Busters," by Michael Alexander, *ComputerWorld,* September 10, 1990, p. 49. "Viruses? Who You Gonna Call? 'Hackbusters'," by Evan I. Schwartz and Jeffrey Rothfeder, *Business Week,* August 6, 1990, p. 72.

together (see Figure 14-18). This is true for both hardware and software products. As a result, data can now move freely from application to application, and devices can move from system to system. This is a major benefit for users. Most organizations now try to buy products that fit the open systems philosophy. Nobody wants to be boxed into a particular vendor's solution. It's better to have the option of picking the best value for the money.

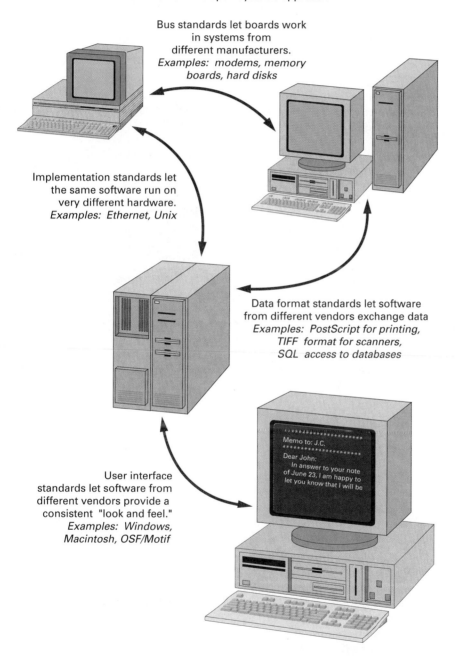

Standards: The open-systems approach

Bus standards let boards work in systems from different manufacturers. *Examples: modems, memory boards, hard disks*

Implementation standards let the same software run on very different hardware. *Examples: Ethernet, Unix*

Data format standards let software from different vendors exchange data *Examples: PostScript for printing, TIFF format for scanners, SQL access to databases*

User interface standards let software from different vendors provide a consistent "look and feel." *Examples: Windows, Macintosh, OSF/Motif*

Memo to: J.C.

Dear John:
In answer to your note of June 23, I am happy to let you know that I will be

FIGURE 14-18

The open-systems approach has revolutionized the computer industry. In the past, vendors used proprietary technology and secret interfaces, protecting themselves from competitors but making life hard for users. Today, many vendors work together to define standards, and strive to build systems that can cooperate.

- **GUI computing.** Graphical user interfaces (GUIs), found on products like the Macintosh and PC's running Windows, have proven to be immensely popular. GUIs offer reduced training, improved integration, and better user service. This approach was pioneered 20 years ago at places like Xerox PARC (Palo Alto Research Center). Today, virtually all new software development relies on the GUI style of user tools.

A CURE FOR THE CIO BLUES

Imagine you're the chief information officer (CIO) for a large corporation with tens of thousands of computers. You make the major purchasing decisions regarding computer hardware, operating systems software, applications software, networking systems, and so forth. Like most CIOs, you dream of the day when all the software you buy will run on all the computers you own, and data from any software program on any computer can be easily transmitted to any other program and any other computer.

You dream, that is, of the perfect "open system." And you wait, and wait, for the computer industry hardware and software giants to agree on standards that will allow for perfectly compatible systems.

John Loewenberg, CIO for Aetna Life & Casualty, is just one of many who have decided to stop waiting and take matters into their own hands. Loewenberg is creating an open system for Aetna's 40,000-plus computers by defining a company-based standard, *Aetna Information Technology Architecture*. Loewenberg's goal is to remove all roadblocks in Aetna's vast collection of computers.

Applications programs such as spreadsheet, word processor, and knowledge-based software will be standard throughout Aetna's 40,000 desktop computers. Operating systems software will be standard too, and the computers themselves will all use compatible hardware.

Aetna's open system will take five years or more to implement. But Loewenberg believes that when they're finished, Aetna will be able to insist that computer and software companies tailor their products to fit Aetna's designs, rather than the reverse.

Another force for open systems and industrywide standards is coming from a highly influential group of U.S. and European corporations that calls itself the X/Open Company, Ltd. X/Open styles itself as a neutral organization that can, over time, set standards for all sorts of computer products. The idea, already beginning to take hold, is that computer manufacturers and software developers will bring their new products to X/Open for their "seal of approval," much as the Good Housekeeping Seal of Approval works for consumer products.

Who will win the race to develop open systems—the vendors who make hardware and software, or their customers, the businesses who buy and use computers on a large scale? Everyone wants powerful computers that are simple to use, and it's now a question of who's in the driver's seat.

John Loewenberg, Aetna Life & Casualty's chief information officer, is working to create an open system for his company's 25,000 computers.

Source: "Computer Confusion," *Business Week*, June 10, 1991, p. 72.

- **Networks.** As more office workers get computers, organizations need networks to enable resource sharing and data exchange. Network technology continues to come down in cost, making departmental and companywide networks increasingly common. Most organizations are evaluating or installing networks to help coordinate office computer use.

- **Portable computers.** Small computers—laptops and notebooks—are getting as powerful as desktop machines. Many aren't much more expensive than their desktop equivalents. As a result, we can expect to see more computers on the go, accompanying workers on trips out of the office. Many new software and hardware tools are making portable computers more practical. In particular, watch for the emergence of *pen-based computers* (see Figure 14-19)—small notebook computers without keyboards that use a penlike stylus for user input. It will be some time before these machines can read your doctor's scrawled prescriptions, but they already can do an excellent job at reading block letters as they are written. They provide an extremely natural interface for selecting items from menus and lists. Such computers are especially useful for workers in the field, such as sales representatives, field technicians, and inspectors.

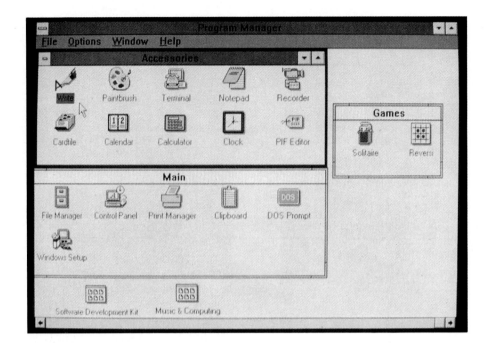

FIGURE 14-19

Pen-based computing is going to change the computer world forever. This photograph shows pen computing under Windows. Instead of using cursor keys, a mouse, and a keyboard, the user simply points a stylus at menu options, icons, or buttons. By writing block letters, text and numbers can be entered as well. In time, more powerful machines will be able to learn your own handwriting and shorthand.

There is no sign of microcomputer progress slowing down. We're about to see another revolution in computer use. As computers get smarter and friendlier, as they get small and cheap enough to fit on a dashboard or a sales counter, and as they break the keyboard barrier by accepting handwriting and voice input, they will make hundreds of new uses possible.

KEEPING YOUR KNOWLEDGE CURRENT

How can you keep up with all this computer progress? There are many good sources of information that won't force you to become a software designer or a hardware engineer.

- We've mentioned several periodicals as sources of information about specific products. These magazines are also excellent guides to industry progress. Pick up an issue every few months. Many of the editors' columns, in particular, offer useful perspectives on the industry as a whole.

- Your local computer store and bookstore stock a wide range of computer books. Watch for new titles that fit your career goals.

- Classes are available on many aspects of computer technology. In addition to traditional curricula at colleges and technical schools, there are many excellent commercial seminars. Most larger vendors also run seminars and classes on their own products.

- Technical conferences and trade shows, held regularly in most major cities, offer exhibition spaces where many vendors show their latest products. Most of these conferences also include tutorial sessions, presentations, papers, and other sources of information. See Figure 14-20.

But perhaps the best way to stay current is to keep experimenting. Tackle new problems. Try new products. Read hardware and software manuals. Explore the more specialized features of your hardware and software.

Experienced computer users develop instincts about how things work. Eventually, they hardly refer to manuals. *This will happen to you.* The more products and techniques you know, the more they'll all have in common, and the more you'll be able to accomplish with computers.

FIGURE 14-20

A PC trade show offers many interesting sights and can help you stay abreast of industry progress.

REVIEW QUESTIONS

1. There are two basic types of business needs that justify a computer purchase: the need to improve employee productivity and the need to automate tasks. Name two computer applications that improve employee productivity. Name two that automate tasks.

2. Computers must pay their way by providing useful services. Besides the cost of purchase, what other costs must be covered by the value a computer offers?

3. What are the three main steps in acquiring new technology?

4. Requirements analysis essentially means answering a series of questions. Suppose you need to pick a computer for a new employee. How would you get the information you need?

5. When identifying alternatives, should you start with overall goals or with details?

6. Where could you get technical information about your alternatives?

7. You have enough information to start evaluating some sample system configurations. How many configurations should you develop, and what guidelines should you use to pick the components?

8. Why is it easier to get technical information based on a specific configuration?

9. What is a learning curve? Is a long learning curve bad?

10. True or false: You can tell whether a computer product will meet your needs by spending an afternoon using it before you buy it.

11. What is a benchmark?

12. What is cost-benefit analysis?

13. Name two aspects of system operations.

14. True or false: You are normally allowed to give copies of software packages to co-workers in the same company.

15. True or false: Most computer systems don't require backups if they have sealed disk drives.

16. Name two situations in which computer security is important.

17. What is the single most effective computer security measure?
18. What is a password?
19. What does open systems mean?
20. True or false: Some computers can use handwriting as input.

TOPICS FOR RESEARCH AND DISCUSSION

1. You are working in a company and need to use a spreadsheet program, but you don't have one on your computer. Your friend in the next office has the spreadsheet program you need. The company purchased the software. Your friend offers to give you the master disks for the spreadsheet program so you can copy it onto your computer. What would you do?

2. Suppose you need to recommend a computer system for printing mailing lists. Using the information you can obtain from magazines, plus telephone calls to different vendors, develop three basic configurations: a low-cost system with a slow dot-matrix printer; a medium-cost system with a fast dot-matrix printer; and a high-cost system with a laser printer. Be sure to include software to maintain and print the lists (a word processor or spreadsheet might do). Also, confirm that the software can support the printer you pick! Once you have the three basic configurations, select one and create a detailed configuration, with model numbers and specific prices.

3. Many different technologies usually can be used to address the same needs. Five major systems are available for microcomputer users: Macintosh systems, MS/DOS text systems, MS/DOS Windows systems, OS/2 systems, and Unix systems. There are many people who are fanatically devoted to each of these systems. Find two technicians who have strong but different opinions about the best technology from this list. Find out why they prefer their favorites. Create a comparison framework showing the strengths and weaknesses of the two systems, and identify the business goals that each one might support best. You can find talkative technicians at places with lots of computers, such as computer stores, desktop publishing centers, and many offices such as banks or manufacturers.

GLOSSARY

absolute cell address In a spreadsheet formula, a cell address that remains constant even if the formula is copied to another range of cells.

access arm The part of a disk drive that moves the read/write head across the disk.

access time The amount of time required to move information from a disk to a computer screen.

access window A cutout window at the center of a floppy disk cover, where the disk drive reads or writes data on the disk.

accounting system A computer system for maintaining financial records.

active cell On a spreadsheet, the cell where the cursor is located.

address register A register that holds the portion of a program which indicates where a piece of data is located.

analog signals Complex sounds that constantly change in pitch, volume, and tone, such as the sound of the human voice.

analysis tools Decision support systems, executive information systems, and other programs that senior staff members use to evaluate alternative ways of using data.

analyst A member of a system design team who evaluates current practices, defines system requirements, and creates specifications for the new system.

animation program Software for creating graphics that move.

application software Computer programs used for work or entertainment, such as accounting programs and computer games.

argument In a spreadsheet, the variable information that follows a function name, such as a range of cells, to be included in a calculation.

arithmetic logic unit (ALU) The area of a central processing unit that performs numerical operations, such as adding numbers, and logical operations, such as comparing numbers.

ascending From last to first, or from least to most, as in from Z to A or from 1 to 99.

ASCII A standard code for microcomputers that assigns a specific byte to each character on a computer keyboard; short for *A*merican *S*tandard *C*haracter *I*nformation *I*nterchange.

A/UX A Macintosh version of the UNIX operating system.

auxiliary storage Permanent storage of data files and software; also called permanent storage or mass storage.

backlit monitor An LCD monitor that has its own light sources, behind the crystals.

backup Copying data from a computer's hard disk onto removable media such as floppy disks or tape cassettes or copying data from one diskette to another. Before using software on a diskette, you always copy (backup) it.

backup cycle A routine for performing backups at regular intervals.

backup utility program Software for copying files from a hard disk onto a floppy diskette or tape cartridge.

bar code A set of black and white stripes, found on most product containers, that represent data such as prices and that can be scanned with an input device.

bar code reader An optical scanning device that reads bar codes.

base-2 A system of mathematics using only two digits: 1, to represent the condition of on, and 0, to represent the condition of off; also called binary.

BASIC A programming language designed to allow beginners to create small programs easily.

basic input/output system (BIOS) A set of programs, mostly contained in ROM chips, that governs all activity to and from a computer's components.

baud In data communications, the number of bits transmitted per second.

benchmark A structured test of a system's performance.

binary Consisting of two states, on or off, which are represented by 1 (on) and 0 (off) in the binary system of mathematics; also called base-2.

BIPS (billions of instructions per second) A unit for measuring the processing speed of a supercomputer.

bit The smallest unit of storage in a computer, represented by a 1 or a 0; short for *bi*nary digi*t*.

bitmapped font A font that must be mapped out, one pixel at a time by the monitor and one dot at a time by a printer and that is usually limited to a specific size.

bitmapping The process of assigning the pixels of an image on the computer screen to bits in the computer's memory.

bits per inch The measurement unit for the linear density of a disk.

blackout A complete loss of power to the microcomputer, which can result in loss of data.

block move The process of highlighting a block of text and moving it to another position with a word processor; also called cut and paste.

block-structured language A programming language that breaks programs visually into blocks that reflect the programs' behavior.

bootstrap loader The first firmware program a computer follows when turned on, which tells the computer how to start and prepares it to perform diagnostic tests of its components.

bridge A connection between two LANs that enables them to exchange data.

bubble-jet printer A lightweight ink-jet printer used with laptop computers.

bulletin board A data communications forum for special-interest groups that allows members to post messages that can be read and answered by other members.

business form generator Graphics software for creating business forms.

byte A string of bits, usually eight bits long, that work together as a group to store characters or digits.

C One of the most popular programming languages for microcomputer software.

cable One or more electrical wires sealed in insulating plastic.

carrier signal The high-pitched tone that a modem uses to send data.

cartridge font A font contained on a microchip and encased in a cartridge that can be plugged into a printer.

CASE (computer-assisted software engineering) tools Automated methods for developing software.

cathode-ray tube (CRT) A large vacuum tube, like the picture tube of a television set, that serves as the display screen in a desktop computer monitor.

CD ROM (compact disk read-only memory) A removable computer storage medium that looks like an audio CD but which stores data instead of music.

cell The intersection of a row and a column on a spreadsheet, where a piece of data can be entered.

cell address The row letter and column number that identify a specific cell on a spreadsheet.

central processing unit (CPU) The area of a microprocessor that schedules and directs the activities of the microcomputer.

CISC (conventional instruction set computing) processor A processor that understands conventional machine language.

clip art Professional art that is stored and sold on microcomputer disks so it can be used with graphics and desktop publishing programs.

clipboard A temporary memory storage area used for storing text and graphics when moving them from one application program to another.

clone A microcomputer modeled after those made by the International Business Machines Corp.; also called an IBM-compatible.

color graphics adapter (CGA) A circuit board and monitor for displaying four colors at a resolution of 320 by 200 pixels.

command area In spreadsheet software, the part of the control panel at the top of the screen where a list of command options appears.

command interpreter The part of the operating system that reviews all input and determines whether it is valid.

command line A type of user interface that accepts input in the form of keyed-in commands.

command processor The part of a kernel program that gets input ready for processing.

commercial database A large collection of data that is available to subscribers or to the general public.

communications software Computer programs that tell a modem how to transfer data between two computers over telephone lines.

compiler A program for translating source code into instructions a computer can execute.

computer An electronic device that can follow instructions to process information automatically.

computer chip A small square of silicon on which circuits containing thousands of miniature electrical switches have been etched; also called a solid state device or an integrated circuit.

computer graphics Pictures that can be created, modified, or viewed on a computer screen.

computer hacker A person who enjoys breaking computer security systems.

computer system All the hardware and software needed for entering data into a computer and producing information from it.

computer virus A program that attaches itself to normal software and replicates itself, moving from system to system through networks, floppy disks, and data communication with bulletin boards.

computer-assisted design (CAD) The process of creating three-dimensional graphics with a computer.

configured Set up for use by a particular organization.

connectivity The ability to link different computer systems so they can share data.

continuous-form paper Sheets of paper that are joined at their ends and that have rows of holes on either side to guide them through a printer's tractor-feed attachment.

control panel The top three or four lines of the screen above the actual spreadsheet.

control unit The area of a central processing unit (CPU) that manages the activity within the CPU by keeping track of all the instructions being processed.

cordless mouse A mouse that has no cable and uses infrared light instead to communicate with a microcomputer.

core programs Programs built in to the kernel that handle the most basic computing tasks, such as copying files.

cost/benefit analysis The process of weighing the costs of a proposed system against the benefits it will provide.

CP/M (Control Program for Microprocessors) The first commercially available operating system for microcomputers, which is now defunct.

cropping The process of trimming off the unnecessary part of a photo.

cursor A spot of light that marks a computer user's working position on the screen; also a small mouse used with a graphics tablet for precise tracing and drawing.

custom application An application program written for use by one organization only.

customer order system A computer system that processes orders and creates invoices, statements, and shipping orders.

cut and paste The process of highlighting a block of text and moving it to another position with a word processor; also called a block move.

cylinder All of the tracks with the same number on a hard disk which has several platters.

daisy-wheel printer An impact printer with a printing element consisting of spokes arranged around a hub, with characters cast in metal or plastic at the ends of the spokes.

data Raw facts, which can take the form of numbers, words, or codes.

data communications The electronic transfer of information by computers at distant locations; also called telecommunications.

data compression A file transfer strategy that squeezes more characters per second into each transfer by using codes to eliminate repetitions. Also used to condense data stored in files.

data dictionary The part of a DBMS that spells out the rules for using a database and controls access to data.

data entry The inputting and modification of data in databases to keep them up to date.

data file A set of records containing the same kinds of data about different entities.

data integrity The certainty that records do not contain conflicting information.

data security The confidentiality and safety of an organization's data.

data transformation The conversion of data from one format to another, such as from IBM-compatible to Macintosh format, during data communication; also called data translation.

data translation The conversion of data from one format to another, such as from IBM-compatible to Macintosh format, during data communication.

database A set of files containing different kinds of information about different entities, such as an employee file that contains various kinds of information about all of an organization's personnel.

database administrator The person who sets up and maintains the data dictionary in a large organization.

database application An application program written with a DBMS package rather than with a standard programming language, which is actually a database tailored for a specific organization or industry.

database management system (DBMS) A set of programs used to store data in files and to retrieve and manipulate that data.

debugger A programmer's tool for testing software.

decision support system An analysis tool that senior staff members use to evaluate alternative ways of using data.

dedicated device A device such as a printer that is controlled by only one microcomputer.

dedicated word processor A computer that does nothing other than word processing.

default prefix In a spreadsheet program, the label prefix that is put in by the program if one has not been entered by the user.

demodulate Convert from analog signals to digital signals.

descending From first to last, or from most to least, as in from A to Z or from 99 to 1.

desk accessories Programs that perform small tasks such as displaying an on-screen clock, calculator, or calendar.

desktop publishing The use of a microcomputer and software to blend text and documents into high-quality, illustrated documents.

digital Consisting of binary digits (ones and zeros, also called bits) that represent the electrical states of on and off.

digital image input Photographs that are stored in digital format for use in a computer or for transmission to a remote location.

digital signals Binary on/off signals that computers can recognize, record, and play back.

digital sound processing The conversion of music and other sounds to digital form so they can be input into a microcomputer, manipulated, and played back.

digitizer A circuit board that enables a computer to convert the human voice to digital signals.

digitizing The process of converting nondigital communications into bits; done by input devices.

direct page makeup A page composition approach in which characteristics are assigned to text and illustrations as they are placed on a page during desktop publishing.

disk drive A computer component that houses a magnetic disk, reads information from it, and writes information onto it.

distributed database A database that includes files stored in different computers.

DOS (Disk Operating System) The first operating system used with IBM PCs and compatibles, and still widely used.

dot-matrix printer An impact printer with a printing element on which pins are arranged so that their ends form individual characters or graphic images.

downloadable font A font that is stored on a computer disk and loaded from the disk drive to the printer as needed; also called a soft font.

drawing area In graphics software, the blank area of the screen where an image is drawn.

drawing program Graphics software that creates images by combining line segments to form outlines.

drive door An opening through which floppy disks are slid into a disk drive; also called a drive gate.

drive gate An opening through which floppy disks are slid into a disk drive; also called a drive door.

drum plotter A plotter that holds paper on a cylindrical drum that rotates as the plotter's pens move around on it.

DS, DD (double-sided, double-density) disk A floppy disk that can hold 360K of data; also called a low density floppy disk.

DS, HD disk A floppy disk that can hold 1.2MB of data; also called a high density floppy disk.

dynamic link A formula in a spreadsheet cell that retrieves data from a cell in another spreadsheet.

EBCDIC A standard code for mainframe computers that assigns specific bits within a byte to store digits, letters of the alphabet, and special characters. It can be used to represent 256 unique digits, letters, or characters..

electroluminescent display (EL) A type of flat-panel display in which an electrical charge causes the monitor to give out light of its own.

electronic mail The exchange of text files, such as letters and memos, between computers.

end users The ultimate users of a computer system, ranging from clerks to executives.

enhanced graphics adapter (EGA) A monitor and circuit board for displaying 16 colors at a resolution of 640 by 350 pixels.

entity A specific person, place, or thing about which data is stored in a file or in a computer.

EPROM (erasable programmable read-only memory) ROM chips that can be erased with ultraviolet light and then reprogrammed.

executable file A file containing a program the computer can run, as opposed to a data file.

executive information system An analysis tool that senior staff members use to evaluate alternative ways of using data.

expansion card A specialized circuit board that plugs into a computer's motherboard to add features to the system.

expansion slot A plug-in connection on a motherboard for accommodating an expansion card.

export Transfer data from one program currently to a file that can be used with another program.

Extended Industry Standard Architecture (EISA) An alternative to Micro Channel Architecture that is based on an extension of ISA to accommodate 32-bit processors.

extended keyboard A keyboard with extra groups of keys, arranged by function, that speed access to commands and reduce the amount of necessary hand movement.

external modem A modem located outside a computer and connected to it by way of a serial or parallel port.

external specifications A listing of what a system will do, based on a defined set of needs.

FAX (facsimile) machine A scanner that converts the image of a document page to a digital format and transmits it over telephone lines.

FAX board A circuit board installed in a microcomputer that enables the computer to send data to a FAX machine.

FAX interface An external device that can be plugged into a microcomputer to enable the computer to send data to a FAX machine.

field An area of a record that contains a specific piece of data.

file In general, a specific collection of bytes, with a name; in a database, a set of records containing the same kinds of data about different entities.

file compression utility program Software for compressing data stored in files so that less space is needed to store the data on a disk or diskette.

file conversion utility program Software for converting files so they can be used with different application programs or microcomputer types.

file integration The linkage of files in a database so that they can share data.

file management utility program Software that helps users keep track of where files are stored in a microcomputer.

file recovery utility program Software for recovering files that have been erased accidentally.

file server A high-speed microcomputer with a large disk drive that can be accessed by all the other microcomputers on a LAN.

file transfer The process of moving files from one computer to another.

file transfer protocol A set of rules for detecting and correcting errors during data communications; also called a modem protocol.

firmware System software that is built into a computer's microprocessor chips so that it is a permanent part of its hardware.

fixed disk A magnetic disk that is not removable from the disk drive.

flatbed plotter A plotter that holds paper flat and steady while the plotter's pens move across it. Also called a table plotter.

flat-file DBMS A database management system that creates files that are completely independent of each other and cannot share data.

flat-panel display A thin, lightweight monitor built into a laptop computer.

floppy disks Removable secondary storage media for computers, usually 5 1/4 or 3 1/2 inches in diameter; also called floppies or floppy diskettes.

flowchart A graphic that illustrates a process, using standard shapes to represent different steps or phases.

flowchart program Graphics software for drawing flowcharts.

font A set of characters of a specific design and size.

font family All variations on a single font, such as bold, italic, bold-italic, and condensed type.

footer Text that appears at the bottom of every page in a document.

format command The part of a computer's operating system that establishes where tracks and sectors are placed on disks.

formatting (a disk) Using a computer's operating system to create tracks and sectors; also called initializing.

formula bar In spreadsheet software, the area where information appears when it is first keyed in.

frame A position marker for text or a picture on a page.

freeware System utility programs available at little or no cost through computer clubs and electronic distribution services.

function In spreadsheet software, a predefined formula for a calculation.

function keys Keys on a keyboard that are labeled F1, F2, and so on, whose functions vary according to the software being used.

gas-plasma display A type of flat-panel display containing gas that emits light when the monitor's electrical current is turned on.

gateway A device that gives network users access to an incompatible computing environment, such as a mainframe or a different kind of network.

general communications software Programs that provide integrated general purpose communications, including telephone dialing, terminal emulation, and file transfer with several protocols.

gigabyte One thousand million bytes.

global command A command that affects an entire document.

graphical user interface (GUI) An interface that allows a user to enter commands by selecting pictures from the screen.

graphics adapter card A circuit board that enables a computer to display graphic images on a monochrome monitor; also called a graphics adapter or graphics card.

graphics conversion program Software for converting computer graphics files from one format to another.

graphics files Files that contain pictures.

graphics software Programs for creating, editing, or displaying graphics with a computer.

graphics tablet A pad, resembling a mouse pad, that is used with a either a stylus or a cursor and that combines pointing and touch-sensitive input techniques.

graphing program A drawing program for creating graphs.

grid The underlying structure of a page in a desktop-published document, appearing on a computer screen as a set of horizontal and vertical lines that divide the page into areas.

grid line A drawing guide on a graphics software screen.

groupware A kind of software that uses a network "actively" by helping users interact using a common pool of shared data.

handwriting recognition tablet A device that allows for inputting information into a computer by writing script on a touch-sensitive pad; also known as a pen-based input device.

hard copy Printed output from a computer.

hard disk A nonremovable storage disk that can hold much more information than a removable disk; also called a fixed disk.

hard disk card A hard disk mounted on an expansion card that fits into a slot on a microcomputer's motherboard.

hard disk cartridge A device resembling a hard disk in a box, which is inserted in an external disk drive with a large door, and which combines the large storage capacity of a hard disk with the convenience of removable floppy disks.

hard-sectored disk Disks, used with older computers, on which sectors are identified by small holes around the perimeter of the disk's center hole.

hardware A computer system's physical components, including its electrical circuitry, screen, keyboard, cables, and so forth.

head crash The scraping off of surface material— and data— from a disk, when a read/write head touches the disk surface.

header Text that appears at the top of every page in a document.

high density floppy disk A floppy disk that can hold 1.2MB of data; also called a DS, HD (short for double-sided, high density) disk.

host computer A mainframe or minicomputer with terminals.

hypermedia applications Applications that let users mix different kinds of data, such as text and graphics.

hypertext A software feature that links documents so you can browse through them on a computer screen to find information on a variety of related subjects.

IBM-compatible A microcomputer modeled after those made by the International Business Machines Corp.; also called a clone.

icon A picture on a computer screen that represents a command in a graphical user interface.

image scanner An optical scanning device for adding printed artwork and photographs to documents and presentations on a microcomputer.

impact printer A printer that strikes its print element against paper.

implementation plan The process of specifying what each program in a system must do; also called system design or internal design.

import In desktop publishing, to transfer graphics or text from a disk to a document that is being laid out.

incremental compiler A programming tool that lets programmers change source code while they are debugging it.

index The part of a DBMS that tells the system where records are located on the computer's storage disk.

index hole A small hole near the center hole of a floppy disk that enables a disk controller to locate disk sectors.

Industry Standard Architecture (ISA) The system data bus design of the original 8-bit IBM Personal Computer.

infected disk A disk containing a virus.

information Data that has been processed and made useful.

information modeling A systems planning process in which a large organization itemizes every piece of data and every business procedure in order to spot and prevent wasteful procedures.

initializing (a disk) Using the computer's operating system to create tracks and sectors.

ink-jet printer A printer that forms characters and graphic images by spraying dots of ink onto paper.

input Data or instructions entered into a computer.

input device A keyboard, a mouse, or another device that translates human communication into binary electrical signals and transfers the signals to a computer's circuitry.

inputting The process of transferring data into a computer.

instruction register A register that holds the part of a program indicating the process the computer is to perform.

integrated circuit A small square of silicon on which circuits containing thousands of miniature electrical switches have been etched.; also called a solid state device or a computer chip.

integrated development environment A set of programming tools that work together and is often tailored to a particular language, database, or operating environment.

interface design The process of matching user requirements to system requirements when planning a system.

internal design The process of specifying what each program in a system must do; also called system design or implementation plan.

internal modem A modem installed in an expansion slot inside a computer.

inventory control system A computer system that records orders and shipments and automatically adjusts inventory data.

item selection menu A menu consisting of a list of options identified by numbers or letters.

kernel A part of the operating system that acts as an interface between BIOS and the central processing unit.

key field A field containing entries that can be indexed in a logical order, such as social security numbers, names, or employee numbers.

keyboard The most commonly used input device for microcomputers, resembling a typewriter keyboard.

keypunching A nearly obsolete data entry method that involves coding cards by punching holes in them. The cards are then read by a card reader and the data transferred into a computer for processing.

kilobyte (K) 1,024 bytes, which equals approximately 1,000 letters or numbers.

knowledge workers End users of a system whose jobs revolve around computer data, such as financial analysts.

label Text that identifies a part of a spreadsheet, such as column or row headings.

label prefix In spreadsheet programs, the indication on the screen that the text entered is a label—that is, text that identifies a part of the spreadsheet, such as a column.

lands Flat areas where data is stored on an optical disk.

laptop A portable microcomputer, generally with all of its components in one small housing.

laser printer A printer that uses a laser to form images on a drum, then coats the drum with toner powder and rolls paper over the drum to transfer the images to the paper.

learning curve A period when users of a new system are becoming familiar with it and are not yet fully proficient.

linear density The closeness of bits to each other on the tracks of a storage disk, which is measured in bits per inch.

linker A programmer's tool using one or more object files to create a program the computer can run.

liquid crystal display (LCD) A type of flat-panel display monitor in which an electrical charge causes liquid crystals to reflect light.

local-area network (LAN) A high-speed pathway for exchanging messages and data among microcomputers.

logging on The process computer users follow to connect to computer networks and identify themselves; also called signing on.

logical disk A partition of a hard disk.

low density floppy disk A disk that can hold 360K of data; also called a DS, DD (for double-sided, double-density) disk.

lower-CASE (computer-assisted software engineering) tools Tools that system developers use for implementing and using systems.

machine language The language of binary numbers the computer understands. Source code is translated into machine language instructions.

Macintosh A popular microcomputer made by Apple Computer, Inc., that has a graphical user interface.

macros A series of commands and/or keystrokes that can be saved and then retrieved when the user wants to execute the commands or enter the keystrokes.

macro utility program Software that lets a user record a sequence of commands, give them an identifier, and activate the sequence by keying in the identifier.

magnetic disk The most common permanent storage device for microcomputers, which can be either a floppy disk or a hard disk.

magnetic-ink character recognition (MICR) The process of scanning characters printed with magnetic ink, such as those found on bank checks.

magnetic scanner An optical scanning device that reads text printed with magnetic ink.

magnetic tape cartridge A storage medium for backing up large amounts of information quickly and conveniently.

mail merge A word processor feature that automates mass mailings of form letters.

mainframe The largest type of modern computer, generally used as the central computer for a very large organization.

mapping program Graphics software for drawing maps, generally containing built-in maps that can be modified.

mass storage Permanent storage of data files and software; also called permanent storage or auxiliary storage.

master page A page layout that can be used with many different documents.

math co-processor A chip designed to perform calculations with precision and speed, which resembles a microprocessor and can usually be plugged into a socket on a motherboard.

mechanical A model for a page of a book, magazine, or other published document, consisting of text and illustrations pasted onto cardboard, that is photographed to make a printing plate.

mechanical mouse A mouse that rolls on a small rubber ball as it is moved across a flat surface.

megabyte (MB) Approximately one million bytes.

megahertz (MHz) A unit for measuring the speed of a system clock or microprocessor.

memory management utility program Software that runs with DOS to provide more RAM than the 640K the operating system normally allows.

menu A type of user interface that allows users to select commands from menus or respond to questions instead of keying in commands.

menu shell utility program Software for adding menus to a command line interface or a graphical interface.

Micro Channel Architecture (MCA) A system data bus specification developed by IBM for 32-bit microprocessors.

micro disk A 3 1/2-inch removable storage disk with a hard plastic covering.

microcomputer The smallest and least powerful computer, typically used by just one person; also called a personal computer (PC).

microcomputer chip A computer chip etched with the circuitry needed to process data; also called a microprocessor.

microprocessor The central processing unit (CPU) and principal components of a microcomputer.

minicomputer A computer smaller than a mainframe but larger than a microcomputer, suitable for use as the main computer of a small company or a department in a large company.

MIPS (millions of instructions per second) A unit for measuring the processing speed of a mainframe computer.

mission-critical systems Systems that are required for running a business.

mode indicator In spreadsheet programs, the line on the screen that gives the current operating mode, or the specific set of conditions under which an operation is taking place.

modem A device for transmitting information between computers by way of telephone lines.

modem protocol A set of rules for detecting and correcting errors during data communications; also called a file transfer protocol.

modulate Convert from digital signals to analog signals.

monitor A device that displays computer output on a video screen; also called video display terminal (VDT).

monochrome monitor A monitor that displays images in only one color against a background of a contrasting color or shade.

motherboard The internal circuit board holding the processing components that enables the computer to accept, store, and act on information; also called a system board.

mouse A small box with buttons on top, usually attached to a microcomputer by a cable, that controls the cursor position and is used for selecting menu options and other items.

mouse pad A rubber pad that sits under a mouse on a desk or other flat surface.

multimedia The combining of data, images, and sound on a single optical disk for playback on microcomputer output devices.

multitasking The process of running several application programs at one time.

needs analysis The identification of ways in which new applications can solve problems.

network A group of computers that are linked so they can share data, hardware components, and software.

network backbone A set of bridges that carry most of the long-distance data communications traffic in a wide-area network.

network-aware application A software application that takes advantage of network services, especially high-speed LAN-based file sharing.

networking The process of linking computers so they can share data, hardware components, and software.

nonvolatile memory A form of computer memory that retains its contents when the computer is turned off; also called permanent memory.

notebook microcomputer A battery operated portable microcomputer the size of a clipboard, with touch pads built in but no keyboard or mouse.

NuBus Apple Computer's 32-bit system bus architecture.

numeric keypad An area on a keyboard, with number keys arranged like those on a calculator, for inputting numbers quickly.

object code Instructions that a central processing unit (CPU) can follow.

object-oriented programming A programming technique that focuses on data rather than on programs and lets developers create better software in less time.

off-the-shelf programs Application software that can be used by many organizations or users.

open system Computer systems whose inner workings are publicized by their creators so that other companies can develop products that work well with them.

operating environment System software that acts as an interface between the user and the operating system and makes it possible to use the operating system without knowing its commands.

operating system System software that gives a user access to the computer's internal resources and also manages all of its components.

operating system utilities Programs that carry out routine tasks such as formatting disks.

optical character recognition (OCR) The process optical scanners use to read letters, numbers, and other symbols in typed or printed documents.

optical disk A secondary storage medium that uses laser light, rather than electromagnetic charges, to read and write data.

optical mark recognition (OMR) The process optical scanners use to read handwritten marks on cards or forms and translate them into characters.

optical mouse A mouse with a light sensor used on a mouse pad imprinted with a grid that controls the cursor position.

optical scanning The process of separating out differing degrees of reflected light to recognize images or characters.

optical scanning device A device, such as a FAX machine or a bar code reader, that scans images and converts them to digital form for computer processing.

organization chart A graphic that shows the formal structure of a business, with boxes representing management levels and lines connecting the boxes.

organization chart program Software for creating organization charts.

orphan The first line of a paragraph that appears at the end of a page, separated from the rest of the paragraph.

OS/2 (Operating System 2) An operating system for IBM-compatibles that has a graphical user interface and allows easy access to commands.

outline font A font that is not limited to one size but can be scaled to any size.

output Documents and other information produced by a computer.

ozone A gas produced by laser printers that can irritate eyes and skin.

page composition The process of laying out document pages; also called page makeup.

page description language A programming language that enables desktop publishing software to communicate efficiently with printers and that tells a printer to reproduce a page exactly as it appears on the screen; also called a printer language.

page makeup The process of laying out document pages; also called page composition.

page printer A printer that prints one page at a time, as contrasted to a line printer.

painting program Graphics software that creates images dot by dot.

parallel port A port for transferring information by sending electrical signals across multiple wires simultaneously, used most often for printing.

parallel test Simultaneous use of an old system and the new system that will replace it.

partitioning Part of a formatting procedure, in which a hard disk is divided into logical units that enable it to act like multiple disks.

Pascal A programming language created for developing structured programs.

password A secret code word that a user must enter into a computer to gain access to it.

pen-based computer A notebook microcomputer that uses a pen-like stylus for input.

pen-based input device A device that allows for inputting information into a computer by writing script on a touch-sensitive pad; also known as a handwriting recognition tablet.

permanent memory A form of computer memory that retains its contents when the computer is turned off; also called nonvolatile memory.

personal computer (PC) The smallest and least powerful computer, typically used by just one person; also called a microcomputer.

pilot project A phase of system installation in which only a small number of users begin working with the new system.

pits Tiny depressions in which data is stored on an optical disk.

pixel One of the thousands of dots that make up an image on a monitor.

plotter An output device that uses pens and a wide range of colors to draw images directly on paper.

point A printer's unit of measurement, equal to 1/72 inch.

pointer A DBMS command that tells the system to retrieve data for a given field from a record in another file.

port A physical connector used to attach external devices to a microcomputer's system unit.

portable language A programming language that enables programs written in it to be moved from one system environment to another — from an IBM-compatible using DOS to one using UNIX or to a Macintosh, for example.

PostScript A page description language, widely used in desktop publishing.

presentation graphics programs Drawing programs used to produce graphics for sales presentations, seminars, and other kinds of meetings.

primary key field A field containing a piece of data that distinguishes an entity from all other entities in a file.

print spooling A network feature that automatically manages the network's printers, scheduling print orders and so forth.

printed circuit (p.c.) board A thin sheet of plastic on which metallic electrical circuits are printed and electronic devices are mounted.

printer language A programming language that enables desktop publishing software to communicate efficiently with printers, and which tells a printer to reproduce a page exactly as it appears on the screen; also called a page description language.

printer network A data communications pathway that enables several microcomputers to share a printer.

process control system Software for operating machinery that manufactures products.

processing cycle The steps involved in a computer's processing of an instruction.

ProDOS The operating system for the Apple II.

program Instructions for a computer; also called software.

programmer A person who writes software.

programming language A language for writing computer programs; examples include BASIC, COBOL, and C.

PROM (programmable read-only memory) ROM chips that can be encoded with specific instructions by manufacturers; often used in scientific equipment.

proprietary Used by only one company or in one product.

protected field A field in a given record that contains information you cannot change, although you might be able to change the same data on another record for the same entity.

prototyping Creating mock-ups of system functions for users to try.

public network A data communications service, such as *CompuServe* or *Prodigy*, that offers electronic mail and commercial database access to the general public.

pull-down menu A menu of command options that appears when a user opens the menu by selecting its title.

punch cards Cards that are coded with data in the keypunching process, and then read by a card reader. The data is then processed by the computer or stored in a file.

quality assurance The process of creating methods to avoid the accidental creation of defects in software.

quality control The process of discovering, diagnosing, and correcting defects.

Query by Example (QBE) A query language developed by IBM for use on mainframes, which is emulated by the proprietary query languages of many microcomputer DBMS products.

query language The part of a DBMS that is used to create reports.

RAM (random access remory) A set of computer chips that hold data temporarily during processing but do not retain the data when the computer is turned off; also called volatile memory or user memory.

random access A data search method in which the disk drive goes directly to the data instead of starting at the beginning of a data collection and working toward it.

range command A command that affects part of a spreadsheet, such as a column, row, or block of cells.

raw data capture A passive file transfer strategy in which a terminal or microcomputer downloads data from a passive remote computer.

RISC (Reduced Instruction Set Computing) processor A microprocessor that can understand a recently developed machine language that uses fewer instructions than conventional machine language.

read/write head The part of a disk drive that reads information from a magnetic disk or writes information onto it.

record A collection of data about a specific person, place, or thing.

record form A form used to fill in the fields of data needed to create a record.

records management system A computer system for maintaining important documents.

register An area on a microprocessor that contains a piece of data required by the current processing instructions.

relational DBMS A database management system that can link files so that they share data.

relative cell address In a spreadsheet, a cell address in a formula that the software adjusts automatically if the formula is copied from one range to another.

report A set of information based on data from several records.

resident font A font that is built into a printer.

resolution The sharpness and clarity of images displayed on a monitor or printed on paper.

ROM (read only memory) Computer chips encoded with essential instructions for start-up and other operations, which the computer can read but cannot alter or erase.

ruler line A guide along the top edge of a graphics software screen that helps a user to draw graphics to precise measurements.

sans serif A typeface in which characters lack decorative details.

scalable fonts A feature that enables a printer to reproduce characters in a given typeface at any specified size.

scan To illuminate a printed image or page and read the light reflected from it.

screen capture program Software that can take a "snapshot" of an image on a computer screen and store it on a disk.

screen saver utility program Software that blanks out or constantly changes the image on a monitor to prevent the image from being permanently burned into the monitor.

script A stored sequence of communication commands, including telephone and modem controls, keystrokes, and other communications operations, that can be replayed for different data communications.

scrolling The movement of text off the screen to make room for text above it or below it in a document.

SCSI (Small Computer Systems Interface) port A port that provides high-speed data transfer and that can be shared by multiple devices; first used on the Macintosh.

search and replace The feature that enables a word processor to search for and replace a specified word throughout a document with another specified word.

secondary sort field A field used for distinguishing between two records with the same data in the primary sort field. For example, if records are sorted by name and the secondary sort field contains social security numbers, records for people with the same name are listed in the order of their social security numbers.

secondary storage Permanent storage of data files and software; also called auxiliary storage.

security The protection of information in a computer system.

security utility program Software for preventing unauthorized users from gaining access to data or application programs.

sector The basic storage division of a disk, usually part of a track.

sequential access A data search method that begins each search at the start of a data collection and works toward the end until the data is found.

serial port A port for sending signals one after another across a single wire, used most often for modem communications.

serif A kind of typeface in which characters have decorative details.

sheet feeder An attachment for dot-matrix printers that feeds individual sheets of paper into the printer automatically.

sidelit monitor An LCD monitor that has its own light source, behind the crystals.

signing on The process computer users follow to connect to computer networks and identify themselves; also called logging on.

sign-making program Graphics software for creating signs.

SIMMs (single in-line memory modules) Groups of RAM chips on small printed circuit boards made to plug into slots in the computer.

single-task Able to run only one application program at a time. DOS is an example of a single-task operating system.

smart text editor A tool that lets programmers check source code for errors while they are keying it in.

soft copy Text and pictures displayed on a monitor, as opposed to printed text and pictures.

soft font A font that is stored on a computer disk and loaded from the disk drive to the printer as needed; also called a downloadable font.

soft-sectored disk A disk on which the sectors and tracks are created and identified by the computer's operating system.

software Instructions for a computer; also called programs.

Software Publishers Association An industry association of major software companies.

solid state device A small square of silicon on which circuits containing thousands of miniature electrical switches have been etched.; also called an integrated circuit or a computer chip.

source code Statements written in a programming language.

special function register A register that contains a specific type of data, such as an instruction or an address.

specialized terminal emulator A device that enables a microcomputer to imitate a specific terminal model during telecommunications.

spreadsheet An electronic version of a financial worksheet.

stand-alone A microcomputer that is used independently of other computers.

star network A network in which microcomputers are linked directly to a mainframe or minicomputer.

status line In some software, an area on the screen that displays information such as error messages and whether the Caps Lock key is turned on.

storage register A register that holds a piece of data being used by the program instruction.

Structured Query Language (SQL) A standard language, developed by IBM, that is used for producing reports with many DBMS products.

style sheet In word processing, a format that has been stored on a disk so it can be used with many different documents; in desktop publishing, an approach to page composition that involves placing text and graphics in frames on the page and assigning tags to text that represent fonts.

stylus An inkless pen used for freehand drawing or writing on a graphics tablet or handwriting recognition tablet.

super VGA A monitor and circuit board for displaying 256 colors at a resolution of at least 800 by 600 pixels and as much as 1,024 by 768 pixels.

supercomputer The fastest and most powerful type of mainframe, used primarily by defense and research organizations for tasks that involve analyzing massive amounts of data.

surge A sudden and potentially damaging rush of electrical current to a microcomputer's power supply.

surge protector A device that guards against sudden increases in electrical current.

System The operating system for the Macintosh.

system architect A designation often given to a senior technician on a system development team; also called a system designer.

system board or pc board A thin sheet of plastic on which metallic electrical circuits are printed and electronic devices are mounted. The electrical circuits that make up the basic processing pathways within the microcomputer.

system clock An internal device that times and synchronizes a microcomputer's operations.

system data bus The data pathway formed by the electrical connections on a motherboard.

system design The process of specifying what each program in a system must do; also called internal design or implementation plan.

system designer A designation often given to a senior technician on a system development team; also called a system architect.

system requirements What a system must do, including the input it must accept and the output it must create.

system software Programs that enable a computer to run software for specific applications.

system startup The series of automatic operations a computer performs when you turn it on.

system unit The central component of a microcomputer, to which all other components are connected.

system utility programs Add-on software that enhances operating systems.

table-driven configuration A configuration method that allows users to change the behavior of a program easily.

tag In desktop publishing, a code that represents a font, which can be assigned to a block of text.

telecommunications The electronic transfer of information between computers and remote devices, including other computers, at distant locations; also called data communications.

telemarketing system A computer system that helps give fast, efficient service to customers over the telephone.

template A model for formatting a page, spreadsheet, or other document with software.

terminal An attachment for getting information into and out of a mainframe or minicomputer, generally consisting of a keyboard and monitor; also called a workstation.

terminal emulation The use of a microcomputer as a terminal to a larger computer.

text editor A simple word processor for programming, which programmers use to create source code files.

text entry The process of keying in text with a word processor.

text file A file that contains text.

3270 board A specialized modem that enables a microcomputer to exchange data with an IBM mainframe.

three-dimensional spreadsheet A spreadsheet that is linked to other spreadsheets, so that a change in one is reflected on the others, as well.

tool bar In some spreadsheet software, an area on the screen that displays icons to represent format options.

toolbox The area on a graphics software screen that contains shapes and line thicknesses that can be used in graphics, as well as icons of drawing tools such as a pen and an eraser.

tools-oriented language A programming language that draws on libraries of prewritten tools for needs such as graphics, statistics, and data management.

top-down design A system design strategy that involves breaking each function performed by the system into smaller pieces, so that the system is defined as the sum of its parts.

touch pad A small, touch-sensitive input device that can be attached to a microcomputer by a cable or built in to a keyboard or notebook computer.

touch screen A computer monitor with a soft overlay which the user touches to select items on the screen.

touch-sensitive device An input device formed in which a pliable surface covers a grid of electrical wires, so that touching the surface transmits signals to the computer.

tpi (tracks per inch) A unit for measuring the number of tracks on a disk, which helps to determine the amount of data the disk can store.

track One of the many invisible concentric rings on a storage disk, which are composed of electromagnetic charges.

trackball A stationary input device containing a ball that is manipulated with a thumb or finger to control the cursor position.

tractor-feed A printer attachment that makes it possible to print on continuous-form paper rather than on individual sheets.

transaction processing system A system with a structured user interface for high-volume processing of transactions.

TSR (terminate and stay resident) A program that waits in RAM to be activated by the user while another program is running.

typeface The design of a font.

typeset Produced by a specialized machine that can produce hard copy of very high resolution.

typesetter A person who operates a typesetting machine.

typesetting machine A specialized machine that can produce hard copy of very high resolution.

universal power supply (UPS) A device that provides battery power to a microcomputer when a blackout occurs and filters out surges before they reach the microcomputer.

UNIX An operating system available for both microcomputers and minicomputers that allows a user to run many programs at once.

upper-CASE (computer-aided software engineering) tools Tools that system developers use for planning and designing systems.

user friendly Easy to use.

user ID A short identifier assigned to each valid user in a computer network; also called a user name.

user interface The part of a program that enables a user to communicate with a computer.

user memory A set of computer chips that hold data temporarily during processing but do not retain the data when the computer is turned off; also called random access memory (RAM) or volatile memory.

user name A short identifier assigned to each valid user in a computer network; also called a user ID.

user requirements What users need in a system in order to do their work.

verified file transfer A file transfer strategy that uses protocols to check the accuracy of the data being transferred.

vertical market application A software package written for use by a whole category of businesses, such as a database that can be used by any medical practice.

video digitizer A process that converts video images into digital form using a videocamera connected to digital input devices.

video display terminal (VDT) A device that displays computer output on a video screen; also called a monitor.

video graphics array (VGA) A circuit board and monitor for displaying 16 colors at a resolution of 720 by 400 pixels or 16 colors at a resolution of 640 by 480 pixels.

virus A computer program that corrupts data or software and interrupts a user's ability to work on a microcomputer.

virus protection utility program Software for preventing viruses and removing them from disks.

voice output The use of a computer to make sounds that resemble human speech.

voice recognition devices Input devices that record spoken language and translate it into commands and data for a microcomputer.

voice-activated systems Computer systems that recognize spoken input.

volatile memory A set of computer chips that hold data temporarily during processing but do not retain the data when the computer is turned off; also called random access memory (RAM) or user memory.

wand reader A magnetic scanner, commonly used in department stores, that reads data from magnetically coded price tags.

warm link A link between a spreadsheet and a word-processing document to which it has been exported, which enables any changes in the spreadsheet to be made in the document automatically.

wide-area network (WAN) A data communications network that generally incorporates several LANs at different locations.

widow The last line of a paragraph that appears at the beginning of a page, separated from the rest of the paragraph.

wildcard A symbol an OCR uses to represent a character it cannot read.

Winchester drive A disk drive in which the disk, the drive, and the read/write head are all sealed in a single box to protect them against dust, smoke, and dirt.

Windows A operating environment for IBM-compatibles that features a graphical user interface and enables a user to run several programs at one time.

window An on-screen frame in which a microcomputer user can display the contents of application files.

word A string of bytes that includes the number of bits a microcomputer can accept at one time.

word processor Software for producing documents that consist mainly of text, such as letters and memos.

word wrap A feature of word processors that moves a word to the next line automatically if it does not fit on the line where a user begins keying it.

workstation An attachment for getting information into and out of a mainframe or minicomputer, generally consisting of a keyboard and monitor; also called a terminal.

WORM (write once, read many times) disk A removable computer storage medium with a capacity of 3 gigabytes, on which data can be written only once.

write-protect notch A square notch in the corner of a floppy disk that can be covered to prevent data from being written onto the disk.

XENIX A version of UNIX sold by Microsoft Corp. for use with IBM-compatibles.

yes-and-no menu A type of menu that presents choices in the form of questions.

zoom A feature of some graphics and desktop publishing software products that enables users to magnify a small portion of the screen to check details.

Copyright Acknowledgments

Registered Trademarks

A/UX	Apple Computer, Inc.
ABC Flowcharter	ROYKORE
Above Disc	Above Software
Adobe Illustrator, Photoshop	Adobe Systems, Inc.
After Dark	Berkeley Systems, Inc.
Applause	Ashton-Tate
Apple	Apple Computer, Inc.
ARC Plus	Systems Enhancement Associates, Inc.
Arts & Letters Graphics Editor	Computer Support Corporation
Aspects	Group Technologies
AT&T Rhapsody	AT&T
AutoCAD, Autodesk Animator	Autodesk, Inc.
BannerMania	Broderbund Software, Inc.
BLAST/PC	Micro Future
Canvas	Deneba Software
Case Master III	Software Technology Inc.
Certus	Foundation Ware
Chart-Master	Ashton-Tate
ClarisCAD	Claris Corporation
ColoRIX	RIX Softworks, Inc.
CompuServe	CompuServe, Inc.
COREfast	CORE International
Corel Draw	Corel Systems Corporation
Cricket Draw, Cricket Paint Cricket Presents	Cricket Software
Crosstalk	Crosstalk Communications
DataShaper	ElseWare Corporation
db Publisher	Digital Composition Systems, Inc.
dBASE, dBASE II, dBASE IV	Ashton-Tate
Digital Darkroom	Silicon Beach Software, Inc.
Direct	Access Delta Technology
DiskFit	SuperMac Technology
Do-It	Kallistra, Inc.
Double Helix	Odesta Corporation
Dow Jones, Dow Jones News/Retrieval	Dow Jones Information Services
dQUERY	Quadbase, Inc.
DrawPerfect	Wordperfect Corporation
Dreams	Innovative Data Designs, Inc.
DynaComm	Future Soft Engineering
Electric Pencil	Michael Shrayer
Excel, Excel 3.0	Microsoft Corporation
EasyFlow	Haventree Software Ltd.
Fastback, Fastback II, Fastback Plus	Fifth Generation Systems, Inc.
FileMaker	Claris Corporation
Finder	Apple Computer, Inc.
FlexQL	Data Access Corporation
FlowMaster	Select Micro Systems, Inc.
Flu Shot	Software Concept Design
Form Filler, FormTool	BLOC Development Corporation
Form Publisher, FormWorx	FormWorx Corporation
FormBase	Ventura Software, Inc.
FormMaker	FormMaker Software, Inc.
FORTRAN	Pecan Software Systems, Inc.
4th Dimension	Acius Inc.
FoxBase+, FoxPro	Fox Software
Free Hand	Aldus Corporation
Front Page	Arrays, Inc.-Continental Software
Fullpaint	Ann Arbor Softworks, Inc.
Genie	New Horizons Software
Grammatik	Reference Software International
Harvard Graphics	Software Publishing Corporation
HiJaak	Inset Systems, Inc.
Hyper-Word	Zaron Software, Inc.
HyperAnimator	Bright Star Technology, Inc.
HyperCard	Logical Operations
Hypertext	Zaron Software Inc.
IBM	International Business Machines Corporation
IconAuthor	AimTech
ImageWriter	Apple Computer, Inc.
INGRES	Relational Technology
IRMA	Dynacomp, Inc.
JetForm Design	JetForm Corporation
KnowledgeSeeker	FirstMark Technologies, Ltd.
LapLink	Traveling Software, Inc.
LaserWriter	Apple Computer, Inc.
Letraset ColorStudio, Letraset DesignStudio	Esselte Pendaflex Corporation
Lexis	Mead Data Central
Lotus Notes, Lotus 1-2-3, Lotus 1-2-3 3.0, Lotus 1-2-3 for Windows, Lotus1-2-3/Graphical	Lotus Development Corporation
Lucid 3-D	Borland International, Inc.
MacDraw, MacPaint, MacWrite	Apple Computer, Inc.
MacLink Plus, MacLink Plus/PC	DataViz, Inc.
Magic Wand	Atari Corporation
Mapmaker	Select Micro Systems, Inc.
MapMaster	Ashton-Tate
MCI Mail	MCI
Micrografx Designer	Micrografx, Inc.
MicroPhone	Software Ventures Corporation

293

Microsoft Chart,	Microsoft Corporation
Microsoft File,	
Microsoft Windows 3.0,	
Microsoft Word,	
Microsoft Works,	
MS-DOS Version 1.0,	
MS-DOS Version 2,	
MS-DOS Version 3,	
MS-DOS Version 3.3,	
MS-DOS Version 4,	
MS-DOS Version 5.0	
New Wave	Hewlett-Packard
Nightwatch	Kent Marsh Ltd.
Norton Commander,	Symantec Corporation
Norton Utilities	
Notes	Layered, Inc.
Omnis	Blyth Software, Inc.
Oracle	Oracle Corporation
Org Plus	Banner Corporation
OS/2	Microsoft Corporation
P.C. Tools Deluxe,	Central Point Software, Inc.
P.C. Tools for the Macintosh	
Pac Man	Atari Corporation
PageAhead	PageAhead Software Corporation
PageMaker	Aldus Corporation
PaintBrush	Microsoft Corporation
Panorama	ProVue Development
Paradox	Borland International, Inc.
PC-File	ButtonWare, Inc.
PerForm,	Technology Inc.
PerForm Pro, PerForm	
Persuasion	Aldus Corporation
Pizazz	Application Techiques, Inc.
PlanPerfect	Borland International, Inc.
PosterMaker	Serider Software
PostScript	Aldus Corporation
Power Point	Microsoft Corporation
Presentation Manager	NEC Technology
The Print Shop	Broderbund Software, Inc.
ProComm	Datastorm Techniques, Inc.
Prodigy	Prodigy Services
ProDos	Apple Computer, Inc.
Professional File	Software Publishing Corporation
Progress	Progress Software Corporation
Protec	Sophco, Inc.
Publish-It	Timeworks
Pyro	Fifth Generation Systems, Inc.
Q & A	Symantec Corporation
QuarkXPress	Quark, Inc.
Quattro Plus, Quattro Pro	Borland International, Inc.

R & R Report Writer	Concentric Data Systems, Inc.
R:base	Microrim, Inc.
Red Ryder	FreeSoft
Reflection Series	Richer & Quinn, Inc.
Report Writer	Clarion Software Corporation
RightWriter	Que Software (a division of Macmillan Computer Publishing/Maxwell Communications Corporation)
SAM	Symantec Corporation
SmartForm Designer	Claris Corporation
Smartcom	Hayes Microcomputer Products, Inc.
Solaris	SunSoft
Space Invaders	Atari Corporation
Stacker	Stac Electronics
Studio 32	Electronic Arts
StuffIt, StuffIt Deluxe	Aladdin Systems
SuperCalc 5, SuperKey	Borland International, Inc.
Super Paint	Silicon Beach Software, Inc.
System 7.0	Apple Computer, Inc.
Tandy	Radio Shack, a Division of Tandy Corporation
Tempo	Affinity Microsystems, Inc.
386 MAX	Qualitas Trading Corporation
ToolBook	Asymnetrix
TransText 90	Maxthink, Inc.
Twin	Mosaic Software
Underground Empire	Personal Software
UNIX	AT&T
Ventura Publisher	Xerox Corporation
Virex	Microcom Inc.
Virtual	Connectix Corporation
Viruscan	Interpath
VisiCalc	VisiCorp.
VP Planner	Paperback Software International
Watchdog	Fischer International
Windows,Window Terminal, Word, Word for Windows	Microsoft Corporation
WordMaster	Wordstar International, Inc.
WordPerfect 2.0, WordPerfect 5.0, WordPerfect 5.1	Wordperfect Corporation
WordStar	MicroPro International Corporation
XENIX	Microsoft Corporation
XTree	XTree Company
Zork	Personal Software

INDEX